CW01630709

PENGUIN BOO[...]

White Teet[...]

'Quirky, sassy and wise . . . a big, splashy, populous production reminiscent of books by Dickens and Salman Rushdie . . . demonstrates both an instinctive storytelling talent and a fully fashioned voice that's street-smart and learned, sassy and philosophical all at the same time . . . In what will surely rank as one of her generation's most precocious débuts, Smith announces herself as a writer of remarkable powers'
The New York Times

'An extraordinarily accomplished first novel, a new voice that will give its readers hope for a multicultural society' *Financial Times*

'Exceptional talent . . . Smith writes like an old hand, and, sometimes, like a dream' *New Yorker*

'Extremely funny . . . witty and fresh with authenticity . . . Smith is not merely telling a story, she is creating a world . . . *White Teeth* is one of the best first novels of recent years, characterized by a sharp intelligence, a love of words and a broad range of allusion, both to literature and pop culture' *Literary Review*

'A great big blast of a novel' *Independent*

'Has energy, pace, humour and fully formed characters; it is blissfully free of the introversion and self-conscious detail that mar many first novels . . . the dialogue is pitch perfect . . . bounding, vibrant, richly imagined and thoroughly enjoyable' *Daily Telegraph*

'The comedy fizzes up through the characters' *Economist*

ABOUT THE AUTHOR

Zadie Smith was born in north-west London in 1975, and continues to live in the area. Her two novels, *White Teeth* and *The Autograph Man*, are published by Penguin.

White Teeth

ZADIE SMITH

PENGUIN BOOKS

PENGUIN BOOKS

Published by the Penguin Group
Penguin Books Ltd, 80 Strand, London WC2R 0RL, England
Penguin Putnam Inc., 375 Hudson Street, New York, New York 10014, USA
Penguin Books Australia Ltd, 250 Camberwell Road, Camberwell, Victoria 3124, Australia
Penguin Books Canada Ltd, 10 Alcorn Avenue, Toronto, Ontario, Canada M4V 3B2
Penguin Books India (P) Ltd, 11 Community Centre, Panchsheel Park, New Delhi – 110 017, India
Penguin Books (NZ), Cnr Rosedale and Airborne Roads, Albany, Auckland, New Zealand
Penguin Books (South Africa) (Pty) Ltd, 24 Sturdee Avenue, Rosebank 2196, South Africa

Penguin Books Ltd, Registered Offices: 80 Strand, London WC2R 0RL, England

www.penguin.com

First published by Hamish Hamilton Ltd 2000
Published in Penguin Books 2001
001

The publisher is grateful for permission to reproduce the following extracts: 'As Time Goes By', words and music by Herman Hupfeld, copyright 1931 by T. B. Harms Company, all rights assigned to Warner Chappell Music Inc., all rights reserved, lyric reproduced by kind permission of Redwood Music Ltd (Carlin), London NW1 8BD, covering the Commonwealth of Nations including Canada, Australasia and Hong Kong, Germany, Austria, Switzerland, South Africa and Spain only; *Where Angels Fear to Tread* by E. M. Forster, Penguin Books, Twentieth-Century Classics edition; *Lolita* by Vladimir Nabokov, Penguin Books, Twentieth-Century Classics edition; 'My Back Pages' by Bob Dylan, copyright © 1964 by Warner Bros. Inc., copyright renewed 1992 by Special Rider Music, all rights reserved, international copyright secured, reprinted by permission; (p. 228) the Koran, Sura 109 and (p. 501) Sura 52.44, translation by N. J. Dawood, first published by Penguin Books 1956; (p. 501) the Koran, Sura 52.44 and (p. 502) Sura 52.49, translation by J. M. Rodwell, first published 1861, Orion Publishing Group, Orion House, 5 Upper St Martin's Lane, London WC2E 9EA; and (p. 502) the Koran, Sura 52.49, translation by Mohammed Marmaduke Pickthall, first published 1930, UBSPD, 5 Ansari Road, New Delhi 110002.

Set in 11/13 pt Monotype Dante
Typeset by Rowland Phototypesetting Ltd, Bury St Edmunds, Suffolk
Printed in England by Clays Ltd, St Ives plc

ISBN: 978–0–241–96559–7

www.greenpenguin.co.uk

MIX
Paper from responsible sources
FSC www.fsc.org FSC™ C018179

Penguin Books is committed to a sustainable future for our business, our readers and our planet. This book is made from paper certified by the Forest Stewardship Council.

ALWAYS LEARNING PEARSON

To my mother and my father
And for Jimmi Rahman

'What's past is prologue'

– *The Tempest*, Act II, scene i

Contents

Acknowledgements

I am grateful to both Lisa and Joshua Appignanesi for contriving between them to get me a room of my own when it was most required. Thanks are due to Tristan Hughes and Yvonne Bailey-Smith for providing two happy homes for this book and its author. I am also indebted to the bright ideas and sharp eyes of the following people: Paul Hilder, friend and sounding-board; Nicholas Laird, fellow *idiot savant*; Donna Poppy, meticulous in everything; Simon Prosser, as judicious an editor as one could hope for; and finally my agent, Georgia Garrett, from whom nothing escapes.

Archie

1974, 1945

'Every little trifle, for some reason, does seem incalculably important today, and when you say of a thing that "nothing hangs on it" it sounds like blasphemy. There's never any knowing – how am I to put it? – which of our actions, which of our idlenesses won't have things hanging on it for ever.'

Where Angels Fear to Tread, E. M. Forster

1 *The Peculiar Second Marriage of Archie Jones*

Early in the morning, late in the century, Cricklewood Broadway. At 06.27 hours on 1 January 1975, Alfred Archibald Jones was dressed in corduroy and sat in a fume-filled Cavalier Musketeer Estate face down on the steering wheel, hoping the judgement would not be too heavy upon him. He lay forward in a prostrate cross, jaw slack, arms splayed either side like some fallen angel; scrunched up in each fist he held his army service medals (left) and his marriage licence (right), for he had decided to take his mistakes with him. A little green light flashed in his eye, signalling a right turn he had resolved never to make. He was resigned to it. He was prepared for it. He had flipped a coin and stood staunchly by its conclusions. This was a decided-upon suicide. In fact it was a New Year's resolution.

But even as his breathing became spasmodic and his lights dimmed, Archie was aware that Cricklewood Broadway would seem a strange choice. Strange to the first person to notice his slumped figure through the windscreen, strange to the policemen who would file the report, to the local journalist called upon to write fifty words, to the next of kin who would read them. Squeezed between an almighty concrete cinema complex at one end and a giant intersection at the other, Cricklewood was no kind of place. It was not a place a man came to die. It was a place a man came in order to go other places via the A41. But Archie Jones didn't want to die in some pleasant, distant woodland, or on a cliff edge fringed with delicate heather. The way Archie saw it, country people should die in the country and city people should die in the city. Only proper. *In death as he was in life* and all that. It made sense that Archibald should die on this nasty urban street where he had ended up, living alone at the age of forty-seven, in a one-bedroom flat above a deserted chip shop. He wasn't the type to make elaborate plans – suicide notes and funeral instructions – he wasn't the type for anything fancy. All he asked for was a bit of silence, a bit of *shush* so he could concentrate. He wanted it to be perfectly quiet and still, like the inside of an empty confessional box or the moment in the brain between thought and speech. He wanted to do it before the shops opened.

Overhead, a gang of the local flying vermin took off from some unseen perch, swooped, and seemed to be zeroing in on Archie's car roof – only to perform, at the last moment, an impressive U-turn, moving as one with the elegance of a curve ball and landing on the Hussein-Ishmael, a celebrated halal butchers. Archie was too far gone to make a big noise about it, but he watched them with a warm internal smile as they deposited their load, streaking white walls purple. He watched them stretch their peering bird heads over the Hussein-Ishmael gutter; he watched them watch the slow and steady draining of blood from the dead things – chickens, cows, sheep – hanging on their hooks like coats around the shop. The Unlucky. These pigeons had an instinct for the Unlucky, and so they passed Archie by. For, though he did not know it, and despite the Hoover tube that lay on the passenger seat pumping from the exhaust pipe into his lungs, luck was with him that morning. The thinnest covering of luck was on him like fresh dew. Whilst he slipped in and out of consciousness, the position of the planets, the music of the spheres, the flap of a tiger-moth's diaphanous wings in Central Africa, and a whole bunch of other stuff that Makes Shit Happen had decided it was second-chance time for Archie. Somewhere, somehow, by somebody, it had been decided that he would live.

The Hussein-Ishmael was owned by Mo Hussein-Ishmael, a great bull of a man with hair that rose and fell in a quiff, then a ducktail. Mo believed that with pigeons you have to get to the root of the problem: not the excretions but the pigeon itself. *The shit is not the shit* (this was Mo's mantra), *the pigeon is the shit*. So the morning of Archie's almost-death began as every morning in the Hussein-Ishmael, with Mo resting his huge belly on the windowsill, leaning out and swinging a meat cleaver in an attempt to halt the flow of dribbling purple.

'Get out of it! Get away, you shit-making bastards! Yes! SIX!'

It was cricket, basically – the Englishman's game adapted by the immigrant, and six was the most pigeons you could get at one swipe.

'Varin!' said Mo, calling down to the street, holding the bloodied cleaver up in triumph. 'You're in to bat, my boy. Ready?'

Below him on the pavement stood Varin – a massively overweight Hindu boy on misjudged work experience from the school round the corner, looking up like a big dejected blob underneath Mo's question mark. It was Varin's job to struggle up a ladder and gather spliced bits of pigeon into a small Kwik Save carrier bag, tie the bag up, and dispose of it in the bins at the other end of the street.

'Come on, Mr Fatty-man,' yelled one of Mo's kitchen staff, poking Varin up the arse with a broom as punctuation for each word. 'Get-your-fat-Ganesh-Hindu-backside-up-there-Elephant-Boy-and-bring-some-of-that-mashed-pigeon-stuff-with-you.'

Mo wiped the sweat off his forehead, snorted, and looked out over Cricklewood, surveying the discarded armchairs and strips of carpet, outdoor lounges for local drunks; the slot-machine emporiums, the greasy spoons and the minicabs – all covered in shit. One day, so Mo believed, Cricklewood and its residents would have cause to thank him for his daily massacre; one day no man, woman or child in the broadway would ever again have to mix one part detergent to four parts vinegar to clean up the crap that falls on the world. *The shit is not the shit*, he repeated solemnly, *the pigeon is the shit*. Mo was the only man in the community who truly understood. He was feeling really very Zen about this – very goodwill-to-all-men – until he spotted Archie's car.

'Arshad!'

A shifty-looking skinny guy with a handlebar moustache, dressed in four different shades of brown, came out of the shop, with blood on his palms.

'Arshad!' Mo barely restrained himself, stabbed his finger in the direction of the car. 'My boy, I'm going to ask you just once.'

'Yes, Abba?' said Arshad, shifting from foot to foot.

'What the hell is this? What is this doing here? I got delivery at 6.30. I got fifteen dead bovines turning up here at 6.30. I got to get it in the back. That's my job. You see? There's *meat* coming. So, I am *perplexed* . . .' Mo affected a look of innocent confusion. 'Because I thought this was clearly marked "Delivery Area".' He pointed to an ageing wooden crate which bore the legend NO PARKINGS OF ANY VEHICLE ON ANY DAYS. 'Well?'

'I don't know, Abba.'

'You're my son, Arshad. I don't employ you not to know. I employ *him* not to know' – he reached out of the window and slapped Varin, who was negotiating the perilous gutter like a tightrope-walker, giving him a thorough cosh to the back of his head and almost knocking the boy off his perch – 'I employ *you* to know things. To compute information. To bring into the light the great darkness of the creator's unexplainable universe.'

'Abba?'

'Find out what it's doing there and get rid of it.'

Mo disappeared from the window. A minute later Arshad returned with the explanation. 'Abba.'

Mo's head sprang back through the window like a malicious cuckoo from a Swiss clock.

'He's gassing himself, Abba.'

'What?'

Arshad shrugged. 'I shouted through the car window and told the guy to move on and he says, "I am gassing myself, leave me alone." Like that.'

'No one gasses himself on my property,' Mo snapped as he marched downstairs. 'We are not licensed.'

Once in the street, Mo advanced upon Archie's car, pulled out the towels that were sealing the gap in the driver's window, and pushed it down five inches with brute, bullish force.

'Do you hear that, mister? We're not licensed for suicides around here. This place halal. Kosher, understand? If you're going to die round here, my friend, I'm afraid you've got to be thoroughly bled first.'

Archie dragged his head off the steering wheel. And in the moment between focusing on the sweaty bulk of a brown-skinned Elvis and realizing that life was still his, he had a kind of epiphany. It occurred to him that, for the first time since his birth, Life had said Yes to Archie Jones. Not simply an 'OK' or 'You-might-as-well-carry-on-since-you've-started', but a resounding affirmative. Life wanted Archie. She had jealously grabbed him from the jaws of death, back to her bosom. Although he was not one of her better specimens, Life wanted Archie and Archie, much to his own surprise, wanted Life.

Frantically, he wound down both his windows and gasped for oxygen from the very depths of his lungs. In between gulps he thanked Mo profusely, tears streaming down his cheeks, his hands clinging on to Mo's apron.

'All right, all right,' said the butcher, freeing himself from Archie's fingers and brushing himself clean, 'move along now. I've got meat coming. I'm in the business of bleeding. Not counselling. You want Lonely Street. This Cricklewood Lane.'

Archie, still choking on thankyous, reversed, pulled out from the curb, and turned right.

Archie Jones attempted suicide because his wife Ophelia, a violet-eyed Italian with a faint moustache, had recently divorced him. But he had not spent New Year's morning gagging on the tube of a vacuum cleaner because he loved her. It was rather because he had lived with her for so long and had *not* loved her. Archie's marriage felt like buying a pair of shoes, taking them home and finding they don't fit. For the sake of appearances, he put up with them. And then, all of a sudden and after thirty years, the shoes picked themselves up and walked out of the house. She left. Thirty years.

As far as he remembered, just like everybody else they began well. The first spring of 1946, he had stumbled out of the darkness of war and into a Florentine coffee house, where he was served by a waitress truly like the sun: Ophelia Diagilo, dressed all in yellow, spreading warmth and the promise of sex as she passed him a frothy cappuccino. They walked into it blinkered as horses. She was not to know that women never stayed as daylight in Archie's life; that somewhere in him he didn't like them, he didn't trust them, and he was able to love them only if they wore haloes. No one told Archie that lurking in the Diagilo family tree were two hysteric aunts, an uncle who talked to aubergines and a cousin who wore his clothes back to front. So they got married and returned to England, where she realized very quickly her mistake, he drove her very quickly mad, and the halo was packed off to the attic to collect dust with the rest of the bric-a-brac and broken kitchen appliances that Archie promised one day to repair. Amongst that bric-a-brac was a Hoover.

*

On Boxing Day morning, six days before he parked outside Mo's halal butchers, Archie had returned to their semi-detached in Hendon in search of that Hoover. It was his fourth trip to the attic in so many days, ferrying out the odds and ends of a marriage to his new flat, and the Hoover was amongst the very last items he reclaimed – one of the most broken things, most ugly things, the things you demand out of sheer bloody-mindedness because you have lost the house. This is what divorce is: taking things you no longer want from people you no longer love.

'So *you* again,' said the Spanish home-help at the door, Santa-Maria or Maria-Santa or something. 'Meester Jones, what now? Kitchen sink, sí?'

'Hoover,' said Archie, grimly. 'Vacuum.'

She cut her eyes at him and spat on the doormat inches from his shoes. '*Welcome*, señor.'

The place had become a haven for people who hated him. Apart from the home-help, he had to contend with Ophelia's extended Italian family, her mental-health nurse, the woman from the council, and of course Ophelia herself, who was to be found in the kernel of this nuthouse, curled up in a foetal ball on the sofa, making lowing sounds into a bottle of Bailey's. It took him an hour and a quarter just to get through enemy lines – and for what? A perverse Hoover, discarded months earlier because it was determined to perform the opposite of every vacuum's objective: spewing out dust instead of sucking it in.

'Meester Jones, why do you come here when it make you so unhappy? Be *reasonable*. What can you want with it?' The home-help was following him up the attic stairs, armed with some kind of cleaning fluid: 'It's broken. You don't *need* this. See? See?' She plugged it into a socket and demonstrated the dead switch. Archie took the plug out and silently wound the cord round the Hoover. If it was broken, it was coming with him. All broken things were coming with him. He was going to fix every damn broken thing in this house, if only to show that he was good for something.

'You good for nothing!' Santa whoever chased him back down the stairs. 'Your wife is ill in her head, and this is all you can do!'

Archie hugged the Hoover to his chest and took it into the crowded living room, where, under several pairs of reproachful eyes, he got out his toolbox and started work on it.

'Look at him,' said one of the Italian grandmothers, the more glamorous one with the big scarves and fewer moles, 'he take everything, capisce? He take-a her mind, he take-a the blender, he take-a the old stereo – he take-a everything except the floorboards. It make-a you sick . . .'

The woman from the council, who even on dry days resembled a long-haired cat soaked to the skin, shook her skinny head in agreement. 'It's disgusting, you don't have to tell me, it's disgusting . . . and naturally, we're the ones left to sort out the mess; it's *muggins* here who has to –'

Which was overlapped by the nurse: 'She can't stay here alone, can she . . . now *he's* buggered off, poor woman . . . she needs a proper home, she needs . . .'

I'm here, Archie felt like saying, *I'm right here you know, I'm bloody right here. And it was my blender*.

But he wasn't one for confrontation, Archie. He listened to them all for another fifteen minutes, mute as he tested the Hoover's suction against pieces of newspaper, until he was overcome by the sensation that Life was an enormous rucksack so impossibly heavy that, even though it meant losing everything, it was infinitely easier to leave all baggage here on the roadside and walk on into the blackness. *You don't need the blender, Archie-boy, you don't need the Hoover. This stuff's all dead weight. Just lay down the rucksack, Arch, and join the happy campers in the sky*. Was that wrong? To Archie – ex-wife and ex-wife's relatives in one ear, spluttering vacuum in the other – it just seemed that The End was unavoidably nigh. Nothing personal to God or whatever.

It just felt like the end of the world. And he was going to need more than poor whisky, novelty crackers and a paltry box of Quality Street – all the strawberry ones already scoffed – to justify entering another annum.

Patiently he fixed the Hoover, and vacuumed the living room with a strange methodical finality, shoving the nozzle into the most difficult corners. Solemnly he flipped a coin (heads, life, tails, death) and felt nothing in particular when he found himself staring at the dancing lion. Quietly he detached the Hoover tube, put it in a suitcase, and left the house for the last time.

But dying's no easy trick. And suicide can't be put on a list of Things to Do in between cleaning the grill pan and levelling the sofa leg with a brick. It is the decision not to do, to un-do; a kiss blown at oblivion. No matter what anyone says, suicide takes guts. It's for heroes and martyrs, truly vainglorious men. Archie was none of these. He was a man whose significance in the Greater Scheme of Things could be figured along familiar ratios:

Pebble: Beach.

Raindrop: Ocean.

Needle: Haystack.

So for a few days he ignored the decision of the coin and just drove around with the Hoover tube. At nights he looked out through the windscreen into the monstropolous sky and had the old realization of his universal proportions, feeling what it was to be tiny and rootless. He thought about the dent he might make on the world if he disappeared, and it seemed negligible, too small to calculate. He squandered spare minutes wondering whether 'Hoover' had become a generic term for vacuum cleaners or whether it was, as others have argued, just a brand name. And all the time the Hoover tube lay like a great flaccid cock on his back seat, mocking his quiet fear, laughing at his pigeon-steps as he approached the executioner, sneering at his impotent indecision.

Then, on the 29th of December, he went to see his old friend Samad Miah Iqbal. An unlikely compadre possibly, but still the oldest friend he had – a Bengali Muslim he had fought alongside back when the fighting had to be done, who reminded him of that war; that war that reminded some people of fatty bacon and painted-on-stockings but recalled in Archie gunshots and card games and the taste of a sharp, foreign alcohol.

'Archie, my dear friend,' Samad had said, in his warm, hearty tones. 'You must forget all this wife-trouble. Try a new life. That is what you need. Now, enough of all this: I will match your five bob and raise you five.'

They were sitting in their new haunt, O'Connell's Pool House, playing poker with only three hands, two of Archie's and one of Samad's – Samad's right hand being a broken thing, grey-skinned and unmoving, dead in every way bar the blood that ran through it. The place they sat in, where they met each evening for dinner, was half café, half gambling den, owned by an Iraqi family, the many members of which shared a bad skin condition.

'Look at me. Marrying Alsana has given me this new lease on living, you understand? She opens up for me the new possibilities. She's so young, so vital – like a breath of fresh air. You come to me for advice? Here it is. Don't live this old life – it's a sick life, Archibald. It does you no good. No good whatsoever.'

Samad had looked at him with a great sympathy, for he felt very tenderly for Archie. Their wartime friendship had been severed by thirty years of separation across continents, but in the spring of 1973 Samad had come to England, a middle-aged man seeking a new life with his twenty-year-old new bride, the diminutive, moon-faced Alsana Begum with her shrewd eyes. In a fit of nostalgia, and because he was the only man Samad knew on this little island, Samad had sought Archie out, moved into the same London borough. And slowly but surely a kind of friendship was being rekindled between the two men.

'You play like a faggot,' said Samad, laying down the winning queens back to back. He flicked them with the thumb of his left hand in one elegant move, making them fall to the table in a fan shape.

'I'm old,' said Archie, throwing his cards in, 'I'm old. Who'd have me now? It was hard enough convincing anybody the first time.'

'That is nonsense, Archibald. You have not even met the right one yet. This Ophelia, Archie, she is not the right one. From what you leave me to understand she is not even for this time –'

He referred to Ophelia's madness, which led her to believe, half of the time, that she was the maid of the celebrated fifteenth-century art lover Cosimo de' Medici.

'She is born, she lives, simply in the wrong time! This is just not her day! Maybe not her millennium. Modern life has caught that woman completely unawares and up the arse. Her mind is gone. Buggered. And you? You have picked up the wrong life in the cloakroom and you must return it. Besides, she has not blessed you with children . . . and life without children, Archie, what is it for? But there are second chances; oh yes, there are second chances in life. Believe me, I know. You,' he continued, raking in the 10p's with the side of his bad hand, 'should never have married her.'

Bloody hindsight, thought Archie. It's always 20/20.

Finally, two days after this discussion, early on New Year's morning, the pain had reached such a piercing level that Archie was no longer able to cling to Samad's advice. He had decided instead to mortify his own flesh, to take his own life, to free himself from a life path that had taken him down numerous wrong turnings, led him deep into the wilderness and finally petered out completely, its breadcrumb course gobbled up by the birds.

Once the car started to fill with gas, he had experienced the obligatory flashback of his life to date. It turned out to be a short, unedifying viewing experience, low on entertainment value, the metaphysical equivalent of the Queen's Speech. A dull childhood, a bad marriage, a dead-end job – that classic triumvirate – they all flicked by quickly, silently, with little dialogue, feeling pretty much the same as they did the first time round. He was no great believer in destiny, Archie, but on reflection it did seem that a special effort of predestination had ensured his life had been picked out for him like a company Christmas present – early, and the same as everyone else's.

There was the war, of course; he had been in the war, only for the last year of it, aged just seventeen, but it hardly counted. Not frontline, nothing like that. He and Samad, old Sam, Sammy-boy, they had a few tales to tell, mind, Archie even had a bit of shrapnel in the leg for anyone who cared to see it – but nobody did. No one wanted to talk about *that* any more. It was like a club-foot, or a disfiguring mole. It was like nose hair. People looked away. If someone said to Archie, *What have you done in life, then,* or *What's your biggest memory*, well, God help him if he mentioned the war; eyes glazed over, fingers tapped, everybody offered to buy the next round. No one really wanted to *know*.

Summer of 1955 Archie went to Fleet Street with his best winkle-pickers on, looking for work as a war correspondent. Poncey-looking bloke with a thin moustache and a thin voice had said, *Any experience, Mr Jones?* And Archie had explained. All about Samad. All about their Churchill tank. Then this poncey one had leant over the desk, all smug, all suited, and said, *We would require something other than merely having fought in a war, Mr Jones. War experience isn't really relevant.*

And that was it, wasn't it. There was no relevance in the war – not in '55, even less now in '74. Nothing he did *then* mattered *now*. The skills you learnt were, in the modern parlance, not relevant, *not transferable.*

Was there anything else, Mr Jones?

But of course there bloody wasn't anything else, the British education system having tripped him up with a snigger many years previously. Still, he had a good eye for the look of a thing, for the shape of a thing, and that's how he had ended up in the job at Morgan*Hero*, twenty years and counting in a printing firm in the Euston Road, designing the way all kinds of things should be *folded* – envelopes, direct mail, brochures, leaflets – not much of an achievement, maybe, but you'll find things need folds, they need to overlap, otherwise life would be like a broadsheet: flapping in the wind and down the street so you lose the important sections. Not that Archie had much time for the broadsheets. If they couldn't be bothered to fold them properly, why should he bother to read them (that's what he wanted to know)?

What else? Well, Archie hadn't always folded paper. Once upon a time he had been a track cyclist. What Archie liked about track cycling was the way you went round and round. Round and round. Giving you chance after chance to get a bit better at it, to make a faster lap, to do it *right*. Except the thing about Archie was he *never did* get any better. 62.8 seconds. Which is a pretty good time, world-class standard, even. But for three years he got precisely 62.8 seconds on every single lap. The other cyclists used to take breaks to watch him do it. Lean their bikes against the incline and time him with the second hand of their wrist watches. 62.8 every time. That kind of inability to improve is really very rare. That kind of consistency is miraculous, in a way.

Archie liked track cycling, he was consistently good at it and it provided him with the only truly great memory he had. In 1948, Archie Jones had participated in the Olympics in London, sharing thirteenth place (62.8 seconds) with a Swedish gynaecologist called Horst Ibelgaufts. Unfortunately this fact had been omitted from the Olympic records by a sloppy secretary who returned one morning after a coffee break with something else on her mind and missed his name as she transcribed one list to another piece of paper. Madam Posterity stuck Archie down the arm of the sofa and forgot about him. His only proof that the event had taken place at all were the periodic letters and notes he had received over the years from Ibelgaufts himself. Notes like:

17 May 1957

Dear Archibald,

I enclose a picture of my good wife and I in our garden in front of a rather unpleasant construction site. Though it may not look like Arcadia, it is here that I am building a crude velodrome – nothing like the one you and I raced in, but sufficient for my needs. It will be on a far smaller scale, but you see, it is for the children we are yet to have. I see them pedalling around it in my dreams and wake up with a glorious smile upon my face! Once it is completed, we insist that you visit us. Who more worthy to christen the track of your earnest competitor,

Horst Ibelgaufts?

And the postcard that lay on the dashboard this very day, the day of his Almost Death:

28 December 1974

Dear Archibald,

I am taking up the harp. A New Year's resolution, if you like. Late in the day, I realize, but you're never too old to teach the old dog in you new tricks, don't you feel? I tell you, it's a heavy instrument to lay against your shoulder, but the sound of it is quite angelic and my wife thinks me quite sensitive because of it. Which is more than she could say for my old cycling obsession! But then, cycling was only ever understood by old boys like you, Archie, and of course the author of this little note, your old contender,

Horst Ibelgaufts

He had not met Horst since the race, but he remembered him affectionately as an enormous man with strawberry-blond hair, orange freckles and misaligned nostrils, who dressed like an international playboy and seemed too large for his bike. After the race Horst had got Archie horribly drunk and procured two Soho whores who seemed to know Horst well ('I make many business trips to your fair capital, Archibald,' Horst had explained). The last Archie had ever seen of Horst was an unwanted glimpse of his humongous pink arse bobbing up and down in the adjoining room of an Olympic chalet. The next morning, waiting at the front desk, was the first letter of his large correspondence:

Dear Archibald,

In an oasis of work and competition, women are truly sweet and easy refreshment, don't you agree? I'm afraid I had to leave early to catch the necessary plane, but I compel you, Archie: Don't be a stranger! I think of us now as two men as close as our finish! I tell you, whoever said thirteenth was unlucky was a bigger fool than your friend,

Horst Ibelgaufts

P.S. Please make sure that Daria and Melanie get home fine and well.

Daria was his one. Terribly skinny, ribs like lobster cages and no chest to speak of, but she was a lovely sort: kind; soft with her kisses and with double-jointed wrists she liked to show off in a pair of long silk gloves – set you back four clothing coupons at least. 'I *like* you,' Archie remembered saying helplessly, as she replaced the gloves and put on her stockings. She turned, smiled. And though she was a professional, he got the feeling she liked him too. Maybe he should have left with her right then, run to the hills. But at the time it seemed impossible, too involved, what with a young wife with one in the oven (an hysterical, fictional pregnancy, as it turned out, a big bump full of hot air), what with his dodgy leg, what with the lack of hills.

Strangely, Daria was the final pulse of thought that passed through Archie just before he blacked out. It was the thought of a whore he met once twenty years ago, it was Daria and her smile which made him cover Mo's apron with tears of joy as the butcher saved his life. He had seen her in his mind: a beautiful woman in a doorway with a *come hither* look; and realized he regretted not coming hither. If there was any chance of ever seeing a look like that again, then he wanted the second chance, he wanted the extra time. Not just this second, but the next and the next – all the time in the world.

Later that morning, Archie did an ecstatic eight circuits of Swiss Cottage roundabout in his car, his head stuck out the window while a stream of air hit the teeth at the back of his mouth like a wind sock. He thought: *Blimey. So this is what it feels like when some bugger saves your life. Like you've just been handed a great big wad of Time*. He drove straight past his flat, straight past the street signs (Hendon 3¾), laughing like a loon. At the traffic lights he flipped ten pence and smiled when the result seemed to agree that Fate was pulling him towards another life. Like a dog on a lead round a corner. Generally, women can't do this, but men retain the ancient ability to leave a family and a past. They just unhook themselves, like removing a fake beard, and skulk discreetly back into society, changed men. Unrecognizable. In this manner, a new Archie is about to emerge. We have caught him on the hop. For he is in a past-tense, future-perfect kind of mood. He is in a *maybe this, maybe that* kind of mood. Approaching a forked road, he slows down, checks his undistinguished face in the wing-mirror, and quite indiscriminately chooses a route he's never taken before, a residential street leading to a place called Queens Park. Go straight past *Go!*, Archie-boy, he tells himself; collect two hundred and don't for gawd's sake look back.

Tim Westleigh (more commonly known as Merlin) finally registered the persistent ringing of a doorbell. He picked himself off the kitchen floor, waded through an ocean of supine bodies, and opened the door to arrive face-to-face with a middle-aged man dressed head-to-toe in grey corduroy, holding a ten pence coin in his open palm. As Merlin was later to reflect when describing the incident, at any time of the day corduroy is a highly stressful fabric. Rent men wear it. Tax men too. History teachers add leather elbow patches. To be confronted with a mass of it, at nine in the a.m., on the first day of a New Year, is an apparition lethal in its sheer quantity of negative vibes.

'What's the deal, man?' Merlin blinked in the doorway at the man in corduroy who stood on his doorstep illuminated by winter sunshine. 'Encyclopedias or God?'

Archie noted the kid had an unnerving way of emphasizing certain words by moving his head in a wide circular movement from the right shoulder to the left. Then, when the circle was completed, he would nod several times.

''Cos if it's encyclopedias we've got enough, like, *information* . . . and if it's God, you've got the wrong house. We're in a mellow place, here. Know what I mean?' Merlin concluded, doing the nodding thing and moving to shut the door.

Archie shook his head, smiled and remained where he was.

'Erm . . . are you all right?' asked Merlin, hand on the doorknob. 'Is there something I can do for you? Are you high on something?'

'I saw your sign,' said Archie.

Merlin pulled on a joint and looked amused. 'That sign?' He bent his head to follow Archie's gaze. The white bedsheet hanging down from an upper window. Across it, in large rainbow-coloured lettering, was painted: WELCOME TO THE 'END OF THE WORLD' PARTY, 1975.

Merlin shrugged. 'Yeah, sorry, man, looks like it wasn't. Bit of a disappointment, that. Or a blessing,' he added amiably, 'depending on your point of view.'

'Blessing,' said Archie, with passion. 'Hundred per cent, bona fide *blessing*.'

'Did you, er, dig the sign, then?' asked Merlin, taking a step back behind the doorstep in case the man was violent as well as schiz. 'You into that kind of scene? It was kind of a joke, you see, more than anything.'

'Caught my eye, you might say,' said Archie, still beaming like a mad man. 'I was just driving along looking for somewhere, you know, somewhere to have another drink, New Year's Day, hair of the dog and all that – and I've had a bit of a rough morning all in all – and it just sort of *struck* me. I flipped a coin and thought: why not?'

Merlin looked perplexed at the turn the conversation was taking. 'Er . . . party's pretty much over, man. Besides, I think you're a little *advanced* in years . . . if you know what I mean . . .' Here Merlin turned gauche; underneath the dakshiki he was at heart a good middle-class boy, instilled with respect for his elders. 'I mean,' he said after a difficult pause, 'it's a bit of a younger crowd than you might be used to. Kind of a commune scene.'

'But I was so much older then,' sang Archie mischievously, quoting a ten-year-old Dylan track, arching his head round the door, *'I'm younger than that now.'*

Merlin took a cigarette from behind his ear, lit it, and frowned. 'Look, man . . . I can't just let anyone in off the street, you know? I mean, you could be the police, you could be a freak, you could –'

But something about Archie's face – huge, innocent, sweetly expectant – reminded Tim what his estranged father, the Vicar of Snarebrook, had to say about Christian charity every Sunday from his pulpit. 'Oh, what the hell. It's New Year's Day, for fuckssake. You best come in.'

Archie sidestepped Merlin, and moved into a long hallway with four open-doored rooms branching off from it, a staircase leading to another storey, and a garden at the end of it all. Detritus of every variety – animal, mineral, vegetable – lined the floor; a great mass of bedding, under which people lay sleeping, stretched from one end of the hallway to the other, a red sea which grudgingly separated each time Archie took a step forward. Inside the rooms, in certain corners, could be witnessed the passing of bodily fluids: kissing, breast-feeding, fucking, throwing up – all the things Archie's Sunday Supplement had informed him could be found in a commune. He toyed for a moment with the idea of entering the fray, losing himself between the bodies (he had all this new *time* on his hands, masses and masses of it, dribbling through his fingers), but decided a stiff drink was preferable. He tackled the hallway until he reached the other end of the house and stepped out into the chilly garden, where some, having given up on finding a space in the warm house, had opted for the cold lawn. With a whisky tonic in mind, he headed for the picnic table, where something the shape and colour of Jack Daniels had sprung up like a mirage in a desert of empty wine bottles.

'Mind if I . . . ?'

Two black guys, a topless Chinese girl, and a white woman wearing a toga were sitting around on wooden kitchen chairs, playing rummy. Just as Archie reached for the Jack Daniels, the white woman shook her head and made the signal of a stubbed-out cigarette.

'Tobacco sea, I'm afraid, darling. Some evil bastard put his fag out in some perfectly acceptable whisky. There's Babycham and some other inexorable shit over here.'

Archie smiled in gratitude for the warning and the kind offer.

He took a seat and poured himself a big glass of Liebfraumilch instead.

Many drinks later, and Archie could not remember a time in his life when he had not known Clive and Leo, Wan-Si and Petronia, intimately. With his back turned and a piece of charcoal, he could have rendered every puckered goosepimple around Wan-Si's nipples, every stray hair that fell in Petronia's face as she spoke. By 11 a.m., he loved them all dearly, they were the children he had never had. In return, they told him he was in possession of a unique soul for a man of his age. Everybody agreed some intensely positive karmic energy was circulating in and around Archie, the kind of thing strong enough to prompt a butcher to pull down a car window at the critical moment. And it turned out Archie was the first man over forty ever invited to join the commune; it turned out there had been talk for some time of the need for an older sexual presence to satisfy some of the more adventurous women. 'Great,' said Archie. 'Fantastic. That'll be me, then.' He felt so close to them that he was confused when around midday their relationship suddenly soured, and he found himself stabbed by a hangover and knee deep in an argument about the Second World War, of all things.

'I don't even know how we got into this,' groaned Wan-Si, who had covered up finally just when they decided to move indoors, Archie's corduroy slung round her petite shoulders. 'Let's not get into this. I'd rather go to bed than get into this.'

'We *are* into it, we *are* into it,' Clive was ranting. 'This is the whole problem with his generation, they think they can hold up the war as some kind of –'

Archie was grateful when Leo interrupted Clive and dragged the argument into some further subset of the original one, which Archie had started (some unwise remark three quarters of an hour ago about military service building up a young man's character) and then immediately regretted when it required him to defend himself at regular interludes. Freed finally of this obligation, he sat on the stairs, letting the row continue above while he placed his head in his hands.

Shame. He would have *liked* to have been part of a commune. If he'd played his cards right instead of starting a ding-dong, he might have had free love and bare breasts all over the gaff; maybe even a portion of allotment for growing fresh food. For a while (around 2 a.m., when he was telling Wan-Si about his childhood) it had looked like his new life was going to be fabulous, and from now on he was always going to say the right thing at the right time, and everywhere he went people would love him. *Nobody's fault*, thought Archie, mulling over the balls-up, *nobody's fault but my own*, but he wondered whether there wasn't some higher pattern to it. Maybe there will always be men who say the right thing at the right time, who step forward like Thespis at just the right moment of history, and then there will be men like Archie Jones who are just there to make up the numbers. Or, worse still, who are given their big break only to come in on cue and die a death right there, centre stage, for all to see.

A dark line would now be drawn underneath the whole incident, underneath the whole sorry day, had not something happened that led to the transformation of Archie Jones in every particular that a man can be transformed; and not due to any particular effort on his part, but by means of the entirely random, adventitious collision of one person with another. Something happened by accident. That accident was Clara Bowden.

But first a description: Clara Bowden was beautiful in all senses except maybe, by virtue of being black, the classical. Clara Bowden was magnificently tall, black as ebony and crushed sable, with hair plaited in a horseshoe which pointed up when she felt lucky, down when she didn't. At this moment it was up. It is hard to know whether that was significant.

She needed no bra – she was independent, even of gravity – she wore a red halterneck which stopped below her bust, underneath which she wore her belly button (beautifully) and underneath that some very tight yellow jeans. At the end of it all were some strappy heels of a light brown suede, and she came striding down the stairs on them like some kind of vision or, as it seemed to Archie as he turned to observe her, like a reared-up thoroughbred.

Now, as Archie understood it, in movies and the like it is common for someone to be so striking that when they walk down the stairs the crowd goes silent. In life he had never seen it. But it happened with Clara Bowden. She walked down the stairs in slow motion, surrounded by afterglow and fuzzy lighting. And not only was she the most beautiful thing he had ever seen, she was also the most comforting woman he had ever met. Her beauty was not a sharp, cold commodity. She smelt musty, womanly, like a bundle of your favourite clothes. Though she was disorganized physically – legs and arms speaking a slightly different dialect from her central nervous system – even her gangly demeanour seemed to Archie exceptionally elegant. She wore her sexuality with an older woman's ease, and not (as with most of the girls Archie had run with in the past) like an awkward purse, never knowing how to hold it, where to hang it or when to just put it down.

'Cheer up, bwoy,' she said in a lilting Caribbean accent that reminded Archie of That Jamaican Cricketer, 'it might never happen.'

'I think it already has.'

Archie, who had just dropped a fag from his mouth which had been burning itself to death anyway, saw Clara quickly tread it underfoot. She gave him a wide grin that revealed possibly her one imperfection. A complete lack of teeth in the top of her mouth.

'Man . . . dey get knock out,' she lisped, seeing his surprise.

'But I tink to myself: come de end of de world, d'Lord won't mind if I have no toofs.' She laughed softly.

'Archie Jones,' said Archie, offering her a Marlboro.

'Clara.' She whistled inadvertently as she smiled and breathed in the smoke. 'Archie Jones, you look justabout exackly how I feel. Have Clive and dem people been talking foolishness at you? Clive, you bin playing wid dis poor man?'

Clive grunted – the memory of Archie had all but disappeared with the effects of the wine – and continued where he left off, accusing Leo of misunderstanding the difference between political and physical sacrifice.

'Oh, no . . . nothing serious,' Archie burbled, useless in the face of her exquisite face. 'Bit of a disagreement, that's all. Clive and I have different views about a few things. Generation gap, I suppose.'

Clara slapped him on the hand. 'Hush yo mout! You're nat dat ol'. I seen older.'

'I'm old enough,' said Archie, and then, just because he felt like telling her, 'You won't believe me, but I almost died today.'

Clara raised an eyebrow. 'You don't say. Well, come and join de club. Dere are a lot of us about dis marnin'. What a *strange* party dis is. You know,' she said brushing a long hand across his bald spot, 'you look pretty djam good for someone come so close to St Peter's Gate. You wan' some advice?'

Archie nodded vigorously. He always wanted advice, he was a huge fan of second opinions. That's why he never went anywhere without a ten pence coin.

'Go home, get some rest. Marnin' de the world new, every time. Man . . . dis life no easy!'

What home? thought Archie. He had unhooked the old life, he was walking into unknown territory.

'Man . . .' Clara repeated, patting him on the back, 'dis life no easy!'

She let off another long whistle and a rueful laugh, and, unless he was really going nuts, Archie saw that *come hither* look; identical to Daria's; tinged with a kind of sadness, disappointment; like she didn't have a great deal of other options. Clara was nineteen. Archibald was forty-seven.

Six weeks later they were married.

2 *Teething Trouble*

But Archie did not pluck Clara Bowden from a vacuum. And it's about time people told the truth about beautiful women. They do not shimmer down staircases. They do not descend, as was once supposed, from on high, attached to nothing other than wings. Clara was *from* somewhere. She had *roots*. More specifically, she was from Lambeth (via Jamaica) and she was connected, through tacit adolescent agreement, to one Ryan Topps. Because before Clara was beautiful she was ugly. And before there was Clara and Archie there was Clara and Ryan. And there is no getting away from Ryan Topps. Just as a good historian need recognize Hitler's Napoleonic ambitions in the east in order to comprehend his reluctance to invade the British in the west, so Ryan Topps is essential to any understanding of why Clara did what she did. Ryan is indispensable. There was Clara and Ryan for eight months before Clara and Archie were drawn together from opposite ends of a staircase. And Clara might never have run into the arms of Archie Jones if she hadn't been running, quite as fast as she could, away from Ryan Topps.

Poor Ryan Topps. He was a mass of unfortunate physical characteristics. He was very thin and very tall, red-headed, flat-footed and freckled to such an extent that his skin was rarer than his freckles. Ryan fancied himself as a bit of a Mod. He wore ill-fitting grey suits with black polo-necks. He wore Chelsea boots after everyone else had stopped wearing them. While the rest of the world discovered the joys of the electronic synthesizer, Ryan swore allegiance to the little men with big guitars: to the Kinks, the Small Faces, the Who. Ryan Topps rode a green Vespa GS scooter which he polished twice a day with a baby's nappy and kept encased in a custom-built corrugated-iron shield. To Ryan's way of thinking, a Vespa was not merely a mode of transport but an ideology, family, friend and lover all rolled into one paragon of late forties engineering.

Ryan Topps, as one might expect, had few friends.

Clara Bowden was gangly, buck-toothed, a Jehovah's Witness, and saw in Ryan a kindred spirit. A typical teenage female panopticon, she knew everything there was to know about Ryan Topps long before they ever spoke. She knew the basics: same school (St Jude's Community School, Lambeth), same height (six foot one); she knew he was, like her, neither Irish nor Roman Catholic, which made them two islands floating surrounded by the popish ocean of St Jude's, enrolled in the school by the accident of their postcodes, reviled by teachers and pupils alike. She knew the name of his bike, she read the tops of his records as they popped up over the brim of his bag. She even knew things about him he didn't know: for example, she knew he was the Last Man on Earth. Every school has one, and in St Jude's, as in other seats of learning, it was the girls who chose this moniker and dished it out. There were, of course, variations:

Mr *Not for a Million Pounds*.

Mr *Not to Save My Mother's Life*.

Mr *Not for World Peace*.

But, generally, the schoolgirls of St Jude's kept to the tried and tested formula. Though Ryan would never be privy to the conversations of the school's female changing rooms, Clara knew. She knew how the object of her affections was discussed, she kept an ear out, she knew what he amounted to when you got down to it, down amongst the sweat and the training bras and the sharp flick of a wet towel.

'Ah, Jaysus, you're not listening. I'm saying, if he was the *last* man on earth!'

'I *still* wouldn't.'

'Ah, bollocks you *would*!'

'But listen: the whole bleedin' world has been hit by the bomb, like in Japan, roight? An' all the good-lookin' men, all the *rides* like your man Nicky Laird, they're all dead. They've all been burnt to a crisp. An' all that's left is Ryan Topps and a bunch of cockroaches.'

'On me life, I'd rather sleep with the cockroaches.'

Ryan's unpopularity at St Jude's was equalled only by Clara's. On her first day at the school her mother had explained to her she was about to enter the devil's lair, filled her satchel with two hundred copies of the *Watchtower* and instructed her to go and do the Lord's work. Week after week she shuffled through the school, head hung to the ground, handing out magazines, murmuring, 'Only Jehovah saves'; in a school where an overexcitable pustule could send you to Coventry, a six-foot black missionary in knee socks attempting to convert six hundred Catholics to the church of the Jehovah's Witnesses equalled social leprosy.

So Ryan was red as a beetroot. And Clara was black as yer boot. Ryan's freckles were a join-the-dots enthusiast's wet dream. Clara could circumnavigate an apple with her front teeth before her tongue got anywhere near it. Not even the Catholics would forgive them for it (and Catholics give out forgiveness at about the same rate politicians give out promises and whores give out); not even St Jude, who got saddled way back in the 1st century with the patronage of hopeless causes (due to the tonal similarity between Jude and Judas), was prepared to get involved.

At five o'clock each day, as Clara sat in her house attending to the message of the gospels or composing a leaflet condemning the heathen practice of blood transfusion, Ryan Topps would scoot by her open window on his way home. The Bowden living room sat just below street level, and had bars on its window, so all views were partial. Generally, she would see feet, wheels, car exhausts, swinging umbrellas. Such slight glimpses were often telling; a lively imagination could squeeze much pathos out of a frayed lace, a darned sock, a low swinging bag that had seen better days. But nothing affected her more deeply than gazing after the disappearing tailpipe of Ryan's scooter. Lacking any name for the furtive rumblings that appeared in her lower abdomen on these occasions, Clara called it the spirit of the Lord. She felt that somehow she was going to save the heathen Ryan Topps. Clara meant to gather this boy close to her breast, keep him safe from the temptation that besets us all around, prepare him for the day of his redemption. (And wasn't there somewhere, lower than her abdomen – somewhere down in the nether region of the unmentionables – was there not the half-conceived hope that Ryan Topps might save *her*?)

If Hortense Bowden caught her daughter sitting wistfully by the barred window, listening to the retreating splutter of an engine while the pages of the *New Bible* flicked over in the breeze, she koofed her up-side her head and thanked her to remember that only 144,000 of the Witnesses of Jehovah would sit in the court of the Lord on Judgement Day. Amongst which number of the Anointed there was no space for nasty-looking so-and-sos on motorcycles.

'But what if we saved –'

'Some people,' Hortense asserted with a snort, 'have done such a hol' heap of sinning, it *late* for dem to be making eyes at Jehovah. It take effort to be close to Jehovah. It take devotion and dedication. *Blessed are the pure in heart for they alone shall see God.* Matthew 5:8. Isn't dat right, Darcus?'

Darcus Bowden, Clara's father, was an odoriferous, moribund, salivating old man entombed in a bug-infested armchair from which he had never been seen to remove himself, not even, thanks to a catheter, to visit the outdoor toilet. Darcus had come over to England fourteen years earlier and spent the whole of that period in the far corner of the living room, watching television. The original intention had been that he should come to England and earn enough money to enable Clara and Hortense to come over, join him and settle down. However, on arrival, a mysterious illness had debilitated Darcus Bowden. An illness that no doctor could find any physical symptoms of, but which manifested itself in the most incredible lethargy, creating in Darcus – admittedly, never the most vibrant of men – a lifelong affection for the dole, the armchair and British television. In 1972, enraged by a fourteen-year wait, Hortense decided finally to make the journey on her own steam. Steam was something Hortense had in abundance. She arrived on the doorstep with the seventeen-year-old Clara, broke down the door in a fury and – so the legend went back in St Elizabeth – gave Darcus Bowden the tongue-whipping of his life. Some say this onslaught lasted four hours, some say she quoted every book of the bible by memory and it took a whole day and a whole night. What is certain is, at the end of it all, Darcus slumped deeper into the recesses of his chair, looked mournfully at the television with whom he had had such an understanding, compassionate relationship – so uncomplicated, so much innocent affection – and a tear squeezed its way out of its duct and settled in a crag underneath his eye. Then he said just one word: Hmph.

Hmph was all Darcus said or ever was to say after. Ask Darcus anything; query him on any subject at any hour of the day and night; interrogate him; chat with him; implore him; declare your love for him; accuse him or vindicate him and he will give you only one answer.

'I say, isn't dat right, Darcus?'

'*Hmph.*'

'An' it not,' exclaimed Hortense, returning to Clara, having received Darcus's grunt of approval, 'dat young man's *soul* you boddrin' yourself wid! How many times must I tell you – you got no time for bwoys!'

For Time was running out in the Bowden household. This

was 1974, and Hortense was preparing for the End of the World, which, in the house diary, she had marked carefully in blue biro: 1 January 1975. This was not a solitary psychosis of the Bowdens. There were eight million Jehovah's Witnesses waiting with her. Hortense was in large, albeit eccentric, company. A personal letter had come to Hortense (as secretary of the Lambeth branch of the Kingdom Halls), with a photocopied signature from William J. Rangeforth of the largest Kingdom Hall in the USA, Brooklyn, confirming the date. The end of the world had been *officially* confirmed with a gold-plated letterhead, and Hortense had risen to the occasion by setting it in an attractive mahogany frame. She had given it pride of place on a doily on top of the television between a glass figurine of Cinderella on her way to the Ball and a tea-cosy embroidered with the Ten Commandments. She had asked Darcus whether he thought it looked nice. He had hmphed his assent.

The end of the world was nigh. And this was not – the Lambeth branch of the church of the Jehovah's Witnesses was to be assured – like the mistakes of 1914 and 1925. They had been promised the entrails of sinners wrapped around the trunks of trees, and this time the entrails of sinners wrapped around the trunks of trees *would* appear. They had waited so long for the rivers of blood to overflow the gutters in the high street, and now their thirst *would* be satiated. The time had come. This was the right date, this was the only date, all other dates that might have been proffered in the past were the result of some bad calculations: someone forgot to add, someone forgot to minus, someone forgot to carry the one. But now was the time. The real thing. 1 January 1975.

Hortense, for one, was glad to hear it. The first morning of 1925 she had wept like a baby when she awoke to find – instead of hail and brimstone and universal destruction – the continuance of daily life, the regular running of the buses and trains. It had been for nothing, then, all that tossing and turning the previous night; waiting for those neighbours, those who failed to listen to your warnings, to sink under a hot and terrible fire that shall separate their skin from their bones, shall melt the eyes in their sockets, and burn the babies that suckle at their mothers' breasts . . . so many of your neighbours shall die that day that their bodies, if lined up side by side, will stretch three hundred times round the earth and on their charred remains shall the true Witnesses of the Lord walk to his side.

– *The Clarion Bell*, issue 245

How bitterly she had been disappointed! But the wounds of 1925 had healed, and Hortense was once again ready to be convinced that apocalypse, just as the right holy Mr Rangeforth had explained, was round the corner. The promise of the 1914 generation still stood: *This generation shall not pass, till all these things be fulfilled* (Matthew 24:34). Those who were alive in 1914 would live to see the Armageddon. It had been promised. Born in 1907, Hortense was getting old now, she was getting tired and her peers were dying off like flies. 1975 looked like the last chance.

Had not two hundred of the church's best intellectuals spent twenty years examining the bible, and hadn't this date been their unanimous conclusion? Had they not read between the lines in Daniel, scanned for the hidden meaning in Revelation, correctly identified the Asian wars (Korea and Vietnam) as the period spoken of by the angel, 'a time, and times, and half a time'? Hortense was convinced these were the sign of signs. These were the final days. There were eight months to the end of the world. Hardly enough time! There were banners to be made, articles to be written ('Will the Lord Forgive the Onanist?'), doorsteps to be trod, bells to be rung. There was Darcus to think about – who could not walk to the fridge without assistance – how was he to make it to the kingdom of the Lord? And in all Clara must lend a hand; there was no time for boys, for Ryan Topps, for skulking around, for adolescent angst. For Clara was not like other teenagers. She was the Lord's child, Hortense's miracle baby.

Hortense was all of forty-eight when she heard the Lord's voice while gutting a fish one morning, Montego Bay, 1955. Straight away she threw down the marlin, caught the trolley car home and submitted to her least favourite activity in order to conceive the child He had asked for. Why had the Lord waited so long? Because the Lord wanted to show Hortense a miracle. For Hortense had been a miracle child herself, born in the middle of the legendary Kingston earthquake, 1907, when everybody else was busy dying – miracles ran in the family. Hortense saw it this way: if she could come into this world in the middle of a ground shaker, as parts of Montego Bay slipped into the sea, and fires came down from the mountains, then nobody had no excuses about nothing no how. She liked to say: 'Bein' *barn* is de hardest part! Once ya done dat – no problems.' So now that Clara was *here*, old enough to help her with doorstepping, administration, writing speeches and all the varied business of the church of the Jehovah's Witnesses, she'd better get on with it. No time for boys. This child's work was just beginning. Hortense – born while Jamaica crumbled – did not accept apocalypse before one's nineteenth birthday as any excuse for tardiness.

Yet strangely, and possibly because of Jehovah's well-documented penchant for moving in a mysterious manner, it was in performing the business of the Lord that Clara eventually met Ryan Topps face to face. The youth group of the Lambeth Kingdom Hall had been sent doorstepping on a Sunday morning, *Separating the sheep from the goats* (Matthew 25:31–46), and Clara, detesting the young Witness men with their bad ties and softly spoken voices, had set off alone with her own suitcase to ring bells along Creighton Road. The first few doors she received the usual pained faces: nice women shooing her away as politely as possible, making sure they didn't get too close, scared they might catch religion like an infection. As she got into the poorer end of the street, the reaction became more aggressive; shouts came from windows or behind closed doors.

'If that's the bloody Jehovah's Witnesses, tell 'em to piss off!'

Or, more imaginatively, 'Sorry, love, don't you know what day it is? It's Sunday, innit? I'm *knackered*. I've spent *all week* creating the land and oceans. It's me day of rest.'

At No. 75 she spent an hour with a fourteen-year-old physics whizz called Colin who wanted to intellectually disprove the existence of God while looking up her skirt. Then she rang No. 87. And Ryan Topps answered.

'Yeah?'

He stood there in all his red-headed, black polo-necked glory, his lip curled in a snarl.

'I . . . I . . .'

She tried desperately to forget what she was wearing: a white shirt complete with throat-ruffle, plaid knee-length skirt and sash that proudly stated NEARER MY GOD TO THEE.

'You want sommink?' said Ryan, taking a fierce drag of a dying cigarette. 'Or sommink?'

Clara tried her widest, buck-toothed smile and went on to auto-pilot. 'Marnin' to you, sir. I am from de Lambet Kingdom Hall, where we, de Witnesses of Jehovah, are waitin' for de Lord to come and grace us wid his holy presence once more; as he did briefly – bot sadly, invisibly – in de year of our farder, 1914. We believe dat when he makes himself known he will be bringing wid 'im de tree-fold fires of hell in Armageddon, dat day when precious few will be saved. Are you int'rested in –'

'Wot?'

Clara, close to tears at the shame of it, tried again. 'Are you int'rested in de teachins of Jehovah?'

'You wot?'

'In Jehovah – in de teachins of d'Lord. You see, it like a staircase.' Clara's last resort was always her mother's metaphor of the holy steps. 'I see dat you walkin' down and der's a missin' step comin'. I'm just tellin' you: watch your step! Me jus wan' share heaven wid you. Me nah wan' fe see you bruk-up your legs.'

Ryan Topps leant against the door frame and looked at her for a long time through his red fringe. Clara felt she was closing in on herself, like a telescope. It was only moments, surely, before she disappeared entirely.

'I 'ave some materials of readin' for your perusal – ' She fumbled with the lock of the suitcase, flipped the catch with her thumb but neglected to hold the other side of the case. Fifty copies of the *Watchtower* spilled over the doorstep.

'Bwoy, me kyant do nuttin' right today – '

She fell to the ground in a rush to pick them up and scraped the skin off her left knee. 'Ow!'

'Your name's Clara,' said Ryan slowly. 'You're from my school, ain't ya?'

'Yes, man,' said Clara, so jubilant he remembered her name that she forgot the pain. 'St Jude's.'

'I *know* wot it's called.'

Clara went as red as black people get and looked at the floor.

'Hopeless causes. Saint of,' said Ryan, picking something surreptitiously from his nose and flicking it into a flowerpot. 'IRA. The lot of 'em.'

Ryan surveyed the long figure of Clara once more, spending an inordinate amount of time on two sizeable breasts, the outline of their raised nipples just discernible through white polyester.

'You best come in,' he said finally, lowering his gaze to inspect the bleeding knee. 'Put somefin' on that.'

That very afternoon there were furtive fumblings on Ryan's couch (which went a good deal further than one might expect of a Christian girl) and the devil won another easy hand in God's poker game. Things were tweaked, and pushed and pulled; and by the time the bell rang for end of school Monday Ryan Topps and Clara Bowden (much to their school's collective disgust) were more or less an item; as the St Jude's phraseology went, they were 'dealing' with each other. Was it everything that Clara, in all her sweaty adolescent invention, had imagined?

Well, 'dealing' with Ryan turned out to consist of three major pastimes (in order of importance): admiring Ryan's scooter, admiring Ryan's records, admiring Ryan. But though other girls might have balked at dates that took place in Ryan's garage and consisted entirely of watching him pore over the engine of a scooter, eulogizing its intricacies and complexities, to Clara there was nothing more thrilling. She learnt quickly that Ryan was a man of painfully few words and that the rare conversations they had would only ever concern Ryan: his hopes, his fears (all scooter-related) and his peculiar belief that he and his scooter would not live long. For some reason, Ryan was convinced of the ageing fifties motto 'Live fast, die young', and, though his scooter didn't do more than 22 m.p.h. downhill, he liked to warn Clara in grim tones not to get 'too involved', for he wouldn't be here long; he was 'going out' early and with a 'bang'. She imagined herself holding the bleeding Ryan in her arms, hearing him finally declare his undying love; she saw herself as Mod Widow, wearing black polo-necks for a year and demanding 'Waterloo Sunset' be played at his funeral. Clara's inexplicable dedication to Ryan Topps knew no bounds. It transcended his bad looks, tedious personality and unsightly personal habits. Essentially, it transcended Ryan, for whatever Hortense claimed, Clara was a teenage girl like any other; the object of her passion was only an accessory to the passion itself, a passion that through its long suppression was now asserting itself with volcanic necessity. Over the ensuing months Clara's mind changed, Clara's clothes changed, Clara's walk changed, Clara's soul changed. All over the world girls were calling this change Donny Osmond or Michael Jackson or the Bay City Rollers. Clara chose to call it Ryan Topps.

There were no dates, in the normal sense. No flowers or restaurants, movies or parties. Occasionally, when more weed was required, Ryan would take her to visit a large squat in North London where an eighth came cheap and people too stoned to make out the features on your face acted like your best friends. Here, Ryan would ensconce himself in a hammock, and, after a few joints, progress from his usual monosyllabic to the entirely catatonic. Clara, who didn't smoke, sat at his feet, admired him, and tried to keep up with the general conversation around her. She had no tales to tell like the others, not like Merlin, like Clive, like Leo, Petronia, Wan-Si and the others. No anecdotes of LSD trips, of police brutality or marching on Trafalgar Square. But Clara made friends. A resourceful girl, she used what she had to amuse and terrify an assorted company of Hippies, Flakes, Freaks and Funky Folk: a different kind of extremity; tales of hellfire and damnation, of the devil's love of faeces, his passion for stripping skin, for red-hot-pokering eyeballs and the flaying of genitals – all the elaborate plans of Lucifer, that most exquisite of fallen angels, that were set for 1 January 1975.

Naturally, the thing called Ryan Topps began to push the End of the World further and further into the back-rooms of Clara's consciousness. So many other things were presenting themselves to her, so much new in life! If it were possible, she felt like one of the Anointed right now, right here in Lambeth. The more blessed she felt on earth, the more rarely she turned her thoughts towards heaven. In the end, it was the epic feat of long division that Clara simply couldn't figure. So many unsaved. Out of eight million Jehovah's Witnesses, only 144,000 men could join Christ in heaven. The good women and good-enough men would gain paradise on earth – not a bad booby prize all things considered – but that still left a few million who failed to make the grade. Add that to the heathens; to the Jews, Catholics, Muslims; to the poor jungle men in the Amazon whom Clara had wept for as a child; so many unsaved. The Witnesses prided themselves on the absence of hell in their theology – the punishment was torture, unimaginable torture on the final day, and then the grave was the grave. But to Clara, this seemed worse – the thought of the Great Crowd, enjoying themselves in earthly paradise, while the tortured, mutilated skeletons of the lost lay just under the topsoil.

On the one side stood all the mammoth quantities of people on the globe, unacquainted with the teachings of the *Watchtower* (some with no access to a postbox), unable to contact the Lambeth Kingdom Hall and receive helpful reading material about the road to redemption. On the other side, Hortense, her hair all wrapped up in iron rollers, tossing and turning in her sheets, gleefully awaiting the rains of sulphur to pour down upon the sinners, particularly the woman at No. 53. Hortense tried to explain: 'Dem dat died widout de knowing de Lord, will be *resurrected* and dem will have anudder chance.' But to Clara, it was still an inequitable equation. Unbalanceable books. Faith is hard to achieve, easy to lose. She became more and more reluctant to leave the impress of her knees in the red cushions in the Kingdom Hall. She would not wear sashes, carry banners or give out leaflets. She would not tell anyone about missing steps. She discovered dope, forgot the staircase and began taking the lift.

1 October 1974. A detention. Held back forty-five minutes after school (for claiming, in a music lesson, that Roger Daltrey was a greater musician than Johann Sebastian Bach) and as a result, Clara missed her four o'clock meeting with Ryan on the corner of Leenan Street. It was freezing cold and getting dark by the time she got out; she ran through piles of putrefying autumn leaves, searched the length and breadth of Leenan, but there was no sign. It was with dread that she approached her own front door, offering up to God a multitude of silent contracts (*I'll never have sex, I'll never smoke another joint, I'll never wear another skirt above the knee*) if only he could assure her that Ryan Topps had not rung her mother's doorbell looking for shelter from the wind.

'Clara! Come out of de cold.'

It was the voice Hortense put on when she had company – an over-compensation of all the consonants – the voice she used for pastors and white women.

Clara closed the front door behind her, and walked in a kind of terror through the living room, past the framed hologram of Jesus who wept (and then didn't), and into the kitchen.

'Dear Lord, she look like someting de cat dragged in, hmm?'

'Mmm,' said Ryan, who was happily shovelling a plate of ackee and saltfish into his mouth on the other side of the tiny kitchen table.

Clara stuttered, her buck teeth cutting shapes into her bottom lip. 'What are you doing *here*?'

'Ha!' cried Hortense, almost triumphant. 'You tink you can hide your friends from me for ever? De bwoy was cold, I let 'im in, we been havin' a nice chat, haven't we young man?'

'Mmm, yes, Mrs Bowden.'

'Well, don' look so shock. You'd tink I was gwan eat 'im up or someting, eh Ryan?' said Hortense, glowing in a manner Clara had never seen before.

'Yeah, right,' smirked Ryan. And together, Ryan Topps and Clara's mother began to laugh.

Is there anything more likely to take the shine off an affair than when the lover strikes up a convivial relationship with the lovee's mother? As the nights got darker and shorter and it became harder to pick Ryan out of the crowd who milled outside the school gates each day at three thirty, a dejected Clara would make the long walk home only to find her lover once more in the kitchen, chatting happily with Hortense, devouring the Bowden household's cornucopia of goodies: ackee and saltfish, beef jerky, chicken-rice-and-peas, ginger cake and coconut ices.

These conversations, lively as they sounded when Clara turned the key in the door, always fell silent as she approached the kitchen. Like children caught out, they would become sullen, then awkward, then Ryan would make his excuses and leave. There was also a look, she noticed, that they had begun to give her, a look of sympathy, of condescension; and not only that – they began to comment on her clothing, which had become steadily more youthful, more colourful; and Ryan – what was happening to Ryan? – shed his polo-neck, avoided her in school, *bought a tie*.

Of course, like the mother of a drug addict or the neighbour of a serial killer, Clara was the last to know. She had once known everything about Ryan – before Ryan himself knew it – she had been a Ryan *expert*. Now she was reduced to overhearing the Irish girls assert that Clara Bowden and Ryan Topps were not dealing with each other – definitively, definitely *not* dealing with each other – oh no, *not any more*.

If Clara realized what was happening, she wouldn't allow herself to believe it. On the occasion she spotted Ryan at the kitchen table, surrounded by leaflets – and Hortense hurriedly gathering them up and shoving them into her apron pocket – Clara *willed* herself to forget it. Later that month, when Clara persuaded a doleful Ryan to go through the motions with her in the disabled toilet, she squinted so she couldn't see what she didn't *want* to see. But it was there, underneath his jumper, there as he leant back on the sink was the glint of silver, its gleam hardly visible in the dismal light – it couldn't be, but it *was* – the silver glint of a tiny silver cross.

It couldn't be, *but it was*. That is how people describe a miracle. Somehow the opposites of Hortense and Ryan had met at their logical extremes, their mutual predilection for the pain and death of others meeting like perspective points on some morbid horizon. Suddenly the saved and the unsaved had come a miraculous full circle. Hortense and Ryan were now trying to save *her*.

'Get on the bike.'

Clara had just stepped out of school into the dusk and it was Ryan, his scooter coming to a sharp halt at her feet.

'Claz, get on the bike.'

'Go ask my mudder if she wan' get on de bike!'

'Please,' said Ryan, proffering the spare scooter helmet. ''Simportant. Need to talk to you. Ain't much time left.'

'Why?' snapped Clara, rocking petulantly on her platform heels. 'You goin' someplace?'

'You and me both,' murmured Ryan. 'The right place, 'opefully.'

'No.'

'Please, Claz.'

'*No.*'

'*Please*. 'Simportant. Life or death.'

'Man . . . all right. But me nah wearin' dat ting' – she passed back the helmet and got astride the scooter – 'not mussin' up me hair.'

Ryan drove her across London and up to Hampstead Heath, the very top of Parliament Hill, where, looking down from that peak on to the sickly orange fluorescence of the city, carefully, tortuously, and in language that was not his own, he put forward his case. The bottom line of which was this: there was only a month until the end of the world.

'And the fing is, herself and myself, we're just –'

'We!'

'Your mum – your mum and myself,' mumbled Ryan, 'we're worried. 'Bout you. There ain't that many wot will survive the last days. You been wiv a bad crowd, Claz –'

'*Man,*' said Clara, shaking her head and sucking her teeth, 'I don' *believe* dis biznezz. Dem were *your* friends.'

'No, no, they ain't. Not no more. The weed – the weed is evil. And all that lot – Wan-Si, Petronia.'

'Dey my friends!'

'They ain't nice girls, Clara. They should be with their families, not dressing like they do and doing things with them men in that house. You yourself shouldn't be doin' that, neither. And dressing like, like, like –'

'Like what?'

'Like a whore!' said Ryan, the word exploding from him like it was a relief to be rid of it. 'Like a loose woman!'

'Oh bwoy, I heard *everyting* now . . . take me home, man.'

'They're going to get theirs,' said Ryan, nodding to himself, his arm stretched and gesturing over London from Chiswick to Archway. 'There's still time for you. Who do you want to be with, Claz? Who d'ya want to be with? With the 144,000, in heaven, ruling with Christ? Or do you want to be one of the Great Crowd, living in earthly paradise, which is all right but . . . Or are you going to be one of them who get it in the neck, torture and death. Eh? I'm just separating the sheep from the goats, Claz, the sheep from the goats. That's Matthew. And I think you yourself are a sheep, innit?'

'Lemme tell you someting,' said Clara, walking back over to the scooter and taking the back seat, 'I'm a goat. I *like* bein' a goat. I *wanna* be a goat. An' I'd rather be sizzling in de rains of sulphur wid my friends than sittin' in heaven, bored to tears, wid Darcus, my mudder and you!'

'Shouldn'ta said that, Claz,' said Ryan solemnly, putting his helmet on. 'I really wish you 'adn't said that. For your sake. *He* can hear us.'

'An' I'm *tired* of hearin' you. Take me home.'

'It's the truth! He can hear us!' he shouted, turning backwards, yelling above the exhaust-pipe noise as they revved up and scooted downhill. 'He can see it all! He watches over us!'

'Watch over where you goin',' Clara yelled back, as they sent a cluster of Hasidic Jews running in all directions. 'Watch de path!'

'Only the few – that's wot it says – only the few. They'll all get it – that's what it says in Dyoot-er-ronomee – they'll all get what's comin' and only the few –'

Somewhere in the middle of Ryan Topps's enlightening biblical exegesis, his former false idol, the Vespa GS, cracked right into a 400-year-old oak tree. Nature triumphed over the presumptions of engineering. The tree survived; the bike died; Ryan was hurled one way; Clara the other.

The principles of Christianity and Sod's Law (also known as Murphy's Law) are the same: *Everything happens to me, for me.* So if a man drops a piece of toast and it lands butter-side down, this unlucky event is interpreted as being proof of an essential truth about bad luck: that the toast fell as it did just to prove to *you*, Mr Unlucky, that there is a defining force in the universe and it is bad luck. It's not random. It could never have fallen on the right side, so the argument goes, because that's Sod's Law. In short, Sod's Law happens to you to prove to you that there is Sod's Law. Yet, unlike gravity, it is a law that does not exist whatever happens: when the toast lands on the *right* side, Sod's Law mysteriously disappears. Likewise, when Clara fell, knocking the teeth out of the top of her mouth, while Ryan stood up without a scratch, Ryan knew it was because God had chosen Ryan as one of the saved and Clara as one of the unsaved. Not because one was wearing a helmet and the other wasn't. And had it happened the other way round, had gravity reclaimed Ryan's teeth and sent them rolling down Primrose Hill like tiny enamel snowballs, well . . . you can bet your life that God, in Ryan's mind, would have done a vanishing act.

As it was, this was the final sign Ryan needed. When New Year's Eve rolled around, he was there in the living room, sitting in the middle of a circle of candles with Hortense, ardently praying for Clara's soul while Darcus pissed into his tube and watched the *Generation Game* on BBC One. Clara, meanwhile, had put on a pair of yellow flares and a red halterneck top and gone to a party. She suggested its theme, helped to paint the banner and hang it from the window; she danced and smoked with the rest of them and felt herself, without undue modesty, to be quite the belle of the squat. But as midnight inevitably came and went without the horsemen of the apocalypse making an appearance, Clara surprised herself by falling into a melancholy. For ridding oneself of faith is like boiling sea-water to retrieve the salt – something is gained but something is lost. Though her friends – Merlin, Wan-Si, et al. – clapped her on the back and congratulated her for exorcizing those fervid dreams of perdition and redemption, Clara quietly mourned the warmer touch she had waited for these nineteen years, the all-enveloping bear hug of the Saviour, the One who was Alpha and Omega, both the beginning and the end; the man who was meant to take her away from all this, from the listless reality of life in a ground-floor flat in Lambeth. What now for Clara? Ryan would find another fad; Darcus need only turn to the other channel; for Hortense another date would of course materialize, along with more leaflets, ever more faith. But Clara was not like Hortense.

Yet a residue, left over from the evaporation of Clara's faith, remained. She still wished for a saviour. She still wished for a man to whisk her away, to choose her above others so that she might *Walk in white with Him: for* [she] *was worthy*. Revelation 3:4.

Perhaps it is not so inexplicable then, that when Clara Bowden met Archie Jones at the bottom of some stairs the next morning she saw more in him than simply a rather short, rather chubby middle-aged white man in a badly tailored suit. Clara saw Archie through the grey-green eyes of loss; her world had just disappeared, the faith she lived by had receded like a low tide, and Archie, quite by accident, had become the bloke in the joke: the last man on earth.

3 *Two Families*

It is better to marry than to burn, says Corinthians I, chapter seven, verse nine.

Good advice. Of course, Corinthians also informs us that we *should not muzzle the ox while it is treading out the grain* – so, go figure.

By February 1975, Clara had deserted the church and all its biblical literalism for Archibald Jones, but she was not yet the kind of carefree atheist who could laugh near altars or entirely dismiss the teachings of St Paul. The second dictum wasn't a problem – having no ox, she was excluded by proxy. But the first was giving her sleepless nights. Was it better to marry? Even if the man was a heathen? There was no way of knowing: she was living without props now, *sans* safety net. More worrying than God was her mother. Hortense was fiercely opposed to the affair, on grounds of colour rather than of age, and on hearing of it had promptly ostracized her daughter one morning on the doorstep.

Clara still felt that deep down her mother would prefer her to marry an unsuitable man rather than live with him in sin, so she did it on impulse and begged Archie to take her as far away from Lambeth as a man of his means could manage – Morocco, Belgium, Italy. Archie had clasped her hand and nodded and whispered sweet nothings in the full knowledge that the furthest a man of his means was going was a newly acquired, heavily mortgaged, two-storey house in Willesden Green. But no need to mention that now, he felt, not right now in the heat of the moment. Let her down gently, like.

Three months later Clara had been gently let down and here they were, moving in. Archie scrabbling up the stairs, as usual cursing and blinding, wilting under the weight of boxes which Clara could carry two, three at a time without effort; Clara taking a break, squinting in the warm May sunshine, trying to get her bearings. She peeled down to a little purple vest and leant against her front gate. What kind of a place *was* this? That was the thing, you see, you couldn't be *sure*. Travelling in the front passenger seat of the removal van, she'd seen the high road and it had been ugly and poor and familiar (though there were no Kingdom Halls or Episcopalian churches), but then at the turn of a corner suddenly roads had exploded in greenery, beautiful oaks, the houses got taller, wider and more detached, she could see parks, she could see libraries. And then abruptly the trees would be gone, reverting back into bus-stops as if by the strike of some midnight bell; a signal which the houses too obeyed, transforming themselves into smaller, stairless dwellings that sat splay opposite derelict shopping arcades, those peculiar lines of establishments that include, without exception,

one defunct sandwich bar still advertising breakfast

one locksmith uninterested in marketing frills (KEYS CUT HERE)

and one permanently shut unisex hair salon, the proud bearer of some unspeakable pun (*Upper Cuts* or *Fringe Benefits* or *Hair Today, Gone Tomorrow*).

It was a lottery driving along like that, looking out, not knowing whether one was about to settle down for life amongst the trees or amidst the shit. Then finally the van had slowed down in front of a house, a nice house somewhere midway between the trees and the shit, and Clara had felt a tide of gratitude roll over her. It was *nice*, not as nice as she had hoped but not as bad as she had feared; it had two small gardens front and back, a doormat, a doorbell, a toilet *inside* . . . And she had not paid a high price. Only love. Just love. And whatever Corinthians might say, love is not such a hard thing to forfeit, not if you've never really felt it. She did not love Archie, but had made up her mind, from that first moment on the steps, to devote herself to him if he would take her away. And now he had; and, though it wasn't Morocco or Belgium or Italy, it was nice – not the promised land – but *nice*, nicer than anywhere she had ever been.

Clara understood that Archibald Jones was no romantic hero. Three months spent in one stinking room in Cricklewood had been sufficient revelation. Oh, he could be affectionate and sometimes even charming, he could whistle a clear, crystal note first thing in the morning, he drove calmly and responsibly and he was a surprisingly competent cook, but romance was beyond him, passion, unthinkable. And if you are saddled with a man as average as this, Clara felt, he should at least be utterly devoted to *you* – to your beauty, to your youth – that's the *least* he could do to make up for things. But not Archie. One month into their marriage and he already had that funny glazed look men have when they are looking through you. He had already reverted back into his bachelorhood: pints with Samad Iqbal, dinner with Samad Iqbal, Sunday breakfasts with Samad Iqbal, every spare moment with the man in that bloody place, *O'Connell's*, in that bloody dive. She tried to be reasonable. She asked him: *Why are you never here? Why do you spend so much time with the Indian?* But a pat on the back, a kiss on the cheek, he's grabbing his coat, his foot's out the door and always the same old answer: *Me and Sam? We go way back*. She couldn't argue with that. They went back to before she was born.

No white knight, then, this Archibald Jones. No aims, no hopes, no ambitions. A man whose greatest pleasures were English breakfasts and DIY. A dull man. An *old* man. And yet . . . good. He was a *good* man. And *good* might not amount to much, *good* might not light up a life, but it is something. She spotted it in him that first time on the stairs, simply, directly, the same way she could point out a good mango on a Brixton stall without so much as touching the skin.

These were the thoughts Clara clung to as she leant on her

garden gate, three months after her wedding, silently watching the way her husband's brow furrowed and shortened like an accordion, the way his stomach hung pregnant over his belt, the whiteness of his skin, the blueness of his veins, the way his 'elevens' were up – those two ropes of flesh that appear on a man's gullet (so they said in Jamaica) when his time was drawing to a close.

Clara frowned. She hadn't noticed these afflictions at the wedding. Why not? He had been smiling and he wore a white polo-neck, but no, that wasn't it – she hadn't been *looking* for them then, *that* was it. Clara had spent most of her wedding day looking at her feet. It had been a hot day, 14 February, but unusually warm, and there had been a wait because the world had wanted to marry that day in a little registry office on Ludgate Hill. Clara remembered slipping off the petite brown heels she was wearing and placing her bare feet on the chilly floor, making sure to keep them firmly planted either side of a dark crack in the tile, a balancing act upon which she had randomly staked her future happiness.

Archie meanwhile had wiped some moisture from his upper lip and cursed a persistent sunbeam that was sending a trickle of salty water down his inside leg. For his second marriage he had chosen a mohair suit with a white polo-neck and both were proving problematic. The heat prompted rivulets of sweat to spring out all over his body, seeping through the polo-neck to the mohair and giving off an unmistakable odour of damp dog. Clara, of course, was all cat. She wore a long brown woollen Jeff Banks dress and a perfect set of false teeth; the dress was backless, the teeth were white, and the overall effect was feline; a panther in evening dress; where the wool stopped and Clara's skin started was not clear to the naked eye. And like a cat she responded to the dusty sunbeam that was coursing through a high window on to the waiting couples. She warmed her bare back in it, she almost seemed to *unfurl*. Even the registrar, who had seen it all – horsy women marrying weaselly men, elephantine men marrying owlish women – raised an eyebrow at this most unnatural of unions as they approached his desk. Cat and dog.

'Hullo, Father,' said Archie.

'He's a registrar, Archibald, you old flake,' said his friend Samad Miah Iqbal, who, along with his wife Alsana, had been called in from the exile of the Wedding Guest Room to witness the contract. 'Not a Catholic priest.'

'Right. Of course. Sorry. Nervous.'

The stuffy registrar said, 'Shall we get on? We've got a lot of you to get through today.'

This and little more had constituted the ceremony. Archie was passed a pen and put down his name (Alfred Archibald Jones), nationality (English) and age (47). Hovering for a moment over the box entitled 'Occupation', he decided upon 'Advertising: (Printed Leaflets)', then signed himself away. Clara wrote down her name (Clara Iphegenia Bowden), nationality (Jamaican) and age (19). Finding no box interested in her occupation, she went straight for the decisive dotted line, swept her pen across it, and straightened up again, a Jones. A Jones like no other that had come before her.

Then they had gone outside, on to the steps, where a breeze lifted second-hand confetti and swept it over new couples, where Clara met her only wedding guests formally for the first time: two Indians, both dressed in purple silk. Samad Iqbal, a tall, handsome man with the whitest teeth and a dead hand, who kept patting her on the back with the one that worked.

'My idea this, you know,' he repeated again and again. 'My idea, all this marriage business. I have known the old boy since – when?'

'1945, Sam.'

'That's what I am trying to tell your lovely wife, 1945 – when you know a man that long, and you've fought alongside him, then it's your mission to make him happy if he is not. And he wasn't! Quite the opposite until you made an appearance! Wallowing in the shit-heap, if you will pardon the French. Thankfully, *she*'s all packed off now. There's only one place for the mad, and that's with others like them,' said Samad, losing steam halfway through the sentence, for Clara clearly had no idea what he was talking about. 'Anyway, no need to dwell on . . . My idea, though, you know, all this.'

And then there was his wife, Alsana, who was tiny and tight-lipped and seemed to disapprove of Clara somehow (though she could only be a few years older); said only 'Oh yes, Mrs Jones' or 'Oh no, Mrs Jones', making Clara so nervous, so *sheepish*, she felt compelled to put her shoes back on.

Archie felt bad for Clara that it wasn't a bigger reception. But there was no one else to invite. All other relatives and friends had declined the wedding invitation; some tersely, some horrified; others, thinking silence the best option, had spent the past week studiously stepping over the mail and avoiding the phone. The only well-wisher was Ibelgaufts, who had neither been invited nor informed of the event, but from whom, curiously, a note arrived in the morning mail:

14 February 1975

Dear Archibald,

Usually, there is something about weddings that brings out the misanthrope in me, but today, as I attempted to save a bed of petunias from extinction, I felt a not inconsiderable warmth at the thought of the union of one man and one woman in lifelong cohabitation. It is truly remarkable that we humans undertake such an impossible feat, don't you think? But to be serious for a moment: as you know, I am a man whose profession it is to look deep inside of 'Woman', and, like a psychiatrist, mark her with a full bill of health or otherwise. And I feel sure, my friend (to extend a metaphor), that you have explored your lady-wife-to-be in such a manner, both spiritually

and mentally, and found her not lacking in any particular, and so what else can I offer but the hearty congratulations of your earnest competitor,
Horst Ibelgaufts

What other memories of that day could make it unique and lift it out of the other 364 that made up 1975? Clara remembered a young black man stood atop an apple crate, sweating in a black suit, who began pleading to his brothers and sisters; an old bag-lady retrieving a carnation from the bin to put in her hair. But then it was all over: the cling-filmed sandwiches Clara had made had been forgotten and sat suffering at the bottom of a bag, the sky had clouded over, and when they walked up the hill to the King Ludd Pub, past the jeering Fleet Street lads with their Saturday pints, it was discovered that Archie had been given a parking ticket.

So it was that Clara spent the first three hours of married life in Cheapside Police Station, her shoes in her hands, watching her saviour argue relentlessly with a traffic inspector who failed to understand Archie's subtle interpretation of the Sunday parking laws.

'Clara, Clara, love –'

It was Archie, struggling past her to the front door, partly obscured by a coffee table.

'We've got the Ick-Balls coming round tonight, and I want to get this house in some kind of order – so mind out the way.'

'You wan' help?' asked Clara patiently, though still half in daydream. 'I can lift someting if –'

'No, no, no, no – I'll manage.'

Clara reached out to take one side of the table. 'Let me jus' –'

Archie battled to push through the narrow frame, trying to hold both the legs and the table's large removable glass top.

'It's man's work, love.'

'But –' Clara lifted a large armchair with enviable ease and brought it over to where Archie had collapsed, gasping for breath on the hall steps. ''Sno prob-lem. If you wan' help: jus' arks farrit.' She brushed her hand softly across his forehead.

'Yes, yes, yes.' He shook her off in irritation, as if batting a fly. 'I'm quite capable, you know –'

'I know dat –'

'It's *man's* work.'

'Yes, yes, I see – I didn't mean –'

'Look, Clara, love, just get out of my way and I'll get on with it, OK?'

Clara watched him roll up his sleeves with some determination, and tackle the coffee table once more.

'If you really want to be of some help, love, you can start bringing in some of your clothes. God knows there's enough of 'em to sink a bloody battleship. How we're going to fit them in what little space we have I'm sure I don't know.'

'I say before – we can trow some dem out, if you tink it best.'

'Not up to me now, not up to me, is it? I mean, is it? And what about the coat-stand?'

This was the man: never able to make a decision, never able to state a position.

'I alreddy say: if ya nah like it, den send da damn ting back. I bought it 'cos I taut you like it.'

'Well, love,' said Archie, cautious now that she had raised her voice, 'it *was* my money – it would have been nice at least to *ask* my opinion.'

'Man! It a coat-stand. It jus' red. An' red is red is red. What's wrong wid red all of a sudden?'

'I'm just trying,' said Archie, lowering his voice to a hoarse, forced whisper (a favourite voice-weapon in the marital arsenal: *Not in front of the neighbours/children*), 'to lift the *tone* in the house a bit. This is a nice neighbourhood, new life, you know. Look, let's not argue. Let's flip a coin; heads it stays, tails . . .'

True lovers row, then fall the next second back into each other's arms; more seasoned lovers will walk up the stairs or into the next room before they relent and retrace their steps. A relationship on the brink of collapse will find one partner two blocks down the road or two countries to the east before something tugs, some responsibility, some memory, a pull of a child's hand or a heart string, which induces them to make the long journey back to their other half. On this Richter scale, then, Clara made only the tiniest of rumbles. She turned towards the gate, walked two steps only and stopped.

'Heads!' said Archie, seemingly without resentment. 'It stays. See? That wasn't too hard.'

'I don' wanna argue.' She turned round to face him, having made a silent renewed resolution to remember her debt to him. 'You said the Iqbals are comin' to dinner. I was just thinkin' . . . if they're going to want me to cook dem some curry – I mean, I can cook curry – but it's *my* type of curry.'

'For God's sake, they're not *those* kind of Indians,' said Archie irritably, offended at the suggestion. 'Sam'll have a Sunday roast like the next man. He serves Indian food all the time, he doesn't want to eat it too.'

'I was just wondering –'

'Well, don't, Clara. *Please.*'

He gave her an affectionate kiss on the forehead, for which she bent downwards a little.

'I've known Sam for years, and his wife seems a quiet sort. They're not the royal family, you know. They're not *those* kind of Indians,' he repeated, and shook his head, troubled by some problem, some knotty feeling he could not entirely unravel.

Samad and Alsana Iqbal, who were not *those* kind of Indians (as, in Archie's mind, Clara was not *that* kind of black), who were, in fact, not Indian at all but Bangladeshi, lived four blocks down on the wrong side of Willesden High Road. It had taken them a year to get there, a year of mercilessly hard graft to make the momentous move from the wrong side of Whitechapel to the wrong side of Willesden. A year's worth of Alsana banging away at the old Singer that sat in the kitchen, sewing together pieces of black plastic for a shop called Domination in Soho (many were the nights Alsana would hold up a piece of clothing she had just made, following the pattern she was given, and wonder what on earth it was). A year's worth of Samad softly inclining his head at exactly the correct deferential angle, pencil in his left hand, listening to the appalling pronunciation of the British, Spanish, American, French, Australian:

Go Bye Ello Sag, please.

Chicken Jail Fret See wiv Chips, fanks.

From six in the evening until three in the morning; and then every day was spent asleep, until daylight was as rare as a decent tip. For what is the point, Samad would think, pushing aside two mints and a receipt to find fifteen pence, what is the point of tipping a man the same amount you would throw in a fountain to chase a wish? But before the illegal thought of folding the fifteen pence discreetly in his napkin hand even had a chance to give itself form, Mukhul – Ardashir Mukhul, who ran the Palace and whose wiry frame paced the restaurant, one benevolent eye on the customers, one ever watchful eye on the staff – Mukhul was upon him.

'Saaamaad' – he had a cloying, oleaginous way of speaking – 'did you kiss the necessary backside this evening, cousin?'

Samad and Ardashir were distant cousins, Samad the elder by six years. With what joy (pure bliss!) had Ardashir opened the letter last January, to find his older, cleverer, handsomer cousin was finding it hard to get work in England and could he possibly . . .

'Fifteen pence, cousin,' said Samad, lifting his palm.

'Well, every little helps, every little helps,' said Ardashir, his dead-fish lips stretching into a stringy smile. 'Into the Piss-Pot with it.'

The Piss-Pot was a black Balti pot that sat on a plinth outside the staff toilets and into which all tips were pooled and then split at the end of the night. For the younger, flashy, good-looking waiters like Shiva, this was a great injustice. Shiva was the only Hindu on the staff – this stood as tribute to his waitering skills, which had triumphed over religious differences. Shiva could make a four quid tip in an evening if the blubberous white divorcee in the corner was lonely enough and he batted his long lashes at her effectively. He could also make his money out of the polo-necked directors and producers (the Palace sat in the centre of London's theatreland, and these were still the days of the Royal Court, of pretty boys and kitchen-sink drama) who flattered the boy, watched his ass wiggle provocatively to the bar and back, and swore that if anyone ever adapted *A Passage to India* for the stage he could have whichever role tickled his fancy. For Shiva, then, the Piss-Pot system was simply daylight robbery and an insult to his unchallenged waitering abilities. But for men like Samad, in his late forties, and for the even older, like the white-haired Muhammed (Ardashir's great-uncle), who was eighty if he was a day, who had deep pathways dug into the sides of his mouth where he had smiled when he was young, for men like this the Piss-Pot could not be complained about. It made more sense to join the collective than pocket fifteen pence and risk being caught (and docked a week's tips).

'You're all on my back!' Shiva would snarl, when he had to relinquish five pounds at the end of the night and drop it into the pot. 'You all live off my back! Somebody get these losers off my back! That was my fiver and now it's going to be split sixty-five-fucking-million ways as a hand-out to these losers! What is this: communism?'

And the rest would avoid his glare and busy themselves quietly with other things, until one evening, one fifteen pence evening,

Samad said, 'Shut up, boy,' quietly, almost under his breath.

'You!' Shiva swung round to where Samad stood, crushing a great tub of lentils for tomorrow's dal. 'You're the worst of them! You're the worst fucking waiter I've ever seen! You couldn't get a tip if you mugged the bastards! I hear you trying to talk to the customer about biology this, politics that – just serve the food, you idiot – you're a waiter, for fuck's sake, you're not Michael Parkinson. "*Did I hear you say Delhi*"' – Shiva put his apron over his arm and began posturing around the kitchen (he was a pitiful mimic) – '"I was there myself, you know, Delhi University, it was most fascinating, yes – and I fought in the war, for England, yes – yes, yes, charming, charming."' Round and round the kitchen he went, bending his head and rubbing his hands over and over like Uriah Heep, bowing and genuflecting to the head cook, to the old man arranging great hunks of meat in the walk-in freezer, to the young boy scrubbing the underside of the oven. 'Samad, *Samad* . . .' he said with what seemed infinite pity, then stopped abruptly, pulled the apron off and wrapped it round his waist. 'You are such a sad little man.'

Muhammed looked up from his pot-scrubbing and shook his head again and again. To no one in particular he said, 'These young people – what kind of talk? What kind of talk? What happened to respect? What kind of talk is this?'

'And you can fuck off too,' said Shiva, brandishing a ladle in his direction, 'you old fool. You're not my father.'

'Second cousin of your mother's uncle,' a voice muttered from the back.

'Bollocks,' said Shiva. 'Bollocks to that.'

He grabbed the mop and was heading off for the toilets, when he stopped by Samad and placed the handle inches from Samad's mouth.

'Kiss it,' he sneered; and then, impersonating Ardashir's sluggish drawl, 'Who knows, cousin, you might get a rise!'

And that's what it was like most nights: abuse from Shiva and others; condescension from Ardashir; never seeing Alsana; never seeing the sun; clutching fifteen pence and then releasing it; wanting desperately to be wearing a sign, a large white placard that said:

I AM NOT A WAITER. I HAVE BEEN A STUDENT, A SCIENTIST, A SOLDIER, MY WIFE IS CALLED ALSANA, WE LIVE IN EAST LONDON BUT WE WOULD LIKE TO MOVE NORTH. I AM A MUSLIM BUT ALLAH HAS FORSAKEN ME OR I HAVE FORSAKEN ALLAH, I'M NOT SURE. I HAVE A FRIEND – ARCHIE – AND OTHERS. I AM FORTY-NINE BUT WOMEN STILL TURN IN THE STREET. SOMETIMES.

But, no such placard existing, he had instead the urge, the need, to speak to every man, and, like the Ancient Mariner, explain constantly, constantly wanting to reassert something, anything. Wasn't that important? But then the heart-breaking disappointment – to find out that the inclining of one's head, poising of one's pen, these were important, so important – it was important to be a good waiter, to listen when someone said –

Lamb Dawn Sock and rice. With chips. Thank you.

And fifteen pence clinked on china. Thank you, sir. Thank you so very much.

∽

On the Tuesday after Archie's wedding, Samad had waited till everyone left, folded his white, flared trousers (made from the same fabric as the tablecloths) into a perfect square, and then climbed the stairs to Ardashir's office, for he had something to ask him.

'Cousin!' said Ardashir, with a friendly grimace at the sight of Samad's body curling cautiously round the door. He knew that Samad had come to inquire about a pay increase, and he wanted his cousin to feel that he had at least considered the case in all his friendly judiciousness before he declined.

'Cousin, come in!'

'Good evening, Ardashir Mukhul,' said Samad, stepping fully into the room.

'Sit down, sit down,' said Ardashir warmly. 'No point standing on ceremony now, is there?'

Samad was glad this was so. He said as much. He took a moment to look with the necessary admiration around the room, with its relentless gold, with its triple-piled carpet, with its furnishings in various shades of yellow and green. One had to admire Ardashir's business sense. He had taken the simple idea of an Indian restaurant (small room, pink tablecloth, loud music, atrocious wallpaper, meals that do not exist in India, sauce carousel) and just made it bigger. He hadn't improved anything; everything was the same old crap, but it was all bigger in a bigger building in the biggest tourist trap in London, Leicester Square. You had to admire it and admire the man, who sat now like a benign locust, his slender insectile body swamped in a black leather chair, leaning over the desk, all smiles, a parasite disguised as a philanthropist.

'Cousin, what can I do for you?'

Samad took a breath. The matter was this . . .

Ardashir's eyes glazed over a little as Samad explained his situation. His skinny legs twitched underneath the desk, and in his fingers he manipulated a paperclip until it looked reasonably like an A. A for Ardashir. The matter was . . . what was the matter? The house was the matter. Samad was moving out of East London (where one couldn't bring up children, indeed, one couldn't, not if one didn't wish them to come to bodily harm, he agreed), from East London with its NF gangs, to North London, north-west, where things were more . . . more . . . liberal.

Was it his turn to speak?

'Cousin . . .' said Ardashir, arranging his face, 'you must

understand . . . I cannot make it my business to buy houses for all my employees, cousin or not cousin . . . I pay a wage, cousin . . . That is business in this country.'

Ardashir shrugged as he spoke as if to suggest he deeply disapproved of 'Business in this country', but there it was. He was forced, his look said, forced by the English to make an awful lot of money.

'You misunderstand me, Ardashir. I have the deposit for the house, it is *our* house now, we have moved in –'

How on earth has he afforded it, he must work his wife like a bloody slave, thought Ardashir, pulling out another paperclip from the bottom drawer.

'I need only a small wage increase to help me finance the move. To make things a little easier as we settle in. And Alsana, well, she is pregnant.'

Pregnant. Difficult. The case called for extreme diplomacy.

'Don't mistake me, Samad, we are both intelligent, frank men and I think I can speak frankly . . . I know you're not a *fucking* waiter' – he whispered the expletive and smiled indulgently after it, as if it were a naughty, private thing that brought them closer together – 'I see your position . . . of course I do . . . but you must understand *mine* . . . If I made allowances for every relative I employ I'd be walking around like bloody Mr Gandhi. Without a pot to piss in. Spinning my thread by the light of the moon. An example: at this very moment that wastrel Fat Elvis brother-in-law of mine, Hussein-Ishmael –'

'The butcher?'

'The butcher, demands that I should raise the price I pay for his stinking meat! "But Ardashir, we are brothers-in-law!" he is saying to me. And I am saying to him, but Mohammed, this is *retail* . . .'

It was Samad's turn to glaze over. He thought of his wife, Alsana, who was not as meek as he had assumed when they married, to whom he must deliver the bad news; Alsana, who was prone to moments, even fits – yes, fits was not too strong a word – of rage. Cousins, aunts, brothers, thought it a bad sign, they worried if there wasn't some 'funny mental history' in Alsana's family, they sympathized with him the way you sympathize with a man who has bought a stolen car with more mileage on it than first thought. In his naivety Samad had simply assumed a woman so young would be . . . easy. But Alsana was not . . . no, she was not easy. It was, he supposed, the way with these young women these days. Archie's bride . . . last Tuesday he had seen something in her eyes that wasn't easy either. It was the new way with these women.

Ardashir came to the end of what he felt was his perfectly worded speech, sat back satisfied, and laid the M for Mukhul he had moulded next to the A for Ardashir that sat on his lap.

'Thank you, sir,' said Samad. 'Thank you so very much.'

That evening there was an awful row. Alsana slung the sewing machine, with the black studded hotpants she was working on, to the floor.

'Useless! Tell me, Samad Miah, what is the point of moving here – nice house, yes, very nice, very nice – but where is the food?'

'It is a nice area, we have friends here.'

'Who are they?' She slammed her little fist on to the kitchen table, sending the salt and pepper flying, to collide spectacularly with each other in the air. 'I don't know them! You fight in an old, forgotten war with some Englishman . . . married to a black! Whose friends are they? These are the people my child will grow up around? Their children – half blacky-white? But tell me,' she shouted, returning to her favoured topic, 'where is our food?' Theatrically, she threw open every cupboard in the kitchen. 'Where is it? Can we eat china?' Two plates smashed to the floor. She patted her stomach to indicate her unborn child and pointed to the pieces. 'Hungry?'

Samad, who had an equally melodramatic nature when prompted, yanked upon the freezer and pulled out a mountain of meat which he piled in the middle of the room. His mother worked through the night preparing meat for her family, he said. His mother did not, he said, spend the household money, as Alsana did, on prepared meals, yoghurts and tinned spaghetti.

Alsana punched him full square in the stomach.

'Samad Iqbal the traditionalist! Why don't I just squat in the street over a bucket and wash clothes? Eh? In fact, what about my clothes? Edible?'

As Samad clutched his winded belly, there in the kitchen she ripped to shreds every stitch she had on and added them to the pile of frozen lamb, spare cuts from the restaurant. She stood naked before him for a moment, the yet small mound of her pregnancy in full view, then put on a long, brown coat and left the house.

But all the same, she reflected, slamming the door behind her, it was true: it was a nice area; she couldn't deny it as she stormed towards the high road, avoiding trees where previously, in Whitechapel, she avoided flung-out mattresses and the homeless. It would be good for the child, she couldn't deny it. Alsana had a deep-seated belief that living near green spaces was morally beneficial to the young, and there to her right was Gladstone Park, a sweeping horizon of green named after the Liberal Prime Minister (Alsana was from a respected old Bengal family and had read her English History; but look at her now; if they could see what depths . . . !), and in the Liberal tradition it was a park without fences, unlike the more affluent Queens Park (Victoria's), with its pointed metal railings. Willesden was not as pretty as Queens Park, but it was a nice area. No denying it. Not like Whitechapel, where that madman E-knock someoneoranother gave a speech that forced them into the basement while kids broke the windows with their steel-capped boots. Rivers of blood silly-billy nonsense. Now she was pregnant she needed a little bit of peace and quiet. Though it was the same here in a way: they all looked at her strangely, this tiny Indian woman stalking the high road in a mackintosh, her plentiful hair flying every which way. *Mali's Kebabs, Mr Cheungs, Raj's, Malkovich Bakeries* – she read the new, unfamiliar signs as she passed. She was shrewd. She saw what this was. 'Liberal? Hosh-kosh nonsense!' No one was more liberal than anyone else anywhere anyway. It was only that here, in Willesden, there was just not enough of any one thing to gang up against any other thing and send it running to the cellars while windows were smashed.

'Survival is what it is about!' she concluded out loud (she spoke to her baby; she liked to give it one sensible thought a day), making the bell above Crazy Shoes tinkle as she opened the door. Her niece Neena worked there. It was an old-fashioned cobblers. Neena fixed heels back on to stilettos.

'Alsana, you look like dog shit,' Neena called over in Bengali. 'What is that horrible coat?'

'It's none of your business, is what it is,' replied Alsana in English. 'I came to collect my husband's shoes, not to chit-chat with Niece-of-Shame.'

Neena was used to this, and now that Alsana had moved to Willesden there would only be more of it. It used to come in longer sentences, i.e., *You have brought nothing but shame* . . . or *My niece, the shameful* . . . but now because Alsana no longer had the time or energy to summon up the necessary shock each time, it had become abridged to Niece-of-Shame, an all-purpose tag that summed up the general feeling.

'See these soles?' said Neena, moving one of her dyed blonde bangs from her eye, taking Samad's shoes off a shelf and handing Alsana the little blue ticket. 'They were so worn through, Auntie Alsi, I had to reconstruct them from the very base. From the base! What does he do in them? Run marathons?'

'He works,' replied Alsana tersely. 'And prays,' she added, for she liked to show people her respectability, and besides she was really very traditional, very religious, lacking nothing except the faith. 'And don't call me Auntie. I am two years older than you.' Alsana swept the shoes into a plastic carrier bag and turned to leave.

'I thought that praying was done on people's knees,' said Neena, laughing lightly.

'Both, both, asleep, waking, walking,' snapped Alsana, as she passed under the tinkly bell once more. 'We are never out of sight of the Creator.'

'How's the new house, then?' Neena called after her.

But she had gone; Neena shook her head and sighed as she watched her young aunt disappear down the road like a little brown bullet. Alsana. She was young and old at the same time, Neena reflected. She acted so sensible, so straight-down-the-line in her long sensible coat, but you got the feeling . . .

'Oi! Miss! There's shoes back here that need your attention,' came a voice from the store room.

'Keep your tits on,' said Neena.

At the corner of the road Alsana popped behind the post office and removed her pinchy sandals in favour of Samad's shoes. (It was an oddity about Alsana. She was small but her feet were enormous. You felt instinctively when looking at her that she had yet more growing to do.) In seconds she whipped her hair into an efficient bun, and wrapped her coat tighter around her to keep out the wind. Then she set off up past the library and up a long green road she had never walked along before. 'Survival is all, little Iqbal,' she said to her bump once more. 'Survival.'

Halfway up the road, she crossed the street, intending to turn left and circle round back to the high road. But then, as she approached a large white van open at the back and looked enviously at the furniture that was piled up in it, she recognized the black lady who was leaning over a garden fence, looking dreamily into the air towards the library (half dressed, though! A lurid purple vest, underwear almost), as if her future lay in that direction. Before she could cross over once more to avoid her, Alsana found herself spotted.

'Mrs Iqbal!' said Clara, waving her over.

'Mrs Jones.'

Both women were momentarily embarrassed at what they were wearing, but, looking at the other, gained confidence.

'Now, isn't that strange, Archie?' said Clara, filling in all her consonants. She was already some way to losing her accent and she liked to work on it at every opportunity.

'What? What?' said Archie, who was in the hallway, becoming exasperated with a bookcase.

'It's just that we were just talking about you – you're coming to dinner tonight, yes?'

Black people are often friendly, thought Alsana, smiling at Clara, and adding this fact subconsciously to the short 'pro' side of the pro and con list she had on the black girl. From every minority she disliked, Alsana liked to single out one specimen for spiritual forgiveness. From Whitechapel, there had been many such redeemed characters. Mr Van, the Chinese chiropodist, Mr Segal, a Jewish carpenter, Rosie, a Dominican woman who continuously popped round, much to Alsana's grievance and delight, in an attempt to convert her into a Seventh-Day Adventist – all these lucky individuals were given Alsana's golden reprieve and magically extrapolated from their skins like Indian tigers.

'Yes, Samad mentioned it,' said Alsana, though Samad had not.

Clara beamed. 'Good . . . good!'

There was a pause. Neither could think of what to say. They both looked downwards.

'Those shoes look truly comfortable,' said Clara.

'Yes. Yes. I do a lot of walking, you see. And with this –' She patted her stomach.

'You're pregnant?' said Clara surprised. 'Pickney, you so small me kyant even see it.'

Clara blushed the moment after she had spoken; she always dropped into the vernacular when she was excited or pleased about something. Alsana just smiled pleasantly, unsure what she had said.

'I wouldn't have known,' said Clara, more subdued.

'Dear me,' said Alsana with a forced hilarity. 'Don't our husbands tell each other anything?'

But as soon as she had said it, the weight of the other possibility rested on the brains of the two girl-wives. That their husbands told each other everything. That it was they themselves who were kept in the dark.

4 *Three Coming*

Archie was at work when he heard the news. Clara was two and a half months up the spout.

'You're not, love!'

'I am!'

'You're not!'

'I am! And I arks de doctor what it will look like, half black an' half white an' all dat bizncss. And 'im say anyting could happen. Dere's even a chance it may be blue-eyed! Kyan you imagine dat?'

Archie couldn't imagine that. He couldn't imagine any piece of him slugging it out in the gene pool with a piece of Clara and *winning*. But what a possibility! What a thing that would be! He dashed out of the office on to the Euston Road for a box of cigars. Twenty minutes later he swaggered back into Morgan*Hero* with a huge box of Indian sweets and started making his way round the room.

'Noel, have a sticky thing. That one's good.'

Noel, the office junior, looked inside the oily box with suspicion. 'What's all this in aid . . . ?'

Archie pounded him on the back. 'Going to have a kid, ain't I? Blue eyes, would you credit it? I'm celebrating! Thing is, you can get fourteen types of dal, but you can't get a bloody cigar in the Euston Road for love nor money. Go on, Noel. How about this one?'

Archie held up a half-white, half-pink one with an unwelcoming odour.

'Erm, Mr Jones, that's very . . . But it's not really my cup of . . .' Noel made as if to return to his filing. 'I'd better get on with . . .'

'Oh, go on, Noel. I'm going to have a kid. Forty-seven and I'm going to *have a little baby*. That calls for a bit of a party, don't it? Go on . . . you won't know till you try. Just give it a nibble.'

'Just them Pakistani foods aren't always . . . I've got a bit of a funny . . .'

Noel patted his stomach and looked desperate. Despite being in the direct mail business, Noel hated to be spoken to directly. He liked being the intermediary at Morgan*Hero*. He liked putting calls through, telling one person what another person said, forwarding letters.

'Bloody hell, Noel . . . it's just a sweet. I'm just trying to celebrate, mate. Don't you hippies eat sweets or something?'

Noel's hair was ever so slightly longer than everyone else's, and he had once bought an incense stick to burn in the coffee room. It was a small office, there was little to talk about, so these two things made Noel second only to Janis Joplin, just as Archie was the white Jesse Owens because he came thirteenth in the Olympics twenty-seven years ago, Gary from Accounts had a French grandmother and blew cigarette smoke out of his nose so he was Maurice Chevalier, and Elmott, Archie's fellow paper-folder, was Einstein because he could manage two thirds of *The Times* crossword.

Noel looked pained. 'Archie . . . Did you get my note from Mr Hero about the folds on the . . . ?'

Archie sighed. 'On the Mothercare account. Yes, Noel, I've told Elmott to move the perforation.'

Noel looked thankful. 'Well, congratulations about the . . . I'll be getting on with . . .' Noel returned to his desk.

Archie left to try Maureen the receptionist. Maureen had good legs for a woman her age – legs like sausages tightly packed in their skins – and she'd always fancied him a bit.

'Maureen, love. I'm going to be a father!'

'Are you, love? Oh, I am *pleased*. Girl or –'

'Too early to tell as yet. Blue eyes, though!' said Archie, for whom these eyes had passed from rare genetic possibility to solid fact. 'Would you credit it!'

'Did you say *blue* eyes, Archie, love?' said Maureen, speaking slowly so she might find a way to phrase it. 'I'm not bein' funny . . . but in't your wife, well, *coloured*?'

Archie shook his head wonderingly. 'I know! Her and me have a child, the genes mix up, and blue eyes! Miracle of nature!'

'Oh yes, miracle,' said Maureen tersely, thinking that was a polite word for what it was.

'Have a sweet?'

Maureen looked dubious. She patted her pitted pink thighs encased in their white tights. 'Oh, Archie, love, I *shouldn't*. Goes straight on the legs and hips, don't it? An' neither of us is getting any younger, are we, eh? Are we, eh? None of us can turn back the clock, can we, eh? That Joan Rivers, I wish I knew how she does it!'

Maureen laughed for a long time, her trademark laugh at Morgan*Hero*: shrill and loud, but with her mouth only slightly open, for Maureen had a morbid dread of laughter lines.

She poked one of the sweets with a sceptical, blood-red fingernail. 'Indian, are they?'

'Yes, Maureen,' said Archie with a blokeish grin, 'spicy and sweet at the same time. Bit like you.'

'Oh, Archie, you *are* funny,' said Maureen sadly, for she had always fancied Archie a *bit* but never more than a bit because of this strange way he had about him, always talking to Pakistanis and Caribbeans like he didn't even notice and now he'd gone and married one and hadn't even thought it worth mentioning what colour she was until the office dinner when she turned up black as anything and Maureen almost choked on her prawn cocktail.

Maureen stretched over her desk to attend to a ringing telephone. 'I don't think I will, Archie, love . . .'

'Please yourself. Don't know what you're missing, though.'

Maureen smiled weakly and picked up the receiver. 'Yes, Mr Hero, he's right here, he's just found out he's going to be a daddy . . . yes, it'll have blue eyes, apparently . . . yes, that's what I said, something to do with genes, I suppose . . . oh yes, all right . . . I'll tell him, I'll send him in . . . Oh, *thank you*, Mr Hero, you're very *kind*.' Maureen stretched her talons across the receiver and spoke in a stage-whisper to Archie, 'Archibald, love, Mr Hero wants to see you. Urgent, he says. You been a naughty boy or sommink?'

'I should cocoa!' said Archie, heading for the lift.

The door said:

Kelvin Hero
Company Director
Morgan*Hero*
Direct Mail Specialists

It was meant to intimidate and Archie responded in kind, rapping the door too lightly and then too hard and then kind of falling through it when Kelvin Hero, dressed in moleskin, turned the handle to let him in.

'Archie,' said Kelvin Hero, revealing a double row of pearly whites that owed more to expensive dentistry than to regular brushing. 'Archie, Archie, Archie, Archie.'

'Mr Hero,' said Archie.

'You puzzle me, Archie,' said Mr Hero.

'Mr Hero,' said Archie.

'Sit down there, Archie,' said Mr Hero.

'Right you are, Mr Hero,' said Archie.

Kelvin wiped a streak of grimy sweat from around his shirt collar, turned his silver Parker pen over a few times in his hand and took a series of deep breaths. 'Now, this is quite delicate . . . and I have never considered myself a racialist, Archie . . .'

'Mr Hero?'

Blimey, thought Kelvin, what an *eye-to-face ratio*. When you want to say something delicate, you don't want that eye-to-face ratio staring up at you. Big eyes, like a child's or a baby seal's; the physiognomy of innocence – looking at Archie Jones is like looking at something that expects to be clubbed round the head any second.

Kelvin tried a softer tack. 'Let me put it another way. Usually, when confronted with this type of delicate situation, I would, as you know, confer with *you*. Because I've always had a lot of *time* for you, Arch. I *respect* you. You're not *flashy*, Archie, you've never been flashy, but you're –'

'Sturdy,' finished Archie, because he knew this speech.

Kelvin smiled: a big gash across his face that came and went with the sudden violence of a fat man marching through swing doors. 'Right, yeah, *sturdy*. People *trust* you, Archie. I know you're getting on a bit, and the old leg gives you a bit of trouble – but when this business changed hands, I kept you on, Arch, because I could see straight off: *people trust you*. That's why you've stayed in the direct mail business so long. And I'm trusting you, Arch, to take what I've got to say in the right way.'

'Mr Hero?'

Kelvin shrugged. 'I could have lied to you, Archie, I could have told you that we'd made a mistake with the bookings, and there just wasn't room for you; I could have fished around in my arse and pulled out a juicy one – but you're a *big boy*, Archie. You'd phone the restaurant, you're not a baboon, Archie, you've got something upstairs, you'd have put two and two together –'

'And made four.'

'And made four, *exactly*, Archie. You would have made *four*. Do you understand what I'm saying to you, Archie?' said Mr Hero.

'No, Mr Hero,' said Archie.

Kelvin prepared to cut to the chase. 'That company dinner last month – it was awkward, Archie, it was unpleasant. And now there's this annual do coming up with our sister company from Sunderland, about thirty of us, nothing fancy, you know, a curry, a lager and a bit of a boogie . . . as I say, it's not that I'm a racialist, Archie . . .'

'A racialist . . .'

'I'd spit on that Enoch Powell . . . but then again he does have a point, doesn't he? There comes a point, a saturation point, and people begin to feel a bit uncomfortable . . . You see, all he was saying –'

'Who?'

'Powell, Archie, Powell – *try and keep up* – all he was saying is enough is enough after a certain point, isn't it? I mean, it's like Delhi in Euston every Monday morning. And there's some people around here, Arch – and I don't include myself here – who just feel your attitude is a little *strange*.'

'Strange?'

'You see the wives don't like it because, let's face it, she's a sort, a real beauty – incredible legs, Archie, I'd like to congratulate you on them legs – and the men, well, the men don't like it 'cos they don't like to think they're wanting a bit of the other when they're sitting down to a company dinner with their lady wives, especially when she's . . . *you know* . . . they don't know what to make of that at all.'

'Who?'

'What?'

'Who are we talking about, Mr Hero?'

'Look, Archie,' said Kelvin, the sweat now flowing freely, distasteful for a man with his amount of chest hair, 'take these.' Kelvin pushed a large wad of Luncheon Vouchers across the table. 'They're left over from that raffle – you remember, for the Biafrans.'

'Oh no – I already won an oven mitt in that, Mr Hero, there's no need –'

'Take them, Archie. There's fifty pounds' worth of vouchers in there, redeemable in over five thousand food outlets nationwide. Take them. Have a few meals on me.'

Archie fingered the vouchers like they were so many fifty pound notes. Kelvin thought for a moment he saw tears of happiness in his eyes.

'Well, I don't know what to say. There's a place I go to, pretty regular like. If they take these I'm made for life. Ta very much.'

Kelvin took a handkerchief to his forehead. 'Think nothing of it, Arch. Please.'

'Mr Hero, could I . . .' Archie gestured towards the door. 'It's just that I'd like to phone some people, you know, give them the news about the baby . . . if we've finished here.'

Kelvin nodded, relieved. Archie lifted himself out of his seat. He had just reached for the handle of the door when Kelvin snatched up his Parker pen once more and said, 'Oh, Archie, one more thing . . . that dinner with the Sunderland team . . . I talked to Maureen and I think we need to cut down on the numbers . . . we put the names in a hat and yours came out. Still, I don't suppose you'll be missing much, eh? These things are always a bit of a bore.'

'Right you are, Mr Hero,' said Archie, mind elsewhere; praying to God that O'Connell's was a 'food outlet'; smiling to himself, imagining Samad's reaction when he copped fifty quids' worth of bloody Luncheon Vouchers.

∽

Partly because Mrs Jones becomes pregnant so soon after Mrs Iqbal and partly because of a daily proximity (by this point Clara is working part time as a supervisor for a Kilburn youth group which looks like the fifteen-man line-up of a ska and roots band – six-inch Afros, Adidas tracksuits, brown ties, Velcro, sun-tinted shades – and Alsana attends an Asian Women's Pre-natal Class in Kilburn High Road round the corner), the two women begin to see more of each other. Hesitant in the beginning – a few lunch dates here and there, the occasional coffee – what begins as a rearguard action against their husbands' friendship soon develops. They have resigned themselves to their husbands' mutual appreciation society and the free time this leaves is not altogether unpleasant; there is time for picnics and outings, for discussion and personal study; for old French movies where Alsana screams and covers her eyes at the suggestion of nudity ('Put it away! We are not wanting to see the dangly bits!') and Clara gets a glimpse of how the other half live: the half who live on romance, passion and *joie de vivre*. The other half who have *sex*. The life that might have been hers had she not been at the top of some stairs one fine day as Archibald Jones waited at the bottom.

Then, when their bumps become too large and cinema seats no longer accommodate them, the women begin to meet up for lunch in Kilburn Park, often with the Niece-of-Shame, the three of them squeezed on to a generous bench where Alsana presses a thermos of P. G. Tips into Clara's hand, without milk, with lemon. Unwraps several layers of cling-film to reveal today's peculiar delight: savoury dough-like balls, crumbly Indian sweets shot through with the colours of the kaleidoscope, thin pastry with spiced beef inside, salad with onion; saying to Clara, 'Eat up! Stuff yourself silly! It's in there, wallowing around in your belly, waiting for the menu. Woman, don't torture it! You want to starve the bump?' For, despite appearances, there are six people on that bench (three living, three coming); one girl for Clara, two boys for Alsana.

Alsana says, 'Nobody's complaining, let's get that straight. Children are a blessing, the more the merrier. But I tell you, when I turned my head and saw that fancy ultra-business thingummybob . . .'

'Ultra*sound*,' corrects Clara, through a mouthful of rice.

'Yes, I almost had the heart attack to finish me off! Two! Feeding one is enough!'

Clara laughs and says she can imagine Samad's face when he saw it.

'No, dearie.' Alsana is reproving, tucking her large feet underneath the folds of her sari. 'He didn't see anything. He wasn't there. I am not letting him see things like that. A woman has to have the private things – a husband needn't be involved in body-business, in a lady's . . . *parts*.'

Niece-of-Shame, who is sitting between them, sucks her teeth.

'Bloody hell, Alsi, he must've been involved in your parts sometime, or is this the immaculate bloody conception?'

'So rude,' says Alsana to Clara in a snooty, English way. 'Too old to be so rude and too young to know any better.'

And then Clara and Alsana, with the accidental mirroring that happens when two people are sharing the same experience, both lay their hands on their bulges.

Neena, to redeem herself: 'Yeah . . . well . . . How are you doing on names? Any ideas?'

Alsana is decisive. 'Meena and Malānā, if they are girls. If boys: Magid and Millat. Ems are good. Ems are strong. Mahatma, Muhammad, that funny Mr Morecambe, from Morecambe and Wise – letter you can trust.'

But Clara is more cautious, because naming seems to her a fearful responsibility, a god-like task for a mere mortal. 'If it's a girl, I tink I like *Irie*. It patois. Means everyting *OK, cool, peaceful*, you know?'

Alsana is horrified before the sentence is finished: '"OK"? This is a name for a child? You might as well call her "*Wouldsirlikeanypoppadomswiththat?*" or "*Niceweatherweare having*".'

'– And Archie likes *Sarah*. Well, dere not much you can argue wid in Sarah, but dere's not much to get happy 'bout either. I suppose if it was good enough for the wife of Abraham –'

'Ibrāhim,' Alsana corrects, out of instinct more than Qur'ānic pedantry, 'popping out babies when she was a hundred years old, by the grace of Allah.'

And then Neena, groaning at the turn the conversation is taking: 'Well, I *like* Irie. It's funky. It's different.'

Alsana *loves* this. 'For pity's sake, what does Archibald know about *funky*. Or *different*. If I were you, dearie,' she says, patting Clara's knee, 'I'd choose Sarah and let that be an end to it. Sometimes you have to let these men have it their way. Anything for a little – how do you say it in the English? For a little' – she puts her finger over tightly pursed lips, like a guard at the gate – '*shush*.'

But in response Niece-of-Shame puts on the thick accent, bats her voluminous eyelashes, wraps her college scarf round her head like purdah. 'Oh yes, Auntie, yes, the little *submissive* Indian woman. You don't talk to him, he talks *at* you. You scream and shout at each other, but there's no communication. And in the end he wins anyway because he does whatever he likes, when he likes. You don't even know where he is, what he does, what he *feels*, half the time. It's 1975, Alsi. You can't conduct relationships like that any more. It's not like back home. There's got to be communication between men and women in the West, they've got to listen to each other, otherwise . . .' Neena mimes a small mushroom cloud going off in her hand.

'What a load of the cod's wallop,' says Alsana sonorously, closing her eyes, shaking her head, 'it is you who do not listen. By Allah, I will always give as good as I get. But you presume I *care* what he does. You presume I want to *know*. The truth is, for a marriage to survive you don't need all this talk, talk, talk; all this "I am this" and "I am really like this" like in the papers, all this *revelation* – especially when your husband is old, when he is wrinkly and falling apart – you do not *want* to know what is slimy underneath the bed and rattling in the wardrobe.'

Neena frowns, Clara cannot raise serious objection, and the rice is handed around once more.

'Moreover,' says Alsana after a pause, folding her dimpled arms underneath her breasts, pleased to be holding forth on a subject close to this formidable bosom, 'when you are from families such as ours you should have learnt that *silence*, what is *not* said, is the very *best* recipe for family life.'

For all three have been brought up in strict, religious families, houses where God appeared at every meal, infiltrated every childhood game, and sat in the lotus position under the bedclothes with a torch to check nothing untoward was occurring.

'So let me get this straight,' says Neena derisively. 'You're saying that a good dose of repression keeps a marriage healthy.'

And as if someone had pressed a button, Alsana is outraged. 'Repression! Nonsense silly-billy word! I'm just talking about common sense. What is my husband? What is yours?' she says, pointing to Clara. 'Twenty-five years they live before we are even *born*. What are they? What are they capable of? What blood do they have on their hands? What is sticky and smelly in their private areas? Who knows?' She throws her hands up, releasing the questions into the unhealthy Kilburn air, sending a troupe of sparrows up with them.

'What you don't understand, my Niece-of-Shame, what none of your generation understands . . .'

At which point Neena cannot stop a piece of onion escaping from her mouth due to the sheer strength of her objection. 'My *generation*? For fuckssake, you're two years older than me, Alsi.'

But Alsana continues regardless, miming a knife slicing through the niece-of-shame tongue-of-obscenity, '. . . is that not everybody wants to see into everybody else's sweaty, secret parts.'

'But Auntie,' begs Neena, raising her voice, because this is what she really wants to argue about, the largest sticking point between the two of them, Alsana's arranged marriage. 'How can you *bear* to live with somebody you don't know from Adam?'

In response, an infuriating *wink*: Alsana always likes to appear jovial at the very moment that her interlocutor becomes hot under the collar. 'Because, *Miss Smarty-pants*, it is by far the easier option. It was exactly because Eve did not know Adam from Adam that they got on so A-OK. Let me explain. Yes, I was married to Samad Iqbal the same evening of the very day I met him. Yes, I didn't know him from Adam. But I liked him well enough. We met in the breakfast room on a steaming Delhi day and he fanned me with *The Times*. I thought he had a good face, a sweet voice, and his backside was high and well formed for a man of his age. Very good. Now, every time I learn something more about him, *I like him less*. So you see, we were better off the way we were.'

Neena stamps her foot in exasperation at the skewed logic.

'Besides, I will never know him well. Getting anything out of my husband is like trying to squeeze water out when you're stoned.'

Neena laughs despite herself. 'Water out of a *stone*.'

'Yes, yes. You think I'm so stupid. But I am wise about things like men. I tell you' – Alsana prepares to deliver her summation as she has seen it done many years previously by the young Delhi lawyers with their slick side partings – 'men are the last mystery. God is easy compared with men. Now, enough of the philosophy: samosa?' She peels the lid off the plastic tub and sits fat, pretty and satisfied on her conclusion.

'Shame that you're having them,' says Neena to her aunt, lighting a fag. 'Boys, I mean. Shame that you're going to have boys.'

'What do you mean?'

This is Clara, who is the recipient of a secret (kept secret from Alsana and Archie) lending library of Neena's through which she reads, in a few short months, Greer's *Female Eunuch*, Jong's *Fear of Flying* and *The Second Sex*, all in a clandestine attempt, on Neena's part, to rid Clara of her 'false consciousness'.

'I mean, I just think men have caused enough chaos this century. There's enough fucking men in the world. If I knew I was going to have a boy' – she pauses to prepare her two falsely conscious friends for this new concept – 'I'd have to seriously consider abortion.'

Alsana screams, claps her hands over one of her own ears and one of Clara's, and then almost chokes on a piece of aubergine. For some reason the remark simultaneously strikes Clara as funny; hysterically, desperately funny; miserably funny; and the Niece-of-Shame sits between the two, nonplussed, while the two egg-shaped women bend over themselves, one in laughter, the other in horror and asphyxiation.

'Are you all right, ladies?'

It is Sol Jozefowicz, the old guy who back then took it upon himself to police the park (though his job as park keeper had long since been swept away in council cuts), Sol Jozefowicz stands in front of them, ready as always to be of aid.

'We are all going to burn in hell, Mr Jozefowicz, if you call that being all right,' explains Alsana, pulling herself together.

Niece-of-Shame rolls her eyes. 'Speak for yourself.'

But Alsana is faster than any sniper when it comes to firing back. 'I do, I do – thankfully Allah has arranged it that way.'

'Good afternoon, Neena, good afternoon, Mrs Jones,' says Sol, offering a neat bow to each. 'Are you sure you are all right? Mrs Jones?'

Clara cannot stop the tears from squeezing out of the corners of her eyes. She cannot work out, at this moment, whether it is crying or laughing.

'I'm fine . . . fine, sorry to have worried you, Mr Jozefowicz . . . really, I'm fine.'

'I do not see what's so very funny-funny,' mutters Alsana. 'The murder of innocents – is this funny?'

'Not in my experience, Mrs Iqbal, no,' says Sol Jozefowicz, in the collected manner in which he said everything, passing his handkerchief to Clara. It strikes all three women – the way history will, embarrassingly, without warning, like a blush – what the ex-park keeper's experience might have been. They fall silent.

'Well, as long as you ladies are fine, I'll be getting on,' says Sol, motioning that Clara can keep the handkerchief and replacing the hat he had removed in the old fashion. He bows his neat little bow once more, and sets off slowly, anti-clockwise round the park.

Once Sol is out of earshot: 'OK, Auntie Alsi, I apologize, I apologize . . . For fuck's sake, what more do you want?'

'Oh, every-bloody-thing,' says Alsana, her voice losing the fight, becoming vulnerable. 'The whole bloody universe made clear – in a little nutshell. I cannot understand a thing any more, and I am just beginning. You understand?'

She sighs, not waiting for an answer, not looking at Neena, but across the way at the hunched, disappearing figure of Sol winding in and out of the yew trees. 'You may be right about Samad . . . about many things. Maybe there are no good men, not even the two I might have in this belly . . . and maybe I do not talk enough with mine, maybe I have married a stranger. You might see the truth better than I. What do I know . . . barefoot country girl . . . never went to the universities.'

'Oh, Alsi,' Neena is saying, weaving in and out of Alsana's words like tapestry; feeling bad. 'You know I didn't mean it like that.'

'But I cannot be worrying-worrying all the time about the *truth*. I have to worry about the truth that can be *lived with*. And that is the difference between losing your marbles drinking the salty sea, or swallowing the stuff from the streams. My Niece-of-Shame believes in the talking cure, eh?' says Alsana, with something of a grin. 'Talk, talk, talk and it will be better. Be honest, slice open your heart and spread the red stuff around. But the past is made of more than words, dearie. We married old men, you see? These bumps' – Alsana pats them both – 'they will always have daddy-long-legs for fathers. One leg in the present, one in the past. No talking will change this. Their roots will always be tangled. And roots get dug up. Just look in my garden – birds at the coriander every bloody day . . .'

Just as he reaches the far gate, Sol Jozefowicz turns round to wave, and three women wave back. Clara feels a little theatrical, flying his cream handkerchief above her head. Like she is seeing someone off for a train journey crossing the border of two countries.

'How did they meet?' asks Neena, trying to lift the cloud that has somehow descended on their picnic. 'I mean Mr Jones and Samad Miah.'

Alsana throws her head back, a dismissive gesture. 'Oh, in the war. Off killing some poor bastards who didn't deserve it, no doubt. And what did they get for their trouble? A broken hand for Samad Miah and for the other one a funny leg. Some use, some use, all this.'

'Archie's *right* leg,' says Clara quietly, pointing to a place in her own thigh. 'A piece of metal, I tink. But he don' really tell me nuttin'.'

'Oh, who cares!' Alsana bursts out. 'I'd trust Vishnu the many-handed pick-pocket before I believed a word those men say.'

But Clara holds dear the image of the young soldier Archie, particularly when the old, flabby Direct Mail Archie is on top of her. 'Oh, come now . . . we don' know what –'

Alsana spits quite frankly on the grass. 'Shitty lies! If they are heroes, where are their hero things? Where are the hero bits and bobs? Heroes – they have things. They have hero stuff. You can spot them ten miles away. I've never seen a medal . . . and not so much as a photograph.' Alsana makes an unpleasant noise at the back of her throat, her signal for disbelief. 'So look at it – no, dearie, it must be done – look at it *close up*. Look at what is left. Samad has one hand; says he wants to find God but the fact is God's given him the slip; and he has been in that curry house for two years already, serving up stringy goat to the whiteys who don't know any better, and Archibald – well, look at the thing close up . . .'

Alsana stops to check with Clara if she could speak her mind further without causing offence or unnecessary pain, but Clara's eyes are closed and she is already looking at the thing close up; a young girl looking at an old man close up; finishing Alsana's sentence with the beginning of a smile spreading across her face,

'. . . folds paper for a living, dear *Jesus*.'

5 *The Root Canals of Alfred Archibald Jones and Samad Miah Iqbal*

A propos: it's all very well, this instruction of Alsana's to look at the thing close up; to look at it dead-straight between the eyes; an unflinching and honest stare, a meticulous inspection that would go beyond the heart of the matter to its marrow, beyond the marrow to the root – but the question is how far back do you want? How far will *do*? The old American question: what do you want – *blood*? Most probably more than blood is required: whispered asides; lost conversations; medals and photographs; lists and certificates, yellowing paper bearing the faint imprint of brown dates. Back, back, *back*. Well, all right, then. Back to Archie spit-clean, pink-faced and polished, looking just old enough at seventeen to fool the men from the medical board with their pencils and their measuring tape. Back to Samad, two years older and the warm colour of baked bread. Back to the day when they were first assigned to each other, Samad Miah Iqbal (row 2, Over here now, soldier!) and Alfred Archibald Jones (Move it, move it, move it), the day Archie involuntarily forgot that most fundamental principle of English manners. He stared. They were standing side by side on a stretch of black dirt-track Russian ground, dressed identically in little triangular caps perched on their heads like paper sailing-boats, wearing the same itchy standard uniform, their ice-pinched toes resting in the same black boots scattered with the same dust. But Archie couldn't help but stare. And Samad put up with it, waited and waited for it to pass, until after a week of being cramped in their tank, hot and suffocated by the airless machine and subjected to Archie's relentless gaze, he had putted-up-with as much as his hot-head ever could put up with anything.

'My friend, what is it you find so darned mysterious about me that it has you in such constant revelries?'

'You what?' said Archie, flustered, for he was not one to have private conversations on army time. 'Nobody, I mean, nothing – I mean, well, what do *you* mean?'

They both spoke under their breath, for the conversation was not private in the other sense, there being two other privates and a captain in their five-man Churchill rolling through Athens on its way to Thessaloníki. It was 1 April 1945. Archie Jones was the driver of the tank, Samad was the wireless operator, Roy Mackintosh was the co-driver, Will Johnson was crunched on a bin as the gunner, and Thomas Dickinson-Smith was sitting on the slightly elevated chair, which, even though it squashed his head against the ceiling, his newly granted captaincy would not permit his pride to relinquish. None of them had seen anyone else but each other for three weeks.

'I mean merely that it is likely we have another two years stuck in this thing.'

A voice crackled through the wireless, and Samad, not wishing to be seen neglecting his duties, answered it speedily and efficiently.

'And?' asked Archie, after Samad had given their coordinates.

'And there is only so much of that eyeballing that a man can countenance. Is it that you are doing some research into wireless operators or are you just in a passion over my arse?'

Their captain, Dickinson-Smith, who *was* in a passion over Samad's arse (but not only that; also his mind; also two slender muscular arms that could only make sense wrapped around a lover; also those luscious light green/brown eyes) silenced the conversation immediately.

'Ick-Ball! Jones! Get on with it. Do you see anyone else here chewing the fat?'

'I was just making an objection, sir. It is hard, sir, for a man to concentrate on his Foxtrot F's and his Zebra Z's and then his dots and his dashes when he has a pug-dog fellow who follows his every move with his pug-dog eyes, sir. In Bengal one would assume such eyes belonged to a man filled with –'

'Shut it, Sultan, you poof,' said Roy, who hated Samad and his poncey-radio-operator-ways.

'*Mackintosh,*' said Dickinson-Smith, 'come now, let's not stop the Sultan. Continue, Sultan.'

To avoid the possible suggestion that he was partial to Samad, Captain Dickinson-Smith made a practice of picking on him and encouraging his hateful Sultan nickname, but he never did it in the right way; it was always too soft, too similar to Samad's own luxurious language and only resulted in Roy and the other eighty Roys under his direct command hating Dickinson-Smith, ridiculing him, openly displaying their disrespect; by April 1945 they were utterly filled with contempt for him and sickened by his poncey-commander-queer-boy-ways. Archie, new to the First Assault Regiment R. E., was just learning this.

'I just told him to shut it, and he'll shut it if he knows what's good for him, the Indian Sultan bastard. No disrespect to you, sir, 'course,' added Roy, as a polite gesture.

Dickinson-Smith knew in other regiments, in other tanks, it simply was not the case that people spoke back to their superiors or even spoke at all. Even Roy's Polite Gesture was a sign of Dickinson-Smith's failure. In those other tanks, in the Shermans, Churchills and Matildas dotted over the waste of Europe like resilient cockroaches, there was no question of respect or disrespect. Only Obey, Disobey, Punish.

'Sultan . . . Sultan . . .' Samad mused. 'Do you know, I wouldn't mind the epithet, Mr Mackintosh, if it were at least *accurate*. It's not historically *accurate*, you know. It is not, even *geographically* speaking, accurate. I am sure I have explained to you that I am from *Bengal*. The word "Sultan" refers to certain men of the *Arab* lands – many hundreds of miles west of Bengal. To call me Sultan is about as accurate, in terms of the mileage, you understand, as if I referred to you as a Jerry-Hun fat bastard.'

'I called you Sultan and I'm calling you it again, all right?'

'Oh, Mr *Mackintosh*. Is it so complex, is it so impossible, that you and I, stuck in this British machine, could find it in ourselves to fight together as British subjects?'

Will Johnson, who was a bit simple, took off his cap as he always did when someone said 'British'.

'What's the poof on about?' asked Mackintosh, adjusting his beer-gut.

'Nothing,' said Samad. 'I'm afraid I was not "on" about anything; I was just talking, talking, just trying the shooting of the breeze as they say, and trying to get Sapper Jones here to stop his staring business, his goggly eyes, just this and only this . . . and I have failed on both counts, it seems.'

He seemed genuinely wounded, and Archie felt the sudden unsoldier-like desire to remove pain. But it was not the place and not the time.

'All right. Enough, all of you. Jones, check the map,' said Dickinson-Smith.

Archie checked the map.

Their journey was a long tiresome one, rarely punctuated by any action. Archie's tank was a bridge-builder, one of the specialist divisions not tied to English county allegiances or to a type of weaponry, but providing service across the army and from country to country, recovering damaged equipment, laying bridges, creating passages for battle, creating routes where routes had been destroyed. Their job was not so much to fight the war as to make sure it ran smoothly. By the time Archie joined the conflict, it was clear that the cruel, bloody decisions would be made by air, not in the 30-centimetre difference between the width of a German armour piercing shell and an English one. The real war, the one where cities were brought to their knees, the war with the deathly calculations of size, detonation, population, went on many miles above Archie's head. Meanwhile, on the ground, their heavy, armour-plated scout-tank had a simpler task: to avoid the civil war in the mountains – a war within a war – between the EAM and the ELAS; to pick their way through the glazed eyes of dead statistics and the 'wasted youth'; to make sure the roads of communication stretching from one end of hell to the other were fully communicable.

'The bombed ammunition factory is twenty miles south-west, sir. We are to collect what we can, sir. Private Ick-Ball has passed to me at 16.47 hours a radio message that informs me that the area, as far as can be seen from the air, sir, is unoccupied, sir,' said Archie.

'This is not war,' Samad had said quietly.

Two weeks later, as Archie checked their route to Sofia, to no one in particular Samad said, 'I should not be here.'

As usual he was ignored; most fiercely and resolutely by Archie, who wanted somehow to listen.

'I mean, I am educated. I am trained. I should be soaring with the Royal Airborne Force, shelling from on high! I am an officer! Not some mullah, some sepoy, wearing out my chappals in hard service. My great-grandfather Mangal Pande' – he looked around for the recognition the name deserved but, being met only with blank pancake English faces, he continued – 'was the great hero of the Indian Mutiny!'

Silence.

'Of 1857! It was he who shot the first hateful pigfat-smeared bullet and sent it spinning off into oblivion!'

A longer, denser silence.

'If it wasn't for this buggery hand' – Samad, inwardly cursing the English goldfish-memory for history, lifted five dead, tightly curled fingers from their usual resting place on his chest – 'this shitty hand that the useless Indian army gave me for my troubles, I would have matched his achievements. And why am I crippled? Because the Indian army knows more about the kissing of arses than it does about the heat and sweat of battle! Never go to India, Sapper Jones, my dear friend, it is a place for fools and worse than fools. Fools, Hindus, Sikhs and Punjabis. And now there is all this murmuring about independence – give *Bengal* independence, Archie, is what I say – leave India in bed with the British, if that's what she likes.'

His arm crashed to his side with the dead weight and rested itself like an old man after an angry fit. Samad always addressed Archie as if they were in league together against the rest of the tank. No matter how much Archie shunned him, those four days of eyeballing had created a kind of silk-thread bond between the two men that Samad tugged whenever he got the opportunity.

'You see, Jones,' said Samad, 'the real mistake the viceroy made was to give the Sikhs any position of power, you see? Just because they have some limited success with the kaffir in Africa, he says Yes, Mr Man, with your sweaty fat face and your silly fake English moustache and your pagri balanced like a large shit on the top of your head, you can be an officer, we will Indianize the army; go, go and fight in Italy, Rissaldar Major Pugri, Daffadar Pugri, with my grand old English troops! Mistake! And then they take me, hero of the 9th North Bengal Mounted Rifles, hero of the Bengal flying corps, and say, "Samad Miah Iqbal, Samad, we are going to confer on you a great honour. You will fight in mainland Europe – not starve and drink your own piss in Egypt or Malaya, no – you will fight the Hun where you find him." On his very doorstep, Sapper Jones, on his very doorstep. So! I went. Italy, I thought, well, this is where I will show the English army that the Muslim men of Bengal can fight like any Sikh. Better! Stronger! And are the best educated and are those with the good blood, we who are truly of Officer Material.'

'Indian officers? That'll be the bloody day,' said Roy.

'On my first day there,' continued Samad, 'I destroyed a Nazi hide-out from the air. Like a swooping eagle.'

'Bollocks,' said Roy.

'On my second day, I shot from the air the enemy as he approached the Gothic Line, breaking the Argenta Gap and pushing the Allies through to the Po Valley. Lord Mountbatten himself was to have congratulated me himself in his own person. He would have shaken this hand. But this was all prevented. Do you know what occurred on my third day, Sapper Jones? Do you know how I was crippled? A young man in his prime?'

'No,' said Archie quietly.

'A bastard Sikh, Sapper Jones, a bastard fool. As we stood in a trench, his gun went off and shot me through the wrist. But I wouldn't have it amputated. Every bit of my body comes from Allah. Every bit will return to him.'

So Samad had ended up in the unfêted bridge-laying division of His Majesty's Army with the rest of the losers; with men like Archie, with men like Dickinson-Smith (whose government file included the phrase 'Risk: Homosexual'), with frontal lobotomy cases like Mackintosh and Johnson. The rejects of war. As Roy affectionately called it: the Buggered Battalion. Much of the problem with the outfit lay with the captain of the First Assault Regiment: Dickinson-Smith was no soldier. And certainly no commander, though commanding was in his genes. Against his will he had been dragged out of his father's college, shaken free of his father's gown, and made to Fight A War, as his father had. And his father before him, and his father before him, ad infinitum. Young Thomas had resigned himself to his fate and was engaged in a concerted and prolonged effort (four years now) to get his name on the ever extending list of Dickinson-Smiths carved on a long slab of death-stone in the village of Little Marlow, to be buried on top of them all in the family's sardine-can tomb that proudly dominated the historic churchyard.

Killed by the Hun, the Wogs, the Chinks, the Kaffirs, the Frogs, the Scots, the Spics, the Zulus, the Indians (South, East and Red), and accidentally mistaken for a darting okapi by a

Swede on a big-game hunt in Nairobi, traditionally the Dickinson-Smiths were insatiable in their desire to see Dickinson-Smith blood spilled on foreign soil. And on the occasions when there wasn't a war the Dickinson-Smiths busied themselves with the Irish Situation, a kind of Dickinson-Smith holiday resort of death, which had been going since 1600 and showed no sign of letting up. But dying's no easy trick. And though the chance to hurl themselves in front of any sort of lethal weaponry had held a magnetic attraction for the family throughout the ages, this Dickinson-Smith couldn't seem to manage it. Poor Thomas had a different kind of lust for exotic ground. He wanted to know it, to nurture it, to learn from it, to love it. He was a simple non-starter at the war game.

The long story of how Samad went from the pinnacle of military achievement in the Bengal corps to the Buggered Battalion was told and retold to Archie, in different versions and with elaborations upon it, once a day for another two weeks, whether he listened or not. Tedious as it was, it was a highlight next to the other tales of failure that filled those long nights, and kept the men of the Buggered Battalion in their preferred state of demotivation and despair. Amongst the well-worn canon was the Tragic Death of Roy's Fiancée, a hairdresser who slipped on a set of rollers and broke her neck on the sink; Archie's Failure to Go to Grammar School because his mother couldn't afford to buy the uniform; Dickinson-Smith's many murdered relatives; as for Will Johnson, he did not speak in the day but whimpered as he slept, and his face spoke eloquently of more miserable miseries than anyone dare inquire into. The Buggered Battalion continued like this for some time, a travelling circus of discontents roaming aimlessly through Eastern Europe; freaks and fools with no audience but each other. Who performed and stared in turns. Until finally the tank rolled into a day that History has not remembered. That Memory has made no effort to retain. A sudden stone submerged. False teeth floating silently to the bottom of a glass. 6 May 1945.

At about 18.00 hours on the 6th of May 1945 something in the tank blew up. It wasn't a bomb noise but an engineering disaster noise, and the tank slowly ground to a halt. They were in a tiny Bulgarian village bordering Greece and Turkey, which the war had got bored with and left, returning the people to almost normal routine.

'Right,' said Roy, having had a look at the problem. 'The engine's buggered and one of the tracks has broken. We're gonna have to radio for help, and then sit tight till it arrives. Nothing we can do.'

'We're going to make no effort at all to repair it?' asked Samad.

'No,' said Dickinson-Smith. 'Private Mackintosh is right. There's no way we could deal with this kind of damage with the equipment we have at hand. We'll just have to wait here until help arrives.'

'How long will this be?'

'A day,' piped up Johnson. 'We're way off from the rest.'

'Are we required, Captain Smith, to remain in the vehicle for these twenty-four hours?' asked Samad, who despaired of Roy's personal hygiene and was loath to spend a stationary, sultry evening with him.

'Bloody right we are – what d'ya think this is, a day off?' growled Roy.

'No, no . . . I don't see why you shouldn't wander a bit – there's no point in us all being holed up here. You and Jones go, report back, and then Privates Mackintosh, Johnson and I will go when you come back.'

So Samad and Archie went into the village and spent three hours drinking Sambucca and listening to the café owner tell of the miniature invasion of two Nazis who turned up in the town, ate all his supplies, had sex with two loose village girls and shot a man in the head for failing to give them directions to the next town swiftly enough.

'In everything they were impatient,' said the old man, shaking his head. Samad settled the bill.

Walking back, Archie said, 'Cor, they don't need many of 'em to conquer and pillage,' in an attempt to make conversation.

'One strong man and one weak is a colony, Sapper Jones,' said Samad.

When Archie and Samad reached the tank, they found Privates Mackintosh and Johnson and Captain Thomas Dickinson-Smith dead. Johnson strangled with cheese wire, Roy shot in the back. Roy's jaw had been forced open, his silver fillings removed; a pair of pliers now sat in his mouth like an iron tongue. It appeared that Thomas Dickinson-Smith had, as his attacker moved towards him, turned from his allotted fate and shot himself in the face. The only Dickinson-Smith to die by English hands.

While Archie and Samad assessed this situation as best they could, Colonel-General Jodl sat in a small red schoolhouse in Reims and shook his fountain pen. Once. Twice. Then led the ink a solemn dance along the dotted line and wrote history in his name. The end of war in Europe. As the paper was whisked away by a man at his shoulder, Jodl hung his head, struck by the full realization of the deed. But it would be a full two weeks before either Archie or Samad were to hear about it.

These were strange times, strange enough for an Iqbal and a Jones to strike up a friendship. That day, while the rest of Europe celebrated, Samad and Archie stood on a Bulgarian roadside, Samad clutching a handful of wires, chipboard and metal casing in his good fist.

'This radio is stripped to buggery,' said Samad. 'We'll need to begin from the beginning. This is a very bad business, Jones. Very bad. We have lost our means of communication, transport and defence. Worst: we have lost our command. A man of war without a commander is a very bad business indeed.'

Archie turned from Samad and threw up violently in a bush. Private Mackintosh, for all his big talk, had shat himself at St Peter's Gate, and the smell had forced itself into Archie's lungs and dragged up his nerves, his fear and his breakfast.

As far as fixing the radio went, Samad knew *how*, he knew the *theory*, but Archie had the hands, and a certain knack when it came to wires and nails and glue. And it was a funny kind of struggle between knowledge and practical ability which went on between them as they pieced together the tiny metal strips that might save them both.

'Pass me the three-ohm resistor, will you?'

Archie went very red, unsure which item Samad was referring to. His hand wavered across the box of wires and bits and bobs. Samad discreetly coughed as Archie's little finger strayed towards the correct item. It was awkward, an Indian telling an Englishman what to do – but somehow the quietness of it, the manliness of it, got them over it. It was during this time that Archie learnt the true power of do-it-yourself, how it uses a hammer and nails to replace nouns and adjectives, how it allows men to communicate. A lesson he kept with him all his life.

'Good man,' said Samad, as Archie passed him the electrode, but then, finding one hand not enough to manipulate the wires or to pin them to the radio board, he passed the item back to Archie and signalled where it was to be put.

'We'll get this done in no time,' said Archie cheerfully.

'Bubblegum! Please, mister!'

By the fourth day, a gang of village children had begun to gather round the tank, attracted by the grisly murders, Samad's green-eyed glamour, and Archie's American bubblegum.

'Mr Soldier,' said one chestnut-hued sparrow-weight boy in careful English, 'bubblegum please thankyou.'

Archie reached into his pocket and pulled out five thin pink strips. The boy distributed them snootily amongst his friends. They began chewing wildly, eyes bursting from their heads with the effort. Then, as the flavour subsided, they stood in silent, awed contemplation of their benefactor. After a few minutes the same scrawny boy was sent up as the People's Representative once more.

'Mr Soldier.' He held out his hand. 'Bubblegum please thankyou.'

'No more,' said Archie, going through an elaborate sign language. 'I've got no more.'

'Please, thankyou. *Please?*' repeated the boy urgently.

'Oh, for God's sake,' snapped Samad. 'We have to fix the radio and get this thing moving. Let's get on with it, OK?'

'Bubblegum, mister, Mr Soldier, bubblegum.' It became a chant, almost; the children mixing up the few words they had learnt, placing them in any order.

'*Please?*' The boy stretched out his arm in such a strenuous manner that it pushed him on to the very tips of his toes.

Suddenly he opened his palm, and then smiled coquettishly, preparing to bargain. There in his open fist four green notes were screwed into a bundle like a handful of grass.

'Dollars, mister!'

'Where did you get this?' asked Samad, making a snatch for it. The boy seized back his hand. He moved constantly from one foot to another – the impish dance that children learn from war. The simplest version of being on your guard.

'First bubblegum, mister.'

'Tell me where you got this. I warn you not to play the fool with me.'

Samad made a grab for the boy and caught him by the arm of his shirt. He tried desperately to wriggle free. The boy's friends began to slink off, deserting their quickly sinking champion.

'Did you kill a man for this?'

A vein in Samad's forehead was fighting passionately to escape his skin. He wished to defend a country that wasn't his and revenge the killing of men who would not have acknowledged him in a civilian street. Archie was amazed. It was his country; in his small, cold-blooded, average way he was one of the many essential vertebrae in its backbone, yet he could feel nothing comparable for it.

'No, mister, no, no. From him. Him.'

He stretched his free arm and pointed to a large derelict house that sat like a fat brooding hen on the horizon.

'Did someone in that house kill our men?' barked Samad.

'What you say, mister?' squeaked the boy.

'Who is there?'

'He is doctor. He is there. But sick. Can't move. Dr Sick.'

A few remaining children excitedly confirmed the name. Dr Sick, mister, Dr Sick.

'What's wrong with him?'

The boy, now enjoying the attention, theatrically mimed a man crying.

'English? Like us? German? French? Bulgarian? Greek?' Samad released the boy, tired from the misplaced energy.

'He no one. He Dr Sick, only,' said the boy dismissively. 'Bubblegum?'

A few days later and still no help had arrived. The strain of having to be continually at war in such a pleasant village began to pull at Archie and Samad, and bit by bit they relaxed more and more into a kind of civilian life. Every evening they ate dinner in the old man Gozan's kitchen-café. Watery soup cost five cigarettes each. Any kind of fish cost a low-ranking bronze medal. As Archie was now wearing one of Dickinson-Smith's uniforms, his own having fallen apart, he had a few of the dead man's medals to spare and with them purchased other niceties and necessities: coffee, soap, chocolate. For some pork Archie handed over a fag-card of Dorothy Lamour that had been pressed against his arse in his back pocket ever since he joined up.

'Go on, Sam – we'll use them as tokens, like food stamps; we can buy them back when we have the means, if you like.'

'I'm a Muslim,' said Samad, pushing a plate of pork away. 'And my Rita Hayworth leaves me only with my own soul.'

'Why don't you eat it?' said Archie, guzzling his two chops down like a madman. 'Strange business, if you ask me.'

'I don't eat it for the same reason you as an Englishman will never truly satisfy a woman.'

'Why's that?' said Archie, pausing from his feast.

'It's in our cultures, my friend.' He thought for a minute. 'Maybe deeper. Maybe in our bones.'

After dinner, they would make a pretence of scouring the village for the killers, rushing through the town, searching the same three disreputable bars and looking in the back bedrooms of pretty women's houses, but after a time this too was abandoned and they sat instead smoking cheap cigars outside the tank, enjoying the lingering crimson sunsets and chatting about their previous incarnations as newspaper boy (Archie) and biology student (Samad). They knocked around ideas that Archie did not entirely understand, and Samad offered secrets into the cool night that he had never spoken out loud. Long, comfortable silences passed between them like those between women who have known each other for years. They looked out on to stars that lit up unknown country, but neither man clung particularly to home. In short, it was precisely the kind of friendship an Englishman makes on holiday, that he can make only on holiday. A friendship that crosses class and colour, a friendship that takes as its basis physical proximity and survives because the Englishman assumes the physical proximity will not continue.

*

A week and a half since the radio had been repaired and there was still no reply to the aid signals they sent bouncing along the airwaves in search of ears to hear them. (By now, the village knew the war was over, but they felt disinclined to reveal the fact to their two visitors, whose daily bartering had proved such a boost to the local economy.) In the stretches of empty time Archie would lever up sections of the wheel track with an iron pole, while Samad investigated the problem. Across continents, both men's families presumed them dead.

'Is there a woman that you have back in Brighton City?' asked Samad, anchoring his head between the lion jaws of track and tank.

Archie was not a good-looking boy. He was dashing if you took a photo and put your thumb over his nose and mouth, but otherwise he was quite unremarkable. Girls would be attracted to his large, sad Sinatra blue eyes, but then be put off by the Bing Crosby ears and the nose that ended in a natural onion-bulb swelling like W. C. Fields's.

'A few,' he said nonchalantly. 'You know, here and there. You?'

'A young lady has already been picked out for me. A Miss Begum – daughter of Mr and Mrs Begum. The "in-laws", as you say. Dear God, those two are so far up the rectums of the establishment in Bengal that even the Lord Governor sits snivelling waiting for his mullah to come in carrying a dinner invitation from them!'

Samad laughed loudly and waited for company, but Archie, not understanding a word, stayed poker-faced as usual.

'Oh, they are the best people,' continued Samad, only slightly dispirited. 'The very best people. Extremely good blood . . . and as an added bonus, there is a propensity amongst their women – traditionally, throughout the ages, you understand – for really enormous melons.'

Samad performed the necessary mime, and then returned his

attention to realigning each tooth of track with its appropriate groove.

'And?' asked Archie.

'And what?'

'Are they . . . ?' Archie repeated the mime, but this time with the kind of anatomical exaggeration that leaves air-traced women unable to stand upright.

'Oh, but I have still some time to wait,' he said, smiling wistfully. 'Unfortunately, the Begum family do not yet have a female child of my generation.'

'You mean your wife's not bloody born yet?'

'What of it?' asked Samad, pulling a cigarette from Archie's top pocket. He scratched a match along the side of the tank and lit it. Archie wiped the sweat off his face with a greasy hand.

'Where I come from,' said Archie, 'a bloke likes to get to know a girl before he marries her.'

'Where you come from it is customary to boil vegetables until they fall apart. This does not mean,' said Samad tersely, 'that it is a good idea.'

Their final evening in the village was absolutely dark, silent. The muggy air made it unpleasant to smoke, so Archie and Samad tapped their fingers on the cold stone steps of a church, for lack of other hand-employment. For a moment, in the twilight, Archie forgot the war that had actually ceased to exist anyway. A past tense, future perfect kind of night.

It was while they were still innocent of peace, during this last night of ignorance, that Samad decided to cement his friendship with Archie. Often this is done by passing on a singular piece of information: some sexual peccadillo, some emotional secret or obscure hidden passion that the reticence of new acquaintance has prevented being spoken. But for Samad, nothing was closer or meant more to him than his blood. It was natural, then, as they sat on holy ground, that he should speak of what was holy to him. And there was no stronger evocation of the blood that ran through him, and the ground which that blood had stained over the centuries, than the story of his great-grandfather. So Samad told Archie the much neglected, 100-year-old, mildewed yarn of Mangal Pande.

'So, he was your grandfather?' said Archie, after the tale had been told, the moon had passed behind clouds, and he had been suitably impressed. 'Your real, blood grandfather?'

'*Great*-grandfather.'

'Well, that *is* something. Do you know: I remember it from school – I *do* – History of the Colonies, Mr Juggs. Bald, bug-eyed, nasty old duffer – Mr Juggs, I mean, not your grandfather. Got the message through, though, even if it took a ruler to the back of your hand . . . You know, you still hear people in the regiments calling each other *Pandies*, you know, if the bloke's a bit of a rebel . . . I never thought where it came from . . . Pande was the rebel, didn't like the English, shot the first bullet of the Mutiny. I remember it now, clear as a bell. And that was your grandfather!'

'*Great*-grandfather.'

'Well, well. That's something, isn't it?' said Archie, placing his hands behind his head and lying back to look at the stars. 'To have a bit of history in your blood like that. Motivates you, I'd imagine. I'm a Jones, you see. 'Slike a "Smith". We're nobody . . . My father used to say: "We're the chaff, boy, we're the chaff." Not that I've ever been much bothered, mind. Proud all the same, you know. Good honest English stock. But in your family you had a hero!'

Samad puffed up with pride. 'Yes, Archibald, that is *exactly* the word. Naturally, you will get these petty English academics trying to discredit him, because they cannot bear to give an Indian his due. But he was a hero and every act I have undertaken in this war has been in the shadow of his example.'

'That's true, you know,' said Archie thoughtfully. 'They don't speak well about Indians back home; they certainly wouldn't like it if you said an Indian was a hero . . . everybody would look at you a bit funny.'

Suddenly Samad grabbed his hand. It was hot, almost fevered, Archie thought. He'd never had another man grab his hand; his first instinct was to move or punch him or something, but then he reconsidered because Indians were emotional, weren't they? All that spicy food and that.

'*Please*. Do me this one, great favour, Jones. If ever you hear anyone, when you are back home – if you, if *we*, get back to our respective homes – if ever you hear anyone speak of the East,' and here his voice plummeted a register, and the tone was full and sad, '*hold your judgement*. If you are told "they are all this" or "they do this" or "their opinions are these", withhold your judgement until all the facts are upon you. Because that land they call "India" goes by a thousand names and is populated by millions, and if you think you have found two men the same amongst that multitude, then you are mistaken. It is merely a trick of the moonlight.'

Samad released his hand and rummaged in his pocket, dabbing his finger into a repository of white dust he kept in there, slipping it discreetly into his mouth. He leant against the wall and drew his fingertips along the stone. It was a tiny missionary church, converted into a hospital and then abandoned after two months when the sound of shells began to shake the windowsills. Samad and Archie had taken to sleeping there because of the thin mattresses and the large airy windows. Samad had taken an interest too (due to loneliness, he told himself; due to melancholy) in the powdered morphine to be found in stray storage cabinets throughout the building; hidden eggs on an addictive Easter trail. Whenever Archie went to piss or to try the radio once more, Samad roved up and down his little church, looting cabinet after cabinet, like a sinner moving from confessional to confessional. Then, having found his little bottle of sin, he would take the opportunity to rub a little into his gums or smoke a little in his pipe, and then lay back on the cool terracotta floor, looking up into the exquisite curve of the church dome. It was covered in words, this church. Words left three hundred years earlier by dissenters, unwilling to pay a burial tax during a cholera epidemic, locked in the church by a corrupt landlord and left to die in there – but not before they covered every wall with letters to family, poems, statements of eternal disobedience. Samad liked the story well enough when he first heard it, but it only truly struck him when the morphine hit. Then every nerve in his body would be alive, and the information, all the information contained in the universe, all the information on walls, would pop its cork and flow through him like electricity through a ground wire. Then his head would open out like a deckchair. And he would sit in it a while and watch his world go by. Tonight, after just more than enough, Samad felt particularly lucid. Like his tongue was buttered and like the world was a polished marble egg. And he felt a kinship with the dead dissenters, they were Pande's brothers – every rebel, it seemed to Samad tonight, was his brother – he wished he could speak with them about the mark they made on the world. Had it been enough? When death came, was it really enough? Were they satisfied with the thousand words they left behind?

'I'll tell you something for nothing,' said Archie, following Samad's eyes and catching the church dome's reflection in them. 'If I'd only had a few hours left, I wouldn't have spent it painting pictures on the ceiling.'

'Tell me,' inquired Samad, irritated to have been dragged from his pleasant contemplation, 'what great challenge would you undertake in the hours before your death? Unravel Fermat's Theorem, perhaps? Master Aristotelian philosophy?'

'What? Who? No . . . I'd – you know . . . make *love* – to a *lady*,' said Archie, whose inexperience made him prudish. 'You know . . . for the *last time*.'

Samad broke into a laugh. 'For the first time, is more likely.'

'Oh, go on, I'm *serious*.'

'All right. And if there were no "ladies" in the vicinity?'

'Well, you can always,' and here Archie went a pillar-box red, this being his own version of cementing a friendship, 'slap the salami, as the GIs say!'

'*Slap*,' repeated Samad contemptuously, '*the salami* . . . and that is it, is it? The last thing you would wish to do before you shuffled off this mortal coil is "slap your salami". Achieve orgasm.'

Archie, who came from Brighton, where nobody ever, *ever* said words like orgasm, began to convulse with hysterical embarrassment.

'Who is funny? Something is funny?' asked Samad, lighting a fag distractedly despite the heat, his mind carried elsewhere by the morphine.

'Nobody,' began Archie haltingly, 'nothing.'

'Can't you see it, Jones? Can't you see . . .' Samad lay half in, half out of the doorway, his arms stretched up to the ceiling, '. . . the *intention*? They weren't slapping their salamis – spreading the white stuff – they were looking for something a little more *permanent*.'

'I can't see the difference, frankly,' said Archie. 'When you're dead, you're dead.'

'Oh *no*, Archibald, *no*,' whispered Samad, melancholic. 'You don't believe that. You must live life with the full knowledge that your actions will *remain*. We are creatures of consequence, Archibald,' he said, gesturing to the church walls. 'They knew it. My great-grandfather knew it. Some day our children will know it.'

'Our children!' sniggered Archie, simply amused. The possibility of offspring seemed so distant.

'Our children will be born of our actions. *Our accidents will become their destinies*. Oh, the actions will remain. It is a simple matter of what you will do when the chips are down, my friend.

When the fat lady is singing. When the walls are falling in, and the sky is dark, and the ground is rumbling. In that moment our actions will define us. And it makes no difference whether you are being watched by Allah, Jesus, Buddha, or whether you are not. On cold days a man can see his breath, on a hot day he can't. On both occasions, the man *breathes*.'

'Do you know,' said Archie, after a pause, 'just before I left from Felixstowe I saw this new drill they have now which breaks in two and you can put different things on the end – spanner, hammer, even a bottle-opener. Very useful in a tight spot, I'd imagine. I tell you, I'd bloody love one of those.'

Samad looked at Archie for a moment and then shook his head. 'Come on, let's get inside. This Bulgarian food. Turns my stomach over. I need a bit of sleep.'

'You look pale,' said Archie, helping him up.

'It's for my sins, Jones, for my sins and yet I am more sinned against than sinning.' Samad giggled to himself.

'You what?'

Archie bore the weight of Samad on one side as they walked inside.

'I have eaten something,' said Samad, putting on a cut-glass English accent, 'that is about to disagree with me.'

Archie knew very well that Samad sneaked morphine from the cabinets, but he could see Samad wanted him not to know, so 'Let's get you into bed,' was all he said, bringing Samad over to a mattress.

'When this is over, we will meet again in England, OK?' said Samad, lunging towards his mattress.

'Yes,' said Archie, trying to imagine walking along Brighton pier with Samad.

'Because you are a rare Englishman, Sapper Jones. I consider you my friend.'

Archie was not sure what he considered Samad, but he smiled gently in recognition of the sentiment.

'You will have dinner with my wife and I in the year 1975. When we are big-bellied men sitting on our money-mountains. Somehow we will meet.'

Archie, dubious of foreign food, smiled weakly.

'We will know each other throughout our lives!'

Archie laid Samad down, got himself a mattress and manoeuvred himself into a position for sleep.

'Goodnight, friend,' said Samad, pure contentment in his voice.

In the morning, the circus came to town. Woken by shouts and whooping laughter, Samad struggled into uniform and wrapped one hand around his gun. He stepped into the sun-drenched courtyard to find Russian soldiers in their dun-coloured uniforms leapfrogging over each other, shooting tin cans off each other's heads and throwing knives at potatoes stuck on sticks, each potato sporting a short black twig moustache. With all the exhaustion of revelation, Samad collapsed on to the front steps, sighed, and sat with his hands on his knees, his face turned up towards the heat. A moment later Archie tripped out, trousers half-mast, waving his gun, looking for the enemy, and shot a frightened bullet in the air. The circus continued, without noticing. Samad pulled Archie wearily by the trouser leg and gestured for him to sit down.

'What's going on?' demanded Archie, watery-eyed.

'Nothing. Nothing absolutely is going on. In fact, it's gone off.'

'But these might be the men who –'

'Look at the potatoes, Jones.'

Archie looked wildly about him. 'What have potatoes got to do with it?'

'They're Hitler potatoes, my friend. They are vegetable dictators. Ex-dictators.' He pulled one off its stick. 'See the little moustaches? It's over, Jones. Someone has finished it for us.'

Archie took the potato in his hand.

'Like a bus, Jones. We have missed the bloody war.'

Archie shouted over to a lanky Russian in mid-spear of a Hitler potato. 'Speak English? How long has it been over?'

'The fighting?' he laughed incredulously. 'Two weeks, comrade! You will have to go to Japan if you want any more!'

'Like a bus,' repeated Samad, shaking his head. A great fury was rising in him, bile blocking his throat. This war was to have been his opportunity. He was expected to come home covered in glory, and then to return to Delhi triumphant. When would he ever have another chance? There were going to be no more wars like this one, everybody knew that. The soldier who had spoken to Archie wandered over. He was dressed in the summer uniform of the Russians: the thin material, high-necked collar and oversized, floppy cap; he wore a belt around a substantial waist, the buckle of which caught the sun and shot a beam into Archie's eye. When the glare passed, Archie focused on a big, open face, a squint in the left eye, and a head of sandy hair that struck off in several directions. He was altogether a rather jolly apparition on a bright morning, and when he spoke it was in a fluent, American-accented English that lapped at your ears like surf.

'The war has been over for two weeks and you were not aware?'

'Our radio . . . it wasn't . . .' Archie's sentence gave up on itself.

The soldier grinned widely and shook each man's hand vigorously. 'Welcome to peace-time, gentlemen! And we thought the Russians were an ill-informed nation!' He laughed his big laugh again. Directing his question to Samad, he asked, 'Now, where are the rest of you?'

'There is no rest of us, comrade. The rest of the men in our tank are dead, and there is no sign of our battalion.'

'You're not here for any purpose?'

'Er . . . no,' said Archie, suddenly abashed.

'Purpose, comrade,' said Samad, feeling quite sick to his

stomach. 'The war is over and so we find ourselves here quite without purpose.' He smiled grimly and shook the Russian's hand with his good hand. 'I'm going in. Sun,' he said, squinting. 'Hurts my little peepers. It was nice to have met you.'

'Yes, indeed,' said the Russian, following Samad with his eyes until he had disappeared into the recesses of the church. Then he turned his attention to Archie.

'Strange guy.'

'Hmm,' said Archie. 'Why are *you* here?' he asked, taking a hand-rolled cigarette the Russian offered him. It turned out the Russian and the seven men with him were on their way to Poland, to liberate the work-camps one heard about sometimes in hushed tones. They had stopped here, west of Tokat, to catch themselves a Nazi.

'But there's no one here, mate,' said Archie affably. 'No one but me and the Indian and some old folk and children from the village. Everyone else is dead or fled.'

'Dead or fled . . . *dead or fled*,' said the Russian, highly amused, turning a matchstick over and over between his finger and thumb. 'Good phrase this . . . funny phrase. No, well, you see, I would have thought the same, but we have reliable information – from your own secret service, in fact – that there is a senior officer, at this very moment, hiding in that house. There.' He pointed to the house on the horizon.

'The Doctor? Some little lads told us about him. I mean, he must be shitting himself with fear if you lot are after him,' said Archie, by way of a compliment, 'but I'm sure they said he's just some sick bloke; they called him Dr Sick. Oi: he ain't English, is he? Traitor or something?'

'Hmm? Oh no. No, no, no, no. Dr Marc-Pierre Perret. A young Frenchman. A prodigy. Very brilliant. He has worked in a scientific capacity for the Nazis since before the war. On the sterilization programme, and later the euthanasia policy. Internal German matters. He was one of the very loyal.'

'Blimey,' said Archie, wishing he knew what it all meant. 'Wotchyagunnadoo?'

'Catch him and take him to Poland, where he will be dealt with by the authorities.'

'Authorities,' said Archie, still impressed but not really paying attention. 'Blimey.'

Archie's attention span was always short, and he had become distracted by the big, amiable Russian's strange habit of looking in two directions at once.

'As the information we received was from your secret service and as you are the highest-ranking officer here Captain . . . Captain . . . Captain . . .'

A glass eye. It was a glass eye with a muscle behind it that would not behave.

'I'm afraid I don't know your name or rank,' said the Russian, looking at Archie with one eye and at some ivy creeping round the church door with the other.

'Who? Me? Jones,' said Archie, following the eye's revolving path: tree, potato, Archie, potato.

'Well, Captain Jones, it would be an honour if you would lead the expedition up the hill.'

'Captain – what? Blimey, no, you've got it arse-ways-up,' said Archie, escaping the magnetic force of the eye, and refocusing on himself, dressed in Dickinson-Smith's shiny buttoned uniform.

'I'm not a bloody –'

'The Lieutenant and I would be pleased to take charge,' broke in a voice behind him. 'We've been out of the action for quite a while. It is about time we got back in the thick of it, as they say.'

Samad had stepped out on to the front steps silently as a shadow, in another of Dickinson-Smith's uniforms and with a cigarette hanging casually off his lower lip like a sophisticated sentence. He was always a good-looking boy, and dressed in the shiny buttons of authority this was only accentuated; in the sharp daylight, framed by the church door, he cut quite an awesome figure.

'What my friend meant,' said Samad in his most charming Anglo-Indian lilt, 'is that he is not the bloody captain. I am the bloody captain. Captain Samad Iqbal.'

'Comrade Nikolai – Nick – Pesotsky.'

Samad and the Russian laughed together heartily, shook hands again. Samad lit a cigarette.

'He is my lieutenant. Archibald Jones. I must apologize if I behaved strangely earlier; the food's been disagreeing with me. Now: we'll set off tonight, after dark shall we? Lieutenant?' said Samad, looking at Archie with a private encoded intensity.

'Yes,' blurted Archie.

'By the way, comrade,' said Samad, striking a match off the wall and lighting up, 'I hope you do not mind if I ask – is that a glass eye? It is most realistic.'

'Yes! I purchased it in St Petersburg. I was separated from my own in Berlin. It's a quite incredible likeness, don't you think?'

The friendly Russian popped the eye out of its socket, and laid the slimy pearl in his palm for Samad and Archie to see. When the war started, thought Archie, all us boys were crowded around a fag-card of Grable's legs. Now the war's ended we're huddled round some poor bastard's eye. Blimey.

For a moment the eye slid up and down each side of the Russian's hand, then came to a restful halt in the centre of his longish, creased life-line. It looked up at Lieutenant Archie and Captain Samad with an unblinking stare.

∽

That evening Lieutenant Jones got his first taste of real war. In two army jeeps, Archie, the eight Russians, Gozan the café owner and Gozan's nephew were led by Samad on a mission up the hill to catch a Nazi. While the Russians swigged away at bottles of Sambucca until not a man among them could remember the first lines of their own national anthem, while Gozan sold roasted chicken pieces to the highest bidders, Samad stood atop the first jeep, high as a kite on his white dust, his arms flailing around, cutting the night into bits and pieces, screaming instructions that his battalion were too drunk to listen to and he himself was too far gone to understand.

Archie sat at the back of the second jeep, quiet, sober, frightened and in awe of his friend. Archie had never had a hero: he was five when his father went out for a proverbial pack of fags and neglected to return, and, never being much of a reader, the many awful books written to provide young men with fatuous heroes had never crossed his path – no swashbucklers, no one-eyed pirates, no fearless rapscallions for Archie. But Samad, as he stood up there with his shiny officer buttons glistening in the moonlight like coins in a wishing-well, had struck the seventeen-year-old Archie full square, an uppercut to the jaw that said: here is a man for whom no life-path is too steep. Here was a raving lunatic standing on a tank, here was a friend, here was a *hero*, in a form Archie had never expected. Three quarters of the way up, however, the ad hoc road the tanks had been following thinned unexpectedly, forcing the tank to brake suddenly and throwing the heroic Captain in a backward somersault over the tank, arse in the air.

'No one comes here for long, long time,' said Gozan's nephew, munching on a chicken bone, philosophically. 'This?' He looked at Samad (who had landed next to him) and pointed to the jeep they sat in. 'No way.'

So Samad gathered his now paralytic battalion around him and began the march up the mountain in search of a war he could one day tell his grandchildren about, as his great-grandfather's exploits had been told to him. Their progress was hampered by large clods of earth, torn from parts of the hill by the reverberation of past bombs and left at intervals along the pathway. From many, the roots of trees shot up impotently and languished in the air; to get by, it was necessary for them to be hacked away with the bayonets of the Russian guns.

'Look like hell!' snorted Gozan's nephew, drunkenly scrambling through one such set of roots. 'Everything look like hell!'

'Pardon him. He feel strongly because he is young. But it is the truth. It was not – how do you say – not *argument of ours*, Lieutenant Jones,' said Gozan, who had been bribed two pairs of boots to keep quiet about his friends' sudden rise in rank. '*What do we have to do with all this?*' He wiped a tear, half inebriated, half overcome with emotion. 'What we have to do with? We peaceful people. We don't want be in war! This hill – once *beautiful*! Flowers, birds, they were singing, you understand? We are from the East. What have the battles of the West to do with us?'

Instinctively, Archie turned to Samad, expecting one of his speeches; but before Gozan had even finished, Samad had suddenly picked up his pace, and within a minute was running, pushing ahead of the intoxicated Russians, who were flailing about with their bayonets. Such was his speed that he was soon out of sight, turning a blind corner and disappearing into the swallowing night. Archie dithered for a few minutes, but then loosened himself from Gozan's nephew's merciless grip (he was just embarking upon the tale of a Cuban prostitute he had met in Amsterdam) and began to run to where he had last seen the flicker of a silver button, another one of the sharp turnings that the mountain path took whenever it liked.

'Captain Ick-Ball! Wait, Captain Ick-Ball!'

He ran on, repeating the phrase, waving his torch, which did nothing but light up the undergrowth in increasingly bizarre anthropomorphisms; here a man, here a woman on her knees, here three dogs howling at the moon. He spent some time like this, stumbling about in the darkness.

'Put your light on! Captain Ick-Ball! Captain Ick-Ball!'

No answer.

'Captain Ick-Ball!'

'Why do you call me that,' said a voice, close, on his right, 'when you know I am no such thing?'

'Ick-Ball?' and as he asked the question, Archie's flash stumbled upon him, sitting on a boulder, head in hands.

'Why – I mean, you are not really so much of an idiot, are you – you do know, I presume you know that I am in fact a *private* of His Majesty's Army?'

''Course. We have to keep it up, though, don't we? Our cover, and that.'

'Our cover? Boy.' Samad chuckled to himself in a way that struck Archie as sinister, and when he lifted his head his eyes were both bloodshot and on the brink of tears. 'What do you think this is? Are we playing silly-buggers?'

'No, I . . . are you all right, Sam? You look out of sorts.'

Samad was dimly aware that he looked out of sorts. Earlier that evening he had put a tiny line of the white stuff in the cup of each eyelid. The morphine had sharpened his mind to a knife edge and cut it open. It had been a luscious, eloquent high while it lasted, but then the thoughts thus released had been left to wallow in a pool of alcohol and had landed Samad in a malevolent trough. He saw his reflection this evening, and it was ugly. He saw where he was – at the farewell party for the end of Europe – and he *longed* for the East. He looked down at his useless hand with its five useless appendages; at his skin, burnt to a chocolate-brown by the sun; he saw into his brain, made stupid by stupid conversation and the dull stimuli of death, and longed for the man he once was: erudite, handsome, light-skinned Samad Miah; so precious his mother kept him in from the sun's rays, sent him to the best tutors and covered him in linseed oil twice a day.

'Sam? Sam? You don't look right, Sam. Please, they'll be here in a minute . . . *Sam*?'

Self-hatred makes a man turn on the first person he sees. But it was particularly aggravating to Samad that this should be Archie, who looked down at him with a gentle concern, with a mix of fear and anger all mingled up in that shapeless face so ill-equipped to express emotion.

'Don't call me Sam,' he growled, in a voice Archie did not recognize, 'I'm not one of your English matey-boys. My name is Samad Miah Iqbal. Not Sam. Not Sammy. And not – God forbid – Samuel. It is Sam*ad*.'

Archie looked crestfallen.

'Well, anyway,' said Samad, suddenly officious and wishing to avoid an emotional scene, 'I am glad you are here because I wanted to tell you that I am the worse for wear, Lieutenant Jones. I am, as you say, out of sorts. I am very much the worse for wear.'

He stood, but then stumbled on to his boulder once more.

'Get up,' hissed Archie between his teeth. 'Get up. What's the *matter* with you?'

'It's true, I am very much the worse for the wearing. But I have been thinking,' said Samad, taking his gun in his good hand.

'Put that away.'

'I have been thinking that I am buggered, Lieutenant Jones. I see no future. I realize this may come as a surprise to you – my upper lip, I'm afraid is not of the required stiffness – but the fact remains. I see only –'

'Put that away.'

'Blackness. I'm a *cripple*, Jones.' The gun did a merry dance in his good hand as he swung himself from side to side. 'And my faith is crippled, do you understand? I'm fit for nothing now, not even Allah, who is all powerful in his mercy. What am I going to do, after this war is over, this war that is already over – what am I going to do? Go back to Bengal? Or to Delhi? Who would have such an Englishman there? To England? Who would have such an Indian? They promise us independence in exchange for the men we were. But it is a devilish deal. What should I do?

Stay here? Go elsewhere? What laboratory needs one-handed men? What am I suited for?'

'Look, Sam . . . *you're making a fool of yourself.*'

'*Really?* And is that how it is to be, friend?' asked Samad, standing, tripping over a stone and colliding back into Archie. 'In one afternoon I promote you from Private Shitbag to lieutenant of the British army and this is my thanks? Where are you in my hour of need? Gozan!' he shouted to the fat café owner, who was struggling round the bend, at the very back, sweating profusely. 'Gozan – my fellow Muslim – in Allah's name, is this right?'

'Shut up,' snapped Archie. 'Do you want everyone to hear you? Put it *down*.'

Samad's gun arm shot out of the darkness and wrapped itself around Archie's neck, so the gun and both their heads were pressed together in an odious group hug.

'What am I good for, Jones? If I were to pull this trigger, what will I leave behind? An Indian, a turncoat English Indian with a limp wrist like a faggot and no medals that they can ship home with me.' He let go of Archie and grabbed his own collar instead.

'Have some of these, for God's sake,' said Archie, taking three from his lapel and throwing them at him. 'I've got loads.'

'And what about that little matter? Do you realize we're deserters? Effectively deserters? Step back a minute, my friend, and look at us. Our captain is dead. We are dressed in his uniforms, taking control of officers, men of higher rank than ourselves, and how? By *deceit*. Doesn't that make us deserters?'

'The war was over! I mean, we made an effort to contact the rest.'

'Did we? Archie, my friend, did we? Really? Or did we sit around on our arses like deserters, hiding in a church while the world was falling apart around our ears, while men were dying in the fields?'

They tussled a little as Archie tried to get the gun from him, Samad lashing out at him with not inconsiderable strength. In the distance, Archie could see the rest of their motley crew turning the corner, a great grey mass in the twilight, pitching from side to side, singing 'Lydia the Tattooed Lady'.

'Look, keep your voice down. And calm down,' said Archie, releasing him.

'We're impostors; turncoats in other people's coats. Did we do our duty, Archibald? Did we? In all honesty? I have dragged you down with me, Archie, and for that I am sorry. The truth is, this was my fate. This was all written for me long ago.'

O Lydia O Lydia O have you met Lydia O Lydia the Taaaatooooed Lady!

Samad put the pistol absent-mindedly in his mouth and cocked the trigger.

'Ick-Ball, listen to me,' said Archie. 'When we were in that tank with the Captain, with Roy and the rest.'

O Lydia the Queen of tattoos! On her back is the battle of Waterloo . . .

'You were always going on about being a hero and all that – like your great-uncle whatsis name.'

Beside it the wreck of the Hesperus too . . .

Samad took the gun out of his mouth.

'*Pande*,' he said. 'Great-*grandfather*,' and put the gun back in.

'And here it is – a chance – it's staring you in the face. You didn't want to miss the bus and we're not going to, not if we do this properly. So don't be such a silly fucker about it.'

And proudly above waves the red, white and bloooo,

You can learn a lot from Lydia!

'Comrade! What in God's name.'

Without them noticing, the friendly Russian had ambled up behind them and was looking in horror at Samad, sucking his gun like a lollipop.

'Cleaning it,' stuttered Samad, clearly shaken, removing the gun from his mouth.

'That's how they do it,' Archie explained, 'in Bengal.'

The war that twelve men expected to find in the grand old house on the hill, the war that Samad wanted pickled in a jar to hand to his grandchildren as a souvenir of his youth, was not there. Dr Sick was as good as his name, sitting in an armchair in front of a wood-burning fire. Sick. Huddled in a rug. Pale. Very thin. In no uniform, just an open-neck white shirt and some dark coloured trousers. He was a young man too, not over twenty-five, and he did not flinch or make any protest when they all burst in, guns at the ready. It was as if they had just dropped in on a pleasant French farmhouse, making the faux pas of coming without invitation and bringing guns to the dinner table. The room was lit entirely by gas lamps in their tiny lady-shaped casings, and the light danced up the wall, illuminating a set of eight paintings that showed a continuous scene of Bulgarian countryside. In the fifth one Samad recognized his church, a blip of sandy paint on the horizon. The paintings were placed at intervals and wrapped round the room in a panoramic. Unframed and in a mawkish attempt at the modern style, a ninth sat a little too close to the fireplace on an easel, the paint still wet. Twelve guns were pointed at the artist. And when the Artist-Doctor turned to face them, he had what looked like blood-tinged tears rolling down his face.

Samad stepped forward. He had had a gun in his mouth and was emboldened by it. He had eaten an absurd amount of morphine, fallen through the hole morphine creates, and survived. You are never stronger, thought Samad as he approached the Doctor, than when you land on the other side of despair.

'Are you Dr Perret?' he demanded, making the Frenchman wince at the anglicized pronunciation, sending more bloody tears down his cheeks. Samad kept his gun pointed at him.

'Yes, I am he.'

'What is that? That in your eyes?' asked Samad.

'I have diabetic retinopathy, monsieur.'

'What?' asked Samad, still pointing the gun, determined not to undermine his moment of glory with an unheroic medical debate.

'It means that when I do not receive insulin, I excrete blood, my friend. Through my eyes. It makes my hobby,' he gestured at the paintings that surrounded him, 'not a little difficult. There were to be ten. A 180-degree view. But it seems you have come to disturb me.' He sighed and stood up. 'So. Are you going to kill me, my friend?'

'I'm not your friend.'

'No, I do not suppose that you are. But is it your intention to kill me? Pardon me if I say you do not look old enough to squash flies.' He looked at Samad's uniform. 'Mon Dieu, you are very young to have got so far in life, Captain.' Samad shifted uncomfortably, catching Archie's look of panic in the corner of his vision. Samad placed his feet a little further apart and stood firm.

'I'm sorry if I seem tiresome on this point but . . . is it your intention, then, to kill me?'

Samad's arm stayed perfectly still, the gun unmoving. He could kill him, he could kill him in cold blood. Samad did not need the cover of darkness or the excuse of war. He could kill him and they both knew it. The Russian, seeing the look in the Indian's eye, stepped forward. 'Pardon me, Captain.'

Samad remained silent, facing the Doctor, so the Russian stepped forward. 'We do not have intentions in this matter,' said the Russian, addressing Dr Sick. 'We have orders to bring you to Poland.'

'And there, will I be killed?'

'That will be for the proper authorities to decide.'

The Doctor cocked his head at an angle and narrowed his

eyes. 'It is just . . . it is just a thing a man likes to be told. It is curiously significant to a man to be told. It is only polite, at the very least. To be told whether he shall die or whether he shall be spared.'

'That will be for the proper authorities to decide,' repeated the Russian.

Samad walked behind the Doctor and stuck the gun into the back of his head. 'Walk,' he said.

'For the proper authorities to decide . . . Isn't peace-time civilized?' remarked Dr Sick, as a group of twelve men, all pointing guns at his head, led him out of the house.

∽

Later that night, at the bottom of the hill, the battalion left Dr Sick handcuffed to the jeep and adjourned to the café.

'You play poker?' asked a very merry Nikolai, addressing Samad and Archie as they entered the room.

'I play anything, me,' said Archie.

'The more pertinent question,' said Samad, taking his seat with a wry smile, 'is: do I play it well?'

'And do you, Captain Iqbal?'

'Like a master,' said Samad, picking up the cards dealt to him and fanning them out in his one hand.

'Well,' said Nikolai, pouring more Sambucca for everyone, 'since our friend Iqbal is so confident, it may be best to start relatively small. We'll start with cigarettes and let's see where that takes us.'

Cigarettes took them to medals, which took them to guns, which took them to radios, which took them to jeeps. By midnight, Samad had won three jeeps, seven guns, fourteen medals, the land attached to Gozan's sister's house, and an IOU for four horses, three chickens and a duck.

'My friend,' said Nikolai Pesotsky, his warm, open manner replaced by an anxious gravity. 'You must give us a chance to win back our possessions. We cannot possibly leave things as they are.'

'I want the Doctor,' said Samad, refusing to catch the eye of Archibald Jones, who sat open-mouthed and drunk in his chair. 'In exchange for the things I have won.'

'What on *earth* for?' said Nikolai, astonished, leaning back in his chair. 'What possible use –'

'My own reasons. I wish to take him tonight and not to be followed, and for the incident to go unreported.'

Nikolai Pesotsky looked at his hands, looked round the table, and then at his hands once more. Then he reached into his pocket and threw Samad the keys.

Once outside, Samad and Archie got into the jeep containing Dr Sick, who was asleep on the dashboard, started the engine and drove into the blackness.

Thirty miles from the village, Dr Sick woke up to a hushed argument concerning his imminent future.

'But *why*?' hissed Archie.

'Because, from my point of view, the very problem is that we need blood on our hands, you see? As an atonement. Do you not see, Jones? We have been playing silly buggers in this war, you and I. There is a great evil that we have failed to fight and now it is too late. Except we have him, this opportunity. Let me ask you: why was this war fought?'

'Don't talk nonsense,' blustered Archie, in lieu of an answer.

'So that in the future we may be *free*. The question was always: *What kind of a world do you want your children to grow up in?* And we have done nothing. We are at a moral crossroads.'

'Look, I don't know what you're on about and I don't want to know,' snapped Archie. 'We're going to dump this one' – he motioned to the semi-conscious Sick – 'at the first barracks we come across, then you and me are going our separate ways and that's the only crossroads I care about.'

'What I have realized, is that the generations,' Samad continued as they sped through miles and miles of unchanging flatlands, 'they speak to each other, Jones. It's not a line, life is not a line – this is not palm-reading – it's a circle, and they speak to us. That is why you cannot *read* fate; you must *experience* it.' Samad could feel the morphine bringing the information to him again – all the information in the universe and all the information on walls – in one fantastic revelation.

'Do you know who this man is, Jones?' Samad grabbed the Doctor by the back of his hair and bent his neck over the back seat. 'The Russians told me. He's a scientist, like me – but what is his science? Choosing who shall be born and who shall not – breeding people as if they were so many chickens, destroying them if the specifications are not correct. He wants to control, to dictate the future. He wants a race of men, a race of indestructible men, that will survive the last days of this earth. But it cannot be done in a laboratory. It must be done, it can only be done, with faith! Only Allah saves! I am no religious man – I have never possessed the strength – but I am not fool enough to deny the truth!'

'Ah, now, but you said, didn't you, you said it *wasn't your argument*. On the hill – that's what you said,' gabbled Archie, excited to have caught Samad out on something. 'So, so, so – so what if this bloke does . . . whatever he does – you said that was *our* problem, us in the *West*, that's what you said.'

Dr Sick, watery eye-blood now streaming like rivers, was still being held by the hair by Samad and was gagging, now, on his own tongue.

'Watch out, you're choking him,' said Archie.

'What of it!' yelled Samad into the echoless landscape. 'Men like him believe that living organs should answer to design. They worship the science of the body, but not who has given it to us! He's a Nazi. The worst kind.'

'But you said –' Archie pressed on, determined to make his

point. 'You said that was nothing to do with you. Not your argument. If anyone in this jeep should have a score to settle with mad Jerry here –'

'French. He's French.'

'All right, French – well if anyone's got a score to settle it'd probably have to be me. It's England's future we've been fighting for. For England. You know,' said Archie, searching his brain, 'democracy and Sunday dinners, and . . . and . . . promenades and piers, and bangers and mash – and the things that are *ours*. Not *yours*.'

'*Precisely*,' said Samad.

'You what?'

'*You* must do it, Archie.'

'I should cocoa!'

'Jones, your destiny is staring you in the face and here you are slapping the salami,' said Samad with a nasty laugh in his voice, and still holding the Doctor by the hair across the front seat.

'Steady on,' said Archie, trying to keep an eye on the road, as Samad bent the Doctor's neck almost to breaking point. 'Look, I'm not saying that he doesn't deserve to die.'

'Then do it. *Do it*.'

'But why's it so bloody important to you that I do it? You know, I've never killed a man – not like that, not face to face. A man shouldn't die in a car . . . I can't do that.'

'Jones, it is simply a question of what you will do *when the chips are down*. This is a question that interests me a great deal. Call tonight the practical application of a long-held belief. An experiment, if you like.'

'I don't know what you're talking about.'

'I want to know what kind of a man you are, Jones. I want to know what you are capable of. Are you a coward, Jones?'

Archie brought the jeep to a shattering halt.

'You're bloody asking for it, you are.'

'You don't stand for anything, Jones,' continued Samad. 'Not for a faith, not for a politics. Not even for your country. How your lot ever conquered my lot is a bloody mystery. You're a cipher, no?'

'A what?'

'And an idiot. What are you going to tell your children when they ask who you are, what you are? Will you know? Will you ever know?'

'What are you that's so bloody fantastic?'

'I'm a Muslim and a Man and a Son and a Believer. I will survive the last days.'

'You're a bloody drunkard, and you're – you're drugged, you're drugged tonight, aren't you?'

'I am a Muslim and a Man and a Son and a Believer. I will survive the last days,' Samad repeated, as if it were a chant.

'And what the bloody hell does that mean?' As he shouted, Archie made a grab for Dr Sick. Pulled his now blood-covered face near his own until their noses touched.

'You,' Archie barked. 'You're coming with me.'

'I would but, monsieur . . .' The Doctor held up his handcuffed wrists.

Archie wrestled them open with the rusty key, pulled the Doctor out of the jeep and started walking away from the road into the darkness, a gun pointed at the base point of Dr Marc-Pierre Perret's cranium.

'Are you going to kill me, boy?' asked Dr Sick as they walked.

'Looks like it, dunnit?' said Archie.

'May I plead for my life?'

'If you like,' said Archie, pushing him on.

Sitting in the jeep, some five minutes later, Samad heard a shot ring out. It made him jump. He slapped dead an insect that had been winding its way round his wrist, looking for enough flesh to bite. Lifting his head, he saw in front of him that Archie was returning: bleeding and limping badly, made visible, then invisible, illuminated, obscured, as he wound in and out of the headlights. He looked his tender age, the lamps making his blond hair translucent, his moon-shaped face lit up like a big baby, head first, entering life.

Samad

1984, 1857

'The cricket test – which side do they cheer for? . . . Are you still looking back to where you came from or where you are?'

Norman Tebbit

6 *The Temptation of Samad Iqbal*

Children. Samad had caught children like a disease. Yes, he had sired two of them willingly – as willingly as a man can – but he had not bargained for this other thing. This thing that no one tells you about. This thing of *knowing* children. For forty-odd years, travelling happily along life's highway, Samad had been unaware that dotted along that road, in the crèche facilities of each service station, there lived a subclass of society, a mewling, puking underclass; he knew nothing of them and it did not concern him. Then suddenly, in the early eighties, he became infected with children; *other people's* children, children who were friends of *his* children, and then *their* friends; then children in children's programmes on children's TV. By 1984 at least 30 per cent of his social and cultural circle was under the age of nine – and this all led, inevitably, to the position he now found himself in. He was a *parent-governor*.

By a strange process of symmetry, being a parent-governor perfectly mirrors the process of becoming a parent. It starts innocently. Casually. You turn up at the annual Spring Fair full of beans, help with the raffle tickets (because the pretty red-haired music teacher asks you to) and win a bottle of whisky (all school raffles are fixed), and, before you know where you are, you're turning up at the weekly school council meetings, organizing concerts, discussing plans for a new music department, donating funds for the rejuvenation of the water-fountains – you're *implicated* in the school, you're *involved* in it. Sooner or later you stop dropping your child at the school gates. You start following them in.

*

'Put your hand down.'

'I will *not* put it down.'

'Put it down, please.'

'Let go of me.'

'Samad, why are you so eager to mortify me? *Put it down.*'

'I have an opinion. I have a right to an opinion. And I have a right to *express* that opinion.'

'Yes, but do you have to express it so often?'

This was the hissed exchange between Samad and Alsana Iqbal, as they sat at the back of a Wednesday school governors meeting in early July '84, Alsana trying her best to force Samad's determined left arm back to his side.

'Get off, woman!'

Alsana put her two tiny hands to his wrist and tried applying a Chinese burn. 'Samad Miah, can't you understand that I am only trying to save you from yourself?'

As the covert wrestling continued, the chairwoman Katie Miniver, a lanky white divorcee with tight jeans, extremely curly hair and buck teeth, tried desperately to avoid Samad's eye. She silently cursed Mrs Hanson, the fat lady just behind him, who was speaking about the woodworm in the school orchard, inadvertently making it impossible to pretend that Samad's persistent raised hand had gone unseen. Sooner or later she was going to have to let him speak. In between nodding at Mrs Hanson, she snatched a surreptitious glance at the minutes which the secretary, Mrs Khilnani, was scribbling away on her left. She wanted to check that it was not her imagination, that she was not being unfair or undemocratic, or worse still *racist* (but she had read *Colour Blind*, a seminal leaflet from the Rainbow Coalition, she had scored well on the self-test), racist in ways that were so deeply ingrained and socially determining that they escaped her attention. But no, no. She wasn't crazy. Any random extract highlighted the problem:

13.0 *Mrs Janet Trott wishes to propose a second climbing frame be built in the playground to accommodate the large number of children who enjoy the present climbing frame but unfortunately have made it a safety risk through dangerous overcrowding. Mrs Trott's husband, the architect Hanover Trott, is willing to design and oversee the building of such a frame at no cost to the school.*

13.1 *Chairwoman can see no objection. Moves to put the proposition to a vote.*

13.2 *Mr Iqbal wishes to know why the Western education system privileges activity of the body over activity of the mind and soul.*

13.3 *The Chairwoman wonders if this is quite relevant.*

13.4 *Mr Iqbal demands the vote be delayed until he can present a paper detailing the main arguments and emphasizes that his sons, Magid and Millat, get all the exercise they need via headstands that strengthen the muscles and send blood to stimulate the somatosensory cortex in the brain.*

13.5 *Mrs Wolfe asks whether Mr Iqbal expects her Susan to undertake compulsory headstands.*

13.6 *Mr Iqbal infers that, considering Susan's academic performance and weight problems, a headstand regime might be desirable.*

'*Yes*, Mr Iqbal?'

Samad forcefully removed Alsana's fingers from the clamp grip they had assumed on his lapel, stood up quite unnecessarily and sorted through a number of papers he had on a clipboard, removing the one he wanted and holding it out before him.

'Yes, yes. I have a motion. I have a motion.'

The subtlest manifestation of a groan went round the group of governors, followed by a short period of shifting, scratching, leg-crossing, bag-rifling and the repositioning of coats-on-chairs.

'*Another* one, Mr Iqbal?'

'Oh yes, Mrs Miniver.'

'Only you've tabled twelve motions already this evening; I think possibly somebody else –'

'Oh, it is much too important to be delayed, Mrs Miniver. Now, if I can just –'

'*Ms* Miniver.'

'Pardon me?'

'It's just . . . it's *Ms* Miniver. All evening you've been . . . and it's, umm . . . actually not Mrs. It's Ms. Ms.'

Samad looked quizzically at Katie Miniver, then at his papers as if to find the answer there, then at the beleaguered chairwoman again.

'I'm sorry? You are not married?'

'Divorced, actually, yes, divorced. I'm keeping the name.'

'I see. You have my condolences, Miss Miniver. Now, the matter I –'

'I'm sorry,' said Katie, pulling her fingers through her intractable hair. 'Umm, it's not Miss, either. I'm sorry. I have *been* married you see, so –'

Ellen Corcoran and Janine Lanzerano, two friends from the Women's Action Group, gave Katie a supportive smile. Ellen shook her head to indicate that Katie mustn't cry (*because you're doing well, really well*); Janine mouthed *Go On* and gave her a furtive thumbs-up.

'I really wouldn't feel comforta – I just feel marital status shouldn't be an issue – it's not that I want to embarrass you, Mr Iqbal. I just would feel more – if you – it's Ms.'

'Mzzz?'

'Ms.'

'And this is some kind of linguistic conflation between the words Mrs and Miss?' asked Samad, genuinely curious and oblivious to the nether wobblings of Katie Miniver's bottom lip. 'Something to describe the woman who has either lost her husband or has no prospect of finding another?'

Alsana groaned and put her head in her hands.

Samad looked at his clipboard, underlined something in pen three times and turned to the parent-governors once more.

'The Harvest Festival.'

Shifting, scratching, leg-crossing, coat-repositioning.

'Yes, Mr Iqbal,' said Katie Miniver. 'What *about* the Harvest Festival?'

'That is precisely what I want to know. What *is* all this about the Harvest Festival? What *is* it? *Why* is it? And why must my children celebrate it?'

The headmistress, Mrs Owens, a genteel woman with a soft face half hidden behind a fiercely cut blonde bob, motioned to Katie Miniver that she would handle this.

'Mr Iqbal, we have been through the matter of religious festivals quite thoroughly in the autumn review. As I am sure you are aware, the school already recognizes a great variety of religious and secular events: amongst them, Christmas, Ramadan, Chinese New Year, Diwali, Yom Kippur, Hanukkah, the birthday of Haile Selassie, and the death of Martin Luther King. The Harvest Festival is part of the school's ongoing commitment to religious diversity, Mr Iqbal.'

'I see. And are there many pagans, Mrs Owens, at Manor School?'

'Pagan – I'm afraid I don't under –'

'It is very simple. The Christian calendar has thirty-seven religious events. *Thirty-seven*. The Muslim calendar has *nine*. Only nine. And they are squeezed out by this incredible rash of Christian festivals. Now my motion is simple. If we removed all the pagan festivals from the Christian calendar, there would be an average of' – Samad paused to look at his clipboard – 'of twenty days freed up in which the children could celebrate Lailat-ul-Qadr in December, Eid-ul-Fitr in January and Eid-ul-Adha in April, for example. And the first festival that must go, in my opinion, is this Harvest Festival business.'

'I'm afraid,' said Mrs Owens, doing her pleasant-but-firm smile and playing her punchline to the crowd, 'removing Christian festivals from the face of the earth is a little beyond my jurisdiction. Otherwise I would remove Christmas Eve and save myself a lot of work in stocking-stuffing.'

Samad ignored the general giggle this prompted and pressed on. 'But this is my whole point. This Harvest Festival is *not* a Christian festival. Where in the bible does it say, *For thou must steal foodstuffs from thy parents' cupboards and bring them into school assembly, and thou shalt force thy mother to bake a loaf of bread in the shape of a fish*? These are pagan ideals! Tell me where does it say, *Thou shalt take a box of frozen fishfingers to an aged crone who lives in Wembley*?'

Mrs Owens frowned, unaccustomed to sarcasm unless it was of the teacher variety, i.e., *Do we live in a barn? And I suppose you treat your own house like that!*

'Surely, Mr Iqbal, it is precisely the *charity* aspect of the Harvest Festival that makes it worth retaining? Taking food to the elderly seems to me a laudable idea, whether it has scriptural support or not. Certainly, nothing in the bible suggests we should sit down to a turkey meal on Christmas Day, but few people would condemn it on those grounds. To be honest, Mr Iqbal, we like to think of these things as more about *community* than *religion* as such.'

'A man's god *is* his community!' said Samad, raising his voice.

'Yes, umm . . . well, shall we vote on the motion?'

Mrs Owens looked nervously around the room for hands. 'Will anyone second it?'

Samad pressed Alsana's hand. She kicked him in the ankle. He stamped on her toe. She pinched his flank. He bent back her little finger and she grudgingly raised her right arm while deftly elbowing him in the crotch with her left.

'Thank you, Mrs Iqbal,' said Mrs Owens, as Janice and Ellen

looked over to her with the piteous, saddened smiles they reserved for subjugated Muslim women.

'All those in favour of the motion to remove the Harvest Festival from the school calendar –'

'On the grounds of its pagan roots.'

'On the grounds of certain pagan . . . connotations. Raise your hands.'

Mrs Owens scanned the room. One hand, that of the pretty red-headed music teacher Poppy Burt-Jones, shot up, sending her many bracelets jangling down her wrist. Then the Chalfens, Marcus and Joyce, an ageing hippy couple both dressed in pseudo-Indian garb, raised their hands defiantly. Then Samad looked pointedly at Clara and Archie, sitting sheepishly on the other side of the hall, and two more hands moved slowly above the crowd.

'All those against?'

The remaining thirty-six hands lifted into the air.

'Motion not passed.'

'I am certain the Solar Covenant of Manor School Witches and Goblins will be delighted with that decision,' said Samad, retaking his seat.

After the meeting, as Samad emerged from the toilets, having relieved himself with some difficulty in a miniature urinal, the pretty red-headed music teacher Poppy Burt-Jones accosted him in the corridor.

'Mr Iqbal.'

'Hmm?'

She extended a long, pale, lightly freckled arm. 'Poppy Burt-Jones. I take Magid and Millat for orchestra and singing.'

Samad replaced the dead right hand she meant to shake with his working left.

'Oh! I'm sorry.'

'No, no. It's not painful. It just does not work.'

'Oh, good! I mean, I'm glad there's no, you know, *pain.*'

She was what you would call effortlessly pretty. About twenty-eight, maybe thirty-two at most. Slim, but not at all hard-bodied, and with a curved ribcage like a child; long, flat breasts that lifted at their tips; an open-neck white shirt, some well-worn Levis and grey trainers, a lot of dark red hair swished up in a sloppy ponytail. Wispy bits falling at the neck. Freckled. A very pleasant, slightly goofy smile which she was showing Samad right now.

'Was there something you wanted to discuss about the twins? A problem?'

'Oh no, no . . . well, you know, they're fine. Magid has a little difficulty, but with his good marks I'm sure playing the recorder isn't high on his list, and Millat has a real flair for the sax. No, I just wanted to say that I thought you made a good point, you know,' she said, chucking her thumb over her shoulder in the direction of the hall. 'In the meeting. The Harvest Festival always seemed so ridiculous to me. I mean, if you want to help old people, you know, well, vote for a different government, don't send them cans of Heinz spaghetti.' She smiled at him again and tucked a piece of hair behind her ear.

'It is a great shame more people do not agree,' said Samad, flattered somehow by the second smile and sucking in his well-toned 57-year-old stomach. 'We seemed very much in the minority this evening.'

'Well, the Chalfens were behind you – they're such *nice* people – *intellectuals,*' she whispered, as if it were some exotic disease of the tropics. 'He's a scientist and she's something in gardening – but both very down to earth with it. I talked to them and they thought you should pursue it. You know, actually, *I* was thinking that maybe we could get together at some point in the next few months and work on a second motion for the September meeting – you know, nearer the actual time, make it a little more coherent, maybe, print out leaflets, that sort of thing. Because you know,

I'm really interested in Indian culture. I just think those festivals you mentioned would be so much more . . . colourful, and we could tie it in with art work, music. It could be *really* exciting,' said Poppy Burt-Jones, getting really excited. 'And I think it would be really good, you know, for the kids.'

It was not possible, Samad knew, for this woman to have any erotic interest in him whatsoever. But still he glanced around for Alsana, still he jangled his car keys nervously in his pockets, still he felt a cold thing land on his heart and knew it was fear of his God.

'I'm not actually *from* India, you know,' said Samad, with infinitely more patience than he had ever previously employed the many times he had been required to repeat this sentence since moving to England.

Poppy Burt-Jones looked surprised and disappointed. 'You're not?'

'No. I'm from Bangladesh.'

'Bangladesh . . .'

'Previously Pakistan. Previous to that, Bengal.'

'Oh, right. Same sort of ball-park, then.'

'Just about the same stadium, yes.'

There was a bit of a difficult pause, in which Samad saw clearly that he wanted her more than any woman he had met in the past ten years. Just like that. Desire didn't even bother casing the joint, checking whether the neighbours were in – desire just kicked down the door and made himself at home. He felt queasy. Then he became aware that his face was moving from arousal to horror in a grotesque parody of the movements of his mind, as he weighed up Poppy Burt-Jones and all the physical and metaphysical consequences she suggested. He must speak before it got any worse.

'Well . . . hmm, it is a good idea, retabling the motion,' he said against his will, for something more bestial than his will was now doing the talking. 'If you could spare the time.'

'Well, we can talk about it. I'll give you a call about it in a few weeks. We could meet after orchestra, maybe?'

'That would be . . . fine.'

'Great! That's agreed, then. You know, your boys are really adorable – they're very unusual. I was saying it to the Chalfens, and Marcus put his finger on it: he said that Indian children, if you don't mind me saying, are usually a lot more –'

'More?'

'*Quiet*. Beautifully behaved but very, I don't know, *subdued*.'

Samad winced inside, imagining Alsana listening to this.

'And Magid and Millat are just so . . . *loud*.'

Samad tried to smile.

'Magid is so impressive intellectually for a nine-year-old – everybody says so. I mean, he's really remarkable. You must be *so* proud. He's like a little adult. Even his clothes . . . I don't think I've ever known a nine-year-old to dress so – so *severely*.'

Both twins had always been determined to choose their own clothes, but where Millat bullied Alsana into purchases of red-stripe Nike, Osh-Kosh Begosh and strange jumpers that had patterns on the inside and the out, Magid could be found, whatever the weather, in grey pullover, grey shirt and black tie with his shiny black shoes and NHS specs perched upon his nose, like some dwarf librarian. Alsana would say, 'Little man, how about the blue one for Amma, hmm?', pushing him into the primary colours section of Mothercare. 'Just one blue one. Go so nice with your eyes. For Amma, Magid. How can you not care for blue? It's the colour of the sky!'

'No, Amma. The sky isn't blue. There's just white light. White light has all of the colours of the rainbow in it, and when it is scattered through the squillions of molecules in the sky, the short-wave colours – blue, violet – they are the ones you see. The sky isn't really blue. It just looks that way. It's called Rayleigh scattering.'

A strange child with a cold intellect.

'You must be *so* proud,' Poppy repeated with a huge smile. 'I would be.'

'Sadly,' said Samad sighing, distracted from his erection by the dismal thought of his second son (by two minutes), 'Millat is a good-for-nothing.'

Poppy looked mortified at this. 'Oh no! No, I didn't mean that at all . . . I mean, I think he's probably a little intimidated by Magid in that way, but he's such a personality! He's just not so . . . academic. But everybody just *loves* him – such a beautiful boy, as well. Of course,' she said, giving him a wink and a knock on the shoulder, 'good genes.'

Good genes? What did she mean, *good genes*?

'Hullo!' said Archie, who had walked up behind them, giving Samad a strong thud on the back. 'Hullo!' he said again, shaking Poppy's hand, with the almost mock-aristocratic manner he used when confronted with educated people. 'Archie Jones. Father of Irie, for my sins.'

'Poppy Burt-Jones. I take Irie for –'

'Music, yes, I know. Talks about you constantly. Bit disappointed you passed her over for first violin, though . . . maybe next year, eh? So!' said Archie, looking from Poppy to Samad, who was standing slightly apart from the other two and had a queer look, Archie thought, a bloody queer look on his face. 'You've met the notorious Ick-Ball! You were a bit much in that meeting, Samad, eh? Wasn't he, eh?'

'Oh, I don't know,' said Poppy sweetly. 'I thought Mr Iqbal made some good points, actually. I was really impressed by a lot of what he said. I'd like to be that knowledgeable on so many subjects. Sadly, I'm a bit of a one-trick pony. Are you, I don't know, a *professor* of some kind, Mr Iqbal?'

'No, no,' said Samad, furious that he was unable to lie because of Archie, and finding the word 'waiter' stopping in his throat. 'No, the fact is I work in a restaurant. I did some study in younger days, but the war came and . . .' Samad shrugged as an end to the sentence, and watched with sinking heart as Poppy Burt-Jones's freckled face contorted into one large, red, perplexed question mark.

'War?' she said, as if he had said wireless or pianola or water-closet. 'The Falklands?'

'No,' said Samad flatly. 'The Second World.'

'Oh, Mr Iqbal, you'd never guess. You must have been ever so young.'

'There were tanks there older than us, love,' said Archie with a grin.

'Well, Mr Iqbal, that is a surprise! But they say dark skin wrinkles less, don't they?'

'Do they?' said Samad, forcing himself to imagine her taut, pink skin, folded over in layer after layer of dead epidermis. 'I thought it was children that kept a man young.'

Poppy laughed. 'That too, I'd imagine. Well!' she said, looking flushed, coy and sure of herself, all at the same time. 'You look very good on it. I'm sure the Omar Sharif comparison's been made before, Mr Iqbal.'

'No, no, no, no,' said Samad, glowing with pleasure. 'The only comparison lies in our mutual love of bridge. No, no, no . . . And it's Samad,' he added. 'Call me Samad, please.'

'You'll have to call him Samad some other time, Miss,' said Archie, who always persisted in calling teachers Miss. 'Because we've got to go. Wives waiting in the driveway. Dinner, apparently.'

'Well, it was nice talking to you,' said Poppy, reaching for the wrong hand again, and blushing as he met her with the left.

'Yes. Goodbye.'

'Come on, come on,' said Archie, fielding Samad out of the door and down the sloping driveway to the front gates. 'Dear God, fit as a butcher's dog, that one! *Phee-yooo*. Nice, very nice. Dear me, you were trying it on . . . And what were you on about

– *mutual love of bridge*. I've known you decades and I've never seen you play bridge. Five-card poker's more your game.'

'Shut up, Archibald.'

'No, no, fair dues, you did very well. It's not like you, though, Samad – having found God and all that – not like you to be distracted by the attractions of the flesh.'

Samad shook Archie's hand from where it was resting on his shoulder. 'Why *are* you so irredeemably vulgar?'

'*I* wasn't the one . . .'

But Samad wasn't listening, he was already reciting in his head, repeating two English phrases that he tried hard to believe in, words he had learnt these past ten years in England, words he hoped could protect him from the abominable heat in his trousers:

To the pure all things are pure. To the pure all things are pure. To the pure all things are pure.

Can't say fairer than that. Can't say fairer than that. Can't say fairer than that.

But let's rewind a little.

1. *To the pure all things are pure*

Sex, at least the temptation of sex, had long been a problem. When the fear of God first began to creep into Samad's bones, circa 1976, just after his marriage to the small-palmed, weak-wristed and disinterested Alsana, he had inquired of an elderly alim in the mosque in Croydon whether it was permitted that a man might . . . with his hand on his . . .

Before he had got halfway through this tentative mime, the old scholar had silently passed him a leaflet from a pile on a table and drawn his wrinkled digit firmly underneath point number three.

There are nine acts which invalidate fast:

(i) Eating and drinking
(ii) Sexual intercourse
(iii) Masturbation (*istimna*), which means self-abuse, resulting in ejaculation
(iv) Ascribing false things to Almighty Allah, or his Prophet, or to the successors of the Holy Prophet
(v) Swallowing thick dust
(vi) Immersing one's complete head in water
(vii) Remaining in Janabat or Haidh or Nifas till the Adhan for Fajr prayers
(viii) Enema with liquids
(ix) Vomiting

'And what, Alim,' Samad had inquired, dismayed, 'if he is not fasting?'

The old scholar looked grave. 'Ibn 'Umar was asked about it and is reported to have answered: *It is nothing except the rubbing of the male member until its water comes out. It is only a nerve that one kneads.*'

Samad had taken heart at this, but the Alim continued. 'However, he answered in another report: *It has been forbidden that one should have intercourse with oneself.*'

'But which is the correct belief? Is it halal or haraam? There are some who say . . .' Samad had begun sheepishly, '*To the pure all things are pure*. If one is truthful and firm in oneself, it can harm nobody else, nor offend . . .'

But the Alim laughed at this. 'And we know who *they* are. Allah have pity on the Anglicans! Samad, when the male organ of a man stands erect, two thirds of his intellect go away,' said the Alim, shaking his head. 'And one third of his religion. There is an hadith of the Prophet Muhammad – peace be upon Him! – it is as follows: *O Allah, I seek refuge in you from the evil of my hearing, of my sight, of my tongue, of my heart, and of my private parts.*'

'But surely . . . surely if the man himself is pure, then –'

'Show me the pure man, Samad! Show me the pure act! Oh, Samad Miah . . . my advice to you is stay away from your right hand.'

Of course. Samad, being Samad, had employed the best of his Western pragmatism, gone home and vigorously tackled the job with his functional left hand, repeating *To the pure all things are pure. To the pure all things are pure*, until orgasm finally arrived: sticky, sad, depressing. And that ritual continued for some five years, in the little bedroom at the top of the house where he slept alone (so as not to wake Alsana) after crawling back from the restaurant at three in the morning each and every morning; secretly, silently; for he was, believe it or not, tortured by it, by this furtive yanking and squeezing and spilling, by the fear that he was not pure, that his acts were not pure, that he would never be pure, and always his God seemed to be sending him small signs, small warnings, small curses (a urethra infection, 1976, castration dream, 1978, dirty, encrusted sheet discovered but misunderstood by Alsana's great-aunt, 1979) until 1980 brought crisis point and Samad heard Allah roaring in his ear like the waves in a conch-shell and it seemed time to make a deal.

2. *Can't say fairer than that*

The deal was this: on 1 January 1980, like a New Year dieter who gives up cheese on the condition that they can have chocolate, Samad gave up masturbation so that he might drink. It was a deal, a business proposition, that he had made with God: Samad being the party of the first part, God being the sleeping partner. And since that day Samad had enjoyed relative spiritual peace and many a frothy Guinness with Archibald Jones; he had even developed the habit of taking his last gulp looking up at the sky like a Christian, thinking: I'm basically a good man. I don't slap the salami. Give me a break. I have the odd drink. *Can't say fairer than that . . .*

But of course he was in the wrong religion for compromises, deals, pacts, weaknesses and *can't say fairer than thats*. He was supporting the wrong team if it was empathy and concessions he wanted, if he wanted liberal exegesis, if he wanted to be *given a break*. His God was not *like* that charming white-bearded bungler of the Anglican, Methodist or Catholic churches. His God was not in the business of *giving people breaks*. The moment Samad set eyes on the pretty red-haired music teacher Poppy Burt-Jones that July of 1984, he knew finally the truth of this. He knew his God was having his revenge, he knew the game was up, he saw that the contract had been broken, and the sanity clause did not, after all, exist, that temptation had been deliberately and maliciously thrown in his path. In short, all deals were off.

Masturbation recommenced in earnest. Those two months, between seeing the pretty red-haired music teacher once and seeing her again, were the longest, stickiest, smelliest, guiltiest fifty-six days of Samad's life. Wherever he was, whatever he was doing, he found himself suddenly accosted by some kind of synaesthetic fixation with the woman: hearing the colour of her hair in the mosque, smelling the touch of her hand on the tube, tasting her smile while innocently walking the streets on his way to work; and this in turn led to a knowledge of every public convenience in London, led to the kind of masturbation that even a fifteen-year-old boy living in the Shetlands might find excessive. His only comfort was that he, like Roosevelt, had made a New Deal: he was going to beat but he wasn't going to *eat*. He meant somehow to purge himself of the sights and smells of Poppy Burt-Jones, of the sin of *istimna*, and, though it wasn't fasting season and these were the longest days of the year, still no substance passed Samad's lips between sunrise and sunset, not even, thanks to a little china spitoon, his own saliva. And because there was no food going in the one end, what came out of the other end was so thin and so negligible, so meagre and translucent, that Samad could almost convince himself that the sin was lessened, that one wonderful day he would be able to massage one-eyed-Jack as vigorously as he liked and nothing would come out but air.

But despite the intensity of the hunger – spiritual, physical, sexual – Samad still did his twelve hours daily in the restaurant. Frankly, he found the restaurant about the only place he could bear to be. He couldn't bear to see his family, he couldn't bear to go to O'Connell's, he couldn't bear to give Archie the satisfaction of seeing him in such a state. By mid August he had upped his working hours to fourteen a day; something in the ritual of it – picking up his basket of pink swan-shaped napkins and following the trail of Shiva's plastic carnations, correcting the order of a knife or fork, polishing a glass, removing the smear of a finger from the china plates – soothed him. No matter how bad a Muslim he might be, no one could say Samad wasn't a consummate waiter. He had taken one tedious skill and honed it to perfection. Here at least he could show others the right path: how to disguise a stale onion bhaji, how to make fewer prawns look like more, how to explain to an Australian that he doesn't want the amount of chilli he thinks he wants. Outside the doors of the Palace he was a masturbator, a bad husband, an indifferent father, with all the morals of an Anglican. But inside here, within these four green and yellow paisley walls, he was a one-handed genius.

'Shiva! Flower missing. Here.'

It was two weeks into Samad's New Deal and an average Friday afternoon at the Palace, setting up.

'You've missed this vase, Shiva!'

Shiva wandered over to examine the empty, pencil-thin, aquamarine vase on table nineteen.

'And there is some lime pickle afloat in the mango chutney in the sauce carousel on table fifteen.'

'Really?' said Shiva drily. Poor Shiva; nearly thirty now; not so pretty; still here. It had never happened for him, whatever he thought was going to happen for him. He did leave the restaurant, Samad remembered vaguely, for a short time in 1979 to start up a security firm, but 'nobody wanted to hire Paki bouncers' and he had come back, a little less aggressive, a little more despairing, like a broken horse.

'Yes, Shiva. Really and truly.'

'And that's what's driving you crazy, is it?'

'I wouldn't go as far as to say crazy, no . . . it is *troubling* me.'

'Because something,' interrupted Shiva, 'has got right up your arse recently. We've all noticed it.'

'We?'

'Us. The boys. Yesterday it was a grain of salt in a napkin. The day before Gandhi wasn't hung straight on the wall. The past week you've been acting like Führer-gee,' said Shiva nodding in Ardashir's direction. 'Like a crazy man. You don't smile. You don't eat. You're constantly on everybody's case. And when the head waiter's not all there it puts everybody off. Like a football captain.'

'I am certain I do not know to what you are referring,' said Samad, tight-lipped, passing him the vase.

'And I'm certain you do,' said Shiva provocatively, placing the empty vase back on the table.

'If I am concerned about something, there is no reason why it should disrupt my work here,' said Samad, becoming panicked, passing him back the vase. 'I do not wish to inconvenience others.'

Shiva returned the vase to the table once more. 'So there *is* something. Come on, man . . . I know we haven't always seen eye to eye, but we've got to stick together in this place. How long have we worked together? Samad Miah?'

Samad looked up suddenly at Shiva, and Shiva saw he was sweating, that he seemed almost dazed. 'Yes, yes . . . there is . . . something.'

Shiva put his hand on Samad's shoulder. 'So why don't we sod the fucking carnation and go and cook you a curry – sun'll be down in twenty minutes. Come on, you can tell Shiva all about it. Not because I give a fuck, you understand, but I have to work here too and you're driving me mad, mate.'

Samad, oddly touched by this inelegant offer of a listening ear, laid down his pink swans and followed Shiva into the kitchens.

'Animal, vegetable, mineral?'

Shiva stood at a work surface and began chopping a breast of chicken into perfect cubes and dousing them in corn flour.

'Pardon me?'

'Is it animal, vegetable or mineral?' repeated Shiva impatiently. 'The thing that's bothering you.'

'Animal, mainly.'

'Female?'

Samad dropped on to a nearby stool and hung his head.

'Female,' Shiva concluded. 'Wife?'

'The shame of it, the pain of it will come to my wife, but no . . . she is not the cause.'

'Another bird. My specialist subject.' Shiva performed the action of rolling a camera, sang the theme to *Mastermind* and jumped into shot. 'Shiva Bhagwati, you have thirty seconds on shagging women other than your wife. First question: is it right? Answer: depends. Second question: shall I go to hell? –'

Samad cut in, disgusted. 'I am not . . . making love to her.'

'I've started so I'll finish: shall I go to hell? Answer –'

'Enough. Forget it. Please, forget that I mentioned anything of this.'

'Do you want aubergine in this?'

'No . . . green peppers are sufficient.'

'Alrighty,' said Shiva, throwing a green pepper up in the air and catching it on the tip of his knife. 'One Chicken Bhuna coming up. How long's it been going on, then?'

'Nothing is going on. I met her only once. I barely know her.'

'So: what's the damage? A grope? A snog?'

'A handshake, only. She is my sons' teacher.'

Shiva tossed the onions and peppers into hot oil. 'You've had the odd stray thought. So what?'

Samad stood up. 'It is more than stray thoughts, Shiva. My whole body is mutinous, nothing will do what I tell it. Never before have I been subjected to such physical indignities. For example: I am constantly –'

'Yeah,' said Shiva, indicating Samad's crotch. 'We noticed that too. Why don't you do the five-knuckle-shuffle before you get to work?'

'I do . . . I am . . . but it makes no difference. Besides, Allah forbids it.'

'Oh, you should never have got religious, Samad. It don't suit you.' Shiva wiped an onion-tear away. 'All that guilt's not healthy.'

'It is not guilt. It is fear. I am fifty-seven, Shiva. When you get to my age, you become . . . concerned about your faith, you don't want to leave things too late. I have been corrupted by England, I see that now – my children, my wife, they too have been corrupted. I think maybe I have made the wrong friends. Maybe I have been frivolous. Maybe I have thought intellect more important than faith. And now it seems this final temptation has been put in front of me. To punish me, you understand. Shiva, you know about women. Help me. How can this feeling be possible? I have known of the woman's existence for no more than a few months, I have spoken to her only once.'

'As you said: you're fifty-seven. Mid-life crisis.'

'Mid-life? What does this mean?' snapped Samad irritably. 'Dammit, Shiva, I don't plan to live for one hundred and fourteen years.'

'It's a *manner of speaking*. You read about it in the magazines these days. It's when a man gets to a certain point in life, he starts feeling he's over the hill . . . and you're as young as the girl you feel, if you get my meaning.'

'I am at a moral crossroads in my life and you are talking nonsense to me.'

'You've got to learn this stuff, mate,' said Shiva, speaking slowly, patiently. 'Female organism, gee-spot, testicle cancer, the menstropause – mid-life crisis is one of them. Information the modern man needs at his fingertips.'

'But I don't wish for such information!' cried Samad, standing up and pacing the kitchen. 'That is precisely the point! I don't wish to be a modern man! I wish to live as I was always meant to! I wish to return to the East!'

'Ah, well . . . we all do, don't we?' murmured Shiva, pushing the peppers and onion around the pan. 'I left when I was three. Fuck knows I haven't made anything of this country. But who's got the money for the air fare? And who wants to live in a shack with fourteen servants on the payroll? Who knows what Shiva Bagwhati would have turned out like back in Calcutta? Prince or pauper? And who,' said Shiva, some of his old beauty returning to his face, 'can pull the West out of 'em once it's in?'

Samad continued to pace. 'I should never have come here – that's where every problem has come from. Never should have brought my sons here, so far from God. Willesden Green! Calling-cards in sweetshop windows, Judy Blume in the school, condom on the pavement, Harvest Festival, teacher-temptresses!' roared Samad, picking items at random. 'Shiva – I tell you, in confidence: my dearest friend, Archibald Jones, is an unbeliever! Now: what kind of a model am I for my children?'

'Iqbal, sit down. Be calm. Listen: you just want somebody. People want people. It happens from Delhi to Deptford. And it's not the end of the world.'

'Of this, I wish I could be certain.'

'When are you next seeing her?'

'We are meeting for school-related business . . . the first Wednesday of September.'

'I see. Is she Hindu? Muslim? She ain't Sikh, is she?'

'That is the worst of it,' said Samad, his voice breaking. 'English. White. English.'

Shiva shook his head. 'I been out with a lot of white birds, Samad. A lot. Sometimes it's worked, sometimes it ain't. Two lovely American girls. Fell head-over-heels for a Parisian stunner. Even spent a year with a Romanian. But never an English girl. Never works. Never.'

'Why?' asked Samad, attacking his thumbnail with his teeth and awaiting some fearful answer, some edict from on high. 'Why not, Shiva Bhagwati?'

'Too much history,' was Shiva's enigmatic answer, as he dished up the Chicken Bhuna. 'Too much bloody history.'

8.30 a.m., the first Wednesday of September, 1984. Samad, lost in thought somewhat, heard the passenger door of his Austin Mini Metro open and close – far away in the real world – and turned to his left to find Millat climbing in next to him. Or at least a Millat-shaped thing from the neck down: the head replaced by a *Tomytronic* – a basic computer game that looked like a large pair of binoculars. Within it, Samad knew from experience, a little red car that represented his son was racing a green car and a yellow car along a three-dimensional road of l.e.d.'s.

Millat parked his tiny backside on the brown plastic seat. 'Ooh! Cold seat! Cold seat! Frozen bum!'

'Millat, where are Magid and Irie?'

'Coming.'

'Coming with the speed of a train or coming with the speed of a snail?'

'Eeek!' squealed Millat, in response to a virtual blockade that threatened to send his red car spinning off into oblivion.

'Please, Millat. Take this off.'

'Can't. Need one, oh, two, seven, three points.'

'Millat, you need to begin to understand numbers. Repeat: ten thousand, two hundred and seventy-three.'

'Men blousand, poo bumdred and weventy-wee.'

'Take it off, Millat.'

'Can't. I'll die. Do you want me to die, Abba?'

Samad wasn't listening. It was imperative that he be at school before nine if this trip were going to have any purpose whatsoever. By nine, she'd be in class. By nine-oh-two, she'd be opening the register with those long fingers, by nine-oh-three she'd be tapping her high-mooned nails on a wooden desk somewhere out of sight.

'Where are they? Do they want to be late for school?'

'Uh-huh.'

'Are they always this late?' asked Samad, for this was not his regular routine – the school run was usually Alsana's or Clara's assignment. It was for a glimpse of Burt-Jones (though their meeting was only seven hours and fifty-seven minutes away, seven hours and fifty-six minutes away, seven hours . . .) that he had undertaken the most odious parental responsibility in the book. And he'd had a hard time convincing Alsana there was nothing peculiar in this sudden desire to participate fully in the educational transportation of his and Archie's offspring:

'But Samad, you don't get in the house 'til three in the morning. Are you going peculiar?'

'I want to see my boys! I want to see Irie! Every morning they are growing up – I never see it! Two inches Millat has grown.'

'But not at eight thirty in the morning. It is very funnily enough that he grows all the time – praise Allah! It must be some kind of a miracle. What is this about, hmm?' She dug her fingernail into the overhang of his belly. 'Some hokery-pokery. I can smell it – like goat's tongue gone off.'

Ah, Alsana's culinary nose for guilt, deceit and fear was without equal in the borough of Brent, and Samad was useless in the face of it. Did she know? Had she guessed? These anxieties Samad had slept on all night (when he wasn't slapping the salami) and then brought to his car first thing so that he might take them out on his children.

'Where in hell's name are they?'

'Hell's bells!'

'Millat!'

'*You* swore,' said Millat, taking lap fourteen and getting a five-oh-oh bonus for causing the combustion of Yellow Car. '*You* always do. So does M'ster Jones.'

'Well, we have special swearing licences.'

Headless Millat needed no face to express his outrage. 'NO SUCH *THING* AS –'

'OK, OK, OK,' back-pedalled Samad, knowing there is no joy to be had in arguing ontology with a nine-year-old, 'I have been caught out. No such thing as a licence to swear. Millat, where's your saxophone? You have orchestra today.'

'In the *boot*,' said Millat, his voice at once incredulous and disgusted: a man who didn't know the saxophone went in the boot on Sunday night was some kind of a social retard. 'Why're *you* picking us up? M'ster *Jones* picks us up on Mondays. You don't know *anything* about picking us up. *Or* taking us in.'

'I'm sure somehow I will muddle through, thank you, Millat. It is hardly rocket science, after all. *Where are those two!*' he shouted, beeping the horn, unhinged by his nine-year-old son's ability to recognize the irregularity in his behaviour. 'And will you *please* be taking that damn thing off!' Samad made a grab for the *Tomytronic* and pulled it down around Millat's neck.

'YOU KILLED ME!' Millat looked back in the *Tomytronic*, horrified, and just in time to witness his tiny red alter-ego swerving into the barriers and disappearing in a catastrophic light show of showering yellow sparks. 'YOU KILLED ME WHEN I WAS WINNING!'

Samad closed his eyes and forced his eyeballs to roll up as far as possible in his head, in the hope that his brain might impact upon them, a self-blinding, if he could achieve it, on a par with that other victim of Western corruption, Oedipus. Think: I want another woman. Think: I've killed my son. I swear. I eat bacon. I regularly slap the salami. I drink Guinness. My best friend is a kaffir non-believer. I tell myself if I rub up and down without using hands it does not count. But oh it does count. It all counts on the great counting board of He who counts. What will happen come Mahshar? How will I absolve myself when the Last Judgement comes?

. . . Click-slam. Click-slam. One Magid, one Irie. Samad opened his eyes and looked in the rear-view mirror. In the back seat were the two children he had been waiting for: both with their little glasses, Irie with her wilful Afro (not a pretty child: she had got her genes mixed up, Archie's nose with Clara's awfully buck teeth), Magid with his thick black hair slicked into an unappealing middle-parting. Magid carrying a recorder, Irie with violin. But beyond these basic details, everything was not as it should be. Unless he was very much mistaken, something was rotten in this Mini Metro – something was *afoot*. Both children were dressed in black from head to toe. Both wore white armbands on their left arms upon which were painted crude renditions of baskets of vegetables. Both had pads of writing paper and a pen tied around their necks with string.

'Who did this to you?'

Silence.

'Was it Amma? And Mrs Jones?'

Silence.

'Magid! Irie! Cat got your tongues?'

More silence; children's silence, so desperately desired by adults yet eerie when it finally occurs.

'Millat, do *you* know what this is about?'

''Sboring,' whined Millat. 'They're just being clever, clever, snotty, dumb-bum, Lord Magoo and Mrs Ugly Poo.'

Samad twisted in his car seat to face the two dissenters. 'Am I meant to ask you what this is about?'

Magid grasped his pen and, in his neat, clinical hand, printed: IF YOU WANT TO, then ripped off the piece of paper and handed it to Samad.

'A Vow of Silence. I see. You too, Irie? I would have thought you were too sensible for such nonsense.'

Irie scribbled for a moment on her pad and passed the missive forward. WE ARE PROSTESTING.

'Pros-testing? What are Pros and why are you testing them? Did your mother teach you this word?'

Irie looked like she was going to burst with the sheer force of her explanation, but Magid mimed the zipping up of her mouth, snatched back the piece of paper and crossed out the first *s*.

'Oh, I *see. Protesting.*'

Magid and Irie nodded maniacally.

'Well, that is indeed fascinating. And I suppose your mothers engineered this whole scenario? The costumes? The notepads?'

Silence.

'You are quite the political prisoners . . . not giving a thing away. All right: may one ask *what it is* that you are protesting about?'

Both children pointed urgently to their armbands.

'Vegetables? You are protesting for the rights of vegetables?'

Irie held one hand over her mouth to stop herself screaming the answer, while Magid set about his writing pad in a flurry. WE ARE PROTESTING ABOUT THE HARVEST FESTIVAL.

Samad growled, 'I told you already. I don't want you participating in that nonsense. It has nothing to do with us, Magid. Why are you always trying to be somebody you are not?'

There was a mutual, silent anger as each acknowledged the painful incident that was being referred to. A few months earlier, on Magid's ninth birthday, a group of very nice-looking white boys with meticulous manners had turned up on the doorstep and asked for Mark Smith.

'Mark? No Mark here,' Alsana had said, bending down to their level with a genial smile. 'Only the family Iqbal in here. You have the wrong house.'

But before she had finished the sentence, Magid had dashed to the door, ushering his mother out of view.

'Hi, guys.'

'Hi, Mark.'

'Off to the chess club, Mum.'

'Yes, M – M – Mark,' said Alsana, close to tears at this final snub, the replacement of 'Mum' for 'Amma'. 'Do not be late, now.'

'I GIVE YOU A GLORIOUS NAME LIKE MAGID MAHFOOZ MURSHED MUBTASIM IQBAL!' Samad had yelled after Magid when he returned home that evening and whipped up the stairs like a bullet to hide in his room. 'AND YOU WANT TO BE CALLED MARK SMITH!'

But this was just a symptom of a far deeper malaise. Magid really wanted to be *in some other family*. He wanted to own cats and not cockroaches, he wanted his mother to make the music of the cello, not the sound of the sewing machine; he wanted to have a trellis of flowers growing up one side of the house instead of the ever growing pile of other people's rubbish; he wanted a piano in the hallway in place of the broken door off cousin Kurshed's car; he wanted to go on biking holidays to France, not day-trips to Blackpool to visit aunties; he wanted the floor of his room to be shiny wood, not the orange and green swirled carpet left over from the restaurant; he wanted his father to be a doctor, not a one-handed waiter; and this month Magid had converted all these desires into a wish to join in with the Harvest Festival like Mark Smith would. Like everybody else would.

BUT WE WANT TO DO IT. OR WE'LL GET A DETENTION. MRS OWENS SAID IT IS TRADITION.

Samad blew his top. 'Whose tradition?' he bellowed, as a tearful Magid began to scribble frantically once more. 'Dammit, you are a Muslim, not a wood sprite! I *told* you, Magid, I told you the condition upon which you would be allowed. You come with me on haj. If I am to touch that black stone before I die I will do it with my eldest son by my side.'

Magid broke the pencil halfway through his reply, scrawling the second half with blunt lead. IT'S NOT FAIR! I CAN'T GO ON HAJ. I'VE GOT TO GO TO SCHOOL. I DON'T HAVE TIME TO GO TO MECCA. IT'S NOT FAIR!

'Welcome to the twentieth century. It's not fair. It's never fair.'

Magid ripped the next piece of paper from the pad and held it up in front of his father's face. YOU TOLD HER DAD NOT TO LET HER GO.

Samad couldn't deny it. Last Tuesday he had asked Archie to show solidarity by keeping Irie at home the week of the festival. Archie had hedged and haggled, fearing Clara's wrath, but Samad had reassured him: *Take a leaf from my book, Archibald. Who wears the trousers in my house?* Archie had thought about Alsana, so often found in those lovely silken trousers with the tapered ankle, and of Samad, who regularly wore a long piece of embroidered grey cotton, a lungi, wrapped round his waist, to all intents and purposes, a skirt. But he kept the thought to himself.

WE WON'T SPEAK IF YOU DON'T LET US GO. WE WON'T SPEAK <u>EVER</u>, <u>EVER</u>, <u>EVER</u>, <u>EVER</u> AGAIN. WHEN WE DIE EVERYONE WILL SAY IT WAS YOU. YOU YOU YOU.

Great, thought Samad, *more blood and sticky guilt on my one good hand.*

∽

Samad didn't know anything about conducting, but he knew what he liked. True, it probably wasn't very complex, the way she did it, just a simple three/four, just a one-dimensional metronome drawn in the air with her index finger – but *aaah*, what a joy it was to watch her do it! Her back to him; her bare feet lifting – on every third beat – out of her slip-on shoes; her backside protruding ever so slightly, pressing up against the jeans each time she lunged forward for one of the orchestra's ham-fisted crescendos – what a joy it was! What a *vision*! It was all he could do to stop himself rushing at her and carrying her off; it frightened him, the extent to which he *could not take his eyes off her*. But he had to rationalize: the orchestra needed her – God knows they were never going to get through this adaptation of *Swan Lake* (more reminiscent of ducks waddling through an oil slick) without her. Yet what a terrific *waste* it seemed – akin to watching a toddler on a bus mindlessly grabbing the breast of the stranger sitting next to him – what a *waste*, that something of such beauty should be at the disposal of those too young to know what to do with it. The second he tasted this thought he brought it back up: *Samad Miah . . . surely a man has reached his lowest when he is jealous of the child at a woman's breast, when he is jealous of the young, of the future . . .* And then, not for the first time that afternoon, as Poppy Burt-Jones lifted out of her shoes once more and the ducks finally succumbed to the environmental disaster, he asked himself: *Why, in the name of Allah, am I here?* And the answer returned once more with the persistence of vomit: *Because I simply cannot be anywhere else.*

Tic, tic, tic. Samad was thankful for the sound of baton hitting on music-stand, which interrupted him from these thoughts, these thoughts that were something close to delirium.

'Now, kids, kids. Stop. *Shhh*, quieten down. Mouths away from instruments, bows down. *Down*, Anita. That's it, *yes*, right on the floor. *Thank* you. Now: you've probably noticed we have a visitor today.' She turned to him and he tried hard to find some part of her on which to focus, some inch that did not heat his troubled blood. 'This is Mr Iqbal, Magid's and Millat's father.'

Samad stood up as if he'd been called to attention, draped his wide-lapelled overcoat carefully over his volatile crotch, waved rather lamely, sat back down.

'Say "Hello, Mr Iqbal."'

'HELLO, MR ICK-BALL,' came the resounding chorus from all but two of the musicians.

'Now: don't we want to play thrice as well because we have an audience?'

'YES, MISS BURT-JONES.'

'And not only is Mr Iqbal our audience for today, but he's a very *special* audience. It's because of Mr Iqbal that next week we won't be playing *Swan Lake* any more.'

A great roar met this announcement, accompanied by a stray chorus of trumpet hoots, drum rolls, a cymbal.

'All right, all right, enough. I didn't expect *quite* so much joyous approval.'

Samad smiled. She had humour, then. There was wit there, a bit of sharpness – but why think the *more* reasons there were to sin, the *smaller* the sin was? He was thinking like a Christian again; he was saying *Can't say fairer than that* to the Creator.

'Instruments down. Yes, *you*, Marvin. *Thank you* very much.'

'What'll we be doin' instead, then, Miss?'

'Well . . .' began Poppy Burt-Jones, the same half-coy, half-daring smile he had noticed before. 'Something *very* exciting. Next week I want to try to experiment with some *Indian* music.'

The cymbal player, dubious of what place he would occupy in such a radical change of genre, took it upon himself to be the first to ridicule the scheme. 'What, you mean that Eeeee EEEAAaaaa EEEeeee AAOoooo music?' he said, doing a creditable impression of the strains to be found at the beginning of a Hindi musical, or in the back-room of an 'Indian' restaurant, along with attendant head movements. The class let out a blast of laughter as loud as the brass section and echoed the gag en masse: *Eeee Eaaaoo OOOAaaah Eeee OOOiiiiiii* . . . This, along with screeching parodic violins, penetrated Samad's deep, erotic half-slumber and sent his imagination into a garden, a garden encased in marble where he found himself dressed in white and hiding behind a large tree, spying on a be-saried, bindi-wearing Poppy Burt-Jones, as she wound flirtatiously in and out of some fountains; sometimes visible, sometimes not.

'I don't think –' began Poppy Burt-Jones, trying to force her voice above the hoo-hah, then, raising it several decibels, 'I DON'T THINK IT IS VERY NICE TO –' and here her voice slipped back to normal as the class registered the angry tone and quietened down. 'I don't think it is very nice to make fun of *somebody else's culture*.'

The orchestra, unaware that this is what they had been doing, but aware that this was the most heinous crime in the Manor School rule book, looked to their collective feet.

'Do *you*? Do *you*? How would *you* like it, Sophie, if someone made fun of Queen?'

Sophie, a vaguely retarded twelve-year-old covered from head to toe in that particular rock band's paraphernalia, glared over a pair of bottle-top spectacles.

'Wouldn't like it, Miss.'

'No, you wouldn't, would you?'

'No, Miss.'

'Because Freddie Mercury is from *your culture*.'

Samad had heard the rumours that ran through the rank and file of the Palace waiters to the effect that this Mercury character was in actual fact a very light-skin Persian called Farookh, whom the head chef remembered from school in Panchgani, near Bombay. But who wished to split hairs? Not wanting to stop the lovely Burt-Jones while she was in something of a flow, Samad kept the information to himself.

'Sometimes we find other people's music strange because their culture is different from *ours*,' said Miss Burt-Jones solemnly. 'But that doesn't mean it isn't equally good, now does it?'

'NO, MISS.'

'And we can learn about each other through each other's culture, can't we?'

'YES, MISS.'

For example, what music do you like, Millat?'

Millat thought for a moment, swung his saxophone to his side and began fingering it like a guitar. 'Bo-orn to ruuun! Da da da da daaa! Bruce Springsteen, Miss! Da da da da daaa! Baby, we were bo-orn –'

'Umm, nothing – nothing else? Something you listen to *at home*, maybe?'

Millat's face fell, troubled that his answer did not seem to be the right one. He looked over at his father, who was gesticulating wildly behind the teacher, trying to convey the jerky head and hand movements of bharata natyam, the form of dance Alsana had once enjoyed before sadness weighted her heart, and babies tied down her hands and feet.

'Thriiiii-ller!' sang Millat, full throated, believing he had caught his father's gist. 'Thriii-ller night! Michael Jackson, Miss! Michael Jackson!'

Samad put his head in his hands. Miss Burt-Jones looked queerly at the small child standing on a chair, gyrating and grabbing his crotch before her. 'OK, thank you, Millat. Thank you for sharing . . . that.'

Millat grinned. 'No problem, Miss.'

While the children queued up to exchange twenty pence for two dry digestives and a cup of tasteless squash, Samad followed the light foot of Poppy Burt-Jones like a predator – into the music cupboard, a tiny room, windowless, with no means of escape, and full of instruments, filing cabinets overbrimming with sheet-music, and a scent Samad had thought hers but now identified as the maturing leather of violin cases mixed with the mellowing odour of cat-gut.

'This,' said Samad, spotting a desk beneath a mountain of paper, 'is where you work?'

Poppy blushed. 'Tiny, isn't it? Music budgets get cut every year until this year there was nothing left to cut *from*. It's got to the point where they're putting desks in cupboards and calling them offices. If it wasn't for the GLC, there wouldn't even be a desk.'

'It is certainly small,' said Samad, scanning the room desperately for some spot where he might stand that would put her out of arm's reach. 'One might almost say, claustrophobic.'

'I know, it's *awful* – but won't you sit down?'

Samad looked for the chair she might be referring to.

'Oh God! I'm sorry! It's *here*.' She swept paper, books and rubbish on to the floor with one hand, revealing a perilous-looking stool. 'I made it – but it's pretty safe.'

'You excel in carpentry?' inquired Samad, searching once again for more good reasons to commit a bad sin. 'An artisan as well as a musician?'

'No, no, no – I went to a few night classes – nothing special. I made that and a foot stool, and the foot stool broke. I'm no – do you know I *can't* think of a single carpenter!'

'There is always Jesus.'

'But I can't very well say "I'm no Jesus" . . . I mean, obviously I'm not, but for other reasons.'

Samad took his wobbly seat as Poppy Burt-Jones went to sit behind her desk. 'Meaning you are not a good person?'

Samad saw that he had flustered her with the accidental solemnity of the question; she drew her fingers through her fringe, fiddled with a small tortoiseshell button on her blouse, laughed shakily. 'I like to think I'm not all bad.'

'And that is enough?'

'Well . . . I . . .'

'Oh my dear, I apologize . . .' began Samad. 'I was not being serious, Miss Burt-Jones.'

'Well . . . Let's say I'm no *Mr Chippendale* – that'll do.'

'Yes,' said Samad kindly, thinking to himself that she had far better legs than a Queen Anne chair, 'that will do.'

'Now: where were we?'

Samad leant a little over the desk, to face her. 'Were we somewhere, Miss Burt-Jones?'

(He used his eyes; he remembered people used to say that it was his eyes – that new boy in Delhi, Samad Miah, they said, he has *eyes to die for*.)

'I was looking – looking – I was looking for my notes – where *are* my notes?'

She began rifling through the catastrophe of her desk, and Samad leant back once more on his stool, taking what little satisfaction he could from the fact that her fingers, if he was not mistaken, appeared to be trembling. Had there been *a moment*, just then? He was fifty-seven – it was a good ten years since he'd had a moment – he was not at all sure he would recognize a moment if one came along. *You old man*, he told himself as he dabbed at his face with a handkerchief, *you old fool*. Leave now – leave before you drown in your own guilty excrescence (for he was sweating like a pig), *leave before you make it worse*. But was it possible? Was it possible that this past month – the month that he had been squeezing and spilling, praying and begging, making deals and thinking, thinking always about her – that she had been thinking of *him*?

'Oh! While I'm looking . . . I remember there was something I wanted to ask you.'

Yes! said the anthropomorphized voice that had taken up residence in Samad's right testicle. Whatever the question the answer is *yes yes yes*. *Yes*, we will make love upon this very table, *yes*, we will burn for it, and *yes*, Miss Burt-Jones, *yes*, the answer is inevitably, inescapably, *YES*. Yet somehow, out there where conversation continued, in the rational world four feet above his ball-bag, the answer turned out to be – 'Wednesday.'

Poppy laughed. 'No, I don't mean what day it is – I don't look that ditsy do I? No, I meant what *day* is it; I mean, for Muslims. Only I saw Magid was in some kind of costume, and when I asked him what it was for he wouldn't speak. I was terribly worried that I'd offended him somehow.'

Samad frowned. It is odious to be reminded of one's children when one is calculating the exact shade and rigidity of a nipple that could so assert itself through bra and shirt.

'Magid? Please do not worry yourself about Magid. I am sure he was not offended.'

'So I was right,' said Poppy gleefully. 'Is it like a type of, I don't know, vocal fasting?'

'Er . . . yes, yes,' stumbled Samad, not wishing to divulge his family dilemma, 'it is a symbol of the Qur'ān's . . . *assertion* that the day of reckoning would first strike us all unconscious. Silent, you see. So, so, so the eldest son of the family dresses in black and, umm, disdains speech for a . . . a period of . . . of *time* as a process of – of *purification*.'

Dear *God*.

'I *see*. That's just *fascinating*. And Magid is the elder?'

'By two minutes.'

Poppy smiled. 'Only just, then.'

'Two minutes,' said Samad patiently, because he was speaking to one with no knowledge of the impact such small periods of time had amounted to throughout the history of the Iqbal family, 'made all the difference.'

'And does the process have a name?'

'*Amar durbol lagche*.'

'What does it mean?'

Literal translation: *I feel weak*. It means, Miss Burt-Jones, that *every strand of me feels weakened by the desire to kiss you*.

'It means,' said Samad aloud, without missing a beat, 'closed-mouth worship of the Creator.'

'*Amar durbol lagche*. Wow,' said Poppy Burt-Jones.

'Indeed,' said Samad Miah.

Poppy Burt-Jones leant forward in her chair. 'I don't know . . . To me, it's just like this *incredible* act of *self-control*. We just don't have that in the West – that sense of sacrifice – I just have so much admiration for the sense your people have of abstinence, of *self-restraint*.'

At which point Samad kicked the stool from under him like a man hanging himself, and met the loquacious lips of Poppy Burt-Jones with his own feverish pair.

7 *Molars*

And the sins of the Eastern father shall be visited upon the Western sons. Often taking their time, stored up in the genes like baldness or testicular carcinoma, but sometimes on the very same day. Sometimes at the very same moment. At least, that would explain how two weeks later, during the old Druid festival of harvest, Samad can be found quietly packing the one shirt he's never worn to mosque (*To the pure all things are pure*) into a plastic bag, so that he might change later and meet Miss Burt-Jones (4.30, Harlesden Clock) without arousing suspicion . . . while Magid and a change-of-heart Millat slip only four cans of past-their-sell-by-date chickpeas, a bag of variety crisps and some apples into two rucksacks (*Can't say fairer than that*), in preparation for a meeting with Irie (4.30, ice-cream van) and a visit to their assigned old man, the one to whom they will offer pagan charity, one Mr J. P. Hamilton of Kensal Rise.

Unbeknownst to all involved, ancient ley-lines run underneath these two journeys – or, to put it in the modern parlance, this is a rerun. We have been here before. This is like watching TV in Bombay or Kingston or Dhaka, watching the same old British sitcoms spewed out to the old colonies in one tedious, eternal loop. Because immigrants have always been particularly prone to repetition – it's something to do with that experience of moving from West to East or East to West or from island to island. Even when you arrive, you're still going back and forth; your children are going round and round. There's no proper term for it – *original sin* seems too harsh; maybe *original trauma* would be better. A trauma is something one repeats and repeats, after all, and this is the tragedy of the Iqbals – that they can't help but re-enact the dash they once made from one land to another, from one faith to another, from one brown mother country into the pale, freckled arms of an imperial sovereign. It will take a few replays before they move on to the next tune. And this is what is happening as Alsana sews loudly on her monstrous Singer machine, double-stitching around the vacancy of a crotchless knicker, oblivious to the father and the sons who are creeping around the house, packing clothes, packing provisions. It is a visitation of repetition. It is a dash across continents. It is a rerun. But one at a time, now, one at a time . . .

Now, how do the young prepare to meet the old? The same way the old prepare to meet the young: with a little condescension; with low expectation of the other's rationality; with the knowledge that the other will find what they say hard to understand, that it will go beyond them (not so much over the head as between the legs); and with the feeling that they must arrive with something the other will like, something suitable. Like Garibaldi biscuits.

'They *like* them,' explained Irie when the twins queried her choice, as the three of them rumbled to their destination on the top of the 52 bus, 'they like the raisins in them. Old people *like* raisins.'

Millat, from under the cocoon of his *Tomytronic*, sniffed, 'Nobody likes raisins. Dead grapes – *bleurgh*. Who wants to eat *them*?'

'*Old people do*,' Irie insisted, stuffing the biscuits back into her bag. 'And they're not dead, *akchully*, they're *dried*.'

'Yeah, *after* they've died.'

'Shut *up*, Millat. Magid, tell him to shut up!'

Magid pushed his glasses up to the bridge of his nose and diplomatically changed the subject. 'What else have you got?'

Irie reached into her bag. 'A coconut.'

'A coconut!'

'For your information,' snapped Irie, moving the nut out of Millat's reach, 'old people *like* coconuts. They can use the milk for their tea.'

Irie pressed on in the face of Millat retching. '*And* I got some crusty French bread and some cheese-singlets and some apples –'

'We *got* apples, you *chief*,' cut in Millat, 'chief', for some inexplicable reason hidden in the etymology of North London slang, meaning *fool, arse, wanker*, a loser of the most colossal proportions.

'Well, I got some *more* and *better* apples, *akchully*, and some Kendal mint cake and some ackee and saltfish.'

'I *hate* ackee and saltfish.'

'Who said *you* were eating it?'

'I don't *want* to.'

'Well, you're not *going* to.'

'Well, good, 'cos I don't *want* to.'

'Well, good, 'cos I wouldn't let you even if you *wanted* to.'

'Well, that's lucky 'cos I *don't*. So *shame*,' said Millat; and, without removing his *Tomytronic*, he delivered shame, as was traditionally the way, by dragging his palm along Irie's forehead. '*Shame* in the *brain*.'

'Well, *akchully*, don't worry 'cos you're not going to get it –'

'Oooh, feel the heat, *feel the heat*!' squealed Magid, rubbing his little palm in. 'You been shamed, man!'

'*Akchully*, I'm not shamed, *you're* shamed 'cos it's for Mr J. P. Hamilton –'

'Our stop!' cried Magid, shooting to his feet and pulling the bell cord too many times.

'*If you ask me*,' said one disgruntled OAP to another, '*they should all go back to their own . . .*'

But this, the oldest sentence in the world, found itself stifled by the ringing of bells and the stamping of feet, until it retreated under the seats with the chewing gum.

'Shame, shame, know your name,' trilled Magid. The three of them hurtled down the stairs and off the bus.

∽

And the 52 bus goes two ways. From the Willesden kaleidoscope, one can catch it west like the children; through Kensal Rise, to Portobello, to Knightsbridge, and watch the many colours shade off into the bright white lights of town; or you can get it east, as Samad did; Willesden, Dollis Hill, Harlesden, and watch with dread (if you are fearful like Samad, if all you have learnt from the city is to cross the road at the sight of dark-skinned men) as white fades to yellow fades to brown, and then Harlesden Clock comes into view, standing like Queen Victoria's statue in Kingston – a tall stone surrounded by black.

Samad had been surprised, yes *surprised*, that it was *Harlesden* she had whispered to him when he pressed her hand after the kiss – that kiss he could still taste – and demanded where it was he might find her, away from here, *far* from here (*'My children, my wife,'* he had mumbled, incoherent); expecting 'Islington' or maybe 'West Hampstead' or at least 'Swiss Cottage' and getting instead, 'Harlesden. I live in Harlesden.'

'Stonebridge Estate?' Samad had asked, alarmed; wide-eyed at the creative ways Allah found to punish him, envisioning himself atop his new lover with a gangster's four-inch knife in his back.

'No – but not far from there. Do you want to meet up?'

Samad's mouth had been the lone gunman on the grassy knoll that day, killing off his brain and swearing itself into power all at the same time.

'Yes. Oh, dammit! *Yes*.'

And then he had kissed her again, turning something relatively chaste into something else, cupping her breast in his left hand and enjoying her sharp intake of breath as he did so.

Then they had the short, obligatory exchange that those who cheat have to make them feel less like those who cheat.

'I really shouldn't –'

'I'm not at all sure how this –'

'Well, we need to meet at least to discuss what has –'

'Indeed, what has happened, it must be discu –'

'Because something has happened here, but –'

'My wife . . . my children . . .'

'Let's give it some time . . . two weeks Wednesday? 4.30? Harlesden Clock?'

He could at least, in this sordid mess, congratulate himself on his timing: 4.15 by the time he got off the bus, which left five minutes to nip into the McDonald's toilets (that had black guards on the door, black guards to keep out the blacks) and squeeze out of the restaurant flares into a dark blue suit, with a wool V-neck and a grey shirt, the pocket of which contained a comb to work his thick hair into some obedient form. By which time it was 4.20, five minutes in which to visit cousin Hakim and his wife Zinat who ran the local £1 + 50p shop (a type of shop that trades under the false premise that it sells no items above this price but on closer inspection proves to be the minimum price of the stock) and whom he meant inadvertently to provide him with an alibi.

'Samad Miah, oh! So smart-looking today – it cannot be without a reason.'

Zinat Mahal: a mouth as large as the Blackwall Tunnel and Samad was relying upon it.

'Thank you, Zinat,' said Samad, looking deliberately disingenuous. 'As for a reason . . . I am not sure that I should say.'

'Samad! My mouth is like the grave! Whatever is told to me dies with me.'

Whatever was told to Zinat invariably lit up the telephone network, rebounded off aerials, radiowaves and satellites along the way, picked up finally by advanced alien civilizations as it bounced through the atmosphere of planets far removed from this one.

'Well, the truth is . . .'

'By Allah, get on with it!' cried Zinat, who was now almost on the other side of the counter, such was her delight in gossip. 'Where are you off to?'

'Well . . . I am off to see a man in Park Royal about life insurance. I want my Alsana well provided for after my death – but!' he said, waggling a finger at his sparkling, jewel-covered interrogator who wore too much eyeshadow, 'I don't want her to know! Thoughts of death are abhorrent to her, Zinat.'

'Do you hear that, Hakim? Some men worry about the future of their wives! Go on – get out of here, don't let me keep you, cousin. And don't worry,' she called after him, simultaneously reaching for the phone with her long curling fingernails, 'I won't say one word to Alsi.'

Alibi done, three minutes were left for Samad to consider what an old man brings a young girl; something an old brown man brings a young white girl at the crossroads of four black streets; something suitable . . .

'A coconut?'

Poppy Burt-Jones took the hairy object into her hands and looked up at Samad with a perplexed smile.

'It is a mixed-up thing,' began Samad nervously. 'With juice like a fruit but hard like a nut. Brown and old on the outside, white and fresh on the inside. But the mix is not, I think, bad. We use it sometimes,' he added, not knowing what else to say, 'in curry.'

Poppy smiled; a terrific smile which accentuated every natural beauty of that face and had in it, Samad thought, something better than this, something with no shame in it, something better and purer than what they were doing.

'It's lovely,' she said.

Out in the street and five minutes from the address on their school sheets, Irie still felt the irritable hot sting of shame and wanted a rematch.

'Tax that,' she said, pointing to a rather beat-up motorbike leaning by Kensal Rise tube. 'Tax that, and that,' indicating two BMXs beside it.

Millat and Magid jumped into action. The practice of 'taxing' something, whereby one lays claims, like a newly arrived colonizer, to items in a street that do not belong to you, was well known and beloved to both of them.

'*Cha*, man! Believe, I don't *want* to tax dat crap,' said Millat with the Jamaican accent that all kids, whatever their nationality, used to express scorn. 'I tax *dat*,' he said, pointing out an admittedly impressive small, shiny, red MG about to turn the corner. 'And *dat*!' he cried, getting there just before Magid as a BMW whizzed past. 'Man, you *know* I tax that,' he said to Magid, who offered no dispute. '*Blatantly*.'

Irie, a little dejected by this turn of events, turned her eyes from the road to the floor, where she was suddenly struck by a flash of inspiration.

'I tax *those*!'

Magid and Millat stopped and looked in awe at the perfectly white Nikes that were now in Irie's possession (with one red tick, one blue; so beautiful, as Millat later remarked, it made you want to kill yourself), though to the naked eye they appeared to be walking towards Queens Park attached to a tall natty-dread black kid.

Millat nodded grudgingly. 'Respect to *that*. I wish I'd seed dem.'

'Tax!' said Magid suddenly, pushing his grubby finger up against some shop glass in the direction of a four-foot-long chemistry set with an ageing TV personality's face on the front. He thumped the window. 'Wow! I tax that!'

A brief silence ensued.

'You tax *that*?' asked Millat, incredulous. '*That*? You tax a chemistry set?'

Before poor Magid knew where he was, two palms had made a ferocious slap on his forehead, and were doing much rubbing for good measure. Magid gave Irie an *et tu Brute* type of pleading look, in the full knowledge that it was useless. There is no honesty amongst almost-ten-year-olds.

'*Shame! Shame! Know your name!*'

'But Mr J. P. Hamilton,' moaned Magid from under the heat of shame. 'We're here now. His house is just there. It's a quiet street, you can't make all this noise. He's *old*.'

'But if he's old, he'll be deaf,' reasoned Millat. 'And if you're deaf you can't hear.'

'It doesn't work like that. It's hard for old people. You don't understand.'

'He's probably too old to take the stuff out of the bags,' said Irie. 'We should take them out and carry them in our hands.'

This was agreed upon, and some time was taken arranging all the foodstuffs in the hands and crevices of the body, so that they might 'surprise' Mr J. P. Hamilton with the extent of their charity when he answered the door. Mr J. P. Hamilton, confronted on his doorstep by three dark-skinned children clutching a myriad of projectiles, was duly surprised. As old as they had imagined but far taller and cleaner, he opened the door only slightly, keeping his hand, with its mountain range of blue veins, upon the knob, while his head curled around the frame. To Irie he was reminiscent of some genteel elderly eagle: tufts of feather-like hair protruded from ear drums, shirt cuffs and the neck, with one white spray falling over his forehead, his fingers lay in a permanent tight spasm like talons, and he was well dressed, as one might expect of an elderly English bird in Wonderland – a suede waistcoat and a tweed jacket, and a watch on a gold chain.

And twinkling like a magpie, from the blue scattering in his eyes undimmed by the white and red surround, to the gleam of a signet ring, four argent medals perched just above his heart, and the silver rim of a Senior Service packet peeping over the breast pocket.

'Please,' came the voice from the bird-man, a voice that even the children sensed was from a different class, a different era. 'I must ask that you remove yourselves from my doorstep. I have no money whatsoever; so be your intention robbing or selling I'm afraid you will be disappointed.'

Magid stepped forward, trying to place himself in the old man's eyeline, for the left eye, blue as Rayleigh scattering, had looked beyond them, while the right was so compacted beneath wrinkles it hardly opened. 'Mr Hamilton, don't you remember, the school sent us, these are –'

He said, 'Goodbye, now,' as if he were bidding farewell to an elderly aunt embarking on a train journey, then once more 'Goodbye', and through two panels of cheap stained-glass on the closed door the children watched the lengthy figure of Mr Hamilton, blurred as if by heat, walking slowly away from them down a corridor until the brown flecks of him merged with the brown flecks of the household furnishings and the former all but disappeared.

Millat pulled his *Tomytronic* down around his neck, frowned, and purposefully slammed his little fist into the doorbell, holding it down.

'Maybe,' suggested Irie, 'he doesn't want the stuff.'

Millat released the doorbell briefly. 'He's got to want it. He asked for it,' he growled, pushing the bell back down with his full force. ''SGod's harvest, innit? Mr Hamilton! Mr J. P. Hamilton!'

And then that slow process of disappearance began to rewind as he reconstituted himself via the atoms of a staircase and a dresser until he was large as life once more, curled around the door.

Millat, lacking patience, thrust his school information sheet into his hand. ''SGod's harvest.'

But the old man shook his head like a bird in a bird-bath. 'No, no, I really won't be intimidated into purchases on my own doorstep. I don't know what you are selling – please God let it not be encyclopedias – at my age it is not *more* information one requires but *less*.'

'But it's free!'

'Oh . . . yes, I see . . . why?'

''S God's harvest,' repeated Magid.

'Helping the local community. Mr Hamilton, you must have spoken to our teacher, because she sent us here. Maybe it slipped your mind,' added Irie in her grown-up voice.

Mr Hamilton touched his temple sadly as if to retrieve the memory and then ever so slowly opened his front door to full tilt and made a pigeon-step forward into the autumn sunlight. 'Well . . . you'd better come in.'

They followed Mr Hamilton into the town house gloom of his hall. Filled to the brim with battered and chipped Victoriana punctuated by signs of more recent life – children's broken bikes, a discarded *Speak-and-Spell*, four pairs of muddy wellies in a family's variant sizes.

'Now,' he said cheerily, as they reached the living room with its beautiful bay windows through which a sweeping garden could be seen, 'what have we got here?'

The children released their load on to a moth-eaten chaise longue, Magid reeling off the contents like items from a shopping list, while Mr Hamilton lit a cigarette and inspected the urban picnic with doddering fingers.

'Apples . . . oh, dear me, no . . . chickpeas . . . no, no, no, potato-chips . . .'

It went on like this, each article being picked up in its turn and chastised, until the old man looked up at them with faint tears in his eyes. 'I can't eat any of this, you see . . . too hard, too bloody hard. The most I could manage is probably the milk in that coconut. Still . . . we will have tea, won't we? You'll stay for tea?'

The children looked at him blankly.

'Go on, my dears, do sit down.'

Irie, Magid and Millat shuffled up nervously on the chaise longue. Then there was a click-clack sound and when they looked up Mr Hamilton's teeth were on his tongue, as if a second mouth had come out of the first. And then in a flash they were back in.

'I simply cannot eat anything unless it has been pulverized beforehand, you see. My own fault. Years and years of neglect. Clean teeth – never a priority in the army.' He signalled himself clumsily, an awkward jab at his own chest with a shaking hand. 'I was an army man, you see. Now: how many times do you young people brush your teeth?'

'Three times a day,' said Irie, lying.

'LIAR!' chorused Millat and Magid. 'PANTS ON FIRE!'

'Two and a half times.'

'Well, dear me, which is it?' said Mr Hamilton, smoothing down his trousers with one hand and lifting his tea with the other.

'Once a day,' said Irie sheepishly, the concern in his voice compelling her to tell the truth. 'Most days.'

'I fear you will come to regret that. And you two?'

Magid was midway through formulating some elaborate fantasy of a toothbrush machine that did it while you slept, but Millat came clean. 'Same. Once a day. More or less.'

Mr Hamilton leant back contemplatively in his chair. 'One sometimes forgets the significance of one's teeth. We're not like the lower animals – teeth replaced regularly and all that – we're of the mammals, you see. And mammals only get two chances, with teeth. More sugar?'

The children, mindful of their two chances, declined.

'But like all things, the business has two sides. Clean white teeth are not always wise, now are they? Par exemplum: when I was in the Congo, the only way I could identify the nigger was by the whiteness of his teeth, if you see what I mean. Horrid business. Dark as buggery, it was. And they died because of it, you see? Poor bastards. Or rather I survived, to look at it in another way, do you see?'

The children sat silently. And then Irie began to cry, ever so quietly.

Mr Hamilton continued, 'Those are the split decisions you make in war. See a flash of white and bang! as it were . . . Dark as buggery. Terrible times. All these beautiful boys lying dead there, right in front of me, right at my feet. Stomachs open, you know, with their guts on my shoes. Like the end of the bloody world. Beautiful men, enlisted by the Krauts, black as the ace of spades; poor fools didn't even know why they were there, what people they were fighting for, who they were shooting at. The decision of the gun. So quick, children. So brutal. Biscuit?'

'I want to go home,' whispered Irie.

'My dad was in the war. He played for England,' piped up Millat, red-faced and furious.

'Well, boy, do you mean the football team or the army?'

'The British army. He drove a tank. A Mr Churchill. With her dad,' explained Magid.

'I'm afraid you must be mistaken,' said Mr Hamilton, genteel as ever. 'There were certainly no wogs as I remember – though you're probably not allowed to say that these days are you? But no . . . no Pakistanis . . . what would we have fed them? No, no,' he grumbled, assessing the question as if he were being given the opportunity to rewrite history here and now. 'Quite out of the question. I could not possibly have stomached that rich food. No Pakistanis. The Pakistanis would have been in the Pakistani army, you see, whatever that was. As for the poor Brits, they had enough on their hands with us old Queens . . .'

Mr Hamilton laughed softly to himself, turned his head and silently admired the roaming branches of a cherry tree that dominated one whole corner of his garden. After a long pause he turned back and tears were visible in his eyes again – fast, sharp tears as if he had been slapped in the face. 'Now, you young men shouldn't tell fibs should you? Fibs will rot your teeth.'

'It's not a lie, Mr J. P. Hamilton, he really was,' said Magid, always the peace-maker, always the negotiator. 'He was shot in the hand. He has medals. He was a hero.'

'And when your teeth rot –'

'It's the truth!' shouted Millat, kicking over the tea-tray that sat on the floor between them. 'You *stupid* fucking old man.'

'And when your teeth rot,' continued Mr Hamilton, smiling at the ceiling, 'aaah, there's no return. They won't look at you like they used to. The pretty ones won't give you a second glance, not for love or money. But while you're still young, the important matter is the third molars. They are more commonly referred to as the wisdom teeth, I believe. You simply must deal with the third molars before anything else. That was my downfall. You won't have them yet, but my great-grandchildren are just feeling them now. The problem with third molars is one is never sure whether one's mouth will be quite large enough to accommodate them. They are the only part of the body that a man must grow into. He must be a big enough man for these teeth, do you see? Because if not – oh dear me, they grow crooked or any which way, or refuse to grow at all. They stay locked up there with the bone – an impaction, I believe, is the term – and terrible, terrible infection ensues. Have them out early, that's what I tell my granddaughter Jocelyn in regard to her sons. You simply must. You can't fight against it. I wish I had. I wish I'd given up early and hedged my bets, as it were. Because they're your father's teeth, you see, wisdom teeth are passed down by the father, I'm certain of it. So you must be big enough for them. God knows, I wasn't big enough for mine . . . Have them out and brush three times a day, if my advice means anything.'

By the time Mr J. P. Hamilton looked down to see whether his advice meant anything, his three dun-coloured visitors had already disappeared, taking with them the bag of apples (apples he had been contemplating asking Jocelyn to put through the food processor); tripping over themselves, running to get to a green space, to get to one of the lungs of the city, some place where free breathing was possible.

∽

Now, the children knew the city. And they knew the city breeds the Mad. They knew Mr White-Face, an Indian who walks the streets of Willesden with his face painted white, his lips painted blue, wearing a pair of tights and some hiking boots; they knew Mr Newspaper, a tall skinny man in an ankle-length raincoat who sits in Brent libraries removing the day's newspapers from his briefcase and methodically tearing them into strips; they knew Mad Mary, a black voodoo woman with a red face whose territory stretches from Kilburn to Oxford Street but who performs her spells from a bin in West Hampstead; they knew Mr Toupee, who has no eyebrows and wears a toupee not on his head but on a string around his neck. But these people *announced* their madness – they were better, less scary than Mr J. P. Hamilton – they flaunted their insanity, they weren't half mad and half not, curled around a door frame. They were properly mad in the Shakespearean sense, talking sense when you least expected it. In North London, where councillors once voted to change the name of the area to *Nirvana*, it is not unusual to walk the streets and be suddenly confronted by sage words from the chalk-faced, blue-lipped or eyebrowless. From across the street or from the other end of a tube carriage they will use their schizophrenic talent for seeing connections in the random (for discerning the whole world in a grain of sand, for deriving narrative from nothing) to riddle you, to rhyme you, to strip you down, to tell you who you are and where you're going (usually Baker Street – the great majority of modern-day seers travel the Metropolitan Line) and why. But as a city we are not appreciative of these people. Our gut instinct is that they intend to embarrass us, that they're out to *shame* us somehow as they lurch down the train aisle, bulbous-eyed and with carbuncled nose, preparing to ask us, inevitably, *what we are looking at*. What the *fuck* are we looking at. As a kind of pre-emptive defence mechanism, Londoners have learnt not to look, never to look, to avoid eyes at all times so that the dreaded question 'What you looking at?' and its pitiful, gutless, useless answer – 'Nothing' – might be avoided. But as the prey evolves (and we are prey to the Mad who are pursuing us, desperate to impart their own brand of truth to the hapless commuter) so does the hunter, and the true professionals begin to tire of that old catchphrase 'What you looking at?' and move into more exotic territory. Take Mad Mary. Oh, the principle's still the same, it's still all about eye contact and the danger of making it, but now she's making eye contact from a hundred, two hundred, even three hundred yards away, and if she catches you doing the same she roars down the street, dreads and feathers and cape afloat, Hoodoo stick in hand, until she gets to where you are, spits on you, and begins. Samad knew all of this – they'd had dealings before, he and red-faced Mad Mary; he'd even suffered the misfortune of having her sit next to him on a bus. Any other day and Samad would have given her as good as he got. But today he was feeling guilty and vulnerable, today he was holding Poppy's hand as the sun crept away; he could not face Mad Mary and her vicious truth-telling, her ugly madness – which of course was precisely why she was stalking him, quite deliberately stalking him down Church Road.

'For your own safety, don't look,' said Samad. 'Just keep on walking in a straight line. I had no idea she travelled this far into Harlesden.'

Poppy snatched the quickest glance at the multicoloured streaming flash galloping down the high street on an imaginary horse.

She laughed. 'Who is *that*?'

Samad quickened the pace. 'She is Mad Mary. And she is not remotely funny. She is dangerous.'

'Oh, don't be ridiculous. Just because she's homeless and has mental health . . . *difficulties*, doesn't mean she wants to hurt anyone. Poor woman, can you imagine what must have happened in her life to make her like that?'

Samad sighed. 'First of all, she is not homeless. She has stolen every wheelie bin in West Hampstead and has built quite a significant structure out of them in Fortune Green. And secondly she is not a "poor woman". Everyone is terrified of her, from the council downwards, she receives free food from every cornershop in North London ever since she cursed the Ramchandra place and business collapsed within the month.' Samad's portly figure was working up quite a sweat now, as he shifted another gear in response to Mad Mary doing the same on the other side of the street.

Breathless, he whispered, 'And she doesn't like white people.'

Poppy's eyes widened. 'Really?' she said, as if such an idea had never occurred to her, and turned round to make the fatal mistake of looking. In a second, Mad Mary was upon them.

A thick globule of spit hit Samad directly between his eyes, on the bridge of his nose. He wiped it away, pulled Poppy to him and tried to sidestep Mad Mary by ducking into the courtyard of St Andrew's Church, but the Hoodoo stick slammed down in front of them both, marking a line in the pebbles and dust that could not be crossed over.

She spoke slowly, and with such a menacing scowl that the left side of her face seemed paralysed. 'You . . . lookin' . . . at . . . some . . . ting?'

Poppy managed a squeak, 'No!'

Mad Mary whacked Poppy's calf with the Hoodoo stick and turned to Samad. 'You, sir! You . . . lookin' . . . at . . . some . . . ting?'

Samad shook his head.

Suddenly she was screaming. 'BLACK MAN! DEM BLOCK YOU EVERYWHERE YOU TURN!'

'Please,' stuttered Poppy, clearly terrified. 'We don't want any trouble.'

'BLACK MAN!' (She liked to speak in rhyming couplets.) 'DE BITCH SHE WISH TO SEE YOU BURN!'

'We are minding our own business –' began Samad, but he was stopped by a second projectile of phlegm, this time hitting him on the cheek.

'Tru hill and gully, dem follow you dem follow you, Tru hill and gully, de devil swallow you 'im swallow you.' This was delivered in a kind of singing stage-whisper, accompanied by a dance from side to side, arms outstretched and Hoodoo stick resting firmly underneath Poppy Burt-Jones's chin.

'What 'as dem ever done for us body bot kill us and enslave us? What 'as dem done for our minds bot hurt us an' enrage us? What's de pollution?'

Mad Mary lifted Poppy's chin with her stick and asked again, 'WHAT'S DE POLLUTION?'

Poppy was weeping. 'Please . . . I don't know what you want me to –'

Mad Mary sucked her teeth and turned her attention once more to Samad. 'WHAT'S DE SOLUTION?'

'I don't know.'

Mad Mary slapped him around the ankles with her stick. 'WHAT'S DE SOLUTION, BLACK MAN?'

Mad Mary was a beautiful, a striking woman: a noble forehead, a prominent nose, ageless midnight skin and a long neck that Queens can only dream about. But it was her alarming eyes, which shot out an anger on the brink of total collapse, that Samad was concentrated on, because he saw that they were speaking to him and him alone. Poppy had nothing to do with this. Mad Mary was looking at him with *recognition*. Mad Mary had spotted a *fellow traveller*. She had spotted the madman in him (which is to say, the *prophet*); he felt sure she had spotted the angry man, the masturbating man, the man stranded in the desert far from his sons, the foreign man in a foreign land caught between borders . . . the man who, if you push him far enough, will suddenly see sense. Why else had she picked him from a street full of people? Simply because she recognized him. Simply because they were from the same place, he and Mad Mary, which is to say: *far away*.

'Satyagraha,' said Samad, surprising himself with his own calmness.

Mad Mary, unused to having her interrogations answered, looked at him in astonishment. 'WHAT'S DE SOLUTION?'

'Satyagraha. It is Sanskrit for "truth and firmness". Gandhi-gee's word. You see, he did not like "passive resistance" or "civil disobedience".'

Mad Mary was beginning to twitch and swear compulsively under her breath, but Samad sensed that in some way this was Mad Mary listening, this was Mad Mary's mind trying to process words other than her own.

'Those words weren't big enough for him. He wanted to show what we call weakness to be a strength. He understood that sometimes not to act is a man's greatest triumph. He was a Hindu. I am a Muslim. My friend here is – '

'A Roman Catholic,' said Poppy shakily. 'Lapsed.'

'And you are?' began Samad.

Mad Mary said *cunt, bitch, rhasclaat* several times and spat on the *floor*, which Samad took as a sign of cooling hostilities.

'What I am trying to say . . .'

Samad looked at the small group of Methodists who, hearing the noise, had begun to gather nervously at the door of St Andrew's. He grew confident. There had always been a manqué preacher in Samad. A know-it-all, a walker-and-a-talker. With a small audience and a lot of fresh air he had always been able to convince himself that all the knowledge in the universe, all the knowledge on walls, was his.

'I am trying to say that life is a broad church, is it not?' He pointed to the ugly red-brick building full of its quivering believers. 'With wide aisles.' He pointed to the smelly bustle of black, white, brown and yellow shuffling up and down the high street. To the albino woman who stood outside the Cash and Carry, selling daisies picked from the churchyard. 'Which my friend and I would like to continue walking along if it is all right with you. Believe me, I understand your concerns,' said Samad, taking his inspiration now from that other great North London street-preacher, Ken Livingstone, 'I am having difficulties myself – we are all having difficulties in this country, this country which is new to us and old to us all at the same time. We are divided people, aren't we.'

And here Samad did what no one had done to Mad Mary for well over fifteen years: he touched her. Very lightly, on the shoulder.

'We are split people. For myself, half of me wishes to sit quietly with my legs crossed, letting the things that are beyond my control wash over me. But the other half wants to fight the holy war. Jihad! And certainly we could argue this out in the street, but I think, in the end, your past is not my past and your truth is not my truth and your solution – it is not my solution. So I do not know what it is you would like me to say. Truth and firmness is one suggestion, though there are many other people you can ask if that answer does not satisfy. Personally, my hope lies in the last days. The prophet Muhammad – peace be upon Him! – tells us that on the Day of Resurrection everyone will be struck unconscious. Deaf and dumb. No chit-chat. Tongueless. And what a *bloody* relief that will be. Now, if you will excuse me.'

Samad took Poppy firmly by the hand and walked on, while Mad Mary stood dumbstruck only briefly before rushing to the church door and spraying saliva upon the congregation.

Poppy wiped away a frightened tear and sighed.

She said, 'Calm in a crisis. Impressive.'

Samad, increasingly given to visions, saw that great-grandfather of his, Mangal Pande, flailing with a musket; fighting against the new, holding on to tradition.

'It runs in the family,' he said.

Later, Samad and Poppy walked up through Harlesden, around Dollis Hill, and then, when it seemed they were hovering too near to Willesden, Samad waited till the sun went down, bought a box of sticky Indian sweets and turned into Roundwood Park; admired the last of the flowers. He talked and talked, the kind of talking you do to stave off the inevitable physical desire, the kind of talking that only increases it. He told her about Delhi circa 1942, she told him about St Albans circa 1972. She complained about a long list of entirely unsuitable boyfriends, and Samad, not able to criticize Alsana or even mention her name, spoke of his children: fear of Millat's passion for obscenities and a noisy TV show about an A-team; worries about whether Magid got enough direct sunlight. What was the country doing to his sons, he wanted to know, what was it doing?

'I like you,' she said finally. 'A lot. You're very funny. Do you know that you're funny?'

Samad smiled and shook his head. 'I have never thought of myself as a great comic wit.'

'No – you *are* funny. That thing you said about camels . . .' She began to laugh, and her laugh was infectious.

'What thing?'

'About camels – when we were walking.'

'Oh, you mean, "Men are like camels: there is barely one in a hundred that you would trust with your life."'

'Yes!'

'That's not comedy, that is the Bukhārī, part eight, page one hundred and thirty,' said Samad. 'And it is good advice. I have certainly found it to be true.'

'Well, it's still funny.'

She sat closer to him on the bench and kissed his ear. 'Seriously, I like you.'

'I'm old enough to be your father. I'm married. I am a Muslim.'

'OK, so Dateline wouldn't have matched our forms. So what?'

'What kind of a phrase is this: "So what?" Is that English? That is not English. Only the immigrants can speak the Queen's English these days.'

Poppy giggled. 'I still say: So –'

But Samad covered her mouth with his hand, and looked for a moment almost as if he intended to hit her. 'So *everything*. So *everything*. There is nothing funny about this situation. There is nothing good about it. I do not wish to discuss the rights or wrongs of this with you. Let us stick to what we are obviously here for,' he spat out. 'The physical, not the metaphysical.'

Poppy moved to the other end of the bench and leant forward, her elbows resting on her knees. 'I know,' she began slowly, 'that this is no more than it is. But I won't be spoken to like that.'

'I am sorry. It was wrong of me –'

'Just because you feel guilty, I've nothing to feel –'

'Yes, I'm sorry. I have no –'

'Because you can go if you –'

Half thoughts. Stick them all together and you have less than you began with.

'I don't want to go. I want you.'

Poppy brightened a bit and smiled her half-sad, half-goofy smile.

'I want to spend the night . . . with you.'

'Good,' she replied. 'Because I bought this for you while you were next door buying those sugary sweets.'

'What is it?'

She dived into her handbag, and in the attenuated minute in which she scrabbled through lipsticks and car-keys and spare change, two things happened.

1.1 Samad closed his eyes and heard the words *To the pure all things are pure* and then, almost immediately afterwards, *Can't say fairer than that.*

1.2 Samad opened his eyes and saw quite clearly by the bandstand his two sons, their white teeth biting into two waxy apples, waving, smiling.

And then Poppy resurfaced, triumphant, with a piece of red plastic in her hand.

'A toothbrush,' she said.

8 *Mitosis*

The stranger who wanders into O'Connell's Pool House at random, hoping for the soft rise and fall of his grandfather's brogue, perhaps, or seeking to rebound a red ball off the side cushion and into the corner pocket, is immediately disappointed to find the place is neither Irish nor a pool house. He will survey the carpeted walls, the reproductions of George Stubbs's racehorse paintings, the framed fragments of some foreign, Eastern script, with not a little confusion. He will look for a snooker table and find instead a tall, brown man with terrible acne standing behind a counter, frying up eggs and mushrooms. His eye will land with suspicion upon an Irish flag and a map of the Arab Emirates knotted together and hung from wall to wall, partitioning him from the rest of the customers. Then he will become aware of several pairs of eyes upon him, some condescending, some incredulous; the hapless stranger will stumble out, warily, backwards, knocking over the life-size cut-out of Viv Richards as he goes. The customers will laugh. O'Connell's is no place for strangers.

O'Connell's is the kind of place family men come to for a different kind of family. Unlike blood relations, it is necessary here to *earn* one's position in the community; it takes years of devoted fucking around, time-wasting, laying-about, shooting the breeze, watching paint dry – far more dedication than men invest in the careless moment of procreation. You need to *know* the place. For example, there are reasons why O'Connell's is an Irish pool house run by Arabs with no pool tables. And there are reasons why the pustule-covered Mickey will cook you chips, egg and beans, or egg, chips and beans, or beans, chips, eggs and mushrooms but not, under any circumstances, chips, beans, eggs and bacon. But you need to hang around for that kind of information. We'll get into that later. For now, suffice to say this is Archie's and Samad's home from home; for ten years they have come here between six (the time Archie finishes work) and eight (the time Samad starts) to discuss everything from the meaning of Revelation to the prices of plumbers. And women. Hypothetical women. If a woman walked past the yolk-stained window of O'Connell's (a woman had never been known to venture inside) they would smile and speculate – depending on Samad's religious sensibilities that evening – on matters as far reaching as whether one would kick her out of bed in a hurry, to the relative merits of stockings or tights, and then on, inevitably, to the great debate: small breasts (that stand up) vs big breasts (that flop to the sides). But there was never any question of real women, real flesh and blood and wet and sticky women. Not until now. And so the unprecedented events of the past few months called for an earlier O'Connell's summit than usual. Samad had finally phoned Archie and confessed the whole terrible mess: he had cheated, he was cheating; he had been seen by the children and now he was seeing the children, like visions, day and night. Archie had been silent for a bit, and then said, 'Bloody hell. Four o'clock it is, then. Bloody hell.' He was like that, Archie. Calm in a crisis.

But come 4.15 and still no sign of him, a desperate Samad had chewed every fingernail he possessed to the cuticle and collapsed on the counter, nose squished up against the hot glass where the battered burgers were kept, eye to eye with a postcard showing the eight different local charms of County Antrim.

Mickey, chef, waiter and proprietor, who prided himself on knowing each customer's name and knowing when each customer was out of sorts, prised Samad's face off the hot glass with an egg slice.

'Oi.'

'Hello, Mickey, how are you?'

'Same old, same old. But enough about me. What's the fucking matter wiv you, mate. Eh? Eh? I've been watching you, Sammy, since the minute you stepped in here. Face as long as shit. Tell your uncle Mickey.'

Samad groaned.

'Oi. No. None of that. You know me. I'm the sympathetic side of the service industry, I'm service with a fucking smile, I'd wear a little red tie and a little red hat like them fuckwits in Mr Burger if my fuckin' head weren't so big.'

This was not a metaphor. Mickey had a very large head, almost as if his acne had demanded more room and received planning permission.

'What's the problem?'

Samad looked up at Mickey's big red head.

'I am just waiting for Archibald, Mickey. Please, do not concern yourself. I will be fine.'

''Sbit early, innit?'

'Pardon?'

Mickey checked the clock behind him, the one with the palaeolithic piece of encrusted egg on the dial. 'I say 'Sbit early, innit? For you and the Archie-boy. Six is when I expect you. One chips, beans, egg and mushroom. And one omelette and mushrooms. With seasonal variations, naturally.'

Samad sighed. 'We have much to discuss.'

Mickey rolled his eyes. 'You ain't starting on that Mangy Pandy whateverthefuckitis again, are you? Who shot who, and who hung who, my grandad ruled the Pakis or whateverthefuckitwas, as if any poor fucker gives a flying fuck. You're driving the custom away. You're creating –' Mickey flicked through his new bible, *Food for Thought: A Guideline for Employers and Employees Working in the Food Service Industry – Customer Strategy and Consumer Relations*. 'You're creating a *repetitive syndrome* that puts all these buggers off their *culinary experience*.'

'No, no. My *great*-grandfather is not up for discussion today. We have other business.'

'Well, thank *fuck*. Repetitive syndrome is what it is.' Mickey patted his book, affectionately. ''Sall in 'ere, mate. Best four ninety-five I ever spent. Talking of moolah, you 'aving a flutter today?' asked Mickey, signalling downstairs.

'I am a Muslim, Mickey, I don't indulge any more.'

'Well, obviously, yeah, we're all Brothers – but a man's gotta live, now. Hasn't he? I mean, hasn't he?'

'I don't know, Mickey, does he?'

Mickey slapped Samad firmly on the back. ''Course he does! I was saying to my brother Abdul –'

'Which Abdul?'

It was a tradition, both in Mickey's wider and nuclear family, to name all sons Abdul to teach them the vanity of assuming higher status than any other man, which was all very well and good but tended to cause confusion in the formative years. However, children are creative, and all the many Abduls added an English name as a kind of buffer to the first.

'Abdul-Colin.'

'Right.'

'So, you know Abdul-Colin went a bit fundamental – EGGS, BEANS, CHIPS, TOAST – big fucking beard, no pig, no drink, no pussy, the fuckin' works, mate – there you are, guvnor.'

Abdul-Mickey pushed a plate of festering carbohydrate to a sunken old man whose trousers were so high up his body they were gradually swallowing him whole.

'Well, where do you think I slap eyes on Abdul-Colin last week? Only in the Mickey Finn, down Harrow Road way, and I says, "Oi, Abdul-Colin, this is a fucking turn-up for the fucking books" and he says, all solemn, you know, all fully bearded, he says –'

'Mickey, Mickey – do you mind very much if we leave the story for later . . . it is just that . . .'

'No, fine, fine. Wish I knew why the fuck I bother.'

'If you could possibly tell Archibald I am sitting in the booth behind the pinball when he comes in. Oh, and my usual.'

'No problemo, mate.'

About ten minutes later the door went and Mickey looked up from Chapter 6, 'There's a Fly in My Soup: Dealing with Frameworks of Hostility Regarding Health Issues', to see Archibald Jones, cheap suitcase in hand, approaching the counter.

'All right, Arch. How's the folding business?'

'Oh, you know. Comme si, comme sar. Samad about?'

'Is he *about*? Is he *about*? He's been hanging round like a bad fucking smell for half a fucking hour. Face as long as shit. Someone wants to get a Poop-a-Scoop and clean him up.'

Archie put his suitcase on the counter and furrowed his brow. 'In a bad way, is he? Between you and me, Mickey, I'm really worried about him.'

'Go tell it to the fucking mountain,' said Mickey, who had been aggravated by Chapter 6's assertion that you should rinse plates in piping hot water. 'Or, alternatively, go to the booth behind the pinball.'

'Thanks, Mickey. Oh, omelette and –'

'I know. Mushrooms.'

Archie walked down the lino aisles of O'Connell's.

'Hello, Denzel, evening, Clarence.'

Denzel and Clarence were two uniquely rude, foul-mouthed octogenarian Jamaicans. Denzel was impossibly fat, Clarence was horribly thin, their families had both died, they both wore trilbies, and they sat in the corner playing dominoes all the hours that were left to them.

'What dat bambaclaat say?'

' 'Im say *evenin'*.'

'Can't 'im see me playin' domino?'

'No man! 'Im 'ave a pussy for a face. How you expec' 'im to see any little ting?'

Archie took it on the chin as it was meant and slipped into the booth, opposite Samad. 'I don't understand,' said Archie, picking up immediately where their phone conversation had terminated. 'Are you saying you're seeing them there in your imagination or you're seeing them there in real life?'

'It is really very simple. The first time, the very first time, they were there. But since then Archie, these past few weeks, I see the twins whenever I am with her – like apparitions! Even when we are . . . I see them there. Smiling at me.'

'Are you sure you're not just overworked.'

'Listen to me, Archie: I *see* them. It is a sign.'

'Sam, let's try and deal with the facts. When they really saw you – what did you do?'

'What could I do? I said, "Hello, sons. Say hello to Miss Burt-Jones.'

'And what did they say?'

'They said hello.'

'And what did you say?'

'Archibald, do you think I could simply tell you what occurred without this constant inane interjection?'

'CHIPS, BEANS, EGG, TOMATO AND MUSHROOM!'

'Sam, that's yours.'

'I resent that accusation. It is not mine. I never order tomato. I do not want some poor peeled tomato boiled to death, then fried to death.'

'Well, it's not mine. I asked for omelette.'

'Well, it is not mine. Now: may I continue?'

'With pleasure.'

'I looked at my boys, Archie . . . I looked at my beautiful boys . . . and my heart cracked – no, more than this – it shattered. It shattered into so many pieces and each piece stabbed me like a mortal wound. I kept thinking: how can I teach my boys anything, how can I show them the straight road when I have lost my own bearings?'

'I thought,' began Archie haltingly, 'that the problem was the woman. If you really don't know what to do about her, well . . . we could flip this coin, heads you stay, tails you go – at least you'd have made a –'

Samad slammed his good fist on the table. 'I don't want to flip a bloody coin! Besides, it is too late for that. Can't you see? What is done is done. I am hell-bound, I see that now. So I must concentrate on saving my sons. I have a choice to make, a choice of *morality*.' Samad lowered his voice, and even before he spoke Archie knew to what he was about to refer. 'You have made hard choices yourself, Archie, many years ago. You hide it well, but I know you have not forgotten what it is like. You have a bit of bullet in the leg to prove it. You struggled with him. You won out. I have not forgotten. I have always admired you because of it, Archibald.'

Archie looked at the floor. 'I'd rather not –'

'Believe me, I take no pleasure from dragging up that which is distasteful to you, my friend. But I am just trying to make you understand my situation. Then, as now, the question is always: *What kind of a world do I want my children to grow up in?* You took action on that matter once. And now it is my turn.'

Archie, making no more sense of Samad's speeches than he had forty years ago, played with a toothpick for a moment.

'Well . . . why don't you just stop, well, seeing her.'

'I try . . . I try.'

'That good is it?'

'No, well, that is not strictly . . . what I mean to say is, it is nice, yes . . . but it is not debauched . . . we kiss, we embrace.'

'But no –'

'Not strictly speaking, no.'

'But some –'

'Archibald, are you concerned about my sons or my sperm?'

'Sons,' said Archie. 'Definitely sons.'

'Because there is rebellion in them, Archie. I can see it – it is small now but it is growing. I tell you, I don't know what is happening to our children in this country. Everywhere you look, it is the same. Last week, Zinat's son was found smoking marijuana. Like a Jamaican!'

Archie raised his eyebrows.

'Oh, I meant no offence, Archibald.'

'None taken, mate. But you shouldn't judge before you've tried it. Being married to a Jamaican has done wonders for my arthritis. But that's by the by. Carry on.'

'Well, take Alsana's sisters – all their children are nothing but trouble. They won't go to mosque, they don't pray, they speak strangely, they dress strangely, they eat all kinds of rubbish, they have intercourse with God knows who. No respect for tradition. People call it assimilation when it is nothing but corruption. Corruption!'

Archie tried to look shocked and then tried disgusted, not knowing what to say. He liked people to get on with things, Archie. He kind of felt people should just live together, you know, in peace or harmony or something.

'CHIPS, BEANS, EGG, MUSHROOM! OMELETTE AND MUSHROOMS!'

Samad raised his hand and turned to the counter. 'Abdul-Mickey!' he yelled, his voice assuming a slight, comic, cockney twinge. 'Over here, my guvnor, please.'

Mickey looked at Samad, leant on the counter, and wiped his nose with his apron.

'Now you know better than that. It's self-service around here, gentlemen. This ain't the fucking Waldorf.'

'I'll get it,' said Archie, sliding out of his seat.

'How is he?' asked Mickey under his breath, as he pushed the plate towards Archie.

Archie frowned. 'Dunno. He's on about tradition again. He's worried about his sons, you see. Easy for children to go off the rails in this day and age, you know. I don't really know what to say to him.'

'Don't have to tell me, mate,' said Mickey, shaking his head. 'I wrote the fucking book, didn't I? Look at my littlest, Abdul-Jimmy. Up in juvenile court next week for swiping fucking VW medallions. I says to 'im, you fucking stupid or sommink? What the fuck is the point of that? At least steal the fucking *car*, if that's the way you feel about it. I mean, why? 'E says it's sommink to do wiv some fucking Beetie Boys or some such bollocks. Well, I says to him, that lot are dead as shit if I get hold of 'em, and I can tell you that for fucking nothing. No sense of tradition, no fucking morality, is the problem.'

Archie nodded and picked up a wad of napkins with which to handle the hot dishes.

'If you want my advice – and you do, 'cos that's part of the special relationship between caff owner and caff customer – you tell Samad he has two options. He can either send them back to the old country, back to India –'

'Bangladesh,' corrected Archie, nicking a chip from Samad's meal.

'Whereverthefuckitis. He can send 'em back there and have 'em brought up proper, by their granddads and grandmums, have 'em learn about their fucking culture, have 'em grow up with some fucking principles. Or – one minute – CHIPS, BEANS, PATTIE AND MUSHROOMS! FOR TWO!'

Denzel and Clarence ever so slowly sidled up to the hot plates.

'Dat pattie look *strange*,' said Clarence.

''Im try to poison us,' said Denzel.

'Dem mushroom look *peculiar*,' said Clarence.

''Im try to infiltrate a good man with de devil's food,' said Denzel.

Mickey slapped his egg slice down on Denzel's fingers, 'Oi.

Morecambe and fucking Wise. Get a new fucking routine, all right?'

'Or what?' persisted Archie.

''Im tryin' to kill an 'ol man. An 'ol, weak man,' muttered Denzel, as the two of them shuffled back to their seats.

'Fucking 'ell, those two. They're only alive 'cos they're too stingy to pay for the fucking cremation.'

'Or what?'

'What?'

'What's the second option?'

'Oh, yeah. Well, second option's obvious, innit?'

'Is it?'

'*Accept* it. He'll have to *accept* it, won't he. We're all English now, mate. Like it or lump it, as the rhubarb said to the custard. And that'll be two fifty, Archibald, my good man. The golden age of Luncheon Vouchers is over.'

The golden age of Luncheon Vouchers ended ten years ago. For ten years Mickey had been saying, 'The golden age of Luncheon Vouchers is over.' And that's what Archie loved about O'Connell's. Everything was remembered, nothing was lost. History was never revised or reinterpreted, adapted or whitewashed. It was as solid and as simple as the encrusted egg on the clock.

When Archie returned to table eight, Samad was like Jeeves: if not exactly disgruntled, then some way from being gruntled.

'Archibald, did you take a wrong turn at the Ganges? Weren't you listening to my dilemma? I am corrupt, my sons are becoming corrupt, we are all soon to burn in the fires of hell. These are problems of some urgency, Archibald.'

Archie smiled serenely and stole another chip. 'Problem solved, Samad, mate.'

'Problem solved?'

'Problem solved. Now, the way I see it, you have two options . . .'

Around the beginning of this century, the Queen of Thailand was aboard a boat, floating along with her many courtiers, manservants, maids, feet-bathers and food tasters, when suddenly the stern hit a wave and the Queen was thrown overboard into the turquoise waters of the Nippon-Kai where, despite her pleas for help, she drowned, for not one person on that boat went to her aid. Mysterious to the outside world, to the Thai the explanation was immediately clear: tradition demanded, as it does to this day, that no man or woman may touch the Queen.

If religion is the opium of the people, tradition is an even more sinister analgesic, simply because it rarely appears sinister. If religion is a tight band, a throbbing vein and a needle, tradition is a far homelier concoction: poppy seeds ground into tea; a sweet cocoa drink laced with cocaine; the kind of thing your grandmother might have made. To Samad, as to the people of Thailand, tradition was culture, and culture led to roots, and these were good, these were untainted principles. That didn't mean he could live by them, abide by them or grow in the manner they demanded, but roots were roots and roots were good. You would get nowhere telling him that weeds too have tubers, or that the first sign of loose teeth is something rotten, something degenerate, deep within the gums. Roots were what saved, the ropes one throws out to rescue drowning men, to Save Their Souls. And the further Samad himself floated out to sea, pulled down to the depths by a siren named Poppy Burt-Jones, the more determined he became to create for his boys roots on shore, deep roots that no storm or gale could displace. Easier said than done. He was in Poppy's poky little flat, going through his own household accounts, when it became obvious to him that he had more sons than money. If he was to send them back, he would need two dowries for the grandparents, two amounts for the schooling, two amounts for the clothes. As it was he could barely cover both air fares. Poppy had said: 'What about your wife? She's from a rich family isn't she?' But Samad had not yet revealed his plan to Alsana. He had only tested the water, mentioning it in a passing, hypothetical way to Clara while she did her gardening. How would she react if someone, acting in Irie's best interest, took the child away to a better life? Clara rose from her flower bed and stared at him in silent concern, and then laughed long and loud. *The man who did that*, she said finally, brandishing a large pair of garden shears inches from his crotch, *chop, chop*. Chop, chop, thought Samad; and it became clear to him what he was going to do.

'*One* of them?'

O'Connell's again. 6.25. One chips, beans, egg and mushroom. And one omelette and mushrooms *with peas* (seasonal variation).

'Just *one* of them?'

'Archibald, please keep your voice down.'

'But – just *one* of them?'

'That is what I said. Chop, chop.' He divided the fried egg on his plate down the middle. 'There is no other way.'

'But –'

Archie was thinking again, as best he could. The same old stuff. You know, why couldn't people just get on with things, just live together, you know, in peace or harmony or something. But he didn't say any of that. He just said, 'But –' And then, 'But –'

And then finally, 'But which *one*?'

And that (if you're counting air fare, dowry, initial schooling fee) was the three thousand, two hundred and forty-five quid question. Once the money was sorted – yes, he remortgaged the house, he risked his land, the greatest mistake an immigrant can make – it was simply a matter of choosing the child. For the first week it was going to be Magid, definitely Magid. Magid had the brains, Magid would settle down quicker, learn the language quicker, and Archie had a vested interest in keeping Millat in the country because he was the best striker Willesden Athletic FC (under fifteens) had seen in decades. So Samad began stealing Magid's clothes away for surreptitious packing, arranged a separate passport (he would be travelling with auntie Zinat on 4 November) and had a word in the ear of the school (long holiday, could he be given some homework to take with him, etc.).

But then the next week there was a change of heart and it was Millat, because Magid was really Samad's favourite, and he wanted to watch him grow older, and Millat was the one more in need of moral direction anyway. So *his* clothes were pilfered, *his* passport arranged, *his* name whispered into the right ears.

The following week it was Magid until Wednesday and then Millat because Archie's old penpal Horst Ibelgaufts wrote the following letter, which Archie, familiar now with the strangely prophetic nature of Horst's correspondence, brought to Samad's attention:

15 September 1984

Dearest Archibald,

It is some time since my last letter, but I felt compelled to write to you about a wonderful development in my garden which has brought me no little pleasure these past few months. To make a long story shorter and sweeter, I have finally gone for the chop and removed that old oak tree from the far corner and I cannot begin to describe to you the difference it has made! Now the weaker seeds are receiving so much more sun and are so healthy I am able even to make cuttings from them – for the first year in my memory each of my children has a vase of peonies on their windowsill. I had been suffering under the misapprehension all these years that I was simply an indifferent gardener – when all the time it was that grand old tree, taking up half the garden with its roots and not allowing anything else to grow.

The letter went on, but Samad stopped there. Irritably he said, 'And I am meant to divine from this precisely . . . what?'

Archie tapped the side of his nose knowingly. 'Chop, chop. It's got to be Millat. An omen, mate. You can trust Ibelgaufts.'

And Samad, who usually had no time for omens or nose tapping, was nervous enough to take the advice. But then Poppy (who was acutely aware that she was fading from Samad's mind in comparison with the question of the boys) suddenly took an interest, claiming to have *just sensed* in a dream that it should be Magid and so it was Magid once more. Samad, in his desperation, even allowed Archie to flip a coin, but the decision was hard to stick by – best out of three, best out of five – Samad couldn't trust it. And this, if you can believe it, was the manner in which Archie and Samad went about playing lottery with two boys, bouncing the issue off the walls of O'Connell's, flipping souls to see which side came up.

In their defence, one thing should be made clear. At no point was the word *kidnap* mentioned. In fact had this been offered as terminology for what he was about to do, Samad would have been appalled and astounded, would have dropped the whole thing like the somnambulist who wakes up to find himself in the master bedroom with a breadknife in his hand. He understood that he had *not yet informed Alsana*. He understood that he had *booked a 3 a.m. flight*. But it was in no way self-evident to him that these two facts were related or would combine to spell out *kidnap*. So it was with surprise that Samad greeted the vision of a violently weeping Alsana, at 2 a.m. on 31 October, hunched over the kitchen table. He did not think, *Ah, she has discovered what I am to do with Magid* (it was finally and for ever Magid), because he was not a moustachioed villain in a Victorian crime novel and besides which he was not conscious of plotting any crime. Rather his first thought was, *So she knows about Poppy*, and in response to this situation he did what every adulterous man does out of instinct: attack first.

'So I must come home to this, must I?' – slam down bag for effect – 'I spend all night in that infernal restaurant and then I am having to come back to your melodramatics?'

Alsana convulsed with tears. Samad noticed too that a gurgle sound was emanating from her pleasant fat which vibrated in the gap between her sari; she waved her hands at him and then put them over her ears.

'Is this really necessary?' asked Samad, trying to disguise his fear (he had expected anger, he didn't know how to deal with tears). 'Please, Alsana: surely this is an overreaction.'

She waved her hand at him once more as if to dismiss him and then lifted her body a little and Samad saw that the gurgling had not been organic, that she had been hunched *over* something. A radio.

'What on earth –'

Alsana pushed the radio from her body into the middle of the table and motioned for Samad to turn it up. Four familiar beeps, the beeps that follow the English into whatever land they conquer, rang round the kitchen, and then in Received Pronunciation Samad heard the following:

This is the BBC World Service at 03.00 hours. Mrs Indira Gandhi, Prime Minister of India, was assassinated today, shot down by her Sikh bodyguards in an act of open mutiny as she walked in the garden of her New Delhi home. There is no doubt that her murder was an act of revenge for 'Operation Blue Star', the storming of the Sikhs' holiest shrine at Amritsar last June. The Sikh community, who feel their culture is being attacked by –

'Enough,' said Samad, switching it off. 'She was no bloody good anyway. None of them is any bloody good. And who cares what happens in that cesspit, India. Dear me . . .' And even before he said it, he wondered why he had to, why he felt so *malevolent* this evening. 'You really are genuinely *pathetic*. I wonder: where would those tears be if *I* died? Nowhere – you care more about some corrupt politician you never met. Do you know you are the perfect example of the ignorance of the masses, Alsi? Do you know that?' he said, talking as if to a child and holding her chin up. 'Crying for the rich and mighty who would disdain to piss upon you. Doubtless next week you will be bawling because Princess Diana broke a fingernail.'

Alsana gathered all the spit her mouth could accommodate and launched it at him.

'*Bhainchute!* I am not crying for her, you *idiot*, I am crying for my *friends*. There will be blood on the streets back home because of this, India *and* Bangladesh. There will be riots – knives, guns. Public death, I have seen it. It will be like Mahshar, Judgement Day – people will die in the streets, Samad. You know and I know. And Delhi will be the worst of it, is always the worst of it. I have some family in Delhi, I have friends, *old lovers* –'

And here Samad slapped her, partly for the old lovers and partly because it was many years since he had been referred to as a *bhainchute* (translation: someone who, to put it simply, fucks their sisters).

Alsana held her face, and spoke quietly. 'I am crying with misery for those poor families and out of *relief* for my own children! Their father ignores them and bullies them, yes, but at least they will not die on the streets like rats.'

So this was going to be one of those rows: the same positions, the same lines, same recriminations, same right hooks. Bare fists. The bell rings. Samad comes out of his corner.

'No, they will suffer something worse, much worse: sitting in a morally bankrupt country with a mother who is going mad. Utterly cuckoo. Many raisins short of the fruitcake. Look at you, look at the state of you! Look how *fat* you are!' He grabbed a piece of her, and then released it as if it would infect him. 'Look how you dress. Running shoes and a sari? And what is that?'

It was one of Clara's African headscarfs, a long, beautiful piece of orange Kenti cloth in which Alsana had taken to wrapping her substantial mane. Samad pulled it off and threw it across the room, leaving Alsana's hair to crash down her back.

'You do not even know what you are, where you come from. We never see family any more – I am ashamed to show you to them. *Why did you go all the way to Bengal for a wife*, that's what they ask. *Why didn't you just go to Putney?*'

Alsana smiled ruefully, shook her head, while Samad made a pretence of calm, filling their metal kettle with water and slamming it down on the stove.

'And that is a beautiful lungi you have on, Samad Miah,' she said bitterly, nodding in the direction of his blue-towelling jogging suit topped off with Poppy's LA Raiders baseball cap.

Samad said, 'The difference is what is in here,' not looking at her, thumping just below his left breast bone. 'You say you are thankful we are in England, that's because you have swallowed it whole. I can tell you those boys would have a better life back home than they ever –'

'Samad Miah! Don't even begin! It will be over my dead body that this family moves back to a place where our lives are in danger! Clara tells me about you, she tells me. How you have asked her strange things. What are you plotting, Samad? I hear from Zinat all this about life insurance . . . who is dying? What can I smell? I tell you, it will be over my dead body –'

'But if you are already dead, Alsi –'

'Shut up! Shut up! I am not mad. You are trying to drive me mad! I phoned Ardashir, Samad. He is telling me you have been leaving work at eleven thirty. *It is two in the morning*. I am not mad!'

'No, it is worse. Your mind is diseased. You call yourself a Muslim –'

Alsana whipped round to face Samad, who was trying to concentrate his attention on the whistling steam emerging from the kettle.

'No, Samad. Oh no. Oh no. I don't call myself anything. I don't make claims. *You* call yourself a Muslim. *You* make the deals with Allah. *You* are the one he will be talking to, come Mahshar. *You*, Samad Miah. You, you, *you*.'

Second round. Samad slapped Alsana. Alsana right hooked him in the stomach and then followed up with a blow to the left cheekbone. She then made a dash to the back door, but Samad caught her by the waist, rugby-tackled her, dragged her down and elbowed her in the coccyx. Alsana, being heavier than Samad, knelt up, lifting him; flipped him over and dragged him out into the garden, where she kicked him twice as he lay on the floor – two short, fierce jabs to the forehead – but the rubber-cushioned sole did little damage and in a moment he was on his knees again. They made a grab for each other's hair, Samad determined to pull until he saw blood. But this left Alsana's knee free and it connected swiftly with Samad's crotch, forcing him to release the hair and swing a blind flier meant for her mouth but catching her ear. Around this time, the twins emerged half awake from their beds and stood at the long glass kitchen window to watch the fight, while the neighbours' security lights came on, illuminating the Iqbal garden like a stadium.

'Abba,' said Magid, after surveying the state of play for a moment. 'Definitely Abba.'

'*Cha*, man. No *way*,' said Millat, blinking in the light. 'I bet you two orange lollies Amma's going to kick the shit out of him.'

'Ooooooo!' cried the twins in unison, as if it were a firework display, and then, 'Aaaaaah!'

Alsana had just ended the fight with a little help from the garden rake.

'Now maybe *some* of us, who have to *work* in the morning, can get a *decent night's kip*! *Bloody* Pakis,' shouted a neighbour.

A few minutes later (because they always *held* each other after these fights, a hug somewhere between affection and collapse)

Samad came in from the garden, still mildly concussed and said, 'Go to bed,' before brushing a hand through each son's thick black hair.

As he reached the door, he stopped. 'You'll thank me,' he said, turning to Magid, who smiled faintly, thinking maybe Abba was going to get him that chemistry set after all. 'You'll thank me in the end. This country's no good. We tear each other apart in this country.'

Then he walked up the stairs and phoned Poppy Burt-Jones, waking her up to tell her there would be no more kisses in the afternoon, no more guilty walks, no more furtive taxis. End of affair.

Maybe all the Iqbals were prophets because Alsana's nose for trouble was more right than it had ever been. Public decapitations, families cremated in their sleep, hanging bodies outside the Kashmir gate, people stumbling around dazed missing pieces of themselves; body parts taken from Muslim by Sikh, from Sikh by Hindu; legs, fingers, noses, toes and teeth, teeth everywhere, scattered throughout the land, mingling with the dust. A thousand people had died by 4 November when Alsana emerged from under the bathwater to hear the crackling voice of Our Man in Delhi telling her about it from the top of the medicine cabinet.

Terrible business. But, as Samad saw it, some of us have the luxury of sitting in the bath and listening to the foreign news while some of us have a living to make, and an affair to forget, and a child to abduct. He squeezed into the white flares, checked the air ticket, phoned Archie to go over the plan, and left for work.

On the tube there was a youngish, prettyish girl, dark, Spanish-looking, mono-browed, crying. Just sitting opposite him, in a pair of big, pink leg-warmers, crying quite openly. Nobody said anything. Nobody did anything. Everybody hoped she was getting off at Kilburn. But she kept on like that, just sitting, crying;

West Hampstead, Finchley Road, Swiss Cottage, St John's Wood. Then at Bond Street she pulled a photo of an unpromising-looking young man out of her rucksack, showed it to Samad and some of the other passengers.

'Why he leave? He break my heart . . . Neil, he say his name, Neil. Neil, *Neil.*'

At Charing Cross, end of the line, Samad watched her cross the platform and get the train going straight back to Willesden Green. Romantic, in a way. The way she said 'Neil' as if it were a word bursting at the seams with past passion, with loss. That kind of flowing, feminine misery. He had expected something similar of Poppy, somehow; he had picked up the phone expecting gentle, rhythmic tears and later on letters, maybe, scented and stained. And in *her* grief *he* would have grown, as Neil was probably doing at this moment; her grief would have been an epiphany bringing him one step closer to his own redemption. But instead he had got only, 'Fuck you, you fucking *fuck.*'

'Told you,' said Shiva, shaking his head and passing Samad a basket of yellow napkins to be shaped like castles. 'I told you not to fuck with that business, didn't I? Too much history there, man. You see: it ain't just you she's angry with, is it?'

Samad shrugged and began on the turrets.

'No, man, history, history. It's all brown man leaving English woman, it's all Nehru saying See-Ya to Madam Britannia.' Shiva, in an effort to improve himself, had joined the Open University. 'It's all complicated, complicated shit, it's all about pride. Ten quid says she wanted you as a servant boy, as a wallah peeling the grapes.'

'No,' protested Samad. 'It wasn't that way. This is not the dark ages, Shiva, this is 1984.'

'Show's how much you know. From what you've told me, she's a classic case, mate, classic.'

'Well, I have other concerns now,' muttered Samad (privately calculating that his children would by now be safely tucked in at the Joneses' sleepover, that it was two more hours before Archie would need to wake Magid, leaving Millat to sleep on). 'Family concerns.'

'No time!' cried Ardashir, who had crept up from behind, imperceptibly as ever, to examine the battlements of Samad's castles. 'No time for family concerns, cousin. Everyone's concerned, everybody's trying to get their family out of that mess back home – I myself am forking out one thousand big ones for a ticket for my big-mouth sister – but I still have to come to work, I still have to get on with things. Busy night tonight, cousin,' called Ardashir, as he exited the kitchen to pace around the restaurant floor in a black tuxedo. 'Don't let me down.'

It was the busiest night in the week, Saturday, the night when the crowds come in waves: pre-theatre, post-theatre, post-pub, post-club; the first polite and conversational, the second humming show-tunes, the third rowdy, the fourth wide-eyed and abusive. The theatre crowds were naturally the favourite of the waiters; they were even tempered and tipped big and inquired after the geography of the food – its Eastern origin, its history – all of which would be happily fabricated by the younger waiters (whose furthest expedition East was the one they made daily, back home to Whitechapel, Smithfield's, the Isle of Dogs) or rendered faithfully and proudly by the elders in black biro on the back of a pink napkin.

I'll Bet She Is! was the show at the National these past few months, a rediscovered mid fifties musical set in the thirties. It was about a rich girl who runs away from her family and meets a poor boy on the road, who is himself off to fight the Civil War in Spain. They fall in love. Even Samad, who had no particular ear for a tune, picked up enough discarded programmes and heard enough tables burst into song to know most of the songs; he liked them, in fact they took his mind off the drudgery (even better – tonight they were sweet relief from worrying whether

Archie would manage to get Magid outside the Palace at 1 a.m. on the dot); he murmured them along with the rest of the kitchen in a kind of working rhythm as they chopped and marinaded, sliced and crushed.

I've seen the Paris op'ra and the wonders of the East

'Samad Miah, I'm looking for the Rajah mustard seeds.'

Spent my summers by the Nile and my winters on the piste

'Mustard seeds . . . I think I saw Muhammed with them.'

I've had diamonds, rubies, furs and velvet capes

'Accusations, accusations . . . I have seen no mustard seeds.'

I've had Howard Hughes peel me a grape

'I'm sorry, Shiva, if the old man doesn't have them, then I haven't seen them.'

But what does it mean without love?

'Then what are these?' Shiva walked over from his place next to chef and picked up a packet of mustard seeds by Samad's right elbow. 'Come on, Sam – get it together. Head in the clouds this evening.'

'I'm sorry . . . I have a lot on my mind . . .'

'That lady friend of yours, eh?'

'Keep your voice down, Shiva.'

'They tell me I'm spoilt, a rich broad who means trouble,' sang Shiva in the strangest of Hindified transatlantic accents. 'Oi-oi, my chorus. *But whatever love I'm given I pay it back double.'*

Shiva grabbed a small aquamarine vase and sang his big finale into its upturned end. *'But no amount of money, will make my honey mine* . . . You should take that advice, Samad Miah,' said Shiva, who was convinced Samad's recent remortgage was funding his illicit affair, 'it's good advice.'

A few hours later Ardashir appeared once more through the swing doors, breaking up the singing to deliver his second-phase pep-talk. 'Gentlemen, gentlemen! That is more than enough of that. Now, listen up: it's ten-thirty. They've seen the show.

They're hungry. They got only one pitiful tub of ice-cream in the interval and plenty of Bombay gin, which, as we all know, brings on the need for curry and that, gentlemen, is where we come in. Two tables of fifteen just came in and sat at the back. Now: when they ask for water what do you do? What do you do, Ravind?'

Ravind was brand new, nephew of the chef, sixteen, nervy. 'You tell them – '

'No, Ravind, even before you speak, what do you do?'

Ravind bit his lip. 'I don't know, Ardashir.'

'*You shake your head,*' said Ardashir, shaking his head. 'Simultaneous with a look of concern and fear for their well-being.' Ardashir demonstrated the look. 'And then you say?'

'"Water does not help the heat, sir."'

'But what helps the heat, Ravind? What will aid the gentleman with the burning sensation he is presently feeling?'

'More rice, Ardashir.'

'And? And?'

Ravind looked stumped and began to sweat. Samad, who had been belittled by Ardashir too many times to enjoy watching someone else play the victim, leant over to whisper the answer in Ravind's clammy ear.

Ravind's face lit up in gratitude. 'More naan bread, Ardashir!'

'Yes; because it soaks up the chilli and more importantly water is free and naan bread is one pound twenty. Now cousin,' said Ardashir, turning to Samad and waggling a bony finger, 'how will the boy learn? Let the boy answer for himself next time. You have your own business: a couple of ladies on table twelve requested the head waiter specifically, to be served only by him, so – '

'Requested me? But I thought I might stay in the kitchen this evening. Besides, I cannot be requested like some personal butler, there is too much to do – that is not policy, cousin.'

And at this moment Samad feels panicky. His thoughts are so

taken up with the 1 a.m. abduction, with the prospect of splitting his twins, that he does not trust himself with hot plates and steaming bowls of dal, with the spitting fat of clay-oven chicken, with all the dangers that accost a one-handed waiter. His head is full of his sons. He is half in dream this evening. He has once again bitten every nail beyond the cuticle and is fast approaching the translucent high-moons, the bleeding hubs.

He is saying, he hears himself saying, 'Ardashir, I have a million things to do here in the kitchens. And why should –'

And the answer comes, 'Because the head waiter is the best waiter and naturally they tipped me – us – for the privilege. No quibbling, please, cousin. Table twelve, Samad Miah.'

And perspiring lightly, throwing a white towel over his left arm, Samad begins tunelessly to hum the show-stopper as he pushes through the doors.

What won't a guy do for a girl? How sweet the scent, how huge the pearl?

It is a long walk to table twelve. Not in distance, it is only twenty metres in distance, but it is a long walk through the thick smells and the loud voices and the demands; through the cries of Englishmen; past table two, where the ashtray is full and must be cupped by another ashtray, lifted silently and switched for the new ashtray with perfect insouciance; stopping at table four, where there is an unidentifiable dish that was not ordered; debating with table five, who wish to be joined with table six, no matter the inconvenience; and table seven wants egg fried rice whether or not it is a Chinese dish; and table eight wobbles and more wine! More beer! It is a long walk if you are to negotiate the jungle; attending to the endless needs and needless ends, the desires, the demands of the pink faces that strike Samad now as pith-helmet-wearing gentlemen, feet up on the table with guns across their laps; as tea-slurping ladies on verandas cooling themselves under the breeze of the brown boys who beat the ostrich feathers –

What lengths won't he travel, how many hits of the gavel

By Allah, how *thankful* he is (*yes, madam, one moment, madam*), how *gladdened* by the thought that Magid, Magid at least, will, in a matter of four hours, be flying east from this place and its demands, its constant cravings, this place where there exists neither patience nor pity, where the people want what they want *now*, right now (*We've been waiting twenty minutes for the vegetables*), expecting their lovers, their children, their friends and even their gods to arrive at little cost and in little time, just as table ten expect their tandoori prawns . . .

At the auction of her choosing, how many Rembrandts, Klimts, De Koonings?

These people who would exchange all faith for sex and all sex for power, who would exchange fear of God for self-pride, knowledge for irony, a covered, respectful head for a long, strident shock of orange hair –

It is Poppy at table twelve. It is Poppy Burt-Jones. And just the name would be enough right now (for he is at his most volatile, Samad; he is about to split his own sons in two like that first nervous surgeon wielding his clumsy spit-wet knife over the clodded skin of the twins of Siam), just the name would be enough to explode his mind. The name alone is a torpedo heading for a tiny fishing boat, blowing his thoughts out of the water. But it is more than the name, the echo of a name spoken by some thoughtless fool or found at the bottom of an old letter, it is Poppy Burt-Jones herself in the freckled flesh. Sitting cold and determined with her sister, who seems, like all siblings of those we have desired, an uglier, mis-featured version.

'Say something, then,' says Poppy abruptly, fiddling with a Marlboro packet. 'No witty rejoinder? No crap about camels or coconuts? Nothing to say?'

Samad doesn't have anything to say. He merely stops humming his tune, inclines his head at exactly the correct deferential angle, and puts the nib of his pen preparedly to paper. It is like a dream.

'All right, then,' Poppy is saying tartly, looking Samad up and down, lighting up a fag. 'Have it your way. Right. To start with we'll have lamb samosas and the yoghurt whatdyamacallit.'

'And for the main,' the shorter, plainer, oranger, snub-nosed sister is saying, 'Two Lamb Dawn Sock and rice, with chips, *please*, waiter.'

∽

At least Archie is right on time; right year, right date, right hour; 1984, 5 November, 1 a.m. Outside the restaurant, dressed in a long trench-coat, standing in front of his Vauxhall, one hand tickling some spanking new Pirelli tyres, the other pulling hard on a fag like Bogart or a chauffeur or Bogart's chauffeur. Samad arrives, clasps Archie's right hand in his own and feels the coldness of his friend's fingers, feels the great debt he owes him. Involuntarily, he blows a cloud of frozen breath into his face. 'I won't forget this, Archibald,' he is saying, 'I won't forget what you do for me tonight, my friend.'

Archie shuffles about awkwardly. 'Sam, before you – there's something I have to –'

But Samad is already reaching for the door, and Archie's explanation must follow the sight of three shivering children in the back seat like a limp punchline.

'They *woke up*, Sam. They were all sleeping in the same room – a sleepover, like. Nothing I could do. I just put coats over their pyjamas – I couldn't risk Clara hearing – I *had* to bring them.'

Irie asleep; curled up with her head on the ashtray and her feet resting on the gearbox, but Millat and Magid reaching out for their father gleefully, pulling at his flares, chucking him on the chin.

'Hey, Abba! Where we going, Abba? To a secret disco party? Are we really?'

Samad looks severely at Archie; Archie shrugs.

'We're going on a trip to an airport. To Heathrow.'

'Wow!'

'And then when we get there, Magid – Magid –'

It is like a dream. Samad feels the tears before he can stop them; he reaches out to his eldest-son-by-two-minutes and holds him so tight to his chest that he snaps the arm of his glasses. 'And then Magid is going on a trip with auntie Zinat.'

'Will he come back?' It is Millat. 'It would be *cool* if he didn't come back!'

Magid prises himself from his father's headlock. 'Is it far? Will I be back in time for Monday – only I've got to see how my photosynthesis is for science – I took two plants: put one in the cupboard and one in the sunlight – and I've got to *see*, Abba, *I've got to see which one* –'

Years from now, even hours after that plane leaves, this will be history that Samad tries not to remember. That his memory makes no effort to retain. A sudden stone submerged. False teeth floating silently to the bottom of a glass.

'Will I get back for school, Abba?'

'Come on,' says Archie, solemnly from the front seat. 'We've got to get cracking if we're going to make it.'

'You'll be in a school on Monday, Magid. I promise. Now sit back in your seats, go on. For Abba, please.'

Samad closes the car door and crouches to watch his twin sons blow their hot breath on to the window. He puts his one hand up, applying a false touch to their lips, raw pink against the glass, their saliva mingling in the grimy condensation.

9 *Mutiny!*

To Alsana's mind the real difference between people was not colour. Nor did it lie in gender, faith, their relative ability to dance to a syncopated rhythm or open their fists to reveal a handful of gold coins. The real difference was far more fundamental. It was in the earth. It was in the sky. You could divide the whole of humanity into two distinct camps, as far as she was concerned, simply by asking them to complete a very simple questionnaire, of the kind you find in *Woman's Own* on a Tuesday:

(a) Are the skies you sleep under likely to open up for weeks on end?
(b) Is the ground you walk on likely to tremble and split?
(c) Is there a chance (and please tick the box, no matter how small that chance seems) that the ominous mountain casting a midday shadow over your home might one day erupt with no rhyme or reason?

Because if the answer is yes to one or all of these questions, then the life you lead is a midnight thing, always a hair's breadth from the witching hour; it is volatile, it is threadbare; it is carefree in the true sense of that term; it is light, losable like a keyring or a hairclip. And it is lethargy: why not sit all morning, all day, all year, under the same cypress tree drawing the figure of eight in the dust? More than that, it is disaster, it is *chaos*: why not overthrow a government on a whim, why not blind the man you hated, why not go mad, go gibbering through the town like a loon, waving your hands, tearing your hair? There's nothing to stop you – or rather *anything* could stop you, any hour, any minute. *That* feeling. *That's* the real difference in a life. People who live on solid ground, underneath safe skies, know nothing of this; they are like the English POWs in Dresden who continued to pour tea and dress for dinner, even as the alarms went off, even as the city became a towering ball of fire. Born of a green and pleasant land, a temperate land, the English have a basic inability to conceive of disaster, even when it is man-made.

It is different for the people of Bangladesh, formerly East Pakistan, formerly India, formerly Bengal. They live under the invisible finger of random disaster, of flood and cyclone, hurricane and mud-slide. Half the time half their country lies under water; generations wiped out as regularly as clockwork; individual life expectancy an optimistic fifty-two, and they are coolly aware that when you talk about apocalypse, when you talk about random death en masse, well, they are leading the way in that particular field, they will be the first to go, the first to slip Atlantis-like down to the seabed when the pesky polar ice-caps begin to shift and melt. It is the most ridiculous country in the world, Bangladesh. It is God's idea of a *really good wheeze*, his stab at black comedy. You don't need to give out questionnaires to Bengalis. The facts of disaster are the facts of their lives. Between Alsana's sweet sixteenth birthday (1971), for example, and the year she stopped speaking directly to her husband (1985), more people died in Bangladesh, more people perished in the winds and the rain, than in Hiroshima, Nagasaki and Dresden *put together*. A million people lost lives that they had learnt to hold lightly in the first place.

And this is what Alsana really held against Samad, if you want the truth, more than the betrayal, more than the lies, more than the basic facts of a kidnap: that Magid should *learn to hold his life lightly*. Even though he was relatively safe up there in the Chittagong Hills, the highest point of that low-lying, flatland country, still she hated the thought that Magid should be as she had once been: holding on to a life no heavier than a paisa coin, wading thoughtlessly through floods, shuddering underneath the weight of black skies . . .

Naturally, she became hysterical. Naturally, she tried to get him back. She spoke to the relevant authorities. The relevant authorities said things like, 'To be honest, love, we're more worried about them coming *in*' or 'To tell you the truth, if it was your *husband* who arranged the trip, there's not a great deal that we –', so she put the phone down. After a few months she stopped ringing. She went to Wembley and Whitechapel in despair and sat in the houses of relatives for epic weekends of weeping and eating and commiserations, but her gut told her that though the curry was sound, the commiserations were not all they seemed. For there were those who were quietly pleased that Alsana Iqbal, with her big house and her blacky-white friends and her husband who looked like Omar Sharif and her son who spoke like the Prince of Wales, was now living in doubt and uncertainty like the rest of them, learning to wear misery like old familiar silk. There was a certain *satisfaction* in it, even as Zinat (who never revealed her role in the deed) reached over the chair arm to take Alsana's hand in her sympathetic claws. 'Oh, Alsi, I just keep thinking what a *shame* it is that he had to take the good one! He was so very clever and so *beautifully* behaved! You didn't have to worry about drugs and dirty girls with that one. Only the price of spectacles with all that reading.'

Oh, there was a certain *pleasure*. And don't ever underestimate people, don't ever underestimate the pleasure they receive from viewing pain that is not their own, from delivering bad news, watching bombs fall on television, from listening to stifled sobs from the other end of a telephone line. Pain by itself is just Pain. But Pain + Distance can = entertainment, voyeurism, human interest, *cinéma vérité*, a good belly chuckle, a sympathetic smile, a raised eyebrow, disguised contempt. Alsana sensed all these and more at the other end of her telephone line as the calls flooded in – 28 May 1985 – to inform her of, to offer *commiserations* for, the latest cyclone.

'Alsi, I simply had to call. They say there are so many bodies floating in the Bay of Bengal . . .'

'I just heard the latest on the radio – ten thousand!'

'And the survivors are floating on rooftops while the sharks and crocodiles snap at their heels.'

'It must be terrible, Alsi, not knowing, not being sure . . .'

For six days and six nights, Alsana did not know, was not sure. During this period she read extensively from the Bengali poet Rabindranath Tagore and tried hard to believe his assurances (*Night's darkness is a bag that bursts with the gold of the dawn*), but she was, at heart, a practical woman and found poetry no comfort. For those six days her life was a midnight thing, a hair's breadth from the witching hour. But on the seventh day came light: the news arrived that Magid was fine, suffering only a broken nose delivered by a vase which had fallen from its perilous station on a high shelf in a mosque, blown over in the first breath of the first winds (and keep one eye on that vase, please, it is the same vase that will lead Magid by the nose to his vocation). It was only the servants, having two days earlier taken a secret supply of gin and piled into the family's dilapidated transit van on a pleasure trip to Dhaka, who were now floating belly-up in the Jamuna River as fish finned-silver stared up at them, pop-eyed and bemused.

Samad was triumphant. 'You see? He'll come to no harm in Chittagong! Even better news, he was in a *mosque*. Better he break his nose in a mosque than in a Kilburn fight! It is exactly as I had hoped. He is learning the old ways. Is he not learning the old ways?'

Alsana thought for a moment. Then she said: 'Maybe, Samad Miah.'

'What do you mean, "maybe"?'

'Maybe, Samad Miah, maybe not.'

Alsana had decided to stop speaking directly to her husband. Through the next eight years she would determine never to say *yes* to him, never to say *no* to him, but rather to force him to live like she did – never *knowing*, never being *sure*, holding Samad's sanity to ransom, until she was paid in full with the return of her number-one-son-eldest-by-two-minutes, until she could once more put a chubby hand through his thick hair. That was her promise, that was her curse upon Samad, and it was *exquisite* revenge. At times it very nearly drove him to the brink, to the kitchen-knife stage, to the medicine cabinet. But Samad was the kind of person too stubborn to kill himself if it meant giving someone else satisfaction. He hung on in there. Alsana turning over in her sleep, muttering, 'Just bring him back, Mr Idiot . . . if it's driving you nutso, just bring my baby back.'

But there was no money to bring Magid back even if Samad had been inclined to wave the white dhoti. He learnt to live with it. It got to the point where if somebody said 'yes' or 'no' to Samad in the street or in the restaurant, he hardly knew how to respond, he had come to forget what those two elegant little signifiers meant. He never heard them from Alsana's lips. Whatever the question in the Iqbal house, there would never again be a straight answer:

'Alsana, have you seen my slippers?'

'Possibly, Samad Miah.'

'What time is it?'

'It could be three, Samad Miah, but Allah knows it could also be four.'

'Alsana, where have you put the remote control?'

'It is as likely to be in the drawer, Samad Miah, as it is behind the sofa.'

And so it went.

Sometime after the May cyclone, the Iqbals received a letter from their elder-son-by-two-minutes, written in a careful hand on exercise paper and folded around a recent photograph. It was not the first time he had written, but Samad saw something different in this letter, something that excited him and validated the unpopular decision he had made; some change of tone, some suggestion of maturity, of growing Eastern wisdom; and, having read it carefully in the garden first, he took great pleasure in bringing it back to the kitchen and reading it aloud to Clara and Alsana, who were drinking peppermint tea.

'Listen: here he says, "Yesterday, grandfather hit Tamim (he is the houseboy) with a belt until his bottom was redder than a tomato. He said Tamim had stolen some candles (it's true. I saw him do it!), and this was what he got for it. He says sometimes Allah punishes and sometimes men have to do it, and it is a wise man who knows if it is Allah's turn or his own. I hope one day I will be a wise man." Do you hear that? He wants to be a wise man. How many kids in that school do you know who want to be wise men?'

'Maybe none, Samad Miah. Maybe all.'

Samad scowled at his wife and continued, 'And here, here where he talks about his nose: "It seems to me that a vase should not be in such a silly place where it can fall and break a boy's nose. It should be somebody's fault and somebody should be punished (but not a bottom smack unless they were *small and not a grown-up*. If they were younger than twelve). When I grow up I think I should like to make sure vases are not put in such silly places where they can be dangerous and I would complain about other dangerous things too (by the way, *my nose is fine now*!)." See?'

Clara frowned. 'See what?'

'Clearly he disapproves of iconography in the mosque, he dislikes all heathen, unnecessary, dangerous decoration! A boy like that is destined for greatness, isn't he?'

'Maybe, Samad Miah, maybe not.'

'Maybe he'll go into government, maybe the law,' suggested Clara.

'Rubbish! My son is for God, not men. He is not fearful of his duty. He is not fearful to be a real Bengali, a proper Muslim.

Here he tells me the goat in the photograph is dead. "I helped to kill the goat, Abba," he says. "It kept on moving some time after we had split it in two." Is that a boy who is fearful?'

It clearly being incumbent upon someone to say no, Clara said it with little enthusiasm and reached for the photograph Samad was passing her. There was Magid, dressed in his customary grey, standing next to the doomed goat with the old house behind him.

'Oh! Look at his nose! Look at the break. He's got a Roman nose, now. He looks like a little aristocrat, like a little Englishman. Look, Millat.' Clara put the photo under Millat's smaller, flatter nose. 'You two don't look so much like twins any more.'

'He looks,' said Millat after a cursory glance, 'like a *chief*.'

Samad, never au fait with the language of the Willesden streets, nodded soberly and patted his son's hair. 'It is good that you see the difference between you two boys, Millat, now rather than later.' Samad glared at Alsana as she spun an index finger in a circle by her temple, as she tapped the side of her head: *crazee, nutso*. 'Others may scoff, but you and I know that your brother will lead others out of the wilderness. He will be a leader of tribes. He is a natural *chief*.'

Millat laughed so loud at this, so hard, so uncontrollably, that he lost his footing, slipped on a wash cloth and broke his nose against the sink.

∽

Two sons. One invisible and perfect, frozen at the pleasant age of nine, static in a picture frame while the television underneath him spewed out all the shit of the eighties – Irish bombs, English riots, transatlantic stalemates – above which mess the child rose untouchable and unstained, elevated to the status of ever smiling Buddha, imbued with serene Eastern contemplation; capable of anything, a natural leader, a natural Muslim, a natural chief – in short, nothing but an apparition. A ghostly daguerreotype formed from the quicksilver of the father's imagination, preserved by the salt solution of maternal tears. This son stood silent, distant and was 'presumed well', like one of Her Majesty's colonial island outposts, stuck in an eternal state of original naivety, perpetual pre-pubescence. This son Samad could not see. And Samad had long learnt to worship what he could not see.

As for the son he *could* see, the one who was under his feet and in his hair, well, it is best not to get Samad started up on that subject, the subject of *The Trouble with Millat*, but *here goes*: he is the second son, late like a bus, late like cheap postage, the slowcoach, the catch-up-kid, losing that first race down the birth canal, and now simply a follower by genetic predisposition, by the intricate design of Allah, the loser of two vital minutes that he would never make up, not in those all-seeing parabolic mirrors, not in those glassy globes of the godhead, not *in his father's eyes*.

Now, a more melancholy child than Millat, a more deep-thinking child, might have spent the rest of his life hunting these two minutes and making himself miserable, chasing the elusive quarry, laying it finally at his father's feet. But what his father said about him did not concern Millat all that much: he knew himself to be no follower, no chief, no wanker, no sell-out, no fuckwit – no matter what his father said. In the language of the street Millat was a rudeboy, a badman, at the forefront, changing image as often as shoes; sweet-as, safe, *wicked*, leading kids up hills to play football, downhill to rifle fruit machines, out of schools, into video shops. In Rocky Video, Millat's favourite haunt, run by an unscrupulous coke-dealer, you got porn when you were fifteen, 18s when you were eleven, and snuff movies under the counter for five quid. Here was where Millat really learnt about fathers. Godfathers, blood-brothers, pacinodeniros, men in black who looked good, who talked fast, who never waited a (mutherfuckin') table, who had two, fully functioning, gun-toting hands. He learnt that you don't need to live under flood, under cyclone, to get a little danger, to be a wise man. You go looking for it. Aged twelve, Millat went out looking for it, and though Willesden Green is no Bronx, no South Central, he found a little, he found enough. He was arsey and mouthy, he had his fierce good looks squashed tightly inside him like a jack-in-a-box set to spring aged thirteen, at which point he graduated from leader of zit-faced boys to leader of women. The Pied Piper of Willesden Green, smitten girls trailing behind him, tongues out, breasts pert, falling into pools of heartbreak . . . and all because he was the BIGGEST and the BADDEST, living his young life in CAPITALS: he smoked first, he drank first, he even lost it – IT! – aged thirteen and a half. OK, so he didn't FEEL much or TOUCH much, it was MOIST and CONFUSING, he lost IT without even knowing where IT went, but he still lost IT because there was no doubt, NONE, that he was the best of the rest, on any scale of juvenile delinquency he was the shining light of the teenage community, the DON, the BUSINESS, the DOG'S GENITALIA, a street boy, a leader of tribes. In fact, the only trouble with Millat was that he *loved* trouble. And he was *good* at it. Wipe that. He was *great*.

Still, there was much discussion – at home, at school, in the various kitchens of the widespread Iqbal/Begum clan – about *The Trouble with Millat*, mutinous Millat aged thirteen, who farted in mosque, chased blondes and smelt of tobacco, and not just Millat but *all* the children: Mujib (fourteen, criminal record for joyriding), Khandakar (sixteen, white girlfriend, wore mascara in the evenings), Dipesh (fifteen, marijuana), Kurshed (eighteen, marijuana and very baggy trousers), Khaleda (seventeen, sex before marriage with Chinese boy), Bimal (nineteen, doing a diploma in Drama); *what was wrong with all the children*, what had gone wrong with these first descendants of the great ocean-crossing experiment? Didn't they have everything they could want? Was there not a substantial garden area, regular meals, clean clothes from Marks 'n' Sparks, A-class top-notch education?

Hadn't the elders done their best? Hadn't they all come to this island for a reason? To be safe. Weren't they *safe*?

'*Too* safe,' Samad explained, patiently consoling one or other weeping, angry ma or baba, perplexed and elderly dadu or dida, 'they are too safe in this country, accha? They live in big plastic bubbles of our own creation, their lives all mapped out for them. Personally, you know I would spit on Saint Paul, but the wisdom is correct, the wisdom is really Allah's: *put away childish things*. How can our boys become men when they are never challenged like men? Hmm? No doubt about it, on reflection, sending Magid back was the best thing. I would recommend it.'

At which point, the assembled weepers and moaners all look mournfully at the treasured picture of Magid and goat. They sit mesmerized, like Hindus waiting for a stone cow to cry, until a visible aura seems to emanate from the photo: goodness and bravery through adversity, through hell and high water; the true Muslim boy; the child they never had. Pathetic as it was, Alsana found it faintly amusing, the tables having turned, no one weeping for her, everyone weeping for themselves and their children, for what the terrible eighties were doing to them both. These gatherings were like last-ditch political summits, they were like desperate meetings of government and church behind closed doors while the mutinous mob roamed wild on the streets, smashed windows. A distance was establishing itself, not simply between *fathersons, oldyoung, borntherebornhere*, but between those who stayed indoors and those who ran riot outside.

'Too safe, too easy,' repeated Samad, as great-aunt Bibi wiped Magid lovingly with some Mr Sheen. 'A month back home would sort each and every one of them out.'

But the fact was Millat didn't need to go back home: he stood schizophrenic, one foot in Bengal and one in Willesden. In his mind he was as much there as he was here. He did not require a passport to live in two places at once, he needed no visa to live his brother's life and his own (he was a twin after all). Alsana was the first to spot it. She confided to Clara: *By God, they're tied together like a cat's cradle, connected like a see-saw, push one end, other goes up, whatever Millat sees, Magid saw and vice versa!* And Alsana only knew the incidentals: similar illnesses, simultaneous accidents, pets dying continents apart. She did not know that while Magid watched the 1985 cyclone shake things from high places, Millat was pushing his luck along the towering wall of the cemetery in Fortune Green; that on 10 February 1988, as Magid worked his way through the violent crowds of Dhaka, ducking the random blows of those busy settling an election with knives and fists, Millat held his own against three sotted, furious, quick-footed Irishmen outside Biddy Mulligan's notorious Kilburn public house. Ah, but you are not convinced by coincidence? You want fact fact fact? You want brushes with the Big Man with black hood and scythe? OK: on the 28th of April, 1989, a tornado whisked the Chittagong kitchen up into the sky, taking everything with it except Magid, left miraculously curled up in a ball on the floor. Now, segue to Millat, five thousand miles away, lowering himself down upon legendary sixth-former Natalia Cavendish (whose body is keeping a dark secret from her); the condoms are unopened in a box in his back pocket; but somehow he will not catch it; even though he is moving rhythmically now, up and in, deeper and sideways, dancing with death.

Three days:

15 October 1987

Even when the lights went out and the wind was beating the shit out of the double glazing, Alsana, a great believer in the oracle that is the BBC, sat in a nightie on the sofa, refusing to budge.

'If that Mr Fish says it's OK, it's damn well OK. He's BBC, for God's sake!'

Samad gave up (it was almost impossible to change Alsana's mind about the inherent reliability of her favoured English institutions, amongst them: Princess Anne, Blu-Tack, Children's Royal Variety Performance, Eric Morecambe, *Woman's Hour*). He got the torch from the kitchen drawer and went upstairs, looking for Millat.

'Millat? Answer me, Millat! Are you there?'

'Maybe, Abba, maybe not.'

Samad followed the voice to the bathroom and found Millat chin-high in dirty pink soap suds, reading *Viz*.

'Ah, Dad, wicked. Torch. Shine it over here so I can read.'

'Never mind that.' Samad tore the comic from his son's hands. 'There's a bloody hurricane blowing and your crazy mother intends to sit here until the roof falls in. Get out of the bath. I need you to go to the shed and find some wood and nails so that we can –'

'But Abba, I'm butt-naked!'

'Don't split the hairs with me – this is an emergency. I want you to –'

An almighty ripping noise, like something being severed at the roots and flung against a wall, came from outside.

Two minutes later and the family Iqbal were standing regimental in varying states of undress, looking out through the long kitchen window on to a patch in the lawn where the shed used to be. Millat clicked his heels three times and hammed it up with cornershop accent, 'O me O my. There's no place like home. There's no place like home.'

'*All right*, woman. Are you coming *now*?'

'Maybe, Samad Miah, maybe.'

'*Dammit!* I'm not in the mood for a referendum. We're going to Archibald's. Maybe they still have light. And there is safety in numbers. Both of you – get dressed, grab the essentials, *the life or death things*, and get in the car!'

Holding the car boot open against a wind determined to bring it down, Samad was first amused and then depressed by the items his wife and son determined essential, life or death things:

Millat	*Alsana*
Born to Run (album) – Springsteen	Sewing machine
Poster of De Niro in 'You talkin' to me' scene from *Taxi Driver*	Three pots of tiger balm
Betamax copy of *Purple Rain* (rock movie)	Leg of lamb (frozen)
Shrink-to-fit Levis 501 (red tab)	Foot bath
Pair of black converse baseball shoes	*Linda Goodman's Starsigns* (book)
A Clockwork Orange (book)	Huge box of beedi cigarettes
	Divargiit Singh in *Moonshine over Kerala* (musical video)

Samad slammed the boot down.

'No pen knife, no edibles, no light sources. Bloody great. No prizes for guessing which one of the Iqbals is the war veteran. Nobody even thinks to pick up the Qur'ān. Key item in emergency situation: spiritual support. I am going back in there. Sit in the car and don't move a muscle.'

Once in the kitchen Samad flashed his torch around: kettle, oven hob, teacup, curtain and then a surreal glimpse of the shed sitting happy like a treehouse in next door's horsechestnut. He picked up the Swiss army knife he remembered leaving under the sink, collected his gold-plated, velvet-fringed Qur'ān from the living room and was about to leave when the temptation to feel the gale, to see a little of the formidable destruction, came over him. He waited for a lull in the wind and opened the kitchen door, moving tentatively into the garden, where a sheet of lightning lit up a scene of suburban apocalypse: oaks, cedars, sycamores, elms felled in garden after garden, fences down, garden furniture demolished. It was only his own garden, often ridiculed for its corrugated-iron surround, treeless interior and bed after bed of sickly smelling herbs, that had remained relatively intact.

He was just in the process of happily formulating some allegory regarding the bending Eastern reed versus the stubborn Western oak, when the wind reasserted itself, knocking him sideways and continuing along its path to the double glazing, which it cracked and exploded effortlessly, blowing glass inside, regurgitating everything from the kitchen out into the open air. Samad, a recently airborne collander resting on his ear, held his book tight to his chest and hurried to the car.

'What are *you* doing in the driving seat?'

Alsana held on to the wheel firmly and talked to Millat via the rear-view mirror. 'Will someone please tell my husband that *I* am going to drive. *I* grew up by the Bay of Bengal. I watched my mother drive through winds like these while my husband was poncing about in Delhi with a load of fairy college boys. I suggest my husband gets in the passenger seat and doesn't fart unless I tell him to.'

Alsana drove at three miles an hour through the deserted, blacked-out high road while winds of 110 m.p.h. relentlessly battered the tops of the highest buildings.

'England, this is meant to be! I moved to England so I wouldn't have to do this. Never again will I trust that Mr Crab.'

'Amma, it's Mr Fish.'

'From now on, he's Mr Crab to me,' snapped Alsana with a dark look. 'BBC or no BBC.'

The lights *had* gone out at Archie's, but the Jones household was prepared for every disastrous eventuality from tidal wave to nuclear fallout; by the time the Iqbals got there the place was lit with dozens of gas lamps, garden candles and night lights, the front door and windows had been speedily reinforced with hardboard, and the garden trees had their branches roped together.

'It's all about preparation,' announced Archie, opening the door to the desperate Iqbals and their armfuls of belongings, like a DIY king welcoming the dispossessed. 'I mean, you've got to protect your family, haven't you? Not that you've failed in that depar – you know what I mean – 'sjust the way I see it: it's me against the wind. If I've told you once, Ick-Ball, I've told you a million times: *check the supporting walls*. If they're not in tip-top condition, you're buggered, mate. You really are. And you've got to keep a pneumatic spanner in the house. Essential.'

'That's fascinating, Archibald. May we come in?'

Archie stepped aside. ''Course. Tell the truth, I was expecting you. You never did know a drill bit from a screw handle, Ick-Ball. Good with the theory, but never got the hang of the practicalities. Go on, up the stairs, mind the night lights – good idea that, eh? Hello, Alsi, you look lovely as ever; hello, Millboid, yer scoundrel. So Sam, out with it: what have you lost?'

Samad sheepishly recounted the damage so far.

'Ah, now you see, that's not your glazing – that's fine, *I* put that in – it's the *frames*. Just ripped out of that crumbling wall, I'll bet.'

Samad grudgingly acknowledged this to be the case.

'There'll be worst to come, mark mine. Well, what's done is done. Clara and Irie are in the kitchen. We've got a Bunsen burner going, and grub's up in a minute. But what a bloody storm, eh? Phone's out. 'Lectricity's out. Never seen the likes of it.'

In the kitchen, a kind of artificial calm reigned. Clara was stirring some beans, quietly humming the tune to *Buffalo Soldier*. Irie was hunched over a notepad, writing her diary obsessively in the manner of thirteen-year-olds:

8.30 p.m. Millat just walked in. He's sooo gorgeous but ultimately irritating! Tight jeans as usual. Doesn't look at me (as usual, except in a FRIENDLY way). I'm in love with a fool (stupid me)! If only he had his brother's brains . . . oh well, blah blah. I've got puppy love and puppy fat – aaaagh! Storm still crazy. Got to go. Will write later.

'All right,' said Millat.

'All right,' said Irie.

'Crazy this, eh?'

'Yeah, mental.'

'Dad's having a fit. House is torn to shit.'

'Ditto. It's been madness around here too.'

'I'd like to know where you'd be without me, young lady,' said Archie, banging another nail into some hardboard. 'Best-protected house in Willesden, this is. Can't hardly tell there's a storm going on from here.'

'Yeah,' said Millat, sneaking a final thrilling peek through the window at the apoplectic trees before Archie blocked out the sky entirely with wood and nails. 'That's the problem.'

Samad clipped Millat round the ear. 'Don't you start in on the cheekiness. We know what we're doing. You forget, Archibald and I have coped with extreme situations. Once you have fixed a five-man tank in the middle of a battlefield, your life at risk at every turn, bullets whizzing inches from your arse, while simultaneously capturing the enemy in the harshest possible conditions, let me be telling you, hurricane is little tiny small fry. You could do a lot worse than – yes, yes, very amusing I'm sure,' muttered Samad, as the two children and the two wives feigned narcolepsy. 'Who wants some of these beans? I'm dishing out.'

'Someone tell a story,' said Alsana. 'It's going to get oh so boring if we have to listen to old warhorse big mouths all night.'

'Go on, Sam,' said Archie with a wink. 'Give us the one about Mangal Pande. That's always good for a laugh.'

A clamour of *Nooo*'s, mimed slitting of throats and self-asphyxiation went round the assembled company.

'The story of Mangal Pande,' Samad protested, 'is no laughing matter. He is the tickle in the sneeze, he is why we are the way we are, the founder of modern India, the big historical cheese.'

Alsana snorted. 'Big fat nonsense. Every fool knows Gandhi-gee is the big cheese. Or Nehru. Or maybe Akbar, but he was crook-backed, and huge-nosed, I never liked him.'

'Dammit! Don't talk nonsense, woman. What do you know about it? Fact is: it is simply a matter of market economy, publicity, movie rights. The question is: are the pretty men with the big white teeth willing to play you, et cetera. Gandhi had Mr Kingsley – bully for him – but who will do Pande, eh? Pande's not pretty enough, is he? Too Indian-looking, big nose, big eyebrows. That's why I am always having to tell you ingrates a thing or two about Mangal Pande. Bottom line: if I don't, nobody will.'

'Look,' said Millat, 'I'll do the short version. Great-grandfather –'

'*Your* great-*great*-grandfather, stupid,' corrected Alsana.

'What*ever*. Decides to fuck the English –'

'Millat!'

'To *rebel* against the English, all on his Jack-Jones, spliffed up to the eyeballs, tries to shoot his captain, misses, tries to shoot himself, misses, gets hung –'

'Hanged,' said Clara absent-mindedly.

'Hanged or hung? I'll get the dictionary,' said Archie, laying down his hammer and climbing off the kitchen counter.

'What*ever*. End of story. *Bor*-ing.'

And now a mammoth tree – the kind endemic to North London, the ones that sprout three smaller trees along the trunk before finally erupting into glorious greenery, city-living for whole diaspora of magpie – a tree of this kind tore itself from the dog shit and the concrete, took one tottering step forward, swooned and collapsed; through the guttering, through the double glazing, through the hardboard, knocked over a gas lamp, and then landed in an absence that was Archie-shaped, for he had just left it.

Archie was the first to leap into action, throwing a towel on the small fire progressing along the cork kitchen tiles, while everyone else trembled and wept and checked each other for injury. Then Archie, visibly shaken by this blow to his DIY supremacy, reclaimed control over the elements, tying some of the branches with kitchen rags and ordering Millat and Irie to go around the house, putting out the gas lamps.

'We don't want to burn ourselves to death, now do we? I better find some black plastic and gaffer tape. Do something about this.'

Samad was incredulous. '*Do something about it*, Archibald? I fail to see how some gaffer tape will change the fact there is a half a tree in the kitchen.'

'Man, I'm terrified,' stuttered Clara, after a few minutes' silence, as the storm lulled. 'The quiet is always a bad sign. My grandmother – God rest her – she always said that. The quiet is just God pausing to take a breath before he shouts all over again. I think we should go into the other room.'

'That was the only tree on this side. Best stay in here. Worst's done here. Besides,' said Archie, touching his wife's arm affectionately, 'you Bowdens have seen worse than this! Your mother was born in a bloody earthquake, for Christ's sake. 1907, Kingston's falling apart and Hortense pops into the world. You wouldn't see a little storm like this worrying her. Tough as nails, that one.'

'Not toughness,' said Clara quietly, standing up to look through the broken window at the chaos outside, 'luck. Luck and faith.'

'I suggest we pray,' said Samad, picking up his novelty Qur'ān. 'I suggest we acknowledge the might of the Creator as he does his worst this evening.'

Samad began flicking through and, finding what he wanted, brought it patrician-like under his wife's nose, but she slammed it shut and glared at him. Ungodly Alsana, who was yet a nifty hand with the word of God (good schooling, proper parents, oh yes), lacking nothing but the faith, prepared to do what she did only in emergency: recite: 'I do not serve what you worship, nor do you serve what I worship. I shall never serve what you worship, nor will you ever serve what I worship. You have your own religion, and I have mine. Sura 109, translation N. J. Dawood.' Now, will someone,' said Alsana, looking to Clara, 'please remind my husband that he is not Mr Manilow and he does not have the songs that make the whole world sing. He will whistle his tune and I will whistle mine.'

Samad turned contemptuously from his wife and placed both hands rigidly on his book. 'Who will pray with me?'

'Sorry, Sam,' came a muffled voice (Archie had his head in the cupboard and was searching for the bin bags). 'Not really my cup of tea, either. Never been a church man. No offence.'

Five more minutes passed without the wind. Then the quiet burst and God shouted just as Ambrosia Bowden had told her granddaughter he would. Thunder went over the house like a dying man's bile, lightning followed like his final malediction, and Samad closed his eyes.

'Irie! Millat!' called Clara, then Alsana. No answer. Standing bolt upright in the cupboard, smashing his head against the spice shelf, Archie said, 'It's been ten minutes. Oh blimey. *Where are the kids?*'

One kid was in Chittagong, being dared by a friend to take off his lungi and march through a renowned crocodile swamp; the other two had sneaked out of the house to feel the eye of the storm, and were walking against the wind as if thigh-high in water. They waded into Willesden recreation ground, where the following conversation took place.

'This is *incredible*!'

'Yeah, *mental*!'

'*You're* mental.'

'What do you mean? I'm fine!'

'No, you're not. You're always *looking* at me. And what were you writing? You're such a nerd. You're always writing.'

'Nothing. Stuff. You know, diary stuff.'

'You've got the blatant hots for me.'

'I can't hear you! Louder!'

'THE HOTS! BLATANTLY! YOU CAN HEAR ME.'

'I have not! *You're* an egomaniac.'

'You want my arse.'

'Don't be a wanker!'

'Well, it's no good, anyway. You're getting a bit big. I don't like big. You can't have me.'

'I wouldn't want to, *Mr* Egomaniac.'

'Plus: imagine what our kids would look like.'

'I think they'd look *nice*.'

'Browny-black. Blacky-brown. Afro, flat nose, rabbit teeth and freckles. They'd be freaks!'

'You can talk. I've seen that picture of your grandad –'

'GREAT-GREAT-GRANDAD.'

'Massive nose, horrible eyebrows –'

'That's an artist's impression, you chief.'

'And they'd be crazy – *he* was crazy – your whole family's crazy. It's genetic.'

'Yeah, yeah. What*ever*.'

'And for your information, I don't fancy you, anyway. You've got a bent nose. And you're trouble. Who wants trouble?'

'Well, watch out,' said Millat, leaning forward, colliding with some buck teeth, slipping a tongue in momentarily, and then pulling back. ''Cos that's all the trouble you're getting.'

14 January 1989

Millat spread his legs like Elvis and slapped his wallet down on the counter. 'One for Bradford, yeah?'

The ticket-man put his tired face close up to the glass. 'Are you asking me, young man, or telling me?'

'I just say, yeah? One for Bradford, yeah? You got some problem, yeah? Speaka da English? This is King's Cross, yeah? One for Bradford, innit?'

Millat's Crew (Rajik, Ranil, Dipesh and Hifan) sniggered and shuffled behind him, joining in on the *yeahs* like some kind of backing group.

'*Please?*'

'Please *what*, yeah? One for Bradford, yeah? You get me? One for Bradford. *Chief.*'

'And would that be a return? For a child?'

'Yeah, man. I'm fifteen, yeah? 'Course I want a return, I've got a bāṛii to get back to like everybody else.'

'That'll be seventy-five pounds, then, please.'

This was met with displeasure by Millat and Millat's Crew.

'You what? Takin' liberties! Seventy – *chaaaa*, man. That's *moody*. I ain't payin' no seventy-five pounds!'

'Well, I'm afraid that's the price. Maybe next time you mug some poor old lady,' said the ticket-man, looking pointedly at the chunky gold that fell from Millat's ears, wrists, fingers and from around his neck, 'you could stop in here first *before* you get to the jewellery store.'

'Liberties!' squealed Hifan.

'He's cussin' you, yeah?' confirmed Ranil.

'You better tell 'im,' warned Rajik.

Millat waited a minute. Timing was everything. Then he turned around, stuck his arse in the air, and farted long and loud in the ticket-man's direction.

The Crew, on cue: '*Somokāmi!*'

'What did you call me? You – what did you say? You little bastards. Can't tell me in English? Have to talk your Paki language?'

Millat slammed his fist so hard on the glass that it reverberated down the booths to the ticket-man down the other end selling tickets to Milton Keynes.

'First: I'm not a Paki, you ignorant fuck. And second: you don't need translator, yeah? I'll give it to you straight. You're a fucking faggot, yeah? Queer boy, poofter, batty-rider, shit-dick.'

There was nothing Millat's Crew prided themselves on more than the number of euphemisms they could offer for homosexuality.

'Arse-bandit, fairy-fucker, toilet-trader.'

'You want to thank God for the glass between us, boy.'

'Yeah, yeah, yeah. I thank Allah, yeah? I hope he fucks you up wicked, yeah? We're going to Bradford to sort out the likes of you, yeah? *Chief!*'

Halfway up platform 12, about to board a train they had no tickets for, a King's Cross security guy stopped Millat's Crew to ask them a question. 'You boys not looking for any trouble, are you?'

The question was fair. Millat's Crew looked like trouble. And, at the time, a crew that looked like trouble in this particular way had a name, they were of a breed: *Raggastani*.

It was a new breed, just recently joining the ranks of the other street crews: Becks, B-boys, Indie kids, wide-boys, ravers, rude-boys, Acidheads, Sharons, Tracies, Kevs, Nation Brothers, Raggas and Pakis; manifesting itself as a kind of cultural mongrel of the last three categories. Raggastanis spoke a strange mix of Jamaican patois, Bengali, Gujarati and English. Their ethos, their manifesto, if it could be called that, was equally a hybrid thing: Allah *featured*, but more as a collective big brother than a supreme being, a hard-as-fuck *geezer* who would fight in their corner if necessary; Kung Fu and the works of Bruce Lee were also central to the philosophy; added to this was a smattering of Black Power (as embodied by the album *Fear of a Black Planet*, Public Enemy); but mainly their mission was to put the Invincible back in Indian, the Bad-aaaass back in Bengali, the P-Funk back in Pakistani. People had fucked with Rajik back in the days when he was into chess and wore V-necks. People had fucked with Ranil, when he sat at the back of the class and carefully copied all teacher's comments into his book. People had fucked with Dipesh and Hifan when they wore traditional dress in the playground. People had even fucked with Millat, with his tight jeans and his white rock. But no one fucked with any of them any more because they looked like trouble. They looked like trouble in stereo. Naturally, there was a uniform. They each dripped gold and wore bandanas, either wrapped around their foreheads or tied at the joint of an arm or leg. The trousers were enormous, swamping things, the left leg always inexplicably rolled up to the knee; the trainers were equally spectacular, with tongues so tall they obscured the entire ankle; baseball caps were compulsory, low slung and irremovable, and everything, everything, everything was *Nike*™; wherever the five of them went the impression they left behind was of one gigantic swoosh, one huge mark of corporate approval. And they *walked* in a very particular way, the left side of their bodies assuming a kind of loose paralysis that needed carrying along by the right side; a kind of glorified, funky limp like the slow, padding movement that Yeats imagined for his rough millennial beast. Ten years early, while the happy acid heads danced through the Summer of Love, Millat's Crew were slouching towards Bradford.

'No trouble, yeah?' said Millat to the security guy.

'Just going –' began Hifan.

'To Bradford,' said Rajik.

'For business, yeah?' explained Dipesh.

'See-ya! Bidāyo!' called Hifan, as they slipped into the train, gave him the finger, and shoved their arses up against the closing doors.

'Tax the window seat, yeah? Nice. I've *blatantly* got to have a fag in here, yeah? I'm fuckin' *wired*, yeah? This whole business, man. This fuckin' geezer, man. He's a fuckin' coconut – I'd like to fuck him up, yeah?'

'Is he actually gonna be there?'

All serious questions were always addressed to Millat, and Millat always answered the group as a whole. 'No way. He ain't going to be there. Just brothers going to be there. It's a fucking protest, you chief, why's he going to go to a protest against himself?'

'I'm just saying,' said Ranil, wounded, 'I'd fuck him up, yeah? If he was there, you know. Dirty fucking book.'

'It's a fucking insult!' said Millat, spitting some gum against the window. 'We've taken it too long in this country. And now we're getting it from our own, man. Rhas clut! He's a fucking bādor, white man's puppet.'

'My uncle says he can't even spell,' said a furious Hifan, the most honestly religious of the lot. 'And he dares to talk about Allah!'

'Allah'll fuck him up, yeah?' cried Rajik, the least intelligent, who thought of God as some kind of cross between Monkey-Magic and Bruce Willis. 'He'll kick him in the balls. Dirty book.'

'You read it?' asked Ranil, as they whizzed past Finsbury Park.

There was a general pause.

Millat said, 'I haven't exackly read it exackly – but I know all about that shit, yeah?'

To be more precise, Millat hadn't read it. Millat knew nothing about the writer, nothing about the book; could not identify the book if it lay in a pile of other books; could not pick out the writer in a line-up of other writers (irresistible, this line-up of offending writers: Socrates, Protagoras, Ovid and Juvenal, Radclyffe Hall, Boris Pasternak, D. H. Lawrence, Solzhenitsyn, Nabokov, all holding up their numbers for the mug shot, squinting in the flashbulb). But he knew other things. He knew that he, Millat, was a Paki no matter where he came from; that he smelt of curry; had no sexual identity; took other people's jobs; or had no job and bummed off the state; or gave all the jobs to his relatives; that he could be a dentist or a shop-owner or a curry-shifter, but not a footballer or a film-maker; that he should go back to his own country; or stay here and earn his bloody keep; that he worshipped elephants and wore turbans; that no one who looked like Millat, or spoke like Millat, or felt like Millat, was ever on the news unless they had recently been murdered. In short, he knew he had no face in this country, no voice in the country, until the week before last when suddenly people like Millat were on every channel and every radio and every newspaper and they were angry, and Millat recognized the anger, thought it recognized him, and grabbed it with both hands.

'So . . . you ain't read it?' asked Ranil nervously.

'Look: you best believe I ain't buying that shit, man. No way, star.'

'Me neither,' said Hifan.

'True star,' said Rajik.

'Fucking nastiness,' said Ranil.

'Twelve ninety-five, you know!' said Dipesh.

'Besides,' said Millat, with a tone of finality despite his high-rising terminals, 'you don't have to read shit to know that it's blasphemous, you get me?'

~

Back in Willesden, Samad Iqbal was expressing the very same sentiment loudly over the evening news.

'I don't *need* to read it. The relevant passages have been photocopied for me.'

'Will someone remind my husband,' said Alsana, speaking to the newsreader, 'that he does not even know what the bloody book is about because the last thing he read was the bloody *A–Z*.'

'I'm going to ask you one more time to shut up so I can watch the news.'

'I can hear screaming but it does not appear to be my voice.'

'Can't you understand, woman? This is the most important thing to happen to us in this country, ever. It's crisis point. It's the tickle in the sneeze. It's big time.' Samad hit the volume button a few times with his thumb. 'This woman – Moira whateverhernameis – she mumbles. Why is she reading news if she can't speak properly?'

Moira, turned up suddenly in mid-sentence, said, '. . . the writer denies blasphemy, and argues that the book concerns the struggle between secular and religious views of life.'

Samad snorted. 'What struggle! I don't see any struggle. I get on perfectly OK. All grey cells in good condition. No emotional difficulties.'

Alsana laughed bitterly. 'My husband fights the Third World War every single bloody day in his head, so does everybody –'

'No, no, no. No struggle. What's he on about, eh? He can't wangle out of it by being rational. Rationality! Most overrated Western virtue! Oh no. Fact is, he is simply offensive – he has offended –'

'Look,' Alsana cut in. 'When my little group get together, if we disagree about something, we can sort it out. Example: Mohona Hossain hates Divargiit Singh. Hates all his movies. Hates him with a passion. She likes that other fool with the eyelashes like a lady! But we compromise. Never once have I burned a single video of hers.'

'Hardly the same thing, Mrs Iqbal, hardly the same kettle with fish in it.'

'Oh, passions are running high at the Women's Committee – shows how much Samad Iqbal knows. But I am not like Samad Iqbal. I restrain myself. I live. I let live.'

'It is not a matter of letting others live. It is a matter of protecting one's culture, shielding one's religion from abuse. Not that you'd know anything about that, naturally. Always too busy with this Hindi brain popcorn to pay any attention to your own culture!'

'My *own* culture? And what is that please?'

'You're a Bengali. Act like one.'

'And what is a Bengali, husband, please?'

'Get out of the way of the television and look it up.'

Alsana took out BALTIC–BRAIN, number three of their 24-set *Reader's Digest Encyclopedia*, and read from the relevant section:

The vast majority of Bangladesh's inhabitants are Bengalis, who are largely descended from Indo-Aryans who began to migrate into the country from the west thousands of years ago and who mixed within Bengal with indigenous groups of various racial stocks. Ethnic minorities include the Chakma and Mogh, Mongoloid peoples who live in the Chittagong Hill Tracts District; the Santal, mainly descended from migrants from present-day India; and the Biharis, non-Bengali Muslims who migrated from India after the partition.

'Oi, mister! Indo-*Aryans*. . . it looks like I am Western after all! Maybe I should listen to Tina Turner, wear the itsy-bitsy leather skirts. Pah. It just goes to show,' said Alsana, revealing her English tongue, 'you go back and back and back and it's still easier to find the correct Hoover bag than to find one pure person, one pure faith, on the globe. Do you think anybody is English? Really English? It's a fairy-tale!'

'You don't know what you're talking about. You're out of your depth.'

Alsana held up the encyclopedia. 'Oh, *Samad Miah*. You want to burn this too?'

'Look: I've no time to play right now. I am trying to listen to a very important news story. Serious goings on in Bradford. So, if you don't mind –'

'Oh dear God!' screamed Alsana, the smile leaving her face,

falling to her knees in front of the television, tracing her finger past the burning book to the face she recognized, smiling up at her through light tubes, her pixilated second-son beneath her picture-framed first. 'What is he doing? Is he crazy? Who does he think he is? What on earth is he doing there? He's meant to be in school! Has the day come when the babies are burning the books, *has it*? I don't believe it!'

'Nothing to do with me. Tickle in the sneeze, Mrs Iqbal,' said Samad coolly, sitting back in his armchair. 'Tickle in the sneeze.'

When Millat came home that evening, a great bonfire was raging in the back garden. All his secular stuff – four years' worth of cool, pre- and post-Raggastani, every album, every poster, special-edition t-shirts, club fliers collected and preserved over two years, beautiful Air Max trainers, copies 20–75 of *2000 AD Magazine*, signed photo of Chuck D., impossibly rare copy of Slick Rick's *Hey Young World, Catcher in the Rye*, his guitar, *Godfather I* and *II, Mean Streets, Rumblefish, Dog Day Afternoon* and *Shaft in Africa* – all had been placed on the funeral pyre, now a smouldering mound of ashes that was giving off fumes of plastic and paper, stinging the boy's eyes that were already filled with tears.

'Everyone has to be taught a lesson,' Alsana had said, lighting the match with heavy heart some hours earlier. 'Either everything is sacred or nothing is. And if he starts burning other people's things, then he loses something sacred also. Everyone gets what's coming, sooner or later.'

10 November 1989

A wall was coming down. It was something to do with history. It was *an historic occasion*. No one really knew quite who had put it up or who was tearing it down or whether this was good, bad or something else; no one knew how tall it was, how long it was, or why people had died trying to cross it or whether they would stop dying in future, but it was educational all the same; as good an excuse for a get-together as any. It was a Thursday night, Alsana and Clara had cooked, and everybody was watching history on TV.

'Who's for more rice?'

Millat and Irie held out their plates, jostling for prime position.

'What's happening now?' asked Clara, rushing back to her seat with a bowl of Jamaican fried dumplings, from which Irie snatched three.

'Same, man,' Millat grumbled. 'Same. Same. Same. Dancing on the wall, smashing it with a hammer. Whatever. I wanna see what else is on, yeah?'

Alsana snatched the remote control and squeezed in between Clara and Archie. 'Don't you dare, mister.'

'It's *educational,*' said Clara deliberately, her pad and paper on the arm rest, waiting to leap into action at the suggestion of anything edifying. 'It's the kind of thing we all should be watching.'

Alsana nodded and waited for two awkward-shaped bhajis to go down the gullet. 'That's what I try and tell the boy. Big business. Tip-top historic occasion. When your own little Iqbals tug at your trousers and ask you where you were when –'

'I'll say I was bored shitless watching it on TV.'

Millat got a thwack round the head for 'shitless' and another one for the impertinence of the sentiment. Irie, looking strangely like the crowd on top of the wall in her everyday garb of CND badges, graffiti-covered trousers and beaded hair, shook her head in saddened disbelief. She was that *age*. Whatever she said burst like genius into centuries of silence. Whatever she touched was the first stroke of its kind. Whatever she believed was not formed by faith but carved from certainty. Whatever she thought was the first time such a thought had ever been thunk.

'That's *totally* your problem, Mill. No interest in the outside world. I think this is *amazing*. They're all free! After all this time, don't you think that's *amazing*? That after years under the dark cloud of Eastern communism they're coming into the light of Western democracy, united,' she said, quoting *Newsnight* faithfully. 'I just think democracy is man's *greatest* invention.'

Alsana, who felt personally that Clara's child was becoming impossibly pompous these days, held up the head of a Jamaican fried fish in protest. 'No, dearie. Don't make that mistake. Potato peeler is man's greatest invention. That or Poop-a-Scoop.'

'What they want,' said Millat, 'is to stop pissing around wid dis hammer business and jus' get some Semtex and blow de djam ting up, if they don't like it, you get me? Be quicker, innit?'

'Why do you talk like that?' snapped Iric, devouring a dumpling. 'That's not your voice. You sound ridiculous!'

'And you want to watch dem dumplings,' said Millat, patting his belly. 'Big ain't beautiful.'

'Oh, get lost.'

'You know,' murmured Archie, munching on a chicken wing, 'I'm not so sure that it's such a good thing. I mean, you've got to remember, me and Samad, *we were there*. And believe me, there's a good reason to have it split in two. Divide and conquer, young lady.'

'Jesus *Christ*, Dad. What are you *on*?'

'He's not on anything,' said Samad severely. 'You younger people forget why certain things were done, you forget their significance. We were there. Not all of us think fondly upon a united Germany. They were different times, young lady.'

'What's wrong with a load of people making some noise about their freedom? Look at them. Look at how *happy* they are.'

Samad looked at the happy people dancing on the wall and felt contempt and something more irritating underneath it that could have been jealousy.

'It is not that I disagree with rebellious acts *per se*. It is simply that if you are to throw over an old order, you must be sure that you can offer something of substance to replace it; that is what Germany needs to understand. As an example, take my great-grandfather, Mangal Pande –'

Irie sighed the most eloquent sigh that had ever been sighed. 'I'd rather not, if it's all the same.'

'Irie!' said Clara, because she felt she should.

Irie huffed. And puffed.

'Well! He goes on like he knows everything. Everything's always about *him* – and *I'm* trying to talk about now, *today*, Germany. I bet you,' she said, turning to Samad, 'I know more about it than you do. Go on. Try me. I've been studying it all term. Oh, and by the way: you *weren't* there. You and Dad left in 1945. They didn't do the wall until *1961*.'

'Cold War,' said Samad sourly, ignoring her. 'They don't talk about hot war any more. The kind where men get killed. That's where I learnt about Europe. It cannot be found in books.'

'Oi-oi,' said Archie, trying to diffuse a row. 'You do know *Last of the Summer Wine*'s on in ten minutes? BBC Two.'

'Go on,' persisted Irie, kneeling up and turning around to face Samad. 'Try me.'

'The gulf between books and experience,' intoned Samad solemnly, 'is a lonely ocean.'

'Right. You two talk such a load of sh –'

But Clara was too quick with a slap round the ear. 'Irie!'

Irie sat back down, not so much defeated as exasperated and turned up the TV volume.

The 28-mile-long scar – the ugliest symbol of a divided world, East and West – has no meaning any more. Few people, including this reporter, thought to see it happen in their lifetimes, but last night, at the stroke of midnight, thousands lingering both sides of the wall gave a great roar and began to pour through checkpoints and to climb up and over it.

'Foolishness. Massive immigration problem to follow,' said Samad to the television, dipping a dumpling into some ketchup. 'You just can't let a million people into a rich country. Recipe for disaster.'

'And who does he think he is? Mr Churchill-gee?' laughed Alsana scornfully. 'Original whitecliffsdover piesnmash jellyeels royalvariety britishbulldog, heh?'

'Scar,' said Clara, noting it down. 'That's the right word, isn't it?'

'Jesus *Christ*. Can't any of you understand the enormity of what's going on here? These are the last days of a regime. Political apocalypse, meltdown. It's an historic occasion.'

'So everyone keeps saying,' said Archie, scouring the *TV Times*. 'But what about *The Krypton Factor*, ITV? That's always good, eh? 'Son now.'

'And stop sayin' "an historic",' said Millat, irritated at all the poncey political talk. 'Why can't you just say "a", like everybody else, man? Why d'you always have to be so la di da?'

'Oh, for fuck's sake!' (She loved him, but he was *impossible*.) 'What possible fucking difference can it make?'

Samad rose out of his seat. 'Irie! This is my house and you are still a guest. I won't have that language in it!'

'Fine! I'll take it to the streets with the rest of the proletariat.'

'That girl,' tutted Alsana as her front door slammed. 'Swallowed an encyclopedia and a gutter at the same time.'

Millat sucked his teeth at his mother. 'Don't *you* start, man. What's wrong with "a" encyclopedia? Why's everyone in this house always puttin' on fuckin' airs?'

Samad pointed to the door. 'OK, mister. You don't speak to your mother like that. You out too.'

'I don't think,' said Clara quietly, after Millat had stormed up to his room, 'that we should discourage the kids from having an opinion. It's good that they're free-thinkers.'

Samad sneered, 'And you would know . . . what? You do a

great deal of free-thinking? In the house all day, watching the television?'

'Ex*cuse* me?'

'With respect: the world is complex, Clara. If there's one thing these children need to understand it is that one needs *rules* to survive it, not *fancy*.'

'He's right, you know,' said Archie earnestly, ashing a fag in an empty curry bowl. 'Emotional matters – then yes, that's your department –'

'Oh – women's work!' squealed Alsana, through a mouth full of curry. 'Thank you *so much*, Archibald.'

Archie struggled to continue. 'But you can't beat experience, can you? I mean, you two, you're young women still, in a way. Whereas *we*, I mean, we are, like, *wells of experience* the children can use, you know, when they feel the need. We're like encyclopedias. You just can't offer them what we can. In all fairness.'

Alsana put her palm on Archie's forehead and stroked it lightly. 'You *fool*. Don't you know you're left behind like carriage and horses, like candlewax? Don't you know to them you're old and smelly like yesterday's fishnchip paper? I'll be agreeing with your daughter on one matter of importance.' Alsana stood up, following Clara, who had left at this final insult and marched tearfully into the kitchen. 'You two gentlemen talk a great deal of the youknowwhat.'

Left alone, Archie and Samad acknowledged the desertion of both families by a mutual rolling of eyes, wry smiles. They sat quietly for a moment while Archie's thumb flicked adeptly through *An Historic Occasion*, *A Costume Drama Set in Jersey*, *Two Men Trying to Build a Raft in Thirty Seconds*, *A Studio Debate on Abortion*, and back once more to *An Historic Occasion*.

Click.

Click.

Click.

Click.

Click.

'Home? Pub? O'Connell's?'

Archie was about to reach into his pocket for a shiny ten pence when he realized there was no need.

'O'Connell's?' said Archie.

'O'Connell's' said Samad.

10 *The Root Canals of Mangal Pande*

Finally, O'Connell's. *Inevitably*, O'Connell's. Simply because you could be without family in O'Connell's, without possessions or status, without past glory or future hope – you could walk through that door with nothing and be exactly the same as everybody else in there. It could be 1989 outside, or 1999, or 2009, and you could still be sitting at the counter in the V-neck you wore to your wedding in 1975, 1945, 1935. Nothing changes here, things are only retold, remembered. That's why old men love it.

It's all about time. Not just its stillness but the pure, brazen amount of it. Quantity rather than Quality. This is hard to explain. If only there was some equation . . . something like:

$$\frac{\text{TIME SPENT HERE}}{\text{TIME THAT I COULD HAVE USEFULLY SPENT ELSEWHERE}} \;\text{ENJOYMENT} \times \text{MASOCHISM} = \text{Reason why I am a regular}$$

Something to rationalize, to explain, why one would keep returning, like Freud's grandson with his *fort-da* game, to the same miserable scenario. But *time* is what it comes down to. After you've spent a certain amount, invested so much of it in one place, your credit rating booms and you feel like breaking the chronological bank. You feel like staying in the place until it pays you back all the time you gave it – even if it never will.

And with the time spent, comes the knowledge, comes the history. It was at O'Connell's that Samad had suggested Archie's remarriage, 1974. Underneath table six in a pool of his own vomit, Archie celebrated the birth of Irie, 1975. There is a stain on the corner of the pinball machine where Samad first spilt civilian blood, with a hefty right hook to a racist drunk, 1980. Archie was downstairs the night he watched his fiftieth birthday float up through fathoms of whisky to meet him like an old shipwreck, 1977. And this is where they both came, New Year's Eve, 1989 (neither the Iqbal nor Jones families having expressed a desire to enter the 90s in their company), happy to take advantage of Mickey's special New Year fry-up: £2.85 for three eggs, beans, two rounds of toast, mushrooms and a generous slice of seasonal turkey.

The seasonal turkey was a bonus. For Archie and Samad, it was really all about being the witness, being the *expert*. They came here because they *knew* this place. They knew it inside and out. And if you can't explain to your kid why glass will shatter at certain impacts but not others, if you can't understand how a balance can be struck between democratic secularism and religious belief within the same state, or you can't recall the circumstances in which Germany was divided, then it feels good – no, it feels *great* – to know at least one particular place, one particular period, from first-hand experience, eyewitness reports; to be the authority, to have time on your side, for once, *for once*. No better historians, no better experts in the *world* than Archie and Samad when it came to *The Post-War Reconstruction and Growth of O'Connell's Pool House*.

1952 Ali (Mickey's father), and his three brothers arrive at Dover with thirty old pounds and their father's gold pocket-watch. All suffer from disfiguring skin condition.

1954–1963 Marriages; odd-jobs of all varieties; births of Abdul-Mickey, the five other Abduls and their cousins.

1968 After working for three years as delivery boys in a Yugoslavian dry-cleaning outfit, Ali and his brothers have a small lump sum with which they set up a cab service called Ali's Cab Service.

1971 Cab venture a great success. But Ali is dissatisfied. He decides what he really wants to do is 'serve food, make people happy, have some face to face conversations once in a while'. He buys the disused Irish pool house next to the defunct railway station on the Finchley Road and sets about renovating it.

1972 In the Finchley Road only Irish establishments do any real business. So despite his Middle Eastern background and the fact that he is opening a café and not a pool house, Ali decides to keep the original Irish name. He paints all the fittings orange and green, hangs pictures of racehorses and registers his business name as 'Andrew O'Connell Yusuf'. Out of respect, his brothers encourage him to hang fragments of the Qur'ān on the wall, so that the hybrid business will be 'kindly looked upon'.

13 May 1973 O'Connell's opens for business.

2 November 1974 Samad and Archie stumble upon O'Connell's on their way home and pop in for a fry-up.

1975 Ali decides to carpet the walls to limit food stains.

May 1977 Samad wins fifteen bob on fruit machine.

1979 Ali has a fatal heart attack due to cholesterol build-up around the heart. Ali's remaining family decide his death is a result of the unholy consumption of pork products. Pig is banned from the menu.

1980 Momentous year. Abdul-Mickey takes over O'Connell's. Institutes underground gambling room to make up for the money lost on sausages. Two large pool tables are used: the 'Death' table and the 'Life' table. All those who want to play for money play on the 'Death' table. All those who object for religious reasons or because out of pocket play on the friendly 'Life' table. Scheme a great success. Samad and Archie play on the 'Death' table.

December 1980 Archie gets highest ever recorded score on pinball: 51,998 points.

1981 Archie finds unwanted cut-out of Viv Richards on Selfridges shop floor and brings it to O'Connell's. Samad asks to have his great-grandfather Mangal Pande's picture on the wall. Mickey refuses, claiming his 'eyes are too close together'.

1982 Samad stops playing on the 'Death' table for religious reasons. Samad continues to petition for the picture's installation.

31 October 1984 Archie wins £268.72 on the 'Death' table. Buys beautiful new set of Pirelli tyres for clapped-out car.

New Year's Eve 1989, 10.30 p.m. Samad finally persuades Mickey to hang portrait. Mickey still thinks it 'puts people off their food'.

'I still think it puts people off their food. And on New Year's Eve. I'm sorry, mate. No offence meant. 'Course my opinion's not the fucking word of God, as it were, but it's still my opinion.'

Mickey attached a wire round the back of the cheap frame, gave the dusty glass a quick wipe-down with his apron, and reluctantly placed the portrait on its hook above the oven.

'I mean, he's so bloody *nasty*-looking. That moustache. He looks like a right *nasty* piece of work. And what's that earring about? He's not a queer, is he?'

'No, no, no. It wasn't unusual, then, for men to wear jewellery.'

Mickey was dubious, giving Samad the look he gave to people who claimed to have got no game of pinball for their 50p and came seeking a refund. He got out from behind the counter and took a look at the picture from this new angle. 'What d'you think, Arch?'

'Good,' said Archie solidly. 'I think: *good*.'

'Please. I would consider it a great personal favour if you would allow it to stay.'

Mickey tilted his head to one side and then the other. 'As I said, I don't mean no offence or nothing, I just think he looks a bit bloody *shady*. Haven't you got another picture of him or sommink?'

'That is the only one that survives. I would consider it a great personal favour, very great.'

'Well . . .' ruminated Mickey, flipping an egg over, 'you being a regular, as it were, and you going on about it so bloody much, I suppose we'll have to keep it. How about a public survey? What d'you think Denzel? Clarence?'

Denzel and Clarence were sitting in the corner as ever, their only concession to New Year's Eve a few pieces of mangy tinsel hanging off Denzel's trilby and a feathered kazoo sharing mouth space with Clarence's cigar.

'Was dat?'

'I said, what d'you think of this bloke Samad wants up? It's his grandfather.'

'*Great*-grandfather,' corrected Samad.

'You kyan see me playing dominoes? You tryin' to deprive an ol'man of his pleasure? What picture?' Denzel grudgingly turned to look at it. 'Dat? Hmph! I don' like it. He look like one of Satan's crew!'

'He a relative of you?' squeaked Clarence to Samad in his woman's voice. 'Dat explain much, my friend, much! He got some face like a donkey's pum-pum.'

Denzel and Clarence exploded into their dirty laughter. 'Nuff to put my belly off its digesting, true sur!'

'There you are!' exclaimed Mickey, victorious, turning back to Samad. 'Puts the clientele off their food – that's what I said right off.'

'Assure me you are not going to listen to those two.'

'I don't know . . .' Mickey twisted and turned in front of his cooking; hard thought always enlisted the involuntary help of his body. 'I respect you and that, and you was mates with my dad, but – no disrespect or nuffin' – you're getting a bit fucking long-in-the-tooth, Samad mate, some of the younger customers might not – '

'*What* younger customers?' demanded Samad, gesturing to Clarence and Denzel.

'Yeah, point taken . . . but the customer is always right, if you get my drift.'

Samad was genuinely hurt. '*I* am a customer. *I* am a customer. I have been coming to your establishment for fifteen years, Mickey. A very long time in any man's estimation.'

'Yeah, but it's the majority wot counts, innit? On most other fings I defer, as it were, to your opinion. The lads call you "The Professor" and, fair dues, it's not without cause. I am a respecter of your judgement, six days out of every seven. But bottom line is: if you're one captain and the rest of the crew wants a bloody mutiny, well . . . you're fucked, aren't you?'

Mickey sympathetically demonstrated the wisdom of this in his frying pan, showing how twelve mushrooms could force one mushroom over the edge and on to the floor.

With the cackles of Denzel and Clarence still echoing in his ears, a current of anger worked its way through Samad and rose to his throat before he was able to stop it.

'Give it to me!' He reached over the counter to where Mangal Pande was hanging at a melancholy angle above the stove. 'I should never have asked . . . it would be a dishonour, it would cast into *ignominy* the memory of Mangal Pande to have him placed here in this – this irreligious house of shame!'

'You what?'

'Give it to me!'

'Now look . . . wait a minute –'

Mickey and Archie reached out to stop him, but Samad, distressed and full of the humiliations of the decade, kept struggling to overcome Mickey's strong blocking presence. They tussled for a bit, but then Samad's body went limp and, covered in a light film of sweat, he surrendered.

'Look, Samad,' and here Mickey touched Samad's shoulders with such affection that Samad thought he might weep. 'I didn't realize it was such a bloody big deal for you. Let's start again. We'll leave the picture up for a week and see how it goes, right?'

'Thank you, my friend.' Samad pulled out a handkerchief and drew it over his forehead. 'It is appreciated. It is appreciated.'

Mickey gave him a conciliatory pat between the shoulder blades. 'Fuck knows, I've heard enough about him over the years. We might as well 'ave him up on the bloody wall. It's all the same to me, I suppose. Comme-See-Comme-Sar, as the Frogs say. I mean, bloody *hell*. Blood-ee-*hell*. And that extra turkey requires hard cash, Archibald, my good man. The golden days of Luncheon Vouchers is over. Dear oh dear, what a *palaver* over nuffin' . . .'

Samad looked deep into his great-grandfather's eyes. They had been through this battle many times, Samad and Pande, the battle for the latter's reputation. Both knew all too well that modern opinion on Mangal Pande weighed in on either side of two camps:

An unrecognized hero	**A palaver over nuffin'**
Samad Iqbal	Mickey
A. S. Misra	Magid and Millat
	Alsana
	Archie
	Irie
	Clarence and Denzel
	British scholarship from 1857 to the present day

Again and again he had argued the toss with Archie over this issue. Over the years they had sat in O'Connell's and returned to the same debate, sometimes with new information gleaned from Samad's continual research into the matter – but ever since Archie found out the 'truth' about Pande, circa 1953, there was no changing his mind. Pande's only claim to fame, as Archie was at pains to point out, was his etymological gift to the English language by way of the word 'Pandy', under which title in the *OED* the curious reader will find the following definition:

Pandy /ˈpandi/ *n.* 2 *colloq.* (now *Hist.*) Also **-dee**. M19 [Perh. f. the surname of the first mutineer amongst the high-caste sepoys in the Bengal army.] **1** Any sepoy who revolted in the Indian Mutiny of 1857–9 **2** Any mutineer or traitor **3** Any fool or coward in a military situation.

'Plain as the pie on your face, my friend.' And here Archie would close the book with an exultant slam. 'And I don't need a dictionary to tell me that – but then neither do you. It's common parlance. When you and me were in the army: same. You tried to put one over on me once, but the truth will out, mate. "Pandy" only ever meant one thing. If I were you, I'd start playing down the family connection, rather than bending everybody's ear twenty-four hours a bloody day.'

'Archibald, just because the word exists, it does not follow that it is a correct representation of the character of Mangal Pande. The first definition we agree on: my great-grandfather was a mutineer and I am proud to say this. I concede matters did not go quite according to plan. But traitor? Coward? The dictionary you show me is old – these definitions are now out of currency. Pande was no traitor and no coward.'

'Ahhh, now, you see, we've been through this, and my thought is this: *there's no smoke without fire*,' Archie would say, looking impressed by the wisdom of his own conclusion. 'Know what I mean?' This was one of Archie's preferred analytic tools when confronted with news stories, historical events and the tricky day-to-day process of separating fact from fiction. *There's no smoke without fire.* There was something so vulnerable in the way he relied on this conviction, that Samad had never had the heart to disabuse him of it. Why tell an old man that there can be smoke without fire as surely as there are deep wounds that draw no blood?

'Of course, I see your point of view, Archie, I do. But my point is, and has always been, from the very first time we discussed the subject; my point is that this is not the *full story*. And, yes, I realize that we have several times thoroughly investigated the matter, but the fact remains: full stories are as rare as honesty, precious as diamonds. If you are lucky enough to uncover one, a full story will sit on your brain like lead. They are difficult. They are long-winded. They are epic. They are like the stories God tells: full of impossibly particular information. You *don't* find them in the dictionary.'

'All right, all right, Professor. Let's hear *your* version.'

Often you see old men in the corner of dark pubs, discussing and gesticulating, using beer mugs and salt-cellars to represent long-dead people and far-off places. At that moment they display a vitality missing in every other area of their lives. They light up. Unpacking a full story on to the table – here is Churchill-fork, over there is Czechoslovakia-serviette, here we find the accumulation of German troops represented by a collection of cold peas – they are reborn. But when Archie and Samad had these table-top debates during the eighties, knives and forks were not enough. The whole of the steamy Indian summer of 1857, the whole of that year of mutiny and massacre would be hauled into O'Connell's and brought to semi-consciousness by these two makeshift historians. The area stretching from the jukebox to the fruit machine became Delhi; Viv Richards silently complied as Pande's English superior, Captain Hearsay; Clarence and Denzel continued to play dominoes while simultaneously being cast as the restless sepoy hordes of the British army. Each man brought the pieces of his argument, laid them out and assembled them for the other to see. Scenes were set. Paths of bullets traced. Disagreement reigned.

According to the legend, during the spring of 1857 in a factory in Dum-Dum, a new kind of British bullet went into production. Designed to be used in English guns by Indian soldiers, like most bullets at the time they had a casing that must be bitten in order to fit the barrel. There seemed nothing exceptional about them, until it was discovered by some canny factory worker that they were covered in a grease – a grease made from the fat of pigs, monstrous to Muslims, and the fat of cows, sacred to Hindus. It was an innocent mistake – as far as anything is innocent on stolen land – an infamous British blunder. But what a feverish turmoil must have engulfed the people on first hearing the news! Under the specious pretext of new weaponry, the English were intending to destroy their caste, their honour, their standing in the eyes of Gods and men – everything, in short, that made life worth living. A rumour like this could not be kept secret; it spread like wildfire through the dry lands of India that summer, down the production line, out on to the streets, through town houses and country shacks, through barrack after barrack, until the whole country was ablaze with the desire for a mutiny. The rumour reached the large unsightly ears of Mangal Pande, an unknown sepoy in the small town of Barrackpore, who swaggered into his parade ground – 29 March 1857 – stepping forward from the throng to make a certain kind of history. 'Make a fool of himself, more like,' Archie will say (for these days he does not swallow Pandy-ology as gullibly as he once did).

'You totally misunderstand his sacrifice,' Samad will reply.

'What sacrifice? He couldn't even kill himself properly! The problem with you, Sam, is you won't listen to the evidence. I've read up on it all. The truth is the truth, no matter how nasty it may taste.'

'*Really*. Well, please, my friend, since you are apparently an expert in the doings of my family, please, enlighten me. Let us hear your version.'

*

Now, the average school student nowadays is aware of the complex forces, movements and deep currents that motivate wars and spark revolutions. But when Archie was in school the world seemed far more open to its own fictionalization. History was a different business then: taught with one eye on narrative, the other on drama, no matter how unlikely or chronologically inaccurate. According to this schema, the Russian Revolution began because everyone hated Rasputin. The Roman Empire declined and fell because Antony was having it off with Cleopatra. Henry V triumphed at Agincourt because the French were too busy admiring their own outfits. And the Great Indian Mutiny of 1857 began when a drunken fool called Mangal Pande shot a bullet. Despite Samad's opposition, each time Archie read the following he found himself more convinced:

The scene is Barrackpore, the date 29 March 1857. It is Sunday afternoon; but on the dusty floor of the parade ground a drama is being enacted which is suggestive of anything but Sabbath peace. There chatters and sways and eddies a confused mass of Sepoys, in all stages of dress and undress; some armed, some unarmed; but all fermenting with excitement. Some thirty yards in front of the line of the 34th swaggers to and fro a Sepoy named Mangal Pande. He is half drunk with bhang, and wholly drunk with religious fanaticism. Chin in air, loaded musket in hand, he struts backwards and forwards, at a sort of half dance, shouting in shrill and nasal monotone, 'Come out, you blackguards! Turn out, all of you! The English are upon us. Through biting these cartridges we shall all be made infidels!'

The man, in fact, is in that condition of mingled bhang and 'nerves' which makes a Malay run amok; and every shout from his lips runs like a sudden flame through the brains and along the nerves of the listening crowd of fellow Sepoys, as the crowd gets bigger, the excitement more intense. A human powder magazine, in a word, is about to explode.

And explode it did. Pande shot at his lieutenant and missed him. Then he took out a large sword, a tulwar, and cowardly lunged while his lieutenant's back was turned, catching him on the shoulder. A sepoy tried to restrain him, but Pande battled on. Then came reinforcements: one Captain Hearsay rushed forward, his son at his side, both armed and honourable and prepared to die for their country. ('Hear-say is precisely what it is! Rubbish. Fabrication!') At which point Pande saw the game was up, pointed his enormous gun at his own head and dramatically pulled the trigger with his left foot. He missed. A few days later, Pande stood trial and was found guilty. From the other side of the country, on a chaise longue in Delhi, his execution was ordered by one General Henry Havelock (a man honoured, much to Samad's fury, by a statue just outside the Palace Restaurant, Trafalgar Square, to the right of Nelson), who added – in a postscript to his written instruction – that he *did* hope that this would put an end to all the rash talk of mutiny one kept hearing recently. But it was too late. As Pande swung in the sultry breeze, hanging from a makeshift gallows, his disbanded comrades from the 34th were heading for Delhi, determined to join the rebel forces of what was to become one of the bloodiest failed mutinies of this or any century.

This version of events – by a contemporary historian named Fitchett – was enough to send Samad into spasms of fury. When a man has nothing but his blood to commend him, each drop of it matters, matters terribly; it must be jealously defended. It must be protected against assailants and detractors. It must be fought for. But like a Chinese whisper, Fitchett's intoxicated, incompetent Pande had passed down a line of subsequent historians, the truth mutating, bending, receding as the whisper continued. It didn't matter that bhang, a hemp drink taken in small doses for medicinal purposes, was extremely unlikely to cause intoxication of this kind or that Pande, a strict Hindu, was extremely unlikely to drink it. It didn't matter that Samad could find not one piece of corroborating evidence that Pande had taken bhang that morning. The story still clung, like a gigantic misquote, to the Iqbal reputation, as solid and seemingly irremovable as the misconception that Hamlet ever said he knew Yorick 'well'.

'Enough! It makes no difference how many times you read these things to me, Archibald.' (Archie usually came armed with a plastic bag full of Brent Library books, anti-Pande propaganda, misquotes galore.) 'It is like a gang of children caught with their hands in an enormous honey jar: they are all going to tell me the same lie. I am not interested in this kind of slander. I am not interested in puppet theatre or tragic farce. Action interests me, friend.' And here Samad would mime the final zipping up of his lips, the throwing away of a key. 'True action. Not words. I tell you, Archibald, Mangal Pande sacrificed his life in the name of justice for India, not because he was intoxicated or insane. Pass me the ketchup.'

It was the 1989 New Year's Eve shift in O'Connell's, and the debate was in full swing.

'True, he was not a hero in the way you in the West like your heroes – he did not succeed except in the manner of his honourable death. But imagine it: there he sat.' Samad pointed to Denzel, about to play his winning domino. 'At the trial, knowing death was upon him, refusing ever to reveal the names of his fellow conspirators –'

'Now, *that*,' said Archie, patting his pile of sceptics, Michael Edwardes, P. J. O. Taylor, Syed Moinul Haq and the rest, 'depends what you read.'

'No, Archie. That is a common mistake. The truth does *not* depend on what you read. Please let us not get into the nature of truth. Then you do not have to draw with my cheese and I can avoid eating your chalk.'

'All right, then: Pande. What did he achieve? Nothing! All he did was start a mutiny – too early, mind, before the agreed date – and excuse my French, but that's a fucking disaster in military terms. You *plan*, you don't act on instinct. He caused unnecessary casualties. English *and* Indian.'

'With respect, I don't believe that to be the case.'

'Well, you're wrong.'

'With respect, I believe I am right.'

'It's like this, Sam: imagine here' – he gathered a pile of dirty plates that Mickey was about to put in the dishwasher – 'are all the people who have written about your Pande in the last hundred-and-whatever years. Now: here's the ones that agree with me.' He placed ten plates on his side of the table and pushed one over to Samad. 'And that's the madman on your side.'

'A. S. Misra. Respected Indian civil servant. *Not* a madman.'

'Right. Well, it would take you at least another hundred-and-whatever years to get as many plates as I have, even if you were going to make them all yourself, and the likelihood is, once you had them, no bugger would want to eat off them anyway. Metaphorically speaking. Know what I mean?'

Which left only A. S. Misra. One of Samad's nephews, Rajnu, had written to him in the spring of '81 from his Cambridge college, mentioning casually that he had found a book which might be of some interest to his uncle. In it, he said, could be found an eloquent defence of their shared ancestor, one Mangal Pande. The only surviving copy was in his college library, it was by a man named Misra. Had he heard of it already? If not, might it not serve (Rajnu added in a cautious P. S.) as a pleasant excuse to see his uncle again?

Samad arrived on the train the very next day and stood on the platform, warmly greeting his soft-spoken nephew in the pouring rain, shaking his hand several times and talking as if it were going out of fashion.

'A great day,' he repeated over and over, until both men were soaked to the skin. 'A great day for our family, Rajnu, a great day for the *truth*.'

Wet men not being allowed in college libraries, they spent the morning drying off in a stuffy upstairs café, full of the right type of ladies having the right type of tea. Rajnu, ever the good listener, sat patiently as his uncle babbled wildly – Oh, the *importance* of the discovery, Oh, how *long* he had waited for this moment – nodding in all the right places and smiling sweetly as Samad brushed tears from the corners of his eyes. 'It is a great book, isn't it, Rajnu?' asked Samad pleadingly, as his nephew left a generous tip for the sour-faced waitresses who did not appreciate overexcited Indians spending three hours over one cream tea and leaving wet prints all over the furniture. 'It is recognized, isn't it?'

Rajnu knew in his heart that the book was an inferior, insignificant, forgotten piece of scholarship, but he loved his uncle, so he smiled, nodded and smiled firmly again.

Once in the library, Samad was asked to fill in the visitors' book:

> *Name*: Samad Miah Iqbal
> *College*: Educated elsewhere (Delhi)
> *Research project*: Truth

Rajnu, tickled by this last entry, picked up the pen, adding 'and Tragedy'.

'Truth and Tragedy,' said a deadpan librarian, turning the book back round. 'Any particular kind?'

'Don't worry,' said Samad genially. 'We'll find it.'

It took a stepladder to reach it but it was well worth the stretch. When Rajnu passed the book to his uncle, Samad felt his fingers tingle and, looking at its cover, shape and colour, saw that it was all he had dreamt of. It was heavy, many paged, bound in a tan leather and covered in the light dust that denotes something incredibly precious, something rarely touched.

'I left a marker in it. There is much to read but there is

something I thought you'd like to see first,' said Rajnu, laying it down on a desk. The heavy thud of one side of the book hit the table, and Samad looked at the appointed page. It was more than he could have hoped for.

'It's only an artist's impression, but the similarity between –'

'Don't speak,' said Samad, tracing his fingers across the picture. 'This is our *blood*, Rajnu. I never thought I would see . . . What eyebrows! What a nose! I have his nose!'

'You have his face, Uncle. More dashing, naturally.'

'And what – what does it say underneath. Damn! Where are my reading glasses . . . read it for me, Rajnu, it is too small.'

'The caption? *Mangal Pande fired the first bullet of the 1857 movement. His self-sacrifice gave the siren to the nation to take up arms against an alien ruler, culminating in a mass-uprising with no parallel in world history. Though the effort failed in its immediate consequences, it succeeded in laying the foundations of the Independence to be won in 1947. For his patriotism he paid with his life. But until his last breath he refused to disclose the names of those who were preparing for, and instigating, the great uprising.*'

Samad sat down on the bottom rung of the stepladder and wept.

'So. Let me get this straight. Now you're telling me that without Pande there'd be no Gandhi. That without your mad grandad there'd be no bloody Independence –'

'Great-grandad.'

'No, let me finish, Sam. Is that what you're seriously asking *us*' – Archie clapped an uninterested Clarence and Denzel on the back – 'to believe? Do *you* believe it?' he asked Clarence.

'Me kyan believe dat!' said Clarence, having no idea of the topic.

Denzel blew his nose into a napkin. 'Troof be tol, me nah like to believe any ting. Hear no evil, see no evil, speak no evil. Dat my motto.'

'He was the tickle in the sneeze, Archibald. It is as simple as that. I *do* believe that.'

There was quiet for a minute. Archibald watched three sugar cubes dissolve in his teacup. Then, rather tentatively, he said, 'I've got my own theory, you know. Separate from the books, I mean.'

Samad bowed. 'Please enlighten us.'

'Don't get angry, now . . . But just *think* for a minute. Why is a strict religious man like Pande drinking bhang? Seriously, I know I tease you about it. But why is he?'

'You know my opinion on that. He isn't. He didn't. It was English propaganda.'

'And he was a good shot . . .'

'No doubt about it. A. S. Misra produces a copy of a record stating that Pande trained in a special guard for one year, specially trained in the use of muskets.'

'OK. So: why does he miss? Why?'

'It is my belief that the only possible explanation is that the gun was faulty.'

'Yes . . . there is that. But, maybe, maybe something else. Maybe he was being bullied into going out there and making a row, you know, goaded, by the other guys. And he didn't want to kill anyone in the first place, you know. So he *pretended* to be drunk, so the boys in the barracks room would believe he missed the shot.'

'That is quite the stupidest theory I have ever heard,' sighed Samad, as the second hand of Mickey's egg-stained clock started the thirty-second countdown to midnight. 'The kind only you could come up with. It's absurd.'

'Why?'

'Why? Archibald, these Englishmen, these Captain Hearsays, Havelocks and the rest, were every Indian's mortal enemy. Why should he spare lives he despised?'

'Maybe he just couldn't do it. Maybe he wasn't the type.'

'Do you really believe there is a type of man who kills and a type of man who doesn't?'

'Maybe Sam, maybe not.'

'You sound like my wife,' groaned Samad, mopping up a final piece of egg, 'let me tell you something, Archibald. A man is a man is a man. His family threatened, his beliefs attacked, his way of life destroyed, his whole world coming to an end – he will kill. Make no mistake. He won't let the new order roll over him without a struggle. There will be people he will kill.'

'And there will be people he will save,' said Archie Jones, with a cryptic look his friend would have thought an impossible feat for those sagging, chubby features. 'Trust me.'

'Five! Four! Tree! Two! One! Jamaica Irie!' said Denzel and Clarence, raising hot Irish coffees to each other in a toast, then immediately resuming round nine of the dominoes.

'HAPPY FUCKING NEW YEAR!' bellowed Mickey, from behind the counter.

Irie

1990, 1907

In this wrought-iron world of criss-cross cause and effect, could it be that the hidden throb I stole from them did not affect their future?

– *Lolita*, Vladimir Nabokov

11 *The Miseducation of Irie Jones*

There was a lamp-post, equidistant from the Jones house and Glenard Oak Comprehensive, that had begun to appear in Irie's dreams. Not the lamp-post exactly, but a small, handmade advert which was sellotaped round its girth at eye level. It said:

> ***LOSE WEIGHT TO EARN MONEY***
>
> ***081 555 6752***

Now, Irie Jones, aged fifteen, was big. The European proportions of Clara's figure had skipped a generation, and she was landed instead with Hortense's substantial Jamaican frame, loaded with pineapples, mangoes and guavas; the girl had weight; big tits, big butt, big hips, big thighs, big teeth. She was thirteen stone and had thirteen pounds in her savings account. She knew she was the target audience (if ever there was one), she knew full well, as she trudged schoolwards, mouth full of doughnut, hugging her spare tyres, that the advert was speaking to her. It was *speaking* to her. LOSE WEIGHT (it was saying) TO EARN MONEY. You, you, *you*, Miss Jones, with your strategically placed arms and cardigan, tied around the arse (the endless mystery: how to diminish that swollen enormity, the Jamaican posterior?), with your belly-reducing knickers and breast-reducing bra, with your meticulous lycra corseting – the much lauded nineties answer to whalebone – with your elasticated waists. She knew the advert was talking to *her*. But she didn't know quite what it was saying. What were we talking about here? Sponsored slim? The earning capacity of thin people? Or something altogether more Jacobean, the brain-child of some sordid Willesden Shylock, a pound of flesh for a pound of gold: *meat for money*?

Rapid. Eye. Movement. Sometimes she'd be walking through school in a bikini with the lamp-post enigma written in chalk over her brown bulges, over her various ledges (shelf space for books, cups of tea, baskets or, more to the point, children, bags of fruit, buckets of water), ledges genetically designed with another country in mind, another climate. Other times, the sponsored slim dream: knocking on door after door, butt-naked with a clipboard, drenched in sunlight, trying to encourage old men to pinch-an-inch and pledge-a-pound. Worst times? Tearing off loose, white-flecked flesh and packing it into those old curvaceous Coke bottles; she is carrying them to the cornershop, passing them over a counter; and Millat is the bindi-wearing, V-necked cornershopkeeper, he is adding them up, grudgingly opening the till with blood-stained paws, handing over the cash. *A little Caribbean flesh for a little English change.*

Irie Jones was obsessed. Occasionally her worried mother cornered her in the hallway before she slunk out of the door, picked at her elaborate corsetry, asked, 'What's up with you? What in the Lord's name are you wearing? How can you breathe? Irie, my love, you're fine – you're just built like an honest-to-God Bowden – don't you know you're fine?'

But Irie didn't know she was fine. There was England, a gigantic mirror, and there was Irie, without reflection. A stranger in a stranger land.

Nightmares and daydreams, on the bus, in the bath, in class. Before. After. Before. After. Before. *After.* The mantra of the make-over junkie, sucking it in, letting it out; unwilling to settle for genetic fate; waiting instead for her transformation from Jamaican hourglass heavy with the sands that gather round Dunn

River Falls, to *English Rose* – oh, you know her – she's a slender, delicate thing not made for the hot suns, a surfboard rippled by the wave:

Before: After:

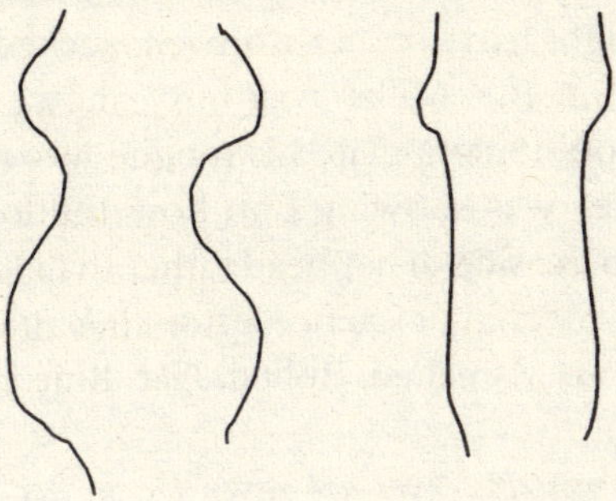

Mrs Olive Roody, English teacher and expert doodle-spotter at distances of up to twenty yards, reached over her desk to Irie's exercise book and tore out the piece of paper in question. Looked dubiously at it. Then inquired with melodious Scottish emphasis, 'Before and after *what*?'

'Er . . . what?'

'Before and after *what*?'

'Oh. Nothing, Miss.'

'Nothing? Oh, come now, Ms Jones. No need for modesty. It is obviously more interesting than Sonnet 127.'

'Nothing. It's *nothing*.'

'Absolutely certain? You don't wish to delay the class any more? Because . . . some of the class need to listen to – *nae*, are even a wee bit *interested in* – what I have to say. So if you could spare some time from your doooodling –'

No one but no one said 'doodling' like Olive Roody.

'– and join the rest of us, we'll continue. Well?'

'Well what?'

'Can you? Spare the time?'

'Yes, Mrs Roody.'

'Oh, *good*. That's cheered me up. Sonnet 127, please.'

'In the old age black was not counted fair,' continued Francis Stone in the catatonic drone with which students read Elizabethan verse. *'Or if it were, it bore not beauty's name.'*

Irie put her right hand on her stomach, sucked in and tried to catch Millat's eye. But Millat was busy showing pretty Nikki Tyler how he could manipulate his tongue into a narrow roll, a flute. Nikki Tyler was showing him how the lobes of her ears were attached to the side of her head rather than loose. Flirtatious remnants of this morning's science lesson: *Inherited characteristics. Part One (a)*. Loose. Attached. Rolled. Flat. Blue eye. Brown eye. Before. After.

'Therefore my mistress' eyes are raven black, her brows so suited, and they mourners seem . . . My mistress' eyes are nothing like the sun; Coral is far more red than her lips' red; If snow be white, why then her breasts are dun . . .'

Puberty, real full-blown puberty (not the slight mound of a breast, or the shadowy emergence of fuzz), had separated these old friends, Irie Jones and Millat Iqbal. Different sides of the school fence. Irie believed she had been dealt the dodgy cards: mountainous curves, buck teeth and thick metal retainer, impossible Afro hair, and to top it off mole-ish eyesight which in turn required bottle-top spectacles in a light shade of pink. (Even those blue eyes – the eyes Archie had been so excited about – lasted two weeks only. She had been born with them, yes, but one day Clara looked again and there were brown eyes staring up at her, like the transition between a closed bud and an open flower, the exact moment of which the naked, waiting eye can never detect.) And this belief in her ugliness, in her *wrongness*, had subdued her; she kept her smart-ass comments to herself these days, she kept her right hand on her stomach. She was all *wrong*.

Whereas Millat was like youth remembered in the nostalgic

eyeglass of old age, beauty parodying itself: broken Roman nose, tall, thin; lightly veined, smoothly muscled; chocolate eyes with a reflective green sheen like moonlight bouncing off a dark sea; irresistible smile, big white teeth. In Glenard Oak Comprehensive, black, Pakistani, Greek, Irish – these were races. But those with sex appeal lapped the other runners. They were a species all of their own.

'If hairs be wires, black wires grow on her head . . .'

She loved him, of course. But he used to say to her: 'Thing is, people rely on me. They need me to be Millat. Good old Millat. Wicked Millat. Safe, sweet-as, Millat. They need me to be cool. It's *practically* a responsibility.'

And it practically was. Ringo Starr once said of the Beatles that they were never bigger than they were in Liverpool, late 1962. They just got more countries. And that's how it was for Millat. He was so big in Cricklewood, in Willesden, in West Hampstead, the summer of 1990, that nothing he did later in his life could top it. From his first Raggastani crowd, he had expanded and developed tribes throughout the school, throughout North London. He was simply too big to remain merely the object of Irie's affection, leader of the Raggastanis, or the son of Samad and Alsana Iqbal. He had to please all of the people all of the time. To the cockney wide-boys in the white jeans and the coloured shirts, he was the joker, the risk-taker, respected lady-killer. To the black kids he was fellow weed-smoker and valued customer. To the Asian kids, hero and spokesman. Social chameleon. And underneath it all, there remained an ever present anger and hurt, the feeling of belonging nowhere that comes to people who belong everywhere. It was this soft underbelly that made him most beloved, most adored by Irie and the nice oboe-playing, long-skirted middle-class girls, most treasured by these hair-flicking and fugue-singing females; he was their dark prince, occasional lover or impossible crush, the subject of sweaty fantasy and ardent dreams . . .

And he was also their *project*: what *was* to be done about Millat? He simply *must* stop smoking weed. We *have* to try and stop him walking out of class. They worried about his 'attitude' at sleep-overs, discussed his education hypothetically with their parents (*Just say there was this Indian boy, yeah, who was always getting into . . .*), even wrote poems on the subject. Girls either wanted him or wanted to improve him, but most often a combination of the two. They wanted to improve him until he justified the amount they wanted him. Everybody's bit of rough, Millat Iqbal.

'But you're different,' Millat Iqbal would say to the martyr Irie Jones, 'you're *different*. We go way back. We've got history. You're a *real* friend. They don't really *mean* anything to me.'

Irie liked to believe that. That they had history, that she was different in a good way.

'*Thy black is fairest in my judgement's place . . .*'

Mrs Roody silenced Francis with a raised finger. 'Now, what is he saying there? Annalese?'

Annalese Hersh, who had spent the lesson so far plaiting red and yellow thread into her hair, looked up in blank confusion.

'*Anything*, Annalese, dear. Any little idea. No matter how small. No matter how paltry.'

Annalese bit her lip. Looked at the book. Looked at Mrs Roody. Looked at the book.

'Black? . . . Is? . . . Good?'

'Yes . . . well, I suppose we can add that to last week's contribution: Hamlet? . . . Is? . . . Mad? Anybody else? What about this? *For since each hand hath put on nature's power, Fairing the foul with art's false borrow'd face*. What might that mean I wonder?'

Joshua Chalfen, the only kid in class who volunteered opinions, put his hand up.

'Yes, Joshua?'

'Make-up.'

'Yes,' said Mrs Roody, looking close to orgasm. 'Yes, Joshua, that's it. What about it?'

'She's got a dark complexion which she's trying to lighten by means of make-up, artifice. The Elizabethans were very keen on a pale skin.'

'They would've loved you, then,' sneered Millat, for Joshua was pasty, practically anaemic, curly-haired and chubby, 'you would have been Tom bloody Cruise.'

Laughter. Not because it was funny, but because it was Millat putting a nerd where a nerd should be. In his place.

'One more word from you Mr Ick-Ball and you are out!'

'Shakespeare. Sweaty. Bollocks. That's three. Don't worry, I'll let myself out.'

This was the kind of thing Millat did so expertly. The door slammed. The nice girls looked at each other in *that* way. (He's just *so* out of control, *so* crazy . . . he *really* needs some help, some close one-to-one *personal* help from a *good friend* . . .) The boys belly-laughed. The teacher wondered if this was the beginning of a mutiny. Irie covered her stomach with her right hand.

'Marvellous. Very adult. I suppose Millat Iqbal is some kind of hero.' Mrs Roody, looking round the gormless faces of 5F, saw for the first time and with dismal clarity that this was exactly what he was.

'Does anyone else have anything to say about these sonnets? Ms Jones! Will you *stop* looking mournfully at the door! He's gone, all right? Unless you'd like to join him?'

'No, Mrs Roody.'

'All right, then. Have you anything to say about the sonnets?'

'Yes.'

'What?'

'Is she black?'

'Is who black?'

'The dark lady.'

'No, dear, she's *dark*. She's not black in the modern sense. There weren't any . . . well, Afro-Carri-bee-yans in England at that time, dear. That's more a modern phenomenon, as I'm sure you know. But this was the 1600s. I mean I can't be sure, but it does seem terribly unlikely, unless she was a slave of some kind, and he's unlikely to have written a series of sonnets to a lord and then a slave, is he?'

Irie reddened. She had thought, just then, that she had seen something like a reflection, but it was receding; so she said, 'Don't know, Miss.'

'Besides, he says very clearly, *In nothing art thou black, save in thy deeds* . . . No, dear, she just has a dark complexion, you see, as dark as mine, probably.'

Irie looked at Mrs Roody. She was the colour of strawberry mousse.

'You see, Joshua is quite right: the preference was for women to be excessively pale in those days. The sonnet is about the debate between her natural colouring and the make-up that was the fashion of the time.'

'I just thought . . . like when he says, here: *Then will I swear, beauty herself is black* . . . And the curly hair thing, black wires –'

Irie gave up in the face of giggling and shrugged.

'No, dear, you're reading it with a modern ear. Never read what is old with a modern ear. In fact, that will serve as today's principle – can you all write that down please.'

5F wrote that down. And the reflection that Irie had glimpsed slunk back into the familiar darkness. On the way out of class, Irie was passed a note by Annalese Hersh, who shrugged to signify that she was not the author but merely one of many handlers. It said: 'By William Shakespeare: ODE TO LETITIA AND ALL MY KINKY-HAIRED BIG-ASS BITCHEZ.'

The cryptically named P. K.'s Afro Hair: Design and Management sat between Fairweather Funeral Parlour and Raakshan Dentists, the convenient proximity meaning it was not at all uncommon for a cadaver of African origin to pass through all three establishments on his or her final journey to an open casket. So when you phoned for a hair appointment, and Andrea or Denise or Jackie told you *three thirty Jamaican time*, naturally it meant come late, but there was also a chance it meant that some stone-cold church-going lady was determined to go to her grave with long fake nails and a weave-on. Strange as it sounds, there are plenty of people who refuse to meet the Lord with an Afro.

Irie, ignorant of all this, turned up for her appointment three thirty on the dot, intent upon transformation, intent upon fighting her genes, a headscarf disguising the bird's nest of her hair, her right hand carefully placed upon her stomach.

'You wan' some ting, pickney?'

Straight hair. Straight straight long black sleek flickable tossable shakeable touchable finger-through-able wind-blowable hair. With a fringe.

'Three thirty,' was all Irie managed to convey of this, 'with Andrea.'

'Andrea's next door,' replied the woman, pulling at a piece of elongated gum and nodding in the direction of Fairweather's, 'having fun with the dearly departed. You better come sit down and wait and don' bodder me. Don' know how long she'll be.'

Irie looked lost, standing in the middle of the shop, clutching her chub. The woman took pity, swallowed her gum and looked Irie up and down; she felt more sympathetic as she noted Irie's cocoa complexion, the light eyes.

'Jackie.'

'Irie.'

'Pale, sir! Freckles an' every ting. You Mexican?'

'No.'

'Arab?'

'Half Jamaican. Half English.'

'Half-*caste*,' Jackie explained patiently. 'Your mum white?'

'Dad.'

Jackie wrinkled her nose. 'Usually de udder way roun'. How

curly is it? Lemme se what's under dere –' She made a grab for Irie's headscarf. Irie, horrified at the possibility of being laid bare in a room full of people, got there before her and held on tight.

Jackie sucked her teeth. 'What d'you 'spec us to do wid it if we kyant see it?'

Irie shrugged. Jackie shook her head, amused.

'You ain't been in before?'

'No, never.'

'What is it you want?'

'Straight,' said Irie firmly, thinking of Nikki Tyler. 'Straight and dark red.'

'Is dat a fact! You wash your hair recent?'

'Yesterday,' said Irie, offended. Jackie slapped her up-side her head.

'Don' wash it! If you wan' it straight, don' wash it! You ever have ammonia on your head? It's like the devil's having a party on your scalp. You crazy? Don' wash it for two weeks an' den come back.'

But Irie didn't have two weeks. She had it all planned; she was going to go round to Millat's this very evening with her new mane, all tied up in a bun, and she was going to take off her glasses and shake down her hair and he was going to say *why Miss Jones, I never would have supposed . . . why Miss Jones, you're –*

'I have to do it *today*. My sister's getting married.'

'Well, when Andrea get back she going to burn seven shades of shit out of your hair an' you'll be lucky if you don' walk out of here with a ball 'ed. But den it *your* funeral. Ear,' she said thrusting a pile full of magazines into Irie's hands. 'Dere,' she said, pointing to a chair.

P. K.'s was split into two halves, male and female. In the male section, as relentless Ragga came unevenly over a battered stereo, young boys had logos cut into the back of their heads at the hands of slightly older boys, skilful wielders of the electric trimmers. ADIDAS. BADMUTHA. MARTIN. The male section was all laughter, all talk, all play; there was an easiness that sprang from no male haircut ever costing over six pounds or taking more than fifteen minutes. It was a simple enough exchange and there was joy in it: the buzz of the revolving blade by your ear, a rough brush-down with a warm hand, mirrors front and back to admire the transformation. You came in with a picky head, uneven and coarse, disguised underneath a baseball cap, and you left swiftly afterwards a new man, smelling sweetly of coconut oil and with a cut as sharp and clean as a swear word.

In comparison, the female section of P. K.'s was a deathly thing. Here, the impossible desire for straightness and 'movement' fought daily with the stubborn determination of the curved African follicle; here ammonia, hot combs, clips, pins and simple fire had all been enlisted in the war and were doing their damnedest to beat each curly hair into submission.

'Is it straight?' was the only question you heard as the towels came off and the heads emerged from the drier pulsating with pain. 'Is it straight, Denise? Tell me is it straight, Jackie?'

To which Jackie or Denise, having none of the obligations of white hairdressers, no need to make tea or kiss arse, flatter or make conversation (for these were not customers they were dealing with but desperate wretched *patients*), would give a sceptical snort and whip off the puke-green gown. 'It as straight as it ever going to be!'

Four women sat in front of Irie now, biting their lips, staring intently into a long, dirty mirror, waiting for their straighter selves to materialize. While Irie flicked nervously through American black hair magazines, the four women sat grimacing in pain. Occasionally one said to another, 'How long?' To which the proud reply came, 'Fifteen minutes. How long for you?' 'Twenty-two. This shit's been on my head twenty-two minutes. It *better* be straight.'

It was a competition in agony. Like rich women in posh restaurants ordering ever smaller salads.

Finally there would come a scream, or a 'That's it! Shit, I can't take it!' and the head in question was rushed to the sink, where the washing could never be quick enough (you cannot get ammonia out of your hair quick enough) and the quiet weeping began. It was at this point that animosity arose; some people's hair was 'kinkier' than others', some Afros fought harder, some survived. And the animosity spread from fellow customer to hairdresser, to inflicter of this pain, for it was natural enough to suspect Jackie or Denise of something like sadism: their fingers were too slow as they worked the stuff out, the water seemed to trickle instead of gush, and meanwhile the devil had a high old time burning the crap out of your hairline.

'Is it straight? Jackie, is it straight?'

The boys arched their heads round the partition wall, Irie looked up from her magazine. There was little to say. They all came out straight or straight enough. But they also came out dead. Dry. Splintered. Stiff. All the spring gone. Like the hair of a cadaver as the moisture seeps away.

Jackie or Denise, knowing full well that the curved African follicle will, in the end, follow its genetic instructions, put a philosophic slant on the bad news. 'It as straight as it ever going to be. Tree weeks if you lucky.'

Despite the obvious failure of the project, each woman along the line felt that it would be different for her, that when their own unveiling came, straight straight flickable, wind-blowable locks would be theirs. Irie, as full of confidence as the rest, returned to her magazine.

Malika, vibrant young star of the smash hit sitcom *Malika's Life*, explains how she achieves her loose and flowing look: 'I hot wrap it each evening, ensuring that the ends are lightly waxed in *African Queen Afro Sheen*™, then, in the morning, I put a comb on the stove for approximately –'

The return of Andrea. The magazine was snatched from her hands, her headscarf unceremoniously removed before she could stop it, and five long and eloquent fingernails began to work their way through her scalp.

'Ooooh,' murmured Andrea.

This sign of approval was a rare-enough occurrence for the rest of the shop to come round the partition to have a look.

'Oooooh,' said Denise, adding her fingers to Andrea's. 'So loose.'

An older lady, wincing with pain underneath a drier, nodded admiringly.

'Such a loose curl,' cooed Jackie, ignoring her own scalded patient to reach into Irie's wool.

'That's half-caste hair for you. I wish mine were like that. That'll relax beautiful.'

Irie screwed up her face. 'I *hate* it.'

'She hates it!' said Denise to the crowd. 'It's light brown in places!'

'I been dealing with a corpse all morning. Be nice to get my hands into somefing sof',' said Andrea, emerging from her reverie. 'You gonna relax it, darlin'?'

'Yes. Straight. Straight and red.'

Andrea tied a green gown round Irie's neck and lowered her into a swivelling chair. 'Don't know about red, baby. Can't dye and relax on the same day. Kill the hair dead. But I can do the relax for you, no problem. Should come out beautiful, darlin'.'

The communication between hairdressers in P. K.'s being poor, no one told Andrea that Irie had washed her hair. Two minutes after having the thick white ammonia gloop spread on to her head, she felt the initial cold sensation change to a terrific fire. There was no dirt there to protect the scalp, and Irie started screaming.

'I jus' put it on! You want it straight, don' you? Stop making that noise!'

'But it hurts!'

'Life hurts,' said Andrea scornfully, 'beauty hurts.'

Irie bit her tongue for another thirty seconds until blood appeared above her right ear. Then the poor girl blacked out.

She came to with her head over the sink, watching her hair, which was coming out in clumps, shimmy down the plughole.

'You should have told me,' Andrea was grumbling. 'You should have told me that you washed it. It's got to be dirty first. Now look.'

Now look. Hair that had once come down to her mid vertebrae was only a few inches from her head.

'See what you've done,' continued Andrea, as Irie wept openly. 'I'd like to know what Mr Paul King is going to say about this. I better phone him and see if we can fix this up for you for free.'

Mr Paul King, the P. K. in question, owned the place. He was a big white guy, in his mid fifties, who had been an entrepreneur in the building trade until Black Wednesday and his wife's credit card excesses took away everything but some bricks and mortar. Looking for a new idea, he read in the lifestyle section of his breakfast paper that black women spend five times as much as white women on beauty products and nine times as much on their hair. Taking his wife Sheila as an archetypal white woman, Paul King began to salivate. A little more research in his local library uncovered a multi-million pound industry. Paul King then bought a disused butcher's on Willesden High Road, head-hunted Andrea from a Harlesden salon, and gave black hairdressing a shot. It was an instant success. He was amazed to discover that women on low income were indeed prepared to spend hundreds of pounds per month on their hair and yet more on nails and accessories. He was vaguely amused when Andrea first explained to him that physical pain was also part of the process. And the best part of it was there was no question of suing – they *expected* the burns. Perfect business.

'Go on, Andrea, love, give her a freebie,' said Paul King,

shouting on a brick-shaped mobile over the construction noise of his new salon, opening in Wembley. 'But don't make a habit of it.'

Andrea returned to Irie with the good tidings. ''Sall right, darlin'. This one's on us.'

'But what –' Irie stared at her Hiroshima reflection. 'What can you –'

'Put your scarf back on, turn left out of here and go down the high road until you get to a shop called Roshi's Haircare. Take this card and tell them P. K.'s sent you. Get eight packets of no. 5 type black hair with a red glow and come back here quick style.'

'Hair?' repeated Irie through snot and tears. '*Fake* hair?'

'Stupid girl. It's not fake. It's real. And when it's on your head it'll be your real hair. Go!'

Blubbing like a baby, Irie shuffled out of P. K.'s and down the high road, trying to avoid her reflection in the shop windows. Reaching Roshi's, she did her best to pull herself together, put her right hand over her stomach and pushed through the doors.

It was dark in Roshi's and smelt strongly of the same scent as P. K.'s: ammonia and coconut oil, pain mixed with pleasure. From the dim glow given off by a flickering strip light, Irie could see there were no shelves to speak of but instead hair products piled like mountains from the floor up, while accessories (combs, bands, nail varnish) were stapled to the walls with the price written in felt-tip alongside. The only display of any recognizable kind was placed just below the ceiling in a loop around the room, taking pride of place like a collection of sacrificial scalps or hunting trophies. Hair. Long tresses stapled a few inches apart. Underneath each a large cardboard sign explaining its pedigree:

2 Metres. Natural Thai. Straight. Chestnut.
1 Metre. Natural Pakistani. Straight with a wave. Black.
5 Metres. Natural Chinese. Straight. Black.
3 Metres. Synthetic hair. Corkscrew curl. Pink.

Irie approached the counter. A hugely fat woman in a sari was waddling to the cash till and back again to hand over twenty-five pounds to an Indian girl whose hair had been shorn haphazardly close to the scalp.

'And please don't be looking at me in that manner. Twenty-five is very reasonable price. I tell you I can't do any more with all these split ends.'

The girl objected in another language, picked up the bag of hair in question from the counter and made as if to leave with it, but the elder woman snatched it away.

'Please, don't embarrass yourself further. We both have seen the ends. Twenty-five is all I can give you for it. You won't get more some other place. Please now,' she said, looking over the girl's shoulder to Irie, 'other customers I have.'

Irie saw hot tears, not unlike her own, spring to the girl's eyes. She seemed to freeze for a moment, vibrating ever so slightly with anger; then she slammed her hand down on the counter, swept up her twenty-five pounds and headed for the door.

The fat lady shook her chins in contempt after the disappearing girl. 'Ungrateful, she is.'

Then she unpeeled a sticky label from its brown paper backing and slapped it on the bag of hair. It said: '6 Metres. Indian. Straight. Black/red.'

'Yes, dear. What is it I can do?'

Irie repeated Andrea's instruction and handed over the card.

'Eight packets? That is about six metres, no?'

'I don't know.'

'Yes, yes, it is. You want it straight or with a wave?'

'Straight. Dead straight.'

The fat lady did a silent calculation and then picked up the bag of hair that the girl had just left. 'This is what you're looking for. I haven't been able to package it, you understand. But it is absolutely clean. You want?'

Irie looked dubious.

'Don't worry about what I said. No split ends. Just silly girl trying to get more than she deserves. Some people got no understanding of simple economics . . . It hurts her to cut off her hair so a million pounds she expects or something crazy. Beautiful hair, she has. When I was young, oh, mine was beautiful too, eh?' The fat lady erupted into high-pitched laughter, her busy upper lip making her moustache quiver. The laugh subsided.

'Tell Andrea that will be thirty-seven fifty. We Indian women have the beautiful hair, hey? Everybody wants it!'

A black woman with children in a twin buggy was waiting behind Irie with a packet of hairpins. She sucked her teeth. 'You people think you're all Mr Bigstuff,' she muttered, half to herself. 'Some of us are happy with our African hair, thank you very much. I don't want to buy some poor Indian girl's hair. And I wish to God I could buy black hair products from black people for once. How we going to make it in this country if we don't make our own business?'

The skin around the fat lady's mouth became very tight. She began talking twelve to the dozen, putting Irie's hair in a bag and writing her out a receipt, addressing all her comments to the woman via Irie, while doing the best to ignore the other woman's interjections: 'You don't like shopping here, then please don't be shopping here – is forcing you anybody? No, is anybody? It's amazing: people, the rudeness, I am not a racist, but I can't understand it, I'm just providing a service, a service. I don't need abuse, just leave your money on the counter, if I am getting abuse, I'm not serving.'

'No one's givin' you abuse. Jesus Christ!'

'Is it my fault if they want the hair that is straight – and paler skin sometimes, like Michael Jackson, my fault he is too? They tell me not to sell the Dr Peacock Whitener – local paper, my God, what a fuss! – and then they buy it – take that receipt to Andrea, will you, my dear, please? I'm just trying to make a living in this country like the rest of everybody. There you are, dear, there's your hair.'

The woman reached around Irie and delivered the right change to the counter with an angry smash. 'For fuck's sake!'

'I can't help it if that's what they want – supply, demand. And bad language, I won't tolerate! Simple economics – mind your step on the way out, dear – and *you*, no, don't come back, please, I will call the police, I won't be threatened, the police, I will call them.'

'Yeah, yeah, *yeah*.'

Irie held the door open for the double buggy, and took one side to help carry it over the front step. Outside the woman put her hairpins in her pocket. She looked exhausted.

'I hate that place,' she said. 'But I need hairpins.'

'I need hair,' said Irie.

The woman shook her head. 'You've *got* hair,' she said.

Five and a half hours later, thanks to an arduous operation that involved plaiting somebody else's hair in small sections to Irie's own two inches and sealing it with glue, Irie Jones had a full head of long, straight, reddish-black hair.

'Is it straight?' she asked, disbelieving the evidence of her own eyes.

'Straight as hell,' said Andrea, admiring her handiwork. 'But honey, you're going to have to plait it properly if you want it to stay in. Why won't you let me plait it? It won't stay in if it's loose like that.'

'It will,' said Irie, bewitched by her own reflection. 'It's got to.'

He – Millat – need only see it once, after all, just once. To ensure she reached him in pristine state, she walked all the way to the Iqbal house with her hands on her hair, terrified that the wind would displace it.

Alsana answered the door. 'Oh, hello. No, he's not here. Out.

Don't ask me where, he doesn't tell me a thing. I know where Magid is more of the time.'

Irie walked into the hallway and caught a sneaky glance of herself in the mirror. Still there and all in the right place.

'Can I wait in here?'

'Of course. You look different, dearie. Lost weight?'

Irie glowed. 'New haircut.'

'Oh yes . . . you look like a newsreader. Very nice. Now in the living room, please. Niece-of-Shame and her nasty friend are in there, but try not to let that bother you. I'm working in the kitchen and Samad is weeding, so keep the noise down.'

Irie walked into the lounge. 'Bloody hell!' screeched Neena at the approaching vision. 'What the fuck do you look like!'

She looked beautiful. She looked straight, un-kinky. Beautiful.

'You look like a freak! Fuck me! Maxine, man, check this out. Jesus Christ, Irie. What exactly were you aiming for?'

Wasn't it obvious? Straight. Straightness. Flickability.

'I mean, what was the grand plan? The Negro Meryl Streep?' Neena folded over like a duvet and laughed herself silly.

'Niece-of-Shame!' came Alsana's voice from the kitchen. 'Sewing requires concentration. Shut it up, Miss Big-Mouth, please!'

Neena's 'nasty friend', otherwise known as Neena's girlfriend, a sexy and slender girl called Maxine with a beautiful porcelain face, dark eyes and a lot of curly brown hair, gave a pull to Irie's peculiar bangs. 'What have you done? You had *beautiful hair*, man. All curly and wild. It was gorgeous.'

Irie couldn't say anything for a moment. She had not considered the possibility that she looked anything less than terrific.

'I just had a haircut. What's the big deal?'

'But that's not *your* hair, for fuck's sake, that's some poor oppressed Pakistani woman who needs the cash for her kids,' said Neena, giving it a tug and being rewarded with a handful of it. 'OH SHIT!'

Neena and Maxine had a hysteria relapse.

'Just get *off* it, OK?' Irie retreated to an armchair and tucked her knees up under her chin. Trying to sound offhand, she asked, 'So . . . umm . . . where's Millat?'

'Is that what all this is in aid of?' asked Neena, astonished. 'My shit-for-brains cousin-gee?'

'No. Fuck off.'

'Well, he's not here. He's got some new bird. Eastern-bloc gymnast with a stomach like a washboard. Not unattractive, spectacular tits, but tight-assed as hell. Name . . . name?'

'Stasia,' said Maxine, looking up briefly from *Top of the Pops*. 'Or some such bollocks.'

Irie sank deeper into the ruined springs of Samad's favourite chair.

'Irie, will you take some advice? Ever since I've known you, you've been following that boy around like a lost dog. And in that time he's snogged everyone, *everyone* apart from you. He's even snogged *me*, and I'm his first cousin, for fuck's sake.'

'And me,' said Maxine, 'and I'm not that way inclined.'

'Haven't you ever wondered why he hasn't snogged you?'

'Because I'm ugly. And fat. With an Afro.'

'No, fuckface, because you're all he's *got*. He *needs* you. You two have history. You really *know* him. Look how confused he is. One day he's Allah this, Allah that. Next minute it's big busty blondes, Russian gymnasts and a smoke of the sinsemilla. He doesn't know his arse from his elbow. Just like his father. He doesn't know who he is. But *you* know him, at least a little, you've known all the sides of him. And he needs that. You're different.'

Irie rolled her eyes. Sometimes you want to be different. And sometimes you'd give the hair on your head to be the same as everybody else.

'Look: you're a smart cookie, Irie. But you've been taught all kinds of shit. You've got to re-educate yourself. Realize your value, stop the slavish devotion, and get a life, Irie. Get a girl, get a guy, but get a life.'

'You're a very sexy girl, Irie,' said Maxine sweetly.

'Yeah. Right.'

'Trust her, she's a raving dyke,' said Neena, ruffling Maxine's hair affectionately and giving her a kiss. 'But the truth is the Barbra Streisand cut you've got there ain't doing shit for you. The Afro was cool, man. It was wicked. It was *yours*.'

Suddenly Alsana appeared at the doorway with an enormous plate of biscuits and a look of intense suspicion. Maxine blew her a kiss.

'Biscuits, Irie? Come and have some biscuits. With me. In the kitchen.'

Neena groaned. 'Don't panic, Auntie. We're not enlisting her into the cult of Sappho.'

'I don't *care* what you're doing. I don't *know* what you're doing. I don't *want* to know such things.'

'We're watching *television*.'

It was Madonna on the TV screen, working her hands around two conically shaped breasts.

'Very nice, I'm sure,' sniped Alsana, glaring at Maxine. 'Biscuits, Irie?'

'*I'd* like some biscuits,' murmured Maxine with a flutter of her extravagant eyelashes.

'I am certain,' said Alsana slowly and pointedly, translating code, 'I don't have the kind *you* like.'

Neena and Maxine fell about all over again.

'Irie?' said Alsana, indicating the kitchen with a grimace. Irie followed her out.

'I'm as liberal as the next person,' complained Alsana, once they were alone. 'But why do they always have to be laughing and making a song-and-dance about everything? I cannot believe homosexuality is that much fun. Heterosexuality certainly is not.'

'I don't think I want to hear that word in this house again,' said Samad deadpan, stepping in from the garden and laying his weeding gloves on the table.

'Which one?'

'Either. I am trying my level best to run a godly house.'

Samad spotted a figure at his kitchen table, frowned, decided it was indeed Irie Jones and began on the little routine the two of them had going. 'Hello, Miss Jones. And how is your father?'

Irie shrugged on cue. 'You see him more than we do. How's God?'

'Perfectly fine, thank you. Have you seen my good-for-nothing son recently?'

'Not recently.'

'What about my good son?'

'Not for years.'

'Will you tell the good-for-nothing he's a good-for-nothing when you find him?'

'I'll do my best, Mr Iqbal.'

'God bless you.'

'Gesundheit.'

'Now, if you will excuse me.' Samad reached for his prayer mat from the top of the fridge and left the room.

'What's the matter with *him*?' asked Irie, noticing that Samad had delivered his lines with less than enthusiasm. 'He seems, I don't know, *sad*.'

Alsana sighed. 'He *is* sad. He feels like he has screwed everything up. Of course, he *has* screwed everything up, but then again, who will cast the first stone, et cetera. He prays and prays. But he will not look straight at the facts: Millat hanging around with God knows what kind of people, always with the white girls, and Magid . . .'

Irie remembered her first sweetheart encircled by a fuzzy halo of perfection, an illusion born of the disappointments Millat had afforded her over the years.

'Why, what's wrong with Magid?'

Alsana frowned and reached up to the top kitchen shelf, where she collected a thin airmail envelope and passed it to Irie. Irie removed the letter and the photograph inside.

The photo was of Magid, now a tall, distinguished-looking young man. His hair was the deep black of his brother's but it was not brushed forward on his face. It was parted on the left side, slicked down and drawn behind the right ear. He was dressed in a tweed suit and what looked – though one couldn't be sure, the photo was not good – like a cravat. He held a large sun hat in one hand. In the other he clasped the hand of the eminent Indian writer Sir R. V. Saraswati. Saraswati was dressed all in white, with his broad-rimmed hat on his head and an ostentatious cane in his free hand. The two of them were posed in a somewhat self-congratulatory manner, smiling broadly and looking for all the world as if they were about to pat each other roundly on the back or had just done so. The midday sun was out and bouncing off Dhaka University's front steps, where the whole scene had been captured.

Alsana inched a smear off the photo with her index finger. 'You know Saraswati?'

Irie nodded. Compulsory GCSE text: *A Stitch in Time* by R. V. Saraswati. A bitter-sweet tale of the last days of Empire.

'Samad hates Saraswati, you understand. Calls him colonial-throwback, English licker-of-behinds.'

Irie picked a paragraph at random from the letter and read aloud.

As you can see, I was lucky enough to meet India's very finest writer one bright day in March. After winning an essay competition (my title: 'Bangladesh – To Whom May She Turn?'), I travelled to Dhaka to collect my prize (a certificate and a small cash reward) from the great man himself in a ceremony at the university. I am honoured to say he took a liking to me and we spent a most pleasant afternoon together; a long, intimate tea followed by a stroll through Dhaka's more appealing prospects. During our lengthy conversations Sir Saraswati commended my mind, and even went so far as to say (and I quote) that I was 'a first-rate young man' – a comment I shall treasure! He suggested my future might lie in the law, the university, or even his own profession of the creative pen! I told him the first-mentioned vocation was closest to my heart and that it had long been my intention to make the Asian countries sensible places, where order prevailed, disaster was prepared for, and a young boy was in no danger from a falling vase (!) New laws, new stipulations, are required (I told him) to deal with our unlucky fate, the natural disaster. But then he corrected me: 'Not fate,' he said. 'Too often we Indians, we Bengalis, we Pakistanis, throw up our hands and cry "Fate!" in the face of history. But many of us are uneducated, many of us do not understand the world. We must be more like the English. The English fight fate to the death. They do not listen to history unless it is telling them what they wish to hear. We say "It had to be!" It does not have to be. Nothing does.' In one afternoon I learnt more from this great man than –

'He learns nothing!'

Samad marched back into the kitchen in a fury and threw the kettle on the stove. 'He learns nothing from a man who knows nothing! Where is his beard? Where is his khamise? Where is his humility? If Allah says there will be storm, there will be storm. If he says earthquake, it will be earthquake. Of course it has to be! That is the very reason I sent the child there – to understand that essentially we are weak, that we are not in control. What does Islam mean? What does the word, the very word, mean? *I surrender*. I surrender to God. I surrender to him. This is not my life, this is his life. This life I call mine is his to do with what he will. Indeed, I shall be tossed and turned on the wave, and there shall be nothing to be done. Nothing! Nature itself is Muslim, because it obeys the laws the creator has ingrained in it.'

'Don't you preach in this house, Samad Miah! There are places for that sort of thing. Go to mosque, but don't do it in the kitchen, people have to be eating in here –'

'But we, we do not automatically obey. We are tricky, we are the tricky bastards, we humans. We have the evil inside us, the free will. We must *learn* to obey. That is what I sent the child Magid Mahfooz Murshed Mubtasim Iqbal to discover. Tell me, did I send him to have his mind poisoned by a Rule-Britannia-worshipping Hindu old Queen?'

'Maybe, Samad Miah, maybe not.'

'Don't, Alsi, I warn you –'

'Oh, go on, you old pot-boiler!' Alsana gathered her spare tyres around her like a sumo wrestler. 'You say we have no control, yet you always try to control everything! Let *go*, Samad Miah. Let the boy go. He is second generation – he was born here – naturally he will do things differently. You can't plan everything. After all, what is so awful – so he's not training to be an alim, but he's educated, he's clean!'

'And is that all you ask of your son? That he be clean?'

'Maybe, Samad Miah, maybe –'

'And don't speak to me of second generation! One generation! Indivisible! Eternal!'

Somewhere in the midst of this argument, Irie slipped out of the kitchen and headed for the front door. She caught an unfortunate glimpse of herself in the scratch and stain of the hall mirror. She looked like the love child of Diana Ross and Engelbert Humperdinck.

'*You have to let them make their own mistakes* . . .' came Alsana's voice from the heat of battle, travelling through the cheap wood of the kitchen door and into the hallway, where Irie stood, facing her own reflection, busy tearing out somebody else's hair with her bare hands.

Like any school, Glenard Oak had a complex geography. Not that it was particularly labyrinthine in design. It had been built in two simple stages, first in 1886 as a workhouse (result: large red monstrosity, Victorian asylum) and then added to in 1963 when it became a school (result: grey monolith, Brave New Council Estate). The two monstrosities were then linked in 1974 by an enormous perspex tubular footbridge. But a bridge was not enough to make the two places one, or to slow down the student body's determination to splinter and factionalize. The school had learnt to its cost that you cannot unite a thousand children under one Latin tag (school code: *Laborare est Orare*, To Labour is to Pray); kids are like pissing cats or burrowing moles, marking off land within land, each section with its own rules, beliefs, laws of engagement. Despite every attempt to suppress it, the school contained and sustained patches, hang-outs, disputed territories, satellite states, states of emergency, ghettos, enclaves, islands. There were no maps, but common sense told you, for example, not to fuck with the area between the refuse bins and the craft department. There had been casualties there (notably some poor sod called Keith who had his head placed in a vice), and the scrawny, sinewy kids who patrolled this area were not to be messed with – they were the thin sons of the fat men with vicious tabloids primed in their back pockets like handguns, the fat men who believe in rough justice – *a life for a life, hanging's too good for them*.

Across from there: the Benches, three of them in a line. These were for the surreptitious dealing of tiny tiny amounts of drugs. Things like £2.50 of marijuana resin, so small it was likely to be lost in your pencil case and confused with a shredded piece of eraser. Or a quarter of an E, the greatest use of which was soothing particularly persistent period pains. The gullible could also purchase a variety of household goods – jasmine tea, garden grass, aspirin, liquorice, flour – all masquerading as Class A intoxicants to be smoked or swallowed round the back, in the hollow behind the drama department. This concave section of wall, depending where you stood, provided low teacher-visibility for smokers too young to smoke in the smoker's garden (a concrete garden for those who had reached sixteen and were allowed to smoke themselves silly – are there any schools *like this* any more?). The drama hollow was to be avoided. These were hard little bastards, twelve, thirteen-year-old chain-smokers; they didn't give a shit. They *really* didn't give a shit – your health, their health, teachers, parents, police – whatever. Smoking was their answer to the universe, their 42, their *raison d'être*. They were passionate about fags. Not connoisseurs, not fussy about brand, just fags, any fags. They pulled at them like babies at teats, and when they were finally finished they ground them into the mud with wet eyes. They fucking loved it. Fags, fags, fags. Their only interest outside fags was politics, or more precisely, this fucker, the chancellor, who kept on putting up the price of fags. Because there was never enough money and there were never enough fags. You had to become an expert in bumming, cadging, begging, stealing fags. A popular ploy was to blow a week's pocket money on twenty, give them out to all and sundry, and spend the next month reminding those with fags about that time when you gave them a fag. But this was a high-risk policy. Better to have an utterly forgettable face, better to be able to cadge a fag and come back five minutes after for another without being remembered. Better to cultivate a cipher-like persona, be a little featureless squib called Mart, Jules, Ian. Otherwise you had to rely on charity and fag *sharing*. One fag could be split in a myriad of ways. It worked like this: someone (whoever had actually bought a pack of fags) lights up. Someone shouts 'halves'. At the halfway point the fag is passed over. As soon as it reaches the second person we hear 'thirds', then 'saves' (which is half a third) then 'butt!', then, if the day is cold and the need for a fag overwhelming, 'last toke!' But last toke is only for the desperate; it is beyond the perforation, beyond the brand name of the cigarette, beyond what could reasonably be described as the butt. Last toke is the yellowing fabric of the roach, containing the stuff that is less than tobacco, the stuff that collects in the lungs like a time-bomb, destroys the immune system and brings permanent, sniffling, nasal flu. The stuff that turns white teeth yellow.

Everyone at Glenard Oak was at work; they were Babelians of every conceivable class and colour speaking in tongues, each in their own industrious corner, their busy censer mouths sending the votive offering of tobacco smoke to the many gods above them (Brent Schools Report 1990: 67 different faiths, 123 different languages).

Laborare est Orare:

Nerds by the pond, checking out frog sex,

Posh girls in the music department singing French rounds, speaking pig Latin, going on grape diets, suppressing lesbian instincts,

Fat boys in the PE corridor, wanking,

High-strung girls outside the language block, reading murder casebooks,

Indian kids playing cricket with tennis rackets on the football ground,

Irie Jones looking for Millat Iqbal,

Scott Breeze and Lisa Rainbow in the toilets, fucking,

Joshua Chalfen, a goblin, an elder and a dwarf, behind the science block playing *Goblins and Gorgons*,

And everybody, everybody smoking fags, fags, fags, working hard at the begging of them, the lighting of them and the inhaling of them, the collecting of butts and the remaking of them, celebrating their power to bring people together across cultures and faiths, but mostly just smoking them – *gis a fag, spare us a fag* – chuffing on them like little chimneys till the smoke grows so thick that those who had stoked the chimneys here back in 1886, back in the days of the workhouse, would not have felt out of place.

And through the fog, Irie was looking for Millat. She had tried the basketball court, the smoking garden, the music department, the cafeteria, the toilets of both sexes and the graveyard that backed on to the school. She had to warn him. There was going to be a raid, to catch all illicit smokers of weed or tobacco, a combined effort from the staff and the local constabulary. The seismic rumblings had come from Archie, angel of revelation; she had overheard his telephone conversation and the holy secrets of the Parent-Teacher Association; now Irie was landed with a burden far heavier than the seismologist, landed, rather, with the burden of the prophet, for she knew the day and time of the quake (today, two thirty), she knew its power (possible expulsion), and she knew who was likely to fall victim to its fault line. She had to save him. Clutching her vibrating chub and sweating through three inches of Afro hair, she dashed through the grounds, calling his name, inquiring of others, looking in all the usual places, but he was not with the cockney barrow-boys, the posh girls, the Indian posse or the black kids. She trudged finally to the science block, part of the old workhouse and a much loved blind-spot of the school, its far wall and Eastern corner affording thirty precious yards of grass, where a pupil indulging in illicit acts was entirely hidden from the common view. It was a fine, crisp autumn day, the place was full; Irie had to walk through the popular tonsil-tennis/groping championships, step over Joshua Chalfen's *Goblins and Gorgons* game ('Hey, watch your feet! Mind the Cavern of the Dead!') and furrow through a tight phalanx of fag smokers before she reached Millat at the epicentre of it all, pulling laconically on a cone-shaped joint, listening to a tall guy with a mighty beard.

'Mill!'

'Not right now, Jones.'

'But Mill!'

'Please, Jones. This is Hifan. Old friend. I'm trying to listen to him.'

The tall guy, Hifan, had not paused in his speech. He had a deep, soft voice like running water, inevitable and constant, requiring a force stronger than the sudden appearance of Irie, stronger maybe, than gravity, to stop it. He was dressed in a sharp black suit, a white shirt and a green bow-tie. His breast pocket was embroidered with a small emblem, two hands cupping a flame, and something underneath it, too small to see. Though no older than Millat, his hair-growing capacity was striking, and his beard aged him considerably.

'. . . and so marijuana weakens one's abilities, one's power, and takes our best men away from us in this country: men like you, Millat, who have natural leadership skills, who possess within them the ability to take a people by the hand and lift them up. There is an hadith from the Bukhārī, part five, page two: *The best people of my community are my contemporaries and supporters*. You are my contemporary, Millat, I pray you will also become my supporter; there is a war going on, Millat, a war.'

He continued like this, one word flowing from another, with no punctuation or breath and with the same chocolatey delivery – one could almost climb into his sentences, one could almost fall asleep in them.

'Mill. *Mill*. 'Simportant.'

Millat looked drowsy, whether from the hash or Hifan wasn't clear. Shaking Irie off his sleeve, he attempted an introduction. 'Irie, Hifan. Him and me used to go about together. Hifan –'

Hifan stepped forward, looming over Irie like a bell tower. 'Good to meet you, sister. I am Hifan.'

'Great. *Millat*.'

'Irie, man, *shit*. Could you just chill for *one* minute?' He passed her the smoke. 'I'm trying to listen to the guy, yeah? Hifan is the don. Look at the suit . . . gangster stylee!' Millat ran a finger down Hifan's lapel, and Hifan, against his better instinct, beamed with pleasure. 'Seriously, Hifan, man, you look wicked. Crisp.'

'Yeah?'

'Better than that stuff you used to go around in back when we used to hang, eh? Back in them Kilburn days. 'Member when we went to Bradford and –'

Hifan remembered himself. Reassumed his previous face of pious determination. 'I am afraid I don't remember the Kilburn days, brother. I did things in ignorance then. That was a different person.'

'Yeah,' said Millat sheepishly. ''Course.'

Millat gave Hifan a joshing punch on the shoulder, in response to which Hifan stood still as a gate post.

'So: there's a fucking spiritual war going on – that's fucking crazy! About time – we need to make our mark in this bloody country. What was the name, again, of your lot?'

'I am from the Kilburn branch of the Keepers of the Eternal and Victorious Islamic Nation,' said Hifan proudly.

Irie inhaled.

'*Keepers of the Eternal and Victorious Islamic Nation*,' repeated Millat, impressed. 'That's a wicked name. It's got a wicked kung-fu kick-arse sound to it.'

Irie frowned. 'KEVIN?'

'We are aware,' said Hifan solemnly, pointing to the spot underneath the cupped flame where the initials were minutely embroidered, 'that we have an acronym problem.'

'Just a bit.'

'But the name is Allah's and it cannot be changed . . . but to continue with what I was saying: Millat, my friend, you could be the head of the Cricklewood branch –'

'*Mill.*'

'You could have what I have, instead of this terrible confusion you are in, instead of this reliance on a drug specifically imported by governments to *subdue* the black and Asian community, to *lessen* our powers.'

'Yeah,' said Millat sadly, in mid-roll of a new spliff. 'I don't really look at it like that. I guess I *should* look at it like that.'

'*Mill.*'

'Jones, *give it a rest*. I'm having a fucking debate. Hifan, what school you at now, mate?'

Hifan shook his head with a smile. 'I left the English education system some time ago. But my education is far from over. If I can quote to you from the Tabrīzī, hadith number 220: *The person who goes in search of knowledge is on active service for God until he returns and the –*'

'Mill,' whispered Irie, beneath Hifan's flow of mellifluous sound. '*Mill.*'

'For *fuck's sake*. *What*? Sorry, Hifan, mate, one minute.'

Irie pulled deeply on her joint and relayed her news. Millat sighed. 'Irie, they come in one side and we go out the other. No biggie. It's a regular deal. All right? Now why don't you go and play with the kiddies? Serious business here.'

'It was good to meet you, Irie,' said Hifan, reaching out his hand and looking her up and down. 'If I might say so, it is refreshing to see a woman who dresses demurely, wearing her hair short. KEVIN believes a woman should not feel the need to pander to the erotic fantasies of Western sexuality.'

'Er, ye-ah. Thanks.'

Feeling sorry for herself and more than a bit stoned, Irie made her way back through the wall of smoke and stepped through Joshua Chalfen's *Goblins and Gorgons* game once more.

'Hey, we're trying to play here!'

Irie whipped round, full of swallowed fury. 'AND?'

Joshua's friends – a fat kid, a spotty kid and a kid with an abnormally large head – shrank back in fear. But Joshua stood his ground. He played oboe behind Irie's second viola in the excuse for a school orchestra, and he had often observed her strange hair and broad shoulders and thought he might have half a chance there. She was clever and not entirely un-pretty, and there was something in her that had a strongly nerdy flavour about it, despite that boy she spent her time with. The Indian one. She hung around him, but she wasn't *like* him. Joshua Chalfen strongly suspected her of being *one of his own*. There was something innate in her that he felt he could bring out. She was a nerd-immigrant who had fled the land of the fat, facially challenged and disarmingly clever. She had scaled the mountains of Caldor, swum the River Leviathrax, and braved the chasm Duilwen, in the mad dash away from her true countrymen to another land.

'I'm just *saying*. You seem pretty keen to step into the land of Golthon. Do you want to play with us?'

'No, I don't want to play with you, you fucking prick. I don't even *know* you.'

'Joshua Chalfen. I was in Manor Primary. And we're in English together. *And* we're in orchestra together.'

'No, we're *not*. I'm in orchestra. You're in orchestra. In no sense are we there *together*.'

The goblin, the elder and the dwarf, who appreciated a good play on words, had a snivelly giggle at that one. But insults meant nothing to Joshua. Joshua was the Cyrano de Bergerac of taking insults. He'd taken insults (from the affectionate end, *Chalfen the Chubster, Posh Josh, Josh-with-the-Jewfro*; from the other, *That Hippy Fuck, Curly-haired Cocksucker, Shit-eater*), he'd taken never-ending insults all his damn life, and survived, coming out the other side to smug. An insult was but a pebble in his path, only proving the intellectual inferiority of she who threw it. He continued regardless.

'I like what you've done with your hair.'

'Are you taking the piss?'

'No, I like short hair on girls. I like that androgyny thing. Seriously.'

'What is your fucking problem?'

Joshua shrugged. 'Nothing. The vaguest acquaintance with basic Freudian theory would suggest you are the one with the problem. Where does all that aggression come from? I thought smoking was meant to chill you out. Can I have some?'

Irie had forgotten the burning joint in her hand. 'Oh, yeah, right. Regular puff-head, are we?'

'I dabble.'

The dwarf, elder and goblin emitted some snorts and liquid noises.

'Oh, sure,' sighed Irie reaching down to pass it to him. 'Whatever.'

'Irie!'

It was Millat. He had forgotten to take his joint off Irie and was now running over to retrieve it. Irie, about to hand it over to Joshua, turning around in mid-action, at one and the same time spotted Millat coming towards her and felt a rumble in the ground, a tremor that shook Joshua's tiny cast-iron goblin army to their knees and then swept them off the board.

'What the –' said Millat.

It was the raid committee. Taking the suggestion of Parent-Governor Archibald Jones, an ex-army man who claimed expertise in the field of ambush, they had resolved to come from *both sides* (never before tested), their hundred-strong party utilizing the element of surprise, giving no pre-warning bar the sound of their approaching feet; simply boxing the little bastards in, thus cutting off any escape route for the enemy and catching the likes of Millat Iqbal, Irie Jones and Joshua Chalfen in the very act of marijuana consumption.

∽

The headmaster of Glenard Oak was in a continual state of implosion. His hairline had gone out and stayed out like a determined tide, his eye sockets were deep, his lips had been sucked backwards into his mouth, he had no body to speak of, or rather he folded what he had into a small, twisted package, sealing it with a pair of crossed arms and crossed legs. As if to counter this personal, internal collapse, the headmaster had the seating arranged in a large circle, an expansive gesture he hoped would help everybody speak to and see each other, allowing everybody to *express their point* and *make themselves heard* so together they could work towards *problem solving* rather than *behaviour chastisement*. Some parents worried the headmaster was a bleeding-heart liberal. If you asked Tina, his secretary (not that no one ever *did* ask Tina a bloody thing, oh no, no fear, only questions like *So, what are these three scallywags up for, then?*), it was more like a haemorrhage.

'So,' said the headmaster to Tina with a doleful smile, 'what are these three scallywags up for, then?'

Wearily, Tina read out the three counts of 'mari-jew-ana' possession. Irie put her hand up to object, but the headmaster silenced her with a gentle smile.

'I see. That'll be all, Tina. If you could just leave the door ajar on your way out, yes, that's it, bit more . . . *fine* – don't want anyone to feel boxed in, as it were. OK. Now. I think the most *civilized* way to do this,' said the headmaster laying his hands palm up and flat on his knees to demonstrate he was packing no weapons, 'so we don't have everybody talking over each other, is if I say my bit, you each then say your bit, starting with you, Millat, and ending with Joshua, and then once we've taken on board all that's been said, I get to say my final bit and that's it. Relatively painless. All right? All right.'

'I need a fag,' said Millat.

The headmaster rearranged himself. He uncrossed his right leg and slung his skinny left leg over instead, he brought his two forefingers up to his lips in the shape of a church spire, he retracted his head like a turtle.

'Millat, *please*.'

'Have you got a fag-tray?'

'No, now, Millat come *on* . . .'

'I'll just go an' have one at the gates, then.'

In this manner, the whole school held the headmaster to ransom. He couldn't have a thousand kids lining the Cricklewood streets, smoking fags, bringing down the tone of the school. This was the age of the league table. Of picky parents nosing their way through *The Times Educational Supplement*, summing up schools in letters and numbers and inspectors' reports. The headmaster was forced to switch off the fire alarms for terms at a time, hiding his thousand smokers within the school's confines.

'Oh . . . look, just move your chair closer to the window. Come on, come on, don't make a song and dance about it. That's it. All right?'

A Lambert & Butler hung from Millat's lips. 'Light?'

The headmaster rifled about in his own shirt pocket, where a packet of German rolling tobacco and a lighter were buried amidst a lot of tissue paper and biros.

'There you go.' Millat lit up, blowing smoke in the headmaster's direction. The headmaster coughed like an old woman. 'OK, Millat, you first. Because I expect this of *you*, at least. Spill the legumes.'

Millat said, 'I was round there, the back of the science block, on a matter of spiritual growth.'

The headmaster leant forward and tapped the church spire against his lips a few times. 'You're going to have to give me a little more to work on, Millat. If there's some religious connection here, it can only work in your favour, but I need to know about it.'

Millat elaborated, 'I was talking to my mate. Hifan.'

The headmaster shook his head. 'I'm not following you, Millat.'

'He's a spiritual leader. I was getting some advice.'

'Spiritual leader? Hifan? Is he in the school? Are we talking cult here, Millat? I need to know if we're talking cult.'

'No, it's not a bloody cult,' barked Irie exasperated. 'Can we get on with it? I've got viola in ten minutes.'

'Millat's speaking, Irie. We're listening to Millat. And hopefully when we get to you, Millat will give you a bit more respect than you've just showed him. OK? We've *got* to have communication. OK, Millat. Go on. What *kind* of spiritual leader?'

'Muslim. He was helping me with my faith, yeah? He's the head of the Cricklewood branch of the Keepers of the Eternal and Victorious Islamic Nation.'

The headmaster frowned. 'KEVIN?'

'They are aware they have an acronym problem,' explained Irie.

'So,' continued the headmaster eagerly, 'this guy from KEVIN. Was he the one who was supplying the gear?'

'No,' said Millat, stubbing his fag out on the windowsill. 'It was my gear. He was talking to me, and I was smoking it.'

'Look,' said Irie, after a few more minutes of circular conversation. 'It's very simple. It was Millat's gear. I smoked it without really thinking, then I gave it to Joshua to hold for a second while I tied my shoelace but he really had nothing to do with it. OK? Can we go now?'

'Yes, I did!'

Irie turned to Joshua. '*What?*'

'She's trying to cover for me. Some of it was my marijuana. I was dealing marijuana. Then the pigs jumped me.'

'Oh, Jesus Christ. Chalfen, you're nuts.'

Maybe. But in the past two days, Joshua had gained more respect, been patted on the back by more people, and generally lorded it around more than he ever had in his life. Some of the glamour of Millat seemed to have rubbed off on him by association, and as for Irie – well, he'd allowed a 'vague interest' to develop, in the past two days, into a full-blown crush. Wipe that. He had a full-blown crush on both of them. There was something compelling about them. More so than Elgin the dwarf or Moloch the sorcerer. He liked being connected with them, however tenuously. He had been plucked by the two of them out of nerddom, accidentally whisked from obscurity into the school spotlight. He wasn't going back without a struggle.

'Is this true, Joshua?'

'Yes . . . umm, it started small, but now I believe I have a real problem. I don't *want* to deal drugs, obviously I don't, but it's like a *compulsion* –'

'Oh, for *God's* sake . . .'

'Now, Irie, you have to let Joshua have his say. His say is as valid as your say.'

Millat reached over to the headmaster's pocket and pulled out his heavy packet of tobacco. He poured the contents out on to the small coffee table.

'Oi. Chalfen. Ghetto-boy. Measure out an eighth.'

Joshua looked at the stinking mountain of brown. 'A European eighth or an English eighth?'

'Could you just do as Millat suggests,' said the headmaster irritably, leaning forward in his chair to inspect the tobacco. 'So we can settle this.'

Fingers shaking, Joshua drew a section of tobacco on to his palm and held it up. The headmaster brought Joshua's hand up under Millat's nose for inspection.

'Barely a five-pound draw,' said Millat scornfully. 'I wouldn't buy shit from you.'

'OK, Joshua,' said the headmaster, putting the tobacco back in its pouch. 'I think we can safely say the game's up. Even *I* knew that wasn't anywhere near an eighth. But it does concern me that you felt the need to lie and we're going to have to schedule a time to talk about that.'

'Yes, sir.'

'In the meantime, I've talked to your parents, and in line with the school policy move *away* from behaviour chastisement and *towards* constructive conduct management, they've very generously suggested a two-month programme.'

'Programme?'

'Every Tuesday and Thursday, you, Millat, and you, Irie, will go to Joshua's house and join him in a two-hour after-school study group split between maths and biology, your weaker subjects and his stronger.'

Irie snorted, 'You're not serious?'

'You know, I *am* serious. I think it's a really interesting idea. This way Joshua's strengths can be shared equally amongst you, and the two of you can go to a stable environment, and one with the added advantage of keeping you both off the streets. I've talked to your parents and they are happy with the, you know, *arrangement*. And what's really exciting is that Joshua's father is something of an eminent scientist and his mother is a horticulturalist, I believe, so, you know, you'll really get a lot out of it. You two have a lot of potential, but I feel you're getting caught up with things that really are damaging to that potential – whether that's family environment or personal hassles, I don't know – but this is a really good opportunity to escape those. I hope you'll see that it's more than punishment. It's constructive. It's people helping people. And I really hope you'll do this wholeheartedly, you know? This kind of thing is very much in the history, the spirit, the whole *ethos* of Glenard Oak, ever since Sir Glenard himself.'

∽

The history, spirit and ethos of Glenard Oak, as any Glenardian worth their salt knew, could be traced back to Sir Edmund Flecker Glenard (1842–1907), whom the school had decided to remember as their kindly Victorian benefactor. The official party line stated that Glenard had donated the money for the original building out of a devoted interest in the social improvement of the disadvantaged. Rather than *workhouse*, the official PTA booklet described it as a 'shelter, workplace and educational institute' used in its time by a mixture of English and Caribbean people. According to the PTA booklet, the founder of Glenard Oak was an educational philanthropist. But then, according to the PTA booklet, 'post-class aberration consideration period' was a suitable replacement for the word 'detention'.

A more thorough investigation in the archives of the local Grange Library would reveal Sir Edmund Flecker Glenard as a successful colonial who had made a pretty sum in Jamaica farming tobacco, or rather overseeing great tracts of land where tobacco was being farmed. At the end of twenty years of this, having acquired far more money than was necessary, Sir Edmund sat back in his impressive leather armchair and asked himself if there were not something he could *do*. Something to send him into his dotage cushioned by a feeling of goodwill and worthiness. Something for the people. The ones he could see from his window. Out there in the field.

For a few months Sir Edmund was stumped. Then one Sunday, while taking a leisurely late afternoon stroll through Kingston, he heard a familiar sound that struck him differently. Godly singing. Hand-clapping. Weeping and wailing. Noise and heat and ecstatic movement coming from church after church and moving through the thick air of Jamaica like a choir invisible. Now, *there* was something, thought Sir Edmund. For, unlike many of his ex-patriot peers, who branded the singing caterwauling and accused it of being heathen, Sir Edmund had always been touched by the devotion of Jamaican Christians. He liked the idea of a jolly church, where one could sniff or cough or make a sudden movement without the vicar looking at one queerly. Sir Edmund felt certain that God, in all his wisdom, had never meant church to be a stiff-collared miserable affair as it was in Tunbridge Wells, but rather a joyous thing, a singing and dancing thing, a foot-stamping hand-clapping thing. The Jamaicans understood this. Sometimes it seemed to be the only thing they *did* understand. Stopping for a moment outside one particularly vibrant church, Sir Edmund took the opportunity to muse upon this conundrum: the remarkable difference between a Jamaican's devotion to his God in comparison to his devotion towards his employer. It was a subject he'd had cause to consider many times in the past. Only this month, as he sat in his study trying to concentrate on the problem he had set himself, his wardens came to him with news of three strikes, various men found asleep or drugged while at work, and a whole collective of mothers (Bowden women amongst them) complaining about low pay, refusing to work. Now you see, that was the rub of it, right there. You could get a Jamaican to pray any hour of the day or night, they would roll into church for any date of religious note, even the most obscure – but if you took your eye off 'em for one minute in the tobacco fields, then work ground to a halt. When they worshipped they were full of energy, moving like jumping beans, bawling in the aisles . . . yet when they worked they were sullen and uncooperative. The question so puzzled him he had written a letter on the subject to the *Gleaner* earlier in the year inviting correspondence, but received no satisfactory replies. The more Edmund thought about it, the more it became clear to him that the situation was quite the opposite in England. One was impressed by the Jamaican's faith but despairing of his work ethic and education. Vice versa, one admired the Englishman's work ethic and education but despaired of his poorly kept faith. And now, as Sir Edmund turned to go back to his estate, he realized that he was in a position to influence the situation – nay, more than that – transform it! Sir Edmund, who was a fairly corpulent man, a man who looked as if he might be hiding another man within him, practically skipped all the way home.

The very next day he wrote an electrifying letter to *The Times* and donated forty thousand pounds to a missionary group on the condition that it went towards a large property in London. Here Jamaicans could work side by side with Englishmen packaging

Sir Edmund's cigarettes and taking general instruction from the Englishmen in the evening. A small chapel was to be built as an annex to the main factory. And on Sundays, continued Sir Edmund, the Jamaicans were to take the Englishmen to church and show them what worship should look like.

The thing was built, and, after hastily promising them streets of gold, Sir Edmund shipped three hundred Jamaicans to North London. Two weeks later, from the other side of the world, the Jamaicans sent Glenard a telegraph confirming their safe arrival and Glenard sent one back suggesting a Latin motto be put underneath the plaque already bearing his name. *Laborare est Orare*. For a while, things went reasonably well. The Jamaicans were optimistic about England. They put the freezing climate to the back of their minds and were inwardly warmed by Sir Edmund's sudden enthusiasm and interest in their welfare. But Sir Edmund had always had difficulties retaining enthusiasm and interest. His mind was a small thing with big holes through which passions regularly seeped out, and *The Faith of Jamaicans* was soon replaced in the inverse sieve of his consciousness by other interests: *The Excitability of the Military Hindoo*; *The Impracticalities of the English Virgin*; *The Effect of Extreme Heat on the Sexual Proclivities of the Trinidadian*. For the next fifteen years, apart from fairly regular cheques sent by Sir Edmund's clerk, the Glenard Oak factory heard nothing from him. Then, in the 1907 Kingston earthquake, Glenard was crushed to death by a toppled marble madonna while Irie's grandmother looked on. (These are old secrets. They will come out like wisdom teeth when the time is right.) The date was unfortunate. That very month he had planned to return to British shores to see how his long-neglected experiment was doing. A letter he had written, giving the details of his travelling plans, arrived at Glenard Oak around the same time a worm, having made the two-day passage through his brain, emerged from the poor man's left ear. But though a vermiculous meal was made of him, Glenard was saved a nasty ordeal, for his experiment was doing badly. The overheads involved in shipping damp, heavy tobacco to England were impractical from the start; when Sir Edmund's subsidies dried up six months previous, the business went under, the missionary group discreetly disappeared, and the Englishmen left to go to jobs elsewhere. The Jamaicans, unable to get work elsewhere, stayed, counting down the days until the food supplies ran out. They were, by now, entirely sensible of the subjunctive mood, the nine times table, the life and times of William the Conqueror and the nature of an equilateral triangle, but they were hungry. Some died of that hunger, some were jailed for the petty crimes hunger prompts, many crept awkwardly into the East End and the English working class. A few found themselves seventeen years later at the British Empire Exhibition of 1924, dressed up as Jamaicans in the Jamaican exhibit, acting out a horrible simulacrum of their previous existence – tin drums, coral necklaces – for they were English now, more English than the English by virtue of their disappointments. All in all, then, the headmaster was wrong: Glenard could not be said to have passed on any great edifying beacon to future generations. A legacy is not something you can give or take by choice, and there are no certainties in the sticky business of inheritance. Much though it may have dismayed him, Glenard's influence turned out to be personal, not professional or educational: it ran through people's blood and the blood of their families; it ran through three generations of immigrants who could feel both abandoned and hungry even when in the bosom of their families in front of a mighty feast; and it even ran through Irie Jones of Jamaica's Bowden clan, though she didn't know it (but then somebody should have told her to keep a backward eye on Glenard; Jamaica is a small place, you can walk around it in a day, and everybody who lived there rubbed up against everybody else at one time or another).

'Do we *really* have a choice?' asked Irie.

'You've been honest with me,' said the headmaster, biting his colourless lip, 'and I want to be honest with you.'

'We don't have a choice.'

'Honestly, no. It's really that or two months of post-class aberration consideration periods. I'm afraid we have to please the people, Irie. And if we can't please all of the people all of the time, we can at least please some of – '

'Yeah, great.'

'Joshua's parents are really fascinating people, Irie. I think this whole experience is going to be really educational for you. Don't you think so, Joshua?'

Joshua beamed. 'Oh yes, sir. I really think so.'

'And you know, the exciting thing is, this could be a kind of guinea-pig project for a whole range of programmes,' said the headmaster, thinking aloud. 'Bringing children of disadvantaged or minority backgrounds into contact with kids who might have something to offer them. And there could be an exchange, vice versa. Kids teaching kids basketball, football et cetera. We could get *funding*.' At the magic word *funding*, the headmaster's sunken eyes began to disappear beneath agitated lids.

'Shit, man,' said Millat, shaking his head in disbelief. 'I need a fag.'

'Halves,' said Irie, following him out.

'See you guys on Tuesday!' said Joshua.

12 *Canines: The Ripping Teeth*

If it is not too far-fetched a comparison, the sexual and cultural revolution we have experienced these past two decades is not a million miles away from the horticultural revolution that has taken place in our herbaceous borders and sunken beds. Where once we were satisfied with our biennials, poorly coloured flowers thrusting weakly out of the earth and blooming a few times a year (if we were lucky), now we are demanding both variety and continuity in our flowers, the passionate colours of exotic blooms 365 days a year. Where once gardeners swore by the reliability of the self-pollinating plant in which pollen is transferred from the stamen to the stigma of the same flower (autogamy), now we are more adventurous, positively singing the praises of cross-pollination where pollen is transferred from one flower to another on the same plant (geitonogamy), or to a flower of another plant of the same species (xenogamy). The birds and the bees, the thick haze of pollen – these are all to be encouraged! Yes, self-pollination is the simpler and more certain of the two fertilization processes, especially for many species that colonize by copiously repeating the same parental strain. But a species cloning such uniform offspring runs the risk of having its entire population wiped out by a single evolutionary event. In the garden, as in the social and political arena, change should be the only constant. Our parents and our parents' petunias have learnt this lesson the hard way. The March of History is unsentimental, tramping over a generation and its annuals with ruthless determination.

The fact is, cross-pollination produces more varied offspring that are better able to cope with a changed environment. It is said cross-pollinating plants also tend to produce more and better-quality seeds. If my one-year-old son is anything to go by (a cross-pollination between a lapsed-Catholic horticulturalist feminist, and an intellectual Jew!), then

I can certainly vouch for the truth of this. Sisters, the bottom line is this: if we are to continue wearing flowers in our hair into the next decade, they must be hardy and ever at hand, something only the truly mothering gardener can ensure. If we wish to provide happy playgrounds for our children, and corners of contemplation for our husbands, we need to create gardens of diversity and interest. Mother Earth is great and plentiful, but even she requires the occasional helping hand!

– Joyce Chalfen, from *The New Flower Power*, pub. 1976, Caterpillar Press

Joyce Chalfen wrote *The New Flower Power* in a poky attic room overlooking her own rambling garden during the blistering summer of '76. It was an ingenuous beginning for a strange little book – more about relationships than flowers – that went on to sell well and steadily through the late seventies (not a coffee table essential by any means, but a close look at any baby-boomer's bookshelves will reveal it lying dusty and neglected near those other familiars, Dr Spock, Shirley Conran, a battered Women's Press copy of *The Third Life of Grange Copeland* by Alice Walker). The popularity of *The New Flower Power* surprised no one more than Joyce. It had practically written itself, taking only three months, most of which she spent dressed in a tiny t-shirt and a pair of briefs in an attempt to beat the heat, breast-feeding Joshua intermittently, almost absent-mindedly, and thinking to herself, between easy-flowing paragraphs, that this was *exactly* the life she had hoped for. This was the future she dared to envisage when she first saw Marcus's intelligent little eyes giving her big white legs the once-over as she crossed the quad of his Oxbridge college, miniskirted, seven years earlier. She was one of those people who knew *immediately*, at first sight, even as her future spouse opened his mouth to say an initial, nervous hello.

A very happy marriage. That summer of '76, what with the heat and the flies and the endless melodies of ice-cream vans, things happened in a haze – sometimes Joyce had to pinch herself to make sure this was real. Marcus's office was down the hall on the right; twice a day she'd pace down the corridor, Joshua on one substantial hip, nudging open the door with the other, just to check he was still there, *that he really existed*, and, leaning lustily over the desk, she'd grab a kiss from her favourite genius, hard at work on his peculiar helixes, his letters and numbers. She liked to pull him away from all that and show him the latest remarkable thing that Joshua had done or learnt; sounds, letter recognition, coordinated movement, imitation: *just like you*, she'd say to Marcus, *good genes*, he'd say to her, patting her behind and luxurious thighs, weighing each breast in his hand, patting her small belly, generally admiring his English Pear, his earth goddess . . . and then she'd be satisfied, padding back to her office like a big cat with a cub in its jaws, covered in a light layer of happy sweat. In an aimless happy way, she could hear herself murmuring, an oral version of the toilet-door doodles of adolescents: Joyce and Marcus, Marcus and Joyce.

Marcus was also writing a book that summer of '76. Not so much a book (in Joyce's sense) as a study. It was called *Chimeric Mice: An Evaluation and Practical Exploration of the Work of Brinster (1974) Concerning the Embryonic Fusion of Mouse Strains at the Eight-cell Stage of Development*. Joyce had read biology in college, but she didn't attempt to touch the many-paged manuscript that was growing like a molehill at her husband's feet. Joyce knew her limitations. She had no great desire to read Marcus's books. It was enough just to know they were being written, somehow. It was enough to know the man she had married was writing them. Her husband didn't just make money, he didn't just make things, or sell things that other people had made, he *created* beings. He went to the edges of his God's imagination and made mice Yahweh could not conceive of: mice with rabbit genes, mice with webbed feet (or so Joyce imagined, she didn't ask), mice who year after year expressed more and more eloquently

Marcus's designs: from the hit-or-miss process of selective breeding, to the chimeric fusion of embryos, and then the rapid developments that lay beyond Joyce's ken and in Marcus's future – DNA microinjection, retrovirus-mediated transgenesis (for which he came within an inch of the Nobel, 1987), embryonic stem cell-mediated gene transfer – all processes by which Marcus manipulated ova, regulated the over or under expression of a gene, planting instructions and imperatives in the germ line to be realized in physical characteristics. Creating mice whose very bodies did exactly what Marcus told them. And always with humanity in mind – a cure for cancer, cerebral palsy, Parkinson's – always with the firm belief in the *perfectibility* of all life, in the possibility of making it more efficient, more logical (for illness was, to Marcus, nothing more than bad logic on the part of the genome, just as capitalism was nothing more than bad logic on the part of the social animal), more effective, more *Chalfenist* in the way it proceeded. He expressed contempt equally towards the animal-rights maniacs – horrible people Joyce had to shoo from the door with a curtain pole when a few extremists caught wind of Marcus's dealings in mice – or the hippies or the tree people or anyone who failed to grasp the simple fact that social and scientific progress were brothers-in-arms. It was the Chalfen way, handed down the family for generations; they had a congenital inability to suffer fools gladly or otherwise. If you were arguing with a Chalfen, trying to put a case for these strange French men who think truth is a function of language, or that history is interpretive and science metaphorical, the Chalfen in question would hear you out quietly, then wave his hand, dismissive, feeling no need to dignify such bunkum with a retort. Truth was truth to a Chalfen. And Genius was genius. *Marcus created beings.* And Joyce was his wife, industrious in creating smaller versions of Marcus.

∽

Fifteen years later and Joyce would still challenge anyone to show her a happier marriage than hers. Three more children had followed Joshua: Benjamin (fourteen), Jack (twelve) and Oscar (six), bouncy, curly-haired boys, all articulate and amusing. *The Inner Life of Houseplants* (1984) and a college chair for Marcus had seen them through the eighties boom and bust, financing an extra bathroom, a conservatory and life's pleasures: old cheese, good wine, winters in Florence. Now there were two new works-in-progress: *The Secret Passions of the Climbing Rose* and *Transgenic Mice: A Study of the Inherent Limitations of DNA Microinjection (Gordon and Ruddle, 1981) in Comparison with Embryonic Stem (ES) Cell-mediated Gene Transfer (Gossler et al., 1986)*. Marcus was also working on a 'pop science' book, against his better judgement, a collaboration with a novelist that he hoped would finance at least the first two children well into their university years. Joshua was a star maths pupil, Benjamin wanted to be a geneticist just like his father, Jack's passion was psychiatry, and Oscar could checkmate his father's king in fifteen moves. And all this despite the fact that the Chalfens had sent their kids to Glenard Oak, daring to take the ideological gamble their peers guiltily avoided, those nervous liberals who shrugged their shoulders and coughed up the cash for a private education. And not only were they bright children, they were happy, not hot-housed in any way. Their only after-school activity (they despised sport) was the individual therapy five times a week at the hands of an old-fashioned Freudian called Marjorie who did Joyce and Marcus (separately) on weekends. It might appear extreme to non-Chalfens, but Marcus had been brought up with a strong respect for therapy (in his family therapy had long supplanted Judaism) and there was no arguing with the result. Every Chalfen proclaimed themselves mentally healthy and emotionally stable. The children had their oedipal complexes early and in the right order, they were all fiercely heterosexual, they adored their mother and admired their father, and, unusually, this feeling only increased as they reached adolescence. Rows were rare, playful and only ever over political or intellectual topics (the importance of anarchy, the need for higher taxes, the problem of South Africa, the soul/body dichotomy), upon which they all agreed anyway.

The Chalfens had no friends. They interacted mainly with the Chalfen extended family (the *good genes* which were so often referred to: two scientists, one mathematician, three psychiatrists and a young cousin working for the Labour Party). Under sufferance and on public holidays, they visited Joyce's long-rejected lineage, the Connor clan, *Daily Mail* letter-writers who even now could not disguise their distaste for Joyce's Israelite love-match. Bottom line: the Chalfens didn't need other people. They referred to themselves as nouns, verbs and occasionally adjectives: *It's the Chalfen way, And then he came out with a real Chalfenism, He's Chalfening again, We need to be a bit more Chalfenist about this.* Joyce challenged anyone to show her a happier family, a more Chalfenist family than theirs.

And yet, and yet . . . Joyce pined for the golden age when she was the linchpin of the Chalfen family. When people couldn't eat without her. When people couldn't dress without her assistance. Now even Oscar could make himself a snack. Sometimes there seemed nothing to improve, nothing to cultivate; recently she found herself pruning the dead sections from her rambling rose, wishing she could find some fault of Joshua's worthy of attention, some secret trauma of Jack's or Benjamin's, a perversion in Oscar. But they were all perfect. Sometimes, when the Chalfens sat round their Sunday dinner, tearing apart a chicken until there was nothing left but a tattered ribcage, gobbling silently, speaking only to retrieve the salt or the pepper – the boredom was *palpable*. The century was drawing to a close and the Chalfens were bored. Like clones of each other, their dinner table was an exercise in mirrored perfection, Chalfenism and all its principles reflecting itself infinitely, bouncing from Oscar to Joyce, Joyce to Joshua, Joshua to Marcus, Marcus to Benjamin, Benjamin to Jack ad nauseam across the meat and veg. They were still the same remarkable family they always had been. But having cut all ties with their Oxbridge peers – judges, TV execs, advertisers, lawyers, actors and other frivolous professions Chalfenism sneered at – there was no one left to admire Chalfenism itself. Its gorgeous logic, its compassion, its intellect. They were like wild-eyed passengers of *The Mayflower* with no rock in sight. Pilgrims and prophets with no strange land. They were bored, and none more than Joyce.

To fill long days left alone in the house (Marcus commuted to his college), Joyce's boredom often drove her to flick through the Chalfens' enormous supply of delivered magazines (*New Marxism, Living Marxism, New Scientist, Oxfam Report, Third World Action, Anarchist's Journal*) and feel a yearning for the bald Romanians or beautiful pot-bellied Ethiopians – yes, she knew it was *awful*, but there it was – children crying out from glossy paper, *needing* her. She needed to be needed. She'd be the first to admit it. She *hated* it, for example, when one after the other her children, pop-eyed addicts of breast milk, finally kicked the habit. She usually stretched it to two or three years, and, in the case of Joshua, four, but though the supply never ended, the demand did. She lived in dread of the inevitable moment when they moved from soft drugs to hard, the switch from calcium to the sugared delights of Ribena. It was when she finished breast-feeding Oscar that she threw herself back into gardening, back into the warm mulch where tiny things relied on her.

Then one fine day Millat Iqbal and Irie Jones walked reluctantly into her life. She was in the back garden at the time, tearfully examining her Garter Knight delphiniums (heliotrope and cobalt-blue with a jet-black centre, like a bullet hole in the sky) for signs of thrip – a nasty pest that had already butchered her bocconia. The doorbell rang. Tilting her head back, Joyce waited till she could hear the slippered feet of Marcus running down the stairs from his study and then, satisfied that he would answer it, delved back into the thick. With raised eyebrow she inspected the mouthy double blooms which stood to attention along the delphinium's eight-foot spine. *Thrip*, she said to herself out loud, acknowledging the dog-eared mutation on every other flower; *thrip*, she repeated, not without pleasure, for it would need seeing to now, and might even give rise to a book or at least a chapter; *thrip*. Joyce knew a thing or two about thrip:

Thrips, common name for minute insects that feed on a wide range of plants, enjoying in particular the warm atmosphere required for an indoor or exotic plant. Most species are no more than 1.5 mm (0.06 inch) long as adults; some are wingless, but others have two pairs of short wings fringed with hairs. Both adults and nymphs have sucking, piercing mouth parts. Although thrips pollinate some plants and also eat some insect pests, they are both boon and bane for the modern gardener and are generally considered pests to be controlled with insecticides, such as Lindex. ***Scientific classification:*** thrips make up the order Thysanoptera.

– Joyce Chalfen, *The Inner Life of Houseplants*, from the index on pests and parasites

Yes. Thrips have good *instincts*: essentially they are charitable, productive organisms which help the plant in its development. Thrips *mean well*, but thrips go too far, thrips go beyond pollinating and eating pests; thrips begin to eat the plant itself, to eat it from within. Thrip will infect generation after generation of delphiniums if you let it. What can one do about thrip if, as in this case, the Lindex hadn't worked? What can you do but prune hard, prune ruthlessly and begin from the beginning? Joyce took a deep breath. She was doing this for the delphinium. She was doing this because without her the delphinium had no chance. Joyce slipped the huge garden scissors out of her apron pocket, grabbed the screaming orange handles firmly and placed the exposed throat of a blue delphinium bloom between two slices of silver. Tough love.

'Joyce! Ja-*oyce*! Joshua and his marijuana-smoking friends are here!'

Pulchritude. From the Latin, *pulcher*, beautiful. That was the word that first struck Joyce when Millat Iqbal stepped forward on to the steps of her conservatory, sneering at Marcus's bad jokes, shading his violet eyes from a fading winter sun. Pulchritude: not just the concept but the whole physical word appeared before her as if someone had typed it on to her retina – `Pulchritude` – beauty where you would least suspect it, hidden in a word that looked like it should signify a belch or a skin infection. Beauty in a tall brown young man who should have been indistinguishable to Joyce from those she regularly bought milk and bread from, gave her accounts to for inspection, or passed her chequebook to from behind the thick glass of a bank till.

'Mill-yat Ick-Ball,' said Marcus, making a performance of the foreign syllables. 'And Irie Jones, apparently. Friends of Josh's. I was just saying to Josh, these are the best-looking friends of his we've ever seen! They're usually small and weedy, so long-sighted they're short-sighted, and with club-feet. And they're *never* female. Well!' continued Marcus jovially, dismissing Joshua's look of horror. 'It's a damn good thing you turned up. We've been looking for a woman to marry old Joshua . . .'

Marcus was standing on the garden steps, quite openly admiring Irie's breasts (though, to be fair, Irie was a good head and shoulders taller than him). 'He's a good sort, smart, a bit weak on fractals but we love him anyway. Well . . .'

Marcus paused for Joyce to come out of the garden, take off her gloves, shake hands with Millat and follow them all into the kitchen. 'You *are* a big girl.'

'Er . . . thanks.'

'We like that around here – a healthy eater. All Chalfens are healthy eaters. I don't put on a pound, but Joyce does. In all the right places, naturally. You're staying for dinner?'

Irie stood dumb in the middle of the kitchen, too nervous to speak. These were not any species of parent she recognized.

'Oh, don't worry about Marcus,' said Joshua with a jolly wink. 'He's a bit of an old letch. It's a Chalfen joke. They like to bombard you the minute you get in the door. Find out how sharp you are. Chalfens don't think there's any point in pleasantries. Joyce, this is Irie and Millat. They're the two from behind the science block.'

Joyce, partially recovered from the vision of Millat Iqbal, gathered herself together sufficiently to play her designated role as Mother Chalfen.

'So *you're* the two who've been corrupting my eldest son. I'm Joyce. Do you want some tea? So *you're* Josh's *bad crowd*. I was just pruning the delphiniums. This is Benjamin, Jack – and that's Oscar in the hallway. Strawberry and mango or normal?'

'Normal for me, thanks, Joyce,' said Joshua.

'Same, thanks,' said Irie.

'Yeah,' said Millat.

'Three normal and one mango, please, Marcus, darling, *please*.'

Marcus, who was just heading out the door with a newly packed tobacco pipe, backtracked with a weary smile. 'I'm a slave to this woman,' he said, grabbing her around the waist, like a gambler collecting his chips in circled arms. 'But if I wasn't, she might run off with any pretty young man who rolled into the house. I don't fancy falling victim to Darwinism this week.'

This hug, explicit as a hug can be, was directed front-ways-on, seemingly for the appreciation of Millat. Joyce's big milky-blue eyes were on him all the time.

'That's what you want, Irie,' said Joyce in a familial stage whisper, as if they'd known each other for five years rather than five minutes, 'a man like Marcus for the long term. These fly-by-nights are all right for fun, but what kind of fathers do they make?'

Joshua coloured. 'Joyce, she just stepped into the house! Let her have some tea!'

Joyce feigned surprise. 'I haven't embarrassed you, have I? You have to forgive Mother Chalfen, my foot and mouth are on intimate terms.'

But Irie wasn't embarrassed; she was fascinated, enamoured after five minutes. No one in the Jones household made jokes about Darwin, or said 'my foot and mouth are on intimate terms', or offered choices of tea, or let speech flow freely from adult to child, child to adult, as if the channel of communication between these two tribes was untrammelled, unblocked by history, *free*.

'Well,' said Joyce, released by Marcus and planting herself down at the circular table, inviting them to do the same, 'you look very exotic. Where are you from, if you don't mind me asking?'

'Willesden,' said Irie and Millat simultaneously.

'Yes, yes, of course, but where *originally*?'

'*Oh*,' said Millat, putting on what he called a *bud-bud-ding-ding* accent. 'You are meaning where from am I *originally*.'

Joyce looked confused. 'Yes, *originally*.'

'Whitechapel,' said Millat, pulling out a fag. 'Via the Royal London Hospital and the 207 bus.'

All the Chalfens milling through the kitchen, Marcus, Josh, Benjamin, Jack, exploded into laughter. Joyce obediently followed suit.

'Chill out, man,' said Millat, suspicious. 'It wasn't that fucking funny.'

But the Chalfens carried on. Chalfens rarely made jokes unless they were exceptionally lame or numerical in nature or both: What did the zero say to the eight? *Nice belt*.

'Are you going to smoke that?' asked Joyce suddenly when the laughter died down, a note of panic in her voice. 'In here? Only, we hate the smell. We only like the smell of German tobacco. And if we smoke it we smoke it in Marcus's room, because it upsets Oscar otherwise, doesn't it, Oscar?'

'No,' said Oscar, the youngest and most cherubic of the boys, busy building a Lego empire, 'I don't care.'

'It upsets Oscar,' repeated Joyce, in that stage-whisper again. 'He hates it.'

'I'll . . . take . . . it . . . to . . . the . . . garden,' said Millat slowly, in the kind of voice you use on the insane or foreign. 'Back . . . in . . . a . . . minute.'

As soon as Millat was out of earshot, and as Marcus brought over the teas, the years seemed to fall like dead skin from Joyce and she bent across the table like a schoolgirl. 'God, he's *gorgeous*, isn't he? Like Omar Sharif thirty years ago. Funny Roman nose. Are you and he . . . ?'

'Leave the girl alone, Joyce,' admonished Marcus. 'She's hardly going to tell you about it, is she?'

'No,' said Irie, feeling she'd like to tell these people everything. 'We're not.'

'Just as well. His parents probably have something arranged for him, no? The headmaster told me he was a Muslim boy. I suppose he should be thankful he's not a girl, though, hmm? Unbelievable what they do to the girls. Remember that *Time* article, Marcus?'

Marcus was foraging in the fridge for a cold plate of yesterday's potatoes. 'Mmm. Unbelievable.'

'But you know, just from the little I've seen, he doesn't seem at all like most Muslim children. I mean, I'm talking from personal experience, I go into a lot of schools with my gardening, working with kids of all ages. They're usually so silent, you know, terribly meek – but he's so full of . . . spunk! But boys like that want the tall blondes, don't they? I mean, that's the bottom line, when they're that handsome. I know how you feel . . . I used to like the troublemakers when I was your age, but you learn later, you really do. Danger isn't really sexy, take my word for it. You'd do a lot better with someone like Joshua.'

'Mum!'

'He's been talking about you non-stop all week.'

'Mum!'

Joyce faced her reprimand with a little smile. 'Well, maybe I'm being too frank for you young people. I don't know . . . in my day, you just were a lot more direct, you *had* to be if you wanted to catch the right man. Two hundred girls in the university and two thousand men! They were fighting for a girl – but if you were smart, you were *choosy*.'

'My, you were choosy,' said Marcus, shuffling up behind her and kissing her ear. 'And with such good *taste*.'

Joyce took the kisses like a girl indulging her best friend's younger brother.

'But your mother wasn't sure, was she? She thought I was too intellectual, that I wouldn't want children.'

'But you convinced her. Those hips would convince anyone!'

'Yes, in the end . . . but she underestimated me, didn't she? She didn't think I was Chalfen material.'

'She just didn't know you then.'

'Well, we surprised her, didn't we!'

'A lot of hard copulation went into pleasing that woman!'

'Four grandchildren later!'

During this exchange, Irie tried to concentrate on Oscar, now creating an ouroboros from a big pink elephant by stuffing the trunk into its own rear end. She'd never been so *close* to this strange and beautiful thing, the *middle class*, and experienced the kind of embarrassment that is actually intrigue, fascination. It was both strange and wondrous. She felt like the prude who walks through a nudist beach, examining the sand. She felt like Columbus meeting the exposed arawaks, not knowing where to look.

'Excuse my parents,' said Joshua. 'They can't keep their hands off each other.'

But even this was said with pride, because the Chalfen children knew their parents were rare creatures, a *happily married couple*, numbering no more than a dozen in the whole of Glenard Oak. Irie thought of her own parents, whose touches were now virtual, existing only in the absences where both sets of fingers had previously been: the remote control, the biscuit tin lid, the light switches.

She said, 'It must be great to feel that way after twenty years or whatever.'

Joyce swivelled round as if someone had released a catch. 'It's marvellous! It's incredible! You just wake up one morning and realize monogamy isn't a bind – it sets you free! And children need to grow up around that. I don't know if you've ever experienced it – you read a lot about how Afro-Caribbeans seem to find it hard to establish long-term relationships. That's terribly sad, isn't it? I wrote about one Dominican woman in *The Inner Life of Houseplants* who had moved her potted azalea through six different men's houses; once by the windowsill, then in a dark corner, then in the south-facing bedroom, etc. You just can't do that to a plant.'

This was a classic Joyce tangent, and Marcus and Joshua rolled their eyes, affectionately.

Millat, fag finished, sloped back in.

'Are we going to get some studying done, yeah? This is all very nice but I want to go out this evening. At some point.'

While Irie had been lost in her reveries assessing the Chalfens like a romantic anthropologist, Millat had been out in the garden, looking through the windows, casing the joint. Where Irie saw culture, refinement, class, intellect, Millat saw money, lazy money, money that was just hanging around this family not doing anything in particular, money in need of a good cause that might as well be him.

'So,' said Joyce, clapping her hands, trying to keep them all in the room a little longer, trying to hold off, for as long as possible, the reassertion of Chalfen silence, 'you're all going to be studying together! Well, you and Irie are really welcome. I was saying to your headmaster, wasn't I, Marcus, that this really shouldn't feel like punishment. It's not exactly a heinous crime. Between us, I used to be a pretty good marijuana gardener myself at one time . . .'

'Way *out*,' said Millat.

Nurture, thought Joyce. Be patient, water regularly and don't lose your temper when pruning.

'. . . and your headmaster explained to us how your own home environments aren't exactly . . . well . . . I'm sure you'll find it easier to work here. Such an important year, the GCSEs. And it's so obvious that you're both bright – anyone can tell that just by looking at your eyes. Can't they, Marcus?'

'Josh, your mother's asking me whether IQ expresses itself in the secondary physical characteristics of eye colour, eye shape, etc. Is there a sensible answer to this inquiry?'

Joyce pressed on. Mice and men, genes and germs, that was Marcus's corner. Seedlings, light sources, growth, nurture, the buried heart of things – that was *hers*. As on any missionary vessel, tasks were delegated. Marcus on the prow, looking for the storm. Joyce beneath deck, checking the linen for bedbugs.

'Your headmaster knows how much I hate to see potential wasted – that's why he sent you to *us*.'

'And because he knows most of the Chalfens are four hundred times smarter than him!' said Jack, doing a star jump. He was still young and hadn't yet learnt to demonstrate his pride in his family in a more socially acceptable manner. 'Even Oscar is.'

'No, I'm not,' said Oscar, kicking in a Lego garage he had recently made. 'I'm the stupidest in the world.'

'Oscar's got an IQ of 178,' whispered Joyce. 'It's a bit daunting, even when you're his mum.'

'Wow,' said Irie, turning, with the rest of the room, to appreciate Oscar trying to ingest the head of a plastic giraffe. 'That's remarkable.'

'Yes, but he's had everything, and so much of it is nurture, isn't it? I really believe that. We've just been lucky enough to give him so much and with a daddy like Marcus – it's like having a strong sunbeam shining on him twenty-four hours a day, isn't it, darling? He's so fortunate to have that. Well, they all are. Now, you may think this sounds strange, but it was always my aim to marry a man cleverer than me.' Joyce put her hands on her hips and waited for Irie to think that sounded strange. 'No, I really did. And I'm a staunch feminist, Marcus will tell you.'

'She's a staunch feminist,' said Marcus from the inner sanctum of the fridge.

'I don't suppose you can understand that – your generation have different ideas – but I knew it would be liberating. And I knew what kind of father I wanted for my children. Now, that's surprised you, hasn't it? I'm sorry, but we really *don't* do small talk around here. If you're going to be here every week, I thought it best you got a proper dose of the Chalfens now.'

All the Chalfens who were in earshot for this last comment smiled and nodded.

Joyce paused and looked at Irie and Millat the way she had looked at her Garter Knight delphinium. She was a quick and experienced detector of illness, and there was damage here. There was a quiet pain in the first one (*Irieanthus negressium marcusilia*), a lack of a father figure perhaps, an intellect untapped, a low self-esteem; and in the second (*Millaturea brandolidia joyculatus*) there was a deeper sadness, a terrible loss, a gaping wound. A hole that needed more than education or money. That needed love. Joyce longed to touch the site with the tip of her Chalfen greenfinger, close the gap, knit the skin.

'Can I ask? Your father? What does he –?'

(Joyce wondered what the parents did, what they had done.

When she found a mutated first bloom, she wanted to know where the cutting had come from. Wrong question. It wasn't the parents, it wasn't just one generation, it was the whole century. Not the bud but the bush.)

'Curry-shifter,' said Millat. 'Bus-boy. Waiter.'

'Paper,' began Irie. 'Kind of folding it . . . and working on things like perforations . . . kind of direct mail advertising but not really advertising, at least not the *ideas* end . . . kind of folding –' She gave up. 'It's hard to explain.'

'Oh yes. Yes, yes, *yes*. When there's a lack of a male role model you see . . . that's when things really go awry, in my experience. I wrote an article for *Women's Earth* recently. I described a school I worked in where I gave all the children a potted Busy Lizzie and told them to look after it for a week like a daddy or mummy looks after a baby. Each child chose which parent they were going to emulate. This lovely little Jamaican boy, Winston, chose his daddy. The next week his mother phoned and asked why I'd asked Winston to feed his plant Pepsi and put it in front of the television. I mean, it's just *terrible*, isn't it. But I think a lot of these parents just don't appreciate their children sufficiently. Partly, it's the culture, you know? It just makes me so angry. The only thing I allow Oscar to watch is *Newsround* for half an hour a day. That's more than enough.'

'Lucky Oscar,' said Millat.

'Anyway, I'm just really excited about you being here because, because, the Chalfens, I mean – it may sound peculiar, but I really wanted to persuade your headmaster this was the best idea, and now I've met you both I'm even more certain – because the *Chalfens* –'

'Know how to bring the right things out in people,' finished Joshua, 'they did with me.'

'Yes,' said Joyce, relieved her search for the words was over, radiating pride. '*Yes*.'

Joshua pushed his chair back from the table and stood up.

'Well, we'd better get down to some study. Marcus, could you come up and help us a bit later on the biology? I'm really bad at reducing the reproductive stuff in bite-size chunks.'

'Sure. I'm working on my FutureMouse, though.' This was the family joke name for Marcus's project, and the younger Chalfens sang *FutureMouse!* after him, imagining an anthropomorphic rodent in red shorts. 'And I've got to play a bit of piano with Jack first. Scott Joplin. Jack's the left hand, I'm the right. Not quite Art Tatum,' he said, ruffling Jack's hair. 'But we get by.'

Irie tried her hardest to imagine Mr Iqbal playing the right hand of Scott Joplin with his dead grey digits. Or Mr Jones turning anything into bite-size chunks. She felt her cheeks flush with the warm heat of Chalfenist revelation. So there existed fathers who dealt in the present, who didn't drag ancient history around like a chain and ball. So there were men who were not neck-high and sinking in the quagmire of the past.

'You'll stay for dinner, won't you?' pleaded Joyce. 'Oscar really wants you to stay. Oscar loves having strangers in the house, he finds it really stimulating. Especially brown strangers! Don't you, Oscar?'

'No, I don't,' confided Oscar, spitting in Irie's ear. 'I hate brown strangers.'

'He finds brown strangers really stimulating,' whispered Joyce.

∽

This has been the century of strangers, brown, yellow and white. This has been the century of the great immigrant experiment. It is only this late in the day that you can walk into a playground and find Isaac Leung by the fish pond, Danny Rahman in the football cage, Quang O'Rourke bouncing a basketball, and Irie Jones humming a tune. Children with first and last names on a direct collision course. Names that secrete within them mass exodus, cramped boats and planes, cold arrivals, medical checks.

It is only this late in the day, and possibly only in Willesden, that you can find best friends Sita and Sharon, constantly mistaken for each other because Sita is white (her mother liked the name) and Sharon is Pakistani (her mother thought it best – less trouble). Yet, despite all the mixing up, despite the fact that we have finally slipped into each other's lives with reasonable comfort (like a man returning to his lover's bed after a midnight walk), despite all this, it is still hard to admit that there is no one more English than the Indian, no one more Indian than the English. There are still young white men who are *angry* about that; who will roll out at closing time into the poorly lit streets with a kitchen knife wrapped in a tight fist.

But it makes an immigrant laugh to hear the fears of the nationalist, scared of infection, penetration, miscegenation, when this is small fry, *peanuts*, compared to what the immigrant fears – dissolution, *disappearance*. Even the unflappable Alsana Iqbal would regularly wake up in a puddle of her own sweat after a night visited by visions of Millat (genetically *BB*; where *B* stands for Bengali-ness) marrying someone called Sarah (aa where 'a' stands for Aryan), resulting in a child called Michael (*B*a), who in turn marries somebody called Lucy (aa), leaving Alsana with a legacy of unrecognizable great-grandchildren (Aaaaaa!), their Bengali-ness thoroughly diluted, genotype hidden by phenotype. It is both the most irrational and natural feeling in the world. In Jamaica it is even in the grammar: there is no choice of personal pronoun, no splits between *me* or *you* or *they*, there is only the pure, homogenous *I*. When Hortense Bowden, half white herself, got to hearing about Clara's marriage, she came round to the house, stood on the doorstep, said, 'Understand: I and I don't speak from this moment forth,' turned on her heel and was true to her word. Hortense hadn't put all that effort into marrying black, into dragging her genes back from the brink, just so her daughter could bring yet more high-coloured children into the world.

Likewise, in the Iqbal house the lines of battle were clearly drawn. When Millat brought an Emily or a Lucy back home, Alsana quietly wept in the kitchen, Samad went into the garden to attack the coriander. The next morning was a waiting game, a furious biting of tongues until the Emily or Lucy left the house and the war of words could begin. But with Irie and Clara the issue was mostly unspoken, for Clara knew she was not in a position to preach. Still, she made no attempt to disguise her disappointment or the aching sadness. From Irie's bedroom shrine of green-eyed Hollywood idols to the gaggle of white friends who regularly trooped in and out of her bedroom, Clara saw an ocean of pink skins surrounding her daughter and she feared the tide that would take her away.

It was partly for this reason that Irie didn't mention the Chalfens to her parents. It wasn't that she intended to *mate* with the Chalfens . . . but the instinct was the same. She had a nebulous fifteen-year-old's passion for them, overwhelming, yet with no real direction or object. She just wanted to, well, kind of, *merge* with them. She wanted their Englishness. Their Chalfishness. The *purity* of it. It didn't occur to her that the Chalfens were, after a fashion, immigrants too (third generation, by way of Germany and Poland, née Chalfenovsky), or that they might be as needy of her as she was of them. To Irie, the Chalfens were more English than the English. When Irie stepped over the threshold of the Chalfen house, she felt an illicit thrill, like a Jew munching a sausage or a Hindu grabbing a Big Mac. She was crossing borders, sneaking into England; it felt like some terribly mutinous act, wearing somebody else's uniform or somebody else's skin.

She just said she had netball on Tuesday evenings and left it at that.

∽

Conversation flowed at the Chalfen house. It seemed to Irie that here nobody prayed or hid their feelings in a toolbox or silently stroked fading photographs wondering what might have been. Conversation was the stuff of life.

'Hello, Irie! Come in, come in, Joshua's in the kitchen with Joyce, you're looking well. Millat not with you?'

'Coming later. He's got a *date*.'

'Ah, yes. Well, if there are any questions in your exams on oral communication, he'll fly through them. Joyce! Irie's here! So how's the study going? It's been – what? Four months now? The Chalfen genius rubbing off?'

'Yeah, not bad, not bad. I never thought I had a scientific bone in my body but . . . it seems to be working. I don't know, though. Sometimes my brain hurts.'

'That's just the right side of your brain waking up after a long sleep, getting back into the swing of things. I'm really impressed; I told you it was possible to turn a wishy-washy arts student into a science student in no time at all – oh, and I've got the FutureMouse pictures. Remind me later, you wanted to see them, no? Joyce, the big brown goddess has arrived!'

'Marcus, chill out, man . . . Hi, Joyce. Hi, Josh. Hey, Jack. Oooh, hell-low, Oscar, you cutie.'

'Hello, Irie! Come here and give me a kiss. Oscar, look, it's Irie come to see us again! Oh, look at his face . . . he's wondering where Millat is, aren't you, Oscar?'

'No, I'm not.'

'Oh dear, yes he is . . . look at his little face . . . he gets very upset when Millat doesn't turn up. Tell Irie the name of the new monkey, Oscar, the one Daddy gave you.'

'George.'

'No, not George – you called it Millat the Monkey, remember? Because monkeys are mischievous and Millat's *just as bad*, isn't he, Oscar?'

'Don't know. Don't care.'

'Oscar gets terribly upset when Millat doesn't come.'

'He'll be along in a while. He's on a *date*.'

'When isn't he on a date! All those busty girls! We might get jealous, mightn't we, Oscar? He spends more time with them than us. But we shouldn't joke. I suppose it's a bit difficult for you.'

'No, I don't mind, Joyce, really. I'm used to it.'

'But everybody loves Millat, don't they, Oscar! It's so hard not to, isn't it, Oscar? We love him, don't we, Oscar?'

'I hate him.'

'Oh, Oscar, don't say silly things.'

'Can we all stop talking about Millat, *please*.'

'Yes, Joshua, all right. Do you hear how he gets jealous? I try to explain to him that Millat needs a little extra care, you know. He's from a very difficult background. It's just like when I give more time to my peonies than my Michaelmas daisies, daisies will grow anywhere . . . you know you can be very selfish sometimes, Joshi.'

'OK, Mum, OK. What's happening with dinner – before study or after?'

'*Before*, I think, Joyce, no? I've got to work on FutureMouse all night.'

'FutureMouse!'

'Shh, Oscar, I'm trying to listen to Daddy.'

'Because I'm delivering a paper tomorrow so best have dinner early. If that's all right with you, Irie, I know how you like your food.'

'That's fine.'

'Don't say things like that, Marcus, dear, she's very touchy about her weight.'

'No, I'm really not –'

'Touchy? About her weight? But everybody likes a big girl, don't they? I know *I* do.'

'Evening all. Door was ajar. Let myself in. One day somebody's going to wander in here and murder the fucking lot of you.'

'Millat! Oscar, look it's Millat! Oscar, you're very happy to see Millat, aren't you, darling?'

Oscar screwed up his nose, pretended to barf and threw a wooden hammer at Millat's shins.

'Oscar gets *so* excited when he sees you. *Well.* You're just in time for dinner. Chicken with cauliflower cheese. Sit down. Josh, put Millat's coat somewhere. *So.* How are things?'

Millat sat down at the table with violence and eyes that looked like they had recently seen tears. He pulled out his pouch of tobacco and little bag of weed.

'Fuckin' awful.'

'Awful how?' inquired Marcus with little attention, otherwise engaged in cutting himself a chunk from an enormous block of Stilton. 'Couldn't get in girl's pants? Girl wouldn't get in your pants? Girl not wearing pants? Out of interest, what kind of pants *was* she –'

'*Dad!* Give it a *rest*,' moaned Joshua.

'Well, if you ever actually *got* in anybody's pants, Josh,' said Marcus, looking pointedly at Irie, 'I'd be able to get my kicks through *you*, but so far –'

'Shhh, the two of you,' snapped Joyce. 'I'm trying to listen to Millat.'

Four months ago, having a cool mate like Millat had seemed to Josh one hell of a lucky break. Having him round his house every Tuesday had upped Josh's ante at Glenard Oak by more than he could have imagined. And now that Millat, encouraged by Irie, had begun to come of his own accord, to come *socially*, Joshua Chalfen, né Chalfen the Chubster, should have felt his star rising. But he didn't. He felt pissed off. For Joshua had not bargained on the power of Millat's attractiveness. His magnet-like qualities. He saw that Irie was still, deep down, stuck on him like a paperclip and even his own mother seemed sometimes to take Millat as her only focus; all her energy for her gardening, her children, her husband, streamlined and drawn to this one object like so many iron filings. It pissed him off.

'I can't talk now? I can't talk in my own house?'

'Joshi, don't be silly. Millat's obviously upset . . . I'm just trying to deal with *that* at the moment.'

'Poor little Joshi,' said Millat in slow, malicious, purring tones. 'Not getting enough attention from his mummy? Want mummy to wipe his bottom for him?'

'Fuck you, Millat,' said Joshua.

'OooooooOOO . . .'

'Joyce, Marcus,' appealed Joshua, looking for an external judgement. 'Tell him.'

Marcus popped a great wedge of cheese in his mouth and shrugged his shoulders. 'I'm afwaid Miyat's oar mu'rer's jurishdicshun.'

'Let me just deal with *this* first, Joshi,' began Joyce. 'And then later . . .' Joyce allowed the rest of her sentence to get jammed in the kitchen door just as her eldest son slammed it.

'Shall I go after . . . ?' asked Benjamin.

Joyce shook her head and kissed Benjamin on the cheek. 'No, Benji. Best leave him to it.'

She turned back to Millat, touching his face, tracing the salt path of an old tear with her finger.

'*Now*. What's been going on?'

Millat began slowly rolling his spliff. He liked to make them wait. You could get more out of a Chalfen if you made them wait.

'Oh, Millat, *don't* smoke that stuff. Every time we see you these days you're smoking. It upsets Oscar *so* much. He's not that young and he understands more than you think. He understands about marijuana.'

'What's mary wana?' asked Oscar.

'You know what it is, Oscar. It's what makes Millat all horrible, like we were talking about today, and it's what kills the little brain cells he has.'

'Get off my fucking back, Joyce.'

'I'm just trying to . . .' Joyce sighed with melodrama, and drew her fingers through her hair. 'Millat, what's the matter? Do you need some money?'

'Yeah, I do, as it happens.'

'Why? What happened? *Millat*. Talk to me. Family again?'

Millat tucked the orange cardboard roach in and stuck the joint between his lips. 'Dad chucked me out, didn't he?'

'Oh God,' said Joyce, tears springing immediately, pulling her chair closer and taking his hand, 'if *I* was your mother, I'd – well, anyway I'm not, am I . . . but she's just *so* incompetent . . . it makes me *so*. . . I mean, imagine letting your husband take away one of your children and do God knows what with the other one, I just –'

'Don't talk about my mother. You've never met her. I wasn't even *talking* about her.'

'Well, she refuses to meet me, doesn't she? As if it were some kind of competition.'

'Shut the fuck up, Joyce.'

'Well, there's no point, is there? Going into . . . it upsets you to . . . I can see that, clearly, it's all too close to the . . . Marcus, get some tea, he *needs* tea.'

'For fuckssake! I don't want any *fucking* tea. All you ever do is drink tea! You lot must piss pure bloody tea.'

'Millat, I'm just try –'

'Well, don't.'

A little hash seed fell out of Millat's joint and stuck on his lips. He picked it off and popped it in his mouth. 'I could do with some brandy, though, if there is any.'

Joyce motioned to Irie with a *what can you do* look and mimed a tiny measure of her thirty-year-old Napoleon brandy between forefinger and thumb. Irie stood on an overturned bucket to get it off the top shelf.

'OK, let's all calm down. OK? OK. *So*. What happened this time?'

'I called him a cunt. He *is* a cunt.' Millat walloped Oscar's creeping fingers that were looking for a plaything and reaching speculatively for his matches. 'I'll need somewhere to stay for a bit.'

'Well, that's not even a question, you can stay at ours, naturally.'

Irie reached between the two of them, Joyce and Millat, to place the big-bottomed brandy glass on the table.

'OK, Irie, give him a little space right now, I think.'

'I was just –'

'Yes, OK, Irie – he just doesn't need crowding right at this moment –'

'He's a bloody hypocrite, man,' Millat cut in with a growl, looking into the middle distance and speaking to the conservatory as much as to anyone, 'he prays five times a day but he still drinks and he doesn't have any Muslim friends, then he has a go at me for fucking a white girl. And then he's pissed off about Magid. He takes all his shit out on me. And he wants me to stop hanging around with KEVIN. I'm more of a fucking Muslim than he is. Fuck him!'

'Do you want to talk about it with all this lot about,' said Joyce, looking meaningfully round the room. 'Or just us?'

'Joyce,' said Millat, downing his brandy in one, 'I don't give a fuck.'

Joyce took that to mean *just us* and ushered the rest of them out of the room with her eyes.

Irie was glad to leave. In the four months that she and Millat had been turning up to the Chalfens, ploughing through Double Science, band I, and eating their selection of boiled food, a strange pattern had developed. The more progress Irie made – whether in her studies, her attempts to make polite conversation or her studied imitation of Chalfenism – the less interest Joyce showed in her. Yet the more Millat veered off the rails – turning up uninvited on a Sunday night, off his face, bringing round girls, smoking weed all over the house, drinking their 1964 Dom

Perignon on the sly, pissing on the rose garden, holding a KEVIN meeting in the front room, running up a three hundred pound phone bill calling Bangladesh, telling Marcus he was queer, threatening to castrate Joshua, calling Oscar a spoilt little shit, accusing Joyce herself of being a maniac – the more Joyce adored him. In four months he already owed her over three hundred pounds, a new duvet and a bike wheel.

'Are you coming upstairs?' asked Marcus, as he closed the kitchen door on the two of them, and bent this way and that like a reed while his children blew past him. 'I've got those pictures you wanted to see.'

Irie gave Marcus a thankful smile. It was Marcus who seemed to keep an eye out for her. It was Marcus who had helped her these four months as her brain changed from something mushy to something hard and defined, as she slowly gained a familiarity with the Chalfen way of thinking. She had thought of this as a great sacrifice on the part of a busy man, but more recently she wondered if there was not some enjoyment in it. Like watching a blind man feeling out the contours of a new object, maybe. Or a laboratory rat making sense of a maze. Either way, in exchange for his attention, Irie had begun to take an interest, first strategic and now genuine, in his FutureMouse. Consequently invitations to Marcus's study at the very top of the house, by far her favourite room, had become more frequent.

'Well, don't stand there grinning like the village idiot. Come on up.'

Marcus's room was like no place Irie had ever seen. It had no communal utility, no other purpose in the house apart from being Marcus's room; it stored no toys, bric-a-brac, broken things, spare ironing boards; no one ate in it, slept in it or made love in it. It wasn't like Clara's attic space, a Xanadu of crap, all carefully stored in boxes and labelled just in case she should ever need to flee this land for another one. It wasn't like the spare rooms of immigrants – packed to the rafters with all that they have ever possessed, no matter how defective or damaged, mountains of odds and ends – that stand testament to the fact that they *have* things now, where before they had nothing.) Marcus's room was purely devoted to Marcus and Marcus's work. A study. Like in Austen or *Upstairs, Downstairs* or Sherlock Holmes. Except this was the first study Irie had ever seen in real life.

The room itself was small and irregular with a sloping floor, wooden eaves that meant it was possible to stand in certain places but not others and a skylight rather than a window which let light through in slices, spotlights for dancing dust. There were four filing cabinets, open-mouthed beasts spitting paper; paper in piles on the floor, on the shelves, in circles around the chairs. The smell of a rich, sweet Germanic tobacco sat in a cloud just above head level, staining the leaves of the highest books yellow, and there was an elaborate smoking set on a side table – spare mouthpieces, pipes ranging from the standard U-bend to ever more curious shapes, snuff boxes, a selection of gauzes – all laid out in a velvet-lined leather case like a doctor's instruments. Scattered about the walls and lining the fireplace were photos of the Chalfen clan, including comely portraits of Joyce in her pert-breasted hippy youth, a retroussé nose sneaking out between two great sheaths of hair. And then a few larger framed centrepieces. A map of the Chalfen family tree. A headshot of Mendel looking pleased with himself. A big poster of Einstein in his American icon stage – Nutty Professor hair, 'surprised' look and huge pipe – subtitled with the quote *God does not play dice with the world*. Finally, Marcus's large oaken armchair backed on to a portrait of Crick and Watson looking tired but elated in front of their model of deoxyribonucleic acid, a spiral staircase of metal clamps, reaching from the floor of their Cambridge lab to beyond the scope of the photographer's lens.

'But where's Wilkins?' inquired Marcus, bending where the ceiling got low and tapping the photo with a pencil. '1962, Wilkins won the Nobel in medicine with Crick and Watson. But no sign of Wilkins in the photos. Just Crick and Watson. Watson and Crick. History likes lone geniuses or double acts. But it's got no time for threesomes.' Marcus thought again. 'Unless they're comedians or jazz musicians.'

''Spose you'll have to be a lone genius, then,' said Irie cheerfully, turning from the picture and sitting down on a Swedish backless chair.

'Ah, but I have a *mentor*, you see.' He pointed to a poster-sized black and white photograph on the other wall. 'And mentors are a whole other kettle of fish.'

It was an extreme close-up of an extremely old man, the contours of his face clearly defined by line and shade, hachures on a topographic map.

'Grand old Frenchman, a gentleman and a scholar. Taught me practically everything I know. Seventy-odd and sharp as a whip. But you see, with a mentor you needn't credit them directly. That's the great thing about them. Now where's this bloody photo . . .'

While Marcus scrabbled about in a filing cabinet, Irie studied a small slice of the Chalfen family tree, an elaborate illustrated oak that stretched back into the 1600s and forward into the present day. The differences between the Chalfens and the Jones/Bowdens were immediately plain. For starters, in the Chalfen family everybody seemed to have a normal number of children. More to the point, everybody knew whose children were whose. The men lived longer than the women. The marriages were singular and long lasting. Dates of birth and death were concrete. And the Chalfens actually *knew* who they were in 1675. Archie Jones could give no longer record of his family than his father's own haphazard appearance on the planet in the back-room of a Bromley public house circa 1895 or 1896 or quite possibly 1897, depending on which nonagenarian ex-barmaid you spoke to. Clara Bowden knew a little about her grandmother, and half believed the story that her famed and prolific Uncle P. had thirty-four children, but could only state definitively that her own mother was born at 2.45 p.m. 14 January 1907, in a Catholic church in the middle of the Kingston earthquake. The rest was rumour, folk-tale and myth:

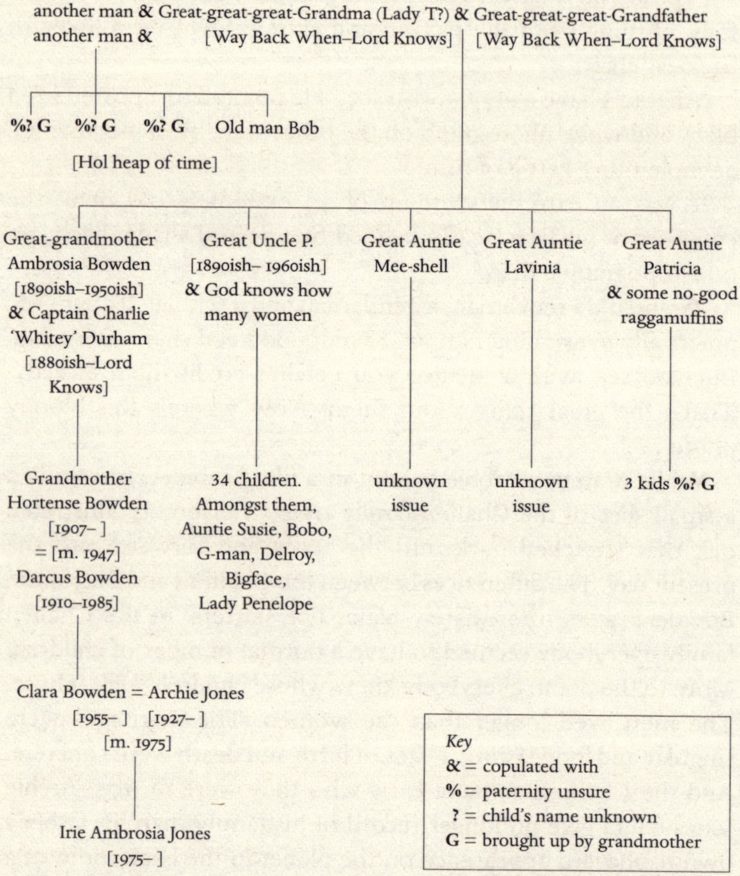

'You guys go so far back,' said Irie, as Marcus came up behind her to see what was of interest. 'It's incredible. I can't imagine what that must feel like.'

'Nonsensical statement. We all go back as far as each other. It's just that the Chalfens have always written things down,' said Marcus thoughtfully, stuffing his pipe with fresh tobacco. 'It helps if you want to be remembered.'

'I guess my family's more of an oral tradition,' said Irie with a shrug. 'But, man, you should ask Millat about his. He's the descendant of –'

'A great revolutionary. So I've heard. I wouldn't take any of that seriously, if I were you. One part truth to three parts fiction in that family, I fancy. Any historical figure of note in your lot?' asked Marcus, and then, immediately uninterested in his own question, returned to his search of filing cabinet number two.

'No . . . no one . . . *significant*. But my grandmother was born in January 1907, during the Kingston –'

'*Here* we are!'

Marcus emerged triumphant from a steel drawer, brandishing a thin plastic folder with a few pieces of paper in it.

'Photographs. Especially for you. If the animal-rights lot saw these, I'd have a contract out on my life. One by one now. Don't grab.'

Marcus passed Irie the first photo. It was of a mouse on its back. Its stomach was littered with little mushroom-like growths, brown and puffy. Its mouth was unnaturally extended, by the prostrate position, into a cry of agony. But not genuine agony, Irie thought, more like theatrical agony. More like a mouse who was making a big show of something. A ham-mouse. A luvvie-mouse. There was something sarcastic about it.

'You see, embryo cells are all very well, they help us understand the genetic elements that may contribute to cancer, but what you really want to know is how a tumour progresses in *living tissue*. I mean, you can't approximate that in a culture, not really. So then you move on to introducing chemical carcinogens in a target organ but . . .'

Irie was half listening, half engrossed in the pictures passed to her. The next one was of the same mouse, as far as she could tell, this time on its front, where the tumours were bigger. There was one on its neck that appeared practically the same size as its ear. But the mouse looked quite pleased about it. Almost as if it had purposefully grown new apparatus to hear what Marcus was saying about him. Irie was aware this was a stupid thing to think about a lab mouse. But, once again, the mouse-face had a mouse-cunning about it. There was a mouse-sarcasm in its mouse-eyes. A mouse-smirk played about its mouse-lips. *Terminal disease?* (the mouse said to Irie) *What terminal disease?*

'. . . slow and imprecise. But if you *re-engineer* the actual genome, so that *specific* cancers are expressed in *specific* tissues at *predetermined* times in the mouse's development, then you're no longer dealing with the *random*. You're *eliminating* the random actions of a mutagen. Now you're talking the *genetic program* of the mouse, a force activating oncogenes *within* cells. Now you see, this particular mouse is a young male . . .'

Now FutureMouse© was being held by his front paws by two pink giant fingers and made to stand vertical like a cartoon mouse, thus forcing his head up. He seemed to be sticking out his little pink mouse-tongue, at the cameraman initially and now at Irie. On his chin the tumours hung like big droplets of dirty rain.

'. . . and he expresses the H-ras oncogene in certain of his skin cells, so he develops multiple benign skin papillomas. Now what's interesting, of course, is young females *don't* develop it, which is . . .'

One eye was closed, the other open. Like a wink. A crafty mouse-wink.

'. . . and why? Because of inter-male rivalry – the fights lead to abrasion. Not a biological imperative but a social one. Genetic result: the same. You see? And it's only with transgenic mice, by adding experimentally to the genome, that you can understand those kind of differences. And this mouse, the one you're looking at, is a *unique* mouse, Irie. I plant a cancer and a cancer turns up precisely when I expect it. Fifteen weeks into the development. Its genetic code is *new*. New breed. No better argument for a patent, if you ask me. Or at least some kind of royalties deal: 80 per cent God, 20 per cent me. Or the other way round, depending on how good my lawyer is. Those poor bastards in Harvard are still fighting the point. I'm not interested in the patent, personally. I'm interested in the *science*.'

'Wow,' said Irie, passing back the pictures reluctantly. 'It's pretty hard to take in. I half get it and I half don't get it at all. It's just amazing.'

'Well,' said Marcus, mock humble. 'It fills the time.'

'Being able to eliminate the random . . .'

'You eliminate the random, you rule the world,' said Marcus simply. 'Why stick to oncogenes? One could program every step in the development of an organism: reproduction, food habits, life expectancy' – automaton voice, arms out like a zombie, rolling eyeballs – 'WORLD DOM-IN-A-SHUN.'

'I can see the tabloid headlines,' said Irie.

'Seriously though,' said Marcus, rearranging his photos in the folder and moving towards the cabinet to refile them, 'the study of isolated breeds of transgenic animals sheds crucial light on the random. Are you following me? One mouse sacrificed for 5.3 billion humans. Hardly mouse apocalypse. Not too much to ask.'

'No, of course not.'

'Damn! This thing is such a bloody mess!'

Marcus tried three times to shut the bottom drawer of his cabinet, and then, losing patience, levelled a kick at its steel sides. 'Bloody thing!'

Irie peered over the open drawer. 'You need more dividers,' she said decidedly. 'And a lot of the paper you're using is A3, A2 or irregular. You need some kind of folding policy; at the moment you're just shoving them in.'

Marcus threw his head back and laughed. 'Folding policy!

Well, I suppose you should know; like father like daughter.'

He crouched down by the drawer and gave it a few more pushes.

'I'm serious. I don't know how you work like that. My school shit is better organized, and I'm not in the business of World Domination.'

Marcus looked up at her from where he was kneeling. She was like a mountain range from that angle; a soft and pillowy version of the Andes.

'Look, how about this: I'll pay you fifteen quid a week if you come round twice a week and get a grip on this filing disaster. You'll learn more, and I'll get something I need done, done. Hey? What about it?'

What about it. Joyce already paid Millat a total of thirty-five quid a week for such diverse activities as baby-sitting Oscar, washing the car, weeding, doing the windows and recycling all the coloured paper. What she was really paying for, of course, was the presence of Millat. That energy around her. And that *reliance*.

Irie knew the deal she was about to make; she didn't run into it drunk or stoned or desperate or confused, as Millat did. Furthermore, she *wanted* it; she *wanted* to merge with the Chalfens, to be of one flesh; separated from the chaotic, random flesh of her own family and transgenically fused with another. A unique animal. A new breed.

Marcus frowned. 'Why all the deliberation? I'd like an answer this millennium, if you don't mind. Is it a good idea or isn't it?'

Irie nodded and smiled. 'Sure is. When do I start?'

∽

Alsana and Clara were none too pleased. But it took them a little while to compare notes and consolidate their displeasure. Clara was in night school three days a week (courses: British Imperialism 1765 to the Present; Medieval Welsh Literature; Black Feminism), Alsana was on the sewing machine all the daylight hours God gave while a family war raged around her. They talked on the phone only occasionally and saw each other even less. But both felt an independent uneasiness about the Chalfens, of whom they had gradually heard more and more. After a few months of covert surveillance, Alsana was now certain that it was to the Chalfens Millat went during his regular absences from the family home. As for Clara, she was lucky to catch Irie in on a week night, and had long ago rumbled her netball excuses. For months now it had been the Chalfens this and the Chalfens that; Joyce said this wonderful thing, Marcus is so terribly clever. But Clara wasn't one to kick up a fuss; she wanted desperately what was *best for Irie*; and she had always been convinced that sacrifice was nine tenths of parenting. She even suggested a meeting, between herself and the Chalfens, but either Clara was paranoid or Irie was doing her best to avoid it. And there was no point looking to Archibald for support. He only saw Irie in flashes – when she came home to shower, dress or eat – and it didn't seem to bother him whether she raved endlessly about the Chalfen children (*They sound nice, love*), or about something Joyce did (*Did she? That's very clever, isn't it, love?*), or something Marcus had said (*Sounds like a right old Einstein, eh, love? Well, good for you. Must dash. Meeting Sammy at O'Connell's at eight*). Archie had skin as thick as an alligator's. Being a father was such a solid genetic position in his mind (the solidest fact in Archie's life), it didn't occur to him that there might be any challenger to his crown. It was left to Clara to bite her lip alone, hope she wasn't losing her only daughter, and swallow the blood.

But Alsana had finally concluded that it was all-out war and she needed an ally. Late January '91, Christmas and Ramadan safely out of the way, she picked up the phone.

'So: you know about these Chaffinches?'

'*Chalfens*. I think the name is Chalfen. Yes, they're the parents of a friend of Irie's, I think,' said Clara disingenuously, wanting to know what Alsana knew first. 'Joshua Chalfen. They sound a nice family.'

Alsana blew air out of her nose. 'I'll call them Chaffinches – little scavenging English birds pecking at all the best seeds! Those birds do the same to my bay leaves as these people do to my boy. But they are *worse*; they are like birds with teeth, with sharp little canines – they don't just steal, they rip apart! What do you know about them?'

'Well . . . nothing, really. They've been helping Irie and Millat with their sciences, that's what she told me. I'm sure there's no harm, Alsi. And Irie's doing very well in school now. She *is* out of the house all the time, but I can't really put my foot down.'

Clara heard Alsana slap the Iqbal bannisters in fury. 'Have you *met* them? Because *I* haven't met them, and yet they feel free to give my son money and shelter as if he had neither – and bad mouth me, no doubt. *God only knows* what he is telling them about me! Who are they? I am not knowing them from Adam or Eve! Millat spends every spare minute with them and I see no particular improvement in his grades and he is still smoking the pot and sleeping with the girls. I try and tell Samad, but he's in his own world; he just won't listen. Just screams at Millat and won't speak to me. We're trying to raise the money to get Magid back and in a good school. I'm trying to keep this family together and these Chaffinches are trying to tear it apart!'

Clara bit her lip and nodded silently at the receiver.

'Are you there, lady?'

'Yes,' said Clara. 'Yes. You see, Irie, well . . . she seems to worship them. I got quite upset at first, but then I thought I was just being silly. Archie says I'm being silly.'

'If you told that potato-head there was no gravity on the moon he'd think you were being silly. We get by without his opinion for fifteen years, we'll manage without it now. Clara,' said Alsana, and her heavy breath rattled against the receiver, her voice sounded exhausted, 'we always *stand by each other* . . . I *need* you now.'

'Yes . . . I'm just thinking . . .'

'Please. Don't think. I booked a movie, old and French, like you like – two thirty today. Meet me in front of the Tricycle Theatre. Niece-of-Shame is coming too. We have tea. We talk.'

The movie was *A Bout de Souffle*. 16 mm, grey and white. Old Fords and boulevards. Turn-ups and handkerchiefs. Kisses and cigarettes. Clara loved it (Beautiful Belmondo! Beautiful Seberg! Beautiful Paris!), Neena found it too French, and Alsana couldn't understand what the bloody thing was about. 'Two young people running around France talking nonsense, killing policemen, stealing vehicles, never wearing bras. If that's European cinema, give me Bollywood every day of the week. Now, ladies, shall we get down to business?'

Neena went and collected the teas and plonked them on the little table.

'So what's all this about a conspiracy of Chaffinches? Sounds like Hitchcock.'

Alsana explained in shorthand the situation.

Neena reached into a bag for her Consulates, lit one up and exhaled minty smoke. 'Auntie, they just sound like a perfectly nice middle-class family who are helping Millat with his studies. Is that what you dragged me from work for? I mean, it's hardly Jonestown, now, is it?'

'No,' said Clara cautiously, 'no, of course not – but all your auntie is saying is that Millat and Irie spend such a lot of time over there, so we'd just like to know a bit more about what they're like, you know. That's natural enough, isn't it?'

Alsana objected. 'That is *not* all I'm saying. I am saying these people are taking my son away from me! Birds with teeth! They're Englishifying him completely! They're deliberately leading him away from his culture and his family and his religion –'

'Since when have you given two shits about his religion!'

'*You*, Niece-of-Shame, *you* don't know how I sweat *blood* for that boy, you *don't know* about –'

'Well, if I don't know anything about anything, why the bloody hell have you brought me here? I've got other fucking things to do, you know.' Neena snatched her bag and made to stand up. 'Sorry about this, Clara. I don't know why this always has to happen. I'll see you soon . . .'

'Sit down,' hissed Alsana, grabbing her by the arm. 'Sit down, all right, point made, Miss Clever Lesbian. Look, we need you, OK? Sit down, apology, apology. OK? Better.'

'All right,' said Neena, viciously stubbing out her fag on a serviette. 'But I'm going to speak my mind and for once just shut that chasm of a mouth while I do it. OK? OK. Right. Now, you just *said* Irie's doing tremendous in school, and if Millat's not doing so well, it's no great mystery – he doesn't do any *work*. At least somebody's trying to help him. And if he's seeing too much of these people, I'm sure that's *his* choice, not *theirs*. It's not exactly Happy Land in your house at the moment, is it? He's running away from himself and he's looking for something as far away from the Iqbals as possible.'

'Ah ha! But they live two roads away!' cried Alsana triumphantly.

'No, Auntie. *Conceptually* far away from you. Being an Iqbal is occasionally a little suffocating, you know? He's using this other family as a refuge. They're probably a good influence or something.'

'Or something,' said Alsana ominously.

'What are you afraid of, Alsi? He's second generation – you always say it yourself – you need to let them go their own way. Yes, and look what happened to me, blah blah blah – I may be Niece-of-Shame to you, Alsi, but I earn a good living out of my shoes.' Alsana looked dubiously at the knee-length black boots that Neena had designed, made and was wearing. 'And I live a pretty good life – you know, I live by principles. I'm just saying.

He's already having a war with uncle Samad. He doesn't need one with you as well.'

Alsana grumbled into her blackberry tea.

'If you want to worry about something, Auntie, worry about these KEVIN people he hangs around with. They're in*sane*. And there's bloody loads of them. All the ones you wouldn't expect. Mo, you know, the butcher – yes, you know – the Hussein-Ishmaels – Ardashir's side of the family. Right, well, he's one. And bloody Shiva, from the restaurant – he's converted!'

'Good for him,' said Alsana tartly.

'But it's nothing to *do* with Islam proper, Alsi. They're a political group. And some politics. One of the little bastards told me and Maxine we were going to roast in the pits of hell. Apparently we are the lowest forms of life, lower than the slugs. I gave his ball-bag a 360-degree twist. *Those* are the people you need to worry about.'

Alsana shook her head and waved Neena off with a hand. 'Can't you understand? I worry about my son being taken away from me. I have lost one already. Six years I have not seen Magid. *Six years*. And I see these people, these Chaffinches – and they spend more time with Millat than I do. Can you understand that, at least?'

Neena sighed, fiddled with a button on her top, and then, seeing the tears forming in her auntie's eyes, conceded a silent nod.

'Millat and Irie often go round there for dinner,' said Clara quietly. 'And Alsana, well, your auntie and I were wondering . . . if once you could go with them – you look young, and you seem young, and you could go and –'

'Report back,' finished Neena, rolling her eyes. 'Infiltrate the enemy. That poor family – they've no idea who they're messing with, have they? They're under surveillance and they don't even know it. It's like the bloody *Thirty-nine Steps*.'

'Niece-of-Shame: yes or no?'

Neena groaned. 'Yes, Auntie. Yes, if I must.'

'Much appreciated,' said Alsana, finishing her tea.

Now, it wasn't that Joyce was a homophobe. She liked gay men. And they liked her. She had even inadvertently amassed a little gay fan club in university, a group of men who saw her as a kind of Barbra Streisand/Bette Davis/Joan Baez hybrid and met once a month to cook her dinner and admire her dress sense. So Joyce couldn't be homophobic. But gay women . . . something confused Joyce about gay women. It wasn't that she disliked them. She just couldn't *comprehend* them. Joyce understood why men would love men; she had devoted her life to loving men, so she knew how it felt. But the idea of women loving women was so far from Joyce's cognitive understanding of the world that she couldn't *process* it. The idea of them. She just didn't *get it*. God knows, she'd made the effort. During the seventies she dutifully read *The Well of Loneliness* and *Our Bodies Ourselves* (which had a small chapter); more recently she had read *and* watched *Oranges Are Not the Only Fruit*, but none of it did her any good. She wasn't offended by it. She just couldn't see the *point*. So when Neena turned up for dinner, arm in arm with Maxine, Joyce just sat staring at the two of them over the starter (pulses on rye bread), utterly fixated. She was rendered dumbstruck for the first twenty minutes, leaving the rest of the family to go through the Chalfen routine minus her own vital bit-part. It was a little like being hypnotized or sitting in a dense cloud, and through the mist she heard snippets of dinner conversation continuing without her.

'So, always the first Chalfen question: what do you do?'

'Shoes. I make shoes.'

'Ah. Mmm. Not the material of sparkling conversation, I fear. What about the beautiful lady?'

'I'm a beautiful lady of leisure. I wear the shoes she makes.'

'Ah. Not in college, then?'

'No, I didn't bother with college. Is that OK?'

Neena was equally defensive. 'And before you ask, neither did I.'

'Well, I didn't mean to embarrass you –'

'You didn't.'

'Because it's no real surprise . . . I know you're not the most academic family in the world.'

Joyce knew things were going badly, but she couldn't find her tongue to smooth it out. A million dangerous double entendres were sitting at the back of her throat, and, if she opened her mouth even a slit (!), she feared one of them was going to come out. Marcus, who was always oblivious to causing offence, chundled on happily. 'You two are terrible temptations for a man.'

'Are we.'

'Oh, dykes always are. And I'm sure certain gentlemen would have half a chance – though you'd probably take beauty over intellect, I suspect, so there go my chances.'

'You seem awfully certain of your intellect, Mr Chalfen.'

'Shouldn't I be? I am terribly clever, you know.'

Joyce just kept looking at them, thinking: *Who relies on whom? Who teaches whom? Who improves whom? Who pollinates and who nurtures?*

'Well, it's great to have another Iqbal round the table, isn't it, Josh?'

'I'm a Begum, not an Iqbal,' said Neena.

'I can't help thinking,' said Marcus, unheeding, 'that a Chalfen man and an Iqbal woman would be a hell of a mix. Like Fred and Ginger. You'd give us sex and we'd give you sensibility or something. Hey? You'd keep a Chalfen on his toes – you're as fiery as an Iqbal. Indian passion. Funny thing about your family: first generation are all loony tunes, but the second generation have got heads just about straight on their shoulders.'

'Umm, look: no one calls my family loony, OK? Even if they are. *I'll* call them loony.'

'Now, you see, try to use the language *properly*. You can say "no one calls my family loony", but that's not a correct statement. Because people do and will. By all means say, "I don't want people to, etc." It's a small thing, but we can all understand each other better when we don't abuse terms and phrases.'

Then, just as Marcus was reaching into the oven to pull out the main course (chicken hotpot), Joyce's mouth opened and for some inexplicable reason this came out: 'Do you use each other's breasts as pillows?'

Neena's fork, which was heading for her mouth, stopped just as it reached the tip of her nose. Millat choked on a piece of cucumber. Irie struggled to bring her lower jaw back into alliance with the upper. Maxine began to giggle.

But Joyce wasn't going to go purple. Joyce was descended from the kind of bloody-minded women who continued through the African swamps even after the bag-carrying natives had dropped their load and turned back, even when the white men were leaning on their guns and shaking their heads. She was cut of the same cloth as the frontier ladies who, armed with only a bible, a shotgun and a net curtain, coolly took out the brown men moving forwards from the horizon towards the plains. Joyce didn't know the meaning of backing down. She was going to stand her ground.

'It's just, in a lot of Indian poetry, they talk about using breasts for pillows, downy breasts, pillow breasts. I just – just – just wondered, if white sleeps on brown, or, as one might expect, brown sleeps on white? Extending the – the – the – pillow metaphor, you see, I was just wondering which . . . way . . .'

The silence was long, broad and malingering. Neena shook her head in disgust and dropped her cutlery on to her plate with a clatter. Maxine tapped her fingers on the tablecloth, marking out a nervous 'William Tell'. Josh looked like he might cry.

Finally, Marcus threw his head back, clapped his hands and let out an enormous Chalfen guffaw. 'I've been wanting to ask that all night. Well *done*, Mother Chalfen!'

ꩠ

And so for the first time in her life Neena had to admit that her auntie was absolutely right. 'You wanted a report, so here's a full report: crazy, nutso, raisins short of a fruitcake, rubber walls, screaming-mad basket-cases. Every bloody one of them.'

Alsana nodded, open-mouthed, and asked Neena to repeat for the third time the bit during dessert when Joyce, serving up a trifle, had inquired whether it was difficult for Muslim women to bake while wearing those long black sheets – didn't the arm bits get covered in cake mixture? Wasn't there a danger of setting yourself alight on the gas hobs?

'Bouncing off the walls,' concluded Neena.

But, as is the way with these things, once confirmation had arrived nobody knew quite what to do with the information. Irie and Millat were sixteen and never tired of telling their respective mothers that they were now of the legal age for various activities and could do whatever, whenever. Short of putting locks on the doors and bars on the windows, Clara and Alsana were powerless. If anything, things got worse. Irie spent more time than ever immersing herself in Chalfenism. Clara noticed her wincing at her own father's conversation, and frowning at the middle-brow tabloid Clara curled up with in bed. Millat disappeared from home for weeks at a time, returning with money that was not his and an accent that modulated wildly between the rounded tones of the Chalfens and the street talk of the KEVIN clan. He infuriated Samad beyond all reason. No, that's wrong. There was a reason. Millat was neither one thing nor the other, this or that, Muslim or Christian, Englishman or Bengali; he lived for the in between, he lived up to his middle name, *Zulfikar*, the clashing of two swords:

'How many times,' Samad growled, after watching his son

purchase the autobiography of Malcolm X, 'is it necessary to say *thank you* in a single transaction? *Thank you* when you hand the book over, *thank you* when she receives it, *thank you* when she tells you the price, *thank you* when you sign the cheque, *thank you* when she takes it! They call it English politeness when it is simply arrogance. The only being who deserves this kind of thanks is Allah himself!'

And Alsana was once again caught between the two of them, trying desperately to find the middle ground. 'If Magid was here, he'd sort you two out. A lawyer's mind, he'd make things straight.' But Magid wasn't here, he was there, and there was still not enough money to change the situation.

Then the summer came and with it exams. Irie came in just behind Chalfen the Chubster, and Millat did far better than anyone, including he, had expected. It could only be the Chalfen influence, and Clara, for one, felt a little ashamed of herself. Alsana just said, 'Iqbal brains. In the end, they triumph,' and decided to mark the occasion with a joint Iqbal/Jones celebration barbecue to be held on Samad's lawn.

Neena, Maxine, Ardashir, Shiva, Joshua, aunties, cousins, Irie's friends, Millat's friends, KEVIN friends and the headmaster, all came and made merry (except for KEVIN, who formed a circle in one corner) with paper cups filled with cheap Spanish bubbly.

It was going well enough until Samad spotted the ring of folded arms and green bow-ties.

'What are *they* doing here? Who let in the infidels?'

'Well, *you're* here, aren't you?' sniped Alsana, looking at the three empty cans of Guinness Samad had already got through, the hotdog juice dribbling down his chin. 'Who's casting the first stone at a barbecue?'

Samad glared and lurched away with Archie to admire their shared handiwork on the reconstructed shed. Clara took the opportunity to pull Alsana aside and ask her a question.

Alsana stamped a foot in her own coriander. 'No! No way at

all. What should I thank her for? If he did well, it was because of his own brains. *Iqbal* brains. Not once, not *once* has that long-toothed Chaffinch even condescended to telephone me. Wild horses will have to drag my dead body, lady.'

'But . . . I just think it would be a nice idea to go and thank her for all the time she's spent with the children . . . I think maybe we misjudged her –'

'By all means, go, Lady Jones, go if you like,' said Alsana scornfully. 'But as for me, wild horses, wild horses could not do it.'

'And that's Dr Solomon Chalfen, Marcus's grandfather. He was one of the few men who would listen to Freud when everybody in Vienna thought they had a sexual deviant on their hands. An incredible face he has, don't you think? There's so much wisdom in it. The first time Marcus showed me that picture, I knew I wanted to marry him. I thought: if my Marcus looks like that at eighty I'll be a very lucky girl!'

Clara smiled and admired the daguerreotype. She had so far admired eight along the mantelpiece with Irie trailing sullenly behind her, and there were at least as many left to go.

'It's a grand old family, and if you don't find it too presumptuous, Clara – is "Clara" all right?'

'Clara's fine, Mrs Chalfen.'

Irie waited for Joyce to ask Clara to call her Joyce.

'Well, as I was saying, it's a grand old family and if you don't find it too presumptuous I like to think of Irie as a kind of addition to it, in a way. She's just *such* a remarkable girl. We've *so* enjoyed having her around.'

'She's enjoyed being around, I think. And she really owes you a lot. We all do.'

'Oh no, no, no. I believe in the Responsibility of Intellectuals . . . besides which, it's been a *joy*. Really. I hope we'll still see her, even though the exams are over. There's still A-levels, if nothing else!'

'Oh, I'm sure she'd come anyway. She talks about you all the time. The Chalfens this, the Chalfens that . . .'

Joyce clasped Clara's hands in her own. 'Oh, Clara, I *am* pleased. And I'm pleased we've finally met as well. Oh now, I hadn't finished. Where were we – oh yes, well here are Charles and Anna – great-uncles and aunts – long buried, sadly. He was a psychiatrist – yes, *another* one – and she was a plant biologist – woman after my own heart.'

Joyce stood back for a minute, like an art critic in a gallery, and put her hands on her hips. 'I mean, after a while, you've got to suspect it's in the genes, haven't you? All these brains. I mean, nurture just won't explain it. I mean, will it?'

'Er, no,' agreed Clara. 'I guess not.'

'Now, out of interest – I mean, I really am curious – which side do you think Irie gets it from, the Jamaican or the English?'

Clara looked up and down the line of dead white men in starched collars, some monocled, some uniformed, some sitting in the bosom of their family, each member manacled into position so the camera could do its slow business. They all reminded her a little of someone. Of her own grandfather, the dashing Captain Charlie Durham, in his one extant photograph: pinched and pale, looking defiantly at the camera, not so much having his picture taken as forcing his image upon the acetate. What they used to call a Muscular Christian. The Bowden family called him Whitey. Djam fool bwoy taut he owned everyting he touched.

'My side,' said Clara tentatively. 'I guess the English in my side. My grandfather was an Englishman, quite la di da, I've been told. His child, my mother, was born during the Kingston earthquake, 1907. I used to think maybe the rumble knocked the Bowden brain cells into place 'cos we been doing pretty well since then!'

Joyce saw that Clara was expecting a laugh and quickly supplied one.

'But seriously, it was probably Captain Charlie Durham. He taught my grandmother all she knew. A good English education. Lord knows, I can't think who else it could be.'

'Well, how fascinating! It's what I say to Marcus – it *is* the genes, whatever he says. He says I'm a simplifier, but he's just too theoretical. I'm proven right *all the time*!'

As the front door closed behind her, Clara bit her own lip once more, this time in frustration and anger. Why had she said Captain Charlie Durham? That was a downright lie. False as her own white teeth. Clara was smarter than Captain Charlie Durham. Hortense was smarter than Captain Charlie Durham. Probably even Grandma Ambrosia was smarter than Captain Charlie Durham. Captain Charlie Durham wasn't smart. He had thought he was, but he wasn't. He sacrificed a thousand people because he wanted to save one woman he never really knew. Captain Charlie Durham was a no-good djam fool bwoy.

13 *The Root Canals of Hortense Bowden*

A little English education can be a dangerous thing. Alsana's favourite example of this was the old tale of Lord Ellenborough, who, upon taking the Sind province from India, sent a telegram of only one word to Delhi: *peccavi*, a conjugated Latin verb, meaning *I have sinned*. 'The English are the only people,' she would say with distaste, 'who want to teach you and steal from you at the same time.' Alsana's mistrust for the Chalfens was no more or less than that.

Clara agreed but for reasons that were closer to home: a family memory; an unforgotten trace of bad blood in the Bowdens. Her own mother, when inside *her* mother (for if this story is to be told, we will have to put them all back inside each other like Russian dolls, Irie back in Clara, Clara back in Hortense, Hortense back in Ambrosia), was silent witness to what happens when all of a sudden an Englishman decides you need an education. For it had not been enough for Captain Charlie Durham – recently posted to Jamaica – to impregnate his landlady's adolescent daughter one drunken evening in the Bowden larder, May 1906. He was not satisfied with simply taking her maidenhood. He had to *teach* her something as well.

'Me? He wan' teach *me*?' Ambrosia Bowden had placed her hand over the tiny bump that was Hortense and tried to look as innocent as possible. 'Why he wan' teach me?'

'Tree times a week,' replied her mother. 'An' don' arks me why. But Lord knows, you could do wid some improvin'. Be tankful for gen'russ-ity. Dere is not required whys and wherefores when a hansum, upright English gentleman like Mr Durham wan' be gen'russ.'

Even Ambrosia Bowden, a capricious, long-legged, maga village-child who had not seen a schoolroom in all of her fourteen years, knew this advice was mistaken. When an Englishman wants to be generous, the *first* thing you ask is why, because there is always a reason.

'You still here, pickney? 'Im wan' see you. Don' let me spit pon de floor and make you get up dere before it dry!'

So Ambrosia Bowden, with Hortense inside her, had dashed up to the Captain's room and returned there three times a week thereafter for instruction. Letters, numbers, the bible, English history, trigonometry – and when that was finished, when Ambrosia's mother was safely out of the house, anatomy, which was a longer lesson, given on top of the student as she lay on her back, giggling. Captain Durham told her not to worry about the baby, he would do no damage to it. Captain Durham told her that their secret child would be the cleverest Negro boy in Jamaica.

As the months flicked by, Ambrosia learnt a lot of wonderful things from the handsome captain. He taught her how to read the trials of Job and study the warnings of Revelation, to swing a cricket bat, to recite 'Jerusalem'. How to add up a column of numbers. How to decline a Latin noun. How to kiss a man's ear until he wept like a child. But mostly he taught her that she was no longer a maidservant, that her education had elevated her, that in her heart she was a lady, though her daily chores remained unchanged. *In here, in here*, he liked to say pointing to somewhere beneath her breastbone, the exact spot, in fact, where she routinely rested her broom. *A maid no more, Ambrosia, a maid no more*, he liked to say, enjoying the pun.

And then one afternoon, when Hortense was five months unborn, Ambrosia sprinted up the stairs in a very loose, disingenuous gingham dress, rapped on the door with one hand, and hid a bunch of English marigolds behind her back with the other. She wanted to surprise her lover with flowers she knew would remind him of home. She banged and banged and called and called. But he was gone.

'Don' arks me why,' said Ambrosia's mother, eyeing her daughter's stomach with suspicion. ''Im jus' get up and go, on de sudden. But 'im leave a message dat he wan' you to be looked after still. He wan' you to go over to de estate quick time and present yourself to Mr Glenard, a good Christian gentleman. Lord knows, you could do wid some improvin'. You still here, pickney? Don' let me spit pon de floor and . . .'

But Ambrosia was out the door before the words hit the ground.

It seemed Durham had gone to control the situation in a printing company in Kingston, where a young man called Garvey was staging a printers' strike for higher wages. And then he intended to be away for three further months to train His Majesty's Trinidadian Soldiers, show them what's what. The English are experts at relinquishing one responsibility and taking up another. But they also like to think of themselves as men of good conscience, so in the interim Durham entrusted the continued education of Ambrosia Bowden to his good friend Sir Edmund Flecker Glenard, who was, like Durham, of the opinion that the natives required instruction, Christian faith and moral guidance. Glenard was charmed to have her – who wouldn't be? – a pretty, obedient girl, willing and able round the house. But two weeks into her stay, and the pregnancy became obvious. People began to talk. It simply wouldn't do.

'Don' arks *me* why,' said Ambrosia's mother, grabbing Glenard's letter of regret from her weeping daughter, 'maybe you kyan be improved! Maybe 'im don' wan' sin around de house. You back here now! Dere's nuttin' to be done now!' But in the letter, so it turned out, there was a consolatory suggestion. 'It say here 'im wan' you to go and see a Christian lady call Mrs Brenton. 'Im say you kyan stay wid her.'

Now, Durham had left instructions that Ambrosia be introduced to the English Anglican Church, and Glenard had suggested the Jamaican Methodist Church, but Mrs Brenton, a fiery Scottish spinster who specialized in lost souls, had her own ideas. 'We are going to *the Truth*,' she said decisively when Sunday came, because she did not care for the word 'church'. 'You and I and the wee innocent,' she said, tapping Ambrosia's belly just inches from Hortense's head, 'are going to hear the words of Jehovah.'

(For it was Mrs Brenton who introduced the Bowdens to the Witnesses, the Russellites, the Watchtower, the Bible Tract Society – in those days they went under many names. Mrs Brenton had met Charles Taze Russell himself in Pittsburgh as the last century turned, and was struck by the knowledge of the man, his dedication, his mighty beard. It was his influence that made her a convert from Protestantism, and, like any convert, Mrs Brenton took great pleasure in the conversion of others. She found two easy, willing subjects in Ambrosia and the child in her belly, for they had nothing to convert *from*.)

The Truth entered the Bowdens that winter of 1906 and flowed through the blood stream directly from Ambrosia to Hortense. It was Hortense's belief that at the moment her mother recognized Jehovah, Hortense herself became conscious, though still inside the womb. In later years she would swear on any bible you put in front of her that even in her mother's stomach each word of Mr Russell's *Millennial Dawn*, as it was read to Ambrosia night after night, passed as if by osmosis into Hortense's soul. Only this would explain why it felt like a 'remembrance' to read the six volumes years later in adult life; why she could cover pages with her hand and quote them from memory, though she had never read them before. It is for this reason that any root canal of Hortense must go right to the very beginning, because she was there; she remembers; the events of 14 January 1907, the day of the terrible Jamaican earthquake, are not hidden from her, but bright and clear as a bell.

'Early will I seek thee . . . My soul thirsteth for thee, my flesh longeth for thee in a dry and thirsty land, where no water is . . .'

So sang Ambrosia as her pregnancy reached full term, and she bounced with her huge bulge down King Street, praying for the return of Christ or the return of Charlie Durham – the two men who could save her – so alike in her mind she had the habit of mixing them up. She was halfway through the third verse, or so Hortense told it, when that rambunctious old rumpot Sir Edmund Flecker Glenard, flushed from one snifter too many at the Jamaica Club, stepped into their path. *Captain Durham's maid!* Hortense recalled him saying, by way of a greeting, and receiving nothing from Ambrosia but a glare, *Fine day for it, eh?* Ambrosia had tried to sidestep him, but he moved his bulk in front of her once more.

So are you a good girl these days, my dear? Gossip informs me Mrs Brenton has introduced you to her church. Very interesting, these Witness people. But are they prepared, I wonder, for this new mulatto member of their flock?

Hortense remembered well the feel of that fat hand landing hot against her mother; she remembered kicking out at it with all her might.

Oh, it's all right, child. The Captain told me your little secret. But naturally secrets have a price, Ambrosia. Just as yams and pimento and my tobacco cost something. Now, have you seen the old Spanish church, Santa Antonia? Have you been inside? It's just here. It's quite a marvel inside, from the aesthetic rather than religious point of view. It will only take a moment, my dear. One should never pass up the opportunity of a little education, after all.

Every moment happens twice: inside and outside, and they are two different histories. Outside of Ambrosia there was much white stone, no people, an altar peeling gold, little light, smoking candles, Spanish names engraved in the floor, and a large marble madonna, her head bowed, standing high upon a plinth. All was preternaturally calm as Glenard began to touch her. But inside, there was a galloping heart-beat, the crush of a million muscles that wanted desperately to repel Glenard's attempts at an education, the clammy fingers that even now were at her breast, slipping between thin cotton and squeezing nipples already heavy with milk, milk never intended for such a rough mouth. Inside she was already running down King Street. But outside Ambrosia was frozen. Rooted to the spot, as feminine a stone as any madonna.

And then the world began to shake. Inside Ambrosia, waters broke. Outside Ambrosia, the floor cracked. The far wall crumbled, the stained-glass exploded, and the madonna fell from a great height like a swooning angel. Ambrosia stumbled from the scene, making it only as far as the confessionals before the ground split once more – a mighty crack! – and she fell down, in sight of Glenard himself, who lay crushed underneath his angel, his teeth scattered on the floor, trousers round his ankles. And the ground continued to vibrate. A second crack came. And a third. The pillars fell, half the roof disappeared. Any other afternoon in Jamaica, the screams of Ambrosia, the screams that followed each contraction of her womb as Hortense pushed out, would have caught somebody's attention, brought somebody to her aid. But the world was ending that afternoon in Kingston. Everybody was screaming.

If this were a fairy-tale, it would now be time for Captain Durham to play hero. He does not seem to lack the necessary credentials. It is not that he isn't handsome, or tall or strong, or that he doesn't want to help her, or that he doesn't love her (oh, he *loves* her; just as the English loved India and Africa and Ireland; it is the love that is the problem, people treat their lovers badly) – all those things are true. But maybe it is just the scenery that is wrong. Maybe nothing that happens upon stolen ground can expect a happy ending.

For when Durham returns, the day after the initial tremors, he finds an island destroyed, two thousand already dead, fire in the hills, parts of Kingston fallen into the sea, starvation, terror, whole streets swallowed up by the earth – and none of this horrifies him as much as the realization that he might never see her again. Now he understands what love means. He stands in the parade ground, lonely and distraught, surrounded by a thousand black faces he does not recognize; the only other white figure is the statue of Victoria, five aftershocks having turned her round by degrees until she appears to have her back to the people. This is not far from the truth. It is the Americans, not the British, who have the resources to pledge serious aid, three warships full of provisions presently snaking down the coast from Cuba. It is an American publicity coup that the British government does not relish, and like his fellow Englishmen Durham cannot help but feel a certain wounded pride. He still thinks of the land as his, his to help or his to hurt, even now when it has proved itself to have a mind all of its own. He still retains enough of his English education to feel slighted when he spots two American soldiers who have docked without permission (all landings must go through Durham or his superiors) standing outside their consulate building, insolently chewing their tobacco. It is a strange feeling, this powerlessness; to discover there is another country more equipped to save this little island than the English. It is a strange feeling, looking out on to an ocean of ebony skins, unable to find the one he loves, the one he thinks he owns. For Durham has orders to stand here and call out the names of the handful of servants, butlers and maids, the chosen few the English will be taking with them to Cuba until the fires die down. If he knew her last name, God knows he would call it out. But in all that teaching, he never learnt it. He never asked.

Yet it was not for this oversight that Captain Durham, the great educator, was remembered as a *fool bwoy* in the annals of the Bowden clan. He found out soon enough where she was; he found little cousin Marlene amongst the throng, and sent her off with a note to the church hall where she had seen Ambrosia last, singing with the Witnesses, offering thanks for the Judgement Day. While Marlene ran as fast as her ashen legs would carry her, Durham walked calmly, thinking the last act was done, to King's House, the residence of Sir James Swettenham, governor of Jamaica. There he asked him to make an exception for Ambrosia—, an 'educated Negress' he wished to marry. She was not like the others. She must have a place with him on the next outgoing ship.

But if you are to rule a land that is not yours, you get used to ignoring exceptions; Swettenham told him frankly there were no spaces on his boats for black whores or livestock. Durham, hurt and vengeful, inferred that Swettenham had no power of his own, that the arrival of American ships was proof of that, and then, as a parting shot, mentioned the two American soldiers he had seen on British soil without permission, presumptuous upstarts on land they didn't own. *Does the baby go out with the bathwater*, demanded Durham, face red as a pillar-box, resorting back to the religion of possession that was his birthright, *is this not still our country? Is our authority so easily toppled by a few rumbles in the ground?*

The rest is that terrible thing: history. As Swettenham ordered the American boats to return to Cuba, Marlene came running back with Ambrosia's reply. One sentence torn from Job: *I will fetch my knowledge from afar*. (Hortense kept the bible it was ripped from and liked to say that from that day forth no Bowden woman took lessons from anyone but the Lord.) Marlene handed the sentence to Durham, and ran off into the parade ground happy as a clam, in search of her mother and father who were injured and weak, on their last legs and waiting for the boats like thousands of others. She wanted to tell them the good news, what Ambrosia had told her: *It soon come, it soon come*. The boats? Marlene had asked, and Ambrosia had nodded, though she was too busy with prayer, too ecstatic to hear the question. *It soon come, it soon come*, she said, repeating what she had learnt from Revelation; what

Durham and then Glenard and then Mrs Brenton had taught her in their different ways; what the fire and earth-cracks and thunder attested to. *It soon come*, she told Marlene, who took her word for gospel. A little English education can be a dangerous thing.

14 *More English than the English*

In the great tradition of English education, Marcus and Magid became penpals. *How* they became penpals was a matter of fierce debate (Alsana blamed Millat, Millat claimed Irie had slipped Marcus the address, Irie said Joyce had sneaked a peek in her address book – the Joyce explanation was correct), but either way they were, and from March '91 onwards letters passed between them with a frequency let down only by the chronic inadequacies of the Bengal postal system. Their combined output was incredible. Within two months they had filled a volume at least as thick as Keats's and by four were fast approaching the length and quantity of the true epistophiles, St Paul, Clarissa, Disgusted from Tunbridge Wells. Because Marcus made copies of all his own letters, Irie had to rearrange her filing system to provide a drawer solely devoted to their correspondence. She split the filing system in two, choosing to file by author primarily, then chronologically, rather than let simple dates rule the roost. Because this was all about people. People making a connection across continents, across seas. She made two stickers to separate the wads of material. The first said: *From Marcus to Magid*. The second said: *From Magid to Marcus*.

An unpleasant mixture of jealousy and animosity led Irie to abuse her secretarial role. She pinched small collections of letters that wouldn't be missed, took them home, slipped them from their sheaths, and then, after close readings that would have shamed F. R. Leavis, carefully returned them to their file. What she found in those brightly stamped airmail envelopes brought her no joy. Her mentor had a new protégé. Marcus and Magid. Magid and Marcus. It even *sounded* better. The way Watson and Crick sounded better than Watson, Crick and Wilkins.

John Donne said *more than kisses, letters mingle souls* and so they do; Irie was alarmed to find such a commingling as this, such a successful merging of two people from ink and paper despite the distance between them. No love letters could have been more ardent. No passion more fully returned, right from the very start. The first few letters were filled with the boundless joy of mutual recognition: tedious for the sneaky mailroom boys of Dhaka, bewildering to Irie, fascinating to the writers themselves:

> *It is as if I had always known you; if I were a Hindu I would suspect we met in some former life.* – Magid.
>
> *You think like me. You're precise. I like that.* – Marcus.
>
> *You put it so well and speak my thoughts better than I ever could. In my desire to study the law, in my longing to improve the lot of my poor country – which is victim to every passing whim of God, every hurricane and flood – in these aims, what instinct is fundamental? What is the root, the dream which ties these ambitions together? To make sense of the world. To eliminate the random.* – Magid.

And then there was the mutual admiration. That lasted a good few months:

> *What you are working on, Marcus – these remarkable mice – it is nothing less than revolutionary. When you delve into the mysteries of inherited characteristics, surely you go straight to the soul of the human condition as dramatically and fundamentally as any poet, except you are armed with something essential the poet does not have: the truth. I am in awe of visionary ideas and visionaries. I am in awe of such a*

man as Marcus Chalfen. I call it an honour to be able to call him friend. I thank you from the bottom of my heart for taking such an inexplicable and glorious interest in my family's welfare. – Magid.

It is incredible to me, the bloody fuss people make about an idea like cloning. Cloning, when it happens (and I can tell you it will be sooner rather than later) is simply delayed twinning, and never in my life have I come across a couple of twins who prove more decidedly the argument against genetic determinism than Millat and yourself. In every area in which he lacks, you excel – I wish I could turn that sentence around for a vice versa effect, but the hard truth is he excels in nothing apart from charming the elastic waistband off my wife's knickers. – Marcus.

And finally, there were the plans for the future, plans made blindly and with amorous speed, like the English nerd who married a nineteen-stone Mormon from Minnesota because she sounded sexy on the chat line:

You must get to England as soon as possible, early '93 at the very latest. I'll stump up some of the cash myself if I have to. Then we can enrol you in the local school, get the exams over and done with and send you off post-haste to whichever of the dreaming spires tickles your fancy (though obviously there's only one real choice) and while you're at it you can hurry up and get older, get to the bar and provide me with the kind of lawyer I need to fight in my corner. My FutureMouse© needs a staunch defender. Hurry up, old chap. I haven't got all millennium. – Marcus.

The last letter, not the last letter they wrote but the last one Irie could stomach, included this final paragraph from Marcus:

Well, things are the same round here except that my files are in excellent order, thanks to Irie. You'll like her: she's a bright girl and she has the most tremendous breasts . . . Sadly, I don't hold out much hope for her aspirations in the field of 'hard science', more specifically in my own biotechnology, which she appears to have her heart set on . . . she's sharp in a way, but it's the menial work, the hard grafting, that she's good at – she'd make a lab assistant maybe, but she hasn't any head for the concepts, no head at all. She could try medicine, I suppose, but even there you need a little bit more chutzpah than she's got . . . so it might have to be dentistry for our Irie (she could fix her own teeth at least), an honest profession no doubt, but one I hope you'll be avoiding . . .

In the end, Irie wasn't offended. She had the sniffles for a while, but they soon passed. She was like her mother, like her father – a great reinventor of herself, a great make-doer. Can't be a war correspondent? Be a cyclist. Can't be a cyclist? Fold paper. Can't sit next to Jesus with the 144,000? Join the Great Crowd. Can't stand the Great Crowd? Marry Archie. Irie wasn't so upset. She just thought, right: dentistry. I'll be a dentist. Dentistry. Right.

∽

And meanwhile Joyce was below deck trying to sort out Millat's problems with white women. Which were numerous. All women, of every shade, from midnight-black to albino, were Millat's. They slipped him phone numbers, they gave him blow jobs in public places, they crossed crowded bars to buy him a drink, they pulled him into taxis, they followed him home. Whatever it was – the Roman nose, the eyes like a dark sea, the skin like chocolate, the hair like curtains of black silk, or maybe just his pure, simple stink – it sure as hell worked. Now, don't be jealous. There's no point. There have always been and always will be people who simply exude sex (who breathe it, who *sweat* it). A few examples from thin air: the young Brando, Madonna, Cleopatra, Pam Grier, Valentino, a girl called Tamara who lives opposite the London Hippodrome, right slap in the middle of town; Imran Khan, Michelangelo's David. You can't fight that kind of marvellous indiscriminate power, for it is not always symmetry or beauty per se that does it (Tamara's nose is ever so slightly bent), and there are no means by which you can gain it. Surely the oldest American sentence is relevant here, pertinent to matters economic, politic and romantic: *you either got it or you don't*. And Millat had it. In spades. He had the choice of the known world, of every luscious female from a size 8 to a 28, Thai or Tongan, from Zanzibar to Zurich, his vistas of available and willing pussy extending in every direction as far as the eye could see. One might reasonably expect a man with such a natural gift to dip into the tun-dishes of a great variety of women, to experiment far and wide. And yet Millat Iqbal's main squeezes were almost all exclusively size 10 white Protestant women aged fifteen to twenty-eight, living in and around the immediate vicinity of West Hampstead.

Initially this neither bothered Millat nor felt unusual to him. His school was full of girls who fitted the general description. By the law of averages – as he was the only guy worth shagging in Glenard Oak – he was going to end up shagging a large proportion of them. And with Karina Cain, the present amour, things were really quite pleasant. He was only cheating on her with three other women (Alexandra Andrusier, Polly Houghton, Rosie Dew), and this was a personal record. Besides which, Karina Cain was different. It wasn't just sex with Karina Cain. He liked her and she liked him, and she had a great sense of humour, which felt like a miracle, and she looked after him when he was down and he looked after her too, in his own way, bringing her flowers and stuff. It was both the law of averages, and a lucky, random thing that had made him happier than he usually was. So that was that.

Except KEVIN didn't see it that way. One evening, after Karina had dropped him off at a KEVIN meeting in her mother's Renault, Brother Hifan and Brother Tyrone crossed Kilburn town hall like two man-mountains, determined to deliver themselves at the feet of Muhammed. They loomed large.

'Hey, Hifan, my speed, Tyrone, my man, why the long faces?'

But brothers Hifan and Tyrone wouldn't tell him why the long faces. Instead they gave him a leaflet. It was called: *Who is truly free? The Sisters of KEVIN or the Sisters of Soho?* Millat thanked them cordially for it. Then he stuffed it in the bottom of his bag.

How was that? they asked him the following week. *Was it a good read, Brother Millat?* Truth was, Brother Millat hadn't got round to reading it (and to be honest, he preferred leaflets called things like *The Big American Devil: How the United States Mafia Rules the World* or *Science versus the Creator: No Contest*), but he could see it seemed to matter to Brother Tyrone and Brother Hifan, so he said he had. They looked pleased and gave him another one. This one was called: *Lycra Liberation? Rape and the Western World*.

'Is light broaching your darkness, Brother Millat?' asked Brother Tyrone eagerly, at the following Wednesday's meeting. 'Are things becoming clearer?'

'Clearer' didn't seem to Millat to be exactly the right adjective. Earlier in the week he had set aside some time, read both leaflets and felt peculiar ever since. In three short days Karina Cain, a darling of a girl, a real good sort who never really irritated him (on the contrary, who made him feel happy! Chuffed!), had irritated him more than she had managed in the whole year they'd been shagging. And no ordinary irritation. A deep unsettleable unsolvable irritation, like an itch on a phantom limb. And it was not clear to him why.

'Yeah, man, Tyrone,' said Millat with a nod and a wide grin. 'Crystal, mate, crystal.'

Brother Tyrone nodded back. Millat was pleased to see he

looked pleased. It was like being in the real life Mafia or a Bond movie or something. Them both in their black and white suits, nodding at each other. *I understand we understand each other.*

'This is Sister Aeyisha,' said Brother Tyrone, straightening Millat's green bow-tie and pushing him towards a tiny, beautiful black girl, with almond eyes and high cheekbones. 'She's an African goddess.'

'Really?' said Millat, impressed. 'Whereabouts you from?'

'Clapham North,' said Sister Aeyisha, with a shy smile.

Millat clapped his hands together and stamped his foot. 'Oh, man, you *must* know the Redback Café?'

Sister Aeyisha the African goddess lit up. '*Yeah*, man, that was my place from way back when! You go there?'

'All the time! Wicked place. Well, maybe I'll see you round them gates sometime. It was nice to meet you, sister. Brother Tyrone, I've got to chip, man, my gal's waiting for me.'

Brother Tyrone looked disappointed. Just before Millat left, he pressed another leaflet into his hand and continued holding his hand until the paper got damp between their two palms.

'You could be a great leader of men, Millat,' said Brother Tyrone (why did everybody keep telling him that?), looking first at him, then at Karina Cain, the curve of her breasts peeping over the car door, beeping her car horn in the street. 'But at the moment you are half the man. We need the whole man.'

'Yeah, wicked, thanks, you too Brother,' said Millat, looking briefly at the leaflet, and pushing open the doors. 'Laters.'

'What's that?' asked Karina Cain, reaching over to open the passenger door and spotting the slightly soggy paper in his hand.

Instinctively, Millat put the leaflet straight in his pocket. Which was weird. He usually showed Karina everything. Now just her asking him grated somehow. And what was she wearing? Same belly top she always wore. Except wasn't it shorter? Weren't the nipples clearer, more deliberate?

He said, 'Nothing.' Grumpily. But it wasn't nothing. It was

the final leaflet in the KEVIN series on Western women. *The Right to Bare: The Naked Truth about Western Sexuality.*

Now, while we're on the subject of nakedness, Karina Cain had a nice little body. All creamy chub and slender extremities. And come the weekend she liked to wear something to show it off. First time Millat noticed her was at some local party when he saw a flash of silver pants, a silver boob-tube, and a bare mound of slightly protruding belly rising up between the two with another bit of silver in the navel. There was something welcoming about Karina Cain's little belly. She hated it, but Millat loved it. He loved it when she wore things that revealed it. But now the leaflets were making things *clearer*. He started noticing what she wore and the way other men looked at her. And when he mentioned it she said, 'Oh, I *hate* that. All those leery old men.' But it seemed to Millat that she was encouraging it; that she positively *wanted* men to look at her, that she was – as *The Right to Bare* suggested – 'prostituting herself to the male gaze'. Particularly white males. Because that's how it worked between Western men and Western women, wasn't it? They liked to do it all in public. The more he thought about it, the more it pissed him off. Why couldn't she cover up? Who was she trying to impress? African goddesses from Clapham North respected themselves, why couldn't Karina Cain? 'I can't respect you,' explained Millat carefully, making sure he repeated the words just as he had read them, 'until you respect yourself.' Karina Cain said she did respect herself, but Millat couldn't believe her. Which was odd, because he'd never known Karina Cain to lie, she wasn't the type.

When they got ready to go out somewhere, he said, 'You're not dressing for me, you're dressing for everybody!' Karina said she didn't dress for him or anybody, she dressed for herself. When she sang 'Sexual Healing' at the pub karaoke, he said, 'Sex is a private thing, between you and me, it's not for everybody!' Karina said she was *singing*, not having sex in front of the Rat and

Carrot regulars. When they made love, he said, 'Don't do that . . . don't offer it to me like a whore. Haven't you heard of unnatural acts? Besides, I'll take it if I want it – and why can't you be a lady, don't make all that noise!' Karina Cain slapped him and cried a lot. She said she didn't know what was happening to him. Problem is, thought Millat, as he slammed the door off its hinges, *neither do I.* And after that row they didn't talk for a while.

About two weeks later, he was doing a shift in the Palace for a little extra money, and he brought the matter up with Shiva, a newish convert to KEVIN and a rising star within the organization. 'Don't talk to me about white women,' groaned Shiva, wondering how many generations of Iqbals he'd have to give the same advice to. 'It's got to the point in the West where the women are men! I mean, they've got the same desires and urges as men – *they want it all the fucking time.* And they dress like they want everyone to *know* they want it. Now is that right? Is it?'

But before the debate could progress, Samad came through the double doors looking for some mango chutney and Millat returned to his chopping.

That evening after work, Millat saw a moon-faced, demure-looking Indian woman through the window of a Piccadilly café who looked, in profile, not unlike youthful pictures of his mother. She was dressed in a black polo-neck, long black trousers and her eyes were partly veiled by long black hair, her only decoration the red patterns of mhendi on the palms of her hands. She was sitting alone.

With the same thoughtless balls he used when chatting up dolly birds and disco brains, with the guts of a man who had no qualms about talking to strangers, Millat went in and started giving her the back page of *The Right to Bare* pretty much verbatim, in the hope that she'd understand. All about soulmates, about self-respect, about women who seek to bring 'visual pleasure' only to the men who love them. He explained: 'It's the liberation of the veil, innit? Look, like here: *Free from the shackles of male scrutiny and the standards of attractiveness, the woman is free to be who she is inside, immune from being portrayed as sex symbol and lusted after as if she were meat on the shelf to be picked at and looked over.* That's what we think,' he said, uncertain if that was what he thought. 'That's our opinion,' he said, uncertain whether it was his opinion. 'You see, I'm from this group –'

The lady screwed up her face and put her forefinger delicately across his lip. 'Oh, darling,' she murmured sadly, admiring his beauty. 'If I give you money, will you go away?'

And then her boyfriend turned up, a surprisingly tall Chinese guy in a leather jacket.

Deep in a blue funk, Millat resolved to walk the eight miles home, beginning in Soho, glaring at the leggy whores and the crotchless knickers and the feather boas. By the time he reached Marble Arch he had worked himself into such a rage he called Karina Cain from a phonebox plastered with tits and ass (whores, whores, whores) and dumped her unceremoniously. He didn't mind about the other girls he was shagging (Alexandra Andrusier, Polly Houghton, Rosie Dew) because they were straight up, posh-totty slags. But he minded about Karina Cain, because she was his *love*, and his love should be his love and nobody else's. Protected like Liotta's wife in *GoodFellas* or Pacino's sister in *Scarface*. Treated like a princess. Behaving like a princess. In a tower. Covered up.

Walking slower now, dragging his heels, there being nobody to go home to, he got waylaid in the Edgware Road, the old fat guys calling him over ('Look, it's Millat, little Millat the Ladies' Man! Millat the Prince of Pussy-pokers! Too big to have a smoke is he, now?') and gave in with a rueful smile. Hookah pipes, halal fried chicken and illegally imported absinthe consumed around wobbling outdoor tables; watching the women hurry by in full purdah, like busy black ghosts haunting the streets, late-night shopping, looking for their errant husbands. Millat liked to watch them go: the animated talk, the exquisite colours of the communicative eyes, the bursts of laughter from invisible lips. He remembered something his father once told him back when they used to speak to each other. You do not know the meaning of the erotic, Millat, you do not know the meaning of *desire*, my second son, until you have sat on the Edgware Road with a bubbling pipe, using all the powers of your imagination to visualize what is beyond the four inches of skin hajib reveals, what is under those great sable sheets.

About six hours later Millat turned up at the Chalfen kitchen table, very, very drunk, weepy and violent. He destroyed Oscar's Lego fire station and threw the coffee machine across the room. Then he did what Joyce had been waiting for these twelve months. He asked her advice.

It seemed like months had been spent across that kitchen table since then, Joyce shooing people out of the room, going through her reading material, wringing her hands; the smell of dope mingling with the steam that rose off endless cups of strawberry tea. For Joyce truly loved him and wanted to help him, but her advice was long and complex. She had read up on the subject. And it appeared Millat was filled with self-revulsion and hatred of his own kind; that he had possibly a slave mentality, or maybe a colour-complex centred around his mother (he was far darker than she), or a wish for his own annihilation by means of dilution in a white gene pool, or an inability to reconcile two opposing cultures . . . and it emerged that 60 per cent of Asian men did *this* . . . and 90 per cent of Muslims felt *that* . . . it was a known fact that Asian families were often . . . and hormonally boys were more likely to . . . and the therapist she'd found him was really very nice, three days a week and don't worry about the money . . . and don't worry about Joshua, he's just sulking . . . and, and, *and*.

Way-back-when in the fuddle of the hash and the talk Millat remembered a girl called Karina Somethingoranother whom he had liked. And she liked him. And she had a great sense of humour which felt like a miracle, and she looked after him when he was down and he looked after her too, in his own way, bringing her flowers and stuff. She seemed distant now, like conker fights and childhood. And that was that.

∽

There was trouble at the Joneses. Irie was about to become the first Bowden or Jones (possibly, maybe, all things willing, by the grace of God, fingers crossed) to enter a university. Her A-levels were chemistry, biology and religious studies. She wanted to study dentistry (white collar! £20k+ !), which everyone was very pleased about, but she also wanted to take a 'year off' in the subcontinent and Africa (Malaria! Poverty! Tapeworm!), which led to three months of open warfare between her and Clara. One side wanted finance and permission, the other side was resolved to concede neither. The conflict was protracted and bitter, and all mediators were sent home empty-handed (*She has made up her mind, there are no arguments to be had with the woman* – Samad) or else embroiled in the war of words (*Why can't she go to Bangladesh if she wants to? Are you saying my country is not good enough for your daughter?* – Alsana).

The stalemate was so pronounced that land had been divided and allocated; Irie claimed her bedroom and the attic, Archie, a conscientious objector, asked only for the spare room, a television and a satellite (state) dish, and Clara took everything else, with the bathroom acting as shared territory. Doors were slammed. The time for talking was over.

On the 25th of October 1991, 01.00 hours, Irie embarked upon a late-night attack. She knew from experience that her mother was most vulnerable when in bed; late at night she spoke softly like a child, her fatigue gave her a pronounced lisp; it was at this point that you were most likely to get whatever it was you'd been pining for: pocket money, a new bike, a later curfew. It was such a well-worn tactic that until now Irie had not considered it worthy of this, her fiercest and longest dispute with her mother. But she hadn't any better ideas.

'Irie? Wha –? Iss sa middle of sa nice . . . Go back koo bed . . .'

Irie opened the door further, letting yet more hall light flood the bedroom.

Archie submerged his head in a pillow. 'Bloody hell, love, it's one in the morning! Some of us have got work tomorrow.'

'I want to talk to Mum,' said Irie firmly, walking to the end of the bed. 'She won't talk to me during the day, so I'm reduced to this.'

'Irie, pleaze . . . I'm exhaushed . . . I'm shrying koo gesh shome shleep.'

'I don't just *want* to have a year off, I *need* one. It's essential – I'm young, I want some experiences. I've lived in this bloody suburb all my life. Everyone's the same here. I want to go and see the people of the world . . . that's what Joshua's doing and *his* parents support him!'

'Well, we can't bloody afford it,' grumbled Archie, emerging from the eiderdown. 'We haven't all got posh jobs in science, now have we?'

'I don't *care* about the money – I'll get a job, somehow or something, but I do want your permission! *Both* of you. I don't want to spend six months away and spend every day thinking you're angry.'

'Well, it's not up to me, love, is it? It's your mother, really, I . . .'

'Yes, Dad. Thanks for stating the bloody obvious.'

'Oh, right,' said Archie huffily, turning to the wall. 'I'll keep my comments to meself, then . . .'

'Oh, *Dad*, I didn't mean . . . Mum? Can you please sit up and speak properly? I'm trying to talk to you? It seems like I'm talking to myself here?' said Irie with absurd intonations, for this was the year Antipodean soap operas were teaching a generation of

English kids to phrase everything as a question. 'Look, I want your permission, yeah?'

Even in the darkness, Irie could see Clara scowl. 'Permishon for *what*? Koo go and share and ogle at poor black folk? Dr Livingshone, I prejume? Iz dat what you leant from da Shalfenz? Because if thash what you want, you can do dat here. Jush sit and look at me for shix munfs!'

'It's nothing to do with that! I just want to see how other people live!'

'An' gek youshelf killed in da proshess! Why don' you go necksh door, dere are uvver people dere. Go shee how dey live!'

Infuriated, Irie grabbed the bed knob and marched round Clara's side of the bed. 'Why can't you just sit up properly and talk to me properly and drop the ridiculous little girl voi –'

In the darkness Irie kicked over a glass and sucked in a sharp breath as the cold water seeped between her toes and into the carpet. Then, as the last of the water ran away, Irie had the strange and horrid sensation that she was being bitten.

'Ow!'

'Oh, for God's sake,' said Archie, reaching over to the side lamp and switching it on. 'What now?'

Irie looked down to where the pain was. In any war, this was too low a blow. The front set of some false teeth, with no mouth attached to them, were bearing down upon her right foot.

'Fucking hell! What the fuck are they?'

But the question was unnecessary; even as the words formed in her mouth, Irie had already put two and two together. The midnight voice. The perfect daytime straightness and whiteness.

Clara hurriedly stretched to the floor and prised her teeth from Irie's foot and, as it was too late for disguise now, placed them directly on the bedside table.

'Shatishfied?' asked Clara wearily. (It wasn't that she had

deliberately not told her. There just never seemed a good time.)

But Irie was sixteen and everything feels deliberate at that age. To her, this was yet another item in a long list of parental hypocrisies and untruths, this was another example of the Jones/Bowden gift for secret histories, stories you never got told, history you never entirely uncovered, rumour you never unravelled, which would be fine if every day was not littered with clues, and suggestions; shrapnel in Archie's leg . . . photo of strange white Grandpa Durham . . . the name 'Ophelia' and the word 'madhouse' . . . a cycling helmet and an ancient mudguard . . . smell of fried food from O'Connell's . . . faint memory of a late night car journey, waving to a boy on a plane . . . letters with Swedish stamps, Horst Ibelgaufts, if not delivered return to sender . . .

Oh what a tangled web we weave. Millat was right: these parents were damaged people, missing hands, missing teeth. These parents were full of information you wanted to know but were too scared to hear. But she didn't want it any more, she was tired of it. She was sick of never getting the whole truth. She was returning to sender.

'Well, don't look so shocked, love,' said Archie amicably. 'It's just some bloody teeth. So now you know. It's not the end of the world.'

But it was, in a way. She'd had enough. She walked back into her room, packed her schoolwork and essential clothes into a big rucksack and put a heavy coat over her nightie. She thought about the Chalfens for half a second, but she knew already there were no answers there, only more places to escape. Besides, there was only one spare room and Millat had it. Irie knew where she had to go, deep into the heart of it, where only the N17 would take her at this time of night, sitting on the top deck, seats decorated with puke, rumbling through 47 bus stops before it reached its destination. But she got there in the end.

Irie 1990, 1907

'Lord a Jesus,' mumbled Hortense, iron-curlers unmoved, bleary-eyed on the doorstep. 'Irie Ambrosia Jones, *is that you?*'

15 *Chalfenism versus Bowdenism*

It was Irie Jones all right. Six years older than the last time they met. Taller, wider, with breasts and no hair and slippers just visible underneath a long duffle coat. And it was Hortense Bowden. Six years older, shorter, wider, with breasts on her belly and no hair (though she took the peculiar step of putting her wig in curlers) and slippers just visible underneath a long, padded baby-pink housecoat. But the real difference was Hortense was eighty-four. Not a littleoldwoman by any means; she was a round robust one, her fat so taut against her skin the epidermis was having a hard time wrinkling. Still, eighty-four is not seventy-seven or sixty-three; at eighty-four there is nothing but death ahead, tedious in its insistence. It was there in her face as Irie had never seen it before. The waiting and the fear and the blessed relief.

Yet though there were differences, walking down the steps and into Hortense's basement flat, Irie was struck by the shock of sameness. Way-back-when, she had been a fairly regular visitor at her grandmother's: sneaky visits with Archie while her mother was at college, and always leaving with something unusual, a pickled fish head, chilli dumplings, the lyrics of a stray but persistent psalm. Then at Darcus's funeral in 1985, ten-year-old Irie had let slip about these social calls and Clara had put a stop to them altogether. They still called each other on the phone, on occasion. And to this day Irie received short letters on exercise paper with a copy of the *Watchtower* slipped inside. Sometimes Irie looked at her mother's face and saw her grandmother: those majestic cheekbones, those feline eyes. But they had not been face to face for six years.

As far as the house was concerned, six seconds seemed to have passed. Still dark, still dank, still underground. Still decorated with hundreds of secular figurines ('Cinderella on her way to the Ball', 'Mrs Tiddlytum shows the little squirrels the way to the picnic'), all balanced on their separate doilies and laughing gaily amongst themselves, amused that anyone would pay a hundred and fifty pounds in fifteen instalments for such inferior pieces of china and glass as they. A huge tripartite tapestry, which Irie remembered the sewing of, now hung on the wall above the fireplace, depicting, in its first strip, the Anointed sitting in judgement with Jesus in heaven. The Anointed were all blond and blue-eyed and appeared as serene as Hortense's cheap wool would allow, and were looking down at the Great Crowd – who were happy-looking, but not as happy as the Anointed – frolicking in eternal paradise on earth. The Great Crowd were in turn looking piteously at the heathens (by far the largest group), dead in their graves, and packed on top of each other like sardines.

The only thing missing was Darcus (whom Irie only faintly remembered as a mixture of smell and texture; naphthalene and damp wool); there was his huge empty chair, still fetid, and there was his television, still on.

'Irie, look at you! Pickney nah even got a gansey on – child must be freezin'! Shiverin' like a Mexico bean. Let me feel you. Fever! You bringin' fever into my house?'

It was important, in Hortense's presence, never to admit to illness. The cure, as in most Jamaican households, was always more painful than the symptoms.

'I'm fine. There's nothing wrong with –'

'Oh, really?' Hortense put Irie's hand on her own forehead. 'That's fever as sure as fever is fever. Feel it?'

Irie felt it. She was hot as hell.

'Come 'ere.' Hortense grabbed a rug from Darcus's chair and wrapped it around Irie's shoulders, 'Now come into the kitchen an' cease an' sekkle. Runnin' roun' on a night like dis, wearin' flimsy nonsense! You're having a hot drink of cerace and den gone a bed quicker den you ever did in your life.'

Irie accepted the smelly wrap and followed Hortense into the tiny kitchen, where they both sat down.

'Let me look at you.'

Hortense leant against the oven with hands on hips. 'You look like Mr Death, your new lover. How you get here?'

Once again, one had to be careful in answering. Hortense's contempt for London Transport was a great comfort to her in her old age. She could take one word like *train* and draw a melody out of it (*Northern Line*), which expanded into an aria (*The Underground*) and blossomed into a theme (*The Overground*) and then grew exponentially into an operetta (*The Evils and Inequities of British Rail*).

'Er . . . Bus. N17. It was cold on the top deck. Maybe I caught a chill.'

'I don' tink dere's any maybes about it, young lady. An' I'm sure I don' know why you come 'pon de bus, when it take tree hours to arrive an' leave you waitin' in de col' an' den' when you get pon it de windows are open anyway an' you freeze half to death.'

Hortense poured a colourless liquid from a small plastic container into her hand. 'Come 'ere.'

'Why?' demanded Irie, immediately suspicious. 'What's that?'

'Nuttin', come 'ere. Take off your spectacles.'

Hortense approached with a cupped hand.

'Not in my eye! There's nothing wrong with my eye!'

'Stop fussin'. I'm not puttin' nuttin' in your eye.'

'Just tell me what it is,' pleaded Irie, trying to work out for which orifice it was intended and screaming as the cupped hand reached her face, spreading the liquid from forehead to chin.

'Aaagh! It burns!'

'Bay rum,' said Hortense matter-of-factly. 'Burns de fever away. No, don' wash it off. Jus' leave it to do its biznezz.'

Irie gritted her teeth as the torture of a thousand pin-pricks faded to five hundred, then twenty-five, until finally it was just a warm flush of the kind delivered by a slap.

'So!' said Hortense, entirely awake now and somewhat triumphant. 'You finally dash from that godless woman, I see. An' caught a flu while you doin' it! Well . . . there are those who wouldn't blame you, no, not at all . . . No one knows better dan me what dat woman be like. Never at home, learnin' all her isms and skisms in the university, leavin' husband and pickney at home, hungry and maga. Lord, naturally you flee! Well . . .' She sighed and put a copper kettle on the stove. 'It is written. *You will flee by my mountain valley, for it will extend to Azel. You will flee as you fled from the earthquake in the days of Uzziah king of Judah. Then the LORD my God will come, and all the holy ones with him.* Zechariah 14:5. In the end the good ones will flee from the evil. Oh, Irie Ambrosia . . . I *knew* you come in de end. All God's children return in de end.'

'Gran, I haven't come to find God. I just want to do some quiet study here and get my head together. I need to stay a few months – at least till the New Year. Oh . . . ugh . . . I feel a bit woozy. Can I have an orange?'

'Yes, dey all return to de Lord Jesus in de end,' continued Hortense to herself, placing the bitter root of cerace into a kettle. 'Dat's not a real orange, dear. All de fruit is plasticated. De flowers are plasticated also. I don't believe de Lord meant me to spend de little housekeeping money I possess on perishable goods. Have some dates.'

Irie grimaced at the shrivelled fruit plonked in front of her.

'So you lef Archibald wid dat woman . . . poor ting. Me always *like* Archibald,' said Hortense sadly, scrubbing the brown scum from a teacup with two soapy fingers. 'Him was never my objection *as such*. He always been a level-headed sort a fellow. Blessed are de peacekeepers. He always strike me as a peacekeeper. But it more de principle of de ting, you know? Black and white never come to no good. De Lord Jesus never meant us to mix it up. Dat's why he made a hol' heap a fuss about de children of men building de tower of Babel. 'Im want everybody to keep tings separate. *And the Lord did confound the language of all the earth and from thence did the Lord scatter them abroad upon the face of all the earth.* Genesis 11:9. When you mix it up, nuttin' good can come. It wasn't *intended*. Except you,' she added as an afterthought. 'You're about de only good ting to come out of dat . . . Bwoy, sometime it like lookin' in a mirror-glass,' she said, lifting Irie's chin with her wrinkled digits. 'You built like me, big, you know! Hip and tie and rhas, and titties. My mudder was de same way. You even named after my mudder.'

'Irie?' asked Irie, trying hard to listen, but feeling the damp smog of her fever pulling her under.

'No, dear, *Ambrosia*. De stuff dat make you live for ever. Now,' she said, clapping her hands together, catching Irie's next question between them, 'you sleepin' in de living room. I'll get a blanket and pillows and den we talk in de marnin'. I'm up at six, 'cos I got Witness biznezz, so don' tink you sleeping none after eight. Pickney, you hear me?'

'Mmm. But what about Mum's old room? Can't I just sleep in there?'

Hortense took Irie's weight half on her shoulder and led her into the living room. 'No, dat's not possible. Dere is a certain situation,' said Hortense mysteriously. 'Dat can wait till de sun is up to be hexplained. *Fear them not therefore: for there is nothing covered that shall not be revealed,*' she intoned quietly, turning to go. '*And nothing hid, that shall not be known.* Dat is Mat-chew, 10:26.'

∽

An autumn morning was the only time worth spending in that basement flat. Between 6 and 7 a.m. when the sun was still low, light shot through the front window, bathed the lounge in yellow, dappled the long thin allotment (7 ft × 30 ft) and gave a healthy veneer to the tomatoes. You could almost convince yourself, at 6 a.m., that you were downstairs in some Continental cabana, or at least street level in Torquay, rather than below ground in Lambeth. The glare was such that you couldn't make out the railway sidings where the strip of green ended, or the busy everyday feet that passed by the lounge window, kicking dust through the grating at the glass. It was all white light and clever shade at six in the morning. Hugging a cup of tea at the kitchen table, squinting at the grass, Irie saw vineyards out there; she saw Florentine scenes instead of the uneven higgledy-piggledy of Lambeth rooftops; she saw a muscular shadowy Italian plucking full berries and crushing them underfoot. Then the mirage, sun reliant as it was, disappeared, the whole scene swallowed by a devouring cloud. Leaving only some crumbling Edwardian housing. Railway sidings named after a careless child. A long, narrow strip of allotment where next to nothing would grow. And a bleached-out bandy-legged red-headed man with terrible posture and wellington boots, stamping away in the mulch, trying to shake the remnants of a squashed tomato from his heel.

'Dat is Mr Topps,' said Hortense, hurrying across the kitchen in a dark maroon dress, the eyes and hooks undone, and a hat in her hand with plastic flowers askew. 'He has been such a help to me since Darcus died. He soothes away my vexation and calms my mind.'

She waved to him and he straightened up and waved back. Irie watched him pick up two plastic bags filled with tomatoes and walk in his strange pigeon-footed manner up the garden towards the back kitchen door.

'An' he de only man who made a solitary ting grow out dere. Such a crop of tomatoes as you never did see! Irie Ambrosia, stop starin' and come an' do up dis dress. Quick before your goggle-eye fall out.'

'Does he live here?' whispered Irie in amazement, struggling to join the two sides of Hortense's dress over her substantial flank. 'I mean, with you?'

'Not in de sense *you* meaning,' sniffed Hortense. 'He is jus' a great help to me in my ol' age. He bin wid me deez six years, God bless 'im and keep 'is soul. Now, pass me dat pin.'

Irie passed her the long hat pin which was sitting on top of a butter dish. Hortense set the plastic carnations straight on her hat and stabbed them fiercely, then brought the pin back up through the felt, leaving two inches of exposed silver sticking up from the hat like a German pickelhaube.

'Well, don' look so shock. It a very satisfactory arrangement. Women need a man 'bout de house, udderwise ting an' ting get messy. Mr Topps and I, we ol' soldiers fightin' the battle of de Lord. Some time ago he converted to the Witness church, an' his rise has been quick an' sure. I've waited fifty years to do someting else in de Kingdom Hall except clean,' said Hortense sadly, 'but dey don' wan' women interfering with real church bizness. Bot Mr Topps do a great deal, and 'im let me help on occasion. He's a very good man. But 'im family are nasty-nasty,' she murmured confidentially. 'The farder is a terrible man, gambler an' whoremonger . . . so after a while, I arks him to come and live with me, seein' how de room empty and Darcus gone. 'Im a very civilized bwoy. Never married, though. Married to de church, yes, suh! An' 'im call me Mrs Bowden deez six years, never any ting else.' Hortense sighed ever so slightly. 'Don' know de meaning of bein' improper. De only ting he wan' in life is to become one of de Anointed. I have de greatest hadmiration for him. He himproved so much. He talk so posh now, you know! And 'im very good wid de pipin' an' plummin' also. How's your fever?'

'Not great. Last hook . . . there that's done.'

Hortense fairly bounced away from her and walked into the hall to open the back door to Ryan.

'But Gran, why does he live –'

'Well, you're going to have to eat up dis marnin' – feed a fever, starve a col'. Deez tomatoes fried wid plantain and some of las' night's fish. I'll fry it up and den pop it in de microwave.'

'I thought it was starve a fe –'

'Good *marnin'*, Mr Topps.'

'Good mornin', Missus Bowden,' said Mr Topps, closing the door behind him and peeling off a protective cagoule to reveal a cheap blue suit, with a tiny gold cross pendant on the collar. 'I trust you is almost of a readiness? We've got to be at the hall on the dot of seven.'

As yet, Ryan had not spotted Irie. He was bent over shaking the mud from his boots. And he did it formidably slowly, just as he spoke, and with his translucent eyelids fluttering like a man in a coma. Irie could only see half of him from where she stood: a red fringe, a bent knee and the shirt cuff of one hand.

But the voice was a visual in itself: cockney yet refined, a voice that had had much work done upon it – missing key consonants and adding others where they were never meant to be, and all delivered through the nose with only the slightest help from the mouth.

'Fine mornin', Mrs B., fine mornin'. Somefing to fank the Lord for.'

Hortense seemed terribly nervous about the imminent likelihood that he should raise his head and spot the girl standing by the stove. She kept beckoning Irie forward and then shooing her back, uncertain whether they should meet at all.

'Oh *yes*, Mr Topps, it is, an' I am ready as ready can be. My hat give me a little trouble, you know, but I just got a pin an –'

'But the Lord ain't interested in the vanities of the flesh, now, is he Mrs B.?' said Ryan, slowly and painfully enunciating each word while crouching awkwardly and removing his left boot. 'Jehovah is in need of your *soul*.'

'Oh yes, surely dat is de holy troot,' said Hortense anxiously, fingering her plasticated carnations. 'But at de same time, surely a Witness lady don' wan' look like a, well, a buguyaga in de house of de Lord.'

Ryan frowned. 'My point is, you must avoid interpretin' scripture by yourself, Mrs Bowden. In future, discuss it wiv myself and my colleagues. Ask us: is pleasant clothing a concern of the Lord's? And myself and my colleagues amongst the Anointed, will look up the necessary chapter and verse . . .'

Ryan's sentence faded into a general *Erhummmm*, a sound he was prone to making. It began in his arched nostrils and reverberated through his slight, elongated, misshapen limbs like the final shiver of a hanged man.

'I don' know why I do it, Mr Topps,' said Hortense shaking her head. 'Sometime I tink I could be one of dem dat teach, you know? Even though I am a woman . . . I feel like the Lord talk to me in a special way . . . It jus' a bad habit . . . but so much in de church change recently, sometimes me kyan keep up wid all de rules and regulations.'

Ryan looked out through the double glazing. His face was pained. 'Nuffin' changes about the word of God, Mrs B. Only people are mistaken. The best thing you can do for the Truth, is just pray that the Brooklyn Hall will soon deliver us with the final date. *Erhummmm.*'

'Oh yes, Mr Topps. I do it day and night.'

Ryan clapped his hands together in a pale imitation of enthusiasm. 'Now, did I 'ear you say plantain for breakfast, Mrs B.?'

'Oh yes, Mr Topps, and dem tomatoes if you will be kind enough to han' dem over to de chef.'

As Hortense had hoped, the passing of the tomatoes coincided with the spotting of Irie.

'Now, dis is my granddarter, Irie Ambrosia Jones. And dis is Mr Ryan Topps. Say hello, Irie, dear.'

Irie did so, stepping forward nervously and reaching out her hand to shake his. But there was no response from Ryan Topps, and the inequality was only increased when on the sudden he seemed to recognize her; there was a pulse of familiarity as his eyes moved over her, whereas Irie saw nothing, not even a *type*, not even a *genre* of face in his; the monstrosity of him was quite unique, redder than any red-head, more freckled than the freckled, more blue-veined than a lobster.

'She's – she's – Clara's darter,' said Hortense tentatively. 'Mr Topps knew your mudder, long time. But it all right, Mr Topps, she come to live wid *us* now.'

'Only for a little time,' Irie corrected hurriedly, noting the look of vague horror on Mr Topps's face. 'Just for a few months maybe, through the winter while I study. I've got exams in June.'

Mr Topps did not move. Moreover nothing on him moved. Like one of China's terracotta army, he seemed poised for battle yet unable to move.

'Clara's darter,' repeated Hortense in a tearful whisper. '*She might have been yours.*'

Nothing surprised Irie about this final, whispered aside; she just added it to the list: Ambrosia Bowden gave birth in an earthquake . . . Captain Charlie Durham was a no-good djam fool bwoy . . . false teeth in a glass . . . *she might have been yours* . . .

Half-heartedly, with no expectation of an answer, Irie asked, 'What?'

'Oh, nuttin', Irie, dear. Nuttin', nuttin'. Let me start fryin'. I can hear bellies rumblin'. You remember Clara, don't you Mr Topps? You and she were quite good . . . friends. Mr Topps?'

For two minutes now Ryan had been fixing Irie with an unwavering stare, his body held absolutely straight, his mouth slightly open. At the question, he seemed to compose himself, closed his mouth and took his seat at the unlaid table.

'Clara's daughter, is it? *Erhummmm . . .*' He removed what looked like a small policeman's pad from his breast pocket and poised a pen upon it as if this would kickstart his memory.

'You see, many of the episodes, people and events from my earlier life have been, as it were, severed from myself by the almighty sword that cut me from my past when the Lord Jehovah saw fit to enlighten me with the Truth, and as he has chosen me for a new role I must, as Paul so wisely recommended in his epistle to the Corinfians, put away childish things, allowing earlier incarnations of myself to be enveloped into a great smog in which,' said Ryan Topps, taking only the smallest breath and his cutlery from Hortense, 'it appears that your mother, and any memory I might 'ave of her, 'ave disappeared. *Erhummmm.*'

'She never mentioned you either,' said Irie.

'Well, it was all a long time ago now,' said Hortense with forced joviality. 'But you did try your best wid 'er, Mr Topps. She was my miracle child, Clara. I was forty-eight! I taut she was God's child. But Clara was bound for evil . . . she never was a godly girl an' in de end dere was nuttin' to be done.'

'He will send down His vengeance, Mrs B.,' said Ryan, with more cheerful animation than Irie had yet seen him display. 'He will send terrible torture to those who 'ave earned it. Three plantain for me, if you please.'

Hortense set all three plates down and Irie, realizing she hadn't eaten since the previous morning, scraped a mountain of plantain on to her plate.

'Ah! It's hot!'

'Better hot dan lukewarm,' said Hortense grimly, with a meaningful shudder. 'Ever so, hamen.'

'Amen,' echoed Ryan, braving the red-hot plantain. 'Amen. So. What exactly is it that you are studyin'?' he asked, looking so intently past Irie that it took a moment before she realized he was addressing her.

'Chemistry, biology and religious studies.' Irie blew on a hot piece of plantain. 'I want to be a dentist.'

Ryan perked up. 'Religious studies? And do they acquaint you with the only true church?'

Irie shifted in her seat. 'Er . . . I guess it's more the big three. Jews, Christians, Muslims. We did a month on Catholicism.'

Ryan grimaced. 'And do you have any uvver in-ter-rests?'

Irie considered. 'Music. I like music. Concerts, clubs, that kind of thing.'

'Yes, *erhummmm*. I used to go in for all that myself at one time. Until the Good News was delivered unto me. Large gatherings of yoof, of the kind that frequent popular concerts, are commonly breeding grounds for devil worship. A girl of your physical . . . assets might find herself lured into the lascivious arms of a sexualist,' said Ryan, standing up from the table and looking at his watch. 'Now that I fink about it, in a certain light you look a lot like your mother. Similar . . . cheekbones.'

Ryan wiped a pearly line of sweat from his forehead. There was a silence in which Hortense stood motionless, clinging nervously to a dishcloth, and Irie had to physically cross the room for a glass of water to remove herself from Mr Topps's stare.

'Well. That's twenty minutes and counting, Mrs B. I'll get the gear, shall I?'

'Oh *yes*, Mr Topps,' said Hortense beaming. But the moment Ryan left the room the beam turned to a scowl.

'Why must you go an' say tings like dat, hmm? You wan' 'im to tink you some devilish heathen gal? Why kyan you say stamp-collecting or some ting? Come on, I gat to clean deez plates – finish up.'

Irie looked at the pile of food left on her plate and guiltily tapped her stomach.

'Cho! Just as I suspeck. Your eyes see more dan your belly can hol'! Give it 'ere.'

Hortense leant against the sink and began popping bits of plantain into her mouth. 'Now, you don' backchat Mr Topps while you here. You gat study to do an' he gat study too,' said Hortense, lowering her voice. 'He's in *consultation* with the Brooklyn gentlemen at de moment . . . *fixing de final date*; no mistakes dis time. You jus' 'ave to look at de trouble goin' on in de world to know we nat far from de appointed day.'

'I won't be any trouble,' said Irie, approaching the washing-up as a gesture of goodwill. 'He just seems a little . . . weird.'

'De ones who are chosen by the Lord always seem peculiar to de heathen. Mr Topps is jus' misunderstood. 'Im mean a lot to me. Me never have nobody before. Your mudder don' like to tell you since she got all hitey-titey, but de Bowden family have had it hard long time. I was barn during an eart-quake. Almost kill fore I was barn. An' den when me a fully grown woman, my own darter run from me. Me never see my only grandpickney. I only have de Lord, all dem years. Mr Topps de first human man who look pon me and take pity an' care. Your mudder was a fool to let 'im go, true sir!'

Irie gave it one last try. 'What? What does that mean?'

'Oh, nuttin, nuttin, dear Lord . . . I and I talking all over de place dis marnin . . . Oh Mr Topps, *dere* you are. We not going to be late now, are we?'

Mr Topps, who had just re-entered the room, was fully adorned in leather from head to toe, a huge motorcycle helmet on his head, a small red light attached to his left ankle and a small white light strapped to his right. He flipped up the visor.

'No, we're all right, by the grace of God. Where's your helmet, Mrs B.?'

'Oh, I've started keepin' it in the oven. Keeps it warm and toasty on de col' marnins. Irie Ambrosia, fetch it for me please.'

Sure enough, on the middle shelf preheated to gas mark 2 sat Hortense's helmet. Irie scooped it out and carefully fitted it over her grandmother's plasticated carnations.

'You ride a motorbike,' said Irie, by way of conversation.

But Mr Topps seemed defensive. 'A GS Vespa. Nuffink fancy. I did fink about givin' it away at one point. It represented a life I'd raaver forget, if you get my meaning. A motorbike is a sexual magnet, an' God forgive me, but I misused it in that fashion. I was all set on gettin' rid of it. But then Mrs B. convinced me that what wiv all my public speaking, I need somefing quick to get around on. An' Mrs B. don't want to be messin' about with buses and trains at her age, do you Mrs B.?'

'No, indeed. He got me dis little buggy –'

'*Side*car,' corrected Ryan tetchily. 'It's called a sidecar. Minetto Motorcycle-combination, 1973 model.'

'Yes, of course, a *sidecar*, an' it is comfortable as a bed. We go everywhere in it, Mr Topps an' I.'

Hortense took down her overcoat from a hook on the door, and reached in the pockets for two Velcro reflector bands which she strapped round each arm.

'Now, Irie, I've got a great deal of bizness to be gettin' on with today, so you're going to have to cook for yourself, because I kyan tell what time we'll be home. But don' worry. Me soon come.'

'No problem.'

Hortense sucked her teeth. '*No problem*. Dat's what her name mean in patois: *Irie*, no problem. Now, what kind of a name is dat to . . . ?'

Mr Topps didn't answer. He was already out on the pavement, revving up the Vespa.

'First I have to keep her from those Chalfens,' growls Clara over the phone, her voice a resonant *tremolando* of anger and fear. 'And now *you* people again.'

On the other end, her mother takes the washing out of the machine and listens silently through the cordless that is tucked between ear and weary shoulder, biding her time.

'Hortense, I don't want you filling her head with a whole load of nonsense. You hear me? Your mother was fool to it, and then you were fool to it, but the buck stopped with me and it ain't going no further. If Irie comes home spouting any of that claptrap, you can forget about the Second Comin' 'cos you'll be dead by the time it arrives.'

Big words. But how fragile is Clara's atheism! Like one of those tiny glass doves Hortense keeps in the lounge cabinet – a breath would knock it over. Talking of which, Clara still holds hers when passing churches the same way adolescent vegetarians scurry by butchers; she avoids Kilburn on a Saturday for fear of streetside preachers on their upturned apple crates. Hortense senses Clara's terror. Coolly cramming in another load of whites and measuring out the liquid with a thrifty woman's eye, she is short and decided: 'Don' you worry about Irie Ambrosia. She in a good place now. She'll tell you herself.' As if she had ascended with the heavenly host rather than entombed herself below ground in the borough of Lambeth with Ryan Topps.

Clara hears her daughter getting on the extension; an initial crackle and then a voice as clear as a carillon. 'Look, I'm not coming home, all right, so don't bother. I'll be back when I'm back, just don't worry about me.' And there *should* be nothing to worry about and there *is* nothing to worry about, except maybe that outside in the streets it is cold packed on cold, even the dogshit has crystallized, there is the first suggestion of ice on the windscreens and Clara has been in that house through the winters. She *knows* what it means. Oh, wonderfully bright at 6 a.m., yes, wonderfully clear for an *hour*. But the shorter the days, the longer the nights, the darker the house, the easier it is, the easier it is, the easier it is, to mistake a shadow for the writing on the wall, the sound of overland footsteps for the distant crack of thunder, and the midnight chime of a New Year clock for the bell that tolls the end of the world.

∽

But Clara needn't have feared. Irie's atheism was robust. It was Chalfenist in its confidence, and she approached her stay with Hortense with detached amusement. She was intrigued by the Bowden household. It was a place of endgames and aftertimes, fullstops and finales; where to count on the arrival of tomorrow was an indulgence, and every service in the house, from the milkman to the electricity, was paid for on a strictly daily basis so as not to spend money on utilities or goods that would be wasted should God turn up in all his holy vengeance the very next day. Bowdenism gave a whole new meaning to the phrase 'hand-to-mouth'. This was living in the eternal instant, ceaselessly teetering on the precipice of total annihilation; there are people who take a great deal of drugs simply to experience something comparable to 84-year-old Hortense Bowden's day-to-day existence. So you've seen dwarfs rip open their bellies and show you their insides, you've been a television switched off without warning, you've experienced the whole world as one Krishna consciousness, free of individual ego, floating through the infinite cosmos of the soul? Big fucking deal. That's all bullshit next to St John's trip when Christ laid the twenty-two chapters of Revelation on him. It must have been a hell of a shock for the apostle (after that thorough spin-job, the New Testament, all those sweet words and sublime sentiments) to discover Old Testament vengeance lurking round the corner after all. *As many as I love, I rebuke and chasten*. That must have been some eye-opener.

Revelation is where all crazy people end up. It's the last stop on the nutso express. And Bowdenism, which was the Witnesses plus Revelation *and then some*, was as left field as they come. *Par exemple*: Hortense Bowden interpreted Revelation 3:15 – *I know thy works, that thou art neither cold nor hot: I would thou wert cold or hot. So then because thou art lukewarm, and neither cold nor hot, I will spue thee out of my mouth* – as a literal mandate. She understood 'lukewarm' to be an evil property in and of itself. She kept a microwave on hand at all times (her sole concession to modern technology – for a long time it was a toss-up between pleasing the Lord and laying oneself open to the United States mind-ray control programme as operated through high-frequency radiowaves) in order to heat every meal to an impossible temperature; she kept whole buckets of ice to chill every glass of water 'colder than cold'. She wore two pairs of knickers at all times like a wary potential traffic-victim; when Irie asked why, she sheepishly revealed that upon hearing the first signs of the Lord (approaching thunder, bellowing voice, Wagner's Ring Cycle), she intended to whip off the one closest to her and replace it with the outer pair, so that Jesus would find her fresh and odourless and ready for heaven. She kept a tub of black paint in the hallway so when the time came she might daub the neighbours' doors with the sign of the Beast, saving the Lord all that trouble of weeding out the baddies, separating sheep from goats. And you couldn't form any sentence in that house which included the words 'end', 'finished', 'done', etc., for these were like so many triggers setting off both Hortense and Ryan with the usual ghoulish relish:

Irie: I finished the washing-up.

Ryan Topps (shaking his head solemnly at the truth of it): As one day we all shall be finished, Irie, my dear; be zealous therefore, and repent.

Or

Irie: It was a such a good film. The end was great!

Hortense Bowden (tearfully): And dem dat expeck such an end to dis world will be sorely disappointed, for He will come trailin' terror and Lo de generation dat witness de events of 1914 shall now witness de turd part of de trees burn, and the turd part of de sea become as blood, and de turd part of de . . .

And then there was Hortense's horror of weather reports. Whoever it was, however benign, honey-voiced and inoffensively dressed, she cursed them bitterly for the five minutes they stood there, and then, out of what appeared to be sheer perversity, proceeded to take the opposite of whatever advice had been proffered (light jacket and no umbrella for rain, full cagoule and rain hat for sun). It was several weeks before Irie understood that weathermen were the secular antithesis of Hortense's life work, which was, essentially, a kind of supercosmic attempt to second-guess the Lord with one almighty biblical exegesis of a weather report. Next to that weathermen were nothing but upstarts . . . *And tomorrow, coming in from the east, we can expect a great furnace to rise up and envelop the area with flames that give no light, but rather darkness visible . . . while I'm afraid the northern regions are advised to wrap up warm against thick-ribbed ice, and there's a fair likelihood that the coast will be beaten with perpetual storms of whirlwind and dire hail which on firm land thaws not . . .* Michael Fish and his ilk were stabbers-in-the-dark, trusting to the tomfoolery of the Met Office, making a mockery of that precise science, eschatology, that Hortense had spent over fifty years in the study of.

'Any news, Mr Topps?' (This question almost invariably asked over breakfast; and girlishly, breathlessly, like a child asking after Santa.)

'No, Mrs B. We are still completing our studies. You must let my colleagues and myself deliberate thoroughly. In this life there are them that are teachers and then there are them that are pupils. There are eight million Witnesses of Jehovah waiting for our decision, waiting for the Judgement Day. But you must learn to leave such fings to them that 'ave the direct line, Mrs B., the direct line.'

∽

After bunking for a few weeks, Irie returned to school. But it seemed so distant; even the journey from South to North each morning felt like an almighty polar trek, and worse, one that stopped short of its goal and ended up instead in the tepid regions, a non-event compared with the boiling maelstrom of the Bowden home. *So then because thou art lukewarm, and neither cold nor hot, I will spue thee out of my mouth.* You become so used to extremity, suddenly nothing else will do.

She saw Millat regularly, but their conversations were brief. He was green-tied now and otherwise engaged. She still did Marcus's filing twice a week, but avoided the rest of the family. She saw Josh fleetingly. He seemed to be avoiding the Chalfens as assiduously as she. Her parents she saw on weekends, icy occasions when everybody called everybody by their first names (*Irie, can you pass the salt to Archie? Clara, Archie wants to know where the scissors are*), and all parties felt deserted. She sensed that she was being whispered about in NW2, the way North Londoners will when they suspect someone of coming down with religion, that nasty disease. So she hurried back to No. 28 Lindaker Road, Lambeth, relieved to be back in the darkness, for it was like hibernating or being cocooned, and she was as curious as everyone else to see what kind of Irie would emerge. It wasn't any kind of prison. That house was an *adventure*. In cupboards and neglected drawers and in grimy frames were the secrets that had been hoarded for so long, as if secrets were going out of fashion. She found pictures of her great-grandmother Ambrosia, a bony, beautiful thing, with huge almond eyes, and one of Charlie 'Whitey' Durham standing in a pile of rubble with a sepia-print sea behind him. She found a bible with one line torn from it. She found photo-booth snaps of Clara in school uniform, grinning maniacally, the true horror of the teeth revealed. She read alternately from *Dental Anatomy* by Gerald M. Cathey and *The Good News Bible*, and raced voraciously through Hortense's small and eclectic library, blowing the red dust of a Jamaican schoolhouse off the covers and often using a pen knife to cut never-before-read pages. February's list was as follows:

An Account of a West Indian Sanatorium, by Geo. J. H. Sutton Moxly. London: Sampson, Low, Marston & Co., 1886. (There was an inverse correlation between the length of the author's name and the poor quality of his book.)

Tom Cringle's Log, by Michael Scott. Edinburgh: 1875.

In Sugar Cane Land, by Eden Phillpotts. London: McClure & Co., 1893.

Dominica: Hints and Notes to Intending Settlers, by His Honour H. Hesketh Bell, CMG. London: A. & C. Black, 1906.

The more she read, the more that picture of dashing Capt. Durham aroused her natural curiosity: handsome and melancholy, surveying the bricks of half a church, looking worldly-wise despite his youth, looking every inch the Englishman, looking like he could tell someone or another a thing or two about something. Maybe Irie herself. Just in case, she kept him under her pillow. And in the mornings it wasn't Italianate vineyards out there any more, it was sugar, sugar, sugar, and next door was nothing but tobacco and she presumptuously fancied that the smell of plantain sent her back to somewhere, somewhere quite fictional, for she'd never been there. Somewhere Columbus called St Jago but the arawaks stubbornly re-named Xaymaca, the name lasting longer than they did. *Well-wooded and Watered*. Not that Irie had heard of those little sweet-tempered pot-bellied victims of their own sweet-tempers. Those were some *other* Jamaicans, fallen short of the attention-span of history. She laid claim to the past – her version of the past – aggressively, as if retrieving misdirected mail. So *this* was where she came from. This all *belonged* to her, her birthright, like a pair of pearl earrings or a post office bond. X marks the spot, and Irie put an X on everything she found, collecting bits and bobs (birth certificates, maps, army reports, news articles) and storing them under the sofa, so that as if by osmosis the richness of them would pass through the fabric while she was sleeping and seep right into her.

As the buds came with the spring, so like any anchoress she was visited. First, by voices. Coming crackling over Hortense's neolithic radio, Joyce Chalfen on *Gardeners' Question Time*:

Foreman: Another question from the audience, I think. Mrs Sally Whitaker from Bournemouth has a question for the panel, I believe. Mrs Whitaker?

Mrs Whitaker: Thank you, Brian. Well, I'm a new gardener and this is my first frost and in two short months my garden's gone from being a real colour explosion to a very bare thing indeed . . . Friends have advised flowers with a compact habit but that leaves me with lots of tiny auricula and double daisies, which look silly because the garden's really quite large. Now, I'd really like to plant something a little more striking, around the height of a delphinium, but then the wind gets it and people look over their fences thinking: *Dear oh dear* (*sympathetic laughter from the studio audience*). So, my question to the panel is, how do you keep up appearances in the bleak midwinter?

Foreman: Thank you, Mrs Whitaker. Well, it's a common problem . . . and it doesn't necessarily get any easier for the seasoned gardener. Personally, I never get it quite right. Well, let's hand the question over to the panel, shall we? Joyce Chalfen, any answers or suggestions for the bleak midwinter?

Joyce Chalfen: Well, first I must say your neighbours sound *very* nosy. I'd tell them to mind their own beeswax if I were you (*laughter from audience*). But to be serious, I think this whole trend for round-the-clock bloom is actually very unhealthy for the garden and the gardener and *particularly* the soil, I really do . . . I think the winter should be a time of *rest*, subdued colours, you know – and then when the late spring does finally arrive the neighbours get a hell of a shock! Boom! There it is, this wonderful explosion of growth. I think the deep winter is really a time for *nurturing* the soil, turning it over, allowing it a rest and plotting its future all the better to *surprise* the nosy people next door. I always think of a

> garden's soil like a woman's body – moving in cycles, you know, fertile at some times and not others, and that's really quite natural. But if you *really* are determined, then Lenten roses – *Helleborus corsicus* – do remarkably well in cold, calcareous soil, even if they're quite in the –

Irie switched Joyce off. It was quite therapeutic switching Joyce off. This was not entirely personal. It just seemed tiring and unnecessary all of a sudden, that struggle to force something out of the recalcitrant English soil. Why bother when there was now this other place? (For Jamaica appeared to Irie as if it were newly made. Like Columbus himself, just by discovering it she had brought it into existence.) This well-wooded and watered place. Where things sprang from the soil riotously and without supervision, and a young white captain could meet a young black girl with no complications, both of them fresh and untainted and without past or dictated future – a place where things simply *were*. No fictions, no myths, no lies, no tangled webs – this is how Irie imagined her homeland. Because *homeland* is one of the magical fantasy words like *unicorn* and *soul* and *infinity* that have now passed into the language. And the particular magic of *homeland*, its particular spell over Irie, was that it sounded like a beginning. The beginningest of beginnings. Like the first morning of Eden and the day after apocalypse. A blank page.

But every time Irie felt herself closer to it, to the perfect blankness of the past, something of the present would ring the Bowden doorbell and intrude. Mothering Sunday brought a surprise visit from Joshua, angry on the doorstep, at least a stone and a half lighter, and much scruffier than usual. Before Irie had a chance to express either concern or shock, he had flounced into the lounge and slammed the door. 'I'm sick of it! Sick to the back fucking teeth with it!'

The vibration of the door knocked Capt. Durham from his perch on Irie's windowsill, and she carefully re-erected him.

'Yeah, nice to see you too, man. Why don't you sit down and slow down. Sick of what?'

'*Them*. They sicken me. They go on about rights and freedoms, and then they eat fifty chickens every fucking week! Hypocrites!'

Irie couldn't immediately see the connection. She took out a fag in preparation for a long story. To her surprise Joshua took one too, and they went to kneel on the window seat, blowing smoke through the grate up into the street.

'Do you *know* how battery chickens live?'

Irie didn't. Joshua explained. Cooped up for most of their poor chicken lives in total chicken darkness, packed together like chicken sardines in their chicken shit and fed the worst type of chicken grain.

And this, according to Joshua, was apparently nothing on how pigs and cows and sheep spent their time. 'It's a fucking *crime*. But try telling Marcus that. Try getting him to give up his Sunday hog-fest. He's so *fucking* ill informed. Have you ever noticed that? He knows this enormous amount about one thing, but there's this whole other world that . . . Oh, before I forget – you should take a leaflet.'

Irie never thought she would see the day when Joshua Chalfen handed her a leaflet. But here it was in her palm. It was called: *Meat is Murder: The Facts and the Fiction*, a publication from the FATE organization.

'It stands for Fighting Animal Torture and Exploitation. They're like the hardcore end of Greenpeace or whatever. Read it – they're not just hippy freaks, they're coming from a solid scientific and academic background and they're working from an anarchist perspective. I feel like I've really found my niche, you know? It's a really incredible group. Dedicated to direct action. The deputy's an ex-Oxford fellow.'

'Mmmm. How's Millat?'

Joshua shook off the question. 'Oh, I don't know. Barmy. Going barmy. And Joyce is still pandering to his every whim. Just don't ask me. They all sicken me. Everything's changed.' Josh ran his fingers anxiously through his hair, which just reached his shoulders now in what Willesdeners affectionately call a Jew-fro Mullet. 'I just can't tell you how everything's changed. I'm having these real . . . *moments of clarity*.'

Irie nodded. She was sympathetic to moments of clarity. Her seventeenth year was proving chock-a-block with them. And she wasn't surprised by Joshua's metamorphosis. Four months in the life of a seventeen-year-old is the stuff of swings and roundabouts; Stones fans into Beatles fans, Tories into Liberal Democrats and back again, vinyl junkies to CD freaks. Never again in your life do you possess the capacity for such total personality overhaul.

'I *knew* you'd understand. I wish I'd talked to you before, but I just can't bear to be in the house these days and when I do see you Millat always seems to be in the way. It's really *good* to see you.'

'You too. You look different.'

Josh gestured dismissively at his clothes, which were distinctly less nerdy than they had been.

'I guess you can't wear your father's old corduroy for ever.'

'I guess not.'

Joshua clapped his hands together. 'Well, I've booked my ticket for Glastonbury and I might not come back. I met these people from FATE and I'm going with them.'

'It's March. Not till the summer, surely.'

'Joely and Crispin – that's these people I met – say we might go up there early. You know, camp out for a bit.'

'And school?'

'If you can bunk, I can bunk . . . it's not as if I'm going to fall behind. I've still got a Chalfen head on my shoulders, I'll just come back for the exams and then fuck off again. Irie, you've just got to meet these people. They're just . . . incredible. He's a Dadaist. And she's an anarchist. A real one. Not like Marcus. I told her about Marcus and his bloody FutureMouse. She thinks he's a dangerous individual. Quite possibly psychopathic.'

Irie thought about this. 'Mmm. I'd be surprised.'

Without stubbing out his fag, he threw it up on to the pavement. 'And I'm giving up all meat. I'm a pescatarian at the moment, but that's just half measures. I'm becoming a fucking vegetarian.'

Irie shrugged, not certain what the right response should be.

'There's a lot to be said for the old motto, you know?'

'Old motto?'

'*Fight fire with fire*. It's only by really fucking extreme behaviour that you can get through to somebody like Marcus. He doesn't even know how *out there* he is. There's no point being reasonable with him because he thinks he *owns* reasonableness. How do you deal with people like that? Oh, and I'm giving up leather – wearing it – and all other animal by-products. Gelatin and stuff.'

After a while of watching the feet go by – leathers, sneakers, heels – Irie said, 'That'll show 'em.'

On April Fool's Day, Samad turned up. He was all in white, on his way to the restaurant, crumpled and creased like a disappointed saint. He looked to be on the brink of tears. Irie let him in.

'Hello, Miss Jones,' said Samad, bowing ever so slightly. 'And how is your father?'

Irie smiled with recognition. 'You see him more than we do. How's God?'

'Perfectly fine, thank you. Have you seen my good-for-nothing son recently?'

Before Irie had a chance to give her next line, Samad broke down in front of her and had to be led into the living room, sat in Darcus's chair and brought a cup of tea before he could speak.

'Mr Iqbal, what's wrong?'

'What is right?'

'Has something happened to Dad?'

'Oh no, no . . . Archibald is fine. He is like the washing-machine advert. He carries on and on as ever.'

'Then what?'

'Millat. He has been missing these three weeks.'

'God. Well, have you tried the Chalfens?'

'He is not with them. I know where he is. Out of the frying pan and into the fire. He is on some retreat with these lunatic green-tie people. In a sports centre in Chester.'

'Bloody hell.'

Irie sat down cross-legged and took out a fag. 'I hadn't seen him in school, but I didn't realize how long it had been. But if you know where he is . . .'

'I didn't come here to find him, I came to ask your advice, Irie. What can I do? You know him – how does one get through?'

Irie bit her lip, her mother's old habit. 'I mean, I don't know . . . we're not as close as we were . . . but I've always thought that maybe it's the Magid thing . . . missing him . . . I mean he'd never admit it . . . but Magid's his twin and maybe if he saw him –'

'No, no. No, no, no. I wish that were the solution. Allah knows how I pinned all my hopes on Magid. And now he says he is coming back to study the English law – paid for by these Chalfen people. He wants to enforce the laws of man rather than the laws of God. He has learnt none of the lessons of Muhammad – peace be upon Him! Of course, his mother is delighted. But he is nothing but a disappointment to me. More English than the English. Believe me, Magid will do Millat no good and Millat will do Magid no good. They have both lost their way. Strayed so far from the life I had intended for them. No doubt they will both marry white women called Sheila and put me in an early grave. All I wanted was two good Muslim boys. Oh, Irie . . .' Samad took her free hand and patted it with sad affection. 'I just don't understand where I have gone wrong. You teach them but they do not listen because they have the "Public Enemy" music on at full blast. You show them the road and they take the bloody path to the Inns of Court. You guide them and they run from your grasp to a Chester sports centre. You try to plan everything and nothing happens in the way that you expected . . .'

But if you could begin again, thought Irie, if you could take them back to the source of the river, to the start of the story, to the homeland . . . But she didn't say that, because he felt it as she felt it and both knew it was as useless as chasing your own shadow. Instead she took her hand from underneath his and placed it on top, returning the stroke. 'Oh, Mr Iqbal. I don't know what to say . . .'

'There are no words. The one I send home comes out a pukka Englishman, white suited, silly wig lawyer. The one I keep here is fully paid-up green bow-tie-wearing fundamentalist terrorist. I sometimes wonder why I bother,' said Samad bitterly, betraying the English inflections of twenty years in the country, 'I really do. These days, it feels to me like you make a devil's pact when you walk into this country. You hand over your passport at the check-in, you get stamped, you want to make a little money, get yourself started . . . but you mean to go back! Who would want to stay? Cold, wet, miserable; terrible food, dreadful newspapers – who would want to stay? In a place where you are never welcomed, only tolerated. Just tolerated. Like you are an animal finally house-trained. Who would want to stay? But you have made a devil's pact . . . it drags you in and suddenly you are unsuitable to return, your children are unrecognizable, you belong nowhere.'

'Oh, that's not true, surely.'

'And then you begin to give up the *very idea* of belonging. Suddenly this thing, this *belonging*, it seems like some long, dirty lie . . . and I begin to believe that birthplaces are accidents, that everything is an *accident*. But if you believe that, where do you go? What do you do? What does anything matter?'

As Samad described this dystopia with a look of horror, Irie was ashamed to find that the land of accidents sounded like *paradise* to her. Sounded like freedom.

'Do you understand, child? I know you understand.'

And what he really meant was: do we speak the same language? Are we from the same place? Are we the same?

Irie squeezed his hand and nodded vigorously, trying to ward off his tears. What else could she tell him but what he wanted to hear?

'Yes,' she said. 'Yes, yes, yes.'

When Hortense and Ryan came home that evening after a late-night prayer meeting, both were in a state of high excitement. Tonight was the night. After giving Hortense a flurry of instructions as to the typesetting and layout of his latest *Watchtower* article, Ryan went into the hallway to make his telephone call to Brooklyn to get the news.

'But I thought he was in consultation *with* them.'

'Yes, yes, he is . . . but de final confirmation, you understand, mus' come from Mr Charles Wintry himself in Brooklyn,' said Hortense breathlessly. 'What a day dis is! What a day! Help me wid liftin' dis typewriter now . . . I need it on de table.'

Irie did as she was told, carrying the enormous old Remington to the kitchen and laying it down in front of Hortense. Hortense passed Irie a bundle of white paper covered in Ryan's tiny script.

'Now you read dat to me, Irie Ambrosia, slowly now . . . an' I'll get it down in type.'

Irie read for half an hour or so, wincing at Ryan's horrible corkscrew prose, passing the whiting fluid when it was required, and gritting her teeth at the author's interruptions as every ten minutes he popped back into the room to adjust his syntax or rephrase a paragraph.

'Mr Topps, did you get trew yet?'

'Not yet, Mrs B., not yet. Very busy, Mr Charles Wintry. I'm going to try again now.'

A sentence, Samad's sentence, was passing through Irie's tired brain. *Sometimes I wonder why I bother.* And now that Ryan was out of the way, Irie saw her opportunity to ask it, though she framed it carefully.

Hortense leant back in her chair and placed her hands on her lap. 'I bin doin' dis a very long time, Irie Ambrosia. I bin' waitin' ever since I was a pickney in long socks.'

'But that's no reason –'

'What d'you know fe reasons? Nuttin' at all. The Witness church is where my roots are. It bin good to me when nobody else has. It was de good ting my mudder gave me, an' I nat going to let it go now we so close to de end.'

'But Gran, it's not . . . you won't ever . . .'

'Lemme tell you someting. I'm not like dem Witnesses jus' scared of dyin'. Jus' scared. Dem wan' everybody to die excep' dem. Dat's not a reason to dedicate your life to Jesus Christ. I gat very different aims. I still hope to be one of de Anointed evan if I am a woman. I want it all my life. I want to be dere wid de Lord making de laws and de decisions.' Hortense sucked her teeth long and loud. 'I gat so tired wid de church always tellin' me I'm a woman or I'm nat heducated enough. Everybody always tryin' to heducate you; heducate you about dis, heducate you about dat . . . Dat's always bin de problem wid de women in dis family. Somebody always tryin' to heducate them about someting, pretendin' it all about learnin' when it all about a battle of de wills. But if I were one of de hundred an' forty-four, no one gwan try to heducate *me*. Dat would be *my* job! I'd make my own laws an' I wouldn't be wanting anybody else's opinions. My mudder was strong-willed deep down, and I'm de same. Lord knows, your mudder was de same. And you de same.'

'Tell me about Ambrosia,' said Irie, spotting a chink in Hortense's armour that one might squeeze through. 'Please.'

But Hortense remained solid. 'You know enough already. De past is done wid. Nobody learn nuttin' from it. Top of page five please – I tink dat's where we were.'

At that moment Ryan returned to the room, face redder than ever.

'What, Mr Topps? Is it? Do you know?'

'God help the heathen, Mrs B., for the day is indeed at hand! It is as the Lord laid out clearly in his book of Revelation. He never intended a third millennium. Now I'll need that article typed up, and then another one that I'll dictate to you off the cuff – you'll need to telephone all the Lambeth members, and leaflet the –'

'Oh, yes, Mr Topps – but jus' let me tyake it in jus' a minute . . . It couldn't be any udder date, could it, Mr Topps? I tol' you I felt it in my bones.'

'I'm not sure as to how much your bones had to do wiv it, Mrs B. Surely more credit is due to the thorough scriptural study done by myself and my colleagues –'

'And God, presumably,' said Irie, cutting him a sharp glare, going over to hold Hortense, who was shaking with sobs. Hortense kissed Irie on both cheeks and Irie smiled at the hot wetness.

'Oh, Irie Ambrosia. I'm so glad you're here to share dis. I live dis century – I came into dis world in an eart-quake at de very beginning and I shall see the hevil and sinful pollution be herased in a mighty rumbling eart-quake once more. Praise de Lord! It is as he promised after all. I knew I'd make it. I got jus' seven years to wait. Ninety-two!' Hortense sucked her teeth contemptuously. 'Cho! My grandmudder live to see one hundered-and-tree an de woman could skip rope till de day she keel over and drop col'. Me gwan make it. I make it dis far. My mudder suffer to get me here – but she knew de true church and she make heffort to push me out in de mos' difficult circumstances so I could live to see that glory day.'

'Amen!'

'Oh, hamen, Mr Topps. Put on de complete suit of armour of God! Now, Irie Ambrosia, witness me as I say it: I'm gwan be dere. An' I'm gwan to be in *Jamaica* to see it. I'm going home that year of our Lord. An' you can come dere too if you learn from me and listen. You wan come Jamaica in de year two thousand?'

Irie let out a little scream and rushed to give her grandmother another hug.

Hortense wiped her tears with her apron. 'Lord Jesus, I live dis century! Well and truly I live dis terrible century wid all its troubles and vexations. And tanks to you, Lord, I'm gwan a feel a rumble at both ends.'

Magid, Millat and Marcus

1992, 1999

fundamental/*a. & n.* lME. *adj.* 1 Of or pertaining to the basis or groundwork; going to the root of the matter. 2 Serving as the base or foundation; essential or indispensable. Also, primary, original; from which others are derived. 3 Of or pertaining to the foundation(s) of a building. 4 Of a stratum: lowest, lying at the bottom.

Fundamentalism *n.* E20 [f. prec. + -ISM.] The strict maintenance of traditional orthodox religious beliefs or doctrines; *esp.* belief in the inerrancy of religious texts.
– *The New Shorter Oxford English Dictionary*

You must remember this, a kiss is still a kiss,
A sigh is just a sigh;
The fundamental things apply,
As time goes by.
– Herman Hupfeld, 'As Time Goes By' (1931 song)

16 *The Return of Magid Mahfooz Murshed Mubtasim Iqbal*

'Excuse me, you're not going to *smoke* that, are you?'

Marcus closed his eyes. He hated the construction. He always wanted to reply with equal grammatical perversity: Yes, I'm not going to smoke that. No, I am going to smoke that.

'Excuse me, I said you're –'

'Yes, I heard you the first time,' said Marcus softly, turning to his right to see the speaker with whom he shared a single arm-rest, each two chairs being assigned only one between them in the long line of moulded plastic. 'Is there a reason why I shouldn't?'

Irritation vanished at the sight of his interlocutor: a slim, pretty Asian girl, with an alluring gap between her front teeth, army trousers and a high ponytail, who was holding in her lap (of all things!) a copy of his collaborative pop science book of last spring (with the novelist Surrey T. Banks), *Time Bombs and Body Clocks: Adventures in Our Genetic Future*.

'Yes, there's a reason, *arsehole*. You can't smoke in Heathrow. Not in this bit of it. And you certainly can't smoke a fucking *pipe*. And these chairs are welded to each other and I've got asthma. Enough reasons?'

Marcus shrugged amiably. 'Yes, more than. Good book?'

This was a new experience for Marcus. Meeting one of his readers. Meeting one of his readers in the waiting lounge of an airport. He had been a writer of academic texts all his life, texts whose audience was tiny and select, whose members he more often than not knew personally. He had never sent his work off into the world like a party-popper, unsure where the different strands would land.

'Pardon?'

'Don't worry, I won't smoke if you don't want me to. I was just wondering, is it a good book?'

The girl screwed up her face, which was not as pretty as Marcus had first thought, the jawline a tad too severe. She closed the book (she was halfway through) and looked at its cover as if she had forgotten which book it was.

'Oh, it's all right, I suppose. Bit bloody weird. Bit of a headfuck.'

Marcus frowned. The book had been his agent's idea: a split-level high/low culture book, whereby Marcus wrote a 'hard science' chapter on one particular development in genetics and then the novelist wrote a twin chapter exploring these ideas from a futuristic, fictional, what-if-this-led-to-this point of view, and so on for eight chapters each. Marcus had university-bound sons plus Magid's law schooling to think about, and he had agreed to the project for pecuniary reasons. To that end, the book had not been the hit that was hoped for or required, and Marcus, when he thought of it at all, thought it was a failure. But weird? A headfuck?

'Umm, in what way *weird*?'

The girl looked suddenly suspicious. 'What is this? An interrogation?'

Marcus shrank back a little. His Chalfenist confidence was always less evident when he strayed abroad, away from the bosom of his family. He was a direct man who saw no point in asking anything other than the direct questions, but in recent years he had become aware that this directness did not always garner direct answers from strangers, as it did in his own small circle. In the outside world, outside of his college and home, one had to add things to speech. Particularly if one was somewhat strange-looking, as Marcus gathered he was; if one was a little old, with eccentric curly hair and spectacles missing their lower rims. You had to add things to your speech to make it more palatable. Niceties, throwaway phrases, pleases and thank yous.

'No, not an interrogation. I was just thinking of reading it myself, you see. I heard it was quite good, you know. And I was wondering why you thought it was weird.'

The girl, deciding at that moment that Marcus was neither mass murderer nor rapist, let her muscles relax and slid back in her chair. 'Oh, I don't know. Not so much weird, I guess, more *scary*.'

'Scary how?'

'Well, it's scary isn't it, all this genetic engineering.'

'Is it?'

'Yeah, you know, messing about with the body. They reckon there's a gene for intelligence, sexuality – practically everything, you know? Recombinant DNA technology,' said the girl, using the term cautiously, as if testing the water to see how much Marcus knew. Seeing no recognition in his face, she continued with more confidence. 'Once you know the restriction enzyme for a particular, like, *bit* of DNA, you can switch anything on or off, like a bloody stereo. That's what they're doing to those poor mice. It's pretty fucking scary. Not to mention, like, the pathogenic, i.e., *disease-producing*, organisms they've got sitting in petri dishes all over the place. I mean, I'm a politics student, yeah, and I'm like: what are they creating? And who do they want to wipe out? You've got to be *seriously* naive if you don't think the West intend to use this shit in the East, on the Arabs. Quick way to deal with the fundamentalist Muslims – no, seriously, man,' said the girl in response to a raised eyebrow from Marcus, 'things are getting scary. I mean, reading this shit you just realize how close science is to science fiction.'

As far as Marcus could see, science and science fiction were like ships in the night, passing each other in the fog. A science fiction robot, for example – even his son Oscar's expectation of a robot – was a thousand years ahead of anything either robotics or artificial intelligence could yet achieve. While the robots in Oscar's mind were singing, dancing and empathizing with his every joy and fear, over at MIT some poor bastard was slowly and painstakingly trying to get a machine to re-create the movements of a single human thumb. On the flip side of the coin, the simplest biological facts, the structure of animal cells for instance, were a mystery to all but fourteen-year-old children and scientists like himself; the former spending their time drawing them in class, the latter injecting them with foreign DNA. In between, or so it appeared to Marcus, flowed a great ocean of idiots, conspiracists, religious lunatics, presumptuous novelists, animal-rights activists, students of politics, and all the other breeds of fundamentalists who professed strange objections to his life's work. In the past few months, since his FutureMouse had gained some public attention, he had been forced to *believe* in these people, believe they actually existed en masse, and this was as hard for him as being taken to the bottom of the garden and told that here lived fairies.

'I mean, they talk about progress,' said the girl shrilly, becoming somewhat excited. 'They talk about leaps and bounds in the field of medicine yada yada yada, but bottom line, if somebody knows how to eliminate "undesirable" qualities in people, do you think some government's not going to do it? I mean, what's undesirable? There's just something a little fascist about the whole deal . . . I guess it's a good book, but at points you do think: where are we going here? Millions of blonds with blue eyes? Mail order babies? I mean, if you're Indian like me you've got something to worry about, yeah? And then they're planting cancers in poor creatures; like, who are you to mess with the make-up of a mouse? Actually creating an animal just so it can die – it's like being God! I mean personally I'm a Hindu, yeah? I'm not religious or nothing, but you know, I believe in the sanctity of life, yeah? And these people, like, *program* the mouse, plot its every move, yeah, when it's going to have kids, when it's going to die. It's just *unnatural*.'

Marcus nodded and tried to disguise his exhaustion. It was exhausting just to listen to her. Nowhere in the book did Marcus even touch upon human eugenics – it wasn't his field, and he had no particular interest in it. And yet this girl had managed to read a book almost entirely concerned with the more prosaic developments in recombinant DNA – gene therapy, proteins to dissolve blood clots, the cloning of insulin – and emerge from it full of the usual neo-fascist tabloid fantasies – mindless human clones, genetic policing of sexual and racial characteristics, mutated diseases, etc. Only the chapter on his mouse could have prompted such an hysterical reaction. It was to his mouse that the title of the book referred (again, the agent's idea), and it was his mouse upon which media attention had landed. Marcus saw clearly now what he had previously only suspected, that if it were not for the mouse there would have been little interest in the book at all. No other work he had been involved with seemed to catch the public imagination like his mice. To determine a mouse's future stirred people up. Precisely because people saw it that way: it wasn't determining the future of a cancer, or a reproductive cycle, or the capacity to age. It was determining the future of *the mouse*. People focused on the mouse in a manner that never failed to surprise him. They seemed unable to think of the animal as a site, a biological site for experimentation into heredity, into disease, into mortality. The mouseness of the mouse seemed inescapable. A picture from Marcus's laboratory of one of his transgenic mice, along with an article about the struggle for a patent, had appeared in *The Times*. Both he and the paper received a ton of hate-mail from factions as disparate as the Conservative Ladies Association, the Anti-Vivisection lobby, the Nation of Islam, the rector of St Agnes's Church, Berkshire, and the editorial board of the far-left *Schnews*. Neena Begum phoned to inform him that he would be reincarnated as a cockroach. Glenard Oak, always acute to a turning media tide, retracted their invitation for Marcus to come to school during National Science week. His own son, his Joshua, still refused to speak to him. The insanity of all of it genuinely *shook* him. The *fear* he had unwittingly provoked. And all because the public were three steps ahead of him like Oscar's robot, they had already played out their endgames, already concluded what the result of his research would be – something he did not presume to imagine! – full of their clones, zombies, designer children, gay genes. Of course, he understood the work he did involved some element of moral luck; so it is for all men of science. You work partly in the dark, uncertain of future ramifications, unsure what blackness your name might yet carry, what bodies will be laid at your door. No one working in a new field, doing truly visionary work, can be certain of getting through his century or the next without blood on his palms. But stop the work? Gag Einstein? Tie Heisenberg's hands? What can you hope to achieve?

'But surely,' Marcus began, more rattled than he expected himself to be, 'surely that's rather the point. All animals are in a sense programmed to die. It's perfectly natural. If it appears random, that's only because we don't clearly understand it, you see. We don't properly understand why some people seem predisposed to cancer. We don't properly understand why some people die of natural causes at sixty-three and some at ninety-seven. Surely it would be interesting to know a little more about these things. Surely the point of something like an oncomouse is that we're given the opportunity to see a life and a death stage by stage under the micro –'

'Yeah, well,' said the girl, putting the book in her bag. 'What*ever*. I've got to get to gate 52. It was nice talking to you. But yeah, you should definitely give it a read. I'm a big fan of Surrey T. Banks . . . he writes some freaky shit.'

Marcus watched the girl and her bouncing ponytail progress down the wide walkway until she merged with other dark-haired girls and was lost. Instantly, he felt relieved and remembered with pleasure his own appointment with gate 32 and Magid Iqbal, who was a different kettle of fish, or a blacker kettle, or whatever the phrase was. With fifteen minutes to spare, he abandoned his coffee which had gone rapidly from scalding to lukewarm, and began to walk in the direction of the lower 50s. The phrase 'a meeting of minds' was running through his head. He knew this was an absurd thing to think of a seventeen-year-old boy, but still he thought it, *felt* it: a certain elation, maybe equal to the feeling his own mentor experienced when the seventeen-year-old Marcus Chalfen first walked into his poky college office. A certain satisfaction. Marcus was familiar with the mutually beneficial smugness that runs from mentor to protégé and back again (ah, but you are brilliant and deign to spend your time with me! Ah, but I am brilliant and catch your attention above all others!). Still, he indulged himself. And he was glad to be meeting Magid for the first time, alone, though he hoped he was not guilty of planning it that way. It was more a series of fortunate accidents. The Iqbals' car had broken down, and Marcus's hatchback was not large. He had persuaded Samad and Alsana that there would not be enough room for Magid's luggage if they came with him. Millat was in Chester with KEVIN and had been quoted as saying (in language reminiscent of his Mafia video days), 'I have no brother.' Irie had an exam in the morning. Joshua refused to get in any car if Marcus was in it; in fact, he generally eschewed cars at present, opting for the environmentally ethical option of two wheels. As far as Josh's decision went, Marcus felt as he did about all human decisions of this kind. One could neither agree nor disagree with them as *ideas*. There was no rhyme nor reason for so much of what people did. And in his present estrangement from Joshua he felt more powerless than ever. It hurt him that even his own son was not as Chalfenist as he'd hoped. And over the past few months he had built up great expectations of Magid (and this would explain why his pace quickened, gate 28, gate 29, gate 30); maybe he had begun to hope, begun to *believe*, that Magid would be a beacon for right-thinking Chalfenism even as it died a death here in the wilderness. They would *save* each other. *This couldn't be faith could it, Marcus?* He questioned himself directly on this point as he scurried along. For a gate and a half the question unnerved him. Then it passed and the answer was reassuring. Not faith, no, Marcus, not the kind with no eyes. Something stronger, something firmer. *Intellectual* faith.

So. Gate 32. It would be just the two of them, then, meeting at last, having conquered the gap between continents; the teacher, the willing pupil, and then that first, historic handshake. Marcus did not think for a second it could or would go badly. He was no student of history (and science had taught him that the past was where we did things through a glass, darkly, whereas the future was always brighter, a place where we did things right or at least right-er), he had no stories to scare him concerning a dark man meeting a white man, both with heavy expectations, but only one with the power. He had brought no piece of white cardboard either, some large banner with a name upon it, like the rest of his fellow waiters, and as he looked around gate 32, that concerned him. How would they know each other? Then he remembered he was meeting a twin, and remembering that made him laugh out loud. It was incredible and sublime, even to him, that a boy should walk out of that tunnel with precisely the same genetic code as a boy he already knew, and yet in every conceivable way be different. He would see him and yet not see him. He would recognize him and yet that recognition would be false. Before he had a chance to think what this meant, whether it meant anything, they were coming towards him, the passengers of BA flight 261; a talkative but exhausted brown mob who rushed towards him like a river, turning off at the last minute as if he were the edge of a waterfall. *Nomoskār . . . sālām ā lekum . . . kamon āchō?* This is what they said to each other and their friends on the other side of the barrier; some women in full purdah, some in saris, men in strange mixtures of fabrics, leather, tweed, wool and nylon, with little boat-hats that reminded Marcus of Nehru; children in jumpers made by the Taiwanese and rucksacks of bright reds and yellows; pushing through the doors to the concourse of gate 32; meeting aunts, meeting drivers, meeting children, meeting officials, meeting sun-tanned white-toothed airline representatives . . .

'You are Mr Chalfen.'

Meeting minds. Marcus lifted his head to look at the tall young man standing in front of him. It was Millat's face, certainly, but it was cleaner cut, and somewhat younger in appearance. The eyes were not so violet, or at least not so violently violet. The hair was floppy in the English public school style and brushed forward. The form was ever so thickly set and healthy. Marcus was no good on clothes, but he could say at least that they were entirely white and that the overall impression was of good materials, well made and soft. And he was handsome, even Marcus could see that. What he lacked in the Byronic charisma of his brother, he seemed to gain in nobility, with a sturdier chin and a dignified jaw. These were all pins in haystacks, however, these were the differences you notice only because the similarity is so striking. They were twins from their broken noses to their huge, ungainly feet. Marcus was conscious of a very faint feeling of disappointment that this was so. But superficial exteriors aside, there was no doubting, Marcus thought, who this boy Magid truly resembled. Hadn't Magid spotted Marcus from a crowd of many? Hadn't they recognized each other, just now, at a far deeper, fundamental level? Not twinned like cities or the two halves of a randomly split ovum, but twinned like each side of an equation: logically, essentially, inevitably. As rationalists are wont, Marcus abandoned rationalism for a moment in the face of the sheer wonder of the thing. This instinctive meeting at gate 32 (Magid had strode across the floor and walked directly to him), finding each other like this in a great swell of people, five hundred at least: what were the chances? It seemed as unlikely as the feat of the sperm who conquer the blind passage towards the egg. As magical as that egg splitting in two. Magid and Marcus. Marcus and Magid.

'Yes! Magid! We finally meet! I feel as if I know you already – well, I do, but then again I don't – but, bloody hell, how did you know it was me?'

Magid's face grew radiant and revealed a lopsided smile of much angelic charm. 'Well, Marcus, my dear man, you are the only white fellow at gate 32.'

The return of Magid Mahfooz Murshed Mubtasim shook the houses of Iqbal, Jones and Chalfen considerably. 'I don't recognize him,' said Alsana to Clara in confidence, after he had spent a few days at home. 'There is something peculiar about him. When I told him Millat was in Chester, he did not say a word. Just a stiff-upper lip. He hasn't seen his brother *in eight years*. But not a little squeak, not a whisperoo. Samad says this is some clone, this is not an Iqbal. One hardly likes to touch him. His teeth, he brushes them six times a day. His underwear, he irons them. It is like sitting down to breakfast with David Niven.'

Joyce and Irie viewed the new arrival with equal suspicion. They had loved the one brother so well and thoroughly for so many years, and now suddenly this new, yet familiar face; like switching on your favourite TV soap only to find a beloved character slyly replaced by another actor with a similar haircut. For the first few weeks they simply did not know what to make of him. As for Samad, if he had had his way, he would have hidden the boy away for ever, locked him under the stairs or sent him to Greenland. He dreaded the inevitable visits of all his relatives (the ones he had boasted to, all the tribes who had worshipped at the altar of the framed photograph) when they caught an eye-load of this Iqbal the younger, with his bow-ties and his Adam Smith and his E. M. bloody Forster and his atheism! The only up-side was the change in Alsana. The *A–Z*? *Yes*, Samad Miah, it is in the top right-hand drawer, *yes*, that's where it is, *yes*. The first time she did it, he almost jumped out of his skin.

The curse was lifted. No more *maybe Samad Miah*, no more *possibly Samad Miah*. Yes, yes, yes. No, no, no. The fundamentals. It was a blessed relief, but it wasn't enough. His sons had failed him. The pain was excruciating. He shuffled through the restaurant with his eyes to the ground. If aunts and uncles phoned, he deflected questions or simply lied. Millat? He is in Birmingham, working in the mosque, yes, renewing his faith. Magid? Yes, he is marrying soon, yes, a very good young man, wants a lovely Bengali girl, yes, upholder of traditions, yes.

So. First came the musical-living-arrangements, as everybody shifted one place to the right or left. Millat returned at the beginning of October. Thinner, fully bearded and quietly determined not to see his twin on political, religious and personal grounds. 'If Magid stays,' said Millat (De Niro, this time), 'I go.' And because Millat looked thin and tired and wild-eyed, Samad said Millat could stay, which left no other option but for Magid to stay with the Chalfens (much to Alsana's chagrin) until the situation could be resolved. Joshua, furious at being displaced in his parents' affections by yet another Iqbal, went to the Joneses', while Irie, though ostensibly having returned to her family home (on the concession of a 'year off'), spent all her time at the Chalfens, organizing Marcus's affairs so as to earn money for her two bank accounts (*Amazon Jungle Summer '93* and *Jamaica 2000*), often working deep into the night and sleeping on the couch.

'The children have left us, they are abroad,' said Samad over the phone to Archie, in so melancholy a fashion that Archie suspected he was quoting poetry. 'They are strangers in strange lands.'

'They've run to the bloody hills, more like,' replied Archie grimly. 'I tell you, if I had a penny for every time I've seen Irie in the past few months . . .'

He'd have about ten pence. She was never home. Irie was stuck between a rock and a hard place, like Ireland, like Israel, like India. A no-win situation. If she stayed home there was Joshua berating her about her involvement with Marcus's mice. Arguments she had no answer for, nor any stomach: *should living organisms be patented? Is it right to plant pathogens in animals?* Irie didn't know and so, with her father's instincts, shut her mouth and kept her distance. But if she was at the Chalfens', working away at what had become a full-time summer job, she had to deal with Magid. Here, the situation was impossible. Her work for Marcus, which had begun nine months earlier as a little light filing, had increased seven fold; the recent interest in Marcus's work meant she was required to deal with the calls of the media, sackfuls of post, organize appointments; her pay had likewise increased to that of a secretary. But that was the problem, she was a *secretary*, whereas Magid was a confidant, an apprentice and disciple, accompanying Marcus on trips, observing him in the laboratory. The golden child. The chosen one. Not only was he brilliant, but he was charming. Not only was he charming, but he was generous. For Marcus, he was an answer to prayers. Here was a boy who could weave the most beautiful moral defences with a professionalism that belied his years, who helped Marcus formulate arguments he would not have had the patience to do alone. It was Magid who encouraged him out of the laboratory, taking him by the hand squinting into the sunlit world where people were calling for him. People wanted Marcus and his mouse, and Magid knew how to give it to them. If the *New Statesman* needed two thousand words on the patent debate, Magid would write while Marcus spoke, translating his words into elegant English, turning the bald statements of a scientist disinterested in moral debates into the polished arguments of a philosopher. If *Channel 4 News* wanted an interview, Magid explained how to sit, how to move one's hands, how to incline one's head. All this from a boy who had spent the greater proportion of his life in the Chittagong Hills, without television or newspaper. Marcus – even though he had a lifelong hatred of the word, even though he hadn't used it since his own father clipped his ear for it when he was three – was tempted to call it a *miracle*. Or, at the very least, extremely fortuitous. The boy was changing his life and that was extremely fortuitous. For the first time in his life, Marcus was prepared to concede faults in himself – small ones, mind – but still . . . *faults*. He had been too insular, perhaps, perhaps. He had been aggressive towards public interest in his work, perhaps, perhaps. He saw room for change. And the genius of it, the master stroke, was that Magid never for a moment let Marcus feel that Chalfenism was being compromised in any way whatsoever. He expressed his undying affection and admiration for it every day. All Magid wanted to do, he explained to Marcus, was bring Chalfenism to the people. And you had to give the people what they wanted in a form *they could understand*. There was something so sublime in the way he said it, so soothing, so *true*, that Marcus, who would have spat on such an argument six months before, gave in without protest.

'There's room for one more chap this century,' Magid told him (this guy was a master in flattery), 'Freud, Einstein, Crick and Watson . . . There is an empty seat, Marcus. The bus is not quite full capacity. Ding! Ding! *Room for one more . . .*'

And you can't beat that for an offer. You can't fight it. Marcus and Magid. Magid and Marcus. Nothing else mattered. The two of them were oblivious to the upset they caused Irie, or to the widespread displacement, the strange seismic ripples, that their friendship had set off in everyone else. Marcus had *pulled out*, like Mountbatten from India, or a satiated teenage boy from his latest mate. He abrogated responsibility, for everything and everybody – Chalfens, Iqbals and Joneses – everything and everyone bar Magid and his mice. All others were fanatics. And Irie bit her tongue because Magid was good, and Magid was kind, and Magid walked through the house in white. But like all manifestations of the Second Coming, all saints, saviours and gurus, Magid Iqbal was also, in Neena's eloquent words, a first-class, one hundred per cent, bona fide, total and utter *pain in the arse*. A typical conversation:

'Irie, I am confused.'

'Not right now, Magid, I'm on the phone.'

'I don't wish to take from your valuable time, but it is a matter of some urgency. I am confused.'

'Magid, could you just – '

'You see. Joyce very kindly bought me these jeans. They are called Levis.'

'Look, could I call you back? Right . . . OK. . . Bye. *What*, Magid? That was an important call. What is it?'

'So you see I have these beautiful American Levi jeans, white jeans, that Joyce's sister brought back from a holiday in Chicago, the Windy City they call it, though I don't believe there is anything particularly unusual about its climate, considering its proximity to Canada. My Chicago jeans. Such a thoughtful gift! I was overwhelmed to receive them. But then I was confused by this label in the inner lining that states that the jeans are apparently "shrink-to-fit". I asked myself, what can this mean: "shrink-to-fit"?'

'They shrink until they fit, Magid. That would be my guess.'

'But Joyce was percipient enough to buy them in precisely the right size, you see? A 32, 34.'

'All right, Magid, I don't want to see them. I believe you. So don't shrink them.'

'That was my original conclusion, also. But it appears there is no separate procedure for shrinking them. If one washes the jeans, they will simply shrink.'

'Fascinating.'

'And you appreciate at some juncture the jeans will require washing?'

'What's your point, Magid.'

'Well, do they shrink by some pre-calculated amount, and if so, by how much? If the amount was not correct, they would open themselves up to a great deal of litigation, no? It is no good if they shrink-to-fit, after all, if they do not shrink-to-fit *me*. There is another possibility, as Jack suggested, that they shrink to the contours of the body. Yet how can such a thing be possible?'

'Well, why don't you get in the fucking bath with the fucking jeans on and see what happens?'

But you couldn't upset Magid with words. He turned the other cheek. Sometimes hundreds of times a day, like a lollipop lady on ecstasy. He had this way of smiling at you, neither wounded nor angry, and then inclining his head (to the exact same angle his father did when taking an order of curried prawns) in a gesture of total forgiveness. He had absolute empathy for everybody, Magid. And it was an unbelievable pain in the arse.

'Umm, I didn't mean to . . . Oh shit. Sorry. Look . . . I don't know . . . you're just so . . . have you heard from Millat?'

'My brother shuns me,' said Magid, that same expression of universal calm and forgiveness unchanged. 'He marks me like Cain because I am a non-believer. At least not in his god or any others with a name. Because of this, he refuses to meet me, even to talk on the telephone.'

'Oh, you know, he'll probably come round. He always was a stubborn bastard.'

'Of course, yes, you love him,' continued Magid, not giving Irie a chance to protest. 'So you know his habits, his manners. You will understand, then, how fiercely he takes my conversion. I have converted to Life. I see his god in the millionth position of *pi*, in the arguments of the Phaedrus, in a perfect paradox. But that is not enough for Millat.'

Irie looked him square in the face. There was something in there she had been unable to put her finger on these four months, because it was obscured by his youth, his looks, his clean clothes and his personal hygiene. Now she saw it clearly. He was touched by it – the same as Mad Mary, the Indian with the white face and the blue lips, and the guy who carried his wig around on a piece of string. The same as those people who walk the Willesden streets with no intention of buying Black Label beer, or stealing a stereo, collecting the dole or pissing in an alleyway. The ones with a wholly different business. *Prophecy*. And Magid had it in his face. He wanted to tell you and tell you and tell you.

'Millat demands complete surrender.'

'Sounds typical.'

'He wants me to join Keepers of the Eternal and –'

'Yeah, KEVIN, I know them. So you *have* spoken to him.'

'I don't need to speak to him to know what he thinks. He is my twin. I don't wish to see him. I don't need to. Do you understand the nature of twins? Do you understand the meaning of the word *cleave*? Or rather, the double meaning that –'

'Magid. No offence, but I've got work to do.'

Magid gave a little bow. 'Naturally. You will excuse me, I have to go and submit my Chicago jeans to the experiment you proposed.'

Irie gritted her teeth, picked up the phone and redialled the number she had cut off. It was a journalist (it was always journalists these days), and she had something to read to him. She'd had a crash course in media relations since her exams, and dealing with them/it had taught her there was no point in trying to deal with each one separately. To give some unique point of view to the *FT* and then to the *Mirror* and then to the *Daily Mail* was impossible. It was their job, not yours, to get the angle, to write their separate book of the huge media bible. Each to their own. Reporters were factional, fanatical, obsessively defending their own turf, propounding the same thing day after day. So it had always been. Who would have guessed that Luke and John would take such different angles on the scoop of the century, the death of the Lord? It just went to prove that you couldn't trust these guys. Irie's job, then, was to give the information as it stood, every time, verbatim from a piece of paper written by Marcus and Magid, stapled to the wall.

'All right,' said the journo. 'Tape's running.'

And here Irie stumbled at the first hurdle of PR: believing in what you sell. It wasn't that she lacked the moral faith. It was more fundamental than that. She didn't believe in it as a *physical fact*. She didn't believe it existed. FutureMouse© was now such an enormous, spectacular, *cartoon* of an idea (in every paper's column, agonized over by journos – *Should it get a patent?* Eulogized by hacks – *Greatest achievement of the century?*), one expected the damn mouse to stand up and speak by itself. Irie took a deep breath. Though she had repeated the words many times, they still seemed fantastical, absurd – fiction on the wings of fantasy – with more of a dash of Surrey T. Banks in them:

PRESS RELEASE: 15 OCTOBER 1992

Subject: Launch of FutureMouse©

Professor Marcus Chalfen, writer, celebrated scientist and leading figure of a group of research geneticists from St Jude's College, intends to 'launch' his latest 'design' in a public space; to increase understanding of transgenics and to raise interest and further investment in his work. The design will demonstrate the sophistication of the work being done on gene manipulation and demystify this much maligned branch of biological research. It will be accompanied by a full exhibition, a lecture hall, a multimedia area and interactive games for children. It will be funded in part by the government's Millennial Science Commission, with additional monies from business and industry.

A two-week-old FutureMouse© is to be put on display at the Perret Institute in London on 31 December 1992. There it will remain on public display until 31 December 1999. This mouse is genetically normal except for a select group of novel genes that are added to the genome. A

DNA clone of these genes is injected into the fertilized mouse egg, thus linking them to the chromosomal DNA in the zygote, which is subsequently inherited by cells of the resulting embryo. Before injection into the germ line, these genes are custom-designed so they can be 'turned on' and expressed only in specific mouse tissue and along a predictable timetable. The mouse will be the site for an experiment into the ageing of cells, the progression of cancer within cells, and a few other matters that will serve as surprises along the way!

The journalist laughed. 'Jesus. What the fuck does that mean?'

'I dunno,' said Irie. 'Surprises, I guess.'

She continued:

The mouse will live the seven years it is on display, roughly double the normal life expectancy of a mouse. The mouse development is retarded, therefore, at a ratio of two years for every one. At the end of the first year the SV40 large-T oncogene, which the mouse carries in the insulin-producing pancreas cells, will express itself in pancreatic carcinomas that will continue to develop at a retarded pace throughout its life. At the end of the second year the H-ras oncogene in its skin cells will begin to express itself in multiple benign papillomas that an observer will be able to see clearly three months later with the naked eye. Four years into the experiment the mouse will begin to lose its ability to produce melanin by means of a slow, programmed eradication of the enzyme tyrosinase. At this point the mouse will lose all its pigmentation and become albino: a white mouse. If no external or unexpected interference occurs, the mouse will live until 31 December 1999, dying within the month after that date. The FutureMouse© experiment offers the

public a unique opportunity to see a life and death in 'close-up'. The opportunity to witness for themselves a technology that might yet slow the progress of disease, control the process of ageing and eliminate genetic defect. The FutureMouse© holds out the tantalizing promise of a new phase in human history where we are not victims of the random but instead directors and arbitrators of our own fate.

'Bloody hell,' said the journo. 'Scary shit.'

'Yeah, I guess,' said Irie vacantly (she had ten more calls to make this morning). 'Do you want me to post on some of the photographic material?'

'Yeah, go on. Save me going through the archive. Cheers.'

Just as Irie put down the phone, Joyce flew into the room like a hippy comet, a great stream of black fringed velvet, kaftan and multiple silk scarves.

'Don't use the phone! I've told you before. We've got to keep the phone free. Millat might be trying to ring.'

Four days earlier Millat had missed a psychiatrist's appointment Joyce had arranged for him. He had not been seen since. Everyone knew he was with KEVIN, and everyone knew he had no intention of ringing Joyce. Everyone except Joyce.

'It's simply *essential* that I talk with him if he rings. We're *so* close to a breakthrough. Marjorie's almost certain it's Attention-Deficit Hyperactivity Disorder.'

'And how come *you* know all this? I thought Marjorie was a doctor. What the fuck happened to doctor–patient privilege?'

'Oh, Irie, don't be silly. She's a *friend* too. She's just trying to keep me informed.'

'Middle-class mafia, more like.'

'Oh *really*. Don't be so hysterical. You're getting more *hysterical* by the day. Look, I need you to keep off the phone.'

'I know. You said.'

'Because if Marjorie's right, and it is ADD, he really needs to get to a doctor and some methylphenidate. It's a very debilitative condition.'

'Joyce, he hasn't got a disorder, he's just a Muslim. There are one billion of them. They can't all have ADD.'

Joyce took in a little gasp of air. 'I think you're being very cruel. That's *exactly* the kind of comment that isn't helpful.'

She stalked over to the bread board, tearfully cut off a huge lump of cheese and said, 'Look. The most important thing is that I get the two of them to face each other. It's time.'

Irie looked dubious. 'Why is it time?'

Joyce popped the lump of cheese into her mouth. 'It's time because they need each other.'

'But if they don't want to, they don't want to.'

'Sometimes people don't know what they want. They don't know what they need. Those boys need each other like . . .' Joyce thought for a moment. She was bad with metaphor. In a garden you never planted something where something else was meant to be. 'They need each other like Laurel and Hardy, like Crick needed Watson –'

'Like East Pakistan needed West Pakistan.'

'Well, I don't think that's very funny, Irie.'

'I'm not laughing, Joyce.'

Joyce cut more cheese from the block, tore two hunks of bread from a loaf, and sandwiched the three together.

'The fact is both these boys have serious emotional problems and it's not helped by Millat refusing to see Magid. It upsets him so much. They've been split by their religions, by their cultures. Can you imagine the *trauma*?'

Irie wished at that moment she had allowed Magid to tell her to tell her to tell her. She would at least have had information. She would have had something to use against Joyce. Because if you listen to prophets, they give you ammunition. The nature of twins. The millionth position of *pi* (do infinite numbers have beginnings?). And most of all, the double meaning of the word *cleave*. Did he know which was worse, which more traumatic: pulling together or tearing apart?

'Joyce, why don't you worry about your own family for once? Just for a change. What about Josh? When's the last time you saw Josh?'

Joyce's upper lip stiffened. 'Josh is in Glastonbury.'

'Right. Glastonbury's been over two months, Joyce.'

'He's doing a little travelling. He said he might.'

'And who's he with? You don't *know* anything about those people. Why don't you worry about *that* for a while, and keep the *fuck* out of everybody else's business.'

Joyce didn't even flinch at this. It is hard to explain just how familiar teenage abuse was to Joyce; she got it so regularly these days from her own children and other people's that a swear-word or a cruel comment just couldn't affect her. She simply weeded them out.

'The reason I don't worry about Josh, as you well know,' said Joyce, smiling broadly and speaking in her Chalfen-guide-to-parenting voice, 'is because he's just trying to get a little bit of attention. Rather like you are at this moment. It's perfectly natural for well-educated middle-class children to act up at his age.' (Unlike many others around this time, Joyce felt no shame about using the term 'middle class'. In the Chalfen lexicon the middle classes were the inheritors of the enlightenment, the creators of the welfare state, the intellectual elite and the source of all culture. Where they got this idea, it's hard to say.) 'But they soon come back into the fold. I'm perfectly confident about Joshua. He's just acting up against his father and it will pass. But Magid has some real problems. I've been doing my research, Irie. And there are just so many *signs*. I can read them.'

'Well, you must be *mis*reading them,' Irie shot back, because a battle was about to begin, she could sense it. 'Magid's *fine*. I was just talking to him. He's a Zen master. He's the most fucking serene individual I ever met in my life. He's working with Marcus, which is what he wants to do, and he's *happy*. How about we all try a policy of non-involvement for once? A little laissez-faire? Magid's *fine*.'

'Irie, darling,' said Joyce, moving Irie along one chair and positioning herself next to the phone. 'What you never understand is that people are *extreme*. It would be wonderful if everyone was like your father, carrying on as normal even if the ceiling's coming down around his ears. But a lot of people can't do that. Magid and Millat display extreme behaviour. It's all very well saying laissez-faire and being terribly clever about it, but the bottom line is Millat's going to get himself into terrible trouble with these fundamentalist people. Terrible trouble. I hardly sleep for worrying about him. You read about these groups in the news . . . And it's putting a terrible mental strain on Magid. Now, am I meant to just sit back and watch them tear themselves apart, just because their parents – no, I will say it, because it's true – just because their parents don't seem concerned? I've only ever had those boys' welfare at heart, you of all people should know that. They need help. I just walked past the bathroom and Magid is sitting in the bath with his jeans on. *Yes*. All right? Now,' said Joyce, serene as a bovine, 'I should think I know a traumatized child when I see one.'

17 *Crisis Talks and Eleventh-hour Tactics*

'Mrs Iqbal? It's Joyce Chalfen. Mrs Iqbal? I can see you quite clearly. It's Joyce. I really think we should talk. Could you . . . umm . . . open the door?'

Yes, she could. *Theoretically*, she could. But in this atmosphere of extremity, with warring sons and disparate factions, Alsana needed a tactic of her own. She'd done silence, and word-strikes and food consumption (the opposite of a hunger-strike; one gets bigger in order to intimidate the enemy), and now she was attempting a sit-down protest.

'Mrs Iqbal . . . just five minutes of your time. Magid's really very upset about all of this. He's worried about Millat and so am I. Just five minutes, Mrs Iqbal, please.'

Alsana didn't rise from her seat. She simply continued along the hem, keeping her eye on the black thread as it shuttled from one cog to the next and down into the PVC, pressing the pedal of the Singer furiously, as if kicking the flank of a horse she wished to ride into the sunset.

'Well, you may as well let her in,' said Samad wearily, emerging from the lounge, where Joyce's persistence had disturbed his appreciation of *The Antiques Roadshow*. (Aside from *The Equalizer*, starring that great moral arbiter Edward Woodward, it was Samad's favourite programme. He had spent fifteen long televisual years waiting for some cockney housewife to pull a trinket of Mangal Pande's out of her handbag. *Oh, Mrs Winterbottom, now this is* very *exciting. What we have here is the barrel of the musket belonging to* . . . He sat with the phone under his right hand so that in the event of such a scenario he could phone the BBC and demand the said Winterbottom's address and asking price. So far only Mutiny medals and a pocket watch belonging to Havelock, but still he watched.)

He peered down the hallway at the shadowy form of Joyce through the glass and scratched his testicles, sadly. Samad was in his television mode: garish V-neck, stomach swelling like a tight hot-water bottle beneath it, long moth-eaten dressing gown, and a pair of paisley boxer-shorts from which two stick legs, the legacy of his youth, protruded. In his television mode action escaped him. The box in the corner of the room (which he liked to think of as an antique of its kind, encased in wood and on four legs like some Victorian robot) sucked him in and sapped all energy.

'Well, why don't you *do* something, Mr Iqbal? Make her go away. Instead of standing there with your flabby gut and your tiny willy on display.'

Samad grunted and tucked the cause of all his troubles, two huge hairy balls and a defeated-looking limp prick, back into the inner lining of his shorts.

'She won't go away,' he murmured. 'And if she does, she will only return with reinforcements.'

'But why? Hasn't she caused enough trouble?' said Alsana loudly, loud enough for Joyce. 'She has her own family, no? Why does she not go and for a change mess them up? She has boys, four boys? How many boys does she want? How bloody many?'

Samad shrugged, went into the kitchen drawer and fished out the earphones that could be plugged into the television and thus short-circuit the outside world. He, like Marcus, had disengaged. *Leave them*, was his feeling. Leave them to their battles.

'Oh *thank* you,' said Alsana caustically, as her husband retreated to his Hugh Scully and his pots and guns. 'Thank you, Samad Miah, for your oh so valuable contribution. This is what the men do. They make the mess, the century ends, and they leave the women to clear up the shit. Thank you, husband!'

She increased the speed of her sewing, dashing out the seam, progressing down the inner leg, while the Sphinx of the letterbox continued to ask unanswerable questions.

'Mrs Iqbal . . . please can we talk? Is there any reason why we shouldn't talk? Do we *have* to behave like children?'

Alsana began to sing.

'Mrs Iqbal? *Please*. What can this possibly achieve?'

Alsana sang louder.

'I must tell you,' said Joyce, strident as ever, even through three panels of wood and double glazing, 'I'm not here for my health. Whether you want me to be *involved* or not, I *am*, you see? I *am*.'

Involved. At least that was the right word, Alsana reflected, as she lifted her foot off the pedal, and let the wheel spin a few times alone before coming to a squeaky halt. Sometimes, here in England, especially at bus-stops and on the daytime soaps, you heard people say 'We're *involved* with each other,' as if this were a most wonderful state to be in, as if one chose it and enjoyed it. Alsana never thought of it that way. *Involved* happened over a long period of time, pulling you in like quicksand. *Involved* is what befell the moon-faced Alsana Begum and the handsome Samad Miah one week after they'd been pushed into a Delhi breakfast room together and informed they were to marry. *Involved* was the result when Clara Bowden met Archie Jones at the bottom of some stairs. *Involved* swallowed up a girl called Ambrosia and a boy called Charlie (yes, Clara had told her *that* sorry tale) the second they kissed in the larder of a guest house. Involved is neither good, nor bad. It is just a consequence of living, a consequence of occupation and immigration, of empires and expansion, of living in each other's pockets . . . one becomes involved and it is a long trek back to being uninvolved. And the woman was right, one didn't do it for one's *health*. Nothing this late in the century was done with *health* in mind. Alsana was no dummy when it came to the Modern Condition. She watched the talk shows, all day long she watched the talk shows – *My wife slept with my brother, My mother won't stay out of my boyfriend's life* – and the microphone holder, whether it be Tanned Man with White Teeth or Scary Married Couple, always asked the same damn silly question: *But why do you feel the need . . . ?* Wrong! Alsana had to explain it to them through the screen. You blockhead; they are not *wanting* this, they are not *willing* it – they are just involved, see? They walk IN and they get trapped between the revolving doors of those two *v*'s. *Involved.* The years pass, and the mess accumulates and here we are. Your brother's sleeping with my ex-wife's niece's second cousin. *Involved.* Just a tired, inevitable fact. Something in the way Joyce said it, *involved* – wearied, slightly acid – suggested to Alsana that the word meant the same thing to her. An enormous web you spin to catch yourself.

'OK, OK, lady, five minutes, only. I have three catsuits to do this morning come hell or high water.'

Alsana opened the door and Joyce walked into the hallway, and for a moment they surveyed their opposite number, guessing each other's weight like nervous prize fighters prior to mounting the scales. They were definitely a match for each other. What Joyce lacked in chest, she made up in bottom. Where Alsana revealed a weakness in delicate features – a thin and pretty nose, light eyebrows – she compensated with the huge pudge of her arms, the dimples of maternal power. For, after all, she was the mother here. The mother of the boys in question. She held the trump card, should she be forced to play it.

'Okey-dokey, then,' said Alsana, squeezing through the narrow kitchen door, beckoning Joyce to follow.

'Is it tea or is it coffee?'

'Tea,' said Joyce firmly. 'Fruit if possible.'

'Fruit not possible. Not even Earl Grey is possible. I come from the land of tea to this godawful country and then I can't afford a proper cup of it. P.G. Tips is possible and nothing else.'

Joyce winced. 'P.G. Tips, please, then.'

'As you wish.'

The mug of tea plonked in front of Joyce a few minutes later was grey with a rim of scum and thousands of little microbes flitting through it, less micro than one would have hoped. Alsana gave Joyce a moment to consider it.

'Just leave it for a while,' she explained gaily. 'My husband hit a water pipe when digging a trench for some onions. Our water is a little funny ever since. It may give you the running shits or it may not. But give it a minute and it clears. See?' Alsana gave it an unconvincing stir, sending yet larger chunks of unidentified matter bubbling up to the surface. 'You see? Fit for Shah Jahan himself!'

Joyce took a tentative sip and then pushed it to one side.

'Mrs Iqbal, I know we haven't been on the best of terms in the past, but –'

'Mrs Chalfen,' said Alsana, putting up her long forefinger to stop Joyce speaking. 'There are two rules that everybody knows, from PM to jinrickshaw-wallah. The first is, never let your country become a trading post. Very important. If my ancestors had followed this advice, my situation presently would be very different, but such is life. The second is, don't interfere in other people's family business. Milk?'

'No, no, thank you. A little sugar . . .'

Alsana dumped a huge heaped tablespoon into Joyce's cup.

'You think I am interfering?'

'I think you have interfered.'

'But I just want the twins to see each other.'

'You are the reason they are apart.'

'But Magid is only living with us because Millat won't live with him here. And Magid tells me your husband can barely stand the sight of him.'

Alsana, little pressure-cooker that she was, blew. 'And *why* can't he? Because *you*, you and your husband, have involved Magid in something so contrary to our culture, to our beliefs, that we barely recognize him! You have done that! He is at odds with his brother now. Impossible conflict! Those green bow-tied bastards: Millat is high up with them now. Very involved. He doesn't tell me, but I hear. They call themselves followers of Islam, but they are nothing but thugs in a gang roaming Kilburn like all the other lunatics. And now they are sending out the – what are they called – folded-paper trouble.'

'Leaflets?'

'*Leaflets*. Leaflets about your husband and his ungodly mouse. Trouble brewing, yes sir. I found them, hundreds of them under his bed.' Alsana stood up, drew a key out of her apron pocket and opened a kitchen cupboard stacked full of green leaflets, which cascaded on to the floor. 'He's disappeared again, three days. I have to put them back before he finds out they are gone. Take some, go on, lady, take them, go and read them to Magid. Show *him* what you have done. Two boys driven to different ends of the world. *You* have made a war between my sons. *You* are splitting them apart!'

A minute earlier Millat had turned the key ever so softly in the front door. Since then he had been standing in the hallway, listening to the conversation and smoking a fag. It was great! It was like listening to two big Italian matriarchs from opposing clans battle it out. Millat loved clans. He had joined KEVIN because he loved clans (and the outfit and the bow tie), and he loved clans at war. Marjorie the analyst had suggested that this desire to be part of a clan was a result of being, effectively, half a twin. Marjorie the analyst suggested that Millat's religious conversion was more likely born out of a need for sameness within a group than out of any intellectually formulated belief in the existence of an all-powerful creator. Maybe. What*ever*. As far as he was concerned, you could analyse it until the cows came home, but nothing beat being all dressed in black, smoking a fag, listening to two mammas battle it out over you in operatic style:

'You claim to want to help my boys, but you have done nothing but drive a wedge between them. It is too late now. I have lost my family. Why don't you go back to yours and leave us alone?'

'You think it's paradise over at my house? My family has been split by this too. Joshua isn't speaking to Marcus. Did you know that? And those two were so close . . .' Joyce looked a bit weepy, and Alsana reluctantly passed her the kitchen roll. 'I'm trying to help *all* of us. And the best way to start is to get Magid and Millat talking before this escalates any further than it has. I think we can both agree on that. If we could find some neutral place, some ground where they both felt no pressures or outside influence . . .'

'But there are no neutral places any more! I agree they should meet, but where and how? You and your husband have made everything impossible.'

'Mrs Iqbal, with all due respect, the problems in your family began long before either my husband or I had any involvement.'

'Maybe, maybe, Mrs Chalfen, but you are the salt in the wound, yes? You are the one extra chilli pepper in the hot sauce.'

Millat heard Joyce draw her breath in sharply.

'Again, with respect, I can't believe that it is the case. I think this has been going on for a very long time. Millat told me that some years ago you burnt all his things. I mean, it's just an example, but I don't think you understand the *trauma* that kind of thing has inflicted on Millat. He's very *damaged*.'

'Oh, we are going to play the tit for the tat. I see. And I am to be the tit. Not that it is any of your big-nose business, but I burnt those things to teach him a lesson – to respect other people's lives!'

'A strange way of showing it, if you don't mind me saying.'

'I do mind! I do mind! What do you know of it?'

'Only what I see. And I see that Millat has a lot of mental scars. You may not be aware, but I've been funding sessions for Millat with my analyst. And I can tell you, Millat's inner life – his karma,

I suppose you might call it in Bengali – the whole *world* of his subconscious shows serious illness.'

In fact, the problem with Millat's subconscious (and he didn't need Marjorie to tell him this) was that it was basically split-level. On the one hand he was trying real hard to live as Hifan and the others suggested. This involved getting his head around four main criteria.

1. To be ascetic in one's habits (cut down on the booze, the spliff, the women).
2. To remember always the glory of Muhammad (peace be upon Him!) and the might of the Creator.
3. To grasp a full intellectual understanding of KEVIN and the Qur'ān.
4. To purge oneself of the taint of the West.

He knew that he was KEVIN's big experiment, and he wanted to give it his best shot. In the first three areas he was doing fine. He smoked the odd fag and put away a Guinness on occasion (can't say fairer than that), but he was very successful with both the evil weed and the temptations of the flesh. He no longer saw Alexandra Andrusier, Polly Houghton or Rosie Dew (though he paid occasional visits to one Tanya Chapman, a very small redhead who understood the delicate nature of his dilemma and would give him a thorough blow job without requiring Millat to touch her at all. It was a mutually beneficial arrangement: she was the daughter of a judge and delighted in horrifying the old goat, and Millat needed ejaculation with no actual active participation on his side). On the scriptural side of things, he thought Muhammad (peace be upon Him!) was a right geezer, a great bloke, and he was in awe of the Creator, in the original meaning of that word: dread, fear, really shit-scared – and Hifan said that was correct, that was how it should be. He understood this idea that his religion was not one based on faith – not like the Christians, the Jews, et al. – but one that could be intellectually proved by the best minds. He understood the *idea*. But, sadly, Millat was far from possessing one of the best minds, or even a reasonable mind; intellectual proof or disproof was beyond him. Still, he understood that to rely on faith, as his own father did, was contemptible. And no one could say he didn't give one hundred per cent to the cause. That seemed enough for KEVIN. They were more than happy with his real forte, which was the *delivery* of the thing. The *presentation*. For instance, if a nervous-looking woman came up to the KEVIN stall in Willesden Library and asked about the faith, Millat would lean over the desk, grab her hand, press it and say: *Not faith, Sister. We do not deal in faith here. Spend five minutes with my Brother Rakesh and he will intellectually prove to you the existence of the Creator. The Qur'ān is a document of science, a document of rational thought. Spend five minutes, Sister, if you care for your future beyond this earth*. And to top it off, he could usually sell her a few tapes (*Ideological Warfare* or *Let the Scholars Beware*), two quid each. Or even some of their literature, if he was on top form. Everyone at KEVIN was mightily impressed. So far so good. As for KEVIN's more unorthodox programmes of direct action, Millat was right in there, he was their greatest asset, he was in the forefront, the first into battle come jihad, cool as fuck in a crisis, a man of action, like Brando, like Pacino, like Liotta. But even as Millat reflected on this with pride in his mother's hallway, his heart sank. For therein lay the problem. Number four. Purging oneself of the West.

Now, he knew, he *knew* that if you wanted an example of *the moribund, decadent, degenerate, over-sexed, violent state of Western capitalist culture and the logical endpoint of its obsession with personal freedoms* (Leaflet: *Way Out West*), you couldn't do much better than Hollywood cinema. And he knew (how many times had he been through it with Hifan?) that the 'gangster' movie, the Mafia genre, was the worst example of that. And yet . . . it was the *hardest* thing to let go. He would give every spliff he'd ever smoked and every woman he'd ever fucked to retrieve the films his mother had burnt, or even the few he had purchased more recently which Hifan had confiscated. He had torn up his *Rocky Video* membership and thrown away the Iqbal video recorder to distance himself from direct temptation, but was it his fault if Channel 4 ran a De Niro season? Could he help it if Tony Bennett's 'Rags to Riches' floated out of a clothes shop and entered his soul? It was his most shameful secret that whenever he opened a door – a car door, a car boot, the door of KEVIN's meeting hall or the door of his own house just now – the opening of *GoodFellas* ran through his head and he found this sentence rolling around in what he presumed was his subconscious:

As far back as I can remember, I always wanted to be a gangster.

He even saw it like that, in that font, like on the movie poster. And when he found himself doing it, he tried desperately not to, he tried to fix it, but Millat's mind was a mess and more often than not he'd end up pushing upon the door, head back, shoulders forward, Liotta style, thinking:

As far back as I can remember, I always wanted to be a Muslim.

He knew, in a way, this was *worse*, but he just couldn't help it. He kept a white handkerchief in his top pocket, he always carried dice, even though he had no idea what a crap game actually was, he loved long camel jackets and he could cook a killer seafood linguine, though a lamb curry was completely beyond him. It was all haraam, he knew that.

Worst of all was the anger inside him. Not the righteous anger of a man of God, but the seething, violent anger of a gangster, a juvenile delinquent, determined to prove himself, determined to run the clan, determined to beat the rest. And if the game was God, if the game was a fight against the West, against the presumptions of Western science, against his brother or Marcus Chalfen, he was determined to win it. Millat stubbed his fag out against the bannister. It pissed him off that these were not pious thoughts. But they were in the right ball park, weren't they? He had the fundamentals, didn't he? Clean living, praying (five times a day without fail), fasting, working for the cause, spreading the message? And that was enough, wasn't it? Maybe. What*ever*. Either way, there was no going back now. Yeah, he'd meet Magid, he'd meet him . . . they'd have a good face-off, he'd come out of it the stronger; he'd call his brother *a little cock-a-roach*, and walk out of that tête-à-tête even more determined to fulfil his destiny. Millat straightened his green bow-tie and slunk forward like Liotta (all menace and charm) and pushed open the kitchen door *(Ever since I can remember . . .)*, waiting for two pairs of eyes, like two of Scorsese's cameras, to pan on to his face and focus.

'Millat!'

'Amma.'

'Millat!'

'Joyce.'

(*Great, supwoib, so we all know each other*, went Millat's inner monologue in Paul Sorvino's voice, *Now let's get down to business*.)

'All right, gentlemen. There is no reason to be alarmed. It is simply my son. Magid, Mickey. Mickey, Magid.'

O'Connell's once more. Because Alsana had eventually conceded Joyce's point, but did not care to dirty her hands. Instead, she demanded Samad take Magid 'out somewhere' and spend an evening persuading him into meeting with Millat. But the only 'out' Samad understood was O'Connell's and the prospect of taking his son there was repellent. He and his wife had a thorough wrestle in the garden to settle the point, and he was confident of success until Alsana fooled him with a dummy trip, then an armlock-knee-groin combination. So here he was: O'Connell's, and it was as bad a choice as he'd suspected. When he, Archie and Magid walked in, trying to make a low-key entrance, there had been widespread consternation amongst both staff and clientele. The last stranger anybody remembered arriving with Arch and Sam was Samad's accountant, a small rat-faced man who tried to talk to people about their savings (as if people in O'Connell's had savings!) and asked not once but twice for blood pudding, though it had been explained to him that pig was unavailable. That had been around 1987 and nobody had enjoyed it. And now what was this? A mere five years later and here comes another one, this time all dressed in white – insultingly clean for a Friday evening in O'Connell's – and way below the unspoken minimum age requirement (thirty-six). What was Samad trying to do?

'Whattareya tryin' to do to us, Sammy?' asked Johnny, a mournful-looking stick of an ex-Orangeman, who was leaning over the hot plate to collect some bubble and squeak. 'Overrun us, are ya or sumthin?'

'Oo 'im?' demanded Denzel, who had not yet died.

'Your batty bwoy?' inquired Clarence, who was also, by God's grace, hanging on in there.

'All right, gentlemen. There is no reason to be alarmed. It is simply my son. Magid, Mickey. Mickey, Magid.'

Mickey looked a little dumbfounded by this introduction, and just stood there for a minute, a soggy fried egg hanging off his spatula.

'Magid Mahfooz Murshed Mubtasim Iqbal,' said Magid serenely. 'It is a great honour to meet you, Michael. I have heard such a great deal about you.'

Which was odd, because Samad had never told him a thing.

Mickey continued to look over Magid's shoulder to Samad for confirmation. 'You what? You mean the one you, er, sent back 'ome? This is Magid?'

'Yes, yes, this is Magid,' replied Samad rapidly, pissed off by all the attention the boy was getting. 'Now, Archibald and I will have our usuals and –'

'Magid Iqbal,' repeated Mickey slowly. 'Well, I bloody never. You know you'd never guess you was an Iqbal. You've got a very trusting, well, kind of *sympathetic* face, if you get me.'

'And yet I *am* an Iqbal, Michael,' said Magid, laying that look of total empathy on Mickey and the other dregs of humanity huddled around the hot counter, 'though I have been gone a long time.'

'Say *that* again. Well, this *is* a turn-up for the books. I've got your . . . wait a minute, let me get this right . . . your great-*great*-grandfather up there, see?'

'I noticed it the moment I came in, and I can assure you, Michael, my soul is very grateful for it,' said Magid, beaming like an angel. 'It makes me feel at home, and, as this place is dear to my father and his friend Archibald Jones I feel certain it shall also be dear to me. They have brought me here, I think, to discuss important matters, and I for one can think of no better place for them, despite your clearly debilitating skin condition.'

Mickey was simply bowled over by that, and could not conceal his pleasure, addressing his reply both to Magid and the rest of O'Connell's.

'Speaks fuckin' nice, don't he? Sounds like a right fuckin' Olivier. Queen's fucking English and no mistake. What a nice fella. You're the kind of clientele I could do wiv in here, Magid, let me tell you. Civilized and that. And don't you worry about my skin, it don't get anywhere near the food and it don't give me much trouble. Cor, what a gentleman. You do feel like you should watch your mouth around him, dontcha?'

'Mine and Archibald's usual, then, please, Mickey,' said Samad.

'I'll leave my son to make up his mind. We will be over by the pinball.'

'Yeah, yeah,' said Mickey, not bothering or able to turn his gaze from Magid's dark eyes.

'Dat a lovely suit you gat dere,' murmured Denzel, stroking the white linen wistfully. 'Dat's what de Englishmen use ta wear back home in Jamaica, remember dat, Clarence?'

Clarence nodded slowly, dribbling a little, struck by the beatific.

'Go on, get out of it, the pair of you,' grumbled Mickey, shooing them away, 'I'll bring it over, all right? I want to talk to Magid here. Growing boy, he's got to eat. So: what is it I can get you, Magid?' Mickey leant over the counter, all concern, like an over-attentive shopgirl. 'Eggs? Mushrooms? Beans? Fried slice?'

'I think,' replied Magid, slowly surveying the dusty chalkboard menus on the wall, and then turning back to Mickey, his face illumined, 'I should like a bacon sandwich. Yes, that is it. I would love a juicy, yet well-done, tomato ketchup-ed bacon sandwich. On brown.'

Oh, the struggle that could be seen on Mickey's kisser at that moment! Oh, the gargoylian contortions! It was a battle between the favour of the most refined customer he had ever had and the most hallowed, sacred rule of O'Connell's Pool House. NO PORK.

Mickey's left eye twitched.

'Don't want a nice plate of scrambled? I do a lovely scrambled eggs, don't I, Johnny?'

'I'd be a liar if I said ya didn't,' said Johnny loyally from his table, even though Mickey's eggs were famously grey and stiff, 'I'd be a terrible liar, on my mother's life, I would.'

Magid wrinkled his nose and shook his head.

'All right – what about mushrooms and beans? Omelette and chips? No better chips in the Finchley Road. Come on, son,' he pleaded, desperate. 'You're a Muslim, int ya? You don't want to break your father's heart with a bacon sandwich.'

'My father's heart will not be broken by a bacon sandwich. It is far more likely that my father's heart will break from the result of a build-up of saturated fat which is in turn a result of eating in your establishment for fifteen years. One wonders,' said Magid evenly, 'if a case could be made, a legal case, you understand, against individuals in the food service industry who fail to label their meals with a clear fat content or general health warning. One wonders.'

All this was delivered in the sweetest, most melodious voice, and with no hint of threat. Poor Mickey didn't know what to make of it.

'Well, of course,' said Mickey nervously, 'hypothetically that is an interesting question. Very interesting.'

'Yes, I think so.'

'Yeah, definitely.'

Mickey fell silent and spent a minute elaborately polishing the top of the hot plate, an activity he indulged in about once every ten years.

'There. See your face in that. Now. Where were we?'

'A bacon sandwich.'

At the sound of the word 'bacon', a few ears began to twitch at the front tables.

'If you could keep your voice down a little . . .'

'*A bacon sandwich*,' whispered Magid.

'Bacon. Right. Well, I'll have to nip next door, 'cos I ain't got none at present . . . but you just sit down wiv your dad and I'll bring it over. It'll cost a bit more, like. What wiv the extra effort, you know. But don't worry, I'll bring it over. And tell Archie not to worry if he ain't got the cash. A Luncheon Voucher will do.'

'You are very kind, Michael. Take one of these.' Magid reached into his pocket and pulled out a piece of folded paper.

'Oh, fuck me, another leaflet? You can't fucking move – pardon my French – but you can't *move* for leaflets in Norf London these days. My brother Abdul-Colin's always loading me wiv 'em an' all. But seein' as it's you . . . go on, hand it over.'

'It's not a leaflet,' said Magid, collecting his knife and fork from the tray. 'It is an invitation to a launch.'

'You what?' said Mickey excitedly (in the grammar of his daily tabloid, *launch* meant lots of cameras, expensive-looking birds with huge tits, red carpets). 'Really?'

Magid passed him the invite. 'Incredible things are to be seen and heard there.'

'Oh,' said Mickey, disappointed, eyeing the expensive piece of card. 'I've heard about this bloke and his mouse.' He had heard about this bloke and his mouse in this same tabloid; it was a kind of filler between the tits and the more tits and it was underneath the byline: ONE BLOKE AND HIS MOUSE.

'Seems a bit dodgy to me, messing wiv God an' all that. 'Sides I ain't that scientifically minded, you see. Go right over my head.'

'Oh, I don't think so. One just has to look at the thing from a perspective that interests you personally. Take your skin, for example.'

'I wish somebody would fuckin' take it,' joked Mickey amiably. 'I've 'ad a-fucking-nuff of it.'

Magid did not smile.

'You suffer from a serious endocrine disorder. By which I mean, it is not simply adolescent acne caused by the over-excretion of sebum, but a condition that comes from a hormonal defect. I presume your family share it?'

'Er . . . yeah, as it happens. All my brothers. And my son, Abdul-Jimmy. All spotty bastards.'

'But you would not like it if your son were to pass on the condition to his sons.'

'Obviously, no. I 'ad terrible trouble in school. I carry a knife to this day, Magid. But I can't see how that can be avoided, to be honest with you. Been goin' on for decades.'

'But you see,' said Magid (and what an expert he was at the personal interest angle!), 'it can certainly be avoided. It would be perfectly simple and much misery would be saved. That is the kind of thing we will be discussing at the launch.'

'Oh, well, if that's the case, you know, count me in. I thought it was just some bloody mutant-mouse or sommink, you see. But if that's the case . . .'

'Thirty-first of December,' said Magid, before walking down the aisle to his father. 'It will be wonderful to see you there.'

'You took your time,' said Archie, as Magid approached their table.

'Did you come by way of the Ganges?' inquired Samad irritably, shifting up to make space for him.

'Pardon me, please. I was just speaking with your friend, Michael. A very decent chap. Oh, before I forget, Archibald, he said that it would be perfectly acceptable to pay in Luncheon Vouchers this evening.'

Archie almost choked on a little toothpick he was chewing on. 'He said *what*? Are you *sure*?'

'Quite sure. Now, Abba, shall we begin?'

'There's nothing to begin,' growled Samad, refusing to look him in the eye. 'I am afraid we are already far into whatever diabolic plot fate has in store for me. And I want you to know, that I am not here of my own volition but because your mother begged me to do this and because I have more respect for that poor woman than either you or your brother ever had.'

Magid released a wry, gentle smile. 'I thought you were here because Amma beat you in the wrestling.'

Samad scowled. 'Oh yes, ridicule me. My own son. Do you never read the Qur'ān? Do you not know the duties a son owes to his father? You *sicken* me, Magid Mubtasim.'

'Oi, Sammy, old man,' said Archie, playing with the ketchup, trying to keep things light. 'Steady on.'

'No, I will not steady on! This boy is a thorn in my foot.'

'Surely "side"?'

'Archibald, stay out of this.'

Archie returned his attention to the pepper and salt cellars, trying to pour the former into the latter.

'Right you are, Sam.'

'I have a message to deliver and I will deliver it and no more. Magid, your mother wants you to meet with Millat. The woman Chalfen will arrange it. It is their opinion that the two of you must talk.'

'And what is your opinion, Abba?'

'You don't want to hear my opinion.'

'On the contrary, Abba, I would very much like to hear it.'

'Simply, I think it is a mistake. I think you two can do no possible good for each other. I think you should go to opposite corners of the earth. I think I have been cursed with two sons more dysfunctional than Mr Cain and Mr Abel.'

'I am perfectly willing to meet with him, Abba. If he will meet with me.'

'Apparently he is willing, this is what I am told. I don't know. I don't talk with him any more than I talk with you. I am too busy at the moment trying to make my peace with God.'

'Er . . .' said Archibald, crunching on his toothpick out of hunger and nerves, and because Magid gave him the heebie-jeebies, 'I'll go and see if the food is ready, shall I? Yes. I'll do that. What am I picking up for you, Madge?'

'A bacon sandwich, please, Archibald.'

'Bac –? Er . . . right. Right you are.'

Samad's face blew up like one of Mickey's fried tomatoes. 'So you mean to *mock* me, is that it? In front of my face you wish to show me the kaffir that you are. Go on, then! Munch on your pig in front of me! You are so bloody clever, aren't you? Mr Smarty-pants. Mr white-trousered Englishman with his stiff-upper-lip and his big white teeth. You know everything, even enough to escape your own judgement day.'

'I am not so clever, Abba.'

'No, no, you are *not*. You are not half as clever as you think. I don't know why I bother to warn you, but I do: you are on a *direct collision course* with your brother, Magid. I keep my ear to the ground, I hear Shiva talking in the restaurant. And there are others: Mo Hussein-Ishmael, Mickey's brother, Abdul-Colin, and his son, Abdul-Jimmy – these are only a few, there are many more, and they are organizing against you. Millat is with them. Your Marcus Chalfen has stirred a great deal of anger and there are some, these green-ties, who are willing to act. Who are crazy enough to do what they believe is right. Crazy enough to start a war. There aren't many people like that. Most of us just follow along once war has been announced. But some people wish to bring things to a head. Some people march on to the parade ground and fire the first shot. Your brother is one of them.'

All through this, as Samad's face contorted from anger, to despair, to near-hysterical grins, Magid had remained blank, his face an unwritten page.

'You have nothing to say? This news does not surprise you?'

'Why don't you reason with them, Abba,' said Magid after a pause. 'Many of them respect you. You are respected in the community. Reason with them.'

'Because I disapprove as strongly as they do, for all their lunacies. Marcus Chalfen has no *right*. No right to do as he does. It is not his business. It is God's business. If you meddle with a creature, the very *nature* of a creature, even if it is a mouse, you walk into the arena that is God's: creation. You infer that the wonder of God's creation can be improved upon. It cannot. Marcus Chalfen *presumes*. He expects to be worshipped when the only thing in the universe that warrants worship is Allah. And you are wrong to help him. Even his own son has disowned him. And so,' said Samad, unable to suppress the drama queen deep within his soul, 'I must disown you.'

'Ah, now, one chips, beans, egg and mushroom for you, Sammy-my-good-man,' said Archibald, approaching the table and passing the plate. 'And one omelette and mushrooms for me . . .'

'And one bacon sandwich,' said Mickey, who had insisted on breaking fifteen years of tradition in bringing this one dish over himself, 'for the young professor.'

'He will *not* eat that at my table.'

'Oh, come on, Sam,' began Archie gingerly. 'Give the lad a break.'

'I say he will *not* eat that at my table!'

Mickey scratched his forehead. 'Stone me, we're getting a bit fundamentalist in our old age, ain't we?'

'I said –'

'As you wish, Abba,' said Magid, with that same infuriating smile of total forgiveness. He took his plate from Mickey, and sat down at the adjacent table with Clarence and Denzel.

Denzel welcomed him with a grin, 'Clarence, look see! It de young prince in white. 'Im come to play domino. I jus' look in his eye and I and I knew 'im play domino. 'Im an hexpert.'

'Can I ask you a question?' said Magid.

'Def-net-lee. Gwan.'

'Do you think I should meet with my brother?'

'Hmm. I don' tink me can say,' replied Denzel, after a spell of thought in which he laid down a five-domino set.

'I would say you look like a young fellow oo can make up 'im own mind,' said Clarence cautiously.

'Do I?'

Magid turned back to his previous table, where his father was trying studiously to ignore him, and Archie was toying with his omelette.

'Archibald! Shall I meet with my brother or not?'

Archie looked guiltily at Samad and then back at his plate.

'Archibald! This is a very significant question for me. Should I or not?'

'Go on,' said Samad sourly. 'Answer him. If he'd rather advice from two old fools and a man he barely knows than from his own father, then let him have it. Well? Should he?'

Archie squirmed. 'Well . . . I can't . . . I mean, it's not for me to say . . . I suppose, if he wants . . . but then again, if you don't think . . .'

Samad thrust his fist into Archie's mushrooms so hard the omelette slithered off the plate altogether and slipped to the floor.

'Make a decision, Archibald. For once in your pathetic little life, make a decision.'

'Um . . . heads, yes,' gasped Archie, reaching into his pocket for a twenty pence piece. 'Tails, no. Ready?'

The coin rose and flipped as a coin would rise and flip every time in a perfect world, flashing its light and then revealing its dark enough times to mesmerize a man. Then, at some point in its triumphant ascension, it began to arc, and the arc went wrong, and Archibald realized that it was not coming back to him at all but going behind him, a fair way behind him, and he turned with the others to watch it complete an elegant swoop towards the pinball machine and somersault straight into the slot. Immediately the huge old beast lit up; the ball shot off and began its chaotic, noisy course around a labyrinth of swinging doors, automatic bats, tubes and ringing bells, until, with no one to assist it, no one to direct it, it gave up the ghost and dropped back into the swallowing hole.

'Bloody hell,' said Archibald, visibly chuffed. 'What are the chances of that, eh?'

A neutral place. The chances of finding one these days are slim, maybe even slimmer than Archie's pinball trick. The sheer *quantity* of shit that must be wiped off the slate if we are to start again as new. Race. Land. Ownership. Faith. Theft. Blood. And more blood. And more. And not only must the *place* be neutral, but the messenger who takes you to the place, and the messenger who sends the messenger. There are no people or places like that left in North London. But Joyce did her best with what she had. First she went to Clara. In Clara's present seat of learning, a red-brick university, South-West by the Thames, there was a room she used for study on Friday afternoons. A thoughtful teacher had loaned her the key. Always empty between three and six. Contents: one blackboard, several tables, some chairs, two anglepoise lamps, an overhead projector, a filing cabinet, a computer. Nothing older than twelve years, Clara could guarantee that. The university itself was only twelve years old. Built on empty waste land – no Indian burial grounds, no Roman viaducts, no interred alien spacecraft, no foundations of a long-gone church. Just earth. As neutral a place as anywhere. Clara gave Joyce the key and Joyce gave it to Irie.

'But why me? I'm not involved.'

'Exactly, dear. And I'm too involved. But you are perfect. Because you know him but you don't *know* him,' said Joyce cryptically. She passed Irie her long winter coat, some gloves and a hat of Marcus's with a ludicrous bobble on the top. 'And because you love him, though he doesn't love you.'

'Yeah, thanks, Joyce. Thanks for reminding me.'

'Love is the reason, Irie.'

'No, Joyce, Love's not the fucking reason.' Irie was standing on the Chalfen doorstep, watching her own substantial breath in the freezing night air. 'It's a four-letter word that sells life insurance and hair conditioner. It's fucking *cold* out here. You owe me one.'

'Everybody owes everybody,' agreed Joyce and closed the door.

Irie stepped out into streets she'd known her whole life, along a route she'd walked a million times over. If someone asked her just then what memory was, what the *purest definition* of memory was, she would say this: the street you were on when you first jumped in a pile of dead leaves. She was walking it right now. With every fresh crunch came the memory of previous crunches.

She was permeated by familiar smells: wet woodchip and gravel around the base of the tree, newly laid turd underneath the cover of soggy leaves. She was moved by these sensations. Despite opting for a life of dentistry, she had not yet lost all of the poetry in her soul, that is, she could still have the odd Proustian moment, note layers upon layers, though she often experienced them in periodontal terms. She got a twinge – as happens with a sensitive tooth, or in a 'phantom tooth', when the nerve is exposed – she felt a *twinge* walking past the garage, where she and Millat, aged thirteen, had passed one hundred and fifty pennies over the counter, stolen from an Iqbal jam-jar, in a desperate attempt to buy a packet of fags. She felt an *ache* (like a severe malocclusion, the pressure of one tooth upon another) when she passed the park where they had cycled as children, where they smoked their first joint, where he had kissed her once in the middle of a storm. Irie wished she could give herself over to these past-present fictions: wallow in them, make them sweeter, longer, particularly the kiss. But she had in her hand a cold key, and surrounding her lives that were stranger than fiction, funnier than fiction, crueller than fiction, and with consequences fiction can never have. She didn't *want* to be involved in the long story of those lives, but she *was*, and she found herself dragged forward by the hair to their denouement, through the high road – *Mali's Kebabs, Mr Cheungs, Raj's, Malkovich Bakeries* – she could reel them off blindfold; and then down under pigeon-shit bridge and that long wide road that drops into Gladstone Park as if it's falling into a green ocean. You could drown in memories like these, but she tried to swim free of them. She jumped over the small wall that fringed the Iqbal house, as she had a million times over, and rang the doorbell. Past tense, future imperfect.

Upstairs, in his bedroom, Millat had spent the past fifteen minutes trying to get his head around Brother Hifan's written instructions concerning the act of prostration (leaflet: *Correct Worship*):

SAJDA: prostration. In the sajda, fingers must be closed, pointing towards the qibla in line with the ears, and the head must be between hands. It is fard to put the forehead on something clean, such as a stone, some earth, wood, cloth, and it is said (by savants) that it is wajib to put the nose down, too. It is not permissible to put only the nose on the ground without a good excuse. It is makruh to put only the forehead on the ground. In the sajda you must say Subhana rabbiyal-ala at least thrice. The Shiis say that it is better to make the sajda on a brick made from the clay of Karbala. It is either fard or wajib to put two feet or at least one toe of each foot on the ground. There are also some savants who say that it is sunnat. That is, if two feet are not put on the ground, namaz will either not be accepted or it will become makruh. If, during the sajda, the forehead, nose or feet are raised from the ground for a short while, it will cause no harm. In the sajda, it is sunnat to bend the toes and turn them towards the qibla. It is written in Radd-ul-mukhtar that those who say

That's as far as he got, and there were three more pages. He was in a cold sweat from trying to recall all that was halal or haraam, fard or sunnat, makruh-tahrima (prohibited with much stress) or makruh-tanzihi (prohibited, but to a lesser degree). At a loss, he had ripped off his t-shirt, tied a series of belts at angles over his spectacular upper body, stood in the mirror and practised a different, easier routine, one he knew in intimate detail:

You lookin' at me? You lookin' at me?
Well, who the fuck else are you looking at, huh?
I can't see anybody else in here.
You lookin' at me?

He was in the swing of it, revealing his invisible sliding guns and knives to the wardrobe door, when Irie walked in.

'Yes,' said Irie, as he stood there sheepish. 'I'm looking at you.'

Quickly and quietly she explained to him about the neutral

place, about the room, about the date, about the time. She made her own personal plea for compromise, peace and caution (everybody was doing it) and then she came up close and put the cold key in his warm hand. Almost without meaning to, she touched his chest. Just at the point between two belts where his heart, constricted by the leather, beat so hard she felt it in her ear. Lacking experience in this field, it was natural that Irie should mistake the palpitations that come with blood restriction for smouldering passion. As for Millat, it had been a very long time since anybody touched him or he touched anybody. Add to that the touch of memory, the touch of ten years of love unreturned, the touch of a long, long history – the result was inevitable.

Before long their arms were involved, their legs were involved, their lips were involved, and they were tumbling on to the floor, involved at the groin (hard to get more involved than that), making love on a prayer mat. But then as suddenly and feverishly as it had begun it was over; they released each other in horror for different reasons, Irie springing back into a naked huddle by the door, embarrassed and ashamed because she could see how much he regretted it; and Millat grabbing his prayer mat and pointing it towards the Kaba, ensuring the mat was no higher than floor level, resting on no books or shoes, his fingers closed and pointing to the quibla in line with his ears, ensuring both forehead and nose touched the floor, with two feet firmly on the ground but ensuring the toes were not bent, prostrating himself in the direction of the Kaba, but not *for* the Kaba, but for Allahu ta'ala alone. He made sure he did all these things perfectly, while Irie wept and dressed and left. He made sure he did all these things perfectly because he believed he was being watched by the great camera in the sky. He made sure he did all these things perfectly because they were fard and 'he who wants to change worships becomes a disbeliever' (leaflet: *The Straight Path*).

∽

Hell hath no fury *et cetera, et cetera*. Irie walked hot-faced from the Iqbal house and headed straight for the Chalfens with revenge on her mind. But not against Millat. Rather in *defence* of Millat, for she had always been his defender, his blacky-white knight. You see, Millat did not love her. And she thought Millat didn't love her because he couldn't. She thought he was so damaged, he couldn't love anybody any more. She wanted to find whoever had *damaged* him like this, damaged him so terribly; she wanted to find whoever had made him *unable to love her*.

It's a funny thing about the modern world. You hear girls in the toilets of clubs saying, 'Yeah, he fucked off and left me. He didn't love me. He just couldn't *deal* with love. He was too fucked up to know *how* to love me.' Now, how did that happen? What was it about this unlovable century that convinced us we were, despite everything, eminently lovable as a people, as a species? What made us think that anyone who fails to love us is damaged, lacking, *malfunctioning* in some way? And particularly if they replace us with a god, or a weeping madonna, or the face of Christ in a ciabatta roll – then we call them crazy. Deluded. Regressive. We are so convinced of the goodness of ourselves, and the goodness of our love, we cannot bear to believe that there might be something more worthy of love than us, more worthy of worship. Greetings cards routinely tell us everybody deserves love. No. Everybody deserves clean water. Not everybody deserves love all the time.

Millat didn't love Irie, and Irie was sure there must be somebody she could blame for that. Her brain started ticking over. What was the root cause? Millat's feelings of inadequacy. What was the root cause of Millat's feelings of inadequacy? Magid. He had been born second because of Magid. He was the lesser son because of Magid.

Joyce opened the door to her and Irie marched straight upstairs, maliciously determined to make Magid the second-son for once, this time by twenty-five minutes. She grabbed him, kissed him and made love to him angrily and furiously, without conversation or affection. She rolled him around, tugged at his hair, dug what fingernails she had into his back and when he came she was gratified to note it was with a little sigh as if something had been taken from him. But she was wrong to think this a victory. It was simply because he knew immediately where she had been, why she was here, and it saddened him. For a long time they lay in silence together, naked, the autumn light disappearing from the room with every minute that passed.

'It seems to me,' said Magid finally, as the moon became clearer than the sun, 'that you have tried to love a man as if he were an island and you were shipwrecked and you could mark the land with an X. It seems to me it is too late in the day for all that.'

Then he gave her a kiss on the forehead that felt like a baptism and she wept like a baby.

∽

3 p.m., 5 November 1992. The brothers meet (at *last*) in a blank room after a gap of eight years and find that their genes, those prophets of the future, have reached different conclusions. Millat is astounded by the differences. The nose, the line of the jaw, the eyes, the hair. His brother is a stranger to him and he tells him so.

'Only because you wish me to be,' says Magid with a crafty look.

But Millat is blunt, not interested in riddles, and in a single shot asks and answers his own question. 'So you're going through with it, yeah?'

Magid shrugs. 'It is not mine to stop or start, brother, but yes, I intend to help where I can. It is a great project.'

'It is an abomination.' (leaflet: *The Sanctity of Creation*)

Millat pulls out a chair from one of the desks and sits on it backwards, like a crab in a trap, legs and arms splayed either side.

'I see it rather as correcting the Creator's mistakes.'

'The Creator doesn't make mistakes.'

'So you mean to continue?'

'You're damn right.'

'And so do I.'

'Well, that's it, then, isn't it? It's already been decided. KEVIN will do whatever is necessary to stop you and your kind. And that's the fucking end of it.'

But contrary to Millat's understanding, this is no movie and there is no fucking end to it, just as there is no fucking beginning to it. The brothers begin to argue. It escalates in moments, and they make a mockery of that idea, a neutral place; instead they cover the room with history – past, present and future history (for there is such a thing) – they take what was blank and smear it with the stinking shit of the past like excitable, excremental children. They cover this neutral room in themselves. Every gripe, the earliest memories, every debated principle, every contested belief.

Millat arranges the chairs to demonstrate the vision of the solar system which is so clearly and remarkably described in the Qur'ān, centuries before Western science (leaflet: *The Qur'ān and the Cosmos*); Magid draws Pande's parade ground on one blackboard with a detailed reconstruction of the possible path of bullets, and on the other board a diagram depicting a restriction enzyme cutting neatly through a sequence of nucleotides; Millat uses the computer as television, a chalk rubber as the picture of Magid-and-goat, then single-handedly impersonates every dribbling babba, great aunt and cousin's accountant who came that year for the blasphemous business of worshipping an icon; Magid utilizes the overhead projector to illuminate an article he has written, taking his brother point-by-point through his argument, defending the patents of genetically altered organisms; Millat uses the filing cabinet as a substitute for another one he despised, fills it with imaginary letters between a scientist Jew and an unbelieving Muslim; Magid puts three chairs together and shines two anglepoise lamps and now there are two brothers in a car, shivering and huddled together until a few minutes later they are separated for ever and a paper plane takes off.

It goes on and on and on.

And it goes to prove what has been said of immigrants many times before now; they are *resourceful*; they make do. They use what they can when they can.

ꝏ

Because we often imagine that immigrants are constantly on the move, footloose, able to change course at any moment, able to employ their legendary resourcefulness at every turn. We have been told of the resourcefulness of Mr Schmutters, or the footloosity of Mr Banajii, who sail into Ellis Island or Dover or Calais and step into their foreign lands as *blank people*, free of any kind of baggage, happy and willing to leave their difference at the docks and take their chances in this new place, merging with the oneness of this greenandpleasantlibertarianlandofthefree.

Whatever road presents itself, they will take, and if it happens to lead to a dead end, well then, Mr Schmutters and Mr Banajii will merrily set upon another, weaving their way through Happy Multicultural Land. Well, good for them. But Magid and Millat couldn't manage it. They left that neutral room as they had entered it: weighed down, burdened, unable to waver from their course or in any way change their separate, dangerous trajectories. They seem to make no progress. The cynical might say they don't even move at all – that Magid and Millat are two of Zeno's headfuck arrows, occupying a space equal to themselves and, what is scarier, equal to Mangal Pande's, equal to Samad Iqbal's. Two brothers trapped in the temporal instant. Two brothers who pervert all attempts to put dates to this story, to track these guys, to offer times and days, because there isn't, wasn't and never will be any *duration*. In fact, nothing moves.

Nothing changes. They are running at a standstill. Zeno's Paradox.

But what was Zeno's *deal* here (everybody's got a deal), what was his *angle*? There is a body of opinion that argues his paradoxes are part of a more general *spiritual* programme. To

(a) first establish multiplicity, the *Many*, as an illusion, and
(b) thus prove reality a seamless, flowing whole. A single, indivisible *One*.

Because if you can divide reality inexhaustibly into parts, as the brothers did that day in that room, the result is insupportable paradox. You are always still, you move nowhere, there is no progress.

But multiplicity is no illusion. Nor is the speed with which those-in-the-simmering-melting-pot are dashing towards it. Paradoxes aside, they are running, just as Achilles was running. And they will lap those who are in denial just as surely as Achilles would have made that tortoise eat his dust. Yeah, Zeno had an angle. He wanted the One, but the world is Many. And yet still that paradox is alluring. The harder Achilles tries to catch the tortoise, the more eloquently the tortoise expresses its advantage. Likewise, the brothers will race towards the future only to find they more and more eloquently express their past, that place where they have *just been*. Because this is the other thing about immigrants ('fugees, émigrés, travellers): they cannot escape their history any more than you yourself can lose your shadow.

18 *The End of History versus The Last Man*

'Look around *you*! And what do you see? What is the result of this so-called *democracy*, this so-called *freedom*, this so-called *liberty*? Oppression, persecution, *slaughter*. Brothers, you can see it on national television every day, every evening, every *night*! Chaos, disorder, *confusion*. They are not ashamed or embarrassed or *self-conscious*! They don't try to hide, to conceal, to *disguise*! They know as we know: the entire world is in a turmoil! Everywhere men indulge in prurience, promiscuity, *profligacy*, vice, corruption and *indulgence*. The entire world is affected by a disease known as *Kufr* – the state of rejection of the oneness of the Creator – refusing to acknowledge the infinite blessings of the Creator. And on this day, 1 December 1992, I bear witness that there is nothing worthy of worship besides the sole *Creator*, no partner unto *Him*. On this day we should know that whosoever the Creator has guided cannot be *misguided*, and whosoever he has *misguided* from the straight path shall not return to the straight path until the Creator puts *guidance* in his heart and brings him to the *light*. I will now begin my third lecture, which I call "Ideological Warfare", and that means – I will explain for those that don't understand – the war of these things . . . these ideologies, against the Brothers of KEVIN. . . ideology means a kind of brainwashing . . . and we are being indoctrinated, fooled and *brainwashed*, my Brothers! So I will try to elucidate, explain and *expound* . . .'

No one in the hall was going to admit it, but Brother Ibrāhīm ad-Din Shukrallah was no great speaker, when you got down to it. Even if you overlooked his habit of using three words where one would do, of emphasizing the last word of such triplets with his see-saw Caribbean inflections, even if you ignored these as everybody tried to, he was still physically disappointing. He had a small sketchy beard, a hunched demeanour, a repertoire of tense, inept gesticulations and a vague look of Sidney Poitier about him which did not achieve quite the similitude to command any serious respect. And he was short. On this point, Millat felt most let down. There was a tangible dissatisfaction in the hall when Brother Hifan finished his fulsome introductory speech and the famous but diminutive Brother Ibrāhīm ad-Din Shukrallah crossed the room to the podium. Not that anyone would require an alim of Islam to be a towering height, or indeed for a moment dare to suggest that the Creator had not made Brother Ibrāhīm ad-Din Shukrallah precisely the height that He, in all his holy omnipotence, had selected. Still, one couldn't help thinking, as Hifan awkwardly lowered the microphone and the Brother Ibrāhīm awkwardly stretched to meet it, you couldn't help thinking, in the Brother's very own style of third-word emphasis: five foot *five*.

The other problem with Brother Ibrāhīm ad-Din Shukrallah, the biggest problem perhaps, was his great affection for tautology. Though he promised explanation, elucidation and exposition, linguistically he put one in mind of a dog chasing its own tail: 'Now there are many types of warfare . . . I will name a few. Chemical warfare is the warfare where them men kill each other *chemically* with warfare. This can be a terrible warfare. Physical warfare! That is the warfare with physical weapons in which people kill each other *physically*. Then there is germ warfare in which a man, he knows that he's carrying the virus of HIV and he goes to the country and spreads his germ on the loose women of that country and creates *germ* warfare. *Psychological* warfare, that is one of the most evil, the war where they try to psychologically defeat you. This is called psychological warfare. But ideological warfare! That is the sixth warfare which is the worst warfare . . .'

And yet Brother Ibrāhīm ad-Din Shukrallah was no less than

the founder of KEVIN, an impressive man with a formidable reputation. Born Monty Clyde Benjamin in Barbados in 1960, the son of two poverty-stricken barefoot Presbyterian dipsomaniacs, he converted to Islam after a 'vision' at the age of fourteen. Aged eighteen he fled the lush green of his homeland for the desert surrounding Riyadh and the books that line the walls of Al-Imam Muhammad ibn Saud Islamic University. There he studied Arabic for five years, became disillusioned with much of the Islamic clerical establishment, and first expressed his contempt for what he called 'religious secularists', those foolish ulama who attempt to separate politics from religion. It was his belief that many radical modern political movements were relevant to Islam and moreover were to be found in the Qur'ān if one looked closely enough. He wrote several pamphlets on this matter, only to find that his own radical opinions were not welcome in Riyadh. He was considered a troublemaker and his life threatened 'numerous, countless, *innumerable* times'. So in 1984, wishing to continue his study, Brother Ibrāhīm came to England, locked himself in his aunt's Birmingham garage and spent five more years in there, with only the Qur'ān and the fascicles of Endless Bliss for company. He took his food in through the cat-flap, deposited his shit and piss in a Coronation biscuit tin and passed it back out the same way, and did a thorough routine of press-ups and sit-ups to prevent muscular atrophy. The *Selly Oak Reporter* wrote regular bylines on him during this period, nicknaming him 'The Guru in the Garage' (in view of the large Birmingham Muslim population, this was thought preferable to the press-desk favoured suggestion, 'The Loony in the Lock-Up') and had their fun interviewing his bemused aunt, one Carlene Benjamin, a devoted member of the Church of Jesus Christ of Latter-Day Saints.

These articles, cruel, mocking and offensive, had been written by one Norman Henshall and were now classics of their kind, distributed amongst KEVIN members throughout England as an example (if example were needed) of the virulent, anti-KEVIN element that bred in the press from even this foetal stage of their movement. Note – KEVIN members were advised – note how Henshall's articles end halfway through May '87, the very month that Brother Ibrāhīm ad-Din Shukrallah succeeded in converting his aunt Carlene through the cat-flap using nothing else but the pure truth as it was delivered by the final prophet Muhammad (peace be upon Him!). Note how Henshall fails to document the queues of people who came to speak with Brother Ibrāhīm ad-Din Shukrallah, so many they stretched three blocks round the centre of Selly Oak, from the cat-flap to the bingo hall! Note the failure of this same Mr Henshall to publish the 637 separate rules and laws that the Brother had spent five years gleaning from the Qur'ān (listing them in order of severity, and then in subgroups according to their nature, i.e., *Regarding Cleanliness and Specific Genital and Oral Hygiene*). Note all this, brothers and sisters, and then *marvel* at the power of word of mouth. Marvel at the dedication and commitment of the young people of Birmingham!

Their eagerness and enthusiasm was so remarkable (extraordinary, outstanding, *unprecedented*) that almost before the Brother emerged from his confinement and announced it himself, the idea of KEVIN had been born within the black and Asian community. A radical new movement where politics and religion were two sides of the same coin. A group that took freely from Garveyism, the American Civil Rights movement and the thought of Elijah Muhammed, yet remained within the letter of the Qur'ān. The Keepers of the Eternal and Victorious Islamic Nation. By 1992 they were a small but widespread body, with limbs as far-flung as Edinburgh and Land's End, a heart in Selly Oak and a soul in the Kilburn High Road. KEVIN: an extremist faction dedicated to direct, often violent action, a splinter group frowned on by the rest of the Islamic community; popular with the sixteen to twenty-five age group; feared and ridiculed in the press; and gathered tonight in the Kilburn Hall, standing on chairs and packed to the rafters, listening to the speech of their founder.

'There are three things,' continued Brother Ibrāhīm, looking briefly at his notes, 'that the colonial powers wish to do to you, brothers of KEVIN. Firstly, they wish to kill you *spiritually* . . . oh yes, they value nothing higher than your *mental slavery*. There are too many of you to fight hand-to-hand! But if they have your minds, then –'

'Hey,' went a fat man's attempt at a whisper. 'Brother Millat.'

It was Mohammed Hussein-Ishmael, the butcher. He was sweating profusely as ever, and had forced his way through a long line of people apparently to sit next to Millat. They were distantly related, and these past few months Mo had been rapidly nearing the inner circle of KEVIN (Hifan, Millat, Tyrone, Shiva, Abdul-Colin and others) by virtue of the money he had put forward and his stated interest in the more 'active' sides of the group. Personally, Millat was still a little suspicious of him and objected to his big slobbery face, the great quiff emerging from his toki and his chicken-breath.

'Late. I have to close up shop. But I been standing at the back for while. Listening. Brother Ibrāhīm is a very impressive man, hmm?'

'Hmm.'

'Very impressive,' repeated Mo, patting Millat's knee conspiratorially, 'a very impressive Brother.' Mo Hussein was partly funding Brother Ibrāhīm's tour around England, so it was in his interest (or at least it made him feel better about donating two thousand quid) to find the Brother impressive. Mo was a recent convert to KEVIN (he had been a reasonably good Muslim for twenty years), and his enthusiasm for the group was two-pronged. Firstly, he was just flattered, downright flattered, that he should be considered sufficiently successful a Muslim businessman to ponce money off. In normal circumstances he would have shown them the door and where they could stuff a freshly bled chicken, but the truth was, Mo was feeling a bit vulnerable at the time, his stringy-legged Irish wife, Sheila, having just left him for a publican; he was feeling a little *emasculated*, so when KEVIN asked Ardashir for five grand and got it, and Nadir from the rival halal place put up three, Mo came over all macho and put up his own stake.

The second reason for Mo's conversion was more personal. Violence. Violence and theft. For eighteen years Mo had owned the most famous halal butchers in North London, so famous that he had been able to buy the next door property and expand into a sweetshop/butchers. And in this period in which he ran the two establishments, he had been a victim of serious physical attacks and robbery, without fail, three times a year. Now, that figure doesn't include the numerous punches to the head, quick smacks with a crowbar, shifty kicks in the groin or anything else that failed to draw blood. Mo didn't even phone his *wife*, no matter the police, to report those. No: *serious* violence. Mo had been knifed a total of five times (*Ah*), lost the tips of three fingers (*Eeeesh*), had both legs and arms broken (*Oaooow*), his feet set on fire (*jiii*), his teeth kicked out (*ka-tooof*) and an air-gun bullet (*ping*) embedded in his thankfully fleshy posterior. *Boof.* And Mo was a big man. A big man with attitude. The beatings had in no way humbled him, made him watch his mouth or walk with a stoop. He gave as good as he got. But this was one man against an army. There was nobody who could help. The very first time, when he received a hammer blow to his ribs in January 1970, he naively reported it to the local constabulary and was rewarded by a late-night visit from five policemen who gave him a thorough kicking. Since then, violence and theft had become a regular part of his existence, a sad spectator sport watched by the old Muslim men and young Muslim mothers who came in to buy their chicken, and hurried out shortly afterwards, scared they might be next. Violence and theft. The culprits ranged from secondary-school children coming in the cornershop side to buy sweets (which is why Mo only allowed one child from Glenard Oak in at a time. Of course it made no difference, they just took turns beating the shit out of him solo), decrepit drunks, teenage thugs, the parents of teenage thugs, general fascists, specific neo-Nazis, the local snooker team, the darts team, the football team and huge posses of mouthy, white-skirted secretaries in deadly heels. These various people had various objections to him: he was a Paki (try telling a huge drunk Office Superworld check-out boy that you're Bangladeshi); he gave half his cornershop up to selling weird Paki meat; he had a quiff; he liked Elvis ('You like Elvis, then? Do yer? Eh, Paki? Do yer?'); the price of his cigarettes; his distance from home ('Why don't you go back to your own country?' 'But then how will I serve you cigarettes?' *Boof*); or just the look on his face. But they all had one thing in common, these people. They were all white. And this simple fact had done more to politicize Mo over the years than all the party broadcasts, rallies and petitions the world could offer. It had brought him more securely within the fold of his faith than even a visitation from the angel Jabrail could have achieved. The last straw, if it could be called that, came a month before joining KEVIN, when three white 'youths' tied him up, kicked him down the cellar steps, stole all his money and set fire to his shop. Double-jointed hands (the result of many broken wrists) got him out of that one. But he was tired of almost dying. When KEVIN gave Mo a leaflet that explained there was a war going on, he thought: no *shit*. At last someone was speaking his language. Mo had been in the frontline of that war for eighteen years. And KEVIN seemed to understand that it wasn't *enough* – his kids doing well, going to a nice school, having tennis lessons, too pale skinned to ever have a hand laid on them in their lives. Good. But not good enough. *He* wanted a little payback. For *himself*. He wanted Brother Ibrāhīm to stand on that podium and dissect Christian culture and Western morals until it was dust in his hands. He wanted the degenerate nature of these people explained to him. He wanted to know the history of it and the politics of it and the root cause. He wanted to see their art exposed and their science exposed, and their tastes exposed and their distastes. But words would never be enough; he'd heard so many words (*If you could just file a report . . . If you wouldn't mind telling us precisely what the attacker looked like*), and they were never as good as action. He wanted to know *why* these people kept on beating the shit out of him. And then he wanted to go and beat the shit out of some of these people.

'Very impressive, Millat, hey? Everything we hope for.'

'Yeah,' said Millat, despondent. 'I s'pose. Less talk, more action, though, if you ask me. The infidel are everywhere.'

Mo nodded vigorously. 'Oh definitely, Brother. We are two birds from the same bush on that matter. I hear there are some others,' said Mo, lowering his voice and putting his fat, sweaty lips by Millat's ear, 'who are very keen on action. Immediate action. Brother Hifan spoke to me. About the 31st of December. And Brother Shiva and Brother Tyrone . . .'

'Yes, yes. I know who they are. They are the beating heart of KEVIN.'

'And they say *you* know the man himself – this scientist. You in good position. I hear you are his friend.'

'Was. *Was*.'

'Brother Hifan says you have the tickets to get in, that you are organizing –'

'Shhh,' said Millat irritably. 'Not everyone can know. If you want to get near the centre, you've got to keep shtoom.'

Millat looked Mo up and down. The kurta-pyjamas that he somehow managed to make look like a late seventies Elvis flared jumpsuit. The huge stomach he rested on his knee like a friend.

Sharply, he asked, 'You're a bit old aren't you?'

'You rude little bastard. I'm strong as a bloody bull.'

'Yeah, well, we don't need strength,' said Millat tapping his temple, 'we need a little of the stuff upstairs. We've got to get in the place discreetly first, innit? The first evening. It'll be crawling.'

Mo blew his nose in his hand. 'I can be discreet.'

'Yeah, but that means keeping shtoom.'

'And the third thing,' said Brother Ibrāhīm ad-Din Shukrallah, interrupting them, suddenly louder and buzzing the PA system, 'the third thing they will try to do, is to convince you that it is human intellect and not Allah that is omnipotent, unlimited, *all-powerful*. They will try to convince you that your minds are not to be used to pronounce the greater glory of the Creator but to raise yourselves up equal to or beyond the Creator! And now we approach the most serious business of this evening. The greatest evil of the infidel is here, in this very borough of Brent. I will tell you, and you will not believe it, Brothers, but there is a man in this very community who believes that he can improve upon the creation of Allah. There is a man who presumes to change, adjust, *modify* what has been decreed. He will take an animal – an animal that Allah has created – and presume to change that creation. To create a new animal that has no name but is simply an abomination. And when he has finished with that small animal, a mouse, Brothers, when he has finished he will move to sheep, and cats and *dogs*. And who in this lawless society will stop him from one day creating a *man*? A man born not of woman but from a man's intellect alone! And he will tell you that it is medicine . . . but KEVIN makes no complaint against medicine. We are a sophisticated community who count many doctors amongst us, my Brothers. Don't be misled, deluded, *fooled*. This is not medicine. And my question to you, Brothers of KEVIN, is who will make the sacrifice and stop this man? Who will stand up alone in the name of the Creator, and show the modernists that the Creator's laws still exist and are eternal? Because they will try and tell you, the modernists, the cynics, the *Orientalists*, that there are no more beliefs, that our history, our culture, *our world* is over. So thinks this scientist. That is why he so confidently presumes. But he will soon understand what is truly meant by *last days*. So who will show him –'

'Yes, shtoom, yes, I understand,' said Mo, speaking to Millat, but looking straight ahead as in a spy movie.

Millat looked around the room and saw that Hifan was giving him the eye, so he gave it to Shiva, who gave it to Abdul-Jimmy and Abdul-Colin, to Tyrone and the rest of the Kilburn crew, who were stationed by the walls as stewards at particular points in the room. Hifan gave Millat the eye once more, then he looked at the back room. Discreet movement began.

'Something is happening?' whispered Mo, spotting the men with the green steward sashes, making their way through the crowds.

'Come into the office,' said Millat.

∽

'OK, so, I think the key thing here is to come at the issue from two sides. Because it *is* a matter of straight laboratory torture and we can certainly play that to the gallery, but the central emphasis *has* to go to the anti-patent argument. Because that's really an angle we can work. And if we lay our emphasis there, then there are a number of other groups we can call upon – the NCGA, the OHNO, etc., and Crispin's been in touch with them. Because, you know, we haven't really dealt in this area extensively before, but it's clearly a key issue – I think Crispin's going to talk to us about that in more depth in a minute – but for now, I just want to talk about the public support we have here. I mean, particularly the recent press, even the tabloid element have really come up trumps on this . . . there's a lot of bad feeling regarding the patenting of living organisms . . . I think people feel very uncomfortable, rightly, with that concept, and it's really up to FATE to *play* on that, and really get a comprehensive campaign together, so if . . .'

Ah, Joely. Joely, Joely, *Joely*. Joshua knew he should be listening, but looking was so *good*. Looking at Joely was *great*. The way she sat (on a table, knees pulled up to chest), the way she looked up from her notes (kittenishly!), the way the air whistled between her gappy front teeth, the way she continuously tucked her straggly blonde hair behind her ear with one hand and tapped out a rhythm on her huge Doc Martens with the other. Blonde hair aside, she looked a lot like his mother when young: those fulsome English lips, ski-jump nose, big hazel eyes. But the face, spectacular as it might be, was mere *decoration* to top off the most luxurious body in the world. Long in all its lines, muscular in the thigh and soft in the stomach, with breasts that had never known a bra but were an utter delight, and a bottom which was the platonic ideal of all English bottomrey, flat yet peachy, wide but welcoming. Plus she was intelligent. Plus she was devoted to her cause. Plus she despised his father. Plus she was ten years older (which suggested to Joshua all kinds of sexual expertise he couldn't even *imagine* without getting an enormous hard-on right now right here in the middle of the meeting). Plus she was the most wonderful woman Joshua had ever met. Oh, Joely!

'As I see it, what we have to impress upon people is this idea of setting a precedent. You know, the "What next?" kind of argument – and I understand Kenny's POV, that that's way too simplistic a take on it – but I have to argue, I think it's necessary, and we'll put it to a vote in a minute. Is that all right, Kenny? If I can just get on . . . right? Right. Where was I . . . precedent. Because, if it can be argued that the animal under experimentation is owned by any group of people, i.e., it is not a cat but effectively an *invention* with-cat-like-qualities, then that very cleverly and very dangerously short-circuits the work of animal rights groups and that leads to a pretty fucking *scary* vision of the future. Umm . . . I want to bring Crispin in here, to talk a little more about that.'

Of course the cunt of it was, Joely was married to Crispin. And the double-cunt of it was, theirs was a marriage of true love, total spiritual bonding and dedicated political union. Fan-fucking-tastic. Even worse, amongst the members of FATE, Joely's and

Crispin's marriage served as a kind of cosmogony, an originating myth that explained succinctly what people could and should be, how the group began and how it should proceed in the future. Though Joely and Crispin didn't encourage ideas of leadership or any kind of icon worship, it had happened anyway, they were *worshipped*. And they were indivisible. When Joshua first joined the group, he had tried to sniff out a little information on the couple, get the low-down on his chances. Were they wobbly? Had the harsh nature of their business driven them apart? Fat chance. He was told the whole depressing fable by two seasoned FATE activists over some pints in the Spotted Dog: a psychotic ex-postal worker called Kenny who as a child had witnessed his father kill his puppy, and Paddy, a sensitive life-time dole collector and pigeon-fancier.

'Everyone begins wanting to shag Joely,' Kenny had explained, sympathetically, 'but you get over it. You realize the best thing you can do for her is dedicate yourself to the struggle. And then the second thing you realize, is that Crispin's just this *incredible* dude –'

'Yeah, yeah, get on with it.'

Kenny got on with it.

It seemed Joely and Crispin met and fell in love at the University of Leeds the winter of 1982, two young student radicals, with Che Guevara on their walls, idealism in their hearts and a mutual passion for all the creatures that fly, trot, crawl and slime across the earth. At the time, they were both active members of a great variety of far-left groups, but political in-fighting, back-stabbing and endless factionalizing soon disillusioned them as far as the fate of *homo erectus* was concerned. At some point they grew tired of speaking up for this species of ours who will so often organize a coup, bitch behind your back, choose another representative and throw it all back in your face. Instead they turned their attention to our mute animal friends. Joely and Crispin upgraded their vegetarianism to veganism, dropped out of college, got married and formed Fighting Animal Torture and Exploitation in 1985. Crispin's magnetic personality and Joely's natural charm attracted other political drifters, and soon they had become a commune of twenty-five (plus ten cats, fourteen dogs, a garden full of wild rabbits, a sheep, two pigs and a family of foxes) living and working from a Brixton bedsit which backed on to a large expanse of unused allotment. They were pioneers in many senses. Recycling before it became the fashion, making a tropical biosphere of their sweaty bathroom, and dedicating themselves to organic food production. Politically they were equally circumspect. From the very beginning their extremist credentials were impeccable, FATE being to the RSPCA what Stalinism is to the Liberal Democrats. For three years FATE conducted a terror campaign against animal testers, torturers and exploiters, sending death threats to personnel at make-up firms, breaking into labs, kidnapping technicians and chaining themselves to hospital gates. They also ruined fox-hunts, filmed battery chickens, burnt down farms, fire-bombed food outlets and smashed up circus tents. Their brief being so broad and so fanatical (any animal in any level of discomfort), they were kept seriously busy, and life for FATE members was difficult, dangerous and punctuated by frequent imprisonment. Through all of this, Joely's and Crispin's relationship grew stronger and served as an example to them all, a beacon in the storm, the ideal example of love between activists ('Yada yada yada. Get on with it'). Then in 1987 Crispin went to jail for three years for his part in fire-bombing a Welsh laboratory and releasing 40 cats, 350 rabbits and 1,000 rats from their captivity. Before being taken down to Wormwood Scrubs, Crispin generously informed Joely that she had his permission to go to other FATE members if she was in need of sexual satisfaction while he was gone ('And did she?' asked Joshua. 'Did she *fuck*,' replied Kenny sadly).

During Crispin's captivity, Joely devoted herself to transforming FATE from a small gang of highly strung friends to a viable underground political force. She began to put less emphasis on terror tactics and, after reading Guy Debord, grew interested in situationism as a political tactic, which she understood to mean the increased use of large banners, costumes, videos and gruesome re-enactments. By the time Crispin emerged from jail, FATE had grown four-fold, and Crispin's legend (lover, fighter, rebel, hero) had grown with it, fuelled by Joely's passionate interpretation of his life and works and a carefully chosen photo of him circa 1980 in which he looked a bit like Nick Drake. But though his image had been airbrushed, Crispin appeared to have lost none of his radicalism. His first act as a free citizen was to mastermind the release of several hundred voles, an event that received widespread newspaper coverage, though Crispin delegated responsibility for the actual act to Kenny, who was sent down for four months of high security ('Greatest moment of my life'). And then last summer, '91, Joely persuaded Crispin to go to California with her to join the other groups fighting the patent on transgenic animals. Though courtrooms weren't Crispin's scene ('Crispin's a front-line dude'), he succeeded in sufficiently disrupting proceedings to officially warrant a mistrial. The couple flew back to England, elated but with funds perilously low, to find they had been turfed out of their Brixton pad and –

Well, Joshua could take the narrative from here. He met them a week later, wandering up and down the Willesden High Road, looking for a suitable squat. They looked lost, and Joshua, emboldened by the summer vibe and Joely's beauty, went up to talk to them. They ended up going for a pint. They drank, as everybody in Willesden drank, in the aforementioned Spotted Dog, a famous Willesden landmark, described in 1792 as 'being a well accostomed Publick house' (*Willesden Past*, by Len Snow), which became a favourite resort for mid-Victorian Londoners wishing a day out 'in the country', then the meeting point for the horse-buses; later still, a watering hole for local Irish builders. By 1992 it had transformed again, this time into the focal point of the huge Australian immigrant population of Willesden, who, for the last five years, had been leaving their silky beaches and emerald seas and inexplicably arriving in NW2. The afternoon Joshua walked in with Joely and Crispin, this community was in a state of high excitement. After a complaint of a terrible smell above Sister Mary's Palm Readers on the high road, the upper flat had been raided by Health Officers and found to be sheltering sixteen squatting Aussies who had dug a huge hole in the floor and roasted a pig in there, apparently trying to re-create the effect of a South Seas underground kiln. Thrown out on the street, they were presently bemoaning their fate to the publican, a huge bearded Scotsman who had little sympathy for his Antipodean clientele ('Is there some fuckin' sign in fuckin' Sydney that says come to fuckin' Willesden?'). Overhearing the story, Joshua surmised the flat must now be empty and took Joely and Crispin to look at it, his mind already ticking over . . . *if I can get her to live near by . . .*

It was a beautiful, crumbling Victorian building, with a small balcony, a roof garden and a large hole in the floor. He advised them to lie low for a month and then move in. They did, and Joshua saw more and more of them. A month later he experienced a 'conversion' after hours of talk with Joely (hours of examining her breasts underneath those threadbare t-shirts), which felt, at the time, as if somebody had taken his little closed Chalfenist head, stuck two cartoon sticks of dynamite through each ear, and just blown a big mutherfucking hole in his consciousness. It became clear to him in a blinding flash that he loved Joely, that his parents were assholes, that he himself was an asshole, and that the largest community of earth, the animal kingdom, were oppressed, imprisoned and murdered on a daily basis with the full knowledge and support of every government in the world. How much of the last realization was predicated and reliant upon the first was difficult to say, but he had given up Chalfenism and had no interest in taking things apart to see how they fitted together. Instead he gave up all meat, ran off to Glastonbury, got a tattoo, became the kind of guy who could measure an eighth with his eyes closed (so fuck *you*, Millat) and generally had a ball . . . until finally his conscience pricked him. He revealed himself to be the son of Marcus Chalfen. This horrified Joely (*and*, Joshua liked to think, slightly *aroused* her – sleeping with the enemy and all that). Joshua was sent away, while FATE had a two-day summit meeting along the lines of: *But he's the very thing we're . . . Ah, but we could use . . .*

It was a protracted process with votes and subclauses and objections and provisos, but in the end it couldn't really come down to anything more sophisticated than: *Whose side are you on?* Joshua said *yours*, and Joely welcomed him with open arms, pressing his head to her exquisite bosom. He was paraded at meetings, given the role of secretary and was generally the jewel in their crown: *the convert from the other side*.

Since then and for six months, Joshua had indulged his growing contempt for his father, seen plenty of his great love and set about a long-term plan of insinuating himself between the famous couple (he needed somewhere to stay anyway; the Joneses' hospitality was growing thin). He *ingratiated* himself with Crispin, deliberately ignoring Crispin's suspicion of him. Joshua acted like his best mate, did all the shit jobs for him (photocopying, postering, leafleting), kipped on his floor, celebrated his seventh wedding anniversary and presented him with a hand-made guitar plectrum for his birthday; while all the time hating him *intensely*, coveting his wife as no man's wife has ever been coveted before, and dreaming up plots for his downfall with a green-eyed jealousy that would make Iago blush.

All this had distracted Joshua from the fact that FATE were busy plotting his own father's downfall. He had approved it in principle when Magid returned, when his rage was hottest and the idea itself seemed hazy – just some big talk to impress new members. Now the 31st was three weeks away, and Joshua had so far failed to question himself in any coherent way, in any *Chalfenist* fashion, regarding the consequences of what was about to happen. He wasn't even clear precisely what *was* going to happen – there had been no final decision; and now as they argued it, the core members of FATE cross-legged and spaced out around the great hole in the floor, now as he *should* have been listening to these fundamental decisions, he had lost the thread of his attention down Joely's t-shirt, down along the athletic dip and curve of her torso, down further to her tie-dyed pants, down –

'Josh, mate, could you just read me the minutes for a couple of minutes ago, if you get my drift?'

'Huh?'

Crispin sighed and tutted. Joely reached down from her table-top and kissed Crispin on the ear. *Cunt.*

'The minutes, Josh. After the stuff Joely was saying about protest strategy. We'd moved on to the hard part. I want to hear what Paddy was saying a few minutes ago about Punishment versus Release.'

Joshua looked at his blank clipboard and placed it over his detumescent erection.

'Umm . . . I guess I missed that.'

'Er, well that was actually really fucking *important*, Josh. You've got to keep up. I mean, what's the *point* of doing all this talking –'

Cunt, cunt, *cunt*.

'He's doing his *best*,' Joely interceded, reaching down from her table-top once more, this time to ruffle Joshua's Jewfro. 'This is probably quite hard for Joshi, you know? I mean this is quite *personal* to him.' She always called him *Joshi* like that. Joshi and Joely. Joely and Joshi.

Crispin frowned. 'Well, you know, I've said *many times* if Joshua doesn't want to be personally involved in this job, because of personal *sympathies*, if he wants *out*, then –'

'I'm *in*,' snapped Josh, barely restraining the aggression. 'I've no intention of wimping *out*.'

'That's why Joshi's our *hero*,' said Joely, with an enormous, supportive smile. 'Mark my words, he'll be the last man standing.'

Ah, Joely!

'All right, well, let's get on. Try to keep minutes from now on, all right? OK. Paddy, can you just repeat what you were saying, so everyone can take it in, because I think what you said perfectly sums up the key decision we have to make now.'

Paddy's head shot up and he fumbled through his notes. 'Umm, well basically . . . *basically*, it's a question of . . . of what our real *aims* are. If it's to punish the perpetrators and educate the public . . . then, well, that involves one sort of approach – an attack directly on, umm, the person in question,' said Paddy, flashing a nervous glance at Joshua. 'But if our interest is the animal itself, as I think it should be, then it's a question of an anti-campaign, and if that doesn't succeed, then the forceful release of the animal.'

'Right,' said Crispin hesitantly, unsure where the Crispin-role-of-glory would fit into freeing one mouse. 'But surely the mouse in this case is a symbol, i.e., this guy's got a lot more of them in his lab – so we have to deal with the bigger picture. We need someone to bust in there –'

'Well, basically . . . *basically*, I think that's the mistake that OHNO make for example. Because, they take the animal itself as simply a symbol . . . and to me that's absolutely the opposite of what FATE is about. If this were a man trapped in a little glass box for six years, he wouldn't be a symbol, you know? And I don't know about you, but there's no difference between mice and men, you know, in my opinion.'

The gathered members of FATE murmured their assent, because this was the kind of sentiment to which they routinely murmured assent.

Crispin was miffed. 'Right, well, obviously I didn't mean that,

Paddy. I just meant there is a bigger picture here, just like choosing between one man's life and many men's lives, right?'

'Point of order!' said Josh, putting his hand in the air for a chance to make Crispin look stupid. Crispin glared.

'Yes, Joshi,' said Joely sweetly. 'Go on.'

'It's just there aren't any more mice. I mean, yeah, there are lots of mice, but he hasn't got any exactly like this one. It's an incredibly expensive process. He couldn't afford loads. Plus, the press goaded him that if the FutureMouse died while on display he could just secretly replace it with another – so he got cocky. He wants to prove that his calculations are correct in front of the world. He's only going to do one and barcode it. There are no others.'

Joely beamed and reached down to massage Josh's shoulders.

'Right, yes, well, I guess that makes sense. So Paddy, I see what you're saying – it is a question of whether we're going to devote our attentions to Marcus Chalfen or to releasing the actual mouse from its captivity in front of the world's press.'

'Point of order!'

'Yes, Josh, what?'

'Well, Crispin, this isn't like the other animals you bust out. It won't make any difference. The damage is done. The mouse carries around its own torture in its genes. Like a time-bomb. If you release it, it'll just die in terrible pain somewhere else.'

'Point of order!'

'Yes, Paddy, go on.'

'Well, basically . . . would you not help a political prisoner to escape from jail just because he had a terminal disease?'

The multiple heads of FATE nodded vigorously.

'Yes, Paddy, yes, that's right. I think Joshua's wrong there and I think Paddy has presented to us the choice we have to make. It's one we've come up against many times before and we've made different choices in different circumstances. We have, in the past, as you know, gone for the perpetrators. Lists have been made and punishments dealt out. Now, I know in recent years we have been moving away from some of our previous tactics, but I think even Joely would agree this is really our biggest, most fundamental test of that. We are dealing with seriously disturbed individuals. Now, on the other side of things, we have also staged large-scale peaceful protests and supervised the release of thousands of animals held captive by this state. In this case, we just won't have the time or opportunity to employ both strategies. It's a very public place and – well, we've been over that. As Paddy said, I think the choice we have on the 31st is quite simple. It's between the mouse and the man. Has anyone got any problem with taking a vote on that? Joshua?'

Joshua sat on his hands to lift himself up and give Joely better purchase on his upper back massage. 'No problem at all,' he said.

On the 20th of December at precisely 00.00 hours, the phone rang in the Jones house. Irie shuffled downstairs in her nightdress and picked up the receiver.

'*Erhummmm*. I would like you yourself to make a mental note of both the *date* and the *time* when I have chosen to ring you.'

'What? Er . . . what? Is that Ryan? Look, Ryan, I don't mean to be rude, but it's midnight, yeah? Is there something you wanted or –'

'Irie? Pickney? You dere?'

'You granmuvver is on the telephone extension. She wished to talk to you also.'

'Irie,' said Hortense excitably. 'You gwan have to speak up, me kyan hear nuttin' –'

'Irie, I repeat: have you noted the *date* and the *time* of our call?'

'What? Look, I can't . . . I'm really tired . . . could this wait until . . .'

'The 20th, Irie. At O hundred hours. Twos and zeros . . .'

'You lissnin', pickney? Mr Topps tryin' to explain someting very im-par-tent.'

'Gran, you're going to have to talk one at a time . . . you just hauled me out of bed . . . I'm, like, totally *knackered*.'

'Twos and zeros, Miss Jones. Signifying the year 2000. And do you know the month of my call?'

'Ryan, it's December. Is this really –'

'The *twelfth* month, Irie. Corresponding to the twelve tribes of the children of Israel. Of which each woz sealed twelve thousand. Of the tribe of Judah woz sealed twelve thousand. Of the tribe of Reuben woz sealed twelve thousand. Of the tribe of Gad –'

'Ryan, Ryan . . . I get the picture.'

'There are certain days when the Lord wishes us to act – certain pre-warning days, designated days –'

'Where we mus' be savin' de souls of de lost. Warnin' dem ahead of time.'

'We are warning *you*, Irie.'

Hortense began softly weeping. 'We only tryin' to warn you, darlin'.'

'OK. Great. I stand warned. Goodnight, all.'

'That is not the end of our warning,' said Ryan solemnly. 'That is simply the first warning. There are more.'

'Don't tell me – eleven more.'

'Oh!' cried Hortense, dropping the phone but still distantly audible. 'She have been visited by de Lord! She know before she be tol'!'

'Look. Ryan. Could you somehow *condense* the other eleven warnings into one – or at least, tell me the most important one? Otherwise, I'm afraid I'm going to have to go back to bed.'

There was a silence for a minute. Then: '*Erhuuummm*. Very well. Do not get involved with this man.'

'Oh, Irie! Please lissen to Mr Topps! Please lissen to 'im!'

'With *what* man?'

'Oh, Miss Jones. Please do not pretend you 'ave no knowledge of your great sin. Open your soul. Let the Lord let myself reach out for yourself, and wash you free of – '

'Look, I'm really fucking tired. *What* man?'

'The scientist, Chalfen. The man you call "friend" when in truth he is an enemy of all humanity.'

'Marcus? I'm not involved with him. I just answer his phone and do his paperwork.'

'And thus are you made the secretary of the devil,' said Ryan, prompting Hortense into more and louder tears, 'thus is you yourself laid low.'

'Ryan, listen to me. I haven't got *time* for this. Marcus Chalfen is simply trying to come up with some answers to shit like – shit like – *cancer*. OK? I don't know where you've been getting your information, but I can assure you he ain't the devil incarnate.'

'Only one of 'im minions!' protested Hortense. 'Only one of 'im frontline troops!'

'Calm yourself, Mrs B. I am afraid your granddaughter is too far gone for us. As I expected, since leaving us, she 'as joined the dark side.'

'Fuck you, Ryan, I'm not Darth Vader. *Gran* . . .'

'Don't tark to me, pickney, don't tark to me. I and I is bitterly disappointed.'

'It appears we will be seein' you on the 31st, then, Miss Jones.'

'Stop calling me Miss Jones, Ryan. The . . . what?'

'The 31st. The event will provide a platform for the Witness message. The world's press will be there. And so will we. We intend – '

'We gwan warn all a dem!' broke in Hortense. 'And we gat it all plan out nice, see? We gwan sing hymns with Mrs Dobson on de accordion, 'cos you kyan shif a piano all de way dere. An' we gwan hunger-strike until dat hevil man stop messin' wid de Lord's beauteous creation an' – '

'Hunger-strike? Gran, when you go without elevenses you get

nauseous. You've never gone without food for more than three hours in your life. You're eighty-five.'

'You forget,' said Hortense with chilling curtness, 'I was born in strife. Me a survivor. A little no-food don' frighten me.'

'And you're going to let her do that, are you, Ryan? She's eighty-five, Ryan. *Eighty-five*. She can't go on a hunger-strike.'

'I'm tellin' you, Irie,' said Hortense, speaking loudly and clearly into the mouthpiece, 'I *want* to do dis. I'm nat boddered by a little lack of food. De Lord giveth wid 'im right hand and taketh away wid 'im left.'

Irie listened to Ryan drop the phone, walk to Hortense's room and slowly ease the receiver from her, persuading her to go to bed. Irie could hear her grandmother singing as she was led down the hallway, repeating the phrase to no one in particular and setting it to no recognizable tune: *De Lord giveth wid 'im right hand and taketh away wid 'im left!*

But most of the time, thought Irie, *he's simply a thief in the night*. He just taketh away. He just taketh the fuck away.

∽

Magid was proud to say he witnessed every stage. He witnessed the custom design of the genes. He witnessed the germ injection. He witnessed the artificial insemination. And he witnessed the birth, so different from his own. One mouse only. No battle down the birth canal, no first and second, no saved and unsaved. No pot-luck. No random factors. No *you have your father's snout and your mother's love of cheese*. No mysteries lying in wait. No doubt as to when death will arrive. No hiding from illness, no running from pain. No question about who was pulling the strings. No doubtful omnipotence. No shaky fate. No question of a journey, no question of greener grass, for wherever this mouse went, its life would be precisely the same. It would not travel through time (and Time's a bitch, Magid knew *that* much now. Time is *the* bitch), because its future was equal to its present which was equal to its past. A Chinese box of a mouse. No other roads, no missed opportunities, no parallel possibilities. No second-guessing, no what-ifs, no might-have-beens. Just certainty. Just certainty in its purest form. And what more, thought Magid – once the witnessing was over, once the mask and gloves were removed, once the white coat was returned to its hook – what more is God than *that*?

19 *The Final Space*

Thursday, 31 December 1992

So said the banner on the top of the newspaper. So proclaimed the revellers who danced through early evening streets with their shrill silver whistles and Union Jacks, trying to whip up the feeling that goes with the date; trying to bring on the darkness (it was only five o'clock) so that England might have its once-a-year party; get fucked up, throw up, snog, grope and impale; stand in the doorways of trains holding them open for friends; argue with the sudden inflationary tactics of Somalian minicab drivers, jump in water or play with fire, and all by the dim, disguising light of the street lamps. It was the night when England stops saying *pleasethankyoupleasesorrypleasedidI?* And starts saying *pleasefuckmefuckyoumotherfucker* (and we *never* say that; the accent is wrong; we sound silly). The night England gets down to the fundamentals. It was New Year's Eve. But Joshua was having a hard time believing it. Where had the time gone? It had seeped between the crack in Joely's legs, run into the secret pockets of her ears, hidden itself in the warm, matted hair of her armpits. And the consequences of what he was about to do, on this the biggest day of his life, a critical situation that three months ago he would have dissected, compartmentalized, weighed up and analysed with Chalfenist vigour – that too had escaped him into her crevices. He had made no real decisions this New Year's Eve, no resolutions. He felt as thoughtless as the young men tumbling out of pubs, looking for trouble; he felt as light as the child sitting astride his father's shoulders heading for a family party. Yet he was not with them, out there in the streets, having fun – he was here, in here, careening into the centre of town, making a direct line for the

Perret Institute like a heat-seeking missile. He was here, cramped in a bright red minibus with ten jumpy members of FATE, hurtling out of Willesden towards Trafalgar Square, half listening to Kenny read his father's name out loud for the benefit of Crispin who was up front, driving.

'"When Dr Marcus Chalfen puts his FutureMouse on public display this evening he begins a new chapter in our genetic future."'

Crispin threw his head back for a loud, 'Ha!'

'Yeah, right, exactly,' continued Kenny, trying unsuccessfully to scoff and read simultaneously, 'like, thanks for the objective reporting. Umm, where was I . . . all right: "More significantly, he opens up this traditionally secretive, rarefied and complex branch of science to an unprecedented audience. As the Perret Institute prepares to open its doors around-the-clock for seven years, Dr Chalfen promises a national event which will be 'crucially unlike the Festival of Britain in 1951 or the 1924 British Empire Exhibition because it has no political agenda'."'

'Ha!' snorted Crispin once more, this time turning right around in his seat so the FATE minibus (which wasn't officially the FATE minibus; it still had KENSAL RISE FAMILY SERVICES UNIT in ten-inch yellow letters on either side; a loan from a social worker with furry animal sympathies) only narrowly missed a gaggle of pissed-up high-heeled girls who were tottering across the road. 'No political agenda? Is he taking the fucking *piss*?'

'Keep your eyes on the road, darling,' said Joely, blowing him a kiss. 'We want to at least *try* to get there in one piece. Umm, left here . . . down the Edgware Road.'

'Fucker,' said Crispin, glowering at Joshua and then turning back. 'What a *fucker* he is.'

'"By 1999,"' read Kenny, following the arrow from the front to page five, '"the year experts predict recombinant DNA procedure will come into its own – approximately fifteen *million* people will have seen the FutureMouse exhibition, and many more worldwide will have followed the progress of the FutureMouse in the international press. By then, Dr Chalfen will have succeeded in his aim of educating a nation, and throwing the ethical ball into the people's court."'

'Pass. Me. The. Fuck. Ing. Buck. Et,' said Crispin, as if the very words were vomit. 'What do the other papers say?'

Paddy held up Middle England's bible so Crispin could see it in the rear-view. Headline: MOUSEMANIA.

'It comes with a free FutureMouse sticker,' said Paddy, shrugging his shoulders and slapping the sticker on his beret. 'Pretty cute, actually.'

'The tabloids are a surprise winner, though,' said Minnie. Minnie was a brand-new convert: a seventeen-year-old Crusty, with matted blonde dreads and pierced nipples, whom Joshua had briefly considered becoming obsessed with. He tried for a while, but found he just couldn't do it; he just couldn't leave his miserable little psychotic world-of-Joely and go out seeking life on a new planet. Minnie, to her credit, had spotted this straight off and gravitated towards Crispin. She wore as little as the winter weather would allow and took every opportunity to thrust her perky pierced nipples into Crispin's personal space, as she did now, reaching over to the driver's cab to show him the front page of the daily rag in question. At one and the same time Crispin tried unsuccessfully to take the Marble Arch roundabout, avoid elbowing Minnie in the tits, and look at the paper.

'I can't see it properly. What is it?'

'It's Chalfen's head with mouse ears, attached to a goat's torso, which is attached to a pig's arse. And he's eating from a trough that says "Genetic Engineering" at one end and "Public Money" at the other. Headline: CHALFEN CHOWS DOWN.'

'Nice. Every little helps.'

Crispin went round the roundabout again, and this time got

the turning he required. Minnie reached over him and propped the paper on the dashboard.

'God, he looks more fucking Chalfenist than ever!'

Joshua bitterly regretted telling Crispin about this little idiosyncracy of his family, their habit of referring to themselves as verbs, nouns and adjectives. It had seemed a good idea at the time; give everybody a laugh; confirm, if there was any doubt, whose side he was on. But he never felt that he'd betrayed his father – the weight of what he was doing never really hit him – until he heard Chalfenism ridiculed out of Crispin's mouth.

'Look at him Chalfening around in that trough. Exploit everything and everybody, that's the Chalfen way, eh Josh?'

Joshua grunted and turned his back on Crispin, in favour of the window and a view of the frost over Hyde Park.

'That's a classic photo, there, see? The one they've used for the head. I remember it; that was the day he gave evidence in the California trial. That look of *total* fucking *superiority*. Very Chalfenesque!'

Joshua bit his tongue. DON'T RISE TO IT. IF YOU DON'T RISE TO IT, YOU GAIN HER SYMPATHY.

'*Don't*, Crisp,' said Joely firmly, touching Joshua's hair. 'Just try to remember what we're about to do. He doesn't *need* that tonight.'

BINGO.

'Yeah, well . . .'

Crispin put his foot down on the accelerator. 'Minnie, have you and Paddy checked that everyone's got everything they need? Balaclavas and that?'

'Yeah, all done. It's cool.'

'Good.' Crispin pulled out a small silver box filled with all the necessaries to roll a fat joint and threw it in Joely's direction, catching Joshua painfully on the shin.

'Make us one, love.'

CUNT.

Joely retrieved the box from the floor. She worked crouching with the Rizla resting on Joshua's knee, her long neck exposed, her breasts falling forward until they were practically in his hands.

'Are you nervous?' she asked him, flicking her head back once the joint was rolled.

'How d'you mean, nervous?'

'About tonight. I mean, talk about conflict of loyalties.'

'Conflict?' murmured Josh hazily, wishing he were out there with the happy people, the conflict-free people, the New Year people.

'God, I really *admire* you. I mean, FATE are dedicated to extreme action . . . And you know, even now, I find some of the stuff we do . . . *difficult*. And we're talking about the most firmly held principle in my life, you know? I mean, Crispin and FATE. . . that's my whole life.'

OH GREAT, thought Joshua, OH FANTASTIC.

'And I'm still *shit scared* about tonight.'

Joely sparked the joint and inhaled. She passed it straight to Joshua, as the minibus took a right past Parliament. 'It's like that quote: "If I had to choose between betraying my friend or my country, I hope I should have the guts to betray my country." The choice between a duty or a principle, you know? You see, I don't feel torn like that. I don't know if I could do what I do if I did. I mean, if it was my *father*. My first commitment is to animals and that's Crispin's first commitment too, so there's no conflict. It's kind of easy for us. But you, Joshi, *you've* made the most extreme decision out of us all . . . and you just seem so *calm*. I mean, it's admirable . . . and I think you've *really* impressed Crispin, because you know, he was a little unsure about whether . . .'

Joely kept on talking, and Josh kept on nodding in the necessary places, but the hardcore Thai weed he was smoking had lassoed one word of hers – *calm* – and reined it in as a question. *Why so calm, Joshi?* You're about to get into some pretty serious shit – *why so calm?*

Because he imagined he *seemed* calm from the outside, preternaturally calm, his adrenalin enjoying an inverse relationship with the rising New Year sap, with the jittery nerves of the FATE posse; and the effect of the skunk on top of it all . . . it was like walking under water, deep under water, while children played above. But it wasn't calm so much as inertia. And he couldn't work out, as the van progressed down Whitehall, whether this was the right reaction – to let the world wash over him, to let events take their course – or whether he should be more like *those* people, those people out there, whooping, dancing, fighting, fucking . . . whether he should be more – what was that horrible late twentieth-century tautology? *Proactive.* More proactive in the face of the future.

But he took another deep hit on the joint and it sent him back to twelve, being twelve; a precocious kid, waking up each morning fully expecting a *twelve hours until nuclear apocalypse* announcement, that old cheesy end-of-the-world scenario. Round that time he had thought a lot about extreme decisions, about the future and its deadlines. Even then it had struck him that he was unlikely to spend those last twelve hours fucking Alice the fifteen-year-old babysitter next door, telling people that he loved them, converting to orthodox Judaism, or doing all the things he wanted and all the things he never dared. It always seemed more likely to him, much more likely, that he would just return to his room and calmly finish constructing Lego Medieval Castle. What else could you do? What other choice could you be certain about? Because choices need time, the *fullness of time*, time being the horizontal axis of morality – you make a decision and then you wait and see, wait and see. And it's a lovely fantasy, this fantasy of no time (TWELVE HOURS LEFT TWELVE HOURS LEFT), the point at which consequences disappear and any action is allowable ('I'm *mad* – I'm fucking *mad for it*!' came the cry from the street). But twelve-year-old Josh was too neurotic, too anal, too *Chalfenist* to enjoy it, even the thought of it. Instead he was there thinking: but what if the world *doesn't* end and what if I fucked Alice Rodwell and she became *pregnant* and what if –

It was the same now. Always the fear of consequences. Always this terrible inertia. What he was about to do to his father was so huge, so *colossal*, that the consequences were inconceivable – he couldn't imagine a moment occurring after that act. Only blankness. Nothingness. Something like the end of the world. And facing the end of the world, or even just the end of the year, had always given Josh a strangely detached feeling.

Every New Year's Eve is impending apocalypse in miniature. You fuck where you want, you puke when you want, you glass who you want to glass – the huge gatherings in the street; the television round-ups of the goodies and baddies of time past; the frantic final kisses; the 10! 9! 8!

Joshua glared up and down Whitehall, at the happy people going about their dress rehearsal. They were all confident that it wouldn't happen or certain they could deal with it if it did. But the world happens to you, thought Joshua, you don't happen to the world. There's nothing you can do. For the first time in his life, he truly believed that. And Marcus Chalfen believed the direct opposite. And there in a nutshell, he realized, is how I got here, turning out of Westminster, watching Big Ben approach the hour when I shall topple my father's house. That is how we all got here. Between rocks and hard places. The frying pan and the fire.

Thursday, December 31st 1992, New Year's Eve
Signalling problems at Baker Street
No Southbound Jubilee Line Trains from Baker Street

Customers are advised to change on to the Metropolitan Line at Finchley Road

Or Change at Baker Street on to the Bakerloo

There is no alternative bus service

Last Train 02.00 hours

All London Underground staff wish you a safe and happy New Year!

Willesden Green Station Manager, Richard Daley

Brothers Millat, Hifan, Tyrone, Mo Hussein-Ishmael, Shiva, Abdul-Colin and Abdul-Jimmy stood stock-still like maypoles in the middle of the station while the dance of the New Year went on around them.

'*Great*,' said Millat. 'What do we do now?'

'Can't you *read*?' inquired Abdul-Jimmy.

'We do what the board suggests, Brothers,' said Abdul-Colin, short-circuiting any argument with his deep, calming baritone. 'We change at Finchley Road. Allah provides.'

The reason Millat couldn't read the writing on the wall was simple. He was stoned. It was the second day of Ramadan and he was cained. Every synapse in his body had clocked out for the evening and gone home. But there was still some conscientious worker going round the treadmill of his brain, ensuring one thought circulated in his skull: *Why? Why get stoned, Millat? Why?* Good question.

At midday he'd found an ageing eighth of hash in a drawer, a little bundle of cellophane he hadn't had the heart to throw away six months ago. And he smoked it all. He smoked some of it out of his bedroom window. Then he walked to Gladstone Park and smoked some more. He smoked the great majority of it in the car park of Willesden Library. He finished it off in the student kitchen of one Warren Chapman, a South African skateboarder he used to hang with back in the day. And as a result, he was so cained now, standing on the platform with the rest, so *cained* that he could not only hear sounds within sounds but sounds within sounds *within* sounds. He could hear the mouse scurrying along the tracks, creating a higher level of harmonious rhythm with the crackle of the tannoy and the off-beat sniff of an elderly woman twenty feet away. Even when the train pulled in, he could still hear these things beneath the surface. Now, there *is* a level of cained that you can be, Millat knew, that is just so *very very* cained that you reach a level of Zen-like sobriety and come out the other side feeling absolutely tip-top as if you'd never sparked up in the first place. Oh, Millat *longed* for that. He only wished he'd got that far. But there just wasn't quite enough.

'Are you all right, Brother Millat?' asked Abdul-Colin with concern as the tube doors slid open. 'You have gone a nasty colour.'

'Fine, fine,' said Millat, and did a credible impression of being fine because hash just isn't like drink; no matter how bad it is, you can always, at some level, pull your shit together. To prove this theory to himself, he walked in a slow but confident fashion down the carriage and took a seat at the very end of the line of Brothers, between Shiva and some excitable Australians heading for the Hippodrome.

Shiva, unlike Abdul-Jimmy, had had his share of wild times and could spot the tell-tale red-eye from a distance of fifty yards.

'Millat, *man*,' he said under his breath, confident he couldn't be heard by the rest of the Brothers above the noise of the train. 'What have you been *doing* to yourself?'

Millat looked straight ahead and spoke to his reflection in the train window. 'I'm preparing myself.'

'By getting messed up?' hissed Shiva. He peered at the photocopy of Sura 52 he hadn't quite memorized. 'Are you crazy? It's hard enough to remember this stuff without being on the planet Mars while you're doing it.'

Millat swayed slightly, and turned to Shiva with a mistimed lunge. 'I'm not preparing myself for *that*. I'm preparing myself for *action*. Because no one else will do it. We lose one man and you all betray the cause. You desert. But I stand firm.'

Shiva fell silent. Millat was referring to the recent 'arrest' of Brother Ibrāhīm ad-Din Shukrallah on trumped up charges of tax evasion and civil disobedience. No one took the charges seriously, but everybody knew it was a not-so gentle warning from the Metropolitan Police that they had their eye trained on KEVIN activities. In the light of this, Shiva had been the first one to beat a retreat from the agreed Plan A, quickly followed by Abdul-Jimmy and Hussein-Ishmael, who, despite his desire to wreak violence upon somebody, *anybody*, had his shop to think about. For a week the argument raged (with Millat firmly defending Plan A), but on the 26th Abdul-Colin, Tyrone and finally Hifan conceded that Plan A might not be in KEVIN's long-term interest. They could not, after all, put themselves in an imprisonment situation unless they were secure in the knowledge that KEVIN had leaders to replace them. So Plan A was off. Plan B was hastily improvised. Plan B involved the seven KEVIN representatives standing up halfway through Marcus Chalfen's press conference and quoting Sura 52, 'The Mountain', first in Arabic (Abdul-Colin alone would do this) and then in English. Plan B made Millat sick.

'And that's it? You're just going to *read* to him? That's his punishment?'

What happened to revenge? What happened to just desserts, retribution, jihad?

'Do you suggest,' Abdul-Colin solemnly inquired, 'that the word of Allah as given to the Prophet Muhammad – *Salla Allahu 'Alaihi Wa Sallam* – is not sufficient?'

Well, *no*. And so even though it sickened him, Millat had to step aside. In place of the questions of honour, sacrifice, duty, the life and death questions that came with the careful plotting of clan warfare, the very reasons Millat joined KEVIN – in place of these, came the question of *translation*. Everybody agreed that no translation of the Qur'ān could claim to be the word of God, but at the same time everybody conceded that Plan B would lose something in the delivery if no one could understand what was being said. So the question was *which* translation and *why*. Would it be one of the untrusty but clear Orientalists: Palmer (1880), Bell (1937–9), Arberry (1955), Dawood (1956)? The eccentric but poetic J. M. Rodwell (1861)? The old favourite, passionate, dedicated Anglican convert par excellence Muhammad Marmaduke Pickthall (1930)? Or one of the Arab brothers, the prosaic Shakir or the flamboyant Yusuf Ali? Five days they argued it. When Millat walked into the Kilburn Hall of an evening he had only to squint to mistake this talkative circle of chairs, these supposed fanatic fundamentalists, for an editorial meeting at the *London Review of Books*.

'But Dawood is a plod!' Brother Hifan would argue vehemently. 'I refer you to 52:44: *If they saw a part of heaven falling down, they would still say: "It is but a mass of clouds!"* Mass of clouds? It is not a rock concert. At least with Rodwell there is some attempt to capture the poetry, the remarkable nature of the Arabic: *And should they see a fragment of the heaven falling down, they would say, "It is only a dense cloud."* Fragment, dense – the effect is far stronger, accha?'

And then, haltingly, Mo Hussein-Ishmael: 'I am just a butcher-stroke-cornershop-owner. I can't claim to know much about it. But I like very much this last line; it is Rodwell . . . er, I think, yes, Rodwell. 52:49: *And in the night-season: Praise him when the stars are setting*. Night-season. I think that is a lovely phrase. It sounds like an Elvis ballad. Much better than the other one, the Pickthall one: *And in the night-time also hymn His praise, and at the setting of the stars*. Night-season is very much lovelier.'

'And is this what we are here for?' Millat had yelled at all of them. 'Is this what we joined KEVIN for? To take no action? To sit around on our arses playing with words?'

But Plan B stuck, and here they were, whizzing past Finchley Road, heading to Trafalgar Square to carry it out. And this was why Millat was stoned. To give him enough guts to do something else.

'I stand firm,' said Millat, in Shiva's ear, slurring his words, 'that is what we're here for. To stand firm. That is why I joined. Why did you join?'

Well, in fact Shiva had joined KEVIN for three reasons. First, because he was sick of the stick that comes with being the only Hindu in a Bengali Muslim restaurant. Secondly, because being Head of Internal Security for KEVIN beat the hell out of being second waiter at the Palace. And thirdly, for the women. (Not the KEVIN women, who were beautiful but chaste in the extreme, but all the women on the outside who had despaired of his wild ways and were now hugely impressed by his new asceticism. They loved the beard, they dug the hat, and told Shiva that at thirty-eight he had finally ceased to be a boy. They were massively attracted by the fact that he had renounced women and the more he renounced them, the more successful he became. Of course this equation could only work so long, and now Shiva was getting more pussy than he ever had as a kaffir.) However, Shiva sensed that the truth was not what was required here, so he said: 'To do my duty.'

'Then we are on the same wavelength, Brother Shiva,' said Millat, going to pat Shiva's knee but just missing it. 'The only question is: will you do it?'

'Pardon me, mate,' said Shiva, removing Millat's arm from where it had fallen between his legs. 'But I think, taking into account your . . . umm . . . present condition . . . the question is, will *you*?'

Now *there* was a question. Millat was half sure that he was possibly maybe going to do something or not that would be correct and very silly and fine and un-good.

'Mill, we've got a Plan B,' persisted Shiva, watching the clouds of doubt cross Millat's face. 'Let's just go with Plan B, yeah? No point in causing trouble. *Man*. You are *just* like your dad. Classic Iqbal. Can't let things go. Can't let sleeping cats die or whatever the fuck the phrase is.'

Millat turned from Shiva and looked at his feet. He had been more certain when he began, imagining the journey as one cold sure dart on the Jubilee Line: Willesden Green → Charing Cross, no changing of trains, not this higgledy-piggledy journey; just a straight line to Trafalgar, and then he would climb the stairs into the square, and come face to face with his great-great-grandfather's enemy, Henry Havelock on his plinth of pigeon-shat stone. He would be emboldened by it; and he would enter the Perret Institute with revenge and revisionism in his mind and lost glory in his heart and he would and he would and he

'I think,' said Millat, after a pause, 'I am going to vomit.'

'Baker Street!' cried Abdul-Jimmy. And with the discreet aid of Shiva, Millat crossed the platform to the connecting train.

Twenty minutes later the Bakerloo Line delivered them into the icy cold of Trafalgar Square. In the distance, Big Ben. In the square, Nelson. Havelock. Napier. George IV. And then the National Gallery, back there near St Martin's. All the statues facing the clock.

'They do love their false icons in this country,' said Abdul-Colin, with his odd mix of gravity and satire, unmoved by the considerable New Year crowd who were presently spitting at, dancing round and crawling over the many lumps of grey stone. 'Now, will somebody please tell me: what is it about the English that makes them build their statues with their backs to their culture and their eyes on the time?' He paused to let the shivering KEVIN Brothers contemplate the rhetorical question.

'Because they look to their future to forget their past. Sometimes you almost feel sorry for them, you know?' he continued, turning full circle to look around at the inebriated crowd.

'They have no faith, the English. They believe in what men make, but what men make crumbles. Look at their empire. This is all they have. Charles II Street and South Africa House and a lot of stupid-looking stone men on stone horses. The sun rises and sets on it in twelve hours, no trouble. This is what is left.'

'I'm bloody cold,' complained Abdul-Jimmy, clapping his mittened hands together (he found his uncle's speeches a big pain in the arse). 'Let's get going,' he said, as a huge beer-pregnant Englishman, wet from the fountains, collided into him, 'out of this bloody madness. It's on Chandos Street.'

'Brother?' said Abdul-Colin to Millat, who was standing some distance from the rest of the group. 'Are you ready?'

'I'll be along in a minute.' He shooed them away weakly. 'Don't worry, I'll be there.'

There were two things he wanted to see first. The first of which was a particular bench, that bench over there, by the far wall. He walked over to it, a long, stumbling journey, trying to avoid an unruly conga line (so much hashish in his head; lead weights on each foot); but he made it. He sat down. And there it was.

IQBAL

Five-inch letters, between one leg of the bench and the other. IQBAL. It wasn't clear, and the colour of it was a murky rust, but it was there. The story of it was old.

A few months after his father arrived in England, he had sat on this bench nursing a bleeding thumb, the top sliced off by a careless, doddering stroke from one of the older waiters. When it first happened, in the restaurant, Samad couldn't feel it because it was his dead hand. So he just wrapped it in a handkerchief to stem the flow and continued work. But the material had become soaked in blood, he was putting the customers off their food and eventually Ardashir sent him home. Samad took his open thumb out of the restaurant, past theatreland and down St Martin's Lane. When he reached the square he stuck it in the fountain and watched his red insides spill out into the blue water. But he was making a mess and people were looking. He resolved instead to sit on the bench, gripping it at the root until it stopped. The blood kept on coming. After a while, he gave up holding his thumb upright and let it hang down to the floor like halal meat, hoping it would quicken the bleeding process. Then, with his head between his legs, and his thumb leaking on to the pavement, a primitive impulse had come over him. Slowly, with the dribbling blood, he wrote IQBAL from one chair leg to the next. Then, in an attempt to make it more permanent, he had gone over it again with a pen knife, scratching it into the stone.

'A great shame washed over me the moment I finished,' he explained to his sons years later. 'I ran from it into the night; I tried to run from myself. I knew I had been depressed in this country . . . but this was different. I ended up clinging on to the railings in Piccadilly Circus, kneeling and praying, weeping and praying, interrupting the buskers. Because I knew what it meant, this deed. It meant *I wanted to write my name on the world*. It meant *I presumed*. Like the Englishmen who named streets in Kerala after their wives, like the Americans who shoved their flag in the moon. It was a warning from Allah. He was saying: Iqbal, you are *becoming like them*. That's what it meant.'

No, thought Millat, the first time he heard this, no, that's not what it meant. It just meant *you're nothing*. And looking at it now, Millat felt nothing but contempt. All his life he wanted a Godfather, and all he got was Samad. A faulty, broken, stupid, one-handed waiter of a man who had spent eighteen years in a strange land and made no more mark than this. *It just means you're nothing,* repeated Millat, working his way through the premature vomit (girls drinking doubles since three o'clock) over to Havelock, to look Havelock in his stony eye. *It means you're nothing and he's something*. And that's it. That's why Pande hung from a tree while Havelock the executioner sat on a chaise longue in Delhi. Pande was no one and Havelock was someone. No need for library books and debates and reconstructions. *Don't you see, Abba*? whispered Millat. *That's it. That's the long, long history of us and them. That's how it was. But no more.*

Because Millat was here to finish it. To revenge it. To turn that history around. He liked to think he had a different attitude, a second generation attitude. If Marcus Chalfen was going to write his name all over the world, Millat was going to write it BIGGER. There would be no misspelling *his* name in the history books. There'd be no forgetting the dates and times. Where Pande misfooted he would step sure. Where Pande chose A, Millat would choose B.

Yes, Millat was stoned. And it may be absurd to us that one Iqbal can believe the breadcrumbs laid down by another Iqbal, generations before him, have not yet blown away in the breeze. But it really doesn't matter what we believe. It seems it won't stop the man who thinks this life is guided by the life he thinks he had before, or the gypsy who swears by the queens in her tarot pack. And it's hard to change the mind of the high-strung woman who lays responsibility for all her actions at the feet of her mother, or the lonely guy who sits in a fold-up chair on a hill in the dead of night waiting for the little green men. Amidst the strange landscapes that have replaced our belief in the efficacy of the stars, Millat's is not such odd terrain. He believes the decisions that are made, come back. He believes we live in circles. His is a simple, neat fatalism. What goes around comes around.

'Ding, ding,' said Millat out loud, tapping Havelock's foot, before turning on his heel to make his hazy way to Chandos Street. 'Round two.'

December 31st 1992
He that increaseth knowledge increaseth sorrow
Eccles. ch. 1, v. 18

When Ryan Topps was asked to assemble the Lambeth Kingdom Hall's *Thought for the Day* desk calendar for 1992, he took especial care to avoid the mistakes of his predecessors. Too often in the past, Ryan noted, when the assembler came to choose quotations for entirely fatuous, secular days, he let sentiment get the better of him, so that on Valentine's Day 1991 we find ***there is no fear in love; but perfect love casteth out fear***, I John 4:18, as if John were thinking of the paltry feeling that prompts people to send each other Milk Tray and cheap teddy bears rather than the love of Jesus Christ, which nothing surpasseth. Ryan took very much the opposite approach. On a day like New Year's Eve, for example, when everybody was running around making their New Year resolutions, assessing their past year and plotting their success for the next, he felt it necessary to bring them to earth with a bump. He wanted to offer a little reminder that the world is cruel and pointless, all human endeavour ultimately meaningless, and no advancement in this world worth making besides gaining God's favour and an entry ticket into the better half of the after-life. And having completed the calendar the previous year and forgotten much of what he'd done, he was pleasantly surprised – when he ripped off the 30th and looked at the crisp white page of the 31st – at just how effective the reminder was. No thought could have been more apt for the day ahead. No warning more propitious. He ripped it from the calendar, squeezed it into the tight leather of his trousers and told Mrs B. to get in the side car.

'He who would valiant be, 'gainst all disaster!' sang Mrs B. as they zipped along Lambeth Bridge, heading for Trafalgar Square. *'Let 'im in constancy, follow de master!'*

Ryan made sure to signal a good minute before turning left so that the Kingdom ladies in the minibus behind wouldn't get confused. He made a quick mental inventory of the things he'd put in the van: songbooks, instruments, banners, *Watchtower* leaflets. All present and correct. They had no actual tickets, but they would make their protest outside, in the cold, suffering like true Christians. Praise be to God! What a glorious day! All portents were good. He even had a dream last night that Marcus Chalfen was the devil himself and they were standing nose to nose. Ryan had said: *Myself and yourself are at war. There can be only one winner.* Then he had quoted the same piece of scripture at him (he couldn't recall precisely what it was now, but it was something from Revelation) over and over and over again, until the devil/Marcus had become smaller and smaller, grown ears and a long forked tail, and finally scurried away, a tiny satanic mouse. As in this vision, so it would be in life. Ryan would remain unbending, unmoving, absolutely constant, and, in the end, the sinner would repent.

That was how Ryan approached all theological, practical and

personal conflicts. He didn't move, not an inch. But then, that had always been his talent; he had a mono-intelligence, an ability to hold on to a single idea with phenomenal tenacity, and he never found anything that suited it as well as the church of Jehovah's Witnesses. Ryan thought in black and white. The problem with his antecedent passions – scootering and pop music – was there were always shades of grey (though possibly the two closest things in secular life to a Witness preacher are boys who send letters to the *New Musical Express* and those enthusiasts who pen articles for *Scooters Today*). There were always the difficult questions of whether one should dilute one's appreciation of the Kinks with a little Small Faces, or whether Italy or Germany were the best manufacturers of spare engine parts. That life seemed so alien to him now he hardly remembered living it. He pitied those who suffered under the weight of such doubts and dilemmas. He pitied Parliament as he and Mrs B. scooted past it; he pitied it because the laws made in there were provisional where his were eternal . . .

'There's no discouragement, shall make 'im once relent, his first avowed intent, to be a Pilgrim!' trilled Mrs B. *'Who so besets him round, with dismal stories . . . do but themselves confound, his strength the more is . . .'*

He relished it. He relished standing nose to nose with evil and saying, 'You yourself: prove it to me. Go on, *prove it*.' He felt he needed no arguments like the Muslims or the Jews. No convoluted proofs or defences. Just his faith. And nothing rational can fight faith. If *Star Wars* (secretly Ryan's favourite film. The Good! The Evil! The Force! So *simple*. So *true*) is truly the sum of all archaic myths and the purest allegory of life (as Ryan believed it was), then faith, unadulterated, ignorant faith, is the biggest fuck-off light sabre in the universe. *Go on, prove it*. He did that every Sunday on the doorsteps and he would do precisely the same to Marcus Chalfen. *Prove to me that you are right. Prove to me that you are more right than God*. Nothing on earth would do it.

Because Ryan didn't believe in or care about anything on earth.

'We almost there?'

Ryan squeezed Mrs B.'s frail hand and sped across the Strand, then wound his way round the back of the National Gallery.

'No foe shall stay his might, though he with giants fight, he will make good his right, to be a Pilgrim!'

Well said Mrs B.! The right to be a pilgrim! Who does not presume and yet inherits the earth! The right to be right, to teach others, to be just at all times because God has ordained that you will be, the right to go into strange lands and alien places and talk to the ignorant, confident that you speak nothing but the truth. The right to be always *right*. So much better than the rights he once held dear: the right to liberty, freedom of expression, sexual freedom, the right to smoke pot, the right to party, the right to ride a scooter sixty-five miles an hour on a main road without a helmet. So much more than all those, Ryan could claim. He exercised a right so rare, at this the fag-end of the century, as to be practically obsolete. The most fundamental right of all. The right to be the good guy.

On: 31/12/1992
London Transport Buses
Route 98
From: Willesden Lane
To: Trafalgar Square
At: 17:35
Fare: Adult Single £0.70
Retain Ticket for Inspection

Cor (thought Archie) *they don't make 'em like they used to*. That's not to say they make them any *worse*. They just make them very, very *different*. So much *information*. The minute you tore one from the perforation you felt stuffed and pinned down by some all-seeing taxidermist, you felt freeze-framed in time, you felt *caught*. Didn't use to be, Archie remembered. Many years ago he had a cousin, Bill, who worked the old 32 route through Oxford Street. Good sort, Bill. Smile and a nice word for everyone. Used to tear off a ticket from one of those chug-chug big-handled mechanical things (and where have they gone? Where's the smudgy ink?) on the sly, like; no money passed over; *there you go, Arch*. That was Bill, always helping you out. Anyway, those tickets, the old ones, they didn't tell you where you were *going*, much less where you came from. He couldn't remember seeing any dates on them either, and there was certainly no mention of time. It was all different now, of course. All this information. Archie wondered why that was. He tapped Samad on the shoulder. He was sitting directly ahead of him, in the front-most seat of the top deck. Samad turned round, looked at the ticket he was being shown, listened to the question and gave Archie a funny look.

'What is it, *precisely*, that you want to know?'

He looked a bit testy. Everyone was a little testy right now. There'd been a bit of a ding-dong earlier in the afternoon. Neena had demanded that they all go to the mouse thing, seeing as how Irie was involved and Magid was involved and the least they could do was go and support family because whatever they thought of it a lot of work had gone into it and young people need affirmation from their parents and she was going to go even if they weren't and it was a pretty poor show if family couldn't turn up for their big day and . . . well, it went on and on. And then the emotional fall-out. Irie burst into tears (What was wrong with Irie? She was always a bit weepy these days), Clara accused Neena of emotional blackmail, Alsana said she'd go if Samad went, and Samad said he'd spent New Year's Eve at O'Connell's for eighteen years and he wasn't going to stop now. Archie, for his part, said he was buggered if he was going to listen to this racket all evening – he'd rather sit on a quiet hill by himself.

They'd all looked at him queerly when he said that. Little did they know he was taking prophetic advice he'd received from Ibelgaufts the day before:

28 December 1992

My dearest Archibald,

'Tis the season to be jolly . . . so it has been claimed, but from my window I see only turmoil. At present six felines, hungry for territory, are warring in my garden. Not content with their autumnal hobby of drenching their plots in urine, the winter has brought out a more fanatical urge in them . . . it is down to claws and flying fur . . . the screeching keeps me up all through the night! I cannot help but think that my own cat, Gabriel, has the right idea, sat atop my shed, having given up his land claims in exchange for a quiet life.

But in the end, Alsana laid down the law. Archie and the rest were going whether they liked it or not. And they didn't. So now they were taking up half the bus in their attempts to sit alone: Clara behind Alsana who was behind Archie who was behind Samad who was sitting across from Neena. Irie was sitting next to Archie, but only because there wasn't any more space.

'I was just saying . . . you know,' said Archie, attempting the first conversation to broach the frosty silence since they left Willesden. 'It's quite interesting, the amount of information they put on bus tickets these days. Compared with, you know, the old days. I was just wondering why. It's quite interesting.'

'I have to be honest, Archibald,' said Samad with a grimace, 'I find it singularly uninteresting. I find it terminally dull.'

'Oh, right,' said Archie. 'Right you are.'

The bus did one of those arching corners where it feels the merest breath will topple it over.

'Umm . . . so you wouldn't know why –'

'No, Jones, I have no intimate friends at the bus garage nor any inside knowledge of the progressive decisions that are no doubt made daily within London Transport. But if you are asking me for my uneducated guess, then I imagine it is part of some huge government monitoring process to track the every movement of one Archibald Jones, to ascertain where and what he is doing on all days and at every moment –'

'Jesus,' Neena cut in irritably, 'why do you have to be such a *bully*?'

'Excuse me? I was not aware you and I, Neena, were having a conversation.'

'He was just asking a question and you have to come over all arsey. I mean, you've been bullying him for half a century. Haven't you had enough? Why don't you just leave him alone?'

'Neena Begum, I swear if you give me one more instruction today I will personally tear your tongue out at the root and wear it as a necktie.'

'Steady on, Sam,' said Archie, perturbed at the fuss he had inadvertently caused, 'I was just –'

'Don't *you* threaten my niece,' Alsana chimed in from further down the bus. 'Don't you take it out on her just because you'd rather be eating your beans and chips' – *Ah!* (thought Archie, wistfully) *Beans and chips!* – 'than going to see your own son actually achieving something and –'

'I can't remember *you* being all that keen,' said Clara, adding her twopence worth. 'You know, you have a very convenient way, Alsi, of forgetting what happened two minutes ago.'

'This from the woman who lives with Archibald Jones!' scoffed Samad. 'I might remind you that people in glass houses –'

'No, Samad,' Clara protested. 'Don't even *begin* to start on me. You're the one who had all the real objections about coming . . . but you never stick to a decision, do you? Always Pandy-ing around. At least Archie's, well, you know . . .' stumbled Clara, unused to defending her husband and unsure of the necessary adjective, 'at least he makes a decision and sticks by it. At least Archie's *consistent*.'

'Oh surely, yes,' said Alsana acidly. 'The same way that a *stone* is consistent, the same way my dear *babba* is consistent for very simple reason that she's been buried underground for –'

'Oh, shut *up*,' said Irie.

Alsana was silenced for a moment, and then the shock subsided and she found her tongue. 'Irie Jones, don't you tell me –'

'No, I *will* tell you,' said Irie, going very red in the face, 'actually. Yeah, I will. Shut *up*. Shut up, Alsana. And shut up the lot of you. All right? Just shut *up*. In case you didn't notice, there are, like, *other people* on this bus and, believe it or not, not everyone in the *universe* wants to listen to you lot. So shut it. Go on. Try it. *Silence. Ah.*' She reached into the air as if trying to touch the quiet she had created. 'Isn't that something? Did you know this is how other families are? They're *quiet*. Ask one of these people sitting here. They'll tell you. They've got families. *This is how some families are all the time*. And some people like to call these families repressed, or emotionally stunted or whatever, but do you know what I say?'

The Iqbals and the Joneses, astonished into silence along with the rest of the bus (even the loud-mouthed Ragga girls on their way to a Brixton dance hall New Year ting), had no answer.

'I say, *lucky fuckers*. Lucky, lucky *fuckers*.'

'Irie Jones!' cried Clara. 'Watch your mouth!' But Irie couldn't be stopped.

'What a peaceful existence. What a *joy* their lives must be. They open a door and all they've got behind it is a bathroom or a lounge. Just neutral spaces. And not this endless maze of present rooms and past rooms and the things said in them years ago and everybody's old historical shit all over the place. They're not constantly making the same old mistakes. They're not always hearing the same old shit. They don't do public performances of angst on public transport. Really, these people exist. I'm telling you. The biggest traumas of their lives are things like recarpeting. Bill-paying. Gate-fixing. They don't mind what their kids do in life as long as they're reasonably, you know, *healthy. Happy.* And every single fucking day is not this huge battle between who they are and who they should be, what they were and what they will be. Go on, ask them. And they'll tell you. No mosque. Maybe a little church. Hardly any sin. Plenty of forgiveness. No attics. No shit in attics. No skeletons in cupboards. No great-grandfathers. I will put twenty quid down *now* that Samad is the only person in here who knows the inside bloody leg measurement of his great-grandfather. And you know *why* they don't know? Because *it doesn't fucking matter.* As far as they're concerned, it's the *past.* This is what it's like in other families. They're not self-indulgent. They don't run around, relishing, *relishing* the fact that they are utterly dysfunctional. They don't spend their time trying to find ways to make their lives more complex. They just *get on with it.* Lucky bastards. Lucky motherfuckers.'

The enormous adrenalin rush that sprang from this peculiar outburst surged through Irie's body, increased her heart-beat to a gallop and tickled the nerve ends of her unborn child, for Irie was eight weeks pregnant and she knew it. What she didn't know, and what she realized she may *never know* (the very moment she saw the ghostly pastel blue lines materialize on the home test, like the face of the madonna in the zucchini of an Italian housewife), was the identity of the father. No test on earth would tell her. Same thick black hair. Same twinkling eyes. Same habit of chewing the tops of pens. Same shoe size. Same deoxyribonucleic acid. She could not know her body's decision, what choice it had made, in the race to the gamete, between the saved and the unsaved. She could not know if the choice would make any difference. Because whichever brother it was, it was the other one too. She would never know.

At first this fact seemed ineffably sad to Irie; instinctively she sentimentalized the biological facts, adding her own invalid syllogism: if it was not somebody's child, could it be that it was nobody's child? She thought of those elaborate fictional cartograms that folded out of Joshua's old sci-fi books, his Fantasy Adventures. That is how her child seemed. A perfectly plotted thing with no real coordinates. A map to an imaginary fatherland. But then, after weeping and pacing and rolling it over and over in her mind, she thought: *whatever*, you know? What*ever*. It was always going to turn out like this, not precisely like this, but *involved* like this. This was the Iqbals we were talking about, here. This was the Joneses. How could she ever have expected anything less?

And so she calmed herself, putting her hand over her palpitating chest and breathing deeply as the bus approached the square and the pigeons circled. She would tell one of them and not the other; she would decide which; she would do it tonight.

'You all right, love?' Archie asked her, after a long period of silence had set in, putting his big pink hand on her knee, dotted with liver-spots like tea stains. 'A lot on your chest, then.'

'Fine, Dad. I'm fine.'

Archie smiled at her, and tucked a stray hair behind her ear.

'Dad.'

'Yes?'

'The thing about the bus tickets.'

'Yes?'

'One theory goes it's because so many people pay less than they should for their journey. Over the past few years the bus companies have been suffering from larger and larger deficits. You see where it says *Retain for Inspection*? That's so they can check later. It's got all the details there, so you can't get away with it.'

And in the past, Archie wondered, was it just that fewer people cheated? Were they more honest, and did they leave their front doors open, did they leave their kids with the neighbours, pay social calls, run up tabs with the butcher? The funny thing about getting old in a country is people always want to hear that from you. They want to hear it really was once a green and pleasant land. They *need* it. Archie wondered if his daughter needed it. She was looking at him funny. Her mouth down-turned, her eyes almost pleading. But what could he tell her? New Years come and go, but no amount of resolutions seem to change the fact that there are bad blokes. There were always plenty of bad blokes.

'When I was a kid,' said Irie softly, ringing the bell for their stop, 'I used to think they were little alibis. Bus tickets. I mean, look: they've got the time. The date. The place. And if I was up in court, and I had to defend myself, and prove I wasn't where they said I was, doing what they said I did, when they said I did it, I'd pull out one of those.'

Archie was silent and Irie, assuming the conversation was over, was surprised when several minutes later, after they had struggled through the happy New Year crowd and tourists standing round aimlessly, as they were walking up the steps of the Perret Institute, her father said, 'Now, I never thought of that. I'll remember that. Because you never know, do you? I mean, do you? Well. There's a thought. You should pick them up off the street, I suppose. Put 'em all in a jar. An alibi for every occasion.'

∽

And all these people are heading for the same room. The final space. A big room, one of many in the Perret Institute; a room separate from the exhibition yet called an Exhibition Room; a corporate place, a clean slate; white/chrome/pure/plain (this was the design brief) used for the meetings of people who want to meet somewhere neutral at the end of the twentieth century; a virtual place where their business (be that rebranding, lingerie or rebranding lingerie) can be done in an emptiness, an uncontaminated cavity; the logical endpoint of a thousand years of spaces too crowded and bloody. This one is pared down, sterilized, made new every day by a Nigerian cleaning lady with an industrial Hoover and guarded through the night by Mr De Winter, a Polish nightwatchman (that's what he calls himself – his job title is Asset Security Coordinator); he can be seen protecting the space, walking the borders of the space with a Walkman playing Polish folk-tunes; you can see him, you can see *it* through a huge glass front if you walk by – the acres of protected vacuity and a sign with the prices per square foot of these square feet of space of space of space longer than it is wide and tall enough to fit head-to-toe three Archies and at least half an Alsana and tonight there are (there will not be tomorrow) two huge, matching posters, slick across two sides of the room like wallpaper and the text says MILLENNIAL SCIENCE COMMISSION in a wide variety of fonts ranging from the deliberate archaism of viking to the modernity of **impact** in order to get a feel of a thousand years in lettering (this was the brief), and all of it in the alternate colours grey, light blue and dark green because these are the colours research reveals people associate with 'science and technology' (purples and reds denote the arts, royal blue signifies 'quality and/or approved merchandise'), because fortunately after years of corporate synaesthesia (salt & vinegarblue, cheese & oniongreen) people can finally give the answers required when a space is being designed, or when something is being rebranded, a room/furniture/Britain (that was the brief: a new British room, a space for Britain, Britishness, space of Britain, British industrial space cultural space space); they know what is meant when asked how matt chrome makes them feel; and they know what is meant by national identity? symbols? paintings? maps? music? air-conditioning? smiling black children or smiling Chinese children or [tick the box]? world music? shag or pile? tile or floorboards? plants? running water?

they know what they want, especially those who've lived this century, forced from one space to another like Mr De Winter (né

Wojciech), renamed, rebranded, the answer to every questionnaire nothing nothing space please just space nothing please nothing space

20 *Of Mice and Memory*

It's just like on TV! And that is the most superlative compliment Archie can think of for any real-life event. Except this is just like on TV but better. It's very *modern*. It's so well designed you wouldn't want to *breathe* in it, no matter fart in it. There's these chairs, plastic but without legs, curved like an *s*; they seem to work by means of their own fold; and they fit together, about two hundred of them in ten rows; and they snake around you when you sit in them – soft yet supportive! Comfy! Modern! And you've got to admire folding like that, Archie thinks, lowering himself into one, a far higher level of folding than he'd ever been involved with. *Very nice*.

The other thing that makes it all better than TV is it's full of people Archie knows. There's Millboid at the very back (scoundrel), with Abdul-Jimmy and Abdul-Colin; Josh Chalfen nearer the middle, and Magid's sitting up at the front with the Chalfen woman (Alsana won't look at her, but Archie waves anyway because it'd be rude not to) and facing them all (near Archie – Archie's got the best seat in the house) sits Marcus at a long long table, just like on TV, with microphones all over it, like a bloody swarm, the huge black abdomens of killer bees. Marcus is sitting next to four other blokes, three his age and one really old bloke, dry-looking – *desiccated*, if that's the word. And they've all got glasses to a man, the way scientists do on the telly. No white coats, though. All very casual: V-necks, ties, loafers. *Bit disappointing*.

Now he's seen a lot of these press conference larks, Archie has (weeping parents, missing child, or, conversely, if it was a foreign-orphan-scenario, weeping child, missing parents), but this is *miles* better because in the centre of the table is something quite interesting (which you don't usually get on TV, just the weeping people): a mouse. Quite a plain mouse, brown, and not with any other mice, but it's very active, scurrying around in this glass box that's about as big as a television with airholes. Archie was a bit worried when he first saw it (seven years in a glass box!), but it turns out it's temporary, just for the photographs. Irie explained there's this huge thing for it in the Institute, full of pipes and secret places, space upon space, so it won't get too bored, and it'll be transferred there later. So that's all right. He's a cunning-looking little blinder too, this mouse. He looks like he's pulling faces a lot of the time. You forget how alert looking mice are. Terrible trouble to look after, of course. That's why he never got one for Irie when she was small. Goldfish are cleaner – with shorter memories. In Archie's experience anything with a long memory holds a grievance and a pet with a grievance (that time you got the wrong food, that time you bathed me) just isn't what you want.

'Oh, you're right there,' agrees Abdul-Mickey, plonking himself down in the seat next to Archie, betraying no reverence for the legless chair. 'You don't want some resentful fucking rodent on your hands.'

Archie smiles. Mickey's the kind of guy you want to watch the footie with, or the cricket, or if you see a fight in the street you want him to be there, because he's kind of a commentator on life. Kind of a philosopher. He's quite frustrated in his daily existence because he doesn't get much opportunity to show that side of himself. But get him free of his apron and away from the oven, give him space to manoeuvre – he really comes into his own. Archie's got a lot of time for Mickey. A lot of time.

'When they gonna get on wiv it, then?' he says to Archie. 'Taking their time, eh? Can't look at a mouse all bloody night, can you? I mean, you get all these people here on New Year's Eve, you want *something* resembling entertainment.'

'Yeah, well,' says Archie, not disagreeing but not completely agreeing either, 'I 'spect they've got to go through their notes and that . . .'Snot like just getting up and telling a few howlers, is it? I mean, it's not just about pleasing all the people all of the time, now, is it? It's *Science.*' Archie says *Science* the same way he says *Modern*, as if someone has lent him the words and made him swear not to break them. '*Science,*' Archie repeats, handling it more firmly, 'is a different kettle of fish.'

Mickey nods at this, seriously considering the proposition, trying to decide how much weight he should allow this counter-argument *Science*, with all its connotations of expertise and higher planes, of places in thought that neither Mickey nor Archie has ever visited (answer: none), how much respect he should give it in the light of these connotations (answer: fuck all. University of Life, innit?), and how many seconds he should leave before tearing it apart (answer: three).

'On the contrary, Archibald, on the bloody contrary. Speeshuss argument, that is. Common fucking mistake, that is. Science ain't no different from nuffink else, is it? I mean, when you get down to it. At the end of the day, it's got to please the people, you know what I mean?'

Archie nods. He knows what Mickey means. (Some people – Samad for example – will tell you not to trust people who overuse the phrase *at the end of the day* – football managers, estate agents, salesmen of all kinds – but Archie's never felt that way about it. Prudent use of said phrase never failed to convince him that his interlocutor was getting to the bottom of things, to the fundamentals.)

'And if you think there's any difference between a place like this and my caff,' Mickey continues, somehow full throated and yet never increasing above a whisper in terms of decibel, 'you're having a laugh. 'Sall the same in the end. 'Sall about the customer in the end. *Exempli fuckin' gratia*: it's no good me putting *Duck à l'orange* on the menu if nobody wants it. *Vis-à-vis*, there's no point this lot spending a lot of money on some clever ideas if they're not going to do some fucking good for someone. *Think about it,*' says Mickey, tapping his temple, and Archie follows the instruction as best he can.

'But that don't mean you don't give it a bloody chance,' continues Mickey, warming to his theme. 'You've got to give these new ideas a *chance*. Otherwise you're just a philistine, Arch. Now, at the end of the day, you know I've always been your cutting-edge type of geezer. That's why I introduced Bubble and Squeak two years ago.'

Archie nods sagely. The Bubble and Squeak had been a revelation of sorts.

'Same goes here. You've got to give these things a chance. That's what I said to Abdul-Colin and my Jimmy. I said: before you jump the gun, come along and give it a chance. And here they are.' Abdul-Mickey flicked his head back, a vicious tick of recognition in the direction of his brother and son, who responded in kind. 'They might not like what they hear, of course, but you can't account for that, can you? But at least they've come along with an *open mind*. Now, me personally, I'm here on good authority from that Magid Ick-Ball – and I trust him, I trust his judgement. But, as I say, we shall wait and see. We live and fucking learn, Archibald,' says Mickey, not to be offensive, but because the F-word acts like padding to him; he can't help it; it's just a filler like beans or peas, 'we live and fucking learn. And I can tell you, if anything said here tonight convinces me that my Jimmy might not have sprogs wiv skin like the surface of the fucking moon, then I'm converted, Arch. I'll say it now. I've not the fucking foggiest what some mouse's got to do with the old Yusuf skin, but I tell you, I'd put my life in that Ick-Ball boy's hands. I just get a good feeling off that lad. Worth a dozen of his brother,' adds Mickey slyly, lowering his voice because Sam's behind them. 'A dozen easy. I mean, what the fuck was he thinking, eh? I know which one I'd've sent away. No fear.'

Archie shrugs. 'It was a tough decision.'

Mickey crosses his arms and scoffs, 'No such thing, mate. You're either *right* or you *ain't*. And as soon as you realize that, Arch, suddenly your life becomes a lot fucking easier. Take my word for it.'

Archie takes Mickey's words gratefully, adding them to the other pieces of sagacity the century has afforded him: *You're either right or you ain't. The golden age of Luncheon Vouchers is over. Can't say fairer than that. Heads or tails?*

'Oi-oi, what this?' says Mickey with a grin. 'Here we go. Movement. Microphone in action. One-two, one-two. Looks like the manneth beginneth.'

ᔕ

'. . . and this work *is* pioneering, it *is* something that deserves public money and public attention, and it is work the significance of which overrides, in any rational person's mind, the objections that have been levied against it. What we need . . .'

What we *need*, thinks Joshua, are seats closer to the front. Typical cuntish planning on the part of Crispin. Crispin asked for seats in the thick of it, so FATE could kind of merge with the crowd and slip the balaclavas on at the last minute, but it was clearly a rubbish idea which relied upon some kind of middle aisle in the seating, which just isn't here. Now they are going to have to make an ungainly journey to the side aisles, like terrorists looking for their seat in the cinema, slowing down the whole operation, when speed and shock tactics are the whole fucking *point*. What a performance. The whole plan pisses Josh off. So elaborate and absurd, all designed for the greater glory of Crispin. Crispin gets to do a bit of shouting, Crispin gets to do some waving-of-gun, Crispin does some pseudo-Jack Nicholson-psycho twitches just for the drama of it. FANTASTIC. All Josh gets to say is *Dad, please. Give them what they want*, though privately he figures he'll have some room for improvisation: *Dad, please. I'm so fucking young. I want to live. Give them what they want, for Chrissake. It's just a mouse . . . I'm your son,* and then possibly a phoney faint in response to a phoney pistol-whip if his father proves to be hesitant. The whole plan's so high on the cheese factor it's practically Stilton. But it will work (Crispin had said), that stuff always *works*. But having spent so much time in the animal kingdom, Crispin is like Mowgli: he doesn't know about the motivations of people. And he knows more about the psychology of a badger than he will ever know about the inner workings of a Chalfen. So looking at Marcus up there with his magnificent mouse, celebrating the great achievement of his life and maybe *of this generation*, Joshua can't stop his own perverse brain from wondering whether it is just possible that he and Crispin and FATE have misjudged *completely*. That they have all royally messed up. That they have underestimated the power of Chalfenism and its remarkable commitment to the Rational. For it is quite possible that his father will not simply and unreflectingly save the thing he loves like the rest of the plebs. It is quite possible that love doesn't even come into it. And just thinking about that makes Joshua smile.

ഗ

'. . . and I'd like to thank you all, particularly family and friends who have sacrificed their New Year's Eve . . . I'd like to thank you all for being here at the outset of what I'm sure everybody agrees is a very exciting project, not just for myself and the other researchers but for a far wider . . .'

Marcus begins and Millat watches the Brothers of KEVIN exchange glances. They're figuring about ten minutes in. Maybe fifteen. They'll take their cue from Abdul-Colin. They're following instructions. Millat, on the other hand, is not following instructions, at least not the kind that are passed from mouth to mouth or written on pieces of paper. His is an imperative secreted in the genes and the cold steel in his inside pocket is the answer to a claim made on him long ago. He's a Pandy deep down. And there's mutiny in his blood.

As for the practicalities, it had been no biggie: two phone calls to some guys from the old crew, a tacit agreement, some KEVIN money, a trip to Brixton and hey presto it was in his hand, heavier than he had imagined, but, aside from that, not such a headfuck of an object. He almost *recognized* it. The effect of it reminded him of a small car-bomb he saw explode, many years ago, in the Irish section of Kilburn. He was only nine, walking along with Samad. But where Samad was shaken, genuinely shaken, Millat hardly blinked. To Millat, it was so *familiar*. He was so *unfazed* by it. Because there aren't any alien objects or events any more, just as there aren't any sacred ones. It's all so familiar. It's all on TV. So handling the cold metal, feeling it next to his skin that first time: it was easy. And when things come to you easily, when things click effortlessly into place, it is so tempting to use the four-letter F-word. Fate. Which to Millat is a quantity very much like TV: an unstoppable narrative, written, produced and directed by somebody else.

Of course, now that he's here, now that he's stoned and *scared*, and it doesn't feel so easy, and the right-hand side of his jacket feels like someone put a fucking cartoon anvil in there – now he sees the great difference between TV and life, and it kicks him right in the groin. Consequences. But even to think *this* is to look to the movies for reference (because he's not like Samad or Mangal Pande; he didn't get a war, he never saw action, he hasn't got any analogies or anecdotes), is to remember Pacino in the first *Godfather*, huddled in the restaurant toilet (as Pande was huddled in the barracks room), considering for a moment what it means to burst out of the men's room and blast the hell out of the two guys at the checkered table. And Millat remembers. He remembers rewinding and freeze-framing and slow-playing that scene countless times over the years. He remembers that no matter how long you pause the split-second of Pacino reflecting, no matter how often you replay the doubt that seems to cross his face, he never does anything else but what he was always going to do.

∽

'. . . and when we consider that the human significance of this technology . . . which will prove, I believe, the equal of this century's discoveries in the field of physics: relativity, quantum mechanics . . . when we consider the choices it affords us . . . not between a blue eye and a brown eye, but between eyes that would be blind and those that might see . . .'

But Irie now believes there are things the human eye cannot detect, not with any magnifying glass, binocular or microscope. She should know, she's tried. She's looked at one and then the other, one and then the other – so many times they don't seem like faces any more, just brown canvases with strange protrusions, like saying a word so often it ceases to make sense. Magid and Millat. Millat and Magid. Majlat. Milljid.

She's asked her unborn child to offer some kind of a sign, but nothing. She's had a lyric from Hortense's house going through her head – Psalm 63 – *early will I seek thee: my soul thirsteth for thee, my flesh longeth for thee* . . . But it asks too much of her. It requires her to go back, back, back to the root, to the fundamental moment when sperm met egg, when egg met sperm – so early in this history it cannot be traced. Irie's child can never be mapped exactly nor spoken of with any certainty. Some secrets are permanent. In a vision, Irie has seen a time, a time not far from now, when roots won't matter any more because they can't because they mustn't because they're too long and they're too tortuous and they're just buried too damn deep. She looks forward to it.

∽

'He who would most valiant be. 'Gainst all disaster . . .'

For a few minutes now, beneath Marcus's talk and the shutters of cameras, another sound (Millat in particular has been attuned to it), a faint singing sound, has been audible. Marcus is doing his best to ignore it and continue, but it has just got considerably louder. He has begun to pause between his words to look around, though the song is clearly not in the room.

'*Let him with constancy, follow the master . . .*'

'Oh God,' murmurs Clara, leaning forward to speak in her husband's ear. 'It's Hortense. It's *Hortense*. Archie, you've *got* to go and sort it out. *Please*. It's easiest for you to get out of your seat.'

But Archie is thoroughly enjoying himself. Between Marcus's talk and Mickey's commentary, it's like watching two TVs at once. Very informative.

'Ask Irie.'

'I can't. She's too far in to get out. *Archie*,' she growls, lapsing into a threatening patois, 'you kyan jus leddem sing trew de whole ting!'

'Sam,' says Archie, trying to make his whisper travel, 'Sam, you go. You don't even want to be *in* here. Go on. You know Hortense. Just tell her to keep it down. 'Sjust I'd quite like to listen to the rest of this, you know. *Very informative*.'

'With pleasure,' hisses Samad, getting out of his seat abruptly, and not troubling to excuse himself as he steps firmly on Neena's toes. 'No need, I think, to save my place.'

Marcus, who is now a quarter of the way through a detailed description of the mouse's seven years, looks up from his paper at the disturbance, and stops to watch the disappearing figure with the rest of the audience.

'I think somebody realized this story doesn't have a happy ending.'

As the audience laughs lightly and settles back into silence, Mickey nudges Archibald in his ribs. 'Now you see, that's a bit more like it,' he says. 'A bit of a comic touch – liven things up a bit. Layman's terms, innit? Not everybody went to the bloody Oxbridge. Some of us went to the –'

'University of Life,' agrees Archie, nodding, because they were both there, though at different times. 'Can't beat it.'

Outside: Samad feels his resolve, strong when the door slammed behind him, weaken as he approaches the formidable Witness ladies, ten of them, all ferociously be-wigged, standing on the front steps, banging away at their percussion as if they wish to beat out something more substantial than rhythm. They are in full voice. Five security guards have already admitted defeat, and even Ryan Topps seems slightly in awe of his choral Frankenstein's monster, preferring to stand at a distance on the pavement, handing out copies of the *Watchtower* to the great crowd heading for Soho.

'Do I get a concession?' inquires one drunken girl, inspecting the kitschy painting of heaven on the cover, adding it to her handful of New Year club fliers. 'Has it got a dress code?'

With misgivings, Samad taps the triangle-player on her rugby-forward shoulders. He tries the full range of vocabulary available to an Indian man addressing potentially dangerous elderly Jamaican women (*ifIcouldplease sorrypossiblypleasesorry* – you learn it at bus stops), but the drums proceed, the kazoo buzzes, the cymbals crash. The ladies continue to crunch their sensible shoes in the frost. And Hortense Bowden, too old for marching, continues to sit on a fold-up chair, resolutely eyeballing the mass of dancing people in Trafalgar Square. She has a banner between her knees that states, simply,

THE TIME IS AT HAND – Rev. 1:3

'Mrs Bowden?' says Samad, stepping forward in a pause between verses. 'I am Samad Iqbal. A friend of Archibald Jones.'

Because Hortense does not look at him or betray any twinge of recognition, Samad feels bound to delve deeper into the intricate web of their relations. 'My wife is a very good friend of your daughter; my step-niece also. My sons are friends with your –'

Hortense kisses her teeth. 'I know fe who you are, man. You know me, I know you. But at dis point, dere are only two kind of people in de world.'

'It is just that we were wondering,' Samad interrupts, spotting a sermon and wanting to sever it at the root, 'if you could possibly reduce the noise somewhat . . . if only –'

But Hortense is already overlapping him, eyes closed, arm raised, testifying to the truth in the old Jamaican fashion: 'Two kind of people: dem who sing for de Lord and dem who rejeck 'im at de peril of dem souls.'

She turns back. She stands. She shakes her banner furiously in the direction of the drunken hordes moving up and down as one in the Trafalgar fountains, and then she is asked to do it again for a cynical photo-journalist with a waiting space to fill on page six.

'Bit higher with the banner, love,' he says, camera held up, one knee in the snow. 'Come on, get angry, that's it. Lovely Jubbly.'

The Witness women raise their voices, sending song up into the firmament. *'Early will I seek thee,'* sings Hortense. *'My soul thirsteth for thee, my flesh longeth for thee in a dry and thirsty land, where no water is . . .'* Samad watches it all and finds himself, to his surprise, unwilling to silence her. Partly because he is tired. Partly because he is old. But mostly because he would do the same, though in a different name. He knows what it is to seek. He knows the dryness. He has felt the thirst you get in a strange land – horrible, persistent – the thirst that lasts your whole life.

Can't say fairer than that, he thinks, *can't say fairer than that*.

∽

Inside: 'But I'm still waiting for him to get to the bit about my skin. Ain't heard nothing yet, have you, Arch?'

'No, nothing yet. I 'spect he's got a lot to get through. Revolutionary, all this.'

'Yeah, naturally . . . But you pays your money, you gets your choice.'

'You didn't pay for your ticket, did you?'

'No. No, I didn't. But I've still got *expectations*. The principle's the same, innit? Oi-oi, shut it a minute . . . I thought I heard *skin* just then . . .'

Mickey did hear skin. Papillomas on the skin, apparently. A good five minutes' worth. Archie doesn't understand a word of it. But at the end of it, Mickey looks satisfied, as if he's got all the information he's been looking for.

'Mmm, now that's why I came, Arch. Very interesting. Great medical breakthrough. Fucking miracle workers, these doctors.'

'. . . and in this,' Marcus is saying, 'he was elemental and indispensable. Not only is he a personal inspiration, but he laid the foundations for so much of this work, particularly in his seminal paper, which I first heard in . . .'

Oh, that's nice. Giving the old bloke some credit. And you can tell, he's chuffed to hear it. Looks a bit tearful. Didn't catch his name. Still, nice not to take all the glory for yourself. But then again, you don't want to overdo it. The way Marcus is going on, sounds like the old bloke did everything.

'Blimey,' says Mickey, thinking the same thing, 'fulsome praise, eh? I thought you said it was this Chalfen who was the Mr Big.'

'Maybe they're partners in crime,' suggests Archie.

'. . . pushing the envelope, when work in this area was seriously underfunded and looked to remain in the realms of science fiction. For that reason alone he has been the guiding spirit, if you like, behind the research group, and is, as ever, my mentor, a position he has filled for twenty years now . . .'

'You know who my mentor is?' says Mickey. 'Muhammad Ali. No question. Integrity of mind, integrity of spirit, integrity of body. Top bloke. Wicked fighter. And when he said he was the greatest, he didn't just say "the greatest".'

Archie says, 'No?'

'Nah, mate,' says Mickey, solemn. 'He said he was the *greatest of all times*. Past, present, future. He was a cocky bastard, Ali. Definitely my mentor.'

Mentor . . . thinks Archie. For him, it's always been Samad. You can't tell Mickey that, obviously. Sounds daft. Sounds queer. But it's the truth. Always Sammy. Through thick and thin. Even if the world were ending. Never made a decision without him in forty years. Good old Sam. Sam the man.

'. . . and so if any one person deserves the lion's share of recognition for the marvel you see before you, it is Dr Marc-Pierre Perret. A remarkable man and a very great . . .'

Every moment happens twice: inside and outside, and they are two different histories. Archie does recognize the name, faintly, somewhere inside, but he is already twisting in his seat by then, trying to see if Samad is returning. He can't see Samad. Instead he spots Millat, who looks funny. Who looks decidedly funny. Peculiar rather than ha-ha. He's swaying ever so slightly in his seat, and Archie can't catch his eye for a you-all-right-mate-look because his eyes are locked on to something and when Archie follows the path of this stare, he finds himself looking at the same peculiar thing: an old man weeping tiny tears of pride. Red tears. Tears Archie recognizes.

But not before Samad recognizes them; *Captain Samad Miah*, who has just stepped soundlessly through the modern door with its silent mechanism; *Captain Samad Miah*, who pauses for a moment on the threshold, peers through his reading glasses, and realizes that he has been lied to by his only friend in the world for fifty years. That the cornerstone of their friendship was made of nothing more firm than marshmallow and soap bubbles. That there is far, far more to Archibald Jones than he had ever imagined. He realizes everything at once like the climax of a bad

Hindi musical. And then, with a certain horrid glee, he gets to the fundamental truth of it, the anagnorisis: *This incident alone will keep us two old boys going for the next forty years*. It is the story to end all stories. It is the gift that keeps on giving.

'Archibald!' He turns from the doctor towards his Lieutenant and releases a short, loud, hysterical laugh; he feels like a new bride looking at her groom with perfect recognition just at the moment when everything between the two of them has changed. 'You two-faced buggering bastard trickster misā mātā, bhainchute, shora-baicha, syut-morāni, haraam jaddā . . .'

Samad tumbles into the Bengali vernacular, so colourfully populated by liars, sister-fuckers, sons and daughters of pigs, people who give their own mothers oral pleasure . . .

But even before this, or at least simultaneous with this, while the audience looks on, bemused by this old brown man shouting at this old white man in a foreign tongue, Archie senses something else going on, some movement in this space, potential movement all over the room (the Indian guys at the back, the kids sitting near Josh, Irie looking from Millat to Magid, Magid to Millat, like an umpire) and sees that Millat will get there first; and Millat is reaching like Pande; and Archie has seen TV and he has seen real-life and he knows what such a reach means, so he stands. So he moves.

So as the gun sees the light, he is *there*, he is there with no coin to help him, he is there before Samad can stop him, he is there with no alibi, he is there between Millat Iqbal's decision and his target, like the moment between thought and speech, like the split-second intervention of memory or regret.

∽ ∽ ∽

At some point in the darkness, they stopped walking through the flatlands and Archie pushed the Doctor forward, made him stand just in front, where he could see him.

'Stay there,' he said, as the Doctor stepped inadvertently into a moonbeam. 'Stay right bloody there.'

Because he wanted to see evil, pure evil; the moment of the great recognition, he *needed* to see it – and then he could proceed as previously arranged. But the Doctor was stooping badly and he looked weak. His face was covered in pale red blood as if the deed had already been done. Archie'd never seen a man so crumpled, so completely vanquished. It kind of took the wind out of his sails. He was tempted to say *You look like I feel*, for if there was an embodiment of his own pounding headache, of the alcoholic nausea rising from his belly, it was standing opposite him now. But neither man spoke; they just stood there for a while, looking at each other across the loaded gun. Archie had the funny sensation that he could *fold* this man instead of killing him. Fold him up and put him in his pocket.

'Look, I'm sorry about it,' said Archie desperately, after thirty long seconds of silence. 'War's over. I've nothing against you personal . . . but my friend, Sam . . . well, I'm in a bit of a situation. So there it is.'

The Doctor blinked several times and seemed to be struggling to control his breathing. Through lips red with his own blood he said, 'When we were walking . . . you said that I might plead . . . ?'

Keeping his hands behind his head, the Doctor made a move to get on his knees, but Archie shook his head and groaned. 'I *know* what I said . . . but there's no . . . it's just better if I –' said Archie sadly, miming the pull of the trigger and the kick-back of the gun. 'Don't you think? I mean, easier . . . all round?'

The Doctor opened his mouth as if to say something, but Archie shook his head again. 'I've never done this before and I'm a bit . . . well, pissed, frankly . . . I drank quite a bit . . . and it wouldn't help . . . you'd be there talking and I probably wouldn't make head nor tail of it, you know, so . . .'

Archie lifted his arms until they were in line with the Doctor's forehead, closed his eyes, and cocked the gun.

The Doctor's voice jumped an octave. 'A cigarette?'

And it was at that moment that it started to go wrong. Like it went wrong for Pande. He should have shot the bloke then and there. Probably. But instead he opened his eyes to see his victim struggling to pull out a battered cigarette packet and a box of matches from his top pocket like a human being.

'Could I – please? Before . . .'

Archie let all the breath he had summoned up to kill a man come out through his nose. 'Can't say no to a last request,' said Archie, because he'd seen the movies. 'I've got a light, if you like.'

The Doctor nodded, Archie struck a match, and the Doctor leaned forward to light up.

'Well, get on with it,' said Archie, after a moment; he never *could* resist a pointless debate, 'if you've got something to say, say it. I haven't got all night.'

'I can speak? We are to have a conversation?'

'I didn't say we were going to have a conversation,' said Archie sharply. Because this was a tactic of Movie Nazis (and Archie should have known; he spent the first four years of the war watching flickering Movie Nazis at the Brighton Odeon), they try to talk their way out of stuff. 'I said you were going to talk and then I was going to kill you.'

'Oh yes, of course.'

The Doctor used his sleeve to wipe his face, and looked at the boy curiously, double-checking to see if he were serious. The boy looked serious.

'Well, then . . . If I may say so . . .' The Doctor's mouth hung open, waiting for Archie to insert a name but none came. 'Lieutenant . . . if I may say so, Lieutenant, it appears to me you are in something of a . . . a . . . moral quandary.'

Archie didn't know what quandary meant. It reminded him of coal, metal and Wales, somewhere between quarry and foundry. At a loss, he said what he always said in these situations. 'I should cocoa!'

'Er . . . Yes, *yes*,' said Dr Sick, gaining some confidence; he had not yet been shot and a whole minute had so far passed. 'It seems to me you have a *dilemma*. On the one hand . . . I do not believe you wish to kill me –'

Archie squared his shoulders. 'Now look, sunshine –'

'And on the other, you have promised your overzealous friend that you will. But it is *more* than that.'

The Doctor's shaking hands tapped his own cigarette inadvertently, and Archie watched the ash fall like grey snow on to his boots.

'On the one hand, you have an obligation to – to – your country and to what you believe is right. On the other hand, I am a *man*. I am speaking to you. I breathe and I bleed as you do. And you do not know, for certain, what type of a man I am. You have only hearsay. So, I understand your difficulty.'

'I don't have a difficulty. *You're* the one with the difficulty, sunshine.'

'And yet, though I am not your friend, you have a duty to me, because I am a man. I think you are caught between duties. I think you find yourself in a very interesting situation.'

Archie stepped forward, and put the muzzle two inches from the Doctor's forehead. 'You finished?'

The Doctor tried to say *yes* but nothing came except a stutter.

'Good.'

'Wait! *Please*. Do you know Sartre?'

Archie sighed, exasperated. 'No, no, no – we haven't any friends in common – I know that, because I've only got one friend and he's called Ick-Ball. Look, I'm going to kill you. I'm sorry about it but –'

'Not a friend. Philosopher. Sartre. Monsieur J. P.'

'Who?' said Archie, agitated, suspicious. 'Sounds French.'

'He is French. A great Frenchman. I met him briefly in '41, when he was imprisoned. But when I met him he posed a problem, which is similar, I think, to yours.'

'Go on,' said Archie slowly. The fact was he could do with some help.

'The problem,' continued Dr Sick, trying to control his hyperventilation, sweating so much there were two little pools in the hollows at the base of his neck, 'is that of a young French student who ought to care for his sick mother in Paris but at the same time ought to go to England to help the Free French fight the National Socialists. Now, remembering that there are many kinds of *ought* – one *ought* to give to charity, for example, but one doesn't always do so; it is *ideal*, but it is not *required* – remembering this, what should he do?'

Archie scoffed, 'That's a bloody stupid question. *Think about it.*' He gesticulated with the gun, moving it from the Doctor's face and tapping his own temple with it. 'At the end of the day, he'll do the one he cares about more. Either he loves his country or his old mum.'

'But what if he cares about both options, equally? I mean, country and "old mum". What if he is obligated to do both?'

Archie was unimpressed. 'Well, he better just do one and get on with it.'

'The Frenchman agrees with you,' said the Doctor, attempting a smile. 'If neither imperative can be overridden, then choose one, and as you say, get on with it. Man makes himself, after all. And he is responsible for what he makes.'

'There you are, then. End of conversation.'

Archie placed his legs apart, spread his weight, ready to take the kick-back – and cocked the gun once more.

'But – but – think – please, my friend – try to think –' The Doctor fell to his knees, sending up a cloud of dust that rose and fell like a sigh.

'Get up,' gulped Archie, horrified by the streams of eye-blood, the hand on his leg and then the mouth on his shoe. 'Please – there's no need for –'

But the Doctor grabbed the back of Archie's knees. 'Think –

please – anything may happen . . . I may yet redeem myself in your eyes . . . or you may be mistaken – your decision may come back to you as Oedipus's returned to him, horrible and mutilated! You cannot say for sure!'

Archie grabbed the Doctor by his skinny arm, hauled him upright and began yelling, 'Look, mate. You've upset me now. I'm not a bloody fortune-teller. The world might end tomorrow for all I know. But I've got to do this *now*. Sam's *waiting* for me. Please,' said Archie, because his hand was shaking and his resolve was doing a runner, '*please* stop talking. I'm not a fortune-teller.'

But the Doctor collapsed once more, like a jack-in-the-box. 'No . . . no . . . we are not fortune-tellers. I could never have predicted my life would end up in the hands of a child . . . Corinthians I, chapter thirteen, verse eight: *Whether there be prophecies, they shall fail; whether there be tongues, they shall cease; whether there be knowledge, it shall vanish away. For we know in part, and we prophesy in part. But when that which is perfect is come, then that which is in part shall be done away*. But when will it come? For myself, I became tired of waiting. It is such a terrible thing, to know only in part. A terrible thing not to have perfection, human perfection, when it is so readily available.' The Doctor lifted himself up, and tried to reach out to Archie just as Archie backed away. 'If only we were brave enough to make the decisions that must be made . . . between those worth saving and the rest . . . Is it a crime to want –'

'Please, *please*,' said Archie, ashamed to find himself crying, not red tears like the Doctor's, but thick and translucent and salty. 'Stay there. Please stop talking. *Please*.'

'And then I think of the perverse German, Friedrich. Imagine the world with no beginning or end, boy.' He spat this last word, *boy*, and it was a thief that changed the balance of power between them, stealing whatever strength was left in Archie and dispersing it on the wind. 'Imagine, if you *can*, events in the world happening repeatedly, endlessly, in the way they always have . . .'

'Stay where you fucking are!'

'Imagine this war over and over a million times . . .'

'No thanks,' said Archie, choking on snot. ''Sbad enough the first time.'

'It is not a serious proposition. It is a test. Only those who are sufficiently strong and well disposed to life to affirm it – even if it will just keep on repeating – have what it takes to endure the worst blackness. I could see the things I have done repeated infinitely. I am one of the confident ones. But you are not one of them . . .'

'Please, just stop talking, *please*, so I can –'

'The decision you make, Archie,' said Dr Sick, betraying a knowledge that he had possessed from the start, the boy's name, which he had been waiting to employ when it would have the most power, 'could you see it repeated again and again, through eternity? Could you?'

'I've got a coin!' yelled Archie, *screamed* it with joy, because he had just remembered it. 'I've got a coin!'

Dr Sick looked confused, and stopped his stumbling steps forward.

'Ha! I have a coin, you bastard. Ha! So balls to you!'

Then another step. His hands reaching out, palms up, innocent.

'Stay back. Stay where you are. Right. This is what we're going to do. Enough talking. I'm going to put my gun down here . . . slowly . . . *here*.'

Archie crouched and placed it on the floor, roughly between the two of them. 'That's so you can trust me. I'll stand by my word. And now I'm going to throw this coin. And if it's heads, I'm going to kill you.'

'But –' said Dr Sick. And for the first time Archie saw something like real fear in his eyes, the same fear that Archie felt so thoroughly he could hardly speak.

'And if it's tails, I won't. No, I don't want to talk about it. I'm not much of a thinker, when you get down to it. That's the best I can offer. All right, here goes.'

The coin rose and flipped as a coin would rise and flip every time in a perfect world, flashing its light and then revealing its dark enough times to mesmerize a man. Then, at some point in its triumphant ascension, it began to arc, and the arc went wrong, and Archibald realized that it was not coming back to him at all but going behind him, a fair way behind him, and he turned round to watch it fall in the dirt. He was bending to pick it up when a shot rang out, and he felt a blistering pain in his right thigh. He looked down. Blood. The bullet had passed straight through, just missing the bone, but leaving a shard of the cap embedded deep in the flesh. The pain was excruciating and strangely distant at the same time. Archie turned back round to see Dr Sick, half bent over, the gun hanging weakly in his right hand.

'For fuckssake, why did you do that?' said Archie furious, grabbing the gun off the Doctor, easily and forcefully. 'It's tails. See? It's tails. Look. Tails. It was tails.'

So Archie is there, there in the trajectory of the bullet, about to do something unusual, even for TV: save the same man twice and with no more reason or rhyme than the first time. And it's a messy business, this saving people lark. Everybody in the room watches in horror as he takes it in the thigh, right in the femur, spins round with some melodrama and falls right through the mouse's glass box. Shards of glass all over the gaff. What a performance. If it were TV you would hear the saxophone around now; the credits would be rolling.

But first the endgames. Because it seems no matter what you think of them, they must be played, even if, like the independence of India or Jamaica, like the signing of peace treaties or the docking of passenger boats, the end is simply the beginning of an even longer story. The same focus group who picked out the colour of this room, the carpet, the font for the posters, the height of the table, would no doubt tick the box that asks to see all these things played to their finish . . . and there is surely a demographic pattern to all those who wish to see the eyewitness statements that identified Magid as many times as Millat, the confusing transcripts, the videotape of uncooperating victim and families, a court case so impossible the judge gave in and issued four hundred hours community service to both twins, which they served, naturally, as gardeners in Joyce's new project, a huge millennial park by the banks of the Thames . . .

And is it young professional women aged eighteen to thirty-two who would like a snapshot seven years hence of Irie, Joshua and Hortense sitting by a Caribbean sea (for Irie and Joshua become lovers in the end; you can only avoid your fate for so long), while Irie's fatherless little girl writes affectionate postcards to *Bad Uncle Millat* and *Good Uncle Magid* and feels free as Pinocchio, a puppet clipped of paternal strings? And could it be that it is largely the criminal class and the elderly who find themselves wanting to make bets on the winner of a blackjack game, the one played by Alsana and Samad, Archie and Clara, in O'Connell's, 31 December 1999, that historic night when Abdul-Mickey finally opened his doors to women?

But surely to tell these tall tales and others like them would be to speed the myth, the wicked lie, that the past is always tense and the future, perfect. And as Archie knows, it's not like that. It's never been like that.

It would make an interesting survey (what kind would be your decision) to examine the present and divide the onlookers into two groups: those whose eyes fell upon a bleeding man, slumped across a table, and those who watched the getaway of a small brown rebel mouse. Archie, for one, watched the mouse. He watched it stand very still for a second with a smug look as if it expected nothing less. He watched it scurry away, over his hand. He watched it dash along the table, and through the hands of those who wished to pin it down. He watched it leap off the end and disappear through an air vent. *Go on my son!* thought Archie.

ZADIE SMITH

THE AUTOGRAPH MAN

Deeply funny, subversive and splendidly entertaining, *The Autograph Man* is a whirlwind tour of celebrity and our fame-obsessed times. Following one Alex-Li Tandem – a twenty-something, Chinese-Jewish autograph dealer turned on by sex, drugs and organized religion – it takes in London and New York, love and death, fathers and sons, as Alex tries to discover how a piece of paper can bring him closer to his heart's desire. Exposing our misconceptions about our idols – about ourselves – *The Autograph Man* is a brilliant, unforgettable tale about who we are and what we really want to be.

'Full of irony, humour, the search for love and the fear of death . . . a touching, thoughtful, deeply-felt rite of passage novel' *Sunday Telegraph*

'Sharp and tender. Her ear for dialogue [is] pitch perfect' *Daily Mail*

'A glorious concoction written by our most beguiling and original prose-wizard'

Independent on Sunday

ZADIE SMITH

ON BEAUTY

Why do we fall in love with the people we do?

Why do we visit our mistakes on our children?

What makes life truly beautiful?

Set in New England mainly and London partly, On Beauty concerns a pair of feuding families – the Belseys and the Kipps – and a clutch of doomed affairs. It puts low morals among high ideals and asks some searching questions about what life does to love. For the Belseys and the Kipps, the confusions – both personal and political – of our uncertain age are about to be brought close to home: right to the heart of family.

'Exceptionally accomplished, wonderfully funny. Confirms Smith as an outstanding novelist with a powerful understanding both of what the brain knows and what love knows' *Observer*

'That rare thing: a novel that is as affecting as it is entertaining, as provocative as it is humane' *The New York Times*

'A rollicking satire. Fun, chummy and big-hearted ... a tremendously good read. Rich, entertaining and beautiful' *Scotland on Sunday*

read more

ZADIE SMITH

NW

Hobbes, Smith, Bentham, Locke and Russell.

Five identical blocks make up the Caldwell housing estate in North West London. If you grew up in this relic of seventies urban design, the plan was to get out and get on, to something better, somewhere else. Thirty years later, Caldwell kids Leah, Natalie, Felix and Nathan have all moved on, with varying degrees of success – whatever that means. Living only streets apart, they occupy separate worlds, and navigate an atomized city in which few care to be their neighbour's keeper.

Then one April afternoon a stranger comes to Leah's door, seeking help, disturbing the peace, and forcing Leah out of her isolation . . .

From private houses to public parks, at work and at play, where the main streets hide the back alleys and taking the high road can sometimes lead you to a dead end, *NW* is a quietly devastating novel of encounters.

Depicting the modern urban zone – familiar to town-dwellers everywhere – Zadie Smith's brilliant tragi-comic new novel is as mercurial and vital as the city itself.

THE NEW NOVEL

AVAILABLE IN SEPTEMBER 2012